Joy Chambers utilised her [...] historical novels during her [...] career in Australia. Over a dozen years on she retains her enthusiasm for storytelling and research and combines her writing with her business life as chairman of a group of companies along with her husband. Joy says, 'My life is in the entertainment business. A skilfully written book can be read on many levels but it should always entertain... I attempt to do that.'

FOR FREEDOM

Joy Chambers

headline

First published in Great Britain in 2007
by HEADLINE PUBLISHING GROUP

First published in paperback in Great Britain in 2007
by HEADLINE PUBLISHING GROUP

I

ISBN 978 0 7553 0940 5

Typeset in Centaur by Palimpsest Book Production Limited,
Grangemouth, Stirlingshire

Printed and bound in Great Britain by
Mackays of Chatham plc, Chatham, Kent

HEADLINE PUBLISHING GROUP
A division of Hachette Livre UK Ltd
338 Euston Road
London NW1 3BH

www.headline.co.uk
www.hodderheadline.com

To my father, Alan Chambers.
Soldier and philosopher.
British Expeditionary Force: No 63645
Australian Imperial Force: No QX24155
In World War One and World War Two he fought,
for freedom.

My thanks to many people but in particular to:
My most gifted brother, John H Chambers, who reads
all that I write and cares deeply about it.

And to my husband, Reg Grundy, a Renaissance man, who
knows and understands all my characters intimately and remains
my love, my inspiration and my refuge.

Author's notes

The servicemen of the Australian Imperial Forces were all volunteers.

When I was growing up in Australia, the battles in the Owen Stanley Ranges in New Guinea were always referred to as having taken place on the 'Kokoda Trail'. There were no exceptions. Returned servicemen who fought there use this term. In recent years I have noticed a penchant by certain Australian historians to refer to it as the 'Kokoda Track'. I disagree with this trend and have used 'Kokoda Trail' throughout my book.

For the sake of my story I have made two minor adjustments:

The brave men of the Coast Watchers were in position in Southern New Britain in 1942. I have placed them further north.

In October 1942, the USS *Pompano* (SS-181) was in the Eastern Pacific and I have used her in the South-West Pacific area.

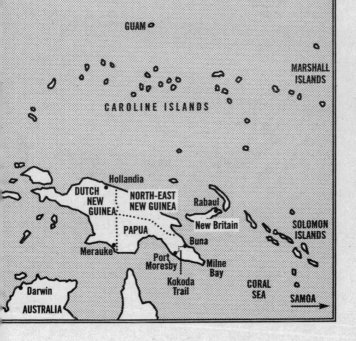

Chapter One

'The streets are more crowded by the day.'

John Drayton Whitby manipulated his car past two bicycles ridden by men in pith helmets and on through a mass of bodies, many black-clothed elderly carrying baskets. They scurried to right and left in front of his vehicle to pour on beneath the coloured signs painted in bright Chinese characters hanging from building to building.

The Austin lurched to the left as he dragged sharply on the wheel to miss the grey cat that squealed and bounded away past an oncoming tram and a host of rickshaws. At his side his wife thudded into his shoulder and he laughed. 'Well, I didn't hit it.'

'Luckily. Though you nearly took a rickshaw with you.'

John Drayton disregarded the reproof as Lexine adjusted her body-hugging robe of beige silk which fell in swathes about her. 'Dr Campbell at the hospital said there are over a hundred thousand refugees from China sleeping in the streets now.'

'Really?'

'Well, he says so. There are certainly hundreds of them in the hospital waiting room every day.'

Her husband's voice was sombre. 'Doesn't that tell you something, Lexi? The Japanese are in China, just across the water; a few miles in a straight line. You know how they dealt with the

I

Koreans and the Manchurians and the Chinese – the atrocities. Why oh why won't you listen to me and leave with your Aunt Della next Sunday?'

'Johnny, dear, we've had this conversation before. I am going. I'll leave after Christmas. That's only a few weeks away, after all.'

John Drayton cleared his throat as he turned through the two pillars bearing the name 'Hydrangea' in slender gold lettering. He replied as they entered the avenue of laburnums leading up to the white citadel which was Lexi's grandparents' home. 'All right, Lexi, but the war in Europe and Africa extends all the time. And there are those of us at the Fort who think the Japs won't wait much longer to move. And the fact that I've been transferred with the liaison team to Singapore makes me worry about you more. How do you think I feel about leaving you here? Can't you understand we're on borrowed time here in Hong Kong?'

'And can't you forget the war for a few hours?' Lexi sighed. 'Oh, I'm sorry. Look, I'm not going to be cross with you. This is such a wonderful occasion. We mustn't have a fight on Grandpa's ninetieth birthday. You know how important it is.'

John Drayton gave a long-suffering sigh as his wife's door was opened and she stepped out of the car. She could see her grandparents standing on the veranda greeting their guests and she spoke quietly as she took her husband's arm. 'Now, dearest, please be good and enjoy the party.'

Lexi dropped his arm and hurried up the path and John Drayton watched her run to her grandfather. For Lexi, coming to Hydrangea was always coming home; she had lived with her grandparents for many of her formative years after her father had drowned.

The night was blanketing the residents of Hong Kong as Brillard Hayes held his granddaughter close in his embrace. His sight was fading and he used an ebony cane during all his waking hours, but his spirit was still that of the boy who had joined the army to see the world seventy-odd years before. As the hard metal of his medals pressed into Lexi through her diaphanous gown he spoke. 'Sweetheart, even with these tired old eyes I know you look exquisite.'

'Thanks, Pa. Happy birthday.'

Colonel Sir Brillard Hayes was legend in Hong Kong's military circles. His personal wealth, which was not inadequate, had been made in the paper trade after his retirement from the army. He was often heard to say, 'The first half of my life I devoted to Queen Victoria's military; the second half to myself.'

He was a prepossessing figure even in great age: his straight back had succumbed only slightly to gravity, bequeathing a gentle rounding to his shoulders. A ruddy glow sat on the cheeks of his large sun-darkened face and his goatee beard appeared like combed white silken threads upon his chin. He smiled indulgently at Lexi as John Drayton stepped up and took his hand. 'Good evening, sir.'

'Evening, son.'

Lexi turned from him to her grandmother. 'You look lovely, Grandma.'

'Thank you, dear.' Helvetia Hayes's powdered face dissolved into a thin smile above the high Chinese collar on her lavender brocade gown. Matching shoes peeped out beneath the skirt which fell to the floor. She was twelve years her husband's junior, mistress of one of Hong Kong's most beautiful houses, and had been at the centre of island society for forty years.

Helvetia gave Lexi a quick hug. 'Everybody's here, you're the last.' This was an admonishment and Lexi replied, 'Sorry, Grandma. We nearly killed a cat trying to be on time,' as she moved on to greet her two uncles: Jasper Hayes and Peter Seaforth.

And now Helvetia turned to John Drayton. Upon him her gaze melted and something akin to genuine pleasure parted her lips. 'Good evening, dear,' she said as she embraced him.

'Hello, darling,' John Drayton replied, kissing her thin cheek.

Helvetia patted his arm. 'You look so handsome in your uniform.' She had always doted on her Australian grandson-in-law and she

3

drew him towards her as Lexi kissed her uncle Jasper — Helvetia and Brillard's only son, a man of fifty-five, quiet and introverted, who seemed to do nothing except sit in the Brillard offices in Kowloon and on Saturdays play polo. He rarely came to family gatherings and was not close to his relatives.

'I'm pleased you came, Uncle Jasper.'

His mouth stretched in a smile. 'It is my father's ninetieth birthday, Lexine.'

Behind them Helvetia clutched John Drayton and spoke confidentially to him. 'Now, dear, have you convinced Lexi not to delay in leaving Hong Kong?'

John Drayton shook his head. 'I'm trying. But she's got a mind of her own, your granddaughter.'

'Brillard's going to talk to her but he wants to speak to you first.'

'Right.' John Drayton moved over to his wife and took her arm, and as they passed along the side of the house, Lexi breathed in the beauty of Hydrangea's grounds: Chinese hanging lanterns decorated with dragons and flowers threw swathes of yellow and rose across the garden. Huge golden Oriental vases overburdened with white orchids and ferns graced pathways and marble tabletops, and tall firebrands planted two by two along the edge of an ornamental pond gently illuminated the huge goldfish swimming beneath the flickering surface. Yes, it was sumptuous, but subdued in comparison to the parties before the European war; every social function these days was scaled down. Instead of the two hundred and fifty guests that a gathering such as this would have seen prior to 1939, there were perhaps sixty and most of them were men in uniform, the majority of the women and children having been repatriated to Australia and New Zealand. The very few females who remained were either in essential services like Lexi or had simply known the right people to avoid the repatriation, like her grandmother.

They passed down a stone walkway covered in dormant allamanda

4

vines and halted to talk to the Chief Justice, Sir Atholl MacGregor, known to many as Sir Alcohol. Kathleen Leigh, Lexi's friend from childhood, joined them. Her glass was almost empty; Sir Atholl's was always empty and he brandished it in the air as he blinked his blood-shot eyes. 'Time for another drink. What's it to be?'

Lexi nodded. 'Yes please, gin and tonic.'

John Drayton looked round for a servant, but as there were none in sight he offered to get the drinks and Kathleen finished her whisky and handed him her glass. 'Another weak one, please,' she said with a warm smile, her oval eyes reflecting the dancing lights like the ocean does the moon.

'I'll come with you,' announced the Chief Justice and the two men strode off to the bar, a long trestle table covered in white linen behind which hovered a dozen Chinese waiters while above their heads the wide leafless branches of a jacaranda tree contorted in octopus manner.

Kathleen lit a cigarette as she turned to Lexi. 'You look lovely, Lex.'

'You too.' Lexi stepped nearer her friend. 'How's your mother?'

Kathleen shrugged and a line of worry settled on her brow. 'The same. She seems to fade more each day.'

Lexi was sympathetic. 'Ah darling, I'm so sorry.'

The two women spoke with the intimacy of a friendship since babyhood and Kathleen lifted her dainty fingers and stroked Lexi's arm. 'So when are your aunt and uncle sailing for Australia?'

'On Sunday. Like me, Aunt Della didn't want to miss Pa's birthday. Otherwise they probably would have gone weeks ago.'

'I suppose your mother will be delighted to have you all in Queensland.'

'No doubt, but Kath, you know my mother, always talking delightful nonsense, playing bridge and drinking gin and inter-ested in nothing beyond who's sleeping with whom and what the latest fashions are. I'm not actually looking forward to that.'

'Oh go on, you'll be all right. Her husband loves you like a daughter. I think she's sensible to enjoy herself, and anyway your Aunt Della will be there, they can entertain each other.'

Lexi nodded. 'True. I love them dearly, but they're just like Grandma, who taught them to be lotus-eaters in the first place.'

Kathleen was amused. 'Now that's a tad cruel. Just because your grandmother was shocked when you became a doctor and actually worked! You forget that most European women here are surrounded by servants and cocooned in lavishness. I don't think they have much option but to succumb to a life of parties and gossip.'

'Very tolerant of you, Kathy.'

'That's the Chinese in me.'

They both laughed at that, and as they did so a hand touched Lexi's back and she turned to find her aunt eyeing her. A dozen rubies twinkled brilliantly at her throat, complementing the scarlet on her mouth; and while the red and white spotted dress pulled here and there, valiantly attempting to cover the corpulence of her midriff, she still made an attractive picture of middle age.

Lexi hugged her relative. 'Oh Aunt Della, I do hope you didn't hear what I said.'

Della Seaforth kissed her niece and spoke with a forbearing tone. 'I'm glad I didn't.' She bent in and brushed Kathleen's cheek with her lips. 'How's your mother?'

'The same.'

'Tell her I'll come over tomorrow.' She grasped Kathleen's forearm affectionately and as she looked past the Eurasian girl she let out a little squeak. 'Oh, there's Chris! You must both meet him. Lovely fellow.' She flashed her vermilion fingernails over a vase of orchids as she rattled on. 'Met him at the yacht club yesterday. He's American and alone in Hong Kong so I invited him. I knew Daddy wouldn't mind.' She herded the two young women towards a man with his back to them, her crimson sandals clicking with importance on the path as she called, 'Chris, Chris?'

The man turned from his companions. 'Yes, Mrs Seaforth?' His

6

face was lit by one of the golden lanterns, and his waving brown hair gleamed as he brought his body round.

Lexi halted; an involuntary sound began and stopped dead in her throat.

Della took the man's arm and drew him forward and in that second he saw Lexi. Just for a heartbeat, surprise registered in his eyes but he instantly covered it with a smile.

'Chris Webster, this is my niece Dr Lexine Whitby, though for some odd reason she still uses her maiden name, Robinson, at the hospital.'

Kathleen glanced at Lexine, who said nothing, so she answered for her. 'It's easier; that's how they knew her before she was married. It saves confusion.' She put out her hand to the American. 'And I'm her friend, Kathleen Leigh. I nurse with Dr Robinson. Have we met before?'

The American grinned. 'I'm sure I would remember if we had.'

Della pressed on. 'As I said, my dears, Chris is American – has been surveying all over the East. He's in Hong Kong now at the behest of one of the banks.' She took a breath and warbled on. 'Lexi's married but Kathleen isn't.' She hesitated and looked around. 'By the way, Lexi, where is your husband?'

As Della said *husband* Chris Webster's gaze lit upon Lexi, but she glanced quickly away, answering abruptly, 'He's gone to get us a drink.'

Lexi felt as if her mind were adrift from her head. She hardly heard what was said, and even though she could see Johnny returning, glasses in hand towards them, she remained motionless.

As her husband approached past the small group of musicians, and Della and Kathleen continued their small talk with the stranger, Lexine remained silent. And when John Drayton arrived, his gaze travelled past his wife and a wide grin of recognition turned up the corners of his mouth. 'Good heavens! Fancy seeing you here.'

This amazed Lexi, and she turned in time to see another expression of fleeting surprise on the newcomer's face before he immediately stepped forward, offering his hand. 'Johnny, how are you?' and he added swiftly as if reminding John Drayton of his name, 'Chris Webster.'

John Drayton met his eyes. 'Yes ... Chris, how are you these days?'

'Fine. Good to see you again.'

They shook hands as Della gazed from one to the other. 'How on earth do you two know one another?'

John Drayton let the American answer.

'We met once in Malaya when I was surveying there for a tin mine.'

Della squeezed Johnny's arm. 'Malaya? Now, darling, what were you doing in Malaya?'

'Same as now: liaison officer. It was late thirty-nine, wasn't it?'

'Yes,' the American confirmed.

Lexi was trying to control the swinging emotions bombarding her. Her mind twisted back to Madura Island and Henaro's bar with the murmur of the sea kneading the beach and the weird thrilling ride through the ebony night with the wind in her hair and her arms tightly about him.

She thanked God for the coloured lanterns, for she knew she must be pale. 'Excuse me ... but I must go to the powder room.' She whirled around and left, even as Kathleen called, 'Do you want me to come with you?'

'No.' Lexi threw the word over her bare shoulder as she hurried away.

She was aware of somebody greeting her but she did not stop, and as she came up the stone path to the long side veranda Captain Quentin Marks in company with George Wright-Nooth of the police force accosted her. 'Now, now, Lexine, don't just race by. We want to talk to the loveliest woman here.' Quentin blocked the path.

She pushed by. 'Sorry, gentlemen, must go.'

'Promise you'll come back?'

She gave no reply and ran up the four wide steps to the veranda, crossed by the bevy of potted palms and rattan chairs and entered the house where servants passed back and forth carrying trays of food. She ran down the corridor to the room she still called her own. Entering it, she closed the door behind her and looked for a key to lock it but there was none. Automatically dropping her silver beaded purse on the bed she moved to the dressing table and sat down resting her head in her hands. The room was dark, only the ambient glow from the garden lanterns illuminating the oversized furniture and the flower-patterned rugs upon the wooden floor.

'Oh God,' she whispered. 'Oh God, oh God, oh God.'

She remained still for a long time until, with a sigh, she stood. She had no idea what to do.

Chris Webster . . . Her aunt had called him that.

He was out there in the garden with her husband. They knew each other! Obviously liked each other. She felt ill.

He was just the same, his expression the same, his face and hair the same, even the way he lifted his hand towards her was the same. Everything about him she remembered. Everything about him played on her mind night and day . . . every day.

Chapter Two

Lexi hesitated at the open door. A flurry from the humid breeze flowing along the veranda made a brief spirited attempt at lifting her red pleated skirt as she looked into the gloom of the interior and then entered the hallway, only to halt again in front of the long, once gilt-framed mirror. The glass was dull and tired from years of heat and humidity; a crack running from top to bottom broke her moody reflection in two. She gazed at herself, narrowing her eyes, and with a swift movement took a lipstick out of her small brocade purse and wiped a smear of crimson on her mouth, exaggerating the cupid's bow of her top lip. She appeared satisfied with the result, for she smiled at her image before pushing her hair back behind her right ear and spinning round to hurry along the hall.

A man loomed before her and she collided with him. Her handbag fell to the floor. 'Oh, sorry.'

He had emerged out of a dark side door and he bent, picked up the purse and stood. She held out her hand for her property but he retained it. He wore civilian clothes, a lightweight jacket over a white shirt open at the neck; this alone was surprising when most of the local Dutch men were in uniform.

They stood looking at each other and an instantaneous wild

10

feeling, immense yet diffused, filled the air. He was neither large nor small, but an energy flowed from him, and as he surveyed her Lexi received the same feeling of potency that might have oozed from one of the large cats: a tiger or a leopard, rippling with power and ever vigilant. She moved slightly away, her hand still outstretched.

Finally, with a consciously disciplined movement of straightening his shoulders, he handed the bag to her; she noticed his long fingers and sun-browned back of his hand.

'Thank you.' She moved further away.

'That's all right.'

'Good evening.' She hurried on by.

He remained watching her. She was aware of his gaze upon her as she passed down the corridor and entered the bar to be greeted by a haze of smoke rising towards the ceiling like steam from a hundred kettles.

Her two friends sat at a round cane table near the open window with a view of the sea and Lexi crossed over and joined them, easing herself into the wicker chair next to Kathleen Leigh. 'God, it's hot.'

Kathleen fanned herself with a newspaper. 'Yes, it is. I feel like I'm melting.'

Mary Barton lit a cigarette and reached for her drink, extending her naked slender arm across the table. 'You were so long out there, Lexi, we wondered what had become of you.'

'Well, there is only one lavatory, you know.' As she spoke, Lexi lifted her gaze and there, through the drifting cigarette smoke, she saw him. He stood in the door opening, leaning on the jamb and looking across the room straight at her. The touch of his gaze was unsettling even at this distance. He nodded. She glanced away.

'Can we buy you a drink, girls?' The thick accent came from a round-faced Dutchman who hovered over them wearing the uniform of the local police. Behind him stood another man.

Mary giggled and Kathleen smiled while the speaker took the

initiative and sat down in the single empty chair between Mary and Lexi and asked, 'What will you have?'

'Until the Real Thing Comes Along' swelled up from the gramophone behind the bar as Mary glanced at Kathleen and a silent consent passed between them. Mary spoke. 'A gin and tonic for me, and Kathleen likes whisky. What about you, Lexi?'

Lexi stood. 'No thanks. I'm on duty at seven in the morning. Second last day and all that. Don't want to spoil a perfect record. I'll say good night.' She kissed Kathleen, picked up her purse, smiled farewell to Mary and disappeared through the smoke. Out in the corridor she glanced again at her image in the broken mirror as she passed. She was half expecting the stranger to be lingering around here somewhere, but the hall was empty and she crossed the threshold of the wide doorway into the hot breeze and the oppressive night. Her footfalls echoed slightly on the veranda and a parrot screeched somewhere in the dark.

She looked around for a 'son of Lakey'. Lakey was a Malay who ran a rickshaw business. He had four grown-up sons, and one could always be relied upon to be waiting outside Henaro's beach bar until closing time. But tonight appeared to be the exception.

She walked ten yards in the moonlight, calling, 'Son of Lakey, are you here?'

There was no reply, and she walked a little further before she paused beneath a palm tree, its fronds rippling in the moist breeze. The moon rode wispy clouds and 'Lady in Red' now carried from the gramophone inside Henaro's, but otherwise all was silent. Towering tropic plants, sombre and mysterious, interlaced their arms along the narrow dirt road before her, and long grass grew knee high at the side of the track which led down to a mangrove swamp and on to a small beach. Lexi fancied she could hear water lapping against the rocks.

'So you're leaving.'

She started, but knew who it was before she turned round.

He was leaning on the trunk of the tallest palm that grew beside a shed across from Henaro's. The collar of his white shirt glimmered in the moonlight.

'You startled me.'

'Sorry.'

Lexi again felt the weight of his gaze. She shivered and a part of her mind thought how ridiculous it was when the temperature must be still over eighty degrees.

He left the obscurity of the palm and walked up to her. 'Where are you going to, lady in red?'

The words of 'Lady in Red' were faint but distinctly sailing along on the damp air.

She realised it was true: her skirt was indeed red. 'I'm going home to the Women's Club.'

'Might I enquire where that is?'

She recognised a slight American accent. She answered, 'Along the waterfront past the pier.'

'I pass that on my way.'

'On your way where?'

'To my lodgings.'

Lexi said nothing and he added, 'I'm staying at Maarten's.'

It was what passed for a hotel on this out-of-the-way isle. She could make out his eyes. 'Who are you?'

There was a pause before he answered. 'Call me Trap.'

'Trap?'

'Yes, my friends call me Trap.'

'Is it a nickname?'

He hesitated. 'Sort of. And what're you called?'

'Lexi.'

'Lexi who?'

'Lexi Robinson.'

'So, Lexi Robinson, can I give you a lift?'

'In what?'

'My vehicle.' He seemed as enigmatic as the mood of the night.

13

A sudden gust of hot wind hit them and a monkey screeched on a branch above their heads. It was so loud and unexpected that Lexi let out a cry and unconsciously moved closer to him. And at the same eerie moment the moon went behind a cloud, 'Lady in Red' swelled more loudly from the distant bar and a number of dark shapes leapt upon them from the undergrowth.

Lexi's mouth formed a scream, but it died in her throat as the heel of a man's hand smashed into the side of her head. She collapsed at the knees and went down, but even as she hit the ground she was aware that her companion sprang forward to meet the attackers.

Feet scuffled near her face as Lexi tried to roll away from them. Loud grunts and groans were followed by a body thudding down upon her back, making her cry out. Someone shouted and a moment later two figures fell into the long grass as she pushed the body from her back and dragged herself away.

She could make out the two forms rising and running into the obscurity of the foliage, and as a boot trod on her hand, she yelped. A man above her slipped and staggered and now, as she sat up, she saw him double up, turn and fall. He hit the ground with a thud.

Silence. The strains of 'Lady in Red' had been replaced by 'All This and Heaven Too'.

The rustling of the trees and the lapping of the water were the same as before.

The body that had fallen upon her now lay an inert black mass beside her. Her heart was pumping and abruptly another dark form loomed towards her as she caught her breath in fear.

'It's me. Are you all right?'

It was Trap. She let out a long sigh. 'Yes, I think so. Who were they?'

He did not reply.

She was shaking. 'God, I think there were four of them.'

He helped her to her feet. 'Yes.' His tone was disinterested and

14

he nudged the nearer prone body with his foot, turned and did the same to the other.

'Are they dead?'

'Yes.'

'You fought them off alone.'

He shrugged.

Her fear still lingered in her voice. 'I've never heard of anyone being attacked on this island before.'

He rubbed his neck and stretched his shoulders, straightening them as he had done in the hallway back at the bar. 'There're some people hereabouts who don't like me, and I'm sorry you got involved.' He turned away. 'Wait here.'

Lexi forced herself to be calm as he strode over to the shed near Henaro's veranda and returned pushing a motorbike and side-car. He halted beside her, stooped down to the closest prone body and hefted it into the side-car.

'What on earth are you doing?' She looked down at the corpse and the head dropped back. She could just make out the face. Her voice revealed her surprise. 'Good Lord, he's the Japanese barber in the village.'

'Yes, it appears he worked two jobs.' He moved to the other body in the gloom and dragged it further off the track into the undergrowth, glancing back to Henaro's just as two men came out on to the veranda. In a slick movement he threw his leg over the bike and sat. 'Come on, Doll, get on. We'd better get out of here.'

Adrenalin shot through Lexi's limbs as she climbed on the vehicle behind him. Her hands slipped around his body and he pulled immediately away through the tunnel of palms and tropic plants into the torpid night.

Lexi's fingers rested on the windowsill as she watched the moon perched on the apex of the tallest palm outside the window. The rustle of the fronds drifted to her as slowly she sipped the Scotch

15

and water she held. Trap had made one for her, and now she was drinking a second she had mixed herself.

She looked at the clock on the wall. It must be an hour since he had disappeared with the words 'Wait for me, I really want you to; I'll be a while, but promise you'll stay here, understand?' She had nodded agreement and the look he cast at her from the doorway was different from any other she had ever received.

And now she was asking herself what she was doing here. Waiting for a man she didn't know; a man who had obviously gone to dispose of the two dead Japanese. He had killed them with his bare hands and fought off two others.

The weird excitement of the bike ride was still with her: streaking through the night with the wind in her hair and her arms holding him. There had been a warm, faint, pleasant scent in her nostrils. Who was this man? He had not taken her to the Women's Club; instead he had brought her here to his room at Maarten's. The surprising element was that she had not even protested. It was as if there had been some unspoken plan which she knew she was party to from the moment of meeting him in the corridor at Henaro's.

Lexi watched the gentle undulation of the sea in the distance beyond the jungle fringe before she finished the last of her Scotch and put down the glass.

Suddenly she stood from the rattan chair and slipped across the bare floorboards. No! She must not stay, this was wrong. Quickly picking up her purse, she moved by a large raffia basket to the door and stretched out her fingers for the handle.

It turned, the door opened and he stood there. In the yellow lamplight she saw his slow smile. 'You waited.'

She stepped two paces away from him. 'I shouldn't have.'

'But you did.'

He closed the door and a moment passed before she asked, 'What have you done with the Japanese men?'

'Best you don't know.'

16

She backed away from him, but he advanced slowly towards her until his body touched hers. She looked up at a scar on the side of his chin and somewhere in the haze of her thoughts, wondered about it. His body heat warmed her skin through the light cotton dress.

He lifted his arms and encompassed her.

The lamplight played across his features as Lexi began a feeble protest, the half-uttered words drowning inside his mouth as it closed over hers. Seconds later he drew her over to the bed.

She came out of a dream to be aware of his hand on her naked stomach, and as she moved it slipped down between her legs and he rose over her again. His lips caressed the side of her neck and he whispered in her hair, 'I've never wanted anything in my life like I want you.'

Lexi turned her head and in reply murmured tender words against the wetness of his mouth.

His voice was hoarse with emotion. 'I'll have to leave this island soon. I'll explain it all to you tomorrow, there's a lot to tell you, but the way I feel about you won't alter.' He drew his finger tenderly down her cheek to the edge of her mouth. 'I've only known you a few hours, Lexi Robinson, but I want you to be my wife. I never want to lose you.'

Lexi closed her eyes. 'Hush,' she whispered. 'Just love me now.'

The horizon line shimmered with the kindling day as the earth maintained its relentless eastward odyssey, and in the bloom of stirring dawn settling on the window near her, Lexi opened her eyes. He was not beside her. She sat up, wide awake immediately. Water was running. He was in the next room bathing.

She slipped from the bed, bent silently and gathered up her shoes and clothes and hardly breathing, turned and tiptoed to the door. It was ajar and she stole into the second room, dressed in haste, not doing up the buttons of her bodice for the sake of

17

speed, picked up her purse, moved with stealth over the floor-boards to the front door, opened it and eased herself out into the hesitant light. All was still, there was no breeze and the only sound was the distant sadness of the rolling sea.

Passing quickly over the veranda, she avoided the path to the front office, and as she moved by the tall palms, straying cattle and rubber plants guarding the back of Maarten's Inn, she halted and glanced back.

The significance of what she had done engulfed her. He was there, fifty yards back, inside the low wooden building surrounded by the coconut palms. She could return now and stay with him . . . always.

The quandary she felt brought stinging tears to her eyes and she hesitated as she wiped them away and murmured, 'No.'

Her vision clouded and new tears welled in her eyes, forcing her to stumble. She righted herself and swiftly put on her shoes, and with a long, deep breath, ran out into the road.

Chapter Three

Lexi stood poised somewhere between reality and illusion in the surreal atmosphere of the bedroom, the melancholy shadows falling about her in counterpoint to the memories in her mind.

He had been Trap and now he was Chris Webster! And he was here, right here in Hong Kong.

A tear slid down her cheek in remembrance of the night she had shared with him; the memory of it lying in wait in her mind, ready for recall at any second of the night or day. She relived that night so often, she felt as if the life blood of him had seeped through her skin right into her mind.

She walked to the stand near the window, where she poured water from the porcelain jug into the dish and taking up the towel at its side, wet it and dabbed her cheeks and forehead. Straightening her gown, she bent in the gloom to the mirror and refreshed her lipstick. She gazed at herself. 'Come on, Lexi, buck up!' Slowly she moved to the door, and out in the hall, Kathleen was coming towards her.

'Darling?' There was concern in her friend's lovely slanting eyes. 'Are you all right?'

'Yes, I felt faint.'

'You rushed away as if the garden were on fire. I was worried.'

'There was no need to be, though I still feel wretched actually. I don't know what it is. I think I'd like to go home.'

Kathleen showed her amazement. 'What? On your grandfather's

19

birthday?' And now she looked more closely at Lexi. 'Come on, what's wrong? Tell me.'

'I don't know.'

Uncertainty showed in Kathleen's face. 'Are you sure? I've never seen you like this before.'

Lexi shook her head.

'Oh heaven, you're not pregnant, are you?'

'Good lord, no.'

'But surely you don't want to leave?'

Lexi took a deep breath. 'I suppose I'll be all right.'

'Come on then, let's go back to the veranda. You can sit down out there — at least there's a tiny breeze now — and I'll go and let John D know you're all right.' She took her friend's arm and steered her back down the hall, but Lexi halted.

'No, Kathy. I'd rather not. I don't want to be caught up with people yet. I still feel odd. Look, I'll go to the rotunda for a while.'

The rotunda was on the far side of the house, away from the garden and the party. Being winter it was bare, but in the solid heat of summer it was wrapped in passion flowers and crisp pink orchids. It was the haven where her grandfather had liked to read the *South China Morning Post* years ago when he had good eyesight, and where he still sat for hours every day.

The two women made their way through the house, and when Kathleen had installed Lexi in amongst soft rosebud cushions and placed a glass of water in her hand and given her an aspirin tablet, she felt her friend's forehead. 'You don't seem to have a temperature. I'll tell John D where you are. Will you be all right for a few minutes?'

Lexi pursed her lips. 'Yes, of course. Good lord, girl, I am a doctor.'

'And I'm a nurse and you've got me worried.' Kathleen patted Lexi's hand and turned away as Lexi sat back and closed her eyes. She could hear the music of the dance band playing near the swimming pool, and it soothed her.

*   *   *

As Kathleen hurried back to John Drayton, she saw him deep in conversation with Chris Webster. They stood together under the jacaranda tree near the bar, both drinking beer, Chris's back resting up against the trunk and his companion's feet planted in grass beneath the outstretched boughs.

A curious look flashed over the American's face, modifying the resident indifference there, as he took a swig of the sweet local beer. He had not expected to see Captain John Drayton Whitby, and it would have been a very pleasant surprise except for the twist of fate that had him married to the Doll. Now that had shocked him, and shock was not an intimate of his. Seeing her again had been bad enough, but realising that she was married to Johnny had knocked him out. But hell, that was life: you messed with everybody, even people you liked ... and you didn't even know you were doing it.

He felt certain the only ones who were aware of anything were himself and the Doll and he had not been surprised when she rushed away. Sure, it had disturbed him seeing her again, he could not deny it. But he wished her to hell all the same.

Johnny had collared him immediately Kathleen and Della Seaforth had left them, and now here they were reminiscing when what he really wanted to do was get out of here. Johnny was obviously so pleased to see him and was still talking about the time they had spent together in Kuala Lumpur. John Drayton's finger wagged in the air. 'And what about the night in the Nyonya family's hut in that kampong on the Ampang Road? Best nasi goreng I ever had. I can still see the luminous face of the man in the moon peering down at us through those blasted glutinous rain clouds. We were soaked just after we left the kampong for the barracks, weren't we?'

'Yes, we were, but it was a swell night.'

'I reckon. You know I went off to that special training course I told you about. Three months in Borneo it was, with some blokes from England. And I raised a commando unit in Malaya this year.

21

Had a bright lieutenant called Wade organising another. They're probably not far from Kuala Lumpur right now, as a matter of fact.' He smiled. 'But I wasn't reckoning on seeing you again.' John Drayon's voice dropped and his tone became confidential. 'You had a different name then.'

Hank Trapperton nodded. The only one here who even knew his nickname of Trap was the Doll. He raised an eyebrow. 'Yeah, that's right, I guess I did.'

'We all reckoned we knew what you were, you know. Spending three months in Tokyo passing yourself off as an Argentinian businessman.'

'Oh you did, huh?'

'Sure. I don't know how much notice the brass took of the intelligence you passed on to us, but it woke me up. I've been expecting the Japs to attack us ever since.'

Trap was looking at Johnny and feeling strangely guilty. It sat oddly with him. Why did he have to like Johnny so damn much? How in Hades could he be married to *her*?

John Drayton went barrelling on. 'You know, I recall telling you in KL that I was going to marry Lexi.' He grinned. 'Hey? What do you think of her?'

What do I think of her? Shit, what a question. Trap took a deep breath. 'She seems great . . . swell. When you told me about her you never mentioned her name.'

'Didn't I? Her real name's Lexine, it's from the old Greek, but she prefers Lexi. You know we decided to marry war or no war; why not have a little happiness?'

'Right. Sure.'

'I've been trying to get her out of here. You know how vulnerable this place is, damned vulnerable. The repatriation of women and children was virtually over eighteen months ago, except for those who pulled strings and got permission to stay like Lexi's grandmother. And of course there are still some in the essential services, like Lexi.'

'I noticed a lot of your military and officials don't exactly seem to mind. The married ones appear to be having a whale of a time with their old ladies away in Australia. Place I was in last night over in the Western District was full of them, most with Chinese girls on their arms.'

John Drayton knew this: the name they gave these local girls was 'adoped daughters'.

'Anyway,' his companion continued, 'you reckon you know my line of business – well the way I see it, it seems the Japs think that Hitler's got the British where he wants them, and that means they won't delay much longer. So do exactly what you just said. Get your wife and anyone else you love out of Hong Kong. Jap spies and informers are all over this place. Their consulate over-looks the naval dockyard, for Christ's sake! They know all there is to know about the defences of Hong Kong. Take it from me, they want all of South-East Asia and more. There'll be no declaration of war. They'll play dirty and simply attack . . . soon.'

John Drayton agreed. It made for a sombre future. 'How soon?'

Trap drew his finger across his throat for emphasis. 'Well, Johnny, I'll answer that by saying, once I've attended to a few things I won't be hanging around here.'

'Right. Exactly what I think. I'm going anyway, I've orders to fly out with the liaison unit to Singapore, so I really must get Lexi out of here with her aunt when she sails on Sunday.'

A flicker of interest appeared in the American's eyes. 'Sails for where? Australia?'

'Yes. Lexi's mother lives in Queensland, married to a man who owns coal mines.'

'Nice.'

'Very.'

'Where exactly?'

'Ipswich. A town in Queensland.'

'I know it. Twenty or so miles from Brisbane.'

'That's right. Gosh, you get around.'

23

'I was there once taking a look at things.'

John Drayton raised an eyebrow. 'Whatever that means.'

'I go lots of places. The Australian communists were very active against the war effort at that time. I was fact-finding.'

At that moment General Charles Maltby, commanding officer of the British forces in Hong Kong, came walking by with his aide and the newly arrived Canadian, Brigadier John Lawson. John Drayton saluted and the generals replied in kind.

Trap watched as Maltby moved out of earshot. 'Lot of big brass here tonight.'

'Indeed. Lexi's grandfather knows them all. Actually he's a fascinating old bloke. Began his military career at nineteen, and at twenty-two he was with General "Chinese" Gordon in Equatoria while he mapped the Upper Nile River and established a line of communication stations.'

'You don't say?'

'Fought in the Zulu war in eighteen seventy-nine too.'

This was certainly an impressive past and Trap turned to glance across at Sir Brillard, who sat with Sek Yau Yu, the film director and actor, as John Drayton took his arm. 'Come on, I'll introduce you.'

'Well, actually, Mrs Seaforth did that on the way in.'

'So now you'll get to have a yarn with him.'

They finished their beers and crossed over to their host and as they approached, his Chinese companion stood and moved away. Sir Brillard smiled up at his granddaughter's husband. He liked John Drayton: he was steady and reliable and was a fine amateur war historian. Sir Brillard enjoyed challenging the younger man on the dates and facts of various battles.

'Sir . . . I know you met my friend earlier, Chris Webster.'

The elderly man rose.

'No need to get up, sir.'

Sir Brillard's colourless eyes sparked. 'Why not? I can get up to speak to you, don't worry about that. My legs haven't gone on me yet. Might have failing eyesight, young fella, but the blasted legs are as good as ever.' He held out his hand and the visitor took it.

'Well, I'm glad to hear that.'

'Me too as they're my legs. I'm ninety today and I'm going to dance later, show you young chaps just how good they really are.' He stepped closer to Trap. 'So, Mr Chris Webster, you sound like an American.'

'I am.'

'Where from?'

'Virginia, sir.'

'Ah, one of the original thirteen colonies. Good place to be born. And what do you do?'

The American met John Drayton's eyes over the knight's shoulder. 'I'm a surveyor, sir.'

'Surveyor, eh? Well I did a bit of that in Equatoria a lifetime ago. Bit dull, eh? Not a lot going on in surveying.'

His guest grinned. 'Actually I like my work, Sir Brillard. Sometimes it's very exciting.'

The elderly man was taken aback. He shook his head. 'Is that so? Surveying, exciting? Well, it must have changed a mighty lot since my time, young fella, that's all I can say.'

Trap's expression of mirth remained. 'I believe you fought the Zulus, sir.'

'Yes. Now there was a warrior race for you. Could run thirty miles and fight a battle afterwards. They'd be a match for the blasted Nazis. I accompanied Chief Cetowayo to London, you know.'

The American shook his head. 'No, I didn't know, there seems no end to the fascinating things you've done.' He could see across the lawn to the dance floor where the Eurasian woman was advancing towards them. 'When was that, sir?'

'Early eighties. Met my darling Helvetia there. Married her two months later and we've lived happily ever after.'

Kathleen arrived beside them. 'I found Lexi. She's not well and I've given her an aspirin. She's resting in the rotunda. I think you should go and see her, John D.' Kathleen often used this shortened form of his name.

'Of course I shall.' He turned to Sir Brillard. 'Excuse me, sir, I'd better see what's wrong.'

The knight's concern was evident. 'What seems to be the matter with her?'

Kathleen replied as John Drayton absently handed his beer glass to her. 'I'm not sure, Sir Brillard. She's just a little off colour.' She held the glass in both hands and watched Lexi's husband closely as he departed, following his progress as he strode away.

Sir Brillard grunted. 'Don't like sickness of any kind. Have to fight it, you know. Lexi's not one to fall ill as a rule.' He eased himself down into a chair. 'Now off you go, you two; don't hang around here. A young man and woman should be dancing.'

He waved them off and the American held out his palm to Kathleen. 'We mustn't disappoint him.' She put down the glass and accompanied him to the dance floor, and as they moved into a waltz Trap tilted his head back to look at his partner. 'How long have you been in love with Johnny?'

Kathleen coloured as she replied, 'What on earth do you mean?'

'What I said. It's unmistakable.'

'It can't be.'

'It is to me.'

'How ridiculous.'

'If you say so. But your secret's safe with me.'

'Mr Webster, if you continue with this silliness, I'll leave the dance floor.'

He held her more tightly. 'Then I'll talk about something else. Tell me, how long have you known his wife?'

As John Drayton advanced towards his wife seated in the rotunda, he noticed her head was leaning back on a white pillar, and as he came closer, his feet silent on the grass, he noticed she stared into space with a faraway, trance-like expression. He had seen a kindred look many times before on Lexine's face and it disturbed him.

'Darling, are you all right?'

She sat upright. 'Oh . . . there you are, dear. I'm feeling a little better.' She realised that if they left the party it would create more than a stir, and she had been thinking that perhaps she could manage to stay and simply keep clear of *him* for the rest of the night.

John Drayton kissed her. 'Perhaps you did too much today. Staying at the hospital for all those hours.'

'Yes, perhaps.'

He kissed her again. 'Well, we'll sit here for a minute. I must say it's a tranquil, nice spot to recover.'

She closed her eyes again. 'Mmm.'

'You know, Lexi, it's just great seeing that Yank again. I couldn't believe it. He's the one I've told you about, the fellow who passed himself off as an Argentinian in Tokyo. He's never admitted it, of course, but he's in the American Secret Service, no doubt about it.'

She did not open her eyes. 'Yes . . . yes, I remember.' It was true, Johnny had spoken often about the American intelligence officer he had met in Malaya. God in heaven! And now she knew exactly who he was.

Just then the rumble of a drum roll swelled around them. It was followed by the loud voice of the new governor, Sir Mark Aitchinson Young. 'Attention, please. You all know why we're gathered tonight. It's to celebrate ninety years of a remarkable life. The life of a man who has been mentor and friend to many of you gathered here tonight as well as patriarch of a wonderful family. He's one of Hong Kong's finest men and I'm delighted to be here. We ask you all to move to the tables and take your seats for the dinner in his honour.'

Lexi opened her eyes. 'Oh Lord. Well, come on, I'll have to be all right.' She stood and straightened her dress.

'You look wonderful.'

She managed a weak smile. 'Thanks.'

Sir Brillard and Lady Hayes sat side-by-side at the head table with their family and the VIPs arranged around them. After the toasts and speeches – kept short by dictate of Sir Brillard – John Drayton changed places with the hostess and leant into his grandfather-in-law's ear.

'Lady Helvetia mentioned you wished to speak to me about Lexine's leaving Hong Kong.'

'I do, son. I want to tell you that I've taken matters into my own hands and booked passage for her and for Della and the rest of the family. They sail on Sunday on the SS *Fortitude*. It's a miracle I got them on. I want your agreement that I've done right.'

'Oh yes, indeed you have, sir. I've been trying to convince her now for a damn year. But it'll come as a surprise to her. How do you propose to get her aboard?'

'Leave it to me. I'll see her tomorrow.' He grinned. 'If she won't go by fair means, I'll use foul.'

'I feel I've failed. I should have been able to persuade her.'

'Now, son, that's not so. Getting Lexi to do anything she has no mind to do is arduous.'

The party was all over by a few minutes after ten p.m. Sir Brillard did not enjoy late nights.

Lexi had managed to avoid the American, who was seated at another table, but she was very aware when he left the party half an hour before it ended. He looked towards her as he departed but she turned away.

Later, as she said good night to her aunt and grandparents, Sir Brillard held her at arm's length, his hands gripping her shoulders. 'Come and see me tomorrow on your way home from the hospital. We'll take tea in the rotunda. I've something special to talk over with you.'

* * *

Lexi and John Drayton drove Kathleen home. She kissed Lexi and stood from the car as the light wind lifted her ebony hair from her shoulders. John Drayton pushed her dancing hair back and kissed her on the cheek and she stood waving while the Austin pulled away, its boot gleaming in the wan light from a single street lamp as it rounded the corner. She sighed and turned to the house she shared with her mother, unlocked the green ornamental gate and slipped through to open her front door.

'Is that you, darling?' The voice came from the top of the narrow staircase to the second floor. 'Come up.'

Kathleen climbed the stairs to the balcony where the limbs of a fiddlewood tree grew in through the latticework of the side wall. She ran her hand across its smooth wood as she passed and the two parakeets that were her mother's pride and joy called from their cage under a golden drape nearby.

Inside the ornately decorated bedroom, Bess Leigh lay propped up with pillows and covered in a rug. An ink drawing of her childhood home in Queensland — a colonial-style house with wide verandas circumnavigating it — hung incongruously amongst the dragons and gold brocade that decorated the wall. Bess's face lit up at the sight of her only child and she opened her arms and hugged her daughter; even such minor exertion making her breathless.

'How . . . did Sir Brillard enjoy his party?'

'He was in fine form. Even danced a short waltz.'

'That's nice . . . Did Della dance?'

'Oh yes, Mama, and she looked lovely. Wore such a pretty dress.'

'Tell me all about it.'

Bess listened with a quiet smile, though her breathing was laboured, and when Kathleen could see her mother was close to sleep she rose, administered the two heart tablets the woman took nightly and kissed her mother's forehead.

Kathleen's gaze rested on the sepia photo in the silver filigreed frame that sat on the cedar table by the bed. It depicted her father

29

standing on the steps of a wooden building beside an elaborately carved veranda post. He had been a Chinese landowner and had met her mother at a mission station in Yunnan province, not far from the city of Kunming where Bess had been one of three Australian volunteers in the Christian mission there. He had died when Kathleen was only a baby. The photo showed a man with clean-shaven face and black eyes, tall for his race. His jet black hair Kathleen had inherited.

Her father's name had been Lee Tain Sen, and when, after his death, her mother had left China and decided to live in the British colony of Hong Kong, she took the Anglicised spelling of Leigh as her own.

When Kathleen had asked why they had not returned to Australia after her father had died, her mother explained that there was nowhere to go. She had been raised in a tiny place called Stanthorpe, where farms of apple orchards dotted the land and the winter landscape was icy with frost, where the flowers of the valley grew in wild profusion and where her parents had died one Michaelmas Eve. 'There was a terrible fire and it took them both. After that I left and became a missionary, my darling. There was nothing to draw me back to Australia and I have preferred to stay here in the Orient, where I have good friends and feel closer to your father.' She would sigh and end with, 'Yes, Hong Kong has been good to us.'

Kathleen's slender fingers stroked the silver of the photo frame. 'Goodnight, Father,' she whispered, and her mother's pale eyes followed her to the door.

Chapter Four

The morning sun insinuated its yellow fingers into the corners of the garden to find Lexi seated on a wicker chair, her thoughts a jumble. She had taken breakfast alone after John Drayton had gone to the Fort, and now paper and pen and ink stood on the low stone table at her side; the letter which she had been writing had been interrupted by her reflections many minutes previously.

Last night had revived the memories she had wanted to lie buried for always.

Johnny had woken this morning and caressed her gently, as the dawn in duplication had stroked Kowloon and Hong Kong. He had drawn her to him and kissed her shoulder, the warmth of his tongue kneading her skin, and as his hands cupped her breasts and his mouth found her nipples, she had rolled from him with the words, 'No, Johnny. I'm sorry, I'm still not feeling right.'

He had lain still and watched her bare back for some seconds before replying. 'All right, sweetheart, I'm sorry you still feel off colour. I insist you rest today. I won't allow you to go into the hospital.'

'Johnny, please. There's so much to do and we're short-staffed. But I promise I'll rest for a few hours and go in a little later.'

He had grudgingly agreed and immediately after breakfast had departed for Fort Stanley.

She had not lied when she said she was still feeling sick. Johnny had talked incessantly about the American last night on the drive home and then again as they readied for bed; he had even suggested they see him again before he left. 'He's staying at the Barnacle Club. And Lexi, you can really talk to him. He's intelligent and well read, went to Brown University and West Point. He's no slouch. You'll love him.' That was the phrase which had really made her stomach turn.

Her eyes were trained on the honeysuckle vine meandering over the stone wall in front of her when abruptly into her vision shot a shoe and a leg, followed by the body that belonged to them. The man jumped to the ground.

She rose to her feet in fright before she saw who it was. 'You!'

'Uh-huh, me.'

'What the devil . . . ?'

'Yes, I suppose you could call me that.' He crossed to her. 'It's taken me a little while to find you.'

Lexi did not speak. She simply watched him.

He eased his body back on to the honeysuckle-covered wall and looked her up and down. 'You haven't altered. Still the same face and hair, same mouth, same body. I remember it all, Doll.'

'What do you want?'

The tone of his voice was like the expression in his eyes, dispassionate and icy, but his answer carried a myriad of emotions. 'Well, Doll, for a start maybe I'd like to hear just why you left me high and dry. Why you made a sucker out of me. A guy who'd never been fooled before in his goddam life.' He gave a caustic laugh. 'Or maybe I wouldn't like to hear it after all. Two years later I find you all married, neat and snug.'

He paused, and a heavy silence hung between them until he broke it. 'Or then perhaps you'd like to know – for your quiet contemplations on afternoons sitting here in the comfortable twilight – that when I came back to the bedroom and found you gone that morning, I went to the Women's Club. There I was informed you were a doctor and that you'd gone to the Javanese hospital on the far side of the island.' Abruptly his voice oozed sarcasm and he stood upright from where he had been leaning. 'And listen to this one, it'll give you a laugh. I rode over to the hospital on what they call a road in that part of the world: a four-hour journey! And you weren't there. But then you know that. You'd caught the noon clipper to Surabaya. Zippo! Gone!'

His tone returned to neutral; it was passionless again. 'The good old Dutch superintendent at the hospital was kind enough to inform me you'd departed the island for good. I can see him now pulling on his goatee and saying something had upset you and he'd granted you and a female friend permission to vacate your positions a day prematurely. Now how about that?

'He was also forthcoming enough to tell me you were returning home to be married . . . And here's the best part: the wedding was just a few weeks away.'

He made the words *married* and *wedding* sound like curses, and immediately dropped again into the disinterested tone. 'Oh, he was a nice old guy, obviously had a soft spot for you. He must have guessed what was on my mind because he asked me not to interfere. Said you'd been engaged to a soldier for two years. His exact words were: "Lexi Robinson's in love. Don't spoil a lot of lives, son, it wouldn't be right. Leave her alone."'

He gave a grating laugh. 'Now like the sucker I was, I then asked where home for you might be, but he wouldn't tell me. I asked a lot of people but there was a code of silence on Madura Island. It took a couple of days and all my skill, but I finally persuaded one of the sons of good old Lakey to spit out the truth. He told me you were to be married in Hong Kong.'

He stepped closer and now the coldness in his tone was like a glacier forming. 'So I took the hint, honey, and left you alone. I went back to what I was supposed to be in Java for, and in any case there were a few pals of the blasted Japs you met who were out looking for me.

'I never would have come to Hong Kong, but the truth is, in my line of work I have no choice. So I arrive and here you are.

And as if that's not enough, you're married to a swell guy I happen to know. Jesus, Doll, how do you do it?'

Lexi could not help it; she said it before she could check herself: 'I've thought about you every single day.'

'Well have you now? So isn't that just something. Gee whiz. Yippee!'

Lexi's hand lifted between them, palm towards him. 'Don't, this isn't fair . . .'

'Fair? What the hell do I care about fair? I was ready to marry you, for Christ's sake!'

Lexi's throat felt like it was closing and tears were hiding just out of sight. 'How could I be sure? It was one night, for heaven's sake.'

'Not to me.' And now the sarcasm was back in his tone. 'But that is inevitably how it turned out.'

'I didn't think I could let Johnny down. I was guilt-ridden. I was brought up to keep my promises. I know it was wrong now.'

'Wrong? Too right it was goddam wrong. So hurt the Yank . . . he doesn't matter.'

'No, please, it wasn't like that. I've told myself a thousand times I stayed with you that night because I was frightened after the attack on us. But I know that's not true. I stayed because I wanted to. If I could do it all again . . . I wouldn't leave you.'

He showed a brief sign of frustration, slamming his hands together and looking away, and in that second a voice sounded behind them. 'Ah there you are, Miss Lexi. I been wonderin' where you are. Been lookin' around for you.'

Lexi spun round and there was Nintuck coming towards them, her small feet stepping lightly over the grass and held firmly in her bony arms was Lexi's fifteen-month-old son, Paul.

Lexi hurried over to the Chinese nanny. 'I'm busy. A friend of Captain Whitby's arrived suddenly and I've been talking to him. Please take Paul inside. I'll be along soon.'

The nanny's eyes narrowed. She did not recall anyone coming

to the front door, and as she cast an interested glance at the visitor the infant cried, 'Mama,' and held out his arms, exposing on the inside of his tiny left wrist a dark birthmark. Lexi kissed him swiftly before gently pushing Nintuck in the direction of the house. 'Go now.'

The nanny glanced back. 'You should leave soon for hospital.'

'I know, I know.'

Nintuck trotted away as Lexi returned across the garden. She was trembling. Mechanically she wrung her hands while Trap stood motionless, his face unreadable as she spoke. 'I think it's best you go, but tell me one thing.'

'What on earth would that be, Doll?'

'Your real name.'

He paused so long that Lexi thought he had not heard her.

He was thinking. He had already broken that particular rule by telling her his real nickname in Madura on the night when he had adored her body and soul.

He moved a step closer to her; he could smell the aroma of her and it disturbed the hell out of him. 'I told you the truth in Java . . . It's Trap.'

She felt comforted, gratified that he had told her the truth two years ago. 'Trap who?'

'Don't do this, Doll . . . that's all I can say.'

'Please.'

He was torn. He hated her; he loved her. Shit! She was looking at him with those blasted blue eyes like an August sky above the Appalachian Trail. 'My name's Hank Trapperton.' He looked past her and added softly, 'As I told you once, my friends call me Trap.'

She repeated it. 'Trap . . . Hank Trapperton.'

He spoke across her words. 'I'm leaving now; I'll go the same way I came. But before I do, it's my turn to ask something.'

'Yes?'

'Don't ever mention my real name to your husband, because nobody here knows it.'

'Of course.'

'He's a good guy.'

'Yes, he is.'

He paused a moment. 'Look, Doll, this is important. Just do like your husband wants you to and leave Hong Kong. With all your British and Canadian troops you total perhaps ten thousand men. Up till now we thought there were about five thousand Japanese on the mainland opposite, but I've learnt this morning that there might in fact be ten times as many . . . It'll be a walkover, no matter how hard the defenders fight. Truth is, I wouldn't want you to be here if . . .' He shrugged before straightening his shoulders. It was somehow a despondent final movement and filled her with despair. 'Goodbye, Doll.'

She made herself reply. 'Goodbye.'

She watched him turn and climb the wall, and within ten seconds she was alone in the corner of the garden, the honeysuckle vine a blur in her misty vision.

At least now when she thought of him she could use his real name.

Her head dropped forward and the tears that had floated in her eyes fell at last. He had not even mentioned her son . . . He had acted as if he hadn't seen the child at all. Perhaps she should be glad.

Chapter Five

Lexi was at the Queen Mary Hospital by 11.30 a.m. It stood solidly on a hill above Pokfu Lam Road, and she and Kathleen had worked in it since its founding in 1937, with one year away in Madura. The hospital corridors were familiar and comfortable. She made her rounds and attended the sick, but she was thinking of all the times Johnny had asked her to leave Hong Kong and take little Paul. At the back of her mind Trap's parting words played a rhythm in her head: We thought there were about five thousand Japanese ... but I've learnt today that there might in fact be ten times as many ... It'll be a walkover ... I wouldn't want you to be here if ... That last phrase had brought her to wishful thinking.

At the end of her shift she left by the front door and saw Kathleen waiting for her on the veranda. In summer the two friends swam together at Repulse Bay after day duty, but as it was winter they usually went shopping or had a cup of green tea at Tina Hung's, a small café on the Pokfu Lam Road past the university. As Lexi approached along the veranda Kathleen rose from a bamboo chair to greet her.

They walked side-by-side to the stone steps. Lexi's Austin was parked down the hill behind a cluster of lantana about fifty yards away, and as they began to descend the steps they heard running footsteps behind them and looked round.

Scuttling along the veranda towards them was Len Sumatu, the only Japanese doctor at the hospital, an orthopaedic surgeon and a good one. He was larger than many of his race, and the only marring of his quite attractive features was a vast series of pockmarks which ran down his throat on the left side of his neck. Kathleen had told Lexi that all the nurses maintained he was notorious for his womanising, and that they tried not to be alone with him.

Sumatu was one who always stopped and talked, but to their surprise he swept by the two women covering the four steps to the ground in one jump, and ran off down the slope. They waited to see who his pursuer was, but no one followed and they watched him disappear in the trees towards the university proper.

'Wonder what's wrong with him?'

Kathleen gave a giggle. 'Some nurse's husband might have turned up.'

An hour later, Lexi left Kathleen outside Tina Hung's and drove off to meet her grandfather, just as he had requested on his birthday.

She drank another cup of sweet green tea with Sir Brillard and ate light fluffy scones with strawberry jam and cream and chatted about the hospital, little Paul and other matters until Sir Brillard placed down his cup, wiped his fingers on his serviette and leant a little forward in his chair to stroke the rich red hair of his aristocratic Irish setter Harold, who lay at the old man's feet.

He looked hard at Lexi as he spoke. 'My darling, John D has told me you are still adamant about not leaving Hong Kong.'

She made to reply but he lifted his hand from Harold for silence. 'Let me finish, then you can say whatever you like.'

'Sorry, Pa.'

'I know your husband has attempted many times to persuade you to take Paul and leave the island sooner than you want to. Lexi, the time has come for me to be brutally honest. You're not thinking of your child. You're a grown-up and have the right to make the decision to remain till January, but you're doing wrong by little

Paul, who has no choice in the matter. You see, my dear, there's every reason to believe the Japanese will attack and the child could die. Time's running out for us. I have no doubt whatever that the Japanese are coming. Ever since they signed that mutual defence pact with Germany and Italy, the writing's been on the wall.

'I've lived many decades and seen much, and I know that in their culture they hold a complete disregard for lower ranks and prisoners; in fact it goes so far as to be contempt. They treat their own soldiers badly so a prisoner has no value at all. They count being vanquished as dishonourable, and one of the first tenets of their belief is that honour is paramount.

'My darling girl, I'm not talking about *if* the Japanese come; I am talking about *when*. I've been a soldier and have seen what soldiers – even those who respect the enemy – are capable of doing. I know there are still many here who are sanguine about whether there will be an assault or not, but that is wishful thinking. For when they do attack this citadel, it will fall. It's not good military strategy to waste more men defending it, and it seems to me that in sending us the two Canadian regiments Mr Churchill has done it merely to make us feel a little safer, for it will mean nothing in the end. They'll be lost along with the British regiments and the Gurkhas and Indians already here.'

His tone had become unequivocal and his Wellington-like face assumed the aspect of an ageing hawk in the fading day.

'And Lexi, we'll put up a spirited defence, but if one doesn't die in the resistance, then one will be a prisoner. A station devoid of dignity if it's the Japanese who are your masters.

'Much of the China coast is occupied by the Japanese. We have only a narrow strip of water between them and us. There are many here who want to get out now and cannot. And you'll have noticed the lack of sampans and fishing craft in the harbour. There's a reason for all that, my girl.'

Lexi went to speak, but he again raised his palm to her. 'On your wedding day I suggested you depart; last Christmas I urged

39

you to go, and now, my lovely girl, I'm telling you!' He gave the suggestion of a sigh. 'I've taken a liberty, my darling, and told Dr Campbell at the hospital that you won't be back, and I've booked passage for you and the family on the only ship available: a little Dutch tub, steamship called *Fortitude*, heading to Borneo, New Guinea and Australia. Your aunt was meant to travel on the SS *Rangoon* but it isn't even coming here because most British and Allied shipping's been diverted to Singapore. That the *Fortitude* is here and leaving on Sunday is a miracle. I only pray it's not too late.' He sat back in his seat.

'But Pa, the Japanese haven't declared war.'

He gave a dismissive shake of his head. 'They never have in all their previous wars, so I'm thinking they won't now.'

His granddaughter reached out and touched his hand. 'Pa, I do understand all you've said. Fact is it's sort of hit me in the last twenty-four hours, so I'm not going to argue. You say you've booked passage for all of us?'

'Yes, even though your Uncle Jasper was at first adamant about not going along.'

'But what about you?'

His faded eyes flickered with an earlier fire. 'I've had many decades upon this earth. Hydrangea is my castle; there is no other life for me.'

'But Pa, you've just told me there's no hope for those who stay in Hong Kong.'

He gave her a rueful smile before he raised his aged veined hand and stroked her cheek. 'Now let's leave that where it lies. Your husband agrees with all I say. So, sweetheart, home you go and start to pack. Don't waste any more time here.'

Lexi hugged him and cried, sobbing like she had as a child upon his still firm shoulder, and as she wept, he told her that four months previously he had transferred all his money from Hong Kong to Sydney. 'It was all for your grandmother, but she has made her choice to remain with me; hence I've made arrangements to divide it between your mother, your Aunt Della and Uncle Peter, Uncle Jasper and yourself.'

Lexi left him when his young friend, the Englishman, George Wright-Nooth, the second-in-command of the Central and Western Divisions of the Royal Hong Kong Police Force arrived for a cup of tea and a chat. They sat on the front porch and waved goodbye to her. On the drive home, the chilling truth had indeed set in for Lexi, and when John Drayton telephoned her that evening she informed him of her altered decision.

'It all makes sense now, I suppose, Pa's adamant that the Japanese are coming. He's frightened the hell out of me.'

'I don't mind, as long as he's convinced you to go.'

'And the dear old so-and-so went and booked passage for me without mentioning it. The *Fortitude*, a Dutch ship. All the family are sailing out on it, except for him and Grandma.'

'I know.'

'So you were in on absolutely everything?'

'Lexi, please ... Haven't I been asking you to leave for over a year?'

'Yes.'

'Then I was doing the right thing, wasn't I?'

'Oh Johnny, I suppose so.'

'I'll be home later. Have to come in for a few hours in the morning, but that's it. I've been given compassionate leave for my final days in Hong Kong. I still wish you and the baby were out of here before me, and not afterwards.'

'God, I don't know how I'll be ready.'

'You'd better be. When will you tell the hospital?'

'Oh, Pa in his wisdom took that licence too. No wonder dear old Campbell looked at me strangely when I left this evening. But I'll go in and say a proper farewell to them all.'

'Right. I'll see you in a few hours. Don't wait up. Good night, sweetheart. You understand I love you, don't you?'

41

'Yes, Johnny. Dear Johnny. Good night, Johnny.'

She went to bed and heard her husband come in around eleven. They were both up by seven and breakfasted together. When he departed she began to pack, but immediately after lunch she kissed Paul and passed him to Nintuck to put down for his nap. Out in the street alone she hailed a rickshaw. Half an hour later she alighted into the winding road that led up from the bottom of the Peak past the Barnacle Club.

Once in front of the two-storey brick building she gazed around. Opposite was a street market where locals sold everything from beer to beads and blankets. She crossed to it and found a vantage point where she kept a view of the front door of the club. With ease she parried the approaches made to her by the Chinese eager to sell their wares and she remained standing between the fragile wooden stalls and a stone wall on their perimeter.

An hour went by and a crisp wind flurried down the hill and as the second hour began she drew her light cardigan more tightly about her. As the time passed she started to think it had been a mistake to come, when all of a sudden she saw him. He appeared carrying a small attaché case from behind a poinciana tree to the left of the building. But he was not alone, for at the same moment, two men who had been seated on the wide veranda stood and marched down the stone steps to meet him. They conversed for some minutes while Lexi watched and to her relief his two companions hailed a rickshaw and left Trap standing alone on the roadside. Briefly he hesitated, then he too hailed a rickshaw.

Instantly she ran across the busy road, avoiding vehicles and bikes, and as he began to step up into the canopied light vehicle she called, 'Trap?'

He halted and turned.

Trap had passed a busy morning. He had been given an assignment to silence a doctor at the Hong Kong hospital: the head of the Japanese agents in Hong Kong. Trap had gone to an address in Kowloon before dawn, only to find an empty apartment and signs of a hasty departure. He had then travelled to the hospital to learn that the man he sought had decamped in haste yesterday. Trap's principal Hong Kong connection had given him a coded message ordering him to leave the colony at 1500 hours; his transport aircraft was ready and waiting at Kowloon airport.

He had returned to the Barnacle Club, packed a single small case with papers and items he must take and left all his clothes hanging in the wardrobe to convince anyone who entered of his intention to remain. He left the club and met briefly in the street with two of his contacts. When they departed he hailed a rickshaw, only to hear her call his name.

He stepped back on to the kerb, handing some coins across to the Chinese rickshaw puller, who grinned widely and departed.

She was gazing up at him as the sun evinced a sheen on his brown hair. Her eyes roamed across his face to the faint scar under his chin; she had first noticed it the night they spent together. She did not feel the sharpness of the wind, but felt flushed and warm.

Trap looked hard at her; staring at her long fair hair resting on the collar of her floral dress, the delicate material pulled taut across her breasts and the blush of colour at her throat. He took a deep breath. 'What the hell are you doing here?'

'I took a chance that I would see you again . . . I wanted to tell you. I'm leaving Hong Kong.'

'When?'

'Sunday.'

'Good.' He wished she were leaving sooner, but did not say so. 'I leave today.'

'Oh.' It was a disappointed sound.

She lifted her hand to shade her eyes, and now she smiled tentatively up at him. 'I wish you luck.' She brought her hand from her brow and touched his sleeve, running her fingers down his arm to rest on the bare skin of his wrist. 'I might never see you again.

Yet I want desperately to see you all the time. Do you understand?'

For a moment he simply lived in the sensation of her skin upon his own. A haze of tenderness almost blurred his vision, but he jolted himself out of that dream as his mouth hardened and roughly he shook off her hand. 'Look, Doll, you're married to a guy I actually like. I said everything I had to say to you yesterday. By all the powers that be, the one and only time I should have seen you was on a grubby, dreary island called Madura where the sun don't shine, but somebody up there is messing with us and so we see each other again. Well that's all it is. Do I understand? Hell no, I don't understand! This is all crazy. I'm leaving . . . you're leaving. We're going in different directions, probably for the rest of eternity. So whether we stand here in the street in Hong Kong getting under each other's skin or not doesn't matter a goddamn.'

She said nothing. Her shoulders drooped with the weight of the truth of all he had said.

'Come on. Get this in perspective. You had your chance with me. Don't do this, Doll. The whole world's a certainty to be at war pretty soon. *Bang!*' She flinched with the impetus he gave the word. 'And what the hell happens to us means nothing.

'Do you know, your husband was here with me this morning? Hey? He wanted to say goodbye. Do you realise what that means? He likes me, damn it, trusts me. For Christ's sake!' He shook his head and momentarily closed his eyes. 'Let's get this straight, Doll . . . this is our final goodbye.'

He stared at her for a heartbeat before he turned away and began walking along the gutter. Her next words stopped him dead. 'He's your son, you know.'

There was a fraction of time when the moving world was suspended for him . . . and then he spun round. His eyes were wide with fury; she thought he was about to strike her down right there in the busy road with the bicycles and rickshaws and bodies streaming all around them. He brought his hand up sharply,

44

threateningly, and she backed away. Then his arm dropped and a strangled sound escaped from his lips. She had never heard anything like it in her life before: soft and quiet though it was, it issued from his mouth like the breath of a thousand tears. 'No! Never speak of it. Never say that again as long as you live! It's not true and I won't hear it. It ... is ... not ... true. You're a liar and a bloody whore, and as far as I'm concerned you can go to hell and take your kid with you!'

And before she could answer he was gone, swiftly lost in the moving bodies of the crowded roadway.

Trap was running now. He had to get out of Hong Kong ... get to the ferry and cross over to Kowloon and meet the transport that was to take him to the Philippines.

This was the last thing he needed. Shit, when he had seen the baby on Sunday, it had given him a real surprise. There in the nanny's arms, the kid with the light brown hair and blue eyes!

Christ, that doll was full of surprises. And sure he had wondered about the baby ... of course he had. The kid was obviously the right age. She had screwed them all up. And poor bloody Johnny, oblivious to the whole stinking mess.

He saw her face in his mind, her lovely, wanton face. He would never forgive her, never. He felt fury gush through him, as if he wanted to kill her.

He was running fast now with the multiplicity of sweet and sour smells of Hong Kong battering his senses, the buildings and markets and trees and people whirling around him. He covered a mile before he slowed down to a walk.

Behind him on the kerb outside the Barnacle Club Lexi stood with the wind lifting her hair. She had told him. Why oh why did I tell him? What good did it do? It was disastrous.

The tears had dried upon her cheeks. She was in love with Trap, a man she would never see again, and she had told him he was the father of her child. The truth had done no good; it had only robbed him of his neutrality. She had betrayed Johnny and betrayed Trap. She felt shrivelled and small and mean and very weary.

Her world was painful, so very painful. She had had her chance. She could have stayed with him. But that had been yesterday, on Madura; this was now, in Hong Kong.

She still watched the road where he had disappeared as if he would reappear; as if he would take her in his arms and tell her he loved her and all would be right.

The wind slapped her hair round into her face, stinging her cheeks, but she did not even lift her hand to stop it. She felt new tears form as she slowly stepped into the street and like an automaton finally raised her arm to call a passing rickshaw.

Chapter Six

Lexi arrived home to find Johnny there. He hugged her close and she returned him a swift kiss with the suggestion they both get on with their packing. For the next few hours, even though she went through the action of choosing those belongings she wanted to take, her thoughts were not on dresses and shoes, hats, handbags and possessions. She felt weak and sad, and every time Johnny passed her with an armful of clothes her guilt was almost too much to stand.

Her mind was possessed by thoughts of Trap and the events of the afternoon, and when Johnny insisted they go out to the Yacht Club for dinner she willed herself to agree. It was a quiet meal, and when halfway through Johnny took up her hand, kissed it and said, 'Where are you, Lexi? Because you aren't here with me', she thought she was going to cry.

She rallied and took a long breath. 'Oh darling, forgive me. I suppose it's just everything. You know . . . I'm finally leaving Hong Kong to go to Australia. And you're off to God knows where and our world is being turned upside down.'

He smiled tenderly. 'I understand.'

The effect of that reply was to make her feel worse.

And later, when they slipped into the ornately carved red sandalwood bed beside the wide window which opened on to the garden, Johnny drew her into his arms and kissed her passionately. He needed her; he was leaving her the day after tomorrow and he did not know when he would hold her again. She was his wife, had borne him a wonderful son and he loved her. He sank into the smell and feel of her, exulting in the taste of her and the smooth undulations of her body. Twice more during the dark hours he reached for her nakedness and loved her greedily again.

Not long after dawn John Drayton was awake and up, and when Lexi rose at seven-thirty she found him already in his uniform and feeding Paul, watched closely by Nintuck. They sat in a sun trap by the kitchen door, the delicate morning light resting on little Paul's pink cheeks. John Drayton left the feeding of his son to Nintuck as he greeted his wife.

'Good morning, sweetheart. I've been asked to attend the Governor's office to give him a report on the Lei Mun Strait defences before I leave. Should be home by lunchtime.'

John Drayton had been in charge of planning parts of the colony's defences. He had blocked the narrow Lei Yue Mun Channel between the colony's north-east end and Devil's Peak on mainland China with booms – floating timber barriers – and would have mined that section of the island's coast if he had had the munitions to do so. He had been perpetually frustrated in his attempts to secure more guns for the coastline of the point facing the Channel and he feared his preparations were inadequate. The areas around the Lei Mun fort and barracks were currently manned by the 5/7 Rajputs, an Indian brigade, and a contingent of the Royal Rifles of Canada, who were game but inexperienced.

John Drayton stood, ruffled his son's hair and kissed Lexi gently on the mouth. She watched his solid straight back disappear into the house and she took over feeding her son.

'You want breakfast, Missus Whitby?'

Lexi did not feel like eating, and her silence brought the request a second time.

'All right, Nintuck, just toast and tea. I'll have it here with Paul.'

The Chinese woman slipped by into the kitchen and Lexi sat staring at Paul hitting the side of the breakfast bowl with his spoon.

Suddenly she was crying, the tears leaked from the corners of her eyes to glide down her cheeks. She felt desperate, but she knew she must be strong and stop allowing this feeling to overwhelm her. 'Buck up, Lexi,' she said aloud, taking a deep breath and blowing her nose on her handkerchief.

By noon two trunks blocked part of the hall outside Lexi's bedroom. The quantity of luggage that passengers could take aboard ship was limited, and later in the week she would wrap those few sentimental items she absolutely could not leave behind. Like the white porcelain goddess that Pa had given her the day of her father's funeral.

Both her mother and grandmother had thought it wrong. 'She's only ten, it's priceless and she'll break it.'

But Sir Brillard had been adamant. 'She needs something special, something important to have completely for her own.'

As he had handed it to her he had spoken softly, 'My sweetheart, this is Kwan Yin, sometimes called Kwannon, she is one of the great bodhisattvas of Chinese Buddhism.'

'What's a body-sat-va, Pa?'

He had tenderly stroked her cheek as he explained, 'Someone who has the opportunity to reach heaven and be forever in glory, but gives it up because of his, or her, great compassion for suffering people.'

Lexi's eyes had widened at such an amazing thing. 'What's compassion, Pa?'

'Pity and caring for the unhappiness of human beings, my darling: fellow feeling, sympathy. Kwan Yin is the perfect goddess for you, my little girl, because she understands your sadness over the loss of your daddy. She's the Chinese Buddhist goddess of mercy and compassion: the two most remarkable of human qualities, which lift us above the common and make us good and special. You would do well to remember them all your life.'

Lexi did remember them; perhaps it was one reason she had become a doctor. And she had not broken the goddess statuette;

she had treasured it. Her Kwan Yin was dressed in sparkling white and sat on a lotus holding a small baby. She had seen numerous depictions of Kwan Yin in the years since, many with multiple arms or eyes and some, just like hers, holding a baby, but none as beautiful as hers, which Pa had told her was from the Ming Dynasty and very precious.

During her formative years Lexi confided her dreams and ideals to Kwan Yin, and even now, as she moved through her bedroom, she lifted the beautiful white figurine from the windowsill and clasped it to her for consolation.

There was a soft sound behind her and she turned to see Nintuck standing in the doorway, her slight figure half hidden in shadow.

'Nintuck, come in. Is everything all right?'

The Chinese woman slipped forward a pace. 'Ah yes, Missus Whitby, little Paul asleep. I come to see if you want lunch?'

Lexi replaced Kwan Yin and beckoned the nanny closer. 'Did Sun Lin come to see you last night?'

Nintuck's eyes lit up and she nodded. Sun Lin was one of the house boys who worked at Hydrangea, and Nintuck was soon to marry him.

Nintuck liked Mrs Whitby very much. She was not one of those Europeans who looked down on the Chinese, and she spoke kindly to all the servants, just the way her husband Captain Whitby did. Nintuck had worked for the Whitbys since their marriage, and she would miss them and baby Paul. But she could not help thinking it would do Mrs Whitby good to be made to be a full-time mother.

'You know the talk is all of the Japanese coming here, don't you?'

Nintuck gave another nod, her voice replete with disgust. '*Loh baak tau!*' she said in Cantonese before she hurried on in her silky smooth voice, 'They long-time enemy of Chinese. If they come they treat us very bad. Treat everyone very bad.'

50

Lexi sighed. 'I wish I could take you with me, Nintuck.'

The Chinese girl gave a benign smile. 'No, Missus Whitby, Nintuck must stay. Must marry Sun Lin. Chinese good at waiting. If enemy come, we wait. We wait, we watch. We try to survive. One day they leave.'

She gave a little bow of her head and began to turn away, but Lexi restrained her. 'I want you to have this.' She took the girl's hand and led her across the tiled floor and the heavy patterned rugs into the handsome living area, where she picked up a large carved ivory box and gave it to the girl. Nintuck's small eyes revealed amazement, for she knew that inside this box was a chess set, and each piece made of solid gold. It was an heirloom from Sir Brillard, and Nintuck would not allow Yun, the maid, to clean the pieces; she did it herself with extreme care.

'I want you to have it, and I know Johnny – Captain Whitby – will too. We cannot take very much with us and this is far too heavy.' Lexi squeezed the girl's hand. 'If . . . if the Japanese do come, this might . . . help you.'

It was plain that Nintuck was uncertain; she stood there holding the box but did not move.

'Nintuck, it's yours. We will see that everyone in this house has something to help them, but this I truly wish you to take for yourself.'

The girl bowed her head over the box. '*Do jey*,' she said quietly, and turned and hastened with tiny steps through the doorway.

That night when the house was quiet Nintuck entered Paul's room through a small rose garden abundant with bushes where the delicate scent of the blooms drifted on the passing breeze.

She crossed to the cot and bent in to the child. He lay on his side with one pudgy baby hand resting on his cheek; she could see the tiny diamond-shaped birthmark on his wrist. He was a beautiful baby with his thick lashes and blue eyes and a crop of light brown curls. He was going out of her life, off on a big ship to Australia, a place so far away she could hardly conceive of it existing at all. She had only ever known Hong Kong and Kowloon, they were the extent of her life vision; anything beyond that seemed unreal.

There was a weight of sadness in her chest as she leant down to him and whispered in Cantonese, 'You are my little one. You have been my charge and I have nurtured you. I bless you, little Paul, with the blessings of my ancestors. I have insight and ability to bestow great gifts or great curses.'

And now a faint melodious incantation followed, before she murmured, 'Upon you I bestow the wondrous elusive gift; it will take care of you in times of trouble and torment.'

She kissed the tips of her fingers and tenderly placed them on the child's body above his heart as she whispered in English, 'I miss you already, little one, for you must go and I must stay.'

Chapter Seven

In the maroon-draped bedroom, decorated with artefacts, figurines, porcelain and vases that had once been for sale in her curio shops, Bess lay on her bed talking to Della Seaforth. On her right side, near the photograph of Lee Tain Sen, stood a ten-inch exquisitely fashioned dragon from the Yuan Dynasty. Bess had been offered fortunes for it but she had refused them. Beside it strutted one of her parakeets; the other was perched on the handle of a silver Buddha-shaped vase. Bess let the birds out of their cages every day and fed them by hand. Confined as she was to sofas and bed, the two parakeets, Liddy and Tot, were a constant source of pleasure to her.

Bess's fingers ran over the dragon, and she spoke to Della, who was sipping black tea. 'You know, these days I often think of when we met.'

Della patted her hand. 'Yes, darling, you'd just come over from China and Kathleen was a wee thing.

'How brave you were to be a missionary. It was only a handful of years after that horrible Boxer Rebellion. I just don't know how you did it. Running up and down that Yellow River in China. It always looked so brown and dirty to me.'

Bess did not say she had never been near the Yellow River; she simply smiled tolerantly as Della prattled on, recalling the day they had met in Bess's shop off the Victoria Road. Lexi had been four and had wandered away from her mother, Marlene, and her

Aunt Della, down the cool dark hall of the shop into the back room where Bess totalled the accounts.

There she and Kathleen, a toddler of three, had begun to play together. On that day, all the friendships had begun.

'And because of you, my Kathleen has always had entrée into the best houses in Hong Kong. How deeply I thank you, dear Della.'

Della's plump fingers patted the back of Bess's thin hand. 'No need. Our friendship has been wonderful, and while I'm looking forward to seeing my sister again, I hate leaving Father and Mother . . . and you.' She leant forward and the tops of her breasts swelled above the neckline of her dress. 'You know, sweetheart, you could come with me.'

Bess shook her head. 'Della dear, be sensible, walking around this small house tires me. I cannot make a journey of any kind. It's my daughter I'd like you to take.'

Della knew this. 'Oh, we'd take her, but she won't leave you.'

Bess leant her head back and closed her eyes. 'I wish there were some way to make her go.'

Della swung her sturdy left leg over her right knee and took up another scone. 'You know, I'm trying to believe that the military are exaggerating things and that the Japanese won't come at all. It's so depressing.'

A few minutes later the mantel clock chimed ten, prompting Della to stand. 'I'll pop in on Saturday evening to say bye bye, darling.'

Bess locked eyes with her friend. 'Thank you for keeping my secret all these years.'

Della obviously knew exactly what Bess meant. 'It's safe, darling, don't worry. Kathleen will never know.'

'You've been wonderful.'

Della looked serious. 'And so have you.'

Liddy and Tot both began to whistle in unison as Della bent forward and clasped her friend's spare body to her rotund bosom.

* * *

Kathleen took a deep breath and removed the black bakelite handset from the tall desk telephone. One lightbulb glowed on the far wall and shadows fell across her desk. The wards were quiet and the six young nurses who reported to her were in another part of the hospital away from the office where she now sat. She rang the telephone exchange and a telephonist answered.

'Number, please?'

Kathleen gave it.

'Putting you through.'

'Good evening, Fort Stanley.'

'Captain Whitby on extension twenty-four, could you put me through please?'

'Who's calling?'

'I'm a friend of his, Kathleen Leigh.'

There was a silence. 'No, he's left the Fort. Won't be back.'

'Oh.' She had hoped he would be at Fort Stanley; it would have been easier talking to him there. She hung up. A few moments later she picked up the telephone receiver again and the same voice asked, 'Number please.'

This time Kathleen gave the Whitby home number.

When John Drayton's voice came over the line she hesitated.

'Good evening, Whitby here . . . Hello. Who's there?'

She hesitated another second. 'John D., it's me, Kathleen.'

His voice registered surprise. 'Kathy! Is everything all right?'

'Oh yes. Hope I'm not calling too late. I just wanted to say . . . Well, you leave on Friday and I hope I'll be seeing you before you go, but in case I don't, I wanted to say goodbye . . .'

'That's nice of you. It's a strange time for all of us.'

Kathleen heard Lexi's voice ask, 'Who is it?'

'Kathy, she's called to say goodbye. I'll put her on to you in a minute, Lex.' He spoke back into the receiver. 'Now, Kathy, you know Lexi wishes you would leave Hong Kong with her.'

'Yes, but I can't go without Mum. She's so ill.'

John Drayton could understand Kathleen's feelings. 'I sympathise with what you're saying, and I don't want to frighten you, but this will be no place for beautiful women like you once . . .' He hesitated. 'Do you understand what I mean?'

'Yes, I do. And while I'm frightened to death, I still can't leave Mum. I'm a nurse after all.'

John Drayton liked Kathy: she was good-natured, a first-rate nurse, a sweet and temperate personality and had been a wonderful friend to Lexi since they were both infants. 'And we all know how much you've done for her.' He paused. 'Look, it isn't my place to talk you round, but I wish I could. In the end it's up to you.'

She nodded into the telephone. 'Yes. Look, John D, thanks anyway. I mean that. It . . . comforts me that you care enough to say all this. And I wish you the best of luck, I really do. I hope . . . the good Lord watches over you and brings you safely through whatever's ahead.'

'And I wish exactly the same for you, Kathy.'

'Time's up. Are you extending, please?'

Kathleen would have gone on talking to him for ever. She attempted to keep her voice light. 'I'd better go then, I'm at work. I've never used the telephone here for a personal call before. Please tell Lexi I'll talk to her tomorrow.'

'I hope I see you before I leave. Goodbye, Kathy.'

The line went dead and Kathleen replaced the receiver in its hook and sat staring at it. She had dared to call him and hear his voice. She hoped with all her heart that he would stay safe and that no harm would come to him. A tear slipped down her cheek and she brushed it away with her fingers.

At the other end of the line Lexi called to her husband. 'Thought she was going to talk to me?'

'Yes, darling, well, time was up.'

It was six a.m. when Kathleen came off duty. A fresh breeze washed straight across the island and the air tasted sweet, though a heavy dew had formed on the plants and grass, and clouds bunched on the horizon threatening rain. She could hear mynah birds calling as she caught her bus and the city woke and vehicles and people – the elderly in black and the youth brighter colours – began to appear.

She descended near her home, walking briskly in the cool morning, and when she gained the entrance of her house she saw movement through the ironwork and recognised Shamoi, her mother's maid. The woman stood from the steps where she had obviously been waiting and hastened forward to slide back the gate.

Shamoi was trembling; her face was wan and her tone the same. 'Oh, Miss Kathleen, your mother . . .' She burst into tears and hung her head.

Kathleen dashed into the house and up the stairs. She took the steps two by two, her heart thumping as she raced by the fiddlewood tree along the balcony and entered her mother's room.

Bess lay dead, her face stiff and strange. Her hands with their long elliptical nails rested outside the coverlet, fingers twined, the gold and jade antique ring on her little finger and the veins dark against the parchment colour of her skin; around her throat lay her favourite dragon pendant. Kathleen had seen many dead people; hundreds during her working life, but they had been patients. This was her mother, her own darling mother!

Liddy and Tot out on the landing screeched wildly as if they too knew full well what had occurred and voiced their suffering.

Kathleen stood transfixed. She was aware that Shamoi had entered the room behind her.

Abruptly she fell to her knees and buried her head in her mother's side. 'Muma, Muma . . .' Minutes passed before she lifted her face to look round at Shamoi standing inertly beside her. 'Did she will it? Did she simply will herself to die?'

The maid did not speak.

Kathleen remained kneeling and lifted her hand to her mother's face to stroke it with trembling fingers. 'Muma darling, it seems you wanted me to leave here very, very badly.'

Chapter Eight

The following day, and a thousand miles to the east, rain spattered on Trap's face while the rising wind caught at his tunic. He strode past a row of coconut palms where all forms of vehicles, both military and private, dotted the landscape, while at his side marched Labratte, a second lieutenant in one of the local intelligence units. Labratte suspected the man he accompanied was important. He knew his visitor was a major, had top priority clearance, had just arrived from Hong Kong and was here to see General MacArthur.

'What was the boat ride from Hong Kong like, sir?'

Trap nodded. 'Like any boat ride in a big sea, Lieutenant. It stank.'

'Yes, sir.'

Trap had not come in by boat, but in his business, hiding the truth was the first law, so whatever the hell Labratte believed to be true was okay by him. He had in fact flown out of Kowloon on Wednesday and arrived here on the lumbering aircraft four hours later.

He kept thinking about her; she drifted at the edges of his perception. For the first time in his life his emotions were having their own way with his mind. Trap hated that. When she had left him that morning in Madura, he had wished her to hell and managed to clear her from his brain in the belief he would never see her again. But fate had betrayed him, and now after Hong

Kong here she was lying in wait in his head at every damn opportunity.

Yesterday morning he had given his verbal report to Colonel Willoughby, General MacArthur's eccentric Chief of Intelligence, and also to Major General Jonathan 'Skinny' Wainwright, the commanding officer in Northern Luzon, a friend of his dead father, a mentor to himself and the officer to whom he reported. After that he had completed his written report and eaten breakfast. Last night he had received orders to travel to General Douglas MacArthur's headquarters, a stone house in the wall of the old city, Victoria Street in Intramuros, Manila, but that order had altered and he had been brought to this camp near Malolos.

Labratte had only recently been commissioned; he was young and keen and he liked shooting the breeze. He rattled on. 'When General MacArthur arrived out of the blue late this afternoon we were all on alert wondering why. You must be really important, sir.'

Trap did not reply.

'It's not much further, just down there.' Labratte pointed to a long, low cement building with a veranda.

Suddenly Trap halted. Labratte turned back to him.

'What's that?' Trap was pointing at a vehicle. It was about 4 feet wide and 8 feet long with a body of rectangular design. He walked over to it and Labratte followed, happy to explain:

'Well, it's what they're calling a GP vehicle, sir.' He waved and shouted to a mechanic who was tinkering with a motorbike near the veranda of one of the buildings. 'Hey, Denham.'

The mechanic approached, wiping his hands on a rag.

'Tell the major about this new reconnaissance vehicle.'

Denham saluted and grinned, showing a dimple in his left cheek. 'Well, sir, it's a government eighty-inch-wheelbase reconnaissance car.' He patted the bonnet affectionately. 'It's out of sight! Can go over all sorts of terrain. This one has four-wheel steering and hydraulic brakes and floating axles, and there's a thirty-calibre machine gun mount on most of them. We've had two dozen just delivered from Stateside, sir.' He sounded proud.

Trap bounded in and sat down. He gave a low whistle. 'Must get some of these,' he said to himself.

'Most of the boys love 'em, sir. I was told by Captain Argus that Ford, Willys and Bantam are making 'em. This one's a Bantam.'

Trap sat for a few moments longer tapping the steering wheel in thought. 'Right!' he remarked as he leapt out. 'Do you know how to maintain one of these, Denham?'

The mechanic beamed. 'I'm learnin' as fast as I can, sir. Study the manual any spare time I get, even gave up goin' to the flicks to do it. The boys are calling them all sorts of names: pigmy, peep, leapin' lena, midget, but the one I like is jeep.'

Trap repeated, 'Jeep.' And, peering at the corporal, asked, 'What's your full name, son?'

'Corporal Thomas Mackim Denham, sir.'

Trap made a mental note. If he could get six or so of these vehicles out of General Wainwright, he would need a good mechanic.

Yesterday when he had reported to General Wainwright, the officer had spoken in grave tones. 'Trap, I want you to go through the units and pick a squad of good, seasoned men. You won't find them in your class, but there are well-trained officers especially in the Twenty-sixth Cavalry and the enlisted men are good, tough Philippine Scouts. Start there.'

'Right. What's the reason, sir?'

The general took his arm. Trap knew Skinny Wainwright intimately, had stayed many a leave with him and his wife Adele and their son Jonathan, whom Skinny called Jack. 'Son, I think you're a hundred per cent right about an imminent invasion, and immediately after your meeting with General MacArthur, I want you to take your chosen troops up to Northen Luzon.'

Trap had this very morning begun to choose his men. He now eyed Denham again.

'What sort of a shot are you, son?'

Labratte replied for him. 'I've seen him on the target range, sir. For a mechanic he's a dead-eye Dick.'

Trap nodded as he moved on. 'Thanks, Corporal.'

'Yes, sir.' Denham gave a smart salute, watched the major cross to the veranda steps, grinned and returned to his bike.

Trap and Labratte passed a sentry; from one of the cement buildings in the vicinity he could hear music, a gramophone was playing 'Lady in Red'.

Why did that damn song continue to haunt him? All it did was bring thoughts of her and the goddam feel of her skin on his. He straightened his shoulders as if to shake the memory off and leapt up the three steps to the veranda, leaving Labratte to hurry up behind him.

They walked twenty yards and the lieutenant pointed to a green door where another sentry barred their way.

'Permission to see the general. He's expecting us. Lieutenant Labratte.'

The sentry saluted. 'Which general? The place is crawling with them.' He poked his thumb over his shoulder.

'The top brass — MacArthur.'

'Who's this?' The sentry pointed at Trap.

'I'm the parcel from Hong Kong.'

The soldier grinned. He appeared to be expecting this, and he turned to an opaque window and tapped on it. It was pushed up a couple of inches from inside. He spoke to the opening. 'Lieutenant Labratte and the parcel from Hong Kong are here.'

The door opened, the sentry stood aside and the two new arrivals entered.

They were escorted along a four-foot-wide corridor. On the walls hung photographs of various Filipino beach scenes in blue-painted frames. They rounded a corner, came to another door, halted and knocked. It opened and Trap and Labratte entered to find themselves in an anteroom with chairs around the wall.

'Wait here.'

They sat.

Four minutes passed while Labratte read an edition of *Newsweek* magazine and by which time Trap had taken in the features of the room: three doors, a brown square rug in the middle of the floor, eleven leather chairs with magazines lying upon them, a white-painted ceiling with three light bulbs in brown shades hanging from it and one manhole in the far corner.

The door nearest the manhole opened and Skinny Wainwright entered. He grinned.

'Major Trapperton, follow me.'

As they traversed a corridor, Skinny spoke confidentially. 'Look, son, General MacArthur doesn't like intelligence operators who are in the direct control of William Donovan and Washington working on his patch, i.e. the Philippines.'

Trap grunted. 'I haven't been in the Philippines until now. I've been in and out of everywhere else in the Orient, but not here.'

'Yes, that's the reason he'll see you. But he doesn't want you operating here, so I've cleared it with Washington and I've informed him that you're returning to active duty under my command and that I'll get you to train some jungle fighters for him.'

'So I'll get no more orders from Washington?'

'I didn't say that, son. I just said you'll stay under my command and train jungle fighters for MacArthur for now.'

Trap looked skywards. 'You're the boss, sir.'

'I am, so follow me.'

Skinny led him into the presence of three other generals. Trap recognised the suntanned individual with the high forehead and imperious expression who wore the uniform of a Lieutenant General in the army of the United States of America. Douglas MacArthur had recently been recalled to active duty after being an adviser to the Philippine government since his retirement as US Chief of Staff in 1937. The saturnine-looking individual beside him Trap knew to be Richard Sutherland, MacArthur's Chief of Staff. The third man wore spectacles and a uniform of a major general in the US Army Air Force. Trap assumed him to be the recently arrived commander of the US Far East Airforce, Lewis Hyde Brereton.

Trap saluted as Wainwright stepped forward and shook hands with MacArthur who said, 'Good to see you, Jonathan.'

'Good to see you too, Douglas. This is Major Hank Trapperton.'

MacArthur, who had been the most highly decorated American soldier in the Great War and who it was often said, lived and breathed the military, gave a sharp nod and stubbed out a black cigar into a rose-patterned china ashtray. Skinny introduced Trap to the others before they all sat and he began to explain.

'I've read Major Trapperton's report, as has General Willoughby, and you each have a copy. We've all suspected for a long time what the real intentions of the Japanese are, and it seems that our negotiations for a peace agreement with them might prove unsuccessful, even though it's our understanding that at this very moment the United States and Japan are still talking.'[1] He lifted his hands palm upwards and dropped them to his lap. 'Major Trapperton is one of our most successful intelligence officers. His information regarding the military build-up on and around the Japanese mainland has been most helpful, and I'd like you gentlemen to hear his recent findings.'

Trap bent slightly forward. 'On the Chinese mainland opposite Hong Kong island, Japanese troops, armaments and tanks are massing. We know there are up to fifty thousand soldiers and the real number could be more. And even with the recent addition of the Canadians to bolster the British defences of Hong Kong, they still only have about ten thousand men.'

Wainwright rubbed his smooth-shaven chin. 'So you believe the Japanese are about to attack Hong Kong?'

'I do. They're poised. It could be any time: today, tomorrow, the next day.'

Wainwright frowned. 'Our British friends in the fortress of Hong Kong can't hold out long against those odds.'

For some reason Trap momentarily pictured the stately Sir Brillard leaning on his cane. 'No, they can't. Nobody there has a chance.' He took a deep breath. 'And the Japs will attack us here, and I would imagine Guam too, probably pretty much at the same time as they land on Hong Kong. They have naval and air bases on Palau and Formosa. Time and time again I saw them practising bomb-dropping on the inland rivers in Formosa when I was there.'

Skinny Wainwright explained: 'Major Trapperton passed himself off as an Argentine businessman in Japan for three months in early forty and he travelled in Formosa as well.'

MacArthur frowned but said nothing, and now Brereton spoke. 'We have detailed reconnaisance intelligence of Formosa's fortifications. We know it's hosting hundreds of Japanese aircraft, perhaps thousands: fighters and bombers.'

Trap agreed. 'Yes, exactly. We noticed unidentified aircraft flying over Clark Field and Fort Stotsenburg yesterday. There's little doubt they were Japs, and probably from Formosa. It's only a two-hundred-and-fifty-mile flight across the strait from Northern Luzon and the same distance again has them right over Manila.'

MacArthur looked across at Brereton, who grinned in condescension. 'We're aware of the geographical distances, Major.'

Trap nodded. 'Sure you are, sir. My point being, it's a simple matter for the Japanese to attack Luzon from Formosa.'

MacArthur spoke irritatedly. 'Yes, Major, well I think we're all aware of that too.'

Trap dared to go on. 'Fact is, I've knowledge that a fleet of aircraft carriers, cruisers and submarines has sailed from Japan proper to a position somewhere further east into the Pacific.'

General MacArthur actually sat up straight. This had his attention. He looked almost affronted that a major could know such a thing. 'Are you sure?'

'Yes, sir.'

'Oh really?' Brereton's tone was disbelieving. 'And where are they headed?'

'I don't know, sir.'

General MacArthur's imperious expression now revealed doubt, even exasperation, as Richard Sutherland gave voice to his standpoint: one that was still held by MacArthur and most of his staff. 'We're all sensitive to the fact that Japan will attack the Philippines, but our intelligence feels it probably won't happen before the spring.'

It was clear to Trap that Douglas MacArthur did not want to hear what was being said. It was diametrically opposed to his theory, yet he was not a fool, and he leant forward on his desk as he eyed the major. 'I can understand the massing of troops and aircraft in Japan and on Formosa and Palau, but a Japanese fleet sailing to an unknown destination in the Western Pacific is a very serious allegation to make, Trapperton.'

'Yes it is, sir. But my sources are impeccable.'

MacArthur frowned again and toyed with an inkwell on his desk. 'What does that mean?'

'I mean my sources are not wrong, sir.'

Brereton and Sutherland spoke as one. 'Now hold on!'

It was General Wainwright who defended Trap. 'It's all in his report. I'd stick my neck out to say the major here is the finest operator the United States has in intelligence in the entire Pacific.'

MacArthur lifted his hand for quiet and accepted this. 'Okay.' He reached over and took a cigar from a glass container at his right hand as Sutherland leant forward and lit it with a Zippo lighter while the commander's gaze flicked from Trap's face down to his feet and back again. 'Anything else to add, Major?'

'The Japs are in earnest. They want the South Pacific and anything else they can grab. Their sidewalk photographers, barbers, bicycle salesmen, prostitutes, you name it, have been sending details about our defences back to Tokyo for years.'

MacArthur's tone was dismissive. 'Yes, yes, we're aware of that.

We know they'll attack. The timing's the thing, that's all.' He made a swift gesture to his forehead, and Trap, understanding it was a salute to end the interview, stood and saluted in return.

Wainwright accompanied Trap out to the anteroom, where Labratte still read a magazine. The young man dropped it and stood.

Skinny Wainwright grasped Trap's shoulder. 'I'm returning north to the fort immediately. Best you accompany me. We can talk on the way.'

'Yes, sir.'

'Oh, and Trap?'

'Yes, sir.'

'Well done in there.' He gestured with his head back to the office they had just exited.

As Trap and Labratte left the building, Wainwright rejoined the generals, who looked up as he entered.

General MacArthur gestured in the air. 'Your man might be right, or he might be exaggerating.'

Wainwright defended Trap again. 'Anything he says has to be taken seriously.'

MacArthur puffed on his cigar. 'What's his upbringing?'

'Actually similar to yours, Commander: West Point, father was a major general.'

MacArthur's dark eyebrow rose and he appeared vaguely interested. 'Not old William Trapperton?'

'Yes.'

'I remember him. He was in France in the Great War. Didn't he die in unusual circumstances?'

Skinny gave a nod. 'Yep. Flying in Alaska in 1925. Never found the aircraft, never found the body. Three of them.' He sighed. 'I was supposed to be the fourth on that fishing trip. Had a tummy bug and couldn't go.'

MacArthur grunted. 'Lucky you.'

'Bill Trapperton was a good man and a close friend, and his

son is one of the new breed. Fluent in three languages, background in intelligence, known for his acuity, first-class shot, agile, can parachute and, I'm told, kills men with his bare hands.'

It was rare to see Douglas MacArthur impressed by anything, but for a heartbeat, his expression exhibited a semblance of admiration. 'I see.' He took another draw on his cigar. 'We all know our instructions from the War Office state that if hostilities with Japan cannot be avoided, then the United States government desires that Japan commit the first overt act.'

Skinny Wainwright grunted affirmatively. 'True, Douglas, but what if Hank Trapperton's right about the unidentified Japanese fleet heading into the Pacific?'

MacArthur shrugged as he glanced from Wainwright to Sutherland to Brereton and back again. 'We'll look damn fools if we report such a thing and it isn't so.' He drummed on the desk with his middle finger. 'He's a bit uppity is Major Trapperton and it could all be his imagination. And while I don't like the sound of it and it seems improbable, I suppose I'll have to read his report and think about it all the same.' He stood. 'But not tonight. I spent hours in Manila early this morning with the British admiral Tom Phillips, and he wants to meet again in the morning. So I'd best be returning to the capital.'

MacArthur, followed by Sutherland, moved to the door, where the commander paused a moment and adjusted his tie in front of a mirror hanging there. Lifting his gaze to Brereton's eyes in the mirror, he spoke as he departed. 'Lewis, I'll see you at the Twenty-Seventh Bombardment Group's gala in your honour on Sunday night. Can't miss that. Now home to Jean and Arthur.' He smiled at the thought and smoothed his hair back with his hand. He had been fifty-seven and childless when he married Jean and now they had a young son, Arthur, whom MacArthur loved with a suffocating adoration.

After their commander's exit, Wainwright lifted his cap from the hook on the back of the door. 'I'm off back up to Fort Stotsenburg.

I'm afraid Trapperton's right in that some sort of an attack's imminent and we're not adequately defended. Many of my troops are untrained and our weapons obsolete. The industrial capacity of our country is only just turning to the production of war material, and unfortunately we're not the first priority.'

Brereton was in accord. 'I've done what I can to reorganise the air forces since I got here, but even with Colonel Eubank's Nineteenth Bombardment Group and their thirty-five B-17s, I've still only got about a hundred and fifty bombers and fighters in the whole country, and an awful lot of them are past it.'

Wainwright opened the door and held it back for Brereton to pass through. 'Yep. Well let's hope we've got more time than Major Trapperton thinks and we can get better prepared.'

Chapter Nine

Saturday 6 December 1941

The convivial sounds drifting to the street from the ballroom of the Grand Peninsula Hotel in Hong Kong caused many locals not fortunate enough to be counted part of the social elite to cast their eyes up to the windows as they passed. Inside, glamorous couples drifted across the floor to the strains of 'A Nightingale Sang in Berkeley Square'.

The Tin Hat Ball was under way and the proceeds were to be sent to the British Government to aid in the buying of bombers.

The guests who had that afternoon attended the Happy Valley race track or watched the Middlesex Regiment play rugby at the cricket club, laughed and cavorted seemingly without a care, but the two leading men of the colony did not even put in a token appearance at the gala affair: Major General Christopher Maltby and the new governor, Sir Mark Young, were conversing in serious tones over a quick drink at Flagstaff House, the beautiful colonial residence of the General Officer Commanding British Troops in China. Currently it was General Maltby's home. He had been working around the clock to create some sort of defensive plan that might deter what he saw as an imminent Japanese assault on the colony. He lit a cigarette as he listened to his companion, the Governor.

These men were newcomers to Hong Kong: both having arrived

as recently as September and both having speedily become aware that they had inherited a time bomb. Chris Maltby MC had seen thirty years active service in the Indian Army. He had served in World War One and had spent years in the Persian Gulf, Salonica, Egypt, Mesopotamia and the North-West Frontier. He was succeeding Major General Edward Grasset CB, a man who had told him that the Japanese were bluffing, that they would not go to war with Great Britain for their interests were best served by remaining neutral. Grasset had smiled with sanguineness as he delivered this message to his successor. At that time Maltby had only been in the colony a week but he did not agree at all, and had wondered at General Grasset's facile attitude.

In fact, the two Canadian battalions which had recently arrived had come as a direct result of Grasset's optimism that they would render the garrison strong enough to withstand an extensive period of siege – when Winston Churchill's opinion had been: 'There is not the slightest chance of holding Hong Kong or relieving it . . . whether there are two or six battalions, they will make no difference.'

The new Governor, Sir Mark Aitchison Young, an ex-Rifle Brigade Officer with an excellent record in various outposts of the Empire, had arrived from Tanganyika and taken over from Sir Geoffrey Northcote, K.G.M.G. who after thirty-seven years serving their Majesties in such debilitating places as the African Gold Coast, had become an ill man. Sir Geoffrey had been invalided home in November and any thoughts he had on the Japanese occupation of mainland China and their obvious intentions in Hong Kong, he had kept to himself. The two newcomers therefore found simpatico in each other's plight. The Governor wore a permanent frown of concern.

'After what we learnt this afternoon, I'm thinking a Japanese invasion is probably imminent.' He was referring to information which had been radioed in that Japanese army transports, escorted by naval vessels, were heading across the Gulf of Siam towards Kota Bharu on the northern coast of Malaya.

71

'Yes.' The general nodded. 'My feeling, as I told my senior officers this afternoon, is that the Japs are obviously heading for Malaya, and that means they'll strike here pretty much at the same time, perhaps in the next forty-eight hours. I'm hoping the report that there are ten to twenty thousand of them poised around Canton is a bit of an exaggeration. My intelligence still maintain there are only perhaps five thousand.'

'Have you told London that?'

'Yes.'

The Governor looked hard at this companion. 'But how many do you think there are?'

General Maltby's high forehead creased as he drew on his cigarette and blew out smoke with a sigh. He smoothed his moustache with his left hand before he answered. 'I'm not sure. I don't believe the naive figure of five thousand, though I'd like to very much. Other reports suggest fifteen to twenty and some actually more.'

'Good lord! We've only got about ten, haven't we?'

'Between ten and fifteen, but many of them are not the sort of battle-hardened fellows I'd like to have. The Canadians have only been here a month, they know nothing of the terrain and much of their heavy equipment hasn't arrived. My two British battalions lack many of their most capable officers, who've been redeployed in Europe, and the aircraft we have are obsolete: two blasted Walrus amphibians and three ancient Wildebeeste torpedo bombers; a joke, I'm afraid. And I'm sorry to say that my investigations show quite inadequate preparations for holding off an invasion. Spoke to a good fellow called Whitby who's done his darnedest to build defences, but he seems to have run into red tape a lot of the time, and anyway he left the colony yesterday.'

Sir Mark expected Hong Kong to fall to the Japanese in the short term and that he and the man with him would be prisoners if they did not die in the attack. He said nothing, he simply took a large mouthful of his drink and contemplated the fine features of the general, who continued speaking.

'I had a meeting with a chap this week who called himself Chris Webster, though my suspicion is it was an alias. He's a Yank — wasn't here officially, though his name came to me through official channels. Now he was much more pessimistic about the number of Japs across the strait; said there could be up to fifty thousand.'

The Governor almost choked on his Scotch. 'Good heavens!' he spluttered.

'Yes. Well, sadly, if I include their air force and naval back-ups in my calculation, I'd guess he's not really far off.'

Sir Mark Young was feeling very uncomfortable. He held his square chin in his hand as he chewed the side of his lip in thought. 'Is there anything else that can be done quickly to defend us?'

The general's tone did not gain in confidence. 'Let's be objective, Governor. The resources aren't here. We've done as much as we can, but it's probably too little and too late. The harbour's closed at night, the Lei Mun Strait's blocked, all troops are on immediate standby. We've units on the mainland and the island and we've armed sentries all over the colony. We've mined the channel where we can.' He cleared his throat. 'Actually, when I finish this drink with you I'm off to tour some of our defences.'

'I'll come with you.' Mark Aitchison Young locked eyes with the colony's commander. 'Another thing you and I have touched on briefly before is that Hong Kong is riddled with agents for the Japanese, who know all there is to know about our defences. Apparently there are Japanese here who make no bones about what they're here for. I'm told there's a Jap barber been here for seven years who cut the hair of the previous two governors as well as the Commissioner for Police, the Colonial Secretary and the chairman of the Hong Kong and Shanghai Bank. Doesn't automatically make him a spy, but one's intellect tells you he almost certainly is.'

General Maltby sighed audibly. 'Yes, your Excellency, that unfortunately sounds right.' He nodded dispiritedly. 'First thing I noticed when I came here was that the Japanese consulate overlooked the harbour. And I learnt from this Webster chap that there was a Japanese doctor, name of Len Sumatu, at the Queen Mary Hospital whom he believed to be the leading agent in Hong Kong. Sumatu disappeared suddenly this week. As the Americans are at war with nobody, I didn't ask the American why he was here, but I received the distinct impression it was something to do with that leading agent.'

The Governor raised his eyebrow. 'You know, that's a bit uppity of the Yanks, coming into our territory, but I suppose, on consideration, they need to look after their own interests. Where's this Webster now?'

'My intelligence people tell me he departed on an American transport aircraft which refuelled here on Wednesday afternoon. I've also asked questions as to why our people didn't know about this Sumatu themselves.' He took a mouthful of his Scotch. 'The more I learn, the worse it gets. There's been a Colonel Suzuki, who was seconded here from the Japanese army well over twelve months ago, ostensibly to learn English. One of our intelligence officers asked him why his English was still so bad when he had nothing else to do except learn the language. Well, this damn Suzuki answered him straight-faced that he really didn't have much time for learning English because his own intelligence duties took up most of his day! He admitted he was here spying! I looked into that immediately I heard about it and found out that this bloody Suzuki left Hong Kong two weeks ago!'

The Governor's kind eyes blinked with feeling and his tone filled with disgust. 'We've inherited a minefield, General.'

'Yes, Governor, deplorable and depressing as it is, I do believe we have.'

The two men separated a little after midnight, having visited Fortress Headquarters and also Brigadier John Lawson[1] and his Canadians. They had crossed over to Kowloon to spend some time with the Royal Scots, the 2/14 Rajputs, and the 5/7 Punjabs who manned the 'Gin Drinkers' Line', a ten-mile fortification stretching across rugged hill country and pocked by trenches and pillboxes. This position was to protect Kowloon, the harbour and the northern part of Hong Kong island from artillery fire from the land, unless the enemy mounted a major offensive. In that event, the mainland positions would provide time to complete demolitions, clear vital supplies and sink shipping in the harbour while the Gin Drinkers' Line was abandoned. The remaining forces were to be concentrated on the island and were to prepare to defend against any Japanese attack from the sea.

The Major General caught the eye of the Governor and gave an odd smile. 'You know my brother Paul[2] is an Air Vice-Marshall and somewhere out here in the east, I hope to heaven he's having a better time of it than we are. Goodnight, Governor.'

'Goodnight, General.'

Major General Chris Maltby went home to Falstaff House, drank a Scotch and went to bed.

On his arrival at Government House, Sir Mark Young's ADC asked if he wanted any supper.

'Yes, I'll have a ham sandwich.'

'Right, sir. I'm sure there's someone in the kitchen who can make it, though quite a few of the staff aren't home from the Tin Hat Ball yet.'

'Ah yes, the ball.' The Governor walked to the window and looked out into the dark sky. He stood there some moments in thought as his forehead dropped to rest on the cool glass. He spoke to himself. 'How dearly I do hope they've had an especially good time . . .'

Chapter Ten

The horn of the *Fortitude* sounded as she swung her bulk around and, on the evening tide, sailed out of Hong Kong.

At the bulwark Lexi clutched Paul in her arms, while beside her ranged Uncle Peter and Aunt Della, their fifteen-year-old son Gregory, Della's brother Jasper, and Kathleen. As they headed towards the South China Sea, everybody's eyes were upon the grey waters swirling along the side of the ship as it cut its way through Victoria Harbour and round the point past tiny Green Island, where tons of explosives for the colony's demolition work were stored.

As the lights of Kowloon and the island faded behind them and the ship rode the swell, Kathleen fingered the golden chain hanging around her neck: a jade pendant in the shape of a small dragon hung from the links. She had never seen another like it, for the image of the dragon had tiny rubies for eyes and a triangular-shaped ruby for the tip of its swirling tail. Her mother had worn it more often than any other jewellery, even though she had collected much more substantial and valuable pieces over the years; she had died wearing it. Kathleen had taken it from her mother's neck an hour before the funeral and clipped it around her own. Touching the pendant now as Hong Kong receded into dimness, she gained a certain solace from it and decided to wear it always.

76

Beside her Della gave a groan. 'Ah dear, so that's the last of Hong Kong. I feel quite odd, I do. And I know I'll just dream about Mother and Father all the time. I hated leaving them.'

Peter squeezed her plump shoulders comfortingly as she turned and spoke to the two young women. 'We'll meet you in the lounge on the main deck at seven.'

'Right, Aunt Della.'

The Seaforth family, with Jasper Hayes two steps behind, walked away along the deck.

It had been a whirlwind five days for them all. Kathleen's mother's death had prompted Lexi to talk her friend into departing. Sir Brillard, who knew all the powerful of the island, had spoken to his friends, and Bess's funeral had been hastily organised for Friday. It took place only three hours before John Drayton had departed on a cargo aircraft from the airport in Kowloon with the other liaison officers bound for Singapore.

The funeral service was conducted in a downpour, ceasing only when the coffin entered the ground. The black umbrellas had been folded as the sun emerged, and afterwards John Drayton had farewelled Kathleen at the gates of the cemetery. In an unusual display of affection, she had clung to him. 'Thank you, John D, for everything. For your friendship and your care towards me.'

He had stroked her cheek affectionately and contemplated her. 'Now, dear, you look after yourself. And take care of my darling Lexi and little Paul for me.'

Through her tears she had gazed up at him with unconcealed affection. 'I will.'

Lexi had seen the exhibition of affection from her friend towards her husband and decided it was due to her unhappy emotional state and she had spoken kindly to her. 'Kathy darling, I'll be back once I see Johnny off. I'll help you finish packing, for we must be quite ready on Sunday.'

Lexi had parted from John Drayton in a dispersal hut on the edge of the field with the solemn grey aircraft a hundred yards distant. As she accompanied him to the door, all at once the impact of his departure struck her. Johnny was actually leaving! She had been so overtaken by seeing Trap again, and the death of Bess Leigh and the rush of organising everything, that she had not actually conceptualised it until now, and a surge of sadness overcame her.

He took her in his arms. 'Darling Lexi. I'll let you know where to write to me. I've got your mother's address in Ipswich.'

A tear welled over her lid and dropped to her chin.

'There, there, sweeheart, don't cry. You've been so brave, and who knows? I might get leave and be down in Queensland with you before long. Anyway, I'll sleep peacefully now I know you'll soon be following me away from Hong Kong.'

Lexi smiled through her tears and he kissed her deeply before he strode away and hastened by the sentry and the barbed wire to cross the airfield. After he had covered about forty yards, he turned and called, 'Look after our lovely little son.'

Suddenly this was all too much for Lexi, and as John Drayton hurried away, his hand high above his head in a wave, a sob broke from her. Quickly covering her mouth with her hands, she saw him enter the troop carrier, and a moment later she spun round and ran out of the small building. She drove back to Kathleen's apartment oppressed by guilt and overcome by tears.

It had been another emotional goodbye when Lexi parted from her grandparents. She had taken little Paul and Nintuck with her. She stood with Pa on the front veranda of Hydrangea while a crisp breeze lifted her skirt as he hugged her and kissed her forehead and took her hands in his. 'Don't ever worry about me, Lexi. Remember always, if you are happy I am happy, no matter where I am.' That alone had made her begin to cry.

'I'll try, Pa.' Her last sight of her grandparents had been as she drove away through the avenue of laburnums to the road with Nintuck beside her nursing her son. She had looked back and there they stood: her grandfather holding his ebony cane pointing to the sky and her grandmother waving a blue handkerchief.

Lexi had felt overwhelmed as she drove up to the white-pillared gateway and halted before entering the road. She reacted with surprise to see two bitterns – Chinese pond herons – perched on a low branch in amongst the reeds that encircled a small pond. As a child she often had played here, but she had never seen even one of the large brown-streaked birds anywhere near Hydrangea before, and as she halted the car, one flew on to the bonnet. Nintuck made a startled sound and it swung its head round to them as if it heard, showing them one blue eye.

Paul woke up and cried out at the same moment the bird let out a booming call. A second later it languidly lifted its wide wings and flew off the car as the second heron followed.

As Lexi brought the car out into the road her hands shook on the wheel, for she was remembering an ancient Chinese story she had heard somewhere about the Yellow Emperor seeing a bittern with one blue eye at his pond and death had followed for many of his household. Lexi looked sideways at Nintuck, who comforted Paul. The Cantonese girl pointed to the disappearing birds with the words 'Bittern bring bitterness.'

Lexi forced herself to give a small laugh. 'Don't be silly, Nintuck.'

The Chinese girl nodded to herself and whispered some sort of incantation over Paul in her arms as Lexi scoffed mentally at it.

But the moment had remained with Lexi, and now as she walked along the deck of the *Fortitude* with Kathleen she thought of it again and felt drained and frightened. She hugged little Paul to her body. It had been hard to leave Nintuck, but the woman had feared the sea voyage. 'No, I must stay and you must go, Missus. It is my fate, and it is your fate.'

She thought of her grandfather: he was the authority in her life, and she had left him behind. She thought of Johnny, the good man she had married: it was possible she would never see him again. And when she thought of Hank Trapperton, the man she admitted she loved, she felt certain he was gone from her life for ever more.

Her shoulders drooped with the mental weight of her anxieties. At her side Kathleen noticed Lexi's depression, but she too was miserable.

Kathleen had been in love with John Drayton for years. That he had married her best friend had been painful, but because she adored Lexi, Kathleen had forced herself to accept it. She had been sustained by the fact that she saw him often and that he classified her as a friend. When he had taken her in his arms after her mother's funeral, it had been the most glorious, yet saddest moment of her life.

She slipped her arm through Lexi's and drew her along the deck. 'Come on, Lex, we'll be all right, darling. Haven't we been together since we were toddlers? And we've got little Paul to take care of; we have to be strong for him.'

Lexi produced a feeble smile. 'Yes, Kathy, of course you're right. I'm just a bit low, that's all, and I shouldn't be, it's you who have lost your mother. Forgive me, I'm so sorry.'

'Don't be silly. Let's go to your cabin and bath Paul, then we'll each take a nice hot bath ourselves.' She managed to brighten her tone. 'Heck, we're off on an adventure, aren't we? Remember when you visited Queensland years ago you really liked it; we might want to stay there for ever.'

Lexi made an effort to brighten, and kissed the soft cheek of her son as he nestled in her arms. 'Yes, Kath darling, we might . . . we might.'

Chapter Eleven

The *Fortitude* skimmed over the calm grey South China Sea at a pleasant ten knots. The passengers were asleep, the wind was from the east and Jan Meer, the wireless operator, glanced towards the door as the night steward entered the radio room and placed down a tray of coffee and cake.

Sidwell, the bearded steward, who took supper each night with 'Sparks', — as radio operators seemed to be called worldwide — poured two coffees from the metal pot and sweetened them as Jan Meer mumbled a thank-you and took his cup to settle back in his worn chair.

Sidwell sipped his drink. 'What's our first port of call, Sparks?'

'The Philippines. Manila.'

'Hang on, I thought we were heading for Jesselton?'

'Borneo?' The wireless operator shook his head. 'No, the route was altered to the Philippines right before we departed Hong Kong.'

Sidwell made a scoffing sound. 'Gawd, we're always the flamin' last to know. Well as long as we end up in Brisbane I don't care how we get there.'

The steward was a boy from Broken Hill in Australia who had been at sea since he was fifteen and had been employed on craft plying in the Dutch East Indies for the last ten years. He had decided it was time to go home and was working his passage to Brisbane this time.

Abruptly Sparks sat up, spilling the liquid in his haste to put it down.

'What?'

'Ssh.' The radio operator held his headphones tightly to his ears while the natural crevice between his eyes deepened as he listened. His tone was urgent. 'Repeat, please. Not understanding. Repeat, please. Over.'

The steward watched as Jan Meer scribbled notes on a pad.

'Yes, got that, but I'm not receiving you clearly. Repeat, please . . . Blast, he's gone.' He took off his earphones and eyed his companion. 'Shi . . . it.' He said it low and long.

'What?'

'I think he said the Japs have attacked Malaya.'

'Gosh! Where?'

'Something about a large Japanese fleet and a landing at Kota Bharu.'[1]

'Where's that?'

'Northern Malaya.' He lifted his hand and pointed to the south-west. 'Over there, on the other side of the South China Sea, about a thousand miles or so.'

Sidwell put down his coffee and tensed. 'Gawd, that ain't far away really!'

'No, it's not. Bastards. No declaration of war.' Jan Meer took off his earphones and stood. 'I better tell Captain Van den Berg straight away.'

'Sure, and I'll make some more coffee. Might be a long night.' The steward pulled on his beard as he watched Sparks head out the doorway to the companionway.

Jan Meer had been back at his post in the radio room about two hours when the second momentous message came through.

He leant into the radio set, pressing the earphones tightly to his head as the captain, seated beside him, watched anxiously, and the mate, who made up the third member of the vigil, tapped with jittery fingers on the desk beside him.

'Yes, receiving. America! . . . Yes.'

82

The captain turned uneasy eyes to the first mate as Jan Meer continued speaking into the microphone. 'Yes . . . Yes . . . Continue . . . Yes, got that. Roger, over and out.'

'What?' uttered the captain and the mate at exactly the same time.

'That was the SS *Manatee* confirming a report they received about half an hour ago. It seems the Japanese have also attacked America. Some place called Pearl Harbor in the Hawaiian islands. Do you know it, Captain?'

'Yes, it's a naval base, lots of battleships and aircraft carriers.'

Jan Meer nodded. 'That's the place then. It was pretty garbled, he was shouting, but that's what he said.'

Captain Van den Berg stood up. 'Japan attacking targets here in the Orient is not unexpected, but to have hit the American naval base surprises me. The long hand of the rising sun is striking out.' He touched his first mate's shoulder. 'Full speed ahead. The sooner we're out of the South China Sea, the better.'

That morning at breakfast the ship's company was agog with the news. Other radio messages had come in during the night, and currently the *Fortitude*'s complement knew more of the facts. By lunchtime they were aware that Japan had launched full-scale assaults against Malaya, followed by Hawaii, the Philippines and Hong Kong, and Wake Island, all within hours.

Uncle Peter woke Lexi and Kathleen with the news and Lexi sat up in bed, shaking her head, her tousled curls swinging on her shoulders. 'Pa and Johnny were right.'

The awful truth of what her husband and her grandfather had been warning her about for nearly two years was now apparent. She pictured Sir Brillard, heard him telling her to leave without delay and saw his rueful smile when she had realised he was not leaving with her. She had said, 'But Pa, you've just told me there's no hope for those who stay in Hong Kong.' How she loved him. What would become of him?

She looked from Kathleen to her uncle. 'Do we know anything of what's happened in Hong Kong?'

Peter shook his head. 'No. All we've been told is that it's been attacked. The captain's going to address us at nine o'clock.'

Kathleen held herself tightly, arms across her waist. 'If my mother hadn't died I'd still be there.' She was remembering friends she had left behind at the hospital, and she was thinking of John Drayton and giving thanks to heaven he was in Singapore.

Lexi reached out to the ledge beside her bed and took up the white porcelain Kwan Yin that Pa had given her all those years ago. With her left hand she held it to her heart as with her right she reached for the palm of her friend.

They all fell quiet, their faces telling the story of their imaginings.

The day passed and the wind rose while the *Fortitude* made good speed in a moving sea.

All the passengers looked disheartened, for the news had given them a lot to think about.

Sixty-seven hours of the journey had passed and the *Fortitude* was sailing down the coast of Luzon when the wind dropped and the captain entered the bridge to stand behind the first mate. The Officer steered the ship and watched the sea washing against the bow and reflecting a gunmetal grey from the lowering clouds gliding menacingly above the swell.

The captain touched the mate's shoulder as he passed him. 'Should see the Cape Bolinao lighthouse twenty minutes after sunset.'

'Aye, sir.'

In the small bar amidships on the main deck a few passengers gathered. Kathleen and Lexi graced a sofa near the door while Jasper Hayes sat alone at the bar a few feet away. Drinks had been delivered by Sidwell the steward, and Lexi sipped lemonade while

Kathleen nursed the sleeping baby Paul. The door beside them opened and in walked Aunt Della along with husband Peter and son Gregory.

Della flopped into a chair beside Jasper, and at the same moment they all felt a heavy thud from below and the ship gave a violent lurch to starboard and remained there. Those standing fell headlong to the floor and those seated were thrown into each other. A conglomerate of sounds surrounded them: bottles and glass broke, trays smashed to the floor, people screamed and objects flew through the air while above the confusion the wail of sirens sharply pierced through the *Fortitude* as she attempted to right herself.

The first person to speak was Uncle Jasper: 'We've been hit!' and a woman on the floor near the bar began to wail.

Kathleen had fallen sideways but had kept hold of Paul, who was now wide awake and adding his frightened cry to the rest of the confusion.

'Get to the lifeboats,' Jasper called out as he disentangled himself from Lexi and tried to help Della, who had skidded on to her knees and hit her head on the side of a small table. Gregory was aiding his father and most people were now up on their knees and trying to stand.

The ship groaned and righted itself and Lexi took Paul from Kathleen as they all struggled out of the exit door on to the deck where sailors ran by yelling and shouting.

Lexi looked around and Jasper pointed up to the crow's nest where above the tumult they heard a shout: 'Torpedoes! Japanese sub!' and in that moment they felt another impact and the *Fortitude* heaved up in the air and pitched forward.

'Oh God, we've been hit again!'

Peter grabbed Della's arm and began to pull her in the direction of the lifeboats as Uncle Jasper surprised them all by waving his arms and yelling, 'Come on, all of you, this way, hurry!'

'But we're a passenger vessel,' Della protested.

Peter pulled her sharply. 'Be sensible. Whatever we damn well are, we've been hit!'

There were cries forward and aft but the family seemed to be alone amidships except for Sidwell the steward, who was right behind them. They had come out on deck near a lifeboat and Jasper urged them towards it, coming to the aid of Lexi and her child and helping them along. They scrambled and slipped over the deck and heard a booming voice over the loudspeaker: '*Verlaat schip!*' Abandon ship!

Fire belched from a companionway about twenty yards distant, and some seconds later a loud explosion rumbled behind them and both Lexi and Kathleen felt a gust of wind lift their hair from their shoulders as the *Fortitude* groaned and listed to starboard again.

'We'll be drowned!'

Gregory pushed his mother towards a lifeboat, but without crew they had no way of getting in and releasing it.

The ship began to lean badly and at the same time dip from the bow. Della, eyes wide with fear, pointed ahead. 'It's sinking!'

Everyone was yelling and clambering around but Jasper acted with deliberation and speed. Later, Lexi recalled how amazed she had been to see her uncle, who until today she had hardly known, take baby Paul from her and coolly jump up into the lifeboat, open the hatch and begin distributing the life jackets. Kathleen strapped Della into hers and then put on her own as the others all swiftly pulled the straps tightly around their bodies.

'We'll have to jump,' Jasper shouted above the din. 'If you can manage to grab some flotsam and use it to help you float, then do so!' And Lexi watched him take a piece of rubber from the hatch and bind it round her baby with his arms out. Hastily he slipped her child inside a life jacket and strapped it firmly around his small form before taking off his own webbed fabric belt and tying it tautly, encircling the jacket and holding baby Paul more safely within. He handed the child down to her, bounded on to the deck and turned away to put on a jacket of his own.

Suddenly there was another shudder through the ship and the deck beneath their feet began to quiver; sailors appeared from forward and ran by as flames kicked out of the door of the bar behind them; and Sidwell yelled and jumped sideways while the *Fortitude* dipped deeper into the South China Sea.

Jasper herded them towards the bulwark. 'Take off your shoes and push them down inside your life jacket, then jump!' he yelled, 'as far out from the ship's side as you can. I can see land over there.' He pointed to the east. 'Swim for that if you can.' He turned to Lexi. 'I'll take Paul.'

She was in the act of handing the child to him when a metal spar crashed down on the deck behind her and the ship gave a sharp lurch. The deck heaved beneath them and Lexi fell backwards, slid across the polished wood, hit her elbow hard against a hatch, dropped her son and screamed. She tried to rise but the angle of the ship was becoming more and more severe so that she kept slipping towards the bulwalk. Della and Uncle Peter lost their balance and came sliding past, arms and legs flailing.

Lexi kept screaming, 'My baby! My baby!' as they all hit the bulwark at the same time. The last thing Lexi saw was Jasper scrambling towards the bundle which was her son as it slid away from him. A second later she, Della and Peter tumbled over the side of the vessel into the sea.

Lexi came to the surface of the water, and instead of swimming away from the ship as she knew she should, she turned back to it. Her mind was not on her own safety but on that of her little son; she knew she was weeping, though her face was covered in salt water and the chop of the sea kept lapping in her face. Her son, her baby boy, had fallen from her arms! She had seen Uncle Jasper attempting to reach him; oh please God that he had done so. Something thumped into her back and she looked round to see Aunt Della suddenly emerge out of the depths beside her. Della tried to speak, but in the wind and chop of the sea Lexi could not hear her, and knowing her aunt was not a good swimmer,

Lexi took hold of the front of her life jacket and kicked hard to move her further away from the sinking vessel.

The moment Kathleen had donned her life jacket she had turned to witness the spar smash down near Lexi, and had watched in horror as the ship abruptly rolled and Lexi fell backwards in the act of handing Paul to her uncle. The siren was still wailing as Kathleen screamed, seeing her friend shoot across the deck, slam into a hatch and drop little Paul.

Kathleen had lost her footing, but grabbed a stay which was lashed to a metal upright at her left hand, and as Jasper stumbled towards the fallen infant she saw Della, Peter and Sidwell lose their balance and plunge down towards the bulwark which was now below them.

She was horrified as baby Paul, wrapped in the life jacket, slid towards the fire which was leaping out of a second door amidships. Jasper, who was trying to reach the baby, kept swaying and then completely lost balance and tumbled towards the others in their plunge over the side towards the sea.

There was a moment when the ship held stable even though it remained on a dire angle, and Kathleen saw Gregory dive overboard along with three sailors who had come down a companionway. The bundle which was Paul, lodged in something on the deck, and flames were now in Kathleen's eyeline as she began to edge along in a desperate effort to reach the infant. She was three yards from the screaming baby when there was a noise from a million nightmares and the ship began to break up. She was still striving to reach the baby when she felt a thump on her head, and as everything went black she was aware she fell.

Lexi and Della appeared to be alone in the dark grey water. Della was spluttering and weeping and trying to speak.

'Don't . . . Aunt Della . . . save your breath.' Lexi saw something floating near them. 'Over here . . . this way.' It was a piece of wood

– not wide but about five feet in length. Lexi pulled her aunt through the mild chop of the sea and stretched her right arm to the limit and grabbed it. 'Here, Aunt Della . . . hold on to this.'

Della locked her plump arm over it and through her tears said, 'I've lost my shoes.'

'Don't worry.' Lexi's reply came as behind them a mighty quake ran through the *Fortitude*. They looked around and watched it plunge nose first into the grey swell. Within a few minutes the burning flames were doused by the surging sea and the superstructure vanished. The water heaved and undulated and where there had been a ship there was nothing at all except metallic grey waves a foot or two high, rising and falling in their eyeline. The vast emptiness of the darkening water lapped around them and the clouds above emptied more rain into the boundless pool of the South China Sea.

The failing light of day showed Lexi two islands in the distance and she began to kick and push Aunt Della towards what seemed the nearer. She kept praying that little Paul would be saved and that they would be reunited on the island. She continued to pray, saying the same words over and over as a litany for her precious son. 'Please, Lord God, save my son. Reunite us. But if there is a choice between him and me, please, Lord God, save him.'

And as the sea continued washing over the two women, Lexi saw about a dozen people in the water some distance to the west, and beyond them a lifeboat – so one had managed to leave the mother ship! Lexi shouted and waved her arm but the swell of the sea hid the boat and they did not see it again.

Lexi kept on towards the island. The sea was cold and they were beginning to feel chilled. As the rain continued to spatter in their faces, they saw a head appear above the water and come towards them.

'I've hurt my left arm.' The new arrival puffed with exertion.

'Hold on to this.' Lexi helped him to clutch the buoyant beam before she kicked herself closer to Della.

He latched his good arm over the floating spar. 'I'm the radio operator. We must make for an island. That nearest one . . . over there . . . doesn't look to be more than half a mile away . . . There are other people in the sea behind us, perhaps forty or more.'

Lexi forced her words out between kicks of her legs. 'I saw . . . a lifeboat earlier.'

'Yes . . . I think . . . two got away. I got a message off to HMS *Resolute* . . . At least they know we were torpeoed. They were . . . about a hundred miles west.'

As they floated on together, Della wept on and off about her husband and son. Lexi thought to herself that the people in the lifeboats might have a chance of being picked up by a ship but did not believe that they had any hope of such a thing.

She kept praying for Paul and hoping that Kathleen and Jasper were in the water somewhere. All the while they headed for the island. At times they thought they were getting closer; at others the rise and fall of the swell appeared to be moving them further away, but as the swift twilight closed upon them they knew they were making progress and Lexi guessed, even though distance at sea was deceptive, that they were only a few hundred yards from shore.

Della was suffering from exposure and was exhausted as dusk fell, but when they heard a sharp, terrible screech behind them in the dark moving sea she snapped her head round to Lexi. 'Oh my God!'

Terror tingled through them.

'What is it?'

'Kick like hell,' Sparks ordered.

Lexi knew exactly what it was and she began to kick insanely towards the land.

Another scream was followed by a sickening shout of *'Haaien!'*

'Oh God! Sharks!'

'Oh no, oh no, oh no.' Della began to make small fearful moans and Lexi automatically kept on kicking like a mad person. Sparks at her side did the same.

Another screech jangled their nerves. It was closer than the others.

'Oh God in heaven, how did this happen?' Della was trembling wildly and near to hysteria.

Lexi's terror forced her on. 'Aunt Della, please. Keep kicking.'

As she spoke, Sparks gave a shriek, his arms flailed, he jerked twice and was pulled downwards to disappear.

'Oh Lord Jesus, he's been taken!'

Della fell silent, the silence of complete horror, and Lexi looked neither right nor left as she just continued the prayer in her head and kicked and pushed towards the land. Her sandals came out from where she had tucked them under her bra strap and slipped into the dark water, but she was unaware of losing them; her whole being was centred on getting to the land.

Five more appalling screams they heard that dusk, sounds that tortured their souls. They expected at every second to feel the ripping razor jaws of death, but there came a moment when Lexi's feet touched solid ground and together the two women dragged themselves through the shallows to fall completely spent upon the island.

Kathleen had regained consciousness as she hit the cold water. She went under a few feet and surfaced to remember what had occurred. The last thing she had seen were the flames coming closer to the baby. She shuddered at the memory.

There were others in the sea, and within minutes she saw the ship sink. Then she remembered the land that Jasper had mentioned and she made out an island in the middle distance. With a prayer for all her companions and a nauseating feeling about the fate of baby Paul, she began swimming strongly towards the land.

Rain fell and spattered on the sea around her as she swam for five hundred strokes and rested treading water for the count of ten. This pattern she kept up in the mildly choppy sea and she was not far off the island when dusk fell and she heard screams over to her left and the shout of '*Haiien!*' She knew no Dutch but her terror forced her on as fast as she could move. When finally her feet touched the bottom of the sea and she staggered through the surf, she thanked God for all the afternoons she and Lexi had swum together in Repulse Bay.

It was completely dark now, and as she stumbled over pebbles, stone and sand, she heard the murmur of voices.

'Who's that?'

'We're over here.'

And twenty seconds later Kathleen fell into Lexi's arms.

Chapter Twelve

Dawn revealed the three women huddled together on the pebble and sand beach. Thick emerald jungle dotted with blooms of crimson and white grew twenty-five yards away and their discarded life-jackets lay nearby. Lexi was the first to wake. Stiff and sore, she sat up and looked around. Out to sea she could make out more land, and surging into her mind came the words that Kathleen had spoken last night in the chill darkness when they had all recovered a little from their exhaustion and Lexi had asked about her baby son.

Kathleen had hugged her. 'I'm so sorry, darling . . . I'm so very sorry. None of us could reach him . . .'

Pain shot through Lexi. 'You mean he's dead . . . ?'

Kathleen had mumbled in the darkness and choked with emotion as she tried to explain, and Della had begun to sob and they had clung to one another in the solid black night and wept together.

They had been cold and wet and shivered through most of the dark hours. And now in the cheerless grey light of morning, tears slid down Lexi's cheeks again. It was retribution. God had taken her little boy away from her because she had committed the sin of sleeping with one man while being engaged to another. She had conceived Paul and had married Johnny and allowed him to believe the child was his. Her innocent baby had suffered, her darling, sweet, innocent little boy. Her culpability swelled up inside her, solidly in her chest; it would never, ever leave her.

Kathleen woke, her mouth was dry and her body ached. Prone beside her was Della, and a few yards beyond, Lexi in tears again. She dragged herself upright and moved to her friend. 'There, there, darling.' She bent down and Lexi lifted her drawn face.

'Did you hear the aeroplanes overhead last night?'

'Yes.' She had just answered when she saw over Lexi's shoulder a number of figures about three hundred yards away beyond a large outcrop of rock. 'Oh Lexi, look!'

At that moment Della opened her eyes and, hearing what Kathleen said, hefted herself up from the beach to gaze along it. Lexi stopped crying and turned to face where Kathleen pointed.

'Come on.' Kathleen headed off towards the others.

As they approached, Kathleen counted twenty people: twelve men and eight women. They all looked bedraggled and none had seen the advancing women until Kathleen called out to them.

Their heads swung round; those sitting gained their feet and those lying sat up. Suddenly Della shouted, 'Peter!' and ran forward to her husband's arms. As Peter hugged and kissed his wife they recognised another man walking back from the jungle. Della's brother Jasper came up to the two young women and stiffly embraced them.

Now Della looked around, eyes searching for her son Gregory, but the males shook their heads. 'We don't know where he is, we didn't see him in the water.' Della's moment of joy at finding her husband and brother faded, and her shoulders slumped and head bowed down.

Six of the survivors were crew, one being Sidwell the steward; the rest were passengers, and even though there had been Chinese men and women aboard the ship there were none here on the beach.

To Lexi's continuing surprise it was her uncle Jasper who suggested that a few of the men should explore the island.

'We need water, food and shelter. Another night out in the chill damp air will tax us all. Some of us must comb the beaches to see if anything of value has washed up from the ship, but before

94

we do I suggest you all go up to the jungle edge where I've just been. There are many large leaves up there quite wet from the morning dew. While the damp still sits on the leaves, wet your mouths as much as you can with the moisture.'

The survivors moved in haste to do as he recommended, some of the men running up the beach ahead, but one person remained unmoving. She was Matilda Ansen, whose husband had been a food and beverage manager at the Peninsula Hotel. 'Oh God, what does it matter? My husband was taken by a shark.' She began to sob. 'I'll never forget his scream, never, never . . .' She mumbled in despair and Jasper bent forward to console her.

She shook her head and Jasper patted her shoulder. 'I shall go and find a leaf or two for you.'

Lexi was astonished by her uncle's actions, just as she had been on the ship when it was sinking. He was like a different man; he was taking charge.

They reached the trees and began to pick the leaves eagerly. When they had moistened their dry mouths and felt a little better, Kathleen inclined her head towards Jasper. 'It's almost as if in leaving Hong Kong and his life there, he's been altered, sort of released or something.'

'Yes, that's what I was thinking.'

'Let's find some more leaves.'

While they searched further into the jungle, Lexi thought about her uncle's metamorphosis. She remembered that the fellows at the hospital used to say he was effeminate; that he liked men. All she knew was that she had never really taken much notice of him, and while she was sure Pa had relied on him in business, it had always been Pa or Uncle Peter who would take charge in a situation like this. Yet in this predicament Peter appeared inadequate.

When the two women ran out of damp plants they returned to the beach to see that Jasper had carried a few dew-covered leaves back to Matilda Ansen, who half-heartedly touched them with her lips.

Jasper moved through the men and women, calling for volunteers to accompany him on his search of the island. 'Only come with me if you still have your footwear.' He halted beside Frans Van Houten, an engineer and the third mate, who spoke English. 'Where do you reckon we are?'

'On one of the islands at the mouth of the Lingayen Gulf in Luzon.'

'That's what I thought.'

'You're right to explore. Must be native Filipinos on some of these.'

Jasper nodded.

'I'll come with you,' Van Houten announced as Sidwell the steward approached them and spoke to Jasper.

'I'd like to accompany you, though I feel like I've been put through a wringer backwards. Me head aches, me body aches and I can hardly feel me legs.'

'We're all a bit like that.' Jasper patted his shoulder. 'I'd be pleased to have you along. Meanwhile we need to leave someone in control here. Let's take a vote.'

Shoerd Amel was decided upon, one of the cooks from the *Fortitude*, and before Jasper and his party moved out he raised his hands for attention. 'It seems pretty clear that we were torpedoed by the Japanese. We believe we're on an island at the mouth of Lingayen Gulf in the Philippines and our only hope is to leave here and make our way south to Manila. There we should be able to get another ship to take us onward. If there are people living here, we might be able to get a craft of some kind. If we find anyone or anything of importance, I'll send Sidwell back.' He pointed along the beach and gave a smile of encouragement. 'If we don't find anything, we'll return by nightfall and begin again in the morning. And Amel?'

'Yes?'

Jasper bent to tie knots in his shoelaces as he continued; his shoes had survived the swim ashore tucked inside his jacket. 'Make sure that you gather a stack of large leaves and soft bracken in case the worst occurs and we have to sleep out again. At least we can lie upon them and cover ourselves. They'll be better than nothing.'

Amel nodded confidently. 'Right. And we'll begin to make a shelter up there near the trees as well.'

Jasper took a deep breath. 'Good idea.'

He stood as Lexi walked over to him. 'Good luck, Uncle Jasper.'

She had a very odd feeling as he bestowed upon her a tender smile. 'Thanks.'

He was studying her with his dark blue eyes, set above his high forehead and straight nose, and suddenly he reminded her of Pa. Even his voice reminded her of Pa. He was not the Uncle Jasper she had known for thirty years.

'You're different.' She could not help but say it.

'Am I?'

'Yes.'

He gave her a strange steady smile. 'Perhaps it's you who are different, Lexi.'

This surprised her, and she had no answer for it.

'I must leave now. Your uncle Peter will look after you.'

She badly wanted to go with him, but she said nothing as he beckoned Van Houten and Sidwell and walked away across the pebbled beach. She felt suddenly lonely as she listened to the survivors call their farewells. Out of the blue she thought of Trap and wondered where he was. Suddenly Kathleen spoke at her side.

'Can you help me tie my hair back?'

Lexi turned and took the piece of string her friend proffered, when abruptly Della screamed. Everybody spun round; even Matilda raised her head, and Jasper and his companions, who were not far down the beach, swung sharply back to the main group.

There, from the opposite direction, running towards them from

97

behind a distant outcrop of rock, were dozens of soldiers in cork sun helmets, bayonets at the ready.

Lexi and Kathleen froze as they recognised the mud-coloured uniform of the Japanese army.

Chapter Thirteen

Within a minute the survivors of the SS *Fortitude* were surrounded.

Jasper, Sidwell and Van Houten were driven back to the main body of Europeans as a captain screamed an order and his troops gestured threateningly for the group to huddle together.

Jasper surprised Lexi once more by speaking loudly in Japanese. She did not know he spoke the language, but she could tell by the tone of his voice that he was making some explanation of their situation. The Japanese captain ignored Jasper and shouted to a sergeant. Within a minute the soldiers began separating the males from the females.

Matilda Ansen had been helped to her feet, and as one of the soldiers pushed her along she screamed and threw off his hand. He smashed her in the back with the butt of his rifle and she fell to the ground.

Matilda cried out and began weeping, and Lexi bent down in an attempt to console her. 'Mrs Ansen, please, just stand up with me. Try not to cry.'

But now Matilda had found her voice. 'You pigs! My husband's dead because of you!'

As Lexi helped her to her feet she hysterically lashed out at the soldier nearest her, who turned and smashed his rifle into her face. Both women screamed in fright and Matilda collapsed to the sand, blood seeping from her nose. It was plain to see it was broken, and as Lexi again attempted to aid her, Jasper protested loudly in

99

Japanese and the soldier nearest him swung his bayonet up to where it almost touched the European's face. '*Damare!*' Jasper did as he had been told and fell silent.

The captives looked at one another in bewilderment: they had no idea what was expected of them.

Kathleen came to assist Lexi with Matilda and they managed to lift the weeping woman to a standing position between them as the soldiers continued to herd them into a group apart from the men.

When they had separated the sexes, ten soldiers stood with fixed bayonets facing the captives, who were now made to line up: the twelve men in one row and the eleven women in the other. Jasper attempted to speak again but the sergeant menaced him with his bayonet and repeated '*Damare!*'

The prisoners were kept standing in two rows without explanation of any kind. Minutes passed and Lexi and Kathleen supported Matilda between them until a sergeant spoke sharply to two privates and they stepped forward and pulled the women apart, making Matilda stand unaided. Her nose continued to bleed and she whimpered constantly.

The sun was ascending and it was not ten minutes before Matilda sank to the beach. As Lexi and Kathleen knelt to aid her, two soldiers thrust them away and dragged the Dutch woman off some yards from the others. Lexi and Kathleen moved again to help her, but the sergeant yelled and gestured wildly for them to rejoin the line of women.

The captain, who watched from a seat on one of a nearby cluster of rocks, shouted an order, and Matilda was taken up again between the two soldiers and pulled over the coarse sand towards him.

'Stop that. What are you doing with her?' Jasper demanded, and for this impertinence he was struck forcibly with a rifle butt hard upon his shoulder.

Matilda was hauled to the far side of the pile of boulders, where they could no longer see her but could hear her sobbing and mumbling.

Lexi and Kathleen stood next to Della. Tears ran down her plump cheeks and she was hunched forward in an attitude of despair, looking far more fragile than the bonny woman of twenty-four hours ago. Her vermilion fingernails glinted absurdly in the sunlight as she caught Lexi's eye. They dared not speak.

Abruptly came a rifle shot. All the survivors flinched.

'Oh my God!'

Della and two others screamed, and Jasper and Van Houten both took an involuntary step forward. 'This is inhuman,' Jasper managed to say, and Van Houten shouted, 'Stop!' before both men were slammed in their chests with rifle butts. They staggered backwards but succeeded in keeping upright.

No more weeping was heard from the other side of the granite outcrop; everybody knew Matilda had been murdered and a pall of horror settled across the captives.

The sun glinted on the green waves of the rolling surf beyond the beach, and sea birds dived and screeched above them as an abrupt shout from the captain brought his men jumping to attention.

All heads turned and the prisoners saw another company of Japanese appear in the distance and approach. As the newcomers passed the rocks where Matilda's body was hidden from sight, the Japanese who were standing there, bowed to, and stepped back from, an individual who wore flared riding breeches and high leather boots. He swaggered across the stony beach and it was only Jasper who recognised the white armband of the dreaded Kempeitai – the Japanese military police. Jasper knew of the utter disregard shown for human life by the Kempeitai, of the abominable tortures perpetrated by them on the Chinese, Korean and Manchurian populations.

In sight of the captives the colonel halted and looked around. The captain, a lieutenant and the sergeant ran forward to his side and he began to ask them a series of questions, during the course of which the captain pointed to Jasper. The colonel dropped his voice and turned his back but still continued speaking to his subordinates. Jasper had a very bad feeling about that.

A few minutes passed and the colonel appeared to be about to leave, but just as Jasper thought he was turning to go he hesitated. 'I will inspect the prisoners,' he announced loudly in English, and marched across to the line of men.

Now Jasper dared to speak again. 'We are not prisoners, we are civilians, none of us are soldiers and according to the Geneva Convention you have no right to hold us or mistreat us, and yet murder has been committed here!'

Lexi gasped as the sergeant whipped his rifle menacingly towards her uncle's face, the bayonet only an inch from his eyes, but the colonel held up his hand for him to restrain himself and stepped closer to Jasper, who stood at least a foot taller than him. 'You speak my language well so you will understand when I say that we Japanese do not hold with the Geneva Convention, so do not mention it again. You are our prisoners, my prisoners. I am fighting a war and you are in my way.' He brushed past Jasper, hand on the sword which hung from his belt and almost dragged in the sand. He crossed the beach to the line of women.

The Japanese colonel stood regarding the women. He had been given his orders and there was much to do. He was commanding a Kempeitai unit linked to the famous Kanno Detachment, named after the commander of the 3rd Battalion, which had landed to the north near Pandan yesterday and already had a controlling foothold around Vigan. There had been no counter attack from the Americans and Filipinos and he felt confident of taking the airfields and therefore sanguine about the success of the offensive. He was reconnoitring for the amphibious landing which was planned to take place within a week or so here in the Gulf.

He was an important man, a commanding officer in the Kempeitai, even the Japanese military were terrified of him. He knew it was unusual to send a man of his rank to do mere reconnaissance but General Homma had wanted someone he could trust implicitly. He had landed here because it seemed uninhabited and he needed to slip into the Gulf, have a look and slip back up the coast. And now these stupid ship survivors had been strewn across his path. They were simply a nuisance. He needed to move on without delay and must keep things tidy. Holding prisoners was not in the equation, but he would look at the women first. He liked to look at women.

He walked slowly down the row of remaining females: plain European faces, fat middle-aged matrons: no use! Ah, two young ones at the end of the row. He halted and eyed them: one probably British, the other Eurasian. Both fine figures, firm breasts. He looked from one to the other and they looked back.

He began to turn away, and as he did he stopped dead and spun back towards Kathleen, his eyes widening noticeably. Both women were aware of his hesitation. They watched as he gazed down Kathleen's body and slowly raised his ebony eyes back up to her face, an inexplicable expression on his own.

'What is your name?' he asked in English.

Kathleen did not answer.

He took a pace towards her. 'I said, what is your name?'

'Kathleen . . .' and from nowhere she found the defiance to add, 'What is yours?' The moment she spoke the words she was overcome with fear and expected him to lash out and strike her, but to her astonishment his face stiffened and he walked away shouting an order.

Jasper, who was at the head of the row of men and the closest to the two young women, had seen what occurred, and when two Japanese crossed to Kathleen and roughly took hold of her, removing her from the line, he called out to her. 'Try not to be afraid, Kathy. For some reason the Jap colonel is taking you with him. Be strong.'

For this brave insolence he was smashed once more on the shoulder with a rifle, causing him to stumble, but again he did not lose his balance and remained standing.

103

Kathleen was resisting, the horror of what had happened to Matilda uppermost in her mind. She began screaming: 'Don't! Stop! Leave me with my friends.' But she was shoved and dragged past Matilda's corpse to be driven along in the direction the colonel had taken.

Twelve of the Japanese troops now began to herd both lines of men and women across the pebble-strewn beach into the surf, and at the same time two soldiers ran up behind them and placed down a light machine gun. Della turned and cried out, 'Peter! Peter!' and her husband shouted, 'Be brave, my love! Be brave!' He turned quickly to his brother-in-law, fear now resident on his face, and asked, 'Are they going to kill us, Jasper?'

Jasper's answer was a single word. 'Yes.' He could see the colonel had halted beyond the boulders and was watching. He had given his brutal orders and now they were being carried out.

The prisoners looked at one another in shock and disbelief; a few even hurried into the water as if they might swim away before the horror began. Some men protested but Jasper, who was at the end of the line of males and closest to Lexi, yelled to her, 'Listen carefully: they will machine-gun us, so when I shout "Now!" dive in front of me into the sea and keep swimming under water as far as you can! I'll try to block the bullets. Do you understand?'

'Yes.' Tears were streaming down Lexi's cheeks, panic shot through her and her throat constricted.

As Jasper pushed through the sea, a wave rolled in and he moved abruptly towards Lexi and at the same time looked sharply back to the Japanese soldiers, who had withdrawn to the beach behind the machine gun. 'Now!' he yelled and raised his arms. Lexi breathed in hard and dived in front of her uncle to the sound of machine gun bullets cutting into the rows of men and women, their screams rending the day.

Sidwell, the steward, had realised what was happening as soon as they had been formed into a line. He knew there was no hope. As they were herded into the water he slipped his right hand deep into his pocket, and in the very moment before the machine gun spat death at him he spun round and threw a long slender dirk straight into the throat of the sergeant. 'You filthy bastard!'

The sergeant dropped to the ground.

Three seconds later Sidwell's chest was shattered and he was floating face down in his own blood; but the boy from Broken Hill who had ridden wild brumbies on the sunburnt plains below the Barrier Range had taken one of the fiends along with him, and as he slipped beneath the waves the firm smile of satisfaction was etched in his face for all time.

Lexi was deep in the water and swimming with all her might out to sea. She felt a sharp stinging pain across her back but she continued on under the waves rolling above, her mind a blur. Swim, Lexi, swim! Don't come to the surface, just keep going. All her years of daily swimming had prepared her for these desperate moments under water. She strove to push on as far as she could without surfacing. She wanted air. Her lungs were bursting, the pain was surging through her, she needed to breathe, but sheer terror gave her even more strength. Keep swimming, Lexi, it's your only chance. Your uncle has just given his life for you. Don't come up for air. Swim!

Behind her the other survivors of the torpedoed SS *Fortitude* were mown down, riddled with bullets. Frans Van Houten had turned to face his death and loudly voiced his hatred of his killers – 'Stinking barbarians!' – as he crumpled into the sea. Jasper had leapt high in the air and thrown his arms up to provide as much cover for Lexi as he could; miraculously he remained vertical, screening her for many seconds, even with eleven bullets in his back. Della had died calling out to Peter and her husband had crumpled beneath the surface of the water with the words 'I love you, Della' on his lips.

Shoerd Amel was the only one who saw Sidwell hit the Japanese sergeant in the throat with his knife, and he pitched forward into the sea exclaiming, 'Well done, Sidwell.'

One woman who was not killed in the first spurt of bullets staggered back towards the shore, arms raised in supplication towards the soldiers. As she tumbled to the edge of the water, blood oozing from the wounds in her stomach, terrified eyes raised in a silent appeal for help, one of the Japanese walked from the line of men, kicked her to the beach and bayoneted her.

As the mutilated bodies floated briefly and began to sink, the morning sun in its innocence highlighted the crimson-stained salt water; sea birds screeched and cried in the sky above and dipped and sped across the surface of the rolling waves, attracted by the chance of the grisly food; and it was not long before dark fins appeared near the corpses to devour the evidence of the atrocity.

The Japanese soldiers did not stay to witness what became of their carnage. They swiftly picked up the machine gun, formed into files of three and retreated along the beach carrying their dying sergeant with them.

Chapter Fourteen

Colonel Tama Ikeda watched his men shoot the captives. At the brittle bark of the machine gun he grunted, and then his fury rose again as he saw one of his men fall from a knife thrown by a prisoner.

He screamed out with anger, his sallow skin flushing. How dare he have a knife! How dare he throw it! Stupid Europeans! They had been uncooperative. It was not right that they die defiantly. They had been prisoners. He cursed and turned sharply away, holding his sword down and striding out as fast as he could in his haste to remove himself.

And that girl, Kathleen, the Eurasian: by all that was sacred, she had shocked him!

He thought of the ancient saying: The water had splashed into the ear of the sleeper and surprised him. He nodded to himself for it seemed that he, Tama, was the sleeper!

He and his men must move on. He would take her with him and think what to do later.

Kathleen watched them fall into the sea; like marionettes they toppled. Those dolls falling forward, reaching at the air, had been her friends. Was that her own voice she heard screaming? Everything was nothing: A blur of pain washed out her mind. Misery and anguish blocked out the light, and she sank towards the sand as her captors held her upright.

* * *

Lexi's lungs were about to explode; she could not hold her breath any longer. She turned on her back and came to the surface, pushing just her mouth above the salt water and inhaling the sweet cool air of life, then she dived again and swam on. She did this seven times before she dared to raise her head and look around. In the distance, perhaps a quarter of a mile away, was the island, but she could see no movement.

She knew she was crying, her tears and the salt water all of a one. She was the lone survivor of the massacre, saved by her wonderful brave uncle whom she had come to know only in these malignant hours.

She became aware of a smudge of pink in the sea around her. She was bleeding! The pain she had felt across her back as she swam away had been a graze from a bullet. Fear grabbed her mind. This sea was full of sharks! She turned in the salt water but could see nothing sinister. Another island loomed not far away. She must make for that. What if she ran into another bunch of Japs? But she could not stay in the water; she had to take the chance. Fighting her exhaustion, she struck out for the new island.

As she carved her way through the South China Sea, she concentrated on her strokes, pushing herself to the extreme of her endurance. Don't think about the sharks. You're in Repulse Bay on a hot afternoon in summer . . . the day is made for swimming. Come on, swim Lexi, swim!

Many minutes later she raised herself from the rolling waves and stood waist deep. She could hardly drag herself through the surf. It had been so long since she had taken any nourishment, so long since she had taken a drink of water. She staggered and fell to her knees, but raised herself again, her whole body trembling.

For a moment her heart raced in panic. What if she had come back to the same beach?

She looked at the jungle. Her head was spinning, and she could not feel her arms and legs; they were numb. Her vision blurred and her legs gave way and the pebbles beneath her feet rose up towards her as she collapsed unconscious to the beach.

Kathleen sobbed, aware of what occurred only in a haze as she was carried along the beach by the soldiers who dragged her between them. They made a sharp turn into the jungle and passed down a narrow path between vines and tall bamboo plants.

Six hundred yards along the track they arrived at a camp in sight of a cove where two patrol boats rode at anchor and two small craft sat at the water's edge. The soldiers' faces turned interestedly towards Kathleen as she was brought by them. A tent flap opened and she was pushed inside to fall upon a reed mat on the ground, where she lay in a stupor.

She did not know how much time had elapsed when finally she sat up and held her head in her hands. What was going on? Why had she been taken when the others had been murdered? What was to become of her? She could see through the open canvas flap two soldiers standing guard, and as she watched a third Japanese came past them and bent into the tent. He placed down a tin container of water and a bowl of rice, motioned for her to eat and drink, and departed.

At the first taste of the water Kathleen's stomach churned. She thought she would be sick but she managed to control herself and gradually, after taking tiny sips for many minutes, she was able to drink the whole container. She ate a little of the rice and sat holding her knees.

Hours went by, and in numb acceptance of her plight she followed the activity of the soldiers through the open canvas. They seemed to be preparing to abandon the camp. NCOs shouted and privates hurried back and forth hastily dumping items in boxes. As the time passed she found herself fingering the jade dragon hanging around her neck. It made her feel closer to her mother, and that brought a certain solace.

Her brain began to work in sequence again and she began

thinking of the others: of Lexi and Della and Peter and Jasper Hayes. This made her feel ill again. They were all dead – all the people who had made up her family, gone, shot to death by the creature who had brought her to this place. Why had she been the one to be spared?

Around sunset her two guards were replaced, and a few minutes later one more tin of water arrived and with it another bowl of rice, this time with a little meat mixed in. She drank all the water and forced herself to eat a little of the food as the light faded and thousands of mosquitoes and other insects appeared.

As day gave up and fires were lit, a long-sleeved jacket and a net to cover her face were handed in and she huddled on the grass mat for what she thought must have been another hour until a shout close by outside caused her to sit straight up, alert.

The beam from a flashlight hit her as the flap of the tent was opened and a soldier barked an order at her.

This was intended to make Kathleen rise and move outside, which she did, fear visible in her face. A sergeant gestured for her to move ahead of him in the beam from the torch. She walked cautiously, and every now and then she was pushed from behind to accelerate her.

She was halted by a large bonfire where the mosquitoes were mercifully fewer. For a few seconds Kathleen did not perceive the colonel, who sat in a portable canvas chair just on the edge of the field of illumination.

She started when he spoke to her. 'Come here to me,' he snapped. His English was excellent though with the usual marked accent of the Oriental speaker. She hated him and in her mind she dubbed him 'Colonel Pig'.

He raised his hand in dismissal to the sergeant who had delivered her, as she glanced right and left. They appeared to be alone; the nearest group of soldiers approximately fifty yards away.

On his head the colonel wore only a cloth cap. He leant forward and she noticed a single deep cleft running between his eyes, which reflected the flames like a line of tiny glow worms on his brow. A fine stubble of beard grew on his chin and the sides of his copious mouth had fallen to form jowls. The top three buttons of his uniform were open and his sleeves were rolled up to show hairless forearms. He had been smoking and stubs of cigarettes lay in the sand around his feet. Now she noticed a second chair beside him and he gestured to it. 'Sit.'

She was terrified but she managed to say, 'I prefer to stand.'

She could see his anger.

'I said sit.'

'I know you did . . . but I prefer to stand.'

'You speak bravely. Some of your companions spoke bravely but it did not save them.'

She could not bear to look at him and she turned her face away, but this action caused him to stand and come to her. He pushed her hard in the back towards the chair. 'Sit or I will cut off your legs.'

She believed him and sat down but kept her face averted.

She felt his fingers remove the mosquito net from her face. He grabbed her chin and roughly turned her head towards him. She closed her eyes.

'You have spirit,' he said, 'but in the end I will break you. So probably best if you cooperate now. Open your eyes.'

She did so but made no reply, her expression speaking to him of the contempt she held for him. He dropped his hands from her face, scratching her chin as his nail scraped across her skin. 'I am Colonel Ikeda, I am an important man.'

She said nothing.

'And your name is Kathleen.'

She nodded.

'Where did you get the jade dragon that hangs around your neck?'

'It was my mother's.'

He did not speak for some moments, and in the silence Kathleen

III

could hear the mosquitoes buzzing above the myriad of other croaking, groaning, whispering sounds of the jungle at night.

'Where did she get it?'

'I don't know. She had it always . . . all my life.'

He cleared his throat and half turned in his chair towards her. 'Where were you born?'

'Why?'

'Where were you born?'

'Southern China. Near the city of Kunming.'

'How old are you?'

'What's so important about me? Tell me why I was not murdered with my friends?'

'Shut up!' He screamed it so loudly she flinched in the chair and many of the soldiers in the distance looked around at them.

His eyes narrowed so that they almost disappeared in the folds of skin encircling them, and his voice dropped to a threatening quiet. 'Do not dare to speak of your friends. Never ask me a question. I ask the questions. Now answer me or you will deeply regret it.'

Kathleen hesitated but she replied as calmly as she could. 'I'm twenty-nine.'

'Where is your family?'

'You killed them.'

She saw the rage rise within him. '*Kimi!*' he shouted and pointed at her. She was to learn this was a Japanese word for 'you'. He poked his finger at her face and reverted to English. 'You will not speak to me this way. You will answer my questions with civility or I will beat you till you beg me to stop.'

She bent her head and fell silent.

'That is better. Is your mother alive?'

'No.'

'When did she die?'

Kathleen choked on the words as she replied, 'A week ago.'

He paused. 'A week ago?' He paused again. 'And her name was . . . ?'

'Bess.'

He frowned. 'Bess? What is that? Bess? Bess?'

She hated to hear her mother's name hissing on his fat lips but she answered, 'Her name was Elizabeth, but she was known as Bess. It is a form of Elizabeth.'

He did not move; he sat stiffly in his chair, as his eyes now closed completely.

Kathleen was amazed, it was unbelievable that this lunatic, this murdering madman, was asking her these questions. It was all insane. She sat petrified, as still as he was, watching him, his formal, frightening face unmoving. He remained this way for over a minute as she sat in confusion beside him, until abruptly he swung his head towards her and opened his eyes.

Alarmed, she sat back in her chair away from him. He continued to stare at her for some time until finally he rose. 'We leave now under cover of darkness,' was all he said, before he spun round and walked away.

Kathleen remained in her chair, gazing at his back as he strode over to a group of soldiers, who jumped to their feet, almost falling down again in their haste to come to attention. He spoke sharply and two detached themselves, picked up a blanket and came in her direction. They placed the blanket around her shoulders and prodded her to stand and move towards one of the small craft beached beyond the camp. There was no point in resisting, so she simply went quietly with them.

In another fifteen minutes Kathleen was aboard one of the Japanese vessels which was anchored in the harbour. She saw the captain who had been on the beach and killed Matilda, but she did not see Colonel Pig again and she was taken to a small cabin and locked inside.

They remained at anchor for perhaps two hours before a soldier entered bearing towels and a pot of green tea with a cup. He placed them down and retreated.

She sipped the tea and thought about all that had happened,

and as she felt the engines start she collapsed on to the bunk with a hopeless feeling in her heart and tears in her eyes.

Colonel Ikeda sat on deck as the patrol boat picked up speed and departed the Lingayen Gulf in a northerly direction. The clouds slipped across the three-quarter moon pursued by the rising wind, and the stars of the firmament watched like thousands of tiny eyes as the craft surged through the oleaginous swell of the South China Sea. He had eaten ashore and would sleep a little soon. There was much to do in conquering the Philippines, then there was Malaya, Borneo, Singapore and Java. Once they had that last island they would have all the oil, tin and tungsten they needed. He smiled. After that came Australia and New Zealand. Part of him had always wanted to visit those countries. He recalled reading an Intelligence report years ago about the deepest harbour in the world being Hobart, a city in the island state of Tasmania in Australia. He would like to see that harbour; and perhaps too he would wish to go to other places . . . or perhaps not.

The furrow on his brow deepened as he remembered the girl called Kathleen who was aboard this very boat.

Lexi felt hands upon her and she struggled to come to consciousness. She sensed being raised and carried but the darkness enveloped her again and she slipped into it.

She was dimly aware of voices and a fire. Something was put in her mouth. It tasted sweet and soothed her dry, cracked tongue. She fought to come to the surface of awareness and she tried to speak, but the pleasant black engulfed her and she slid down into it once more.

Something cool touched her forehead and the sweet taste was repeated in her mouth. This time she realised she was swallowing and she fought again to wake up. She could hear soft sweet music, but she was overcome by the warm, dark sinking feeling once more and she drifted back into sleep.

She dreamt of water all around her; of having to swim for miles in the wide never-ending ocean; of Aunt Della and Kathleen clinging to her in the sea and men in uniform in a lifeboat who would not help them. She saw Uncle Jasper fighting with the men and she realised they were soldiers and she was frightened of them. She knew the soldiers were killing her uncle but she heard him calling out to her to be brave, and yet the water was engulfing her and she had to keep swimming on and on and on . . .

Chapter Fifteen

Lexi felt the touch of a breeze drifting across her bare forearms; then came the music, a sweet haunting sound. For a moment she was seven again and dancing to the lute and recorder at Miss Verner-Smith's School for Girls in Hong Kong.

She opened her eyes and there, through a roughly hewn window, perched on a ledge was a man playing a bamboo flute. He was immersed in his music and sat with one ankle resting on the knee of his other leg. He wore an ill-fitting shirt that a long time previously might have been white but was now a tired grey, and his trousers were torn, showing well-developed calf muscles. Yet his music was soporific and soothing.

She closed her eyes again but suddenly rushing into her mind came all that she had suffered, the loss of her child uppermost. The pain of that awakened her completely. She groaned, and the man, hearing the sound, ceased playing and came to the window.

She sighed and raised herself. 'Don't stop; it's lovely.'

He silently placed his instrument down on the ledge and disappeared.

Lexi glanced around the room. It was a typical traditional rural dwelling, made from the nipa palm, the interior walls being bamboo. The single window revealed the sea some two hundred yards distant, and through the open doorway lay a sort of platform-like small veranda where fishing nets were strung along the rail. She looked up, the roof was straw. She looked down, the floor was covered in a type of hessian. The single decoration was a metal cross above the door.

She sat up feeling slightly giddy and when she put her feet to the floor decided it was better not to stand, so she remained seated on the lumpy mattress. She realised she was wearing a rough warm smock and that the only other items on her body were her diamond engagement ring and her wedding ring. They looked overly large and somehow ridiculous on her hand. She was faintly surprised to think that the jewellery had come through everything with her and sparkled here on her finger. Her other possessions had gone down with the ship, including her lovely Kwan Yin, her silent confidante all these years. Kwan Yin had gone to the bottom of the South China Sea carrying all Lexi's secrets with her: the bodhisattva with all her compassion.

As she hunched forward, the weight of her experience heavy upon her, she wondered where Kathleen was and said a swift silent prayer for her friend, hoping she was alive. A noise outside made her sit up as the man reappeared on the veranda and entered the dwelling with a woman in a similar smock to the one she wore. They halted a yard into the room and the woman crossed herself when she saw Lexi.

'Do you speak English?'

They did not answer, and the man shrugged.

Lexi sighed. 'I suppose not.'

The woman walked over to a table in the corner, poured water from a cracked jug into a cup and handed it to Lexi. She sipped it. It helped and she felt a little better. She smiled at them. 'Thank you.'

They stood looking at her and smiled back. They were friendly and no doubt had saved her life.

She still felt giddy, so she lay back down and closed her eyes. A minute or so later when she opened them she was alone. Well, she believed she was, until she glanced to the window and saw two sets of wide eyes in small faces watching her with interest.

She smiled at them and the heads disappeared. It was not long before she drifted back to sleep.

Some hours later she awakened to fading light and an odd smell assailing her nostrils. It was not a bad smell, just an unusual one, and she raised herself and saw that it came from a smoking pot in the corner of the room. It took her a few minutes before she realised it was to keep the mosquitoes and other insects away.

Lexi suddenly felt very hungry, and a minute later the woman from earlier came in carrying a bowl of rice and fish. At her side was a lean middle-aged lady whose jet-black hair was streaked with grey and who came over to the side of the cot as Lexi sat up.

'I here, speak with you,' the newcomer said, sitting down on a lone stool. She had smooth high cheekbones and wore rosary beads, pale like white crystal, which she fingered as they conversed.

'Oh thank God. You speak English.'

The woman shrugged. 'A little. My big grandson, he out working. He speak little English too. You eat now. Talk after.'

It was good advice, and Lexi ate every morsel while the newcomer watched.

After finishing, she handed the woman the empty bowl. 'I must get to a city. Where am I? Am I in the Philippines?' The woman frowned and Lexi repeated, 'Philippines? Is this place one of the Philippine islands?'

The woman nodded. 'Ah, Philippine . . . Yes. Cabarruyan. We Pangasinan.'

Lexi was not sure what that meant, but it seemed she *was* in the Philippines.

'I must get to a city. Do you understand? A big place with lots of people.'

'No big place here . . . little place called Anda. Big places: Lingayen Dagupan, San Fabian, long way.' She pointed out to sea.

Lexi realised that the towns the woman mentioned were the ones she needed. There would be telephones and means of transport in them, and she could get from one of them to Manila.

Now the woman rose and disappeared for a few minutes before returning with a tin dish of water and a threadbare towel, and through the use of her English and some sign language Lexi understood that her more personal needs would have to be dealt with outside in the trees.

'I fix you hurt,' the Filipina said, and she smiled encouragingly as she slipped the smock down from Lexi's shoulder and rubbed some ointment into the surface wound from the machine gun bullet on her back. Lexi shivered in recollection of the moment she had felt the bullet sting her under water. Her head spun again with the cruel memories.

'I go now, come back after.' The woman departed.

Lexi washed herself as the daylight faded and the moon came up. It threw a glistening silver path across the dark sea to the sandy beach. She shivered in the cool evening and quickly replaced her clothing, and soon she heard sounds of people gaining the veranda.

The man from earlier returned with a lighted candle and placed it on the ledge in the corner. Lexi thanked him and lay back while the family ate at a roughly hewn table outside. She could see a second nipa hut about twenty yards away and she guessed it belonged to the gaunt middle-aged lady.

The man was standing out on the veranda playing his sweet music on the flute again when the woman returned with a youth of about sixteen or seventeen. She introduced him as Carlos. 'This my grandson. He speak some English.' She sat once more on the stool to talk to Lexi. After a time it became clear that her name was Josephine, that the younger woman and man were her daughter Silveria and son-in-law Pitik, and the youth, Carlos and the little ones, their children. Pitik was obviously a fisherman and when Lexi tried to explain she was from a ship which had been sunk by the Japanese, Josephine's face filled with fear and she nodded her head vehemently, saying, 'Japanese bad. Bomb American airfields, bomb everything. Hear aeroplanes in sky. Japanese soldiers sail in gulf.' She pointed to the sea again.

Lexi shivered. 'Have they been here? Have the Japanese been here?'

Josephine shook her head.

'Thank God.'

Josephine pointed inland. 'My cousin grow rice. He have wireless set. Hear all about Japanese.'

'If the Japanese come,' Carlos spoke up, 'I join army . . . Want to fight.'

'Stop!' His grandmother turned to him and spoke sharply in their local tongue. It was evident that his joining the army was not what she wished. She faced back to Lexi with the words, 'He too young for army.'

When they departed, Lexi fell into a troubled sleep, her face towards the shimmering moonbeam which had climbed from the sea to creep over the sand, through the window and trail across the hessian floor to her bed.

The following morning she was well enough to rise and sit for some hours in the warmth of the sun, and as the next few days passed she grew stronger until she felt close to normal, but almost hourly she was plagued by visions of the loss of her loved ones.

From what Josephine and Carlos said, she believed she had been a day unconscious and that she was indeed on an island called Cabarruyan and at the entrance to a body of water called Lingayen Gulf.

Every day at dusk they heard the sounds of aircraft in the sky, and as each night passed Lexi became more anxious to leave. The Japanese were around here somewhere, even if they had not landed in this exact spot. Her best chance was to try and get to one of the bigger places, where she could find out what was happening and go on to Manila. Josephine told her that she had friends called Layosa in the town of San Fabian, which lay on the south-west shore of the Gulf.

'How do you get there? Do you go by boat?'

Josephine nodded.

* * *

Lexi and Josephine had been gathering firewood and were returning along the beach. A breeze had come up and the sand stung Lexi's bare legs as she put down her bundle of sticks and took hold of the woman's bony shoulders and gazed in her eyes.

'Josephine, I would like you to talk to Pitik for me. I must get to a big place, Lingayen or San Fabian. Will he take me in his fishing boat? I will pay him.' She glanced down to her hand. 'I will give him my diamond ring.' She took it off and it glinted as she held it between her thumb and index finger. 'It's the least I can do. Would you ask him to take me, please?'

'I ask.'

That night Lexi sat at table with the family. Pitik, who always was positioned at the head, facing the beach, turned to her. He smiled and showed a broken front tooth. 'Drink? Yes?'

Lexi had learnt in her time with the family that Pitik knew two words of English: yes and drink. He took a stone pitcher and poured her a cup of nipa wine: it seemed to Lexi that most significant items of Pangasinan life came from the nipa palm.

She smiled and sipped the wine as Pitik turned to his mother-in-law and, pointing at Lexi, asked a question. Josephine replied with the words, 'I take you to San Fabian.' Now Pitik pointed to himself and then to Lexi and told her, 'I tek you to San Fabian . . .'

Lexi's relief showed in her face. 'Oh thank you, Pitik.'

The family laughed, and Pitik spoke again at length to Josephine and Carlos, who between them translated for Lexi. It seemed there had been a family meeting where Pitik had decided that with the Japanese patrol boats already in the vicinity, the whole family would be safer in San Fabian where Josephine's friends lived and not out here exposed to the passing soldiers. It was dangerous to cross the Gulf with enemy patrols obviously reconnoitring, but it was also dangerous to remain.

Carlos frowned as he listened to his father and Josephine, and as they completed their translation he spoke up strongly. Lexi only understood the word Hapôn, meaning Japanese, but the way his parents and grandmother reacted, she knew he must have mentioned joining the Filipino army again. Carlos, admonished, fell silent as Pitik took up Lexi's left hand, patted her rings, shook his head and spoke. Lexi glanced to Josephine for explanation.

'He says he not want diamond. You must keep.'

A flood of fondness for this Filipino family who had saved her life rushed through her, and she lifted her cup of nipa wine in the air and from her heart thanked Pitik and Silveria. They all drank a toast – Lexi was not sure what to – but they laughed and patted each other affectionately, and a common bond of warmth and regard flooded around the rustic table to the hum of flying insects.

After dinner Pitik entertained them with his delicate music, and for the first night Lexi slept peacefully; even her dark dreams did not haunt her.

The following morning, under a cloud-filled sky and in a cool breeze, they began to pack. From what Lexi could gather, San Fabian was a seven- or eight-hour sail away, which equated to perhaps fifty miles distance.

She and Josephine were setting boxes in the stern of the boat when suddenly there was a sharp shout and they both whirled round.

Carlos came dashing round a stand of palms and across the sand, screaming, *'Paparating na ang mga Hapôn!'*

Josephine's naturally brown face face blanched; hurriedly she pushed Lexi out of the boat.

'Japanese! They land on beach. Not far away.'

122

Chapter Sixteen

Carlos was waving his arms and shouting: 'They come! Soon!'

Pitik dropped the fishing net he was folding and ran to the nipa hut, yelling for Silveria. It was obvious he was telling her to round up the children.

Josephine grabbed Lexi's hand. 'We and children hide.'

The Filipinos knew the reputation of the Japanese soldiers: they were not about to take any chances with the lives of their children.

There was panic in the air, but suddenly, when Silveria and the two small children appeared, Pitik calmed. Silveria grabbed the toddler, Jimmy, in her arms and her husband wrapped a broad band of material around them, swiftly strapping the child to his mother. He put his finger to his lips for silence and handed his wife a leather water bag. He kissed the children and pointed to the trees, and as if there had been some previous plan, Josephine pulled Lexi towards the jungle. 'Come quick! Pitik and Carlos stay, otherwise soldiers search, find us all and kill. Pitik face soldiers. Hope they go away.'

Into the trees the women and children ran. About a hundred yards in from the beach, beyond forest and banana palms, a bunch of massive mango trees grew covered with lianas, and on the far side of the largest, about three feet from the ground, hidden behind a thick liana was a hole about the size of a foot. Josephine lifted Lessa, her little granddaughter, and from that foothold

Lessa could reach the lower branches. The child climbed the tree with the older woman; Lexi and Silveria with two-year-old Jimmy strapped to her body coming behind. By grabbing branches and lianas they clambered up the tree to a platform where, cramped though they were, they could sit hidden by leaves.

They could see nothing, but they listened.

About half a minute passed before they heard the sound of men running, accompanied by shouting in Japanese and Pitik's voice raised in alarm.

Lexi could feel her heart pumping and she began to shake involuntarily. Tears sprang to Lessa's eyes, and to take her mind from herself, Lexi took the child in her arms and hugged her against her body. 'Hush, darling, hush.' There was comfort in the small body's touch, and Lexi felt her quivering cease as she clasped the child tightly to her breast. She closed her eyes and pretended Lessa was Paul and that they were in the house in Hong Kong and all was right with the world.

They huddled together, hearing another series of yells followed by Pitik's voice again raised in reply. Lessa called out for her father, and as Lexi stiffened, Josephine shot her hand over the girl's mouth whispering that it was imperative they must be silent.

Fear was swamping Lexi's mind but it appeared the soldiers had not heard the child's cry, for no one came in their direction. Josephine kissed the child and put her finger to her lips for silence.

Abruptly in the distance someone screamed an agonising 'No!' and the group in the trees flinched as one. Lexi raised her eyes to Josephine's. Tears were running down the woman's cheeks but she was stone silent, her hand fast across her granddaughter's mouth. The children's eyes were full of fear, and as Josephine and Lexi hugged Lessa, Silveria kissed her son and buried her face in his hair.

They heard no gunshots, but another scream ruptured the air, followed by the sounds of running and thumping and things being thrown or dropped. Soon the smell of burning drifted to Lexi's nostrils. *The nipa huts are on fire!*

The children seemed to realise that complete silence was their only hope now, and they sat rigid with dread while another four or five minutes passed.

They began to hope that the soldiers had gone when the sound of men approaching through the trees reached them. Holding their breath, they looked down through the branches, eyes reflecting their terror, and Lexi saw the dreaded uniform which she would never forget and the cork sun helmets and the blue bayonets. Her mind froze.

The Japanese soldiers trotted by underneath the trees, slashing with their bayonets at undergrowth as they passed. There were perhaps twenty of them.

Lexi and the family sat clutching each other and Silveria, apprehensive about her husband and son, made to climb down, but Josephine restrained her. To their continuing alarm, within a short time five more Japanese moved through the brush and trees below them and followed the others, but that neither Pitik nor Carlos came augured badly.

Finally the children fell asleep and Silveria unstrapped her son and placed him down. Lexi could tell from her agitated movements that the young Filipina mother could wait no longer, and as she spoke softly to Josephine, the older woman nodded and turned to face Lexi. 'We stay with children. Silveria go see.'

As terrified as she was, Lexi could not let Silveria go alone. 'I will accompany Silveria; you stay here with the children.'

With trepidation in their eyes, and trembling fingers, the two young women descended the mango tree.

Tiny beads of sweat appeared on Lexi's temples as she hurried as quietly as possible with her friend back through the trees. As they edged into the clearing all was still. The dwellings had been razed to the ground: constructed of mere sticks and grass, they had made a most effective bonfire. They were now two smouldering heaps of rubble.

125

The two women furtively moved forward and abruptly Silveria's hand shot to her mouth, holding in a broken sound. She fell to her knees, sobbing.

Pitik's head had been lopped off. It lay three or four yards from his body across the blood-soaked ground. His torso had pitched forward into the dirt; his hands were tied behind his back with barbed wire.

Lexi's stomach turned as she stood petrified beside the kneeling Filipina. 'Oh Jesus, dear Lord Jesus in heaven . . .'

Then they saw Carlos. He lay draped across a fishing net ten yards away, face up.

They ran to him and lifted him. His hands were also fastened behind his back with barbed wire and the barbs had cut into his back and made a bloody wound. A big purple lump on his forehead bled, but he was alive. Lexi managed to remove the barbed wire from his bleeding wrists and was about to bathe them with sea water when they heard the sound of a motorboat. Lexi's throat constricted as she whispered, 'It's the same direction the Japs came from.'

They gazed at each other in panic, but through the mind-blanking fear Lexi contrived to think clearly. Carlos had not revived, so she quickly turned him over the way he had been and tucked his hands under his body before grabbing Silveria's arm and drawing her into the undergrowth behind the remains of Josephine's hut.

A minute later a Japanese patrol boat, with hinomaru – the sun ray flag – flapping in the breeze, sailed by a mere seventy or so yards from the shore, heading north out of the Gulf. The women could see the soldiers on the deck looking straight in their direction. Doubtless it was the same unit of troops eyeing their morning's handiwork as they left to return whence they had come.

The women waited until the boat could be heard no more before they dared to run back to Carlos. Now Lexi bathed his wrists with sea water and bandaged them with strips of their clothes while the youth was still unconscious. She tried to explain that she was a doctor, and Silveria appeared to understand.

They realised they must bury Pitik before the small children returned. Lexi used sign language to convey that she would go back to Josephine and tell her to remain with the children and she left Silveria nursing Carlos in her arms and ran back through the trees to report the grisly news to Josephine.

The Filipina woman tried to be strong for the sake of her grandchildren, but she had trouble composing herself and a muscle at the side of her mouth twitched uncontrollably. Finally she caught her breath and managed to say, 'I wait here . . . with little ones. You call me.'

As Lexi returned to Silveria and Carlos she suddenly thought of the fishing boat and she spun round to see that miraculously the Japanese had left it alone. It perched down along the beach at the water's edge, still attached by a rope to the anchor which was wedged into the sand.

Lexi and Silveria carried Carlos and placed him gently under the shade of a tree before they set about burying Pitik's remains. Silveria continued to weep softly during the burial and they were putting the last sods of earth on him when Carlos murmured and opened his eyes.

The women relieved the terror in his eyes by reporting that the soldiers had sailed away, and slowly, stammering and hesitating, the youth related the shocking facts of the morning. He and his father had faced the Japanese and asked to be left in peace. The soldiers had ignored them and taken rice, fruit and other food from the huts and begun to set them on fire. Pitik had objected, and for that impertinence had been forced to his knees and had his hands wired.

The lieutenant in charge had taken his sword and in cursory manner cut off his head in front of Carlos. The horrified boy

127

had screamed when they butchered his father, whereby a soldier had wired his wrists and forced him to the ground. On his knees he had waited to be murdered too but instead he had been smashed with a rifle butt on his buttocks and back and finally on the head, at which point he had screamed again but remembered no more.

When Josephine brought the children from the trees, they ran and hugged and kissed their brother and asked for their father.

The boy wearily shrugged his shoulders and lifted his eyes to his mother and grandmother for explanation.

Josephine's face was tense and drawn. She clasped her daughter in her arms and whispered, 'We will tell the little ones the truth, for they must know, but not now, not yet. When they are older.' And Silveria, torment in her eyes, bent down to her babies and took them in her arms. 'Daddy has gone to heaven, to a wonderful happy place where he will wait for us to come to him a long time from now.'

It was not yet noon, and it was Carlos who said to his grandmother that they should leave now, immediately, for San Fabian Town.

'But are you capable of sailing the boat without your father? And are you well enough after your ordeal? You were unconscious for a long time.'

His bloodshot eyes flashed with new courage. 'I am strong. My father taught me all he knew. I am a good sailor and with a little help from you women, yes, I will take you to San Fabian.' And to the distress of his mother and grandmother, he added, 'I join army now. Kill Japanese.'

They hurriedly moved the babies to the boat, and as Carlos made ready for the voyage, Lexi paused in the stern of the craft and looked to the north-west. Hong Kong was over there across the wide sea, and since her departure so much grief had descended upon her. She could not help but think of the pristine haven of Hydrangea and of Sir Brillard.

Oh my darling Pa, I miss you so. I wonder what is happening to you and Grandmother?

Chapter Seventeen

The morning sun glinted on the brass handle of Sir Brillard's ivory cane as he lifted it and grunted to the young policeman standing beside him on Hydrangea's wide veranda, while Harold the red setter ranged around them sniffing at the breeze.

'I heard about the ridiculous peace mission boat that the Japs sent over yesterday morning from Kowloon.'

The New Territories and Kowloon – as close as a mile across the strait – were now in Japanese hands.

The listener was his friend George Wright-Nooth, whom Sir Brillard had met a year ago when Superintendent Frank Shaftain, the head of CID, had brought him on one of his visits to Hydrangea. There was a frankness to his expression and he spoke his mind. This appealed to Sir Brillard, and George had become a regular visitor to Hydrangea.

He answered the knight as he smoothed his moustache with his fingers.

'Yes, sir. I was there on Queen's Pier with a number of my police when the Japs arrived.'

Brillard gave a chuckle. 'I was told they were accompanied by a pregnant lady almost at full term and along with her was Mrs Lee, the wife of the secretary to the Governor. Is it true she brought over her two fat dachshund dogs on leashes?'

'It is. There were three Jap officers almost falling over their lengthy swords, one carrying a white flag and one with a briefcase.'

'Sounds as if it had all the overtones of musical comedy.'

George grinned and ran his hand through his shock of wavy hair. 'Well it did. They'd brought the women from Kowloon as sort of hostages.'

'I heard Major Boxer met them.' Boxer was a British intelligence officer who spoke fluent Japanese.

'Yes, that's right. He arrived a few minutes after they landed. There were two lone American reporters on the pier as well. They talked to the women until Boxer turned up. It was quite ridiculous. Seems the Japs carried surrender terms to be submitted to the Governor, which of course were sent over to him and rejected out of hand. Then the delegation got back on their craft and departed for Kowloon, and that was that.'

The elderly man patted his visitor's shoulder affectionately. 'Now tell me why you're really here. You didn't just drop by to chat about the blasted peace mission.'

George nodded. 'You're right, I didn't. Fact is, you must leave Hydrangea, sir, there's nothing else for it. We've lost all our positions on the mainland and the last section of our troops who were over there retreated across the Lei Mun Channel thirty-six hours ago. The writing's on the wall.'

Sir Brillard shaded his eyes in the bright early-morning sunshine as the policeman went on: 'There's not a lot of time, sir. This part of the island's one of the first areas the Japanese will pass through when they attack. I know the defence forces have chosen a number of places to make a stand, but Hydrangea is out here all alone. There are lots of places you and Lady Hayes can go.'

'I know what you say is true, George, but I'm not about to leave my castle because some very bad-tempered little yellow men in uniform are coming this way.'

George frowned in concern. It was his duty to try to convince the knight to depart. 'Did you hear that explosion after midnight last night?'

'I did. No doubt the whole island did. Fact is, I thought it was the Japs invading right then.'

'A lot of us thought the same, but it was actually ten tons of our dynamite going up. It was being transferred aboard the steam launch *Jeanette* from the stores on Green Island to the Star Ferry terminal here on the island. Unfortunately the *Jeanette* came in early and to the wrong landing point. God knows why. But apparently one of the Middlesex regiment manning the nearest pillbox mistook the craft for an enemy vessel and opened fire. Up went the whole damn lot! Sub Inspector Hudson and Police Sergeant Donahue were amongst those killed. Reason I tell you this, sir, is that it means we don't have those vital reserves of explosives now and so things are a little more desperate than they were. Which is another reason I'd really like to have you and Lady Hayes moved out of here.'

Sir Brillard nodded tolerantly. 'Son, I understand, but I've lived on this island for nearly forty years. I know our fresh water comes from the New Territories, and because of that alone, with or without the explosives, I'm aware it's only a matter of time before the island falls. I see no point in my moving out of Hydrangea. Though I will try to talk my darling wife into doing as you ask and I'll inform all the household staff that they should return to their homes today.' He made a rueful sound. 'I'm grateful to you for stopping by and for being straight with me, but you go on about your duties now.'

George gave up and sighed in acceptance before saluting, to which Sir Brillard returned a wide smile, straight out of his golden years when he was young and full of life's zest.

'Look after yourself, George. You're a first-class young fellow and I'd like to think you'll make it home to England one day.'

'Thanks, sir. You look after yourself too.'

The young policeman strode down the four stone steps and climbed into his vehicle and drove away. As he passed the pond near the open front gate he glanced into his rear vision mirror to see that the old man had come down from the veranda and now stood upon the gravel drive, cane held high in farewell with his loyal four-legged companion at his side.

He shook his head. 'Goodbye, Sir Brillard,' he said softly as he drove between the two large pillars and turned his vehicle into the road.

The sun was an hour from setting on Saturday 20 December 1941 as Sir Brillard sat drinking a Scotch and gazing over the lawn and down the vista through the avenue of laburnums to the front gate. He could not see the gate itself, for his sight at this distance was blurred, but he could make out the vividness of the two white stone pillars. He was imagining Lexi as a child playing there in the reeds of the pond, her shoes and socks cast aside on the bank and the sound of her merriment drifting to the veranda.

He recalled the first day he had seen this property with Helvetia on his arm. They had strolled through it and stopped at a single bauhinia tree – the Hong Kong orchid. He had reached out, picked a bright rose-coloured flower and tucked it in her hair. She had laughed and kissed his cheek. Since then Helvetia had planted twenty-one of the tall shrub-trees and now they grew throughout the garden. He glanced across to one as he smiled in remembrance of that first day.

A sound behind him made him turn in his chair to see Helvetia coming by the potted palms, pink gin in hand, her face powdered and a bright lipstick on her mouth: the elderly lady who had been his companion for fifty-five years. He had met and married her when he was home on leave in England all those years ago. He knew that he had spoiled her, given her whatever she wanted and that in some ways she had lived a lotus eater's life here in Hong Kong, but that had not always been the way of it. Helvetia had stood by him through the lean years before he had made his money, the times that few knew about except himself and her. Yes, there was more to 'Lady Hayes' than Hong Kong society realised.

Even as late as this morning he had pleaded with her to leave Hydrangea in company with an old friend of his, one of Chiang Kai-shek's Secret Police, who had a boat crossing to Mirs Bay in China and then on to a place of safety. Chiang Kai-shek, the Chinese general, had been fighting the Japanese in China for years and even though the invaders were now in possession of seven of China's largest cities, including Peking, Chiang Kai-shek and his Nationalist Government had retreated further up the Yangtze River Valley to an area of safety where the boat would go. Helvetia had dismissed his appeal with the short reply, 'My place is with you.'

She gave him a gentle smile as she sat down beside him on the veranda sofa and touched his sleeve. He was wearing his old regimental jacket, his crown and pips polished to a brilliant shine. It still fitted him even though it was slightly tight.

'You look wonderful, Brillard dear.'

'Time it was out of mothballs.' He pointed towards the pond and the front gate. 'The sound of the guns comes ever closer, my love, and there's been another air raid on the city and the docks. I could hear the aircraft clearly.'

'Yes, they'll be here very soon. And to think it's almost Christmas.'

There was a portentous rumble of gunfire across the treetops as Brillard answered: 'Just a few days now.' He bent to Harold and rubbed the red setter's head. The old dog responded with a look of adoration.

Helvetia sipped her gin. 'What a strange Yuletide it will be this year. Odd to think all this is going on as the Saviour's birthday approaches.'

'It's odd to us, darling, but not to them.'

'No doubt you're right. It's their emperor who's worshipped as their living God, isn't it?'

Brillard nodded his head. 'It is, but let's not be talking about them. You know, I've been sitting here dwelling upon the past. So

134

much accomplished. Can't complain. We've had a wonderful life together, my sweetheart.'

'We have. I love you, Brillard, I always will.'

He lifted his hand from Harold and turned in the seat to his wife, taking up her free hand and kissing it. 'You know, darling,' he said as he raised his lips from the back of her hand, 'talking about the Saviour's birthday makes me think of my own such a short time ago. Events have moved quite swiftly since that splendid night.'

In response she leant in and touched his cheek with her lips. 'Indeed they have, and I'm only happy that our children are safely out of Hong Kong.'

'Yes, that was a darn good thing.' His voice was thick with emotion now as his faded eyes rested tenderly upon her. 'You know what to do, don't you?'

'Yes, darling, I know *exactly* what to do.'

The first Japanese soldiers to enter Hydrangea came on foot. One unlatched the gate by jumping up on to it and reaching over. He rode it as it swung into the property before he bounded to the ground and, followed by a dozen more all carrying the Arisaka bolt action rifles, loped up the drive towards the house.

They expected no one, believing all residents in this area to have moved back behind the British lines, so when they saw the two figures stand up on the veranda in the dusk they halted abruptly and dropped to the ground. A few moments passed, and perceiving that they were two lone civilians and a dog, the Japanese rose warily and walked towards them fitting their bayonets.

Brillard stood when he saw a movement between the two white columns.

'They're here, my love.'

'Yes, they are.'

They both drained their glasses and placed them neatly on the

135

silver tray on the table by the sofa as they watched the invaders hurrying up the drive.

They saw them halt and drop to the ground and then rise and sidle on. Brillard left his ivory cane leaning against the sofa and walked down the steps with Harold at his heels and his ancient Martini-Henry service rifle in his hands. The dog began to bark and the old man shouted, 'Get off my property! You have no right to be here! You barbarians are trespassing!'

Helvetia saw a soldier raise his rifle, and she screamed at exactly the same time Brillard fired and the nearest soldier fell dead.

There was a moment of complete surprise when no one moved except Helvetia, who raised the handgun she held and squeezed the trigger. A second soldier dropped to the ground as she turned the gun upon herself and fired. Simultaneously the Japanese reply came in a sweeping hail of bullets, and as Brillard fired again, hit another trespasser, and toppled to the drive, Harold leapt growling into the air towards the nearest of the enemy, only to be cut down by more gunfire. The dog fell dead a few yards from his master and the soldiers swarmed over them, up the steps and along the veranda.

As his men entered the house, a lieutenant paused beside the dead form of the knight of the realm. Darkness was descending fast as he nudged the body with his boot and rolled it over. He was surprised when he saw the great age of the man who had challenged them and he took a moment to observe him.

'Strange people, these British,' he said aloud to himself, eyeing the regimental jacket and its shining buttons which the old man wore.

He gave a confused shake of his head as he mounted the veranda and stepped over the dead Lady Helvetia to pass by the handsome specimens of potted palms and follow his men of the Japanese 23rd Army, into the aesthetic sanctums of Hydrangea.

Chapter Eighteen

It was painful for Silveria to leave her husband in the soil outside the remains of their desecrated marital home, but she knew she had no choice and thus the band of 'Lexi and Filipino family' sailed in a strong wind south down the Gulf of Lingayen past the seemingly endless swamps.

During the voyage Lexi took it in turn with the other women to nurse and hug the children, and as the hours passed she taught little Jimmy to say 'boat' and 'water'. She knew she was substituting Jimmy for Paul, and that perhaps she should not, but it was such a solace for her that she could not resist it. Silveria leant across and patted her son's head and her eyes connected with Lexi's. She said something and Josephine translated. 'He two years.'

Lexi smiled tenderly at Silveria and thought of her own baby, who would never see two.

Dusk settled over the fishing boat as they saw the settlement and headed towards it.

San Fabian lay on the pale sand beaches of the eastern shore of the Gulf. They sailed up to a rickety wooden pier on a beach near a collection of stone, wooden and cement buildings which constituted the town and Carlos jumped ashore and tied up the boat. He had done a masterful job. His back and wrists were painful and his head had ached fiercely all the voyage, but he had been determined to bring his family and the British lady to San Fabian.

Beyond the beach people sat in clusters and smoke lifted from a fire smouldering in the distance. None of the townsfolk came to the pier, so Lexi and Josephine determined they had no option but to sleep in the fishing boat for the night and forage out in the daylight. Silveria lay face down in the craft. She was emotionally worn out, and it was Lexi and the older woman who fed the little ones with the rice and potatoes they had stored in the bow before the Japanese had come.

Carlos decided he would do some scouting. He was away perhaps an hour and returned with the news that the settlement was astir with rumours about Japanese landings all around Luzon, and that people in general were very frightened and many had already quit the settlement.

The women looked at each other in despair, but Carlos had much of the strength of his father in him and now in the chaos he was composed. He put his arm around his mother and gave them all a look of confidence. And he took out his father's flute from his trouser pocket and began to play. He had found the instrument lying in the sand before they left the island, and while he did not play as masterfully as Pitik had, there was some strange comfort in hearing the music of the flute again. 'I am strong,' he had said more than once, and Lexi believed it.

The wind died down and the boat undulated gently on the tide as the stars came out. In the distance dogs barked.

This night would live in Lexi's memory. The family's makeshift table – a box on the deck of the fifteen-foot boat; the grown-ups eating by the light of a single candle and listening to the melodies that Carlos elicited from his father's bamboo flute. Silveria wept silently as her son played, and Josephine comforted her, and as the temperature dropped, the young children snuggled together on blankets in the bottom of the boat and the adults cocooned them from the night air and slept as best they could until the dawn.

✻   ✻   ✻

138

With the yellow glow of morning came a priest: a small corpulent man in a Dominican friar's habit. He asked what had brought them to 'the town of Saint Fabian – Pope and martyr' and where they had come from, and Josephine told him about the murder of Pitik and what had happened. He crossed himself and fingered the rope band at his waist upon which hung a metal crucifix. Coughing at intervals he informed them, 'Two patrol boats of the Japanese were seen in the Gulf a few days ago. We have heard many differing reports about amphibious landings by them on the north coast at Aparri and near Vigan. That was over a week ago, I suppose, and we are told they head towards us overland.' He crossed himself again. 'Rumours are rife.'

When Lexi spoke to him in English he answered her haltingly. 'Where you from, daughter?'

'Hong Kong.'

His surprise was evident as she explained, 'I was on a ship sailing for Australia; it was torpedoed by a Japanese submarine.' She did not expand and simply added, 'I must get to Manila.'

He looked doubtful. 'That not easy, my daughter. Many people gone. No buses running here since day before yesterday; no railway.'

Lexi wished he would stop calling her his daughter: yet she was calling him *father* so supposed she should not be irritable about it. She thought of her real father long dead and again wondered what had become of Pa as she eyed the priest. 'I would be grateful for any help you can give me.'

He shook his head.

'But surely there are some soldiers hereabouts?'

'Filipino soldiers in camp . . . that way.' He pointed to the south. 'And American soldiers along river, one, two days ago.' He pointed again, and now Josephine asked if he knew her friends, the family called Layosa.

He replied that he did and he would take them there.

Carlos was keen to leave. His eyes held the look of the zealot:

he must, he would, join the soldiers, he could think of nothing else.

He kissed his mother and small siblings. 'I go to join army.'

The priest studied him. 'You look young for the army, my son.'

'No, I am a man. I go now.' He pushed out his chest in what to Lexi seemed a childish display of bravado, but at the same time she recognised his anger, his passionate indignation at the murder of his father and the beating he himself had taken. He was going to fight the aggressor and there was nothing his mother or grand-mother could do about it.

Silveria began to cry and Josephine remonstrated with him, but he was lost to them. Lexi knew it so she took up his hand. 'Goodbye. Thank you for bringing me here. You are a wonderfully brave young man.'

He nodded stiffly and she stepped in and hugged him.

He turned to his mother and in hesitant but clear English enun-ciated. 'I remember General Del Pilar's words: "I am surrounded by fearful odds that will overcome me and my gallant men. But I am well pleased with the thought that I die fighting for my beloved country. Go you into the hills and defend it to the death."'

He stood rigidly upright on the broken-down wharf, there in the vivid sunlight, the swelling on his forehead and the bandages around his wrists giving him the appearance of an already seasoned soldier. As he delivered his poignant speech, the lines he had learnt from somewhere and which had inspired him, Lexi thought the performance extraordinarily touching and gave a heartfelt sigh as he strode away.

The last they saw of Carlos was his straight back disappearing along the wharf.

Silveria's shoulders slumped with the weight of her son's depar-ture, and Lexi placed her arm around the woman as they waited while Josephine leant down into the vessel and picked up the cloth bag of food and the blankets.

'Who was General Del Pilar?'

Silveria wiped away a tear. 'A Philippine patriot who fought the Americans before they annexed us.'

The little group followed the priest through the streets as the man of religion explained, 'Airfields have been bombed. Many townspeople have withdrawn their money and gone away. We are told of frantic mobs now in the streets of Manila. It is all distressing.'

To Lexi's surprise a few shops were open, but when they arrived at the Layosa house it was empty. Lexi's heart sank and Josephine's eyes brimmed with tears, while Silveria simply slipped to the ground and sat like a broken marionette.

The priest was keen to be away, but Lexi pleaded with him. 'Will you take me to the cable office?' She had no money but she had decided she would use one of her rings as barter.

The priest shook his head. 'It's been closed for two days.'

'In that case, please take me in the direction you last saw the American soldiers. And please come back and see that these people get shelter. I beg you.'

Little Jimmy placed his hands on his cheeks and, looking up with his appealing eyes, said, 'Boat, water.'

Lexi felt like crying. 'Yes, good boy. Boat, water, remember them.'

The priest began to walk away as Lexi said farewell. 'Goodbye, Josephine, goodbye Silveria, goodbye, little ones', but Silveria did not even look up as Lexi turned and followed the flowing brown robe, its frayed hem sweeping the dust.

When she gained the end of the short street, Lexi looked back. Tiny Jimmy stood beside his sister looking forlorn; behind them sat Josephine and Silveria. The family were stock still like a forsaken tableau watching her departure, and she felt sick at heart. Suddenly Jimmy headed towards her, his small feet drumming the cement roadway, and she broke into a run to lift him to her heart. She could not leave them, she just could not.

Her eyes brimmed with tears. 'Josephine, Silveria, do you want to come with me? Leave San Fabian and come along? It means leaving the boat behind.'

Josepine stood up as she answered for them. 'Yes, we come with you.'

Lexi inhaled deeply and her tone became decisive. 'Then come on, let's go. We'll all stay together. We'll leave here and go to wherever that turns out to be.'

Chapter Nineteen

Kathleen lifted her head from the pillow.

The wind was rattling the shutter. It was a cool morning and as she slipped from the bed she draped the blanket around her shoulders and moved to the window. There was no glass — she was in a traditional Filipino house — and she slid back the wooden shutter to be met by the rising dawn light which coated the trunks of the palms with gold. The hills shimmered with the waking day and the sky was a subtlety of apricot and pink as it coaxed the sun from the horizon. The view was so beautiful Kathleen caught her breath. How can the world look like this when it is all such a miserable disaster?

She glanced down and saw movement. Private Hyata, one of her keepers, stepped out from the side of a shed below and looked up. She had six guards. They each watched her for four hours in every twenty-four. This one was the youngest of them all, a boy of about twenty with a smooth face and small ebony eyes that flitted back and forth beneath fine brows. He was the only one of her six wardens who spoke English. She had not realised it until the day before yesterday, when they had been travelling together in the back of a small truck following Colonel Pig in the vehicle ahead.

Suddenly the truck had lurched to a halt and Kathleen had cried out and shot forward. The young Japanese grabbed her and said, 'Are you all right?'

Kathleen turned an amazed face to him. She had hit her head and she put her hand up to it.

'Let me look,' he said. He touched it. 'I think it will be bruised.'

'I'll be all right.'

'Yes, it is not bad. I don't think it will swell.'

She paused. 'Thanks.'

His English was grammatically correct although of course he spoke with a Japanese accent. He had given a sharp bow of his head and that was that.

No one in all the Japanese forces except Ikeda and his henchman, a Captain called Funaki, had spoken English to her and so this had been unexpected. Funaki was the Captain who had been on the beach with Ikeda the day of the massacre.

The young soldier had spoken to her again yesterday. The unit she was travelling with had halted for the night at a deserted village and she sat plaiting a mat. She had begun to weave baskets and mats and small containers using reeds and grasses. She had seen it done when she was a child in Hong Kong and decided that rather than sit out the long, miserable hours of each day, watched by her guards and bored and unhappy, she would do something which at least gave her an interest.

The day had been dying and the young private sat on a log a little distance from her, his rifle between his knees, staring down the dirt road. She regarded him for a time, while he acted as if he did not notice. Suddenly she asked, 'Where did you learn to speak English?'

He continued looking straight ahead and did not reply immediately, but after a few seconds he glanced over his shoulder, and turned and peered along the road before he faced her. 'A religious man, a priest.'

'A shinto priest?'

'Yes. I lived with him. My parents died of a fever when I was six.'

Kathleen had been observing him since the first day he had

144

stood sentry over her. He was different from the others. He did not laugh as loudly and he did not scoff his meals or belch while he ate. He had long fingers and his hands looked soft. All her other custodians frightened her and she believed would shoot her for certain if she ever attempted to escape.

'Where did the shinto priest learn English?'

He took another glance over his shoulder. 'In Australia. He lived there for a period of his life.'

'A shinto priest in Australia? It's hard to believe.' Kathleen had learnt enough about Australia from John Drayton to realise that any Japanese, let alone a shinto priest, would be an oddity there.

'He was a most unusual man and a true scholar.' The young man spoke with pride. 'He worked in a gold mine in a place with the name of Kalgoorlie.' Hyata pronounced the 'l' like an 'r' and Kathleen smiled, but there was no scorn in her expression. 'That's a town all alone out in the desert there. He said there was no settlement for hundreds of miles in any direction. He said there were a few Chinese miners, but he was the only Japanese.'

'My goodness. He does sound like a quite remarkable man. Is he still alive?'

But the young man had suddenly realised that perhaps he had said too much and he rose to his feet, a sharpness in his tone. 'No more talk.'

Yet now, as she looked down from the bedroom of the Filipino *bahay*, she saw that he too had observed her and she dared to wave. There was a brief hesitation from him before he gave a sudden short movement of his hand in reply and looked swiftly away.

She watched him a moment longer before leaving the window.

Since her capture, Kathleen had been unsure what part of the Philippines she was in. The first two days of her abduction she had been aboard the patrol boat, and from it she and her captors had disembarked in part of the Japanese-held Philippines.

As the days had passed she was taken along with the colonel and his men. She knew there were battles being fought, for

145

sometimes she could hear the explosions and the sky to the south was filled with flashing lights. She also realised that the defenders of the island fell back before the invaders for she was on an ever southward journey. She occasionally saw Filipinos, though most had run before the Japanese army. The ones who had remained were in the service of the conquerors.

When she left the window, she washed in a basin on a table near her bed. Female clothes had appeared on the second day of her capture and so had a hairbrush, which had become a prized possession.

The house she currently occupied had been abandoned hurriedly, for there were personal items left behind like clothes and shoes, hair clips and hats and a small hand mirror. Kathleen tried not to use any of them, for she felt like an interloper and thought of how she would not like others touching her possessions. The single thing she occasionally picked up was the hand mirror.

After breakfast – rice and a melon – brought to her by one of the Filipinos who worked for the Japanese, the hours of the morning dragged. The only event she even half-heartedly looked forward to was Private Hyata coming on guard, but as he was on the early morning duty she assumed she would not see him again.

She relived the horror of the murders on the beach and prayed for the souls of Lexi and Aunt Della, Uncle Peter and Jasper. And she prayed for the deliverance of John D from any harm. Now that she had gained some experience of the workings of the Japanese army she implored the powers of the universe to keep John Drayton Whitby out of their hands.

She was surprised when Private Hyata came to guard her again in the afternoon; surprised and pleased. There seemed to be much jubilation in the Japanese ranks, and when they were alone she dared to ask him why. His ebony eyes rested on her moodily before he decided to answer. 'We prepare for a number of landings in a gulf to the south of here. The feeling amongst us is that we will soon possess the Philippines.'

146

Kathleen had no response to that.

Later in the day, as the sun slid in a lustrous orange ball behind the curtain of cloud to the west, Kathleen sat weaving a small oval basket, her back resting against a latticework upright not far from the house she occupied. Three yards away stood Private Hyata, his rifle leaning on the trunk of a nipa palm. The smell of cooking drifted to them on the breeze as a lorry pulled into the short road and came to a halt near a long shed behind a water tank. Two soldiers hopped out of the cabin and opened the back. Nine women, two girls of not more than fourteen, were taken out, marched into the hut and locked in.

There was no one within hearing distance and Kathy spoke quietly to Hyata. 'Who are those girls?'

A long silence followed before his rejoinder. 'Comfort women.'

This was the term used for the females from the countries which Japan had conquered who were coerced into supplying sex for the Japanese armies. It had begun in the armies of occupation in Korea and Manchuria and was now a widespread practice. Wherever the Japanese forces went there were *comfort women in comfort stations*; euphemisms for sexual slavery in government-organised brothels.

Kathleen had first heard about them back in Hong Kong, when the world began to know what the Japanese soldiers were perpetrating in Manchuria and China. The most infamous and shameful episode of their aggression had come to light slowly, but gradually the world learnt of the suffering of the city of Nanking on 13 December, 1937. It remained a scar on the history of the Orient: the mass executions, people hacked to death, the women raped and mutilated and the buildings pillaged. Eventually it was confirmed that over 200,000 civilians had been senselessly massacred. This holocaust became known as the 'rape of Nanking'.

When Ikeda carried her off Kathleen had been terrified of what was to be her fate, but the days had passed and she remained a well-treated prisoner. It confused and troubled her, for she continued to assume that at some point this must alter.

She now knew he was Kempeitai, and she had learnt that the very name was a synonym for merciless cruelty. Kathleen had witnessed the sacking of a Filipino village on the fourth day of her captivity. It had been a settlement of about thirty nipa huts and while half the dwellings were empty there were still people resident. The Japanese convey drove into the centre of the village and alighted and immediately began to set fire to the homes. Soon the whole village was a conflagration. From the back of the truck where she sat caged with her keeper soldier – a man with a thin moustache who had watched the proceedings closely – she saw many of the Filipinos fleeing but one man protested. He was shot through the chest and as he lay on the ground groaning he was beheaded.

In amongst the shrieking and screaming of children and adults, two Filipina women ran by the back of the truck chased by two soldiers. The child had darted into a cluster of ferns and disappeared but the soldiers ran the women down in thick bushes. Kathleen turned her face away and sat shoulders hunched when suddenly her head snapped back!

The guard had grabbed her by her long black hair and was pulling her to him.

She screamed as his hands slid to her shoulders and he forced her from the wooden form, his greedy smile and open mouth filling her world. She kicked and scratched and bit at him but he was young and strong and knocked her to the truck floor.

As Kathleen's horror found voice in another scream she was abruptly free of him. He lurched backwards in the grip of other soldiers who pulled him from her and tossed him over the back of the truck to the ground where he fell heavily. As he tried to rise three jumped down after him and smashed a rifle butt across his mouth. He fell, lips bleeding to the ground and two hauled him up and dragged him away.

Kathleen lay looking up at the remaining soldier in the truck with her. He stood above her, feet wide apart on the boards of the truck, his hand resting on his sword.

'Get up,' said Colonel Ikeda.

She clutched her ripped skirt across her thighs as she rose unsteadily. Ikeda shouted in Japanese to the single soldier remaining near the truck and he saluted and ran off. Abruptly Ikeda rounded back to Kathy. 'Sit here, I have sent for a blanket to cover you.'

Kathy slumped down on the form staring at him as she lifted her trembling hand to point into the bushes where the women and the two soldiers were. She was breathing in shallow gasps and she forced out her words. 'This ... is not what soldiers should do ... No soldiers should do this ... please, help them.'

Anger flashed in his small ruthless eyes, his voice replete with contempt. 'You know nothing. I was here before the war. In Manila they sell their own children as harlots!' He jabbed his index finger at her. 'And *you* shut-up! Concern yourself with yourself.' And he leapt from the truck and was gone.

Kathleen remained smelling the burning huts, tears seeping from her closed eyes, her face averted from what surrounded her. A soldier brought the blanket and she wrapped herself in it with shaking hands. An hour later the military caravan rolled away from the devastated village carrying their single prisoner with them.

Kathleen continued to have no idea why she was a captive of 'Colonel Pig'. Since their first talk that night on the island where he had slaughtered her friends, Ikeda had interviewed her only once more; when he had asked questions about her childhood and her profession as a nurse.

And now, as Private Hyata spoke to her of the nine females who had been brought into the camp, he added, 'We all thought you were one of them at first.'

Kathleen turned to him, her basket resting in her lap.

He continued, 'A comfort woman for the colonel.' He did not

look at her but remained with his face impassively viewing the road.

Her reply was hardly a whisper. 'So did I . . . at first.'

At this he looked round, his pinpoint black eyes finding hers. He paused. She realised he was weighing up whether or not to say more. She simply stared at him and finally he decided. He spoke the words so very quietly: 'I do not like it . . . the practice of using the comfort women.'

Kathleen's expression softened upon him. They were in accord. They contemplated one another for a few seconds before Private Hyata slowly bowed his head to her.

Chapter Twenty

Through the paved streets and dirt byways of San Fabian town lined with palm trees the monk led Lexi and the family. Passing the dominating cathedral with its tall bell tower, he briefly greeted others of his kind before continuing on to the edge of the settlement. Eventually they gained a track where refugees from the town straggled along carrying their belongings in hessian bags, large and small. Vehicles of all kinds were loaded with household goods, trussed pigs and crates of squealing chickens, while at the rear trailed the dogs. To their barking was added the squealing of the pigs and the chatter and cries of children. Everybody watched the skies anxiously for any sign of Japanese aircraft.

After half an hour of tramping along the grass-edged path they came to a junction where a dirt road bordered on one side by mangroves and a swamp, pointed south.

'There, down that way. Last time I saw American soldiers.'

'Oh thank you. Goodbye.'

'Goodbye, my daughter.'

Lexi was glad she had been called that for the last time even though she was truly grateful to him and she touched his arm in thanks and said adieu as the priest automatically blessed them.

They walked carrying Jimmy in turn. Josephine talked but Silveria did not; her gaze remained upon the ground and her slender body moved like an automaton, lifeless, without emotion. Lexi understood the woman's hopelessness.

Lessa complained about being cold and tired and finally Josephine piggybacked her while Lexi did the same for Jimmy. They met two Filipino families heading in the opposite direction, and when Josephine asked them if they had seen American soldiers they confirmed they had at a small airfield some miles ahead.

Three hours passed on the wide plain of inland Luzon with the little group halting now and then for respite. They passed deserted *tribos* – Pangasinán villages – and began to ascend a long low hill where bamboo grew in clumps, and clusters of the ubiquitous coconut and banana palms dotted the landscape. The sound of a vehicle coming from behind made them halt. It was a small army truck. Soldiers! The track was straight at this juncture though they were passing through a stand of palms dotted with pepper trees and bushy undergrowth. They watched as the vehicle advanced.

Suddenly another sound pulsated in the walkers' ears: an aircraft, flying just above the level of the trees. Lexi could see the aeroplane now as it gained on the vehicle and she had a bad feeling this one was not American. When she could make out the dreaded red spot on the wings she shouted, 'Quickly, into the trees!' and the family ran for cover.

The driver of the vehicle accelerated, the speed making the open truck jump and swing up the bumpy incline. Abruptly a burst of gunfire spat from the aircraft and the bullets ripped a furrow along the ground, hitting the rear of the vehicle, which nosed sideways but kept going. The roar of the aeroplane shooting by overhead was deafening. It was Japanese all right, one of the stars of their air fleet, a Mitsubishi A6M Zero naval fighter-bomber, fast and agile.

In the vines and trees the women and children cowered while the truck skidded to a halt right beside them and disgorged five soldiers, who dashed into the palms a few yards away from Lexi and the family.

The exceptionally manoeuvrable Zero had banked and turned

and now the vehicle stood empty on the track: a marker for the human targets crouching nearby under the leaves and branches.

In above the trees the Zero attacked, machine guns pumping bullets, the noise almost unendurable, while Lexi, Silveria and Josephine sheltered the two tiny children with their own bodies. The terrified babies whimpered as bullets spat, cutting through the undergrowth beside them, severing the large leaves of the palms.

Lexi bit her lip to stop herself from crying out, and as the noise of the engine told them the fighter was banking again and coming round, she began to edge them further into the trees. But there was a point beyond which they could not go, for the ground was damp and swampy and began to give way.

Another hail of bullets ripped the green canopy above. The noise was so fierce that Lexi and the family simply huddled together, the staccato menace of bullets all around them, thudding into trunks and splitting more leaves.

The adults sought to soothe the children while a third time the aircraft turned towards them. This time the bullets lacerated the bamboo beside them and Lessa screamed as the truck exploded and pieces of metal rammed into the forest while flames and black smoke speared skywards. This detonation seemed to appease the pilot, for he banked for a look and flew away

Lexi rolled off Jimmy. 'There, there, darling, we're all right.' The little boy jumped to his feet and in apparent disorientation ran over to one of the soldiers, who picked him up and stood looking at Lexi through the veil of dense lianas clinging to the palms.

Lexi climbed to her knees. 'Come on, Josephine, Silveria, the bastard's gone.' But she hesitated as she became aware that Lessa's cries came from beneath Josephine and Silveria, who had both shielded the child.

Lexi crawled over. 'Silveria? Josephine?' But neither of the women moved. 'Say something. Please.' And now her face stiffened, for she could see the blood soaking beneath them into the ground.

153

She immediately comprehended the mother and daughter were dead. She groaned in sorrow as she rolled Silveria away from the crying child and lifted Lessa — her dress covered in blood — up into her arms. She turned wild-eyed to see the soldier holding Jimmy pushing through the undergrowth towards her.

He asked with a southern American accent, 'Are they dead?'

Lexi forced herself to speak. 'I'm almost sure . . . both of them. I'm a doctor, so I need to check their vital signs.'

He came closer and she noticed the sergeant's chevrons on his sleeve. 'Please take the children away.'

Lessa seemed dazed, her eyes glazed with shock, but Jimmy was crying for his mother as the sergeant nodded and moved off with the children through the undergrowth towards the burning vehicle. Lexi turned to the bodies of the women, established they were dead and stood up and walked spiritlessly through the palms to the soldiers and the children.

The sergeant looked at her and Lexi confirmed, 'Yes, as I thought,' as another soldier shouted from about thirty yards away, 'Tate's dead and Sorenson's been hit in the leg.'

The sergeant placed Jimmy on the ground as he spoke. 'Oh hell! Poor Tate. Nice kid.' He lifted his hand and gestured to the bamboo. 'Start making a litter.' Glancing back to Lexi he went on, 'I'm sorry. We'd like to help you bury the women, but we haven't got time. Won't be able to bury my boy either.'

Jimmy continued to weep, his small face mud-stained as he lifted his fist to his eyes. Lexi hurried to the children and drew them to her. No child should have to suffer this . . . no child in the whole bloody world!

The heat from the burning truck blanketed them as she watched the sergeant and his soldiers set to cutting shoots of bamboo with their jungle knives to make the stretcher for the wounded man, who lay thirty yards away, his head in the shade of a banana palm.

The children asked for their mother, crying '*Inay Inay*' but all Lexi could do was wipe their tears and kiss them and attempt to console them. They had just begun to quieten when the sergeant, a stocky man with a barrel chest, returned and stood above Lexi, looking down. 'Are you American?'

'No, British.' She made to stand but swayed and he asked, 'Do you feel all right?'

'Yes.'

He helped her up and she got to her feet, willing herself to be strong. The children clung to her legs as she faced him. 'Look, I'd like to speak to your commanding officer. I must get to Manila.'

He gave a frustrated grunt. 'Hell, lady, everybody must get to Manila. Me included.' He turned away, shouting to his soldiers, 'Come on, you lot, hurry up with that blasted stretcher.'

Lexi bent and took Lessa's palm in her left hand and lifted Jimmy in her right arm as she spoke to the sergeant's back.

'Sergeant, please listen to me.'

He faced round to her. Sergeant Chuck Lister was not a heartless man, but he had to get a move on. A rotten war had begun, and even though he felt sorry for this woman standing here with a child in both hands, he had no time to waste. He bent to the grass and picked up a Colt .44 that had been blown clear of the exploded truck, and as he did he spoke to her again.

'What's a Brit doctor doing out here anyway?'

She gave the back of his head a long-suffering look. 'It's a long story, Sergeant, too long. I was shipwrecked and wound up here, that'll do. Look, I understand what you say about everyone wanting to get to Manila, but I really must.'

'Yeah, well good luck.' He stood up. 'I'm truly sorry about your friends, but you should head back to the main road. Take my advice, you've got the chance of maybe catching a lift from somebody there. This track only goes to a soon-to-be-abandoned airfield; there's not much else down here.'

He turned to his men again and Lexi's mind raced in desperation. Her two women companions were dead! In her hands were the tiny souls who had fallen into her care. She stepped a few

155

paces after the sergeant. 'I suppose you've heard of General MacArthur.'

He glanced at her over his shoulder. 'Come on, lady, what does that mean?'

'He knows me well. He's a close friend of my grandfather's. They met in Singapore, Christmas 1905. He'd be really really mad if he knew I were here, abandoned and alone, and one of his own soldiers was refusing to help me.'

He gave her a close, searching look. 'You kidding me?'

She spoke fast. 'No. It's true. You just asked me yourself what I was doing here. The short form of the long story is I was on my way to Australia on a ship, being evacuated from Hong Kong, and the Japs torpedoed us. A Filipino family took me in. These children are what's left of it. Listen, I know you're in a hurry, and all I'm asking you is to take me along to your commanding officer. Your part ends there.'

He was uncertain what to do, she could sense it. 'Lady, I've got a wounded man and a dead man. I've gotta get going.'

'Listen, Sergeant, I do know General MacArthur. I know him well. I also know his wife Jean, I was at their son's christening in 1938. My grandfather, Sir Brillard Hayes that is, and my grandmother and I, sailed over here for the christening on 2 June that year. It took place in the penthouse at the hotel in Manila where General MacArthur lives. The Episcopalian Bishop christened little Arthur. It was a lovely affair and I think we gave him an antique Chinese silver bowl. Yes, we did, with a gorgeous spoon . . . it had a little emerald in the handle.' She paused and looked him straight in the eye.

Chuck Lister dropped his head to his chest and groaned. 'Shit! Just my luck to run into you.'

'Please take me along. How far is it you're going?'

He took a deep breath. 'About five miles up the road. I report to Lieutenant Nix. He's waiting for us and he ain't gonna like what I've got to tell him.'

156

Lexi stood her ground. 'Just take us along with you, that's all I ask. Please.'

'Now listen to me, lady, Nix ain't the sort of guy to like this. And he's not the sort of guy to help you either, believe me. That ain't his nature. You'd do a lot better back on the main road.'

'Sergeant, just let me try.'

He looked to heaven but there was no answer there.

This woman either knew General MacArthur as she said, or she was a blasted spy and had studied him in minute detail, and eyeing her with the two kids hanging off her, he did not think the latter a possibility. He gave in. 'All right.'

Before Lexi could thank him he strode away to his men, shouting to one of them, 'Get in there to those two women and cover them with whatever you can; do the same for Tate. We've no time for burials. Move it!'

Lexi was drawing on inner reserves of strength she never knew she had. She did not let the children go back near the bodies of Silveria and Josephine but she took Silveria's wedding ring. 'I must keep it for the children,' she kept muttering to herself. 'It will be a precious treasure when we are far from here.'

Lessa and Jimmy were entirely in her care, given to her in some bewildering exchange for Paul.

The sergeant took two chocolate bars out of his pocket and handed them to the children. Jimmy took his silently and Lessa simply let hers fall to the ground. Lexi picked it up and pocketed it for her.

When they moved on, Lexi hefted little Jimmy on her back and took Lessa's hand and trailed out after the soldiers. She was existing on sheer will now.

She looked back and said her silent goodbye to the two women lying in the trees on the green wide plain of Luzon.

She was in grave need; she felt desperate and to steady herself she began to say the 23rd psalm:

The LORD is my shepherd; I shall not want.

He maketh me to lie down in green pastures: he leadeth me beside the still waters.

He restoreth my soul: he leadeth me in the paths of righteousness for his name's sake.

Yea, though I walk through the valley of the shadow of death, I will fear no evil: for thou art with me; thy rod and thy staff they comfort me.

Thou preparest a table before me in the presence of mine enemies: thou anointest my head with oil; my cup runneth over.

Surely goodness and mercy shall follow me all the days of my life: and I will dwell in the house of the LORD for ever.

Chapter Twenty-one

It was half an hour from dusk when the straggling party saw a battered-looking Beech transport and a P-26 Fighter – known as the Peashooter – resting at the edge of the clearing which looked more like a mire than an airfield.

Lexi's feet were covered in dirt and the Filipino raffia shoes that Josephine had given her to wear had made blisters on both her heels.

Earlier, when Lexi had wearied and fallen far behind them, Sergeant Chuck Lister had shown his true disposition and had taken the children from her. The soldiers carried Jimmy and Lessa for the rest of the journey and now, as they reached the airfield and the day ebbed and gloomy darkness wafted through the trees, a thin man in the uniform of a lieutenant in the airborne artillery ran across from the fighter aircraft.

'Where the hell have you been, Lister?' He pointed to Lexi and the children as Chuck placed the little boy on the ground. 'And who the hell are these civilians?'

'We ran into an enemy fighter, sir, got strafed and he blew up the truck. We're lucky to be alive.'

The lieutenant frowned. 'My saddle?'

'Gone, sir, blew up with the vehicle.'

The officer's eyes narrowed and his voice lowered threateningly. 'Jesus H Christ, I sent you back for that. I've waited here for you when I could have been gone. I'm supposed to be in Nielson Field now.' His shadow stretched between them.

Chuck Lister pointed to the man on the litter. 'Sorensen took a hit. Leg's badly injured. Tate's dead.'

'Shit! Well get Sorensen into the transport.' He poked his thumb at the aircraft and eyed Lister. 'I'm holding you personally responsible for the loss of my saddle, Sergeant.'

'Sir? We were hit by a blasted Jap Zero!'

'So you told me. Now move. We've got to get out of here.'

Lister motioned to Lexi. 'Excuse me, sir, this lady needs help. I'd like to request we take her with us. She'll be no trouble.'

The lieutenant blinked. 'Have you lost your mind, Lister?'

'She knows General MacArthur, sir; she needs to reach him in Manila.'

At this point Lexi thought she should speak for herself. 'Lieutenant Nix, please listen, what the sergeant says is true. My grandfather and the general were friends. The sergeant here has been very good to us and has brought—'

His chilling voice cut her off. 'I'm not the least bit interested in who the hell you know, lady. You look like some goddam whore to me. It's bad enough that you've delayed my men.'

'I am not a whore. I'm Lexine Robinson, a doctor. I was on a ship which was torpedoed by the Japs. These children—'

He spoke over her words again. 'Forget it, lady. I don't care. Get it? Don't care! There's a war on and you don't count. Get that? Goodbye.'

He turned his back on her dismissively and Lister tried again. 'Lieutenant Nix, I believe the lady does know General MacArthur. Shouldn't we at least—'

Nix lifted his palm. 'Stay out of it, Lister! You're in enough trouble. Shove off and get everyone into that transport now or I'll report you for insubordination. We're moving out.' He strode away, calling orders for departure.

Lexi watched him go.

'I'm sorry. I knew he wouldn't help,' Chuck Lister announced bleakly at her side.

'You did what you could.'

Lexi looked down at the children, weary and cheerless, their little shoulders drooping as they sat in the dirt at her feet. Her voice was broken and weary. 'Sergeant, just tell me how to get on the right road for Manila.'

Chuck Lister felt bad, really bad. This was a nice lady and she had been in a lot of shit. The lieutenant really was an uncaring bastard.

Nix's voice carried across to them. 'Move it, you scumbags. We're leaving!'

Lister gave a sympathetic grin and attempted to sound encouraging. 'Keep going on this road about a mile; you'll come to a crossroads where there's a small stream and a village of nipa huts. I know a few families remain there and you'll find shelter tonight. Tomorrow take the road that heads to the bridge: you can see it from the village. Eventually it should bring you out on the main road that leads to Manila. There'll be vehicles and refugees and some military movement so that you should get a lift easily.'

Chuck handed the remainder of his chocolate bars to her. 'The capital's about a hundred miles away. Good luck.' In a quick movement he took all his money out of his pocket and gave it to her. 'There might even be some buses still running. This should help.'

Despite her natural reluctance, she took the bank notes. 'Thank you. You're a good man, Sergeant, a really good man. What's your name?'

'Lister, ma'am, Chuck Lister. And yours?'

'Lexi Robinson.' Suddenly and unaccountably she added, 'But my married name is Whitby. She had not worn her rings since she left the island. The night before he had been murdered, Pitik had warned her to hide them while travelling, so they were in a piece of cloth tucked into her brassiere.

Chuck Lister touched her arm. 'He's a lucky man.'

Lexi sighed and lifted her eyes to his. 'Fact is I hope I run into another soldier like you. I'll pray that I do.'

161

He met her gaze with a kind expression. 'I'll pray that you do too.'

The melancholy little group stood together and watched the transport, followed by the Peashooter, lift into the sky until they disappeared into the dusky clouds of twilight.

Lexi was exhausted but she shouted, 'Damn you, Nix, we'll do all right without you!' It was enough to urge her on, and while tears stung her eyes she fought them back and bent down and kissed the children on their grubby cheeks and took up their hands. 'We are lost and bewildered, my little ones, but you are both so very brave and I'll take strength from you. Come on.'

Half an hour later, as the chill of night descended, the moon revealed the village to Lexi, a collection of about fifteen nipa huts. All traditional with living quarters above and swine, goats and fowls below. The first two were dark and obviously empty, but in the third a light glowed and as they headed for it Lexi's nostrils quivered from the stench of an open drain where countless insects in aerial conglomeration were revealed in the gleam ahead. When she called out faces appeared at the windows and the man of the house climbed down the ladder to her and using a little Spanish she made herself understood. She offered one of the Filipino notes that Sergeant Lister had given her and by the glow of the moon she saw the head of the household smile and nod, and he carried Jimmy up the ladder to be followed by Lessa and Lexi.

As the stars blinked in the sky above the huts, Jimmy asked many times for his inay and lola — mother and grandmother — and began to cry. Lexi did her best to comfort him. Lessa remained silent, sitting and staring. She had not spoken since the previous day when her mother and grandmother had been killed. Lexi sat beside the girl and held her close until eventually they all fell asleep.

With the dawn came optimism. She fed Lessa and Jimmy a

substantial breakfast of bananas, rice and pork ribs, and as the sun's strength amplified into a warmer day than the previous one, they bathed in a protected area of the stream where the sun caught them.

As Lexi washed Lessa, the little girl lifted her small snub-nosed face, the morning sun playing on her shiny black hair. She looked straight into Lexi's eyes but still she did not speak.

They left the Filipino family and walked all day, stopping to rest now and then and eat the fruit that Lexi carried with her. They saw horses and carts and occasional motor vehicles going the opposite way, and once they saw a family riding bicycles in the distance. Lexi pushed them on even though the children were quiet and listless, and while occasionally Jimmy prattled away, Lessa continued to stare ahead in silence and apathy.

As the day advanced and became evening, an ox and a calf wandered by, the ox with a short frayed length of rope tied around its neck, and birds twittered on the branches of the occasional trees in the Luzon wilderness, but they saw no more people.

And now Lexi believed she was lost. Aircraft flew high overhead and she had a strong sense they were not American.

As the afternoon waned, she watched the sun approaching the horizon and worked out that she was making her way in a westerly direction. This determined her to take the first turn left in the hope of heading south. She did so and came to a group of bamboo houses where chickens with quite splendid red and orange plumage ranged, but there were no inhabitants.

In the abridged dramatic twilight of the Philippine evening, Lexi drew water from the communal well and fed the children the last of the rice and saved three bananas for breakfast. As the cool night descended, so too did the layer of insects.

Lexi had decided long ago that the Philippine islands were cauldrons of small-winged creatures, which she hated, but at least the fluctuating breeze which drifted now and then through the partly open window helped to move them on.

163

She shivered and felt overwhelmed by gloom. She pictured her exquisite Kwan Yin with her beautiful elliptical eyes of compassion at the bottom of the South China Sea, and wiped away a tear as she lay on a rough pile mattress with the slumbering children beside her, waiting for sleep to come to her in the cool December night.

Chapter Twenty-two

That same night the American forces on the island attempted to deal with the invasion.

Furrows deepened in General Jonathan 'Skinny' Wainwright's forehead as he spoke into the wireless receiver to General Richard Sutherland, MacArthur's Chief of Staff.

'Goddam, Richard! I'm defending an area six hundred and twenty-six miles long by over a hundred wide.' He fell silent, nervously fingering the radio headset with his right hand as he listened. A few seconds later he answered sharply, 'Yes, I know.'

He lifted his long leg encased in its polished cavalry boot up on to a box as he spoke into the telephone inside the shed that was the wireless room at his new field headquarters in Alcala on the Agno River just south of the Lingayen Gulf on the island of Luzon. The telephone system throughout the Philippines gave haphazard service and the call could cut out at any time. As he continued speaking he rested his free hand on his Colt .45 which he wore in a holster on his right hip, reminiscent of the cowboys of the West.

'The Japs are heading down towards us. My North Luzon Force is around twenty-eight thousand men, twenty-five thousand of whom are still untrained, and they're scattered over a mighty big area. The Japs are battle hardened veterans from China. Thousands of them. I've got no air force, no seventy-five-millimetre guns, no anti-tank divisions. I need that Philippine Division and I need it fast.' He listened for a few seconds. 'What am I asking, you say? I'm asking, "Can I have my old Philippine Division?"'

The reply elicited a loud frustrated groan from Wainwright as he finished, 'General, look at the map, work it out for yourself,' and handed the headset back to the operator.

He glanced despondently to his trusted aides, Major Johnny Pugh and Captain Tom Dooley, both slender men who stood some inches shorter than the six-foot-tall, lanky Skinny.

Almost talking to himself, he strode to the map of Luzon tacked on to the hut wall. 'I've requested sixteen standard seven-ton light tanks and my old division. The answer was, "It's highly improbable", so I guess we're on our own, boys.'

'Excuse me, sir!' the radio operator behind him called.

'Yes?'

'Coded Morse communication coming in for you right now, sir.' The young, line-free face of the signalman wrinkled as he listened and took down the message, his pencil speeding over the notepad.

'What is it?'

'"Two cages of monkeys fed and watered. Beetles flying two four six eight. Garlic on the daisy chain. Butter melting. Weather not improving." It was sent in by Demon.'

Pugh grunted. 'Demon is Trapperton's code name, isn't it?'

Wainwright nodded. 'He's been in the north, raiding and harassing, since the enemy landed at Vigan. He's got a platoon of those few seasoned men we actually have and he's pretty much alone up there.' He took a deep breath. 'We'd better get him back here.'

The wireless operator was busy decoding the message, as Wainwright picked up the cup of coffee he had been drinking and drained it while Pugh watched him speculatively. He knew full well who Trapperton was; he and General Wainwright were the only two north of Manila who did know. The general staff thought Major Hank Trapperton was an intelligence officer who, for some reason, reported directly to General Wainwright, which in fact was true, but there was a lot more to know.

Johnny Pugh held a secret file on Hank Trapperton. He was a West Point graduate who had been seconded to a secret army intelligence unit and had worked in the US with William J. 'Wild Bill' Donovan, who was attempting to put together a fourth arm of the US military services along the lines of the British Special Operations. Some thought Trap simply an assassin and a spy, and there was no doubt he qualified as both, but he was more. He was a supreme marksman; Pugh had seen him hit the centre of a moving target at three hundred yards. And Trapperton was classified by Washington itself.

Pugh knew that Wainwright placed great store in Trap, and as Dooley turned away to speak to the wireless operator Pugh spoke quietly to the general. 'It was Trap's father who was one of your commanding officers in France in World War One, wasn't it?'

Wainwright inclined his head. 'I was at his side in the Meuse-Argonne offensive. He was a fine man.'

The General moved over to the wireless operator. 'Decoded that message yet, Sparks?'

The youth spoke up. 'Yes, sir. It reads: "Jap transports, mainly troop buses, heading south Vigan on coastal plain. Two thousand men and counting. Have attacked and delayed. Low on ammunition supplies. Need extra platoon Twenty-sixth to prolong. Request send rendezvous now. Coordinates TWRG."'

Dooley whistled. 'The Twenty-sixth Cavalry, no way.'

The general tapped the signalman on the shoulder. 'Send a coded Morse back to Trapperton. Tell him not to delay. To get out of there immediately with his men and return to Pozorrubio, and make contact from there. Mark that urgent and a direct order from me.'

'Yes, sir, straight away.'

'I've got other things for Trap to do and if he stays there he'll be cut off.' The general moved back to the wall map and stood studying it. 'We'd better work on a plan for a counterattack.'

'With what, sir?' asked Captain Dooley behind him.

'With whatever forces we have, Dooley, with whatever forces we have. Get the Ninety-first combat team from Cabanatuan over to Sison to reinforce the Seventy-first Division.'

Captain Tom Dooley's frown deepened. 'With respect, sir, the positions of the Japanese landings make it pretty obvious that we really need to withdraw behind the Agno river.'

General Wainwright eyed Dooley. 'We're soldiers, son. And soldiers don't like to hear the word "withdraw".'

Dooley looked admonished and Wainwright beckoned both men. 'Follow me outside, you two.'

Into a humid breeze, as a monkey swung down from a branch and ran by screeching, the general strode and faced his two aides. 'We officers are all aware of War Plan Orange even though it's not common knowledge to our troops. Right?' He glanced from one to the other.

'Yes,' Pugh answered. 'It's the retrograde manoeuvre into Bataan.'

Bataan, a Peninsula, was 75 miles to the south, its area of approximately 25 square miles could possibly be secured and held until reinforcements arrived.

'The current draft of the plan being WPO-3,' added Dooley.

'Go on,' prompted the general.

'There are five defensive lines imagined across the route of retreat to Bataan where we will hold the enemy while all forces withdraw. The Agno river being one of the lines.'

Wainwright nodded. 'It'll be a bitter pill to swallow if the order to put WPO-3 in place comes through, though I suppose I'm expecting it.'

Dooley started in surprise. 'You mean *you* can't give it, sir?'

Skinny Wainwright grunted. 'No, it has to come from General MacArthur.'

'Then with complete respect, sir, why hasn't he given it?'

Wainwright was a fair-minded man. 'We're soldiers, son; the commanding officer must have his reasons.' Yet while he spoke, he could not help but be reminded of the way MacArthur had delayed any action for nine hours after the Japanese bombing of Clark Field aerodrome in the initial attack on the Philippines. It was almost as if the commanding officer suffered from shock or disbelief at what had befallen his beloved islands.

But Johnny Pugh dared to say more. 'Might I say something, sir?' he asked.

Wainwright's eyebrow rose. 'Go ahead.'

'We're stretched to the limit now. We've got untrained Filipino recruits who've dropped their Enfields and fled when they encountered the Japs. We're facing superior numbers at all enemy landing points, but if we actually did retire immediately to Bataan and reorganise, it might not be too late. Perhaps we could hold on there indefinitely.'

General Wainwright grunted. 'Do you think you're telling me things I don't know, son?' He saluted, indicating further conversation on that subject was closed. 'Now let's go and have a glass of that bottle of Scotch I saw at chow-down.'

Chapter Twenty-three

'The Japs have landed in the Lingayen Gulf, sir.' Tom Dooley shook Major Johnny Pugh awake with the news.

'Goddam.' He sat up, wiping sleep from his eyes. 'Where?'

Dooley placed a map on the bed in the strip of morning sunlight bursting through the tent flap. His finger ran across the Gulf of Lingayen. 'Here at Bauong and a number of places all the way down to Damortis, we think.'

Pugh leant over the map. 'Phew, that's close. What does the old man say?'

'He still doesn't have orders to put WPO-3 in place.'

Pugh exploded. 'Hell! What the Christ is wrong with MacArthur? If we don't get back into the Bataan peninsula double quick, we've no hope. The bloody Nips are surrounding us!'

Lexi was dreaming. Little Paul was in her arms, stiff and cold, his face the ashen hue of death. His tiny hand lay open and his birthmark glistened blue, the same intense, pure azure that lies within an iceberg. The scar began to pulsate and the colour expanded outwards from the mark and rode up his arm until his whole body pulsated with a deathly blue all over ...

She awoke with a jolt, but the dream was so real she could still feel the icy form in her arms. Yet swiftly she became aware of another small body, not in her arms but at her back: little Jimmy, and he was warm with life. As she opened her eyes, dawn stirred the world and washed over the treetops to sprinkle vague light into the hut, but at the same moment a distant explosion sounded, followed by another and another. She froze. Oh God, the Japs must have landed again nearby. There was a battle starting somewhere not too far away.

'Quickly, up! We must go.'

The children woke and in haste she dressed them, grabbed the bananas she had been saving for breakfast and pushed them into the knapsack.

'We must hurry, little ones.' She rolled up the towels she had taken from an abandoned wayside market and used for bedding, and herded the children to the door, taking up their hands. 'Hurry.'

General Douglas MacArthur bent into the Packard sedan and his aide Colonel Sidney Huff closed the door behind him, strode around the trunk and climbed aboard. He tapped the driver upon his shoulder. 'Let's go!'

Douglas MacArthur's patrician features were tired: he had been visiting camps where he had done all he could to encourage his men, to buoy them up, to give them heart to drive the enemy into the sea, but it seemed to no avail. His confidence in his ability to rally his men had taken a severe battering, something he had trouble admitting even to himself.

His foe, General Masaharu Homma, had made multiple landings now all over the Philippine islands, and his troops were surrounding the defending forces. Some of the assaults had even been unopposed; that knowledge he found hard to swallow.

The latest invasions in the Gulf of Lingayen now forced him to face the reality of a double retrograde manoeuvre: of recalling his North Luzon Army under General Wainwright and his South Luzon Army under General Jones. If he did that it would all need to be timed perfectly to get both armies fighting rearguard actions and to finally cross the Calumpit Bridge north-west of Manila in unison, where the men would flow into the peninsula of Bataan. His advisers had just told him he should wait no longer; they had suggested strongly to him to activate WPO-3. Fact was they had dared to hint that he was vacillating!

Now that had enraged him. He was a strategist. If only President Roosevelt and Chief of Staff George Marshall would support him, send him the relief he so badly needed. He had believed in the fighting qualities of the Philippine army reservists and he had stuck to his conviction that his forces could hold the central Luzon plain, but now, while he hated to admit it, he knew he must revise what appeared to have been his optimistic view.

He knew too that to save Manila from ground and air attack he had to proclaim it an open city the way Paris and Brussels had done against German attack, and remain hopeful that the Japanese would not bomb it. There appeared no option but for him to leave the capital and to persuade his friend, Philippine president Manuel Quezon, to go with him.

He would have to take his darling Jean and little son Arthur and retire the fifty miles across Manila Bay to the fortress island of Corregidor. That was the only thing he could do.

Why oh why had they not sent him the troops and weapons he needed? Roosevelt was overly preoccupied with the European war, he was sure of it.

At his side Sidney Huff turned to him and made to speak, but MacArthur lifted his hand for silence. Huff sank back into his seat and sighed as the general's brow creased and he closed his weary eyes and rested his head back in contemplation while the Packard bumped over the potholed road.

Skinny Wainwright put down his glass on the fold-up table and lifted a wooden pointer to touch the village of Binalonan on the map in front of him. He glanced up at Johnny Pugh. 'Bring the Twenty-sixth Cavalry back here and replace them with the

Seventy-first Division. The cavalry have been fighting nonstop, they're exhausted.'

Pugh agreed. 'They've lost a hundred and fifty men dead and wounded in the fighting from Damortis to the Bued River. Three of their platoons are in Bontoc in the mountains trying to hold the Japs from breaking through to Baguio.'

Pugh's worried expression was fixed on his face as he went on: 'I've just heard we're in trouble in Sison. The Filipinos in the Seventy-first Division broke and fled to the rear; the artillery have retreated south to Pozorrubio. The Japs are right on their tail. The Ninety-first are hard pressed as well.'

At his side Captain Tom Dooley lifted his hand to the map and wiped off a spot of moisture as he spoke. 'Sir, our right flank and the entire line might be strengthened if we do what we said yesterday – immediately withdraw everybody behind the Agno with us.' He ran his hand down the river.

There was a murmur of agreement from the other gathered officers as Wainwright's reply came without enthusiasm. 'Yes, we'll have to. I'll call MacArthur's headquarters for approval.'

Three minutes later he was given immediate permission to withdraw across the Agno but was requested to submit plans for a counterattack. He pushed his luck and once more asked for his old Philippine Division back but he was put off again.

He cursed to himself as he put the phone down. 'Any blasted novice can see there'll be no counterattack if I can't get trained men!'

That night, when 'chow-down' was called General Wainwright ate with his men by the light of a kerosene lamp and the continual noise of aircraft in the distance. 'Bet they aren't ours!' seemed to be the consensus.

After two quick Scotches at the end of his meal, the general walked the short distance from the mess to his broken-down trailer. The smell here in Luzon he would never forget; got into the very nodes of your brain; not a bad smell, just an unforgettable one. For some odd reason he thought of his days at West Point. Hell, this track was a long way from the parade ground. His mind wandered to Little Boy, his thoroughbred stallion. The noble horse was still down at Fort Stotsenburg; how he itched to get back in the saddle. He paused a moment and looked to the sky, the stars were gleaming ... Same stars that could be seen over the whole northern hemisphere ... Over home so far away. A smile stole across his spare mouth as he thought of his wife Adele, whom he called *Kitty* and who had been repatriated to the USA in April; he missed her very badly.

A wild pig grunted somewhere in the night as he stepped up into his trailer, crossed to his desk and began leafing through a stack of maps.

He was drinking a beer and working on his forlorn counter-attack when a noise at the door made him turn. It was Sergeant Carroll, his orderly.

'Excuse me, sir, it's Colonel Irwin from General MacArthur's headquarters calling for you.'

The general's face was clouded as he eyed his staff officers in front of his wall map, his hand on his Colt at his hip. 'It is with great sadness that I inform you that WPO-3 is in effect as of now.'

Dooley gave a low whistle. He knew the general hated the idea of retreat, but he thought it was about blasted time.

Wainwright lifted his fingers to his gaunt chin. 'Give the order to withdraw from all positions and to fall back to Bataan. We'll fight rearguard actions as we go, followed by prompt retirement and the dynamiting of bridges and abandoning and destroying of equipment. We'll move out of here at first light, down to Bamban. Let the war correspondents know.'

The general cleared his throat and added: 'Headquarters in Manila informed me of something else.'

His men all edged slightly forward in expectation.

'General MacArthur himself is about to depart Manila and transfer to the fortress of Corregidor.'

'He must think it's pretty hopeless,' Dooley remarked softly.

A long silence followed and it was General Wainwright who broke it. 'Any news on Trapperton?'

Pugh nodded. 'A Morse code message came in from him in reply to yours, so I'd say he's on his way to Pozorrubio as you ordered.'

'Nothing else?'

'No, sir.'

'See if Signals can raise him. Find out where he is. Send another coded message to tell him to avoid the Gulf, warn him of the enemy landings and make it clear that he must not go to Pozorrubio, but get down to Bamban quick smart.'

'Yes, sir.'

The officers departed and Skinny Wainwright was alone. He stepped across the worn flowered rug that added almost a ludicrous touch of decor to his trailer and halted in front of his map to study the red markers where the enemy had landed. He made a sharp thwarted sound in his throat as he spoke to himself: 'The rat is well and truly in the house.'

Chapter Twenty-four

Trap, his Tommy gun in his lap, travelled south in his GP vehicle, *his jeep*, heading to the township of Pozorrubio, his gaze darting back and forth across the deserted jungle road. Above him pink plumes of dawn light leaked through the clouds bunching on the horizon, and around him dew encrusted the emerald-green foliage like minute sparkling crystals.

On 6 December, with carte blanche from General Wainwright, Trap had picked his squad of men, and on the 7th they had travelled to the far north to begin training certain Filipino divisions in hand-to-hand fighting. He was pleased with his choices; they were the best he could find at Fort Stotsenburg and most of them came from the fighting 26th Cavalry, as Skinny had suggested.

Within twenty-four hours they had heard of the Japanese attack on Hawaii, followed by the bombing of Clark Field down in Southern Luzon. Two days later they knew of the Japanese troop landing at Appari on the northern side of the island.

Trap and his men had fought a few running battles with enemy vanguards from that Appari landing, and when a few days later a small, successful enemy landing was made just north of Vigan, Trap had remained in the vicinity, attempting to harass and hold the enemy if he could.

He was very aware of the elite force which had been raised in Britain the year before. They were called *commandos* and trained in the use of explosives and in unarmed combat, mobility and stealth, infiltration, reconnaissance, and all forms of hit-and-run warfare. He felt strongly that the USA should have a similar type of force and had been involved earlier in the year with the embryo of exactly such a unit. Some of those lethal skills came naturally to the men with him, and he recalled that his old friend John Drayton Whitby had been taught such tactics.

Trap's mouth drew down as he thought of Johnny: he was a good guy, why the hell was he married to *her*? He moved uncomfortably in the seat, straightened his shoulders and looked around.

Since the first run-in with the Japs on the evening of 10 December, four of his boys had been killed outright, and one had died of wounds. The couple of dozen remaining with him were in the vehicles in tandem behind him. They had lost one jeep so were travelling squeezed into five. He and his men had begun to call the new GP vehicles he had wheedled out of General Wainwright by the nickname Corporal Tommy Denham preferred; it seemed the right one to them.

Trap had tried to telephone General Wainwright from the settlements of Luna and San Gabriel but could not get through on the unreliable Philippine telephone system. His short-wave wireless set was on the blink and Private Josh Felix and Lieutenant Jake Williams were working on it whenever they could.

Driving at his side was Caldo, his six-foot tall, Atlas-like half-Filipino sergeant, a Colt .45 thrust in his belt and a green bandanna round his forehead. Behind him, crammed in the back, were three of his men: Privates Ivat, Mangana and Eduardo. Ivat was from Miani, Indiana; the others were local Filipino Scouts.

Lieutenant Jake Williams of the 91st Division brought up the rear in the fifth jeep, and driving alongside him was Denham. Whenever they stopped, the mechanic lovingly looked at his engines, topped up fuel and generally improved where he could. His precious tools in their dark green metal case were attached to the back of the lieutenant's vehicle near the wireless set and alongside the water tank and the spare wheel.

On receipt of General Wainwright's orders, Trap's unit had removed from their hideout on the Vigan road and headed south. Three times they had been strafed by Jap Zero fighter aircraft and they had hidden jeeps and men under the the the canopy of interlaced jungle and branches. The going had been slow because Filipino refugees in all manner of vehicles and carts filled with their animals had often blocked the narrow roadway, but now, as dawn burgeoned, they were alone on an open dirt road.

A growl from Caldo made Trap turn his head. The sergeant's muscles were noticeable under his uniform and his shoulder span was two feet wide. He was indeed memorable for his size but his skin was also a unique colour – a blend of rich ochre brown and gold. His mother had been an educated woman from a black family in North Carolina who had found her way to the Philippines and because of her, Caldo's English was sound. 'This dust and dirt gets everywhere.' He wiped his mouth with the back of his hand. 'I think it's even lodged between my goddam teeth.'

'Yeah, Sarge,' spoke up Terry Ivat, who was polishing his sub-machine gun with a rag. He was the reverse of Caldo, undersized and thin, not a discernible muscle in his frame and his skin was overly pale and blotchy from mosquito bites. 'Though personally I hate the bugs.'

Caldo started to laugh. 'Poor little Ivat, all bug-bitten. Your girlfriend won't recognise you.'

'Whatcha mean? What girlfriend?'

'Girls are nothin' but trouble,' opined Eduardo, coughing and spitting along with the breeze.

Caldo grunted. 'What about the accommodating ones?'

'I knew an accommodatin' one once,' Mangana spoke up, 'but her mother moved the family to another town.'

This elicited a raucous laugh from Caldo, and when it subsided he half turned to Trap. 'What do you reckon about girls, Major?'

Trap's voice was a monotone. 'I avoid them if I can.' He pointed his forefinger to the wheel. 'Two hands, Caldo, and drop the talk about blasted females.' He was remembering a girl in Madura Island and the same Doll in Hong Kong, one he could keep out of his head during the day but who edged her way into his dreams at night. He was thinking of her husband too, that part made him mighty uncomfortable.

Dawn was advancing as they came to a clearing and Trap held up his hand. 'Stop. I want to look at the map.'

'Right.' Caldo lifted his own hand high and the column of jeeps halted. 'Help Denham fill the tanks with juice, boys,' he ordered, and three of his men jumped to do it. Each vehicle carried a spare tank of fuel and two of the jeeps had an extra tank attached to the side.

As Felix lit a cigarette and, overseen by Lieutenant Williams, began to tinker with the wireless set, Cadee, the cook, set about finding firewood and Trap spread a map on the bonnet of his vehicle and took out his compass. A few minutes passed before he realised someone was standing quietly at his side. He looked up. 'Yes, Corporal, what is it?'

Tommy Denham paused and the morning sun caught the sheen in his blond curls as he drew an envelope from his pocket. He looked much younger than his twenty-three years, standing there in the gold of breaking day. 'I'd like you to take this, sir.' He held out the envelope.

'What is it, son?'

'A letter for my mother ... back in Tennessee.' He swallowed. 'In case I don't go home.'

Trap grunted in thought before he answered. 'Now, Denham, firstly, you *are* going back. Secondly, we all have the same chances out here, so I'd like you to return that letter to your pocket and think positively.'

Denham shook his head, continuing to proffer the letter. 'Sure, sir, but I'd still like you to take it, 'cause you're going back for sure.'

Trap frowned. His gaze dropped to the boy's hand holding the

179

envelope and he noticed a scar running down Denham's middle finger. 'What makes you say a thing like that, son?'

Denham screwed up his mouth and the dimple in his cheek deepened. 'I just know, sir.' His hand remained outstretched. 'Please take it for me, sir.'

Trap took it. 'Denham, I want you to understand I'm carrying this for you only temporarily. You'll be getting it back. Now scram.'

'Thanks, sir.'

Trap shook his head and returned his gaze to his map.

Abruptly Caldo yelled, 'Jeez, Major, what's that?'

Trap spun round, his eagle sight picking up movement in the distance. He did not need binoculars to see the troops issuing on to the straight jungle road about a quarter of a mile away. His tone was cold. 'Japs. Hundreds of them. They mightn't have seen us yet. Move!'

Williams snatched the wireless from Felix and ran; Cadee grabbed the canvas cook bag, and threw a tin of coffee to Eduardo, who caught it and kept running, while everybody launched themselves at the jeeps. The vehicles faced towards the Japanese, and as the drivers landed in their seats, pressed the starter buttons and reversed round in the clearing, the enemy in the distance dropped to the ground and began shooting.

They screeched away on the narrow road where bamboo, palms, hardwood trees and banyans grew to the very edges. Trap's jeep brought up the rear, and above the roar he thought he heard the throb of heavy-calibre machine guns. He knew he was right when suddenly bullets ripped into the spare tyre mounted at the back, metal and rubber spat into the air and a round cracked the top of the windscreen on Caldo's driving side.

Ivat yelled but Caldo did not even flinch as he shouted, 'How the hell did the Japs get way down here ahead of us?'

'Must have landed in the Lingayen Gulf!'

'Yeah! Shit.'

They had not travelled a mile when Denham, who was now

driving the first vehicle containing Lieutenant Williams, slammed his foot on the brake and stood up to look down the road. 'Oh no!' he yelled. 'More of them!'

'Shit!' shouted Caldo as Trap bellowed, 'Back up!'

Without room to turn, Caldo reversed the jeep, foot pushing the accelerator to the floor, followed closely by the other four vehicles.

'Make for that side trail about two hundred yards back!'

Caldo nodded, jaw set, foot clamped down. He reached the track and spun into it at speed; the other vehicles did the same. 'Jeez, Major, looks like this whole area's crawling with blasted monkeys.'

'Yeah, Caldo, that's sure how it seems.' Trap roared over the howling engine: 'Heading into Pozorrubio just became a no-no! Stay on this: I've got a feeling we'll join up with another trail that runs into Binalonan. We'll do a wide detour. If the blasted Nips haven't penetrated too far, we should be able to get to Colonel Canten's Asingan camp within a couple of hours.'

It took exactly that. They slowly approached the camp through the ubiquitous nipa palms to find there were no sentries. Smoke hung in the still morning air and signs of withdrawal were all about: empty sheds and shacks, one that had been torched still smouldering; wheels and rusted vehicle parts, abandoned fire sites.

'They've gone,' Ivat declared.

'Don't state the obvious, soldier,' Caldo growled as he alighted beside Trap, whose gaze combed the trees around them while he held his Tommy gun at the ready.

Felix's voice sounded from the back of a vehicle. 'Wireless set's been smashed, sir!'

Caldo made his usual remark: 'Shit!'

Lieutenant Jake Williams edged closer to Trap, his smooth young face wrinkling. 'If this camp's abandoned, sir, it's because there's been a general withdrawal.'

Trap nodded. Most officers knew about WPO-3 and he

181

suddenly had a strong feeling that all their troops were making for Bataan and he and his boys were all alone here.

'I think we might be invited to a party that only the enemy will be attending, sir,' Caldo observed.

Trap lifted his hand for attention. 'Listen up, boys: back into the vehicles; we're going to make for the Agno river.' He took another swift look around as he spoke and his eyes caught something glinting in the undergrowth beyond Felix and Private Abella, who stood near the broken wireless at the back of Lieutenant Williams's jeep.

Trap spun on his heel. 'Get out fast!' But even as the words exploded from his throat, the first volley of rifle fire hit Privates Abella and Felix, who both pitched forward to the muddy ground.

Trap saw instantly that the two soldiers were dead. 'Into the jeeps!' he bawled to the cacophony of a second spate of enemy bullets ripping across the ground.

Trap, Williams, Caldo, Ivat, Mangana and Cadee were the furthest from the jeeps, and Trap shoved Williams behind a smouldering shed wall as he fired a volley from his Tommy gun and dropped down beside the lieutenant. At the same time the other four fell to their knees and returned fire as they surged along behind the protection of the wall.

Three of the five vehicles were partly sheltered from the enemy position by the remains of sheds burnt by the departing US forces. 'Into the jeeps!' Trap repeated, and the others charged across to them and vaulted inside.

Two vehicles sped away with soldiers half in and half out, but the tyres of the third stuck in the loose surface and spun. The delay was only seconds before the rubber grabbed, but two of the soldiers were hit; one lurched to the side but was saved from falling out as the jeep made its escape into the trees.

Trap calculated the distances of the remaining vehicles: one stood alone in the clearing, with bullets raining all around it. The last vehicle was reachable – twenty yards away and half hidden, its nose pushed into a stand of palms.

Trap glanced at the five soldiers with him, returning fire into the trees and undergrowth. His eyes rested on Ivat. 'You're the smallest target, son, so get over to that vehicle near the palms. We'll cover you. Move it forward into protection and we'll follow.'

Ivat looked frightened but mustered, 'Yes, sir.' And while his companions returned as much firepower as possible, the slight soldier streaked away, moving like a sprinter. He reached the jeep unhurt and started it.

'Go, Caldo!'

The big sergeant bolted, bullets lifting the dirt behind him, but he made it. On Caldo's heels, Mangana and Cadee made a dash for it, but now Japanese began emerging from the fronds of undergrowth, firing all the time. Mangana stumbled, and blood spurted from his left knee as Cadee stopped and tried to pull him along.

'Let's go!' Trap yelled as he leapt out from cover, bent over and sweeping the enemy with bullets. At his side came Williams doing the same. One of the Japanese went down and another hesitated, but more cork helmets were issuing from the greenery all the time.

Trap and Williams reached Cadee and Mangana. Mangana lurched from a second hit. He was choking on his own blood and death was moments away. Trap wrenched Cadee from the dying Mangana and pushed him onwards as a bullet zinged off Williams's helmet. 'Run!' howled Trap and they raced and stumbled the last twelve yards to the safety of the jeep hidden by the palms.

Ivat's trembling foot slammed down as the first of the Japanese appeared round the tree behind them and began shooting, but Trap and Caldo were returning fire. Enemy rounds thudded into the rear of the jeep and ricocheted off the bumper bar, but they were away, and to the crackling cadence of bullets razor-cutting palm fronds, the jeep roared down the track, safe from the spitting death behind them.

'Shit!' came Caldo's eternal refrain.

Chapter Twenty-five

The brazen light of afternoon revealed itself through a gap in the clouds and found Lexi trudging along carrying Jimmy and drawing Lessa by the hand.

Earlier they had been caught in a downpour and had sheltered in a deserted nipa hut. It was the dry season and this cloudburst was the first heavy rain Lexi could recall since being shipwrecked. When the tiny spots of rain had begun to fall, little Jimmy, who did not want to get wet, began to brush each droplet off, his fat little fingers dancing across his face, arms and hair until there were so many raindrops coming at speed he began to cry. Lexi had lifted him and pulled Lessa to the meagre hut, which stood atop a short hill.

The rain had stopped and the sun had appeared, and now as she wandered on ever southward praying to find some American troops, thoughts of Trap surfaced in Lexi's head all the time. Thoughts satiated with guilt over her husband Johnny and her dead baby, but they were powerful and would not leave her. She visualised him and wondered where he was and what had become of him. She prayed he was safe. And no sooner had she prayed for Trap than her conscience had her praying for John Drayton.

She could hear shelling in the distance and her fear urged her to keep up the pace even while the children resisted. Most of the time she carried Jimmy and pulled Lessa along, and when Lessa tired she piggy-backed her. She had made herself a sort of waist-pack in which she conveyed the blanket and the few other belongings they had collected. When she was burdened with that and both the children, she thought of herself as a human donkey.

The whole of Luzon was in turmoil: no public transport ran, or certainly not in the areas she had passed through, and people were busy deserting their abodes and heading to Manila: she supposed correctly that those in Manila, on the other hand, were busy leaving the capital for the country. After being unable to find the main road south, Lexi had this morning finally reached what she believed to be an arterial road, for there were people everywhere. Many were in donkey- or horse-drawn carts; others were on foot, but all were heading south. She had asked a number for a lift but their carts were piled high with belongings, domestic animals and children of their own.

The only troops she saw were Filipino soldiers, and they appeared to be fleeing. Some were on motorbikes and in army trucks, but most were on foot, and they paid her no mind. There was massive confusion, and when she did come across people who spoke English she could make no sense of what she was told, for Luzon seemed to be afire with rumours about where the Japanese were.

'They have taken Manila,' she was told by some. 'They are just back over the hill behind us,' said others. One young soldier told her that the US and Filipino forces were withdrawing to the Bataan peninsula. She asked where that was and was informed: 'To the south.' The soldiers were not unsympathetic to her, and some gave her food; it was simply that the army was fighting a rearguard action and had a war on its hands, and one woman and two children were incidental.

One soldier pulled up in a small lorry and gave her a concerned smile indicating that she must get across the Agno river. 'Be over by sunset, lady. We're on general withdrawal and the Japs will be through here pretty soon.'

'How far is the river?'

He pointed. 'About six miles. Take that dirt road; it'll get you there the quickest.' He pointed with a Colt .44. 'You really must get across today.'

Lexi felt an adrenalin rush, and her head spun. There was no hope of travelling six miles before day's end at the pace she and the children moved. She looked down the road he had indicated and saw a few civilians in the distance.

'Can't you take us? Please?'

'Sorry, I can't detour, I'm on orders. Just do as I say, stay on that road.' He pointed again, before leaning out the window and handing her two bananas and a can of beans, 'It's Christmas Day after all.' With a quick salute he drove away.

Christmas Day! She had not even thought about what month it was, let alone the day! She was reminded of the people she loved and she shivered thinking of the massacre, and that led her to thinking of Sir Brillard. In the days since the deaths of Silveria and Josephine she had carried the abiding feeling that her grandfather too was no longer on the world. Always before when she had thought of him she had derived a sense of strength and energy, but now she was overwhelmed with a powerful sadness and a persistent sensation of loss.

She lifted Jimmy and took Lessa's hand. 'Come on, we must walk a lot faster.'

But as the hours passed and the day waned she knew she was not going to reach the river by nightfall. She was mindful that she had not seen anyone for an hour or two; that she and the children were alone on the road. The little girl and boy were worn out, and Jimmy began whimpering.

And now as the shadows of the palms lengthened and the sun almost touched the hilltops her eyes scanned the road behind and into the trees and across to the long rolling slopes covered with knee-high Talahib grass. She thought she saw movement in the distance and electric twinges stabbed through her, but she realised she was wrong and the emerald green hillside was still.

186

She was carrying Jimmy and urging Lessa on when she heard the sound of a motor and her heart accelerated. Moving the children back from a puddle at the side of the road, she turned towards the noise.

Around a bend behind her emerged a beaten-up brown Ford Sedan, being driven at speed, and she raised her hand to halt it. But if anything it accelerated, and she only just had time to pull the children away before it sped straight by. She saw a woman's face at one of the windows as water slopped over her leg, then it was gone. With despair she watched it disappear.

She was frightened now; the lone speeding vehicle was symbolic. It seemed that she and the children were left behind; the defence forces were withdrawing and all the locals had deserted this area as well. She could still hear vague rumbles of battle but was confused about their whereabouts. Around her and the children, the countryside seemed eerily empty, a weird otherworldly mood in the air.

She shook herself into action and, taking a deep breath, she attempted to put a lift in her voice. 'Come on,' she said, hefting Jimmy higher in her right arm and taking Lessa's hand once more. 'We must hurry.'

No sooner had she spoken than she heard a fearful sound. Without hesitation she dragged Lessa and carried Jimmy over the mounds of tall grass into the thickest stand of banana palms, where they lay flat in the grass as the Japanese aircraft skimmed overhead. It boomed and sped on by above them to continue along the course of the road. Jimmy began to cry and Lexi kissed his damp cheek.

Since the day Silveria and Josephine had been killed, Lexi had seen numerous formations of enemy aircraft but had not encountered another fighter at close range. It was an ominous sign.

She urged the children to their feet. 'Come on, my little ones. Dusk is coming, we must travel faster.'

They had gone a little further when she looked to the right and froze.

There across a field, beyond a cluster of tamarind trees and some palms, she saw a man. At first she hoped her eyes had played a trick, but another man appeared beside him. They were not close, perhaps even four hundred yards away, but they were Japanese soldiers. By the very way they moved and carried themselves she knew. The children had not seen them and as she watched she held her breath, for another soldier appeared beside them. They were not facing her, and even as she stood, heart racing, they moved further away in the opposite direction.

Her head shot to right and left, her eyes wild and searching. She looked back to where the soldiers had disappeared and forced herself to calmness; she had to think. She guessed she was still a couple of miles from the river and probably should not stay on the road now the Japanese were in the vicinity. But did she have a choice? This was the only route she knew which led to the river: the river she had to cross today! It would be dark in less than an hour, and even the Japs would have to sleep. If she could keep going she might make the river ... She might make the river ... even in the night.

She began to pull Lessa along as fast as the child could go, but with the burden of the small boy Lexi's own pace suffered, yet terror gave her energy.

'Move, please. Hurry, children.'

They crossed a low hill on the dirt road, and as they reached the dip at the bottom there was suddenly the sound of a motor behind them and Lexi spun round to see a vehicle on the crest of the rise. Fear stabbed through her as another appeared behind the first.

There was a grove of coconut palms beside her and she thought to dart into them but she knew they had seen her. It was too late. The vehicles rolled down towards her — there were four — and she stood helplessly in the middle of the road.

The small trucks were battered and spotted with mud thrown up from the road after the recent rain. The occupants wore dishevelled uniforms. The only objects that did not look grimy were the automatic weapons they held; those looked relatively clean, some even shone in the tiring day.

No! God! She must do something. She could not let them just take her and the babies.

She had half turned to run when she discerned that the soldiers in the jeeps were not Japanese!

The constriction in her throat relaxed and she waited, nursing Jimmy and holding Lessa's hand.

In the first vehicle a big man wearing a green bandanna raised himself from the driver's seat, one hand still on the steering wheel. He called out in Tagalog – the major local language – for her to get off the road, and when she did not move he reverted to Spanish and finally to English.

'Missus, missus, move to the side! We must get by.' He was edging the vehicle closer as he spoke and he looked down to the man who sat next to him. 'Blasted woman must be deaf.'

The man beside him him stepped out and walked forward, shouting, 'Lady? Out of the way.'

Lexi saw the shape of him, the rhythm of his gait, his raised arm, his face under his officer's cap.

He kept coming towards her. 'Look, lady, do you understand English?'

He was about eight yards away, seven yards away, six yards away . . .

She just kept staring at him and no words came. She knew she dropped Lessa's hand and she felt the child move behind her and cling to her legs. Her hand lifted and shot to her mouth.

He kept on coming. He walked right up to her.

Trap had continued travelling southwards through Luzon the best way he could. As time passed he and his men became aware that the Japanese had made a number of landings on the eastern shore of the Lingayen Gulf at dawn on the morning of 22 December.

From what he gathered from local Filipinos the enemy must have landed unopposed at various points between Bauong and Damortis. This meant there were a lot of them ahead of him somewhere.

Last night he and his boys had run into some remnants of the 48th Division and a single tank from the 192nd Tank Division – the only armour in support of the Northern Luzon Forces. They were engaging a vanguard of the enemy near Manoaog. They had no idea where the rest of their forces were and had lost contact with headquarters. Trap and his men fought along with the defenders and held the enemy back till dusk, when the battle lost momentum.

It was from the captain in the tank division that Trap learnt that WPO-3 was in effect and that they were to withdraw across the Agno to the second of the five defensive lines in the fallback to Bataan. The captain was frazzled and exhausted. 'We're too far north, we'll be surrounded if we don't move.'

The defenders left their position under the cover of night and Trap and his boys drove on until they came to an overgrown area which appeared to be a dead end. They halted and caught a few hours' sleep, awakening at dawn on Christmas Day, when they mounted their jeeps and moved cautiously along, attempting to go ever southward. Trap reckoned that by now General Wainwright could have abandoned his field headquarters at Alcala and moved down to Bamban.

Twice they saw the enemy in the distance ahead, once they were fired upon but no one was hurt, and both times they reversed and took circuitous routes to attempt to swing wide round the enemy. This morning Caldo, ever resourceful, had raided what appeared to be a warehouse in a small community and had found a box full of dozens of cans of beans which the whole troop had eaten as they travelled on. Denham had reminded them that this was Christmas Day.

Eventually they found a dirt road that led directly south and Caldo calculated that they were perhaps four or so miles from the

Agno river. They moved with speed, ever vigilant, and when they were hit by a surprise cloudburst they did not halt but kept on moving.

'Perhaps the Japs don't like rain and have gone to ground,' Denham kept saying optimistically.

When they heard an aircraft along the road behind them they drove straight into a grove of palms and watched the enemy Zero zoom by overhead.

They pressed on for another five minutes without incident and cautiously crossed over the crest of a low hill to find a Filipina peasant woman and her children about a hundred and fifty yards ahead in the middle of the road. She made as if to run away at first, but she hesitated and stood still. Caldo began shouting for her to get out of the way.

The woman stood rigidly, an infant in her arms and clutching the hand of a little girl. She was tall for a Filipina and her hair drifted back over her shoulders while the torpid breeze blew her cheap cotton smock between her long, shapely, sun-browned legs. Trap eyed her, feet planted on the damp red soil of the road with her offspring clinging to her as if she were some rustic earth mother. At his side Caldo shouted to her as Trap eased himself out of the jeep and walked towards the female and her kids.

The woman did nothing.

He shouted, 'Lady? Out of the way.'

She did not move or speak, and he walked towards her warily, his gaze searching beyond her into the quickening darkness. She could be a Jap decoy of some kind. Had to be careful. His hand tightened on his Tommy gun as he spoke again. 'Look, lady, do you understand English?'

She let go of the hand of the little girl, who darted behind her to hold her round the knees, and the woman lifted her left palm up towards him. It was an odd movement and reminded him of someone . . . But abruptly she brought her hand sharply back to her face and covered her mouth.

It was in that instant Hank Trapperton knew who she was. He stopped dead a yard away from her.

It was her all right! Looking at him with those pure Virginia sky-blue eyes!

He stifled a strange sound that started in his throat as he actually shook his head in disbelief before he stepped up to her and removed her trembling hand from her mouth.

He knew the touch of these fingers; Jesus, he dreamt about the touch of them!

'Doll, what in the name of God are you doing here?'

Chapter Twenty-six

Lexi's eyes brimmed with tears; her fingers trembled in his.

Without hesitation he stepped forward and took her in his arms, encompassing her and the little boy. From below Lessa looked fearfully up at him, her tiny arms still clutching Lexi around the knees.

Caldo was rarely surprised, let alone shocked, but as he watched his major remove the woman's hand from her mouth and step forward and embrace her, for the first time in his life Caldo admitted he was dumbfounded.

Ivat, seated behind him, gave a long, low whistle. 'Jeez, Sarge, who the hell is that dame?'

'Beats me.'

'The major ain't one for goin' round huggin' strange dames.'

'You can say that again.'

'The major ain't one for goin' round huggi—'

'Shut up, Ivat!'

Silence descended as they continued to witness this oddest of scenes.

Trap held Lexi close while she clung to him with her free hand, living in the touch and feel of him, safe at last in his arms.

For the seconds he held her, Trap's expression softened into tenderness, his lips resting on her forehead, but too quickly he released her. As he stepped away Jimmy regarded him and announced in his baby voice . . . 'soder'.

Lexi tried to smile, but instead a tear slid down the side of her nose. Finally she contrived to speak and she pointed across the fields. 'There are Japs over that way, not far. I saw them only a while ago.'

Trap wheeled in the direction she pointed. All seemed quiet in the haze of afternoon, but they must get out of here. He grabbed her arm and pushed her towards the jeep as she quickly informed him, 'An American soldier told me I had to cross the Agno river before tonight. That they are falling back.'

'Yep, that's right. The Japs are crawling all over the place.' As he spoke, Caldo brought the jeep forward to them and Trap hurried Lexi and the children to its side, his voice matter-of-fact to his men. 'As you can see, I know this lady. We take her with us from here on. Now let's go.'

Not one of his men said anything. The silence seemed to hang heavily in the air and Ivat dug Eduardo in the side when Trap indicated what he wanted. 'One of you three soldiers perch on the back.' For a moment there was hesitation from Eduardo, Ivat and Private Evangelista, who already sat crowded in the rear seat.

'Move!' Trap's tone was unequivocal.

Ivat immediately climbed behind Evangelista to balance on the spare tyre. Eduardo took Jimmy in his arms while Trap helped Lexi into the back seat.

As Lexi entered the jeep Lessa began to punch at Trap's legs in an effort to push past him to follow her. Trap swiftly lifted the child and dropped her into Lexi's lap where the little girl hid her face in the woman's body and Lexi kissed the top of her head while Trap swung aboard thudding down beside Caldo. At the moment his back connected with the seat a volley of bullets spat into the banana palms at the side of the road.

'Shit!' exclaimed Caldo, lunging down on the accelerator as Ivat screamed, 'On the left! Hundreds of them!'

And there they were – Japanese in cork helmets running towards them through the high grass of the emerald-green central Luzon plain.

'Oh not again!' Eduardo cried out, balancing Jimmy and lunging down to pick up his automatic weapon from the floor.

Trap, who had more freedom in the front seat, swung his Tommy gun round and sent a burst off at the approaching enemy, while Ivat, from his precarious perch on the back of the vehicle, attempted to do the same.

All the jeeps were overcrowded and those boys in the other three who had room to use their weapons were firing back as they raced away, when suddenly the jeep behind Trap which held six men slewed sideways off the dirt road. The driver's side of the vehicle had been sprayed with bullets and the soldier at the wheel collapsed over it as it thudded into the trunk of a banana palm.

'Jesus!' shouted Ivat from his perch. 'That jeep's been hit!'

'Stop!' shouted Trap, and Caldo hit the brakes.

'Don't stop, sir, we'll all be killed,' Eduardo cried out, but Caldo had already slammed to a standstill as Trap's arm shot in the air to signal to the other two vehicles to continue on down the road. One sped ahead but Lieutenant Williams's jeep did not move. He vaulted out to join Trap, who had leapt to the ground yelling, 'Hit the floor, Doll, and keep the children down!' Lexi's reaction was immediate, and in the same moment Caldo, Evangelista and Ivat followed Trap and fell down on one knee in the dirt road, firing rapidly to delay the enemy. Eduardo hesitated momentarily before he too jumped down and began shooting.

At the same time the soldiers with the dead driver abandoned their jeep and sprinted towards Trap and their comrades who maintained their battle with the enemy.

The last of the oncoming soldiers, Eddie Black, suddenly stumbled and sank to the ground, blood gushing from his back. Twenty-year-old Dan Clevelly and Cadee the cook stopped and turned

195

back to help him, but a bullet ricocheted off the cook's steel helmet and he staggered and almost fell. Trap ran to them, pulling a grenade from his belt and ripping the pin out with his teeth to hurl it at the closest of the enemy. It exploded with earth and rocks hurtling though the air, to be quickly followed by explosions from two more grenades thrown by Caldo and Ivat. Trap roared his orders. 'Caldo, Denham, get back and start our jeeps!' He wheeled round to his men. 'Come on. One more round and let's get out of here!'

Cadee, who was standing dazed from the bullet which had dinted his helmet, delayed, but Trap looked down at the bleeding soldier. 'Eddie's gone, move!' Clevelly pushed Cadee hard in the back and ran on.

With long strides they raced back. By now Caldo and Denham had their engines running and in ones and twos they leapt aboard, arms and legs entwined and whirling in the air like serpents.

The jeeps were already full, so Ivat and Eduardo scrambled on to the bonnet of Trap's jeep. Ivat held the windscreen on the passenger side and Eduardo wedged his feet on to the bumper and grasped a ledge near the starboard headlight. They retained their weapons as best they could.

As Denham's vehicle sped away, Evangelista, the slowest of the runners, was still some yards from Trap's jeep. Trap jumped up on the rear of the vehicle one leg in, one leg out, while Ivat managed to get a volley off at the Japanese who had rallied and were coming on again. Lexi and the children were stuck in the centre of the vehicle between Caldo's massive right shoulder and Ivat's back as he wielded his gun towards the enemy. Lexi clutched Trap to steady him and he dropped his Tommy gun as he leant out with his hands extended and yelled encouragement to Evangelista. 'Come on, soldier, come on!'

Just then Ivat cried, 'Oh no! More of the bastards!' And like locusts, another unit of Japanese were spreading out through the banana palms about three hundred yards distant.

Eduardo swore. 'Let's go! Let's go!' but Caldo remained motion-less, waiting for his major to order the exit.

As Evangelista made a mighty leap towards Trap and his body slammed on to the stern of the vehicle, his left boot slipped but miraculously lodged under the bumper bar beneath the spare fuel container, where he retained a footing. Trap caught hold of the man's collar but in his own precarious position his grip simply rent the uniform and Evangelista's right hand grabbed thin air. Lexi, with one arm round Trap's waist, lunged forward and managed to take a firm grip on Evangelista's forearm and hold him fast until Trap steadied himself and seized the Filipino.

'Go, Caldo!'

The sergeant stamped on the accelerator. The overloaded vehicle coughed at the weight it carried but it moved, rolled forward and accelerated.

As bullets rammed into the tyre near Trap and cut in the air around them, Evangelista was able to anchor himself on the tail. Caldo was at last making good speed when Evangelista gave a lurch and slumped into Trap's embrace.

'I've been hit, sir.'

Trap slid his arms further round the man's torso as he began to crumple. He held him fast. 'I've got you, soldier, we'll soon be out of here.'

Four minutes later they were at the bridge.

The other two jeeps were already there waiting for them, but instead of smiles came groans of frustration.

There was no bridge over the Agno!

It had been blown up by an efficient demolition unit of the retreating United States Army. The gorge was deep, there was no way down and the river appeared uncrossable.

'Shit,' announced Caldo as usual.

Eduardo was mumbling what they were all thinking. 'All the

freakin' bridges will have been blown. We're stuck on this side with the flamin' Jappos.'

Trap stood near Evangelista, whose lower back wound was being quickly looked at by Lexi. She had explained that she could help and introduced herself as Dr Robinson. Lessa and Jimmy remained silently beside her, the toddler playing with her shoe. The two other wounded soldiers, who had been shot earlier in the escape from the abandoned camp, sat in their jeeps.

But Caldo's frown of concern had become a frown of thought. 'Major, I reckon I know a way across.'

Trap turned his head to his sergeant. 'Right. Shoot.'

'Well, I know exactly where I am, and down there about three miles,' he pointed along the river to the east, 'the river narrows to a certain extent and there's an old railway bridge. Hasn't been used in fifty years. Fact is the rails were lifted when I was a kid and reused somewhere else. It's in a turn of the river and concealed in a cutting from this bank. Unless you knew it was there you probably wouldn't see it because the bend in the river hides it. Now with a bit of luck our boys won't have known anything about it, so I reckon it'll still be standing.'

'But the place is overrun with Japs,' complained Eduardo.

Trap turned to the west. 'It's about half an hour to sunset and we know the Japs we just ran into are heading in this direction, so we can't delay. How do we get to the railway bridge, Caldo?'

The sergeant gestured with his thumb. 'We have to cross this field and the next one. See that grove of banyan trees in the distance? I think there's a track that runs behind them in the direction of the bridge.'

'If the Japs don't get us first,' Clevelly opined, and Eduardo groaned in agreement.

'Drivers, get ready to roll,' Trap announced, his eyes on Lexi, who hurriedly tied a cloth around the middle of the badly wounded Filipino. She stood, and moving away a few paces, beckoned to Trap.

For some seconds there on the river bank with the green Luzon plain behind them and the orange balloon of the sun now subsiding behind the darkening hills, the world did not seem real to Lexi; after all that had happened to her, Trap's turning up was some sort of miracle. But they were in danger and there was no time to indulge herself with such thoughts: she was a doctor.

'Evangelista's not conscious at present — wound's pretty bad; the bullet's close to his spine. We shouldn't move him, but leaving him here . . .' A line fixed itself between her eyes and her mind whirled back to the treatment she had received from the Japanese. She swallowed. 'I don't think we should abandon him, because he's probably got a better chance with us. The other two say they are all right to travel.'

Trap studied her and saw the deep-seated fear. He wanted to hold her and comfort her, to ask what had happened, but she went quickly on, 'Look, moving him is dangerous, but at least he won't feel the pain.'

'Right,' Trap declared and spun round to his men. He noticed the ones who were missing and how his unit was shrinking. He thought of his boys who were dead on the dirt of Luzon. He swallowed hard but his tone was positive and he gave those with him a confident smile. 'Right, we'll make for the railway bridge. It's close to dusk and with a bit of luck most of the Japs will be finding places to camp for the night.' He looked down the road they had come. 'But those Nips back there know about us, so . . .' He slapped Caldo's arm. 'We'll take Evangelista and the woman and children, and you,' he pointed to Ivat, 'can return to your perch on the tail-end of our vehicle. Okay, let's go.'

Everybody did.

The vehicles bumped and rattled as they crossed the field, and Lexi held Evangelista in the rear seat. She was relieved that he could not feel the thumping and shaking. She knew it was risky for him to be jarred like this, but leaving him was not an option.

As Caldo drove past the banyan trees, he grunted knowingly,

'This is it.' They were soon on the narrow dirt path which took them by a collection of abandoned huts sitting at a crossroads. Another mile on they drove down a ditch and up the other side past thick entwined vines and plants and half a dozen banana trees, their vast branches stark; no human beings in sight anywhere. After a few more minutes they came round a bend and saw the river wending its way ahead of them again.

'We're here,' Caldo announced brightly. 'I can see the trees that hide the cutting on this side.'

'Bingo!' proclaimed Ivat from behind.

Chapter Twenty-seven

It was just as Caldo had informed them. The railway lines had been lifted a long time previously and many of the sleepers were gone, but the bridge was still there, stretching about fifty yards over a steep gorge with the river flowing at the bottom.

The track ran down a slope through the cutting, and Trap left Ivat as a lookout at the top.

'I'll drive the last jeep across, Ivat. You can walk ahead of me.'

'Yes, sir.'

The three jeeps bumped down the cutting to the foot of the slope, where Lieutenant Williams slid out of his vehicle. His fair hair had fallen forward in a shock on his forehead and he pushed it back as he came over to Trap, who stood from his seat. 'Major, do you think the bridge will hold the weight of a jeep? Some of those supports look rotten to me and with a driver it'll weigh well over half a ton.'

'With the sarge drivin', the supports ain't got a chance,' remarked Denham, and the men around him laughed.

'Most of us will walk across,' Trap decided, 'then Caldo, Denham and I will each drive a jeep over.'

Lieutenant Williams stepped forward. 'I'd like to take a vehicle instead of you, sir.'

Trap shook his head. 'You're too valuable. If I end up in the drink, you're in charge.'

'With respect, sir, you're the one who is too valuable and I'd still like to do it.'

Trap liked Williams: he was a good officer and had grit. 'I appreciate your offer, son, but the three best drivers are taking the vehicles: the sergeant, the corporal and myself. What you can do right now is walk across and test the supports. Take a man with you. If you get over safely we'll send the woman and children next, then the wounded men, followed by the rest and lastly the vehicles.'

Hank Williams's mouth drew down with disappointment but he knew not to argue. 'Right, sir.' He moved away to the men and detailed Ivat and Cadee to carry Evangelista. 'You, Eduardo, will cross with me right now. We're the guinea pigs.'

Eduardo hung back, half turning away as if he had not heard.

The lieutenant raised his voice. 'Eduardo, come on! Did you hear me, soldier? At the double.'

With obvious reluctance, Eduardo sidled up to the lieutenant's side and they stepped out on to the bridge.

Trap and Caldo crouched down at the edge of the gorge and observed the supports underneath as the two soldiers walking gingerly, traversed the structure without incident.

It was Lexi's turn. She carried Lessa and one of the soldiers carried Jimmy. They passed over easily.

When the whole group except for those driving the vehicles had arrived on the far side, they gravitated together, looking back.

Trap cupped his hands and shouted to Ivat on sentry at the top of the slope: 'See anything, Ivat?'

'No, sir. All clear.'

Caldo contemplated the major with a serious expression in his dark eyes. 'There aren't any grenades or explosives left, sir, so there's no easy way of blowing up the bridge once we're across.'

'I know, Caldo. Just get your vehicle over and leave the rest to me. Now make tracks.'

'Sure, Major.' The sergeant jumped aboard and crossed himself.

'If it holds me and the jeep, it'll take you and Denham no trouble.'

'Good luck, Sarge,' Denham called as Caldo slowly edged his jeep on to the aged wooden structure and Trap crouched eyeing the supports again.

Lexi knelt down on the other side of the gorge, holding the children, round their small bodies, her knees on the coarse grass growing in the solid red earth. She offered a silent prayer to whatever God might be listening. The world was in torment, she had lost many she loved dearly, but she asked for safe passage for the man on the other side of the railway bridge. The moment she had finished her prayer, a deluge of guilt overwhelmed her. What about her husband? What about Johnny? She should pray for him wherever he was.

Tears welled and she wiped them away with the back of her hand as Sergeant Caldo's voice lifted. 'I can feel the bridge swaying a bit, Major!'

'Yes, Caldo, I can see that, but it's holding.' Trap could hear the straining and creaking of the old timber, but nothing splintered and the Filipino brought the vehicle safely over to terra firma.

The soldiers all applauded as the light of day evaporated and dusk descended.

'Shake a leg, Denham!' Trap indicated with his thumb and the corporal followed the same procedure of driving the jeep with infinite care off the land on to the bridge. As he did so, Trap started his own engine, pulled hard on the brake and left his vehicle on the slope of the cutting to stride to the brink of the gorge and crouch down and observe the supports again. When Tommy Denham was halfway across, the bridge trembled and swayed and Trap could hear the timber straining, but there were no signs of the uprights giving way.

But the sudden cry from Ivat sent adrenalin shooting though him.

'Major! Here they come again!' And the soldier abandoned his post and came charging down the slope.

On the far bank Lieutenant Williams called for his men to take cover. 'Get ready to open fire!' Lexi snatched the children and ran to shelter with them behind a lauan tree, the prayer automatically beginning again in her head.

Tommy Denham, who had been edging carefully across the bridge, thumped his foot down on the accelerator in an attempt to speed up, but abruptly the vehicle stalled. With trembling hands he punched the button on the dashboard to restart his motor, but all he heard was a spluttering and whining as the engine refused to turn over.

Ivat was hurtling down the forty-yard incline like an Olympic hurdler, leaping over rocks and debris, and Trap yelled as he launched himself towards his own jeep, 'Get in, Ivat!'

The boy from Indiana did not need a second order: he came like the wind and vaulted into the rear seat, Tommy gun held high, as Trap waved his hand to Denham on the bridge ahead. 'Get out of there, Denham. Leave it!'

The leader released the brake and, picking up speed from the gradient, charged at the stationary vehicle, which was planted two thirds of the way across the old wooden structure, while a phalanx of Japanese emerged over the crown of the slope. A barrage of bullets from Lieutenant Williams's men met them but they were already returning fire.

Trap was still calling to Denham as he came surging across the bridge in his jeep. 'Get out, man!'

Denham got the idea and sprang out of his seat and ran towards his comrades on the far bank, while the cork helmets poured over the hill behind in a mass, firing as they came.

By now Trap had gathered enough speed to smash convincingly into the back of Denham's jeep. With perfect aim he rammed the spare fuel tank. The thud shook the bridge, the tank split and fuel sprayed across the bonnet of the colliding vehicle and all over the stalled one.

Ivat lurched forward but knew what to do: he clambered out and as hastily as possible followed the mechanic towards his buddies on the far bank.

Behind them the first of the Japanese were down the slope and making for the bridge when Trap felt the structure beneath him begin to creak and shudder. He bounded from his seat and edged quickly by Denham's vehicle as the bridge gave another tremble. Running a few paces he spun back and ripped a Zippo lighter from his trouser pocket, lit it and hurled it at the fuel-covered jeeps before he turned and hurtled after Ivat.

Bullets were flying, zinging and whizzing in the air, as Ivat and Denham, with Trap at their heels, threw themselves the last few yards and young Clevelly and Williams ran to help them. At the same time the petrol ignited and the blast of air hit Trap in the back as his jeep exploded and metal spat in all directions. Kaboom! The bridge shook, quivered and swayed as the three soldiers hit the dirt and rolled to a standstill.

The Japanese drew up on the far bank and dropped to the ground as pieces of metal flew into them.

A thick cloud of black smoke discharged skywards into the lowering Philippine dusk, as a loud rumble ran through the elderly wooden railway bridge and a deafening splintering sound rent the fading day. The supports in the middle gave way and that part of the structure began to collapse just as the second vehicle exploded with a deafening boom. More metal sprayed out and everybody, including the enemy, dived as flat to the earth as possible.

A screech from the disintegrating wood echoed along the gorge as one of the burning jeeps slid off the breaking timber and hurtled down into the river. The other remained lodged on the broken section and continued to burn, yellow, blue and red feathers of flame leaping high in the air around the ebony trail of smoke.

Silence fell.

The enemy on the other side of the gorge turned away into

the gathering night as friendly hands pulled Trap and Ivat to their feet with loud congratulations, but Denham did not move.

'Shit!' Caldo exclaimed as he turned the young man over and saw the blood spurting from the artery in his neck. The boy's head fell back at a warped angle, his hazel eyes were glassy and it was evident that he was dead.

Trap knelt beside him. He lifted Tommy's hand and held it for a long time, eyeing the scar he had so recently noticed on the boy's middle finger before he placed it on Tommy's chest and stood. Corporal Thomas Mackim Denham was gone.

'Bring Tommy with us. He's the only one we've lost today whom we'll have time to bury.'

Lexi rose to her feet and stepped out from behind the evergreen arms of the lauan tree. She had taken two steps to hurry towards Trap when she checked herself and halted as his jubilant men swarmed around him. Her shoulders dropped and she turned back to the children, who looked up at her with terrified eyes. 'Oh my darlings,' she said, bending down to take them in her arms. 'We're safe now. Don't be frightened.' And as night surrounded them she hugged them to her heart, and kept thinking, *Can this really be Christmas Day?*

Chapter Twenty-eight

In the cool Christmas night under a tarpaulin stretched between two trees, Lexi brushed her hair and thought of Trap. As she watched the flickering gleam from the hurricane lantern casting its feeble lemon light amongst the trees, she wondered why he did not come to her.

After crossing the river they had found a unit of the 31st Division who were bivouacking for the night. The soldiers had caught some wild fowl and shared passable chicken soup with the arrivals. The children ate ravenously.

Lexi had tended Trap's wounded soldiers and three of the 31st who had shell injuries. Their own regimental doctor had been killed the previous day, so they were very happy to see her. Evangelista had regained consciousness, and from what she could gather, even though he complained of intense pain in his back, he had travelled as well as she had hoped. A corporal in the 31st had brought a medical supply tin to her and she had administered a shot of morphine to him.

The big sergeant had taken care of the children and she had asked him where Trap was. He simply replied that he did not know. He was the one who had brought them here to this spot, and while soldiers had raised the tarpaulin over them and placed a second on the ground, he had found them blankets and rolled-up towels to form makeshift bedding for them. He told her his name was Caldo. 'If you need anything, call out to me.'

Caldo had lit a fire near her and hung the hurricane lantern on the branch of a tree a few yards away. 'Probably best to leave the lantern alight in the trees; it'll warn the boys to keep their distance.' He had given her mosquito netting and told her, 'Don't move more than ten yards from this shelter, ma'am. A soldier will come by later and feed the fire.' With a quick smile he added, 'Happy Christmas,' and took three chocolate bars out of the inside of his jacket. 'Not much of a present, but I got them out of the cook.'

'Bless you,' she said softly as he walked away.

A few minutes later she recognised Lieutenant Williams passing at the edge of the lanternlight. She stood and called out, 'Excuse me. Where is the major? Will I see him tonight?'

Hank Williams halted and shrugged. 'I think he's speaking to General Wainwright.'

'Who is General Wainwright?'

'The commanding officer of the forces here in Northern Luzon.'

'I know General MacArthur.'

Even in the shadowy night she noticed the lieutenant's surprise. 'You do?'

'Yes, and I know his wife, Jean. The general and my grandfather were good friends.'

Williams gave a low whistle. 'Well, I'm sure if you can get to him, ma'am, he'll help you out of here.'

As Williams made to move on, Lexi stepped towards him and put out her hand. 'If you see the major, would you . . . would you please ask him to come and speak with me?'

'Yes, ma'am, if I see him.'

The night wore on and the children in their exhaustion slept deeply, but Lexi clutched the rug round her shoulders and remained watching the movements of the soldiers in the distance around the camp fires, hoping to catch a glimpse of Trap.

She was weary and spent but she kept her vigil until at last fatigue overcame her and she slept.

* * *

Trap had eaten with the captain who was the senior officer of the 31st Division. By the illumination of a half-moon he had heard that the retreat to Bataan was going as planned and for the first time he was able to talk to General Wainwright, who was presently back at his depleted field headquarters in Alcala, on a short-wave radio set.

The general was delighted to hear from him, as he had begun to believe that Trap was caught behind the enemy lines. His sober remark was, 'I think perhaps only you could have removed yourself and your men from that mess.'

'Some good men bought it, sir.'

There was a brief silence before Wainwright replied, 'Yes, I'm afraid a lot of commanders are feeling that way today.'

They kept the conversation brief but the general asked what Trap had eaten for Christmas Dinner and at Trap's rejoinder of chicken soup Wainwright grunted. 'You're better off than us, buddy, the food that was meant to come up from Bamban didn't get here, so it's hungry to bed for us, I'm afraid. But good old Dooley found me a bottle of Scotch somewhere, so all's not lost.'

The general went on, 'Anyway, thank God you're alive, my boy. Get down to my main headquarters as fast as you can. I'm leaving here in the morning. Commandeer any vehicles you can find.'

'Yes, sir. Over and out.'

Trap had given orders to feed Lexi and the children, and he was very aware of the part of the camp where she had been taken. As he walked slowly beneath a canopy of palm leaves, deep in thought, he saw the silhouette of Caldo's wide shoulders coming towards him. His sergeant halted in front of him.

'We've settled the woman and the children over there, sir.' He gestured to where the glow from a hurricane lantern could be seen in the trees beyond.

'Yes, right.'

'We gave them chow earlier and the kids ate pretty well, though the girl didn't speak.'

209

'Yes, right.'

A long silence ensued, which Caldo broke. 'Ah, excuse me, sir, hope I'm not speakin' out of turn, but who is she?'

Trap swallowed hard before he answered. 'She's Dr Robinson from Hong Kong.' He hesitated and then added, 'And the wife of a good friend of mine, that's who she is. And you'd better interview her first thing in the morning and find out why the hell she's here in the Philippines at all.'

When the two men parted, Trap strode thirty yards through the night and paused to look across to where *her* lantern glimmered in the trees. He could just make her out. She was looking down at the sleeping children.

He paused, watching her briefly, before turning and walking away to the edge of the camp where they had buried Tommy Denham. The waxing moon revealed the mound clearly to him. Some distance beyond, the cooks brewed late-night coffee on the fires and he thought he could smell it as he walked up and knelt down on one knee.

He touched the letter in his top pocket as he spoke softly. 'Hell, Tommy, did you foresee this, son?' He gave a weary shake of his head as he listened to the sound of the voices of his men and those of the soldiers of the 31st Division around the fires. 'I'll get it to your mother somehow, don't worry about that.'

In the darkness he reached out and smoothed the moody red earth with his hand as if stroking the boy's hair. He thought of his other boys who had died today, left behind in the soil of Northern Luzon.

Who had said 'Only the dead have seen the last of war'? He could not recall. Well the dead were out of it now, out of the whole bloody mess, but those left were not.

'Rest in peace, my boys,' he said softly. 'Rest in peace, Tommy Denham.'

* * *

Trap left the mound and walked slowly back through the palms. The insects buzzed around him and he suddenly felt the fatigue he had been warding off for many days now.

He made out the burning hurricane lantern hanging on the tree limb over to his left and silently he moved towards it and the suicidal insects fluttering around it. He halted twenty-five yards distant from the pool of light it threw upon the woman beneath the tarpaulin.

She sat on a blanket clasping her knees, beside the two children, who were fast asleep. A fire smouldered nearby and a rug warmed her shoulders. He felt very strange standing there watching her.

She looked tired, and her Virginia sky-blue eyes were lowered to the ground. He wanted to take her in his arms and stroke her and touch her and hold her body to his.

He bit the side of his lip as she opened a box beside her, took out a comb and ran it through her long hair, moving her head so that the waves of bronze drifted in swirling movements on her shoulders. She turned away from him and he fancied he heard her sigh as she put the comb back in the box. She slipped the rug from her shoulders and took off the crude jacket over the threadbare dress which revealed her narrow shoulders and firm body beneath. Taking up another blanket, she draped herself with it and settled down beside the children.

He felt so damn odd, he opened his mouth for air.

What the hell had brought her here? He wanted to ask her right now, to walk into the lamp glow and to bend down on his knee beside her, to touch her hair and talk to her.

No, he must not. Caldo would find out in the morning. Then he would have to make some decisions.

He saw her shoulders moving beneath the blanket and suddenly realised she was weeping, her face averted from the sleeping children. Oh hell! But still he did not move. He just stood in the dark looking at her, listening to her, thinking of that night in

211

Madura. Thinking of the day in the wind near the Peak on Hong Kong island when she had told him her kid was his. Now where was that kid? Well, he supposed he would learn that when Caldo questioned her.

He regarded her now, so close in the black Filipino night, wanting her badly, but remembering Johnny — his friend.

His mouth hardened and he turned and walked away.

He had not gone thirty yards when he saw Caldo looming in front of him again.

'What the hell is it this time, Caldo?'

'Ah, sir, I've told the sentries to leave the woman and kids in peace but to feed the fire every two hours.'

'Yes, yes, all right.'

Caldo did not know much about his commanding officer's personal life, but he had sure seen the way the woman looked at him and it said a mighty lot, and the major seemed mighty crabby every time he spoke of her. 'Ah, Major, just a question. What are we gunna do with her?'

Trap answered immediately. 'Get rid of her as soon as we can.'

Chapter Twenty-nine

Lexi stirred and shivered in the chill winter morning. The air felt damp, and through her mind passed the same thought she had experienced before: this was supposed to be the dry season!

Rolling over, she opened her eyes and saw the fire still burning: the soldiers had fed it during the night just as the sergeant had promised.

What had woken her? Had she heard someone calling? She sat up, pulling the blanket round her.

'Excuse me, Dr Robinson, ma'am, I've some breakfast for you. Can I come in?' The voice came from the cluster of trees beyond the fire.

She looked down at the children lying side-by-side. Jimmy lay on his back, his arm draped across his sister's frame. They were still sleeping.

'All right,' she replied.

It was one of the soldiers she recognised, and he edged out of the foliage and came forward.

Ivat carried a tin bowl and spoke as he came. 'I didn't want to surprise you so thought I'd better call out. We've got beans here mixed with some of that chicken soup from last night. Doesn't taste too bad.' He placed it down on the blanket beside her and handed her three spoons. 'Cadee, he's the cook, is making coffee. We found a stream back there.' He indicated with his thumb over his shoulder. 'I'll bring some to you shortly. The sergeant told me to tell you we have to move out fast. So once you've finished eating, could you get yourself and the kids ready for travelling?'

Lexi nodded and pushed the blanket further up around her chin. 'Who told you my name?'

'Sergeant Caldo, ma'am.'

'Where's the major? I'd like to see him.'

'Oh, he's gone, ma'am.' Ivat scratched his chin. 'He and the lieu-tenant went off not long after first light, I was told. The major commandeered a couple of GP trucks around dawn somewhere and went off in one, leaving the other for us to get down to Bamban in.'

Ivat saw her face stiffen with disappointment and hurried on: 'The sarge told me to tell you that he'll come and talk to you pretty soon.' He pointed at the food. 'But best you eat this, Dr Robinson, because we're to move out as smartly as possible.'

Jimmy murmured and woke and Lessa opened her eyes and sat up beside him, her gaze on the newcomer.

Lexi could not help it: the question just rolled off her tongue. 'Where did the major go? Do you know when he'll be back?'

Ivat shook his head. 'Look, you ask the sergeant . . . he'll know more for sure.'

'Yes, yes, of course. Thank you.'

'And Sarge wants to know if you'll look at the wounded again before we leave. I think they're being moved off somewhere with the Thirty-first.'

Lexi nodded and took a long, deep breath. 'I can see them any time.'

'Right then, I'll be off, but I'll come back with the coffee and I'll bring a bucket of water for you and the kids to wash in.'

He walked away into the palm trees as Jimmy stood up and toddled over to Lexi, who took him in her arms and held him close and buried her face in his dark curls.

* * *

214

They moved out at eight forty-one, escorted by a noisy twittering flock of small brown birds that had been roosting in the banana palms.

Before they drove away, Caldo had asked Lexi to join him and he accompanied her across the still dew-laden grass to a spot in the benign morning sunshine where, occasionally chewing the end of a lead pencil as he wrote down her replies, he had asked her a series of questions.

By the time they left the overnight bivouac, Caldo knew the story of the shipwreck, the death of Lexi's companions and the aftermath which had brought her into the soldiers' company. He could not help but feel sorry for her, and also admire her: she had been through a hell of a lot and here she was taking care of these two kids who were really nothing to her.

Caldo was not a woman's man: he knew he lacked social graces and he was most comfortable when he was surrounded by the boys of his platoon, but this woman had impressed him. She had told her yarn straight, not asking for sympathy or weeping or bemoaning her fate, but simply placing the facts before him. Only twice had she come close to faltering: when she told him how her baby son had drowned and when she spoke of her Uncle Jasper in the sea leaping high in the air to take the machine-gun bullets. She dropped her eyes and gave a tiny shake of her head. 'He was so brave . . . They all were, they all knew they were going to die . . .'

She took up her story, mentioning that the major was a friend of her husband and how she had been relieved to meet up with him on that dirt road the other side of the Agno yesterday. She spoke dispassionately enough about all that, but Caldo had not missed the telltale flush that appeared in her cheeks when she mentioned Major Trapperton. Yeah, she was crazy for the major, he could see that, and she was trying desperately to hide it.

Still, that was not for Caldo to get involved in, so he simply wrote down what she told him without embellishment. And when at the end of his questions she had attempted to lighten her voice

215

and ask impassively, 'When will we join up again with Major Trapperton?' he had hated the reply he had to give her: 'I'm not sure, ma'am. I'm to drive you and the kids and Ivat down to Bamban. The rest of the boys are moving out now to join the major over with Colonel Pierce and the Twenty-sixth Cavalry.'

Lexi did not want to hear that. 'You mean he's gone off to fight the enemy?'

Caldo gave her a hard look. 'There's a war on, Dr Robinson.'

'Of course there is. I'm sorry, silly of me . . . But didn't he say anything specific in regard to me . . . or the children?'

Caldo paused.

Lexi waited.

Caldo eyed the gleam in her hair from the rays of morning light. He glanced away at the trunk of a palm and then back to her, meeting her gaze.

She repeated the words: 'Didn't he?'

Caldo knew what was planned for her all right, because he had heard the major and the lieutenant discussing her this morning before they left. Lieutenant Williams had told Major Trapperton that the doctor knew General MacArthur and his wife. And the major had replied, 'Best news I could have. As soon as we get her down to Bamban we get rid of her. Send her straight to Corregidor. MacArthur can have her with love and kisses.'

Caldo was looking into Lexi's face, her cheeks shining in the morning sun, her eyebrows raised in expectation, a hopeful expression riding in her blue eyes.

He cleared his throat and glanced away. 'No, ma'am, he never really said anything.'

Caldo, Lexi, Lessa, Jimmy and Ivat reached Bamban in the cool of evening.

Lexi had heard enough during the course of the day to realise that once they arrived, there would be no let-up. From what the sergeant had told her, both the northern and southern defending forces were retreating to a place called Calumpit, where there were two bridges across the Pampanga river. From there the troops would flow into the Bataan peninsula, where it seemed they would reorganise their defences and make a stand.

Travelling ever due south across the grassland plain they passed through one deserted town after another: San Manuel, Moncada, Gerona, Tarlac, San Miguel and Santa Rosa until finally they rolled into Bamban. There they proceeded by grassy squares and empty streets, past quiet wells and vacant churches as the misty haze of evening was falling on Boxing Day.

Lexi sat thoughtfully in the front of the truck with the infants between herself and Caldo as they drove up to the sugar mill and beside it the offices and residence of the manager of the Bamban Sugar Central Company – General Wainwright's headquarters.

Caldo and Ivat jumped down to the ground and the sergeant spoke to the sentries. After some minutes he pushed his rugged face through the cabin window and asked Lexi to wait there with Ivat, and he disappeared past a line of palm trees and beyond a couple of heavy vehicles.

She waited in the cabin of the truck while Ivat leant on the bonnet and occasionally spoke to the sentries or kicked stones on the dusty ground.

Day disappeared as groups of soldiers filed past on foot. Finally, as the cloudy moon came up and the children became restless, the lumbering shape of Caldo returned to her.

'Dr Robinson, I finally found someone who knew about you. Please come along.'

The soldiers carried the children and Lexi followed.

That 26 December night she and the children slept in a house, and Lexi had her first real bath since being shipwrecked.

Lexi, Lessa and Jimmy remained in Bamban, while behind them to the north the troops of the North Luzon Force of the United

States Army and the Philippine Army withdrew, fighting bloody rearguard actions most of the way.

They had dug a trench outside her small *bahay* near the wall of the sugar company offices, where she and the children sheltered when the Japanese bombed at dawn, the day after their arrival. The children were resilient as children are and accepted this strange way of existing, surrounded by soldiers and noise, but through it all Lessa remained silent. She still had not spoken a word since her mother's death.

After the bombing, Caldo arrived. He was wearing his bandanna and holding a Colt .45 in his big right hand, and he sniffed and rubbed his nose before he spoke. 'Dr Robinson, ma'am, I'm off to join the major.'

Lexi gave him a steady look. 'Am I allowed to ask where that might be?'

'No, ma'am, you ain't.' He shoved the pistol into his black leather belt as he spoke.

'I thought one of you said the major was coming here?'

Caldo shrugged his mighty shoulders and said nothing to that.

'So what happens now? To me? To us?' She motioned through the doorway to the children playing on the ground outside.

'I'm not sure, ma'am, but I reckon General Wainwright himself knows you're here, and when he gets around to it, well, you and the kids will be taken care of. Meanwhile I've had orders to leave Private Ivat here with you. He'll make sure you're all right. The kids seem to like him, so he copped the soft job.'

Lexi stepped towards the big man and raised her eyes to his. 'Sergeant Caldo, thank you for what you've done for me. But before you leave, will you please be honest with me just once? I think you know that Major Trapperton has no intention of ever seeing me again. I'm right about that, aren't I?'

The physically overwhelming Caldo looked so uncomfortable, he seemed to squirm.

'Please tell me.'

218

'Dr Robinson, I can't possibly answer that question.' He stepped away from her. 'But believe me, the right people know you're here, so you'll be looked after.'

Lexi attempted a smile. 'I suppose I should be grateful for that.'

'Yes, ma'am. Now I gotta go.' He backed out of the door and she followed him. He paused, watching how the morning breeze played about her legs and flapped her skirt.

'When you see him, please tell him I said, I'll always remember Madura . . . all my life . . . He'll know what I mean.'

Caldo studied her, his coal-black eyes squinting as a shaft of morning light hit him through the trees. He nodded his big, dark, craggy head. 'Madura. You'll always remember . . . Right. Got it.' And with lengthy strides he hurried away past Lessa and Jimmy, whom he touched fleetingly in farewell.

Chapter Thirty

On 13 February 1942 the German Admiral Erich Raeder sent a report to Hitler:

'Rangoon, Singapore, and, most likely, also Port Darwin, will be in Japanese hands within a few weeks. Only weak resistance is expected on Sumatra while Java will be able to hold out longer. Japan plans to protect this front in the Indian Ocean, by capturing the key position of Ceylon, and she also plans to gain control of the sea in that area by means of superior naval forces . . .

' . . . With Rangoon Sumatra and Java gone, the last oil-wells between the Persian Gulf and the American continent will be lost . . . Britain will be forced to resort to heavily escorted convoys if she desires to maintain communications with India and the near East and Australia . . .'

As he read this, the self-titled Führer of the German peoples smiled smugly. Nippon would do his work in the Pacific for him.

As February advanced, the conceited predictions by Raeder appeared to be coming true for the tentacles of Japan's aggression spread ever southwards wider and wider to east and west.

On 19 February 1942 Port Darwin in Australia's Northern Territory was bombed by the Japanese from aircraft carriers in the Timor Sea. To the surprise of the defenders, a hospital ship, the *Manunda*, was attacked, and in all, nine ships were lost.[1]

One of the results of this assault was for Prime Minister John Curtin and the Australian Government to harden in their view that they needed two of the Australian Divisions in the Middle East to be returned hastily home. President Roosevelt and Prime Minister Churchill pressed Australia to use them to reinforce the weak Allied resistance in Burma; for Thailand had joined forces with Japan on 25 January, and with their mutual border into Burma, passage through Thailand was the link for the Japanese to take India and the subcontinent.

But John Curtin was adamant that his divisions were needed at home and the consequence was that Winston Churchill ordered the divisions to Australia.

The Australian PM's fears worsened when three more bombing raids on northern Australia occured on the 3rd and 4th of March.

At this juncture a command existed under the supreme authority of British General Archibald Wavell. It was the American-British-Dutch-Australian Command, ABDA and was responsible for a massive area with a thinly spread force from Burma in the west, to New Guinea in the east, and the Philippines in the north.

After a week in Singapore where he picked up three Intelligence liaison officers including Captain John Drayton Whitby, General Wavell moved on to his headquarters in Bandung Java, on 15 January.

As the weeks passed the despairing Wavell presided over the capitulations of Malaya, Singapore, Borneo, Timor, Bali and Sumatra as they joined the fates of Hong Kong, Guam and Wake Islands. The bad news continued with the American forces in the Philippines surrounded by the Japanese in the Peninsula of Bataan and on the island of Corregidor. Java was threatened and Burma was under attack as was Dutch New Guinea. Wavell resigned his post on 25 February and handed control of what remained of the ABDA area to its local commanders.

John Drayton's head hit the broad root of a banyan tree and he rolled over and lay still, his eyes darting to left and right and his mind searching for any pain in his body. There was none and relief flooded though him. He had not been hit! The bullets had gone wide.

A line of ants climbed over the fungus growing on the trunk a few inches from his eyes, and as another burst of fire ripped through the dense foliage of the jungle around him he flicked his gaze round to where five yards away crouched his lieutenant, Ron Howard, dirt on his face and his eyes radiating with the alarm and excitement that comes from an adrenalin surge. Beside Howard squatted Alec Marchant, a freckle-faced twenty-three-year-old. Five others – Parsons, Smith, Wiggers, Bird and Ward – hid in the jungle a few yards behind and were blazing away to the rear.

'The bastards are in front and behind us.' Ron Howard wiped his mouth with his hand.

'I've been hit,' Harry Parsons announced as blood seeped through his shirt. He was a boy from the Barossa Valley in South Australia, from a wine-growing family, and had joined the 2/3rd Machine Gun Battalion within a week of its being formed. He was a soldier of Blackforce, the name given to a number of units from the 7th Division Australian Imperial Forces under Brigadier Arthur Seaforth Blackburn, who had arrived from the Middle East only days ago. Parsons was only twenty-one and as brave as a lion.

John Drayton swiftly took a clean piece of rag from his pocket and began to tie it around Parsons's armpit to stem the blood flow. The bullet appeared to have hit the bone and looked messy but he spoke encouragingly. 'It'll be all right, son.'

Another hail of enemy bullets sliced through the leaves and fronds of fern and they edged further into the jungle together.

'Gawd, they're all around us.'

Ahead on the trail Corporal Dan Lewis, an American with the

131st Field Artillery Regiment, lay dead, and behind on the trail Private Freddie Cassidy, another Australian, lay dead. Both had taken direct hits. Lewis had been the vanguard and Cassidy the rearguard for John Drayton and his small medley of men who were making their escape along this jungle track.

The previous evening they had left the hill camp near Tjikadjang, where every day for the past two weeks the news reaching them had become worse and worse. Each day the Australian British and Allied troops had learnt with growing anxiety of the aerial[2] and sea battles being fought by the ABDA against superior numbers and fleeter, more modern Japanese aircraft and ships. The elderly ships of the ABDA under the command of Dutch Admiral Doorman had fought bravely yet had been defeated continually in the Battle of Makassar Strait; the Battle of Badung Strait; the Battle of Sunda Strait; and finally the harrowing Battle of the Java Sea[3] which had been the last stand against an invasion of Java.

On 5 March Batavia, the capital city of Indonesia on the north of the island, had fallen to the enemy.

The steamy heat was rising from the earth and the afternoon melted into dusk when the commanding officer of the Java hill camp, Major Clifford Cox, 5th Royal Artillery Regiment, came to see John Drayton.

Cox's usually bright eyes were dull with concern.

'More bad news, I'm afraid. The Japs continue flooding ashore.'

John Drayton looked up from the maps he was studying. 'Not what I want to hear, but understandable with four hundred miles of beaches. It's impossible to defend with the tiny number of Dutch, American and British Empire troops here.'

'It gets worse. The commander-in-chief of the Dutch forces has just surrendered to the Japanese, the implication being that all forces on Java — British, Dutch, American and Australian — must therefore surrender.'

Cox fingered his moustache. He was a career soldier, had fought in Palestine and the Somme Valley in the Great War and was approaching fifty. John Drayton had been working with Cox for only a few weeks but he admired him. He and the the major met in what had been General Wavell's headquarters of ABDACOM near the upland town of Bandoeng in the ABDA's last days. John Drayton had been ordered to take his Intelligence unit and accompany him to this fortified area.

The young man grunted painfully; surrender was no surprise. 'Better gather the lads and let them know.'

It was nearing darkness when Clifford Cox lifted the rolled-up map high in the air and cleared his throat and a hush fell over the three platoons in the hill camp.

'Captain Whitby and I have just heard some very bad news. Rangoon fell to the enemy yesterday, so that's Burma gone and the vital road to China lost. And here in Java, even with the magnificent stands made by Blackforce against the overwhelming numbers of the enemy, nothing will now save the island. Our aerodromes have been bombed to the point where they are no longer operational and we've lost the sea war here. Refugees clog the roads and the Japanese advance through the island towards us. The Dutch commander-in-chief is currently busy negotiating terms of surrender with them.'

A loud murmur of disapproval greeted this statement.

Cox gazed around at the men and gave them a strangely intimate smile as he added, 'Negotiating will be a useless exercise: the Japs will do as they please.' He cleared his throat again and paused for a moment. 'Now, the Dutch have definitely ceased fighting everywhere and we do not have the numbers of British and Australians to continue to resist. I have also been informed that the Dutch will not attempt to wage a guerrilla war against the Japs. The hostility amongst the native population prevents it.'

Major Cox had not said it outright, but they all knew the Dutch were not popular masters and that the Javanese would attempt to use the Japanese invasion to get rid of the Dutch government permanently.

'It seems that General Sitwell and Brigadier Blackburn are surrendering. Those troops at headquarters and others including this camp have been today told to display white flags as the enemy approach, to collect arms and to make arrangements to surrender to the nearest Japanese general.'

More loud grumbles of disapproval sounded. Major Cox lifted his map again and another silence fell. 'General Sitwell and Brigadier Blackburn have no choice in the matter, so those, too, are my orders.'

Everybody began to talk at once, and Sergeant Derek Smith, one of half a dozen men of the 2/3rd Machine Gun Battalion AIF lifted his hands in emphasis as he called out, 'Sir? No one asked us if we wanted to surrender.'

'Too bloody right,' was the general consensus.

Major Cox bit the side of his lip under his wide moustache. 'I know exactly how you feel.'

John Drayton read the thoughts that were clearly stamped on all their faces. He turned to the Commanding Officer. 'I think most of us are of a mind to attempt escape, sir.'

Loud affirmative rumblings accompanied his words. Major Cox again lifted his rolled-up map and the boys fell quiet. 'I must surrender as I've been directly ordered to do, but you ... well, there's an argument that you haven't been directly commanded, or perhaps it is that you don't hear what I'm saying ... So while I'm not supposed to tell you this, I'm going to. There's a British lieutenant colonel – a fellow of South African descent – called Laurens van der Post, whom we believe is south of here at this very moment in the mountains near Sindangbarang. He is initiating assembly points down there where bands of men can get down the mountainous coast to the sea. My understanding is he's trying to organise boats for evacuation. If you reach him he might be able to give you supplies.'

The soldiers all began to talk at once, but when Cox spoke again they paused.

'Any of you who wish to stay and surrender to the enemy can remain here with me. To you others I say, may God travel with you.' His voice broke but he completed his statement. 'Grab some rations, get going and don't come back!' He rose to his full height of five feet ten and saluted his men.

In the last rays of day, with the humid breeze ruffling their uniforms, every man present came to attention with parade-ground precision and returned the salute of their commanding officer. An eerie moment of silence hung over them — a memory those who lived would take with them for all time — before the soldiers broke ranks and dispersed.

John Drayton moved across the duckboards placed over the soggy ground and came to Major Cox. 'Sir?'

'Yes, Captain Whitby?'

'I'll be saying goodbye and good luck. Lieutenant Howard, Sergeant Smith and a few of the boys will accompany me; Dian our Javanese interpreter too, I think; but before we leave I want you to know that while it's been brief, I've learnt a lot from you.'

'Thanks for saying that.' Cox tapped the younger man's arm with his rolled-up map. 'You're a fine soldier, and let me tell you, I'm deeply sorry about your family. That was a tragedy. But listen, lad, you get out of here and make it home to good old Australia. Do it in remembrance of your wife and son.'

John Drayton looked straight into the major's eyes. Clifford Cox had been with him when he had made his discovery about the sinking of the SS *Fortitude*.

It occured in Bandoeng before General Wavell's departure. Everybody had been seconded to all manner of odd duties including helping an army surgeon, Major Edward Dunlop, convert a school into a hospital. John Drayton found himself incorporating Dunlop's files into those in the records' office, deciding which would be destroyed and which would go with the departing headquarters' staff. He had been working with Major Cox and the adjutant when he opened a folder of communiqués which listed all Allied shipping destroyed by the enemy from the beginning of hostilities through to 1 February 1942.

It was alphabetical and he flicked through the pages, until he read: SS *Fortitude*:

> SS Fortitude: *torpedoed off coast of Luzon, 9 December 1941. Survivors picked up by light cruiser HMS Resolute.*

The ship's last known position was given but his eyes darted over that and raced down the list of survivors: seventeen people in all. He read the names five times. No Lexi, no Paul, none of the names of his relatives appeared, and no Kathy.

For an optimistic moment he thought that Lexi might have missed the ship! Better for her to be alive, even in Japanese-controlled Hong Kong, than dead at the bottom of the South China Sea! But this hope was dashed as he read the ship's manifest. There they were, recorded under 'W': his wife's name and his son's name.

He swallowed hard and raised his eyes to the listings under 'L': Kathleen, too, was on the manifest.

He read the other names he knew. So they had all been aboard and *all killed by the Japs!*

He stood taut and unmoving, his hands grasping the folder so tightly his knuckles turned white. His brain seemed to refuse to grasp the enormity of his loss. Lexi gone . . . baby Paul gone . . .

He was not sure how long he stood there in disbelief before Clifford Cox's firm right hand had taken a grip on his shoulder. 'Whitby, lad, what's wrong? You're as white as a sheet.'

John Drayton had turned glazed eyes to his superior. 'My wife . . . my son . . . They're dead.'

Chapter Thirty-one

And now, as the acrid dank smell of rotting foliage floated to John Drayton from the nearby swamp, he lurched sideways as another swathe of bullets cut into the banyan tree near his head.

'Jesus, they must be up in the trees!' shouted Ron Howard as they both rolled over and opened fire into the air with their Bren guns while Ken Ward, Charlie Wiggers and Gavin Bird behind them wheeled their rifles up and delivered another volley in the same direction. A shout was followed by a brief silence before they heard the noise of a body hurtling down through the jungle canopy, breaking branches as it came.

'Strewth, I hope there was only one up there.' Ward murmured what everybody thought.

'Hey, Aussie boys! Stop firing. All your mates sullender! We now masters in Java. You come now, hands up, we let you live.'

John Drayton swung his automatic weapon round the trunk of the banyan and fired a burst in the direction of the voice. A few seconds passed and the voice called again, 'Hey, stop that! We let you live if you come now. You defying orders of Aussie general. He sullender! Come out. Hands up!'

John Drayton was speedily reviewing recent events: they had been surprised back and front by the enemy, who had been waiting for them. They had walked into a trap. And how would the Jap who called out have known they were mostly Australian? Calling them 'Aussie boys'. The only way he would know were if he had been told. And the single man who knew where they were and who they were was Dian, the Javanese interpreter! No wonder he had been so keen to go ahead and make contact with his friends who had a boat. Dian had told John Drayton repeatedly that he was sure this trail was absolutely safe!

One thing was favourable: there had not been heavy concentrated fire from the enemy, which led him to believe there might only be ten or twelve of them, a few in front and a few behind. Sure, there had been one up in the trees – the Japanese were good climbers, often wearing split-toed shoes. But thankfully no more gunfire had followed from above.

John Drayton contemplated the jungle around him. It was dense on the other side of the trail, but beside him he could see through the underbrush and mass of leaves at his left hand to where there was a sort of deep fissure in the ground. It led back away from him and appeared wide enough to crawl along.

At the moment of ambush, the two men who had been hit were killed instantly. John Drayton calculated that the enemy to their rear had been close, and he reckoned that if he crawled along this cleft in the jungle floor he just might get past and behind those Japanese back there.

He glanced round the faces of his men – seven now instead of nine – and whispered, 'I'm going through there.' He pointed. 'Reckon if I get far enough along I'll pass the bastards at the rear.'

He pointed to the wounded Parsons. 'You remain here with the lieutenant and Marchant.'

'Yes, sir,' Harry Parsons replied, his alert blue eyes momentarily blinking in a single streak of golden light that found its path through the firmament of dense emerald green.

'Right. Keep the enemy to the front here busy; you others follow me. And Lieutenant, if you hear us open fire, then anticipate that we've done for the Nips behind us, so follow us real fast.'

'Sure, sir.'

With that, John Drayton slithered past the undergrowth and

roots beside the banyan and eased himself into the trench over-hung with masses of leaves, roots, trunks and ferns. Something scuttled past his face and he started, but this only made him move more stealthily. He was aware of his men coming quietly behind him, while he could hear Howard and Marchant returning inter-mittent fire from the enemy.

A small snake shot across in front of him at amazing speed and he paused, heart pumping. There was a movement through the ferns beyond. Three . . . no, four of the enemy, sneaking down the trail, only yards away.

With his mouth set in a hard line, John Drayton signalled his boys and silently they took aim.

'Now!'

They opened fire, cut the ferns to pieces and felled the four Japanese where they stood. They died as instantaneously as Lewis and Cassidy had done ten minutes before. Only one of them made a sound: a gurgling noise.

There was no pity in John Drayton's heart. His mind was full of the dead he had loved. At least he had taken four of the bastards out! He glanced at his men. They were all listening. The jungle was still.

'Reckon we got the lot back here, sir,' Sergeant Smith declared, peering through the undergrowth.

'Let's hope so.'

They heard the crunch of a boot and spun towards it, weapons aimed, but it was only the lieutenant with Marchant helping Parsons to climb up from the trench through the mass of ferns. Ron Howard grinned. 'The Nips near us went quiet, sir.'

'Right, let's see if they're just playing possum. Come on!' John Drayton burst through on to the trail, ran a few yards back along it and opened fire again. He got off one burst before, abruptly, his Bren gun jammed. 'Blast!' He dived to the ground, hit it hard and rolled back into the bracken.

There was no return of fire.

'Perhaps they've really done a bunk, sir.' Howard expressed the hope of them all.

'Yes. But they might have gone for reinforcements, so let's move out fast. I reckon we were set up by Dian and there's no boat waiting for us anywhere.'

'Bloody Dian, I hope we run into him again,' Ward growled, drawing a line across his throat with his finger.

'Yeah, me too,' agreed Alec Marchant. 'We never treated him any way but good. I gave the bugger my fountain pen a few weeks ago.'

John Drayton held up his palm. 'All right boys, save the thoughts of retribution for later. Put your energy into getting out of here.' Sombre-faced, he outlined his plan. 'Remember the shallow stream near the railway line we crossed about an hour ago? Well, if we double back to that I reckon we can follow it down to the coast. Dozens of small fishing villages are scattered along there. We'll buy a boat if we can, or steal one if we can't. It won't be as easy going that way, or as fast as this track, and we'll get wet into the bargain, but I'm pretty sure it'll take us down the mountains.'

'Jeez, I hope there are no crocs,' remarked Parsons, looking down at his wound while Wiggers tied another bandage round it to soak up the blood.

Ward grinned. 'You'll be all right, they don't grow more than about three yards long round here.'

Parsons grunted. 'That's great news, Ward, thanks, real helpful.'

Lieutenant Howard slapped Ward on the shoulder. 'Now let's get ready to move out. Marchant, you bring up the rear and keep looking back, we don't want any surprises.' He glanced at his captain. 'Do you want to lead, sir?'

John Drayton nodded.

Ron Howard herded his men into a group. 'That's it, then, we all move out after Captain Whitby with Parsons in the middle. Can you travel at a trot, Parsons?'

231

The boy's face was covered in perspiration but he effected a grin. 'Yeah, sir, reckon I can ... for a while anyway.'

'Good man.'

John Drayton loped off along the trail, giving his Bren gun a shake. He had noticed that when it jammed, shaking usually got it going again.

They kept up the pace for about fifteen minutes before Parsons, breathing hard, began to slow down. From then on they walked, and when they came to the water the light was receding and shadows and dark patches lodged between the trees. Frogs croaked somewhere nearby, and a solid host of mushrooms coated a moss-covered mound between the mud on the bank of the stream and the edge of the jungle.

Resting briefly by the railway line, John Drayton calculated that they were perhaps six miles from the coast in a straight line. It would be a long sea voyage to Australia. It had to be about a thousand miles to the outpost of Broome, and all open ocean. He made a small ironical sound. He was no Captain Bligh who had made the historic voyage of three thousand six hundred miles in an open boat on sheer will and courage after his men had mutined. But Howard was expert with a compass, and if they could get enough provisions and water he knew these men with him had the pluck for it. Anyway, anything was better than being a prisoner of the Japs!

They were all damp from the exertion, but sweat was still pouring from Parsons and blood seeped through the bandage again. He looked spent and his breathing was laboured. Bird and Ward attempted to cheer him as they squatted down beside the wall of jungle and drank from their canteens.

'Don't worry, Wingy. I'll tie another bandage round your wound, mate.'

'You can make it, and once we get to the boat we'll be on easy street.'

The wounded man closed his eyes as Ward wrapped his already well-bound shoulder again.

John Drayton was looking at the sky. It was not yet quite dusk; they could not afford to dawdle. 'Let's go,' and they set off along the stream.

They moved slowly for a time, and when Harry Parsons faltered Ward slung his wounded mate's good arm over his shoulder and helped him along. The lieutenant carried Parsons's Bren gun.

The party had just climbed over the trunk of a large fallen tree not far from a bend when Marchant at the rear gave a yell. 'Japs!'

Everybody spun round. Swelling out of the jungle on the far side of the railway line about four hundred yards away came a platoon of enemy soldiers, running fast.

'Shit, they went back for their pals all right!'

John Drayton shouted for his men to hurry on round the bend. 'Get on, boys, keep moving.' He dropped behind the solid trunk.

'What about you, sir?' Ron Howard said, remaining at his side.

John Drayton looked up 'I said move, Lieutenant. You take those men on. Without me you're the leader. That's an order.'

As Howard hesitated, Harry Parsons took his automatic weapon back from the lieutenant and eased himself down beside the commanding officer.

'What do you think you're doing, Parsons?' John Drayton raised his eyes to Howard. 'Help him up, Lieutenant.'

'No, sir!' Parsons's voice was adamant. 'I'm hit bad, sir. I can't run. You get going. I'll hold them off as long as I can.'

As he spoke, the first enemy bullets zinged into the mud about four yards in front of them.

'Don't be silly, lad.'

'With respect, I'm not being silly, Captain. I can't make it anyway. They'll get me one way or another. But you and the lieutenant have a chance. Night's falling too, sir: you'll lose them in the dark.'

He was right: the blue night of the jungle was descending. The shadows were lengthening, but the bullets were now spinning by them. Ron Howard was backing slowly away towards the bend and firing at the oncoming enemy.

233

John Drayton yelled at him: 'Get out of here at the double, Lieutenant, that's an order!' And with a last blast of his gun Howard ran round the bend out of sight as Parsons pleaded: 'Please, sir. My right arm's still good. Get going, sir. I've got to do this.'

John Drayton thought of Lexi and Paul and all the family. Did it matter if he lived? Did anything matter at all? He looked round into the overbright eyes of Harry Parsons, now glazed with fever. He couldn't leave him.

'Please, sir. Get back home . . . for me, sir.'

John Drayton's mind raced. He heard Major Cox's words: 'Get out of here and make it home . . . Do it in remembrance of your wife and son.' And now this kid, this bloody brave kid, had said, 'Get back home . . . for me, sir.'

'We'll both go home, son,' John Drayton said with determination, fitting a detachable magazine into the top of his Bren gun and sending a barrage of rounds into the oncoming enemy.

One fell, one screamed and dived for cover, and the others moved into the protection of the jungle. John Drayton was scared but he wore a smile. The gun was working smoothly again! He wished he had the knapsack that Wiggers had been carrying, for it contained six Mills bombs. He had a single one in his breast pocket. He would save that until they got nice and close.

For some minutes John Drayton and young Parsons, in the refuge behind the fallen tree trunk fitted their magazines, fired and held the enemy. There was no doubt they were in a good position. The Japanese had the stream on one side and almost impenetrable jungle on the other, and only a narrow strip of mud to advance upon.

John Drayton prayed they had enough ammunition to hold the Japs off till dark, then he would let them advance, throw his Mills bomb and get the boy out.

The enemy were making dashes from jungle cover to jungle cover and getting closer when suddenly at his side Harry gave a small strange groan and slumped forward on his gun.

234

'What is it, kid?' John Drayton turned to his companion. He touched the boy and his head fell sideways. There was a tiny hole in his forehead. Harry from the green Barossa Valley had a bullet in his brain. The boy died without making another sound.

'Oh Jesus.'

John Drayton flinched as a spate of bullets cut through the wood near his right-hand side. Three Japanese were running forward, emboldened by the hiatus from behind the tree trunk.

It was darkening swiftly now and the moon was appearing. John Drayton took the grenade from his top pocket, and waited till the Japanese were twenty yards away. Then he ripped the pin out, counted two and hurled the Mills bomb. The explosion threw mud, and parts of trees and metal and flesh into the air as John Drayton touched Harry Parsons tenderly on the hole in his forehead. 'Goodbye, kid,' he whispered, and with one last look at him leapt up and ran like hell to the bend in the stream.

Chapter Thirty-two

Same day 10 March 1942

Lexi walked slowly out of the grey concrete arch at the western end of the Malinta Tunnel on the fortress island of Corregidor where Fort Mills was situated, and which was otherwise known as 'the Rock', a tadpole-shaped island at the entrance to Manila Harbour. There had been an air-raid warning which had turned out to be a false alarm. Air attacks were sporadic these days; the intense bombing was occurring two miles to the north across the channel on the Bataan peninsula, where the defending troops were under constant attack.

In the relative calm on Corregidor recently Lexi had taken to walking for exercise, though the northern side of the island still came under long-range shelling and the defending batteries sounded a lot of the day and night. Much of the natural beauty of the island had turned into scarred earth and smashed rock, and the colourful shrubs had all but disappeared.

Early most mornings a single enemy aircraft took photos of the island, but it was always out of range of the island's guns, until yesterday morning when it had come in low and the crew on the I.I-inch automatic gun[1] mounted on top of Malinta Hill had given the pilot a shock and he had climbed away very quickly.

There were a number of tunnels on Corregidor. Malinta was the largest and most secure. It had been dug through solid rock and had taken many years to build. Thirteen lateral passages branched from it on the northern side and eleven on the southern side, with further extensions and a double-track electric trolley running through the concrete-reinforced main tunnel. Even blowers had been installed to allow the circulation of fresh air at certain points, though much of the complex was damp and poorly ventilated and resembled a giant anthill with uniformed men and women ebbing and flowing in and out.

Inside Malinta was the living hub of the island. Command communications, medical units, offices of all sorts and storage sections were located near military living quarters and General MacArthur's USAFFE, United States Army Forces Far East Headquarters. It even contained a hospital. And while people felt safe inside, and Lexi was no exception, it was claustrophobic and weird with the flickering blue mercury lights hanging above. Flies swarmed, and dust hung in the air and clung to everything, even though it was all mopped and wiped twice a day.

A number of news sheets were printed as morale boosters and everyone tried to be optimistic, arduous though it was.

Lexi looked around her as she walked. The island was just under three square miles and it had been home now for her and the children for about nine weeks. They shared it with thousands of military men and a few dozen nurses. She was the only female doctor.

From the day that Sergeant Caldo had left her in Bamban, her journey here had been made in stages. That same morning of his departure, a young corporal called Pulgades had come to her and saluted. 'I've been assigned to you by orders which have come down from General Wainwright himself. I'm to see you to Marivales, ma'am.'

'Where's that?'

'It's a port on the southern tip of Bataan. From there you will be ferried across to the island of Corregidor where General MacArthur is. I've a dispatch order here in my pocket.' He tapped his chest and eyed her with an expression of interest. It was not

237

every day that Corporal Pulgades associated with someone who knew the Commander-in-Chief.

So as the defending forces in Luzon fell back, Lexi and the children were driven south by Corporal Pulgades. They had been caught in a couple of bombing raids but their driver had brought them through. They became used to the way he scratched his chin and delivered the statement, 'The front line is following us, Dr Robinson.'

In due course Joseph Pulgades had deposited Lexi and the children in Marivales, where they lived in a small stone house and waited while 1941 turned into 1942. On 31 December, just as on 25 December, Lexi did not remember what day it was, until one of the soldiers reminded her it was New Year's Eve.

On the morning of Saturday 3 January they said goodbye to Corporal Pulgades on the Marivales dock and to the melancholy echo of booming guns embarked on a small paint-chipped motor launch, which had carried them across the grey water to Corregidor.

At North Dock, the arrival pier, they waited for an hour while the children played in the sand surrounded by scorched rocks and devastated warehouses. There had been an intense bombing raid on 29 December which had blasted much of Corregidor's buildings and defences. Finally two soldiers arrived for them in a small open-backed truck. The men carried the children to the vehicle and they drove up to the centre section of the island known as Middleside and from there along a road beside a railway track to the Malinta Tunnel and General MacArthur's office. But they had found no general; instead there were two Filipino nurses who fed them and helped them settle in. Much later in the day Lexi was taken to General MacArthur, who welcomed her warmly.

They stood together on the porch of the small slate-grey house a quarter of a mile from the eastern end of the Malinta Tunnel that was the MacArthurs' home on Corregidor. They preferred to risk the possibility of bombardment in preference to living in the Malinta Tunnel.

Lexi had almost forgotten the charisma of Douglas MacArthur: standing over six feet tall, with his aquiline good looks, he oozed power. He pushed a Lucky Strike into an ivory cigarette holder and made many references to Sir Brillard and their special friendship, his eyes hidden by sunglasses.

Lexi thought it odd he did not take off his sunglasses as he spoke to her. He was wearing a cap overloaded with braid and set with a large gold American eagle. He had tipped it as she arrived onto the porch. She did not realise it but he was the only American citizen ever to be made a Field Marshal. It had happened here in the Philippines and this cap was part of the uniform he had designed for himself and worn at the inauguration by President Manuel Quezon of the Philippines in 1937. It was a treasured possession.

He lit his Lucky Strike and bestowed a smile upon her. 'My men are calling you Dr Robinson, but aren't you married?'

'Yes, General, I am, but to keep matters simple in a professional sense I continued to use Robinson.'

Perhaps MacArthur thought this avant guarde for he gave her a searching look before he went on, 'Now tell me, what is this I hear of shipwreck and your survival? The little I know is very impressive.'

She gave him a short version of what had happened to her, and how Lessa and Jimmy had come into her care.

'My dear,' he declared, finally taking off his sunglasses to squint in the afternoon sun thrown through the trees, 'what a remarkable young woman you are. Your grandfather will be proud of you. And mothering two of the unfortunate little victims of war the way you have. Well, if you were a military man, I'd recommend you for a silver star.' He gestured to the door. 'Now go on inside, for I know Mrs MacArthur is waiting to receive you.'

And since that first afternoon, Lexi had come and had coffee with Jean twice a week. Jean was ten years Lexi's senior and the last time they had seen each other was Arthur's christening in Manila.

Arthur was now a sweet-faced boy of four. On Mondays and Thursdays, when the women met on the porch of the MacArthur home, Arthur, Jimmy and Lessa would play together, attended by Arthur's Chinese nurse Ah Cheu. Jean's southern accent was particularly pronounced and Lexi smiled to herself when she spoke of her husband as 'Gin-ril'. Jean had confided to Lexi that, 'The Gin-ril gets so upset when he looks across at Manila with his binoculars and sees that huge Japanese flag raised above *our* penthouse.'

The MacArthurs had resided for years in the penthouse atop the Manila Hotel and now it was occupied by General Masaharu Homma, the leader of the Japanese invaders.

As Lexi headed down towards North Dock, where she went each day to sit and look across to Bataan and imagine what Trap might be doing, she halted, because striding towards her along the railway track from Middleside came the commander himself, and, keeping pace with him, his chief of staff, the smooth, dark-haired Major General Richard Sutherland, who rarely left the commander's side. Smoke curled from MacArthur's lips up over his inevitable sunglasses as he puffed on his corncob pipe. Their uniforms were crumpled – there was no laundry on Corregidor – yet the leader's boots were still polished to a high shine and his belt buckle gleamed.

The two men crossed within a dozen yards of Lexi but they did not look in her direction; they were solemn and deep in conversation. They continued on walking close to a team of engineers who were completing construction of reinforced concrete roofs over several 75mm guns as protection from dive bombing attacks.

Lexi watched General MacArthur and General Sutherland stride on by four privates carrying a bulky crate of supplies, but neither of the superior officers even glanced sideways, so intent on their conversation were they. As the leaders disappeared in the direction of the Malinta Tunnel, the men staggered under their load towards the section of railway which ran across the narrow middle of the island from North Dock to South Dock through the small village of San Jose.

Sweat ran off the men as they eased the crate down for a rest a few yards away from Lexi. One of them, a hefty young man, gestured to the back of the disappearing MacArthur. 'Hey, boys, do ya know what they're callin' him over on Bataan now?'

'No, what?'

'Dugout Doug.'

They all broke into laughter.

'Well, you can understand it. The boys over on the peninsula reckon he's hidin' out in the Malinta Tunnel over here, safe and comfy with his cigarettes and three meals a day, while they're on half rations, fast running out of food, ammo, clothing, medicine and the rest of it. Poor bastards!'

'Yeah, I guess we have got it better than them.'

The hefty young soldier wiped his brow with the back of his hand and went on, 'And I know two verses of the latest thing they're singing over on Bataan.' Abruptly he broke into song to the melody of the Battle Hymn of the Republic:

> *Dugout Doug MacArthur lies ashaking on the Rock,*
> *Safe from all the bombers and from any sudden shock*
> *Dugout Doug is eating all the best food on Bataan*
> *And his troops go starving on . . .*

He waved his hands as he continued:

> *Dug out Doug MacArthur lies ashaking on the rock,*
> *With fifty feet of concrete to protect him from the shock;*
> *With patrol boats and his Press Corps waiting stately at the docks,*
> *While his troops go starving on.*

241

Lexi walked away to a reverberation of derisive laughter from the soldiers as they hefted the crate on their shoulders and moved on. Lexi thought that this ditty she had just heard sung must have been born because the general had only been over to visit 'his men' in beleagured Bataan once, on 10 January, and he had been on Corregidor since Christmas Eve nearly three months ago.

She shook her head. So now even some of MacArthur's own men were ridiculing him. Who'd be a general? When she had been travelling down through the Peninsula with Corporal Pulgades Lexi had heard all sorts of stories about Douglas MacArthur: they were rife in this part of the world. People held a multitude of opinions of him: that he admired himself and thought of himself as a great general, that he was vain, arrogant, self-centred and inconsistent; but also that he loved the Philippines and its people; that he was shattered by the turn of events here and the lack of aid he had received from the President; some argued he was a brave man and a conscientious leader.

Lexi took the path down the steep quarter of a mile slope through what had recently been lush green plants and flowers and now was filled with bomb craters. She came out on the shoreline at Bottomside, the lowest part of the island. A couple of ware-houses still stood next to their bombed-out brothers not far from the beach and the broken pier of North Dock where she had landed nine weeks before. Boats still plied the channel from this point across to Marivales on poor battered Bataan.

Over there on the jungle peninsula some eighty thousand men – approximately 60,000 Philippine reserve troops, 10,000 Philippine Scouts and 11,000 Americans – were surrounded and starving and continuing to fight battles. Every day reports came in of how the food was running out and how the lack of medicine, ammunition and other supplies became more and more grave.

And every day Lexi came down here when she took a break from work at the hospital to gaze across the two-mile stretch of dark water in the North Channel and think of Trap over there with his commanding officer General Wainwright. And as she sat and watched, she prayed for their survival.

She gazed about in the early afternoon. The short dry season was almost over and a heavy rain had fallen overnight. She avoided a pool of water and strolled along a path at the bottom of the hill to the road that led to the dock. Part of the cement wharf had been blasted away during the heavy bombing of 29 December, but the pier over from it and a number of warehouses had survived.

A GP vehicle with a sergeant at the wheel waited at the entrance to the wooden pier near the guard house.

She traversed the beach and halted beside a wooden seat not far from the water's edge, where she sat on the unbroken section and looked out to sea. Suddenly Boom-Boom appeared: a black and white demi-fox terrier who was the mascot of the Navy boys in Queen Tunnel. He roamed Corregidor night and day and ran up to her.

'Hello, Boom-Boom.' She looked out to sea, stroking him and thinking of Trap. She had not seen him since the night after they had crossed the Agno river, and she had not seen Sergeant Caldo since he left her early that morning in Bamban.

Recently Lexi had come to know Donald Capinpin, one of the communications officers, and she knew he was in touch with General Wainwright's headquarters over on Bataan on a regular basis. So yesterday, when she had come upon the lieutenant in one of the offshoots of the main tunnel, she had enquired, 'I wonder if it is possible to ask a question next time you speak to Bataan headquarters?'

Lieutenant Capinpin was a good-natured man from Savannah, Georgia. In civilian life he helped his father, a hatter, in a shop on Factor's Walk up from River Street. He was loquacious and quick to grin. 'Well, Dr Robinson, fact is, we are only supposed to carry official messages, but to be honest we often just get to chewing the fat. Why, what's the question?'

'Would it be possible to ask if someone is . . .' She had paused, not sure what exactly to say.

Capinpin waited and she added, '. . . is still alive, I suppose.'

'Sure. We do that all the time. Check on our buddies over there. Who is it?'

'Major Hank Trapperton. He's on General Wainwright's staff.'

'Oh, I know who he is,' Donald declared. 'How do you know him?'

Lexi hoped she hid her relief. 'He was the man who found me north of the Agno and brought me and the children to safety.'

'Really? Now he's a bit of a legend in the ranks, you know. They say he's done all sorts of things: I heard Major Zubay say he can kill with his bare hands.'

She looked at Donald. *Oh yes, he can do that.* She would never forget it. Instantly she was back in Madura in the sultry night being jumped by the Japanese! She blinked to disperse the memories tumbling through her mind as she remarked as casually as possible, 'My goodness, is that right?'

'So they say. Anyway, sure, I'll ask about him for you.'

She could not bear to hear Trap was dead, but at the same time she was almost distracted not knowing, and the weeks were turning into months. She carried an almost constant sensation of guilt. It was wrong to love Trap, but even if she never saw him again she knew she would retain her feelings for him to the grave. She now admitted she should never have married John Drayton: it had been weak, and, yes, even cruel, of her. She truly hoped Johnny was alive: he was a wonderful person and a fine man and she had deceived him. But she had paid for it, hadn't she? With the death of little Paul and her loved ones, and this horrible gnawing sensation she carried inside.

As she sat now gazing out to sea, with the humid breeze stirring the hair on her shoulders Lexi took out of her pocket the small book of poetry she had found lying on the floor in the tunnel and read:

I love thee with a love I seemed to lose
With my lost saints — I love thee with the breath,
Of smiles, tears, of all my life!

She looked up, and there in the rolling swell of the North Channel she caught movement out to sea. Squinting, she recognised the small paint-chipped motorboat which had carried her and the children over from Marivales. It was wending its way here. She slid the poetry book back into the wide pocket of her dress and sat eyeing the craft's approach through the grey water.

Within a few minutes the launch edged along to the dark, partly burnt section of the pier which still remained intact and a sailor jumped out and tied a rope around a bollard on the wharf. A number of soldiers swiftly climbed ashore.

The first to disembark wore the uniform of a general, even though it was grubby and dishevelled. He was tall and thin with a gaunt face, high, wide forehead and an oval chin under his 'tin lid'. She guessed he might be 'Skinny' Wainwright, and sat up straight to view the procession with marked interest. On the heels of the general were two officers who were strangers to her. It was the sight of the third officer who followed which brought her hand to her mouth in shock.

Hank Trapperton, looking weary and far thinner than she remembered, but with his determined, recognisable gait, was striding down the pier towards her.

Chapter Thirty-three

Trap noticed Lexi at the same moment she saw him. She rose from the seat and stood stock still.

She was the only person at hand. The nearest others were a dozen soldiers a hundred yards or so away working on the beach defences.

Trap knew she was here, of course, but had not expected this. For a moment he felt as if the loose collar of his shirt tightened. How the hell was it that on an island of some three square miles, this Doll had to be standing right alongside the landing pier when he arrived? *Jesus, it's uncanny.*

But here she was, the breeze trifling with her colourful skirt, raising it so that it danced around her knees, those legs that he dreamed about, planted on the sand. He watched her hand lift to her mouth in that familiar movement of surprise.

'Skinny' Wainwright halted and so did the small military entourage with him. Skinny glanced around. 'Well, boys, seems like the only welcoming committee is a GP vehicle. We'll go up to the tunnel.'

'Right, sir.'

They moved on towards the lone woman, who dropped her hand from her mouth and remained unmoving on the beach, the bold sunlight of early afternoon kissing her skin and roving in flashes of bronze upon the waves of her hair rippling in the breeze.

As the general drew alongside her and passed by, he smiled at her and touched his cap. So too did Major Johnny Pugh and Captain Tom Dooley. It was only Trap who stared directly ahead and walked on without greeting her.

As the general climbed into the vehicle, Tom Dooley spoke. 'Mighty pretty nurses on the rock, if she's a sample.'

Johnny Pugh beside him was enthusiastic. 'You bet.'

Trap stopped himself from retorting, 'She's not a nurse, she's a doctor,' just at the moment Johnny looked round and remarked, 'A looker, wouldn't you say, Trap?'

Why was it he felt so irritable as he replied, 'I didn't notice.'

Johnny made a mildly disapproving sound. 'Gosh, being hungry must have affected your eyesight.'

Trap said no more and the group fell silent as they climbed the hill to Middleside, their minds leaving women and coming back to wondering why the general had been summoned over from Bataan.

Lexi turned to watch them drive away.

Trap had not given any sign of seeing her. But of course he had, he must have; the other soldiers tipped their caps, even the general.

Why oh why did she love him so much? And why was he here?

When they disappeared from sight she took the same route on foot and returned first to a mess tent near the stockade for a small lunch and then back to the hospital, though her mind was elsewhere and she had to keep reminding herself to stop thinking of him.

Trap and the others entered the Malinta Tunnel. It was the first time he had seen the famous structure and it was pretty much what he had expected: solid reinforced cement, twenty-four feet wide, eighteen feet high at the top of the arches, and about fourteen hundred feet long.

They had come over from Bataan at the request of General MacArthur's Chief of Staff, Major General Richard Sutherland.

He told Skinny Wainwright that MacArthur wished to see him. So the small party headed straight through the tunnel to the Commander's office, only to find he was not there. Sutherland was, however, and he took Skinny aside to speak to him.

As Trap, Johnny and Tom waited, they talked to their brother officers working in the USAFFE headquarters, but Trap's eyes remained on his general, deep in conversation with Sutherland some yards away in a small alcove. He could see Skinny's back and he noted that the general stood rigidly, his hand on his Colt, throughout the exchange.

It was just over five minutes before Skinny came back to them as Sutherland hovered some yards away. The expression on their senior officer's face revealed to his three accompanying staff officers that something of great moment had been told to him by Sutherland, but what it was he did not disclose. He simply said, 'Wait here, I'm going with General Sutherland to see General MacArthur. I think I'll be about an hour or so. I'll meet you back at North Dock.'

As they watched him leave, a captain in the marines spoke. 'Why don't you come and have some lunch while you wait? You all look hungry.'

The three officers from Bataan gazed slowly around at one another. Oh yes, they were hungry. On the Bataan peninsula they were on three-eighths rations and fast running out of food. Any meat came from the horses and mules of the 26th Cavalry or the occasional Philippine beast of burden: the carabao or water buffalo, even monkeys and snakes. They were besieged by the overwhelming might of the Japanese constantly, day and night: blockaded at sea, cut off from any help from outside. The wounded were in vulnerable hospital tents and malaria and dysentery were rampant, and there was a water shortage. They were bombed everyday. The enemy were now bringing cross-fire to bear upon them from the salient they had pushed into the defenders' main line, and most of their anti-aircraft equipment and many guns and batteries had already been destroyed. Ammunition was low and the entire airforce of the besieged amounted to two P-40s. The endurance of the men was beginning to fade, and living over there was nightmarish.

As Trap looked into Johnny Pugh's handsome face, his eyes overbright from a recent bout of malaria, he answered for them, 'No thanks. We'd feel bad for the men. We only eat twice a day over there. Best not to alter the custom.'

The Corregidor officers showed surprise. There was a silence. There was no shortage of food on Corregidor up to now.

'Perhaps you'd like to tour the rock, then?'

'Sure, let's do that.'

And as they headed out of the tunnel Trap began thinking of her and remembering the message that Caldo gave him last December. His sergeant had returned to Trap and the platoon as they fought a defensive action not far from Bamban. That night, in a lull from the fighting, the big sergeant had turned a sheepish expression to his leader. 'Dr Robinson gave me a message for you, Major.'

Trap endeavoured to look uninterested. 'Oh?'

'She said to tell you she'll always remember Madura . . . all her life.'

Trap had not wanted to hear that; not at all. He had grunted and turned away from Caldo.

And just half an hour ago she had been so close he could have touched her. He wondered if she were in the hospital. Should he go and find her? Hell! He had to stop thinking this way.

Suddenly he realised the officer at his side was speaking.

Trap looked round. 'What was that?'

'Do you want to ride or walk, sir?'

'Oh, walk . . . yes, I'd much prefer to walk.'

As Skinny covered the quarter of a mile between the East Tunnel entrance past the water tanks to MacArthur's house his mind whirled with the information the man at his side had just given him.

General MacArthur was leaving Corregidor! In fact, he was leaving the Philippines. He planned to depart around 1830 the following afternoon with his family and personal staff, along with Admiral Rockwell and his 16th Naval District Staff. They would leave by motor torpedo boat for Mindanao, the largest of the southern islands of the Philippines, where some of the USAFFE airfields were still operational and where an aircraft from Australia would land and airlift MacArthur and his family and staff out. That is if they managed to get through. The Japanese navy had blockaded Manila Bay and patrolled the seas around the islands.

Sutherland had told Skinny that MacArthur was going to divide his Philippine forces into four subcommands and retain overall command himself from Australia.

Skinny Wainwright was a soldier. He reported to General MacArthur; he admired the man. If this course of action had been decided, then that was that. Though there was an uneasiness at the back of his mind as to how the leader could continue to command with any effectiveness from a country so far away. Port Darwin, the closest point, was almost two thousand miles distant. And his greatest fear was how the subcommands could continue to exist when the war was going so badly.

He took a loud breath and strode on at Richard Sutherland's side.

Douglas MacArthur glanced through the small front window of the slate-grey house and saw the two generals coming along the path. He left Jean and Arthur inside and came out on to the porch to meet them.

MacArthur looked worried as he held out his hand. 'Jonathan, I'm glad you're here.' MacArthur was the only person who ever called him *Jonathan*. Skinny took the extended hand and the two men sat on the pale blue cushions of two cane chairs as Sutherland disappeared around the corner of the house.

The commander of the Philippines then repeated part of what Skinny already knew: that he was leaving for Australia and taking his family and staff. He explained who was accompanying him and why he had chosen them.

'President Roosevelt has ordered me to leave, and while I've ignored his request up to now, I cannot go on doing so.' He shook his head in obvious discomfort and looked miserable.

Skinny understood. It was a tough thing for a career soldier like MacArthur to have to do. 'I am tortured by this, Jonathan, absolutely tortured. I'm a soldier. I've never left a command in my life.'

Skinny was still taking it all in as MacArthur placed a cigar between his teeth and offered him one. They lit up. MacArthur blew out a trail of smoke. 'Jonathan, you're a cavalryman. Continue to keep hitting the enemy in fast-moving narrow lines.'

Skinny refrained from asking — *With what?*

'Your defence must have depth . . . for extended defence you need depth.'

Skinny met MacArthur's eyes. 'Yes, I'm doing that. As much as the terrain and my number of troops allow.'

Neither man spoke of how long Bataan, or Corregidor, for that matter, would last.

MacArthur cleared his throat. 'I'm placing you in command of all the troops on Bataan. Your new army will include General Jones's I Corps and also General Parker's 2 Corps and those still up in the Cagayan Valley operating in guerrilla fashion.'

Finally General MacArthur repeated that he had to leave. 'A soldier must obey orders,' he announced as he took off his field marshal's cap, turned it in his hands and met Wainwright's eyes. 'I must obey or get out of the army.' There was a silence. 'I'll be back, Jonathan, with as much as I can bring.' It sounded like a solemn promise.

'Yes, I know you will. You'll get through . . . and you'll get back.'

The two men stood and shook hands, hesitating momentarily as they listened to the booming sounds echoing across the North Channel from Bataan. 'I'll make you a lieutenant general if you're still here when I come back, Jonathan.'

Skinny dropped his superior's hand. 'If I'm alive, Douglas, I'll be on Bataan.'

'Jonathan?'

'Yes?'

'You know that message I sent to you and your troops on January fifteen, telling you that help was on the way, that relief and salvation were at hand?'

Skinny nodded.

'Well . . .' He paused a long time, so long that Skinny wondered if he had forgotten what he was about to say. But finally he put his cigar out and went on, 'That's the reason why I never came back to Bataan after my January visit. Because I could not face you or the soldiers over there knowing I had misled them. Not deliberately, you see, for I truly believed what I said at the time, that aid was imminent. But I misled them nevertheless.' For a moment, a fraught, somehow vulnerable expression passed across the commander's features, making Skinny think MacArthur might have been sorry for attempting explanation. Yet the expression was speedily replaced by a thin smile. 'Look here, I've got some things for you.' And MacArthur turned to a table and picked up a box of cigars and two jars of shaving cream. He handed them to Skinny.

There was another pause, before General Wainwright declared, 'I understand all you've said.'

MacArthur gave a weary smile. 'There's a matter regarding the organising of guerrilla fighters in Mindanao. I'll get Richard to discuss it with you before you leave. Trapperton's the man for that.'

'Right.'
They shook hands again.
'Goodbye, Jonathan.'
'Goodbye, Douglas.'

Chapter Thirty-four

We're the battling bastards of Bataan;
No mama, no papa, no Uncle Sam;
No aunts, no uncles, no cousins, no nieces,
No pills, no planes, no artillery pieces.
And nobody gives a damn.
Nobody gives a damn.[1]

Trap, Johnny Pugh and Tom Dooley stood waiting near the North Dock pier in the clammy afternoon. They had taken their brief tour of the rock with three of the USAFFE officers, and now as a languid breeze drifted in from the sea, General Sutherland's car pulled up beyond the cement apron of the dock and Skinny and Sutherland alighted.

Wainwright raised his hand and called, 'Major Trapperton?'

Trap excused himself from his companions and crossed to his superior officer and MacArthur's chief of staff.

'Trap, we're going to tell you something which is classified information until the twelfth.'

That was the day after tomorrow.

'Yes, sir.'

Skinny proceeded to inform him of General MacArthur's impending departure. When he had finished, Richard Sutherland added, 'This affects you.'

Trap looked mildly surprised. 'Well yes, I guess it affects all of us.'

'No, you specifically.'

'How?'

Sutherland scratched his chin. 'You have certain qualifications.'

Trap did not comment and Sutherland continued, 'You have an in-depth knowledge of the Philippines and the Japanese. I believe you were in Tokyo passing yourself off as an Argentine businessman for a time. Right?'

'Right.'

'So you speak Japanese?'

'A smattering only; my Spanish is a whole lot better, hence the Argentine cover.' Trap was frowning. He looked questioningly at Wainwright, and Skinny clarified the matter.

'What General Sutherland is saying is that the Intelligence Department has given specific orders about you. General MacArthur is leaving tomorrow evening in a convoy of four torpedo boats. He wants you to follow on a fifth. The final rendezvous is in Cagayan in Mindanao. Colonel William Donovan specifically named you for the assignment.'

Trap knew Wild Bill Donovan. He was President Roosevelt's Coordinator of Information, a sort of overall chief of the United States intelligence community, a conglomeration of army, navy, FBI, State Department and other interests.

Trap's gaze narrowed as his commanding officer continued: 'While General MacArthur and his party will be airlifted from Del Monte Airfield in Mindanao, you, who are regarded as an expert, are to remain and report on the possibility of setting up a network of guerrilla units. They are to continue warfare against the Japanese on the island of Mindanao in case, heaven forbid, some or all of the Philippines fall to the Japs. You are to report there to Brigadier General Sharp, though you'll remain in wireless contact with me.'

Sutherland broke in: 'We'll be out of it for a while setting up headquarters in Australia. But if need be you can maintain short-wave wireless contact with Hawaii. You'll be given a secret frequency.'

Trap revealed no sign of his feelings. He glanced back to General Wainwright. 'So this is Donovan's idea?'

'Originally, but in your case General MacArthur has had to agree. There's an order in place. If it comes to the point where the Philippines are entirely taken, you'll be repatriated by submarine.'

Trap's forefinger stroked the scar on his chin as a dubious expression crossed his face. 'Repatriated?'

'Yes. A submarine will be dedicated to your removal. You'll be given the coordinates and the dates. Make sure you meet it. You'll be needed elsewhere.'

'But what about my own command, sir? Those boys in my platoon . . . they depend on me.'

Sutherland made a dismissive sound in his throat, and Trap looked helplessly at Skinny. 'Can I speak to you in private, sir?'

The Chief of Staff nodded agreement and Trap and Skinny stepped away a few paces into the shadow of one of the remaining walls of a bombed-out warehouse, where Trap appealed to his general. 'Couldn't I remain here and do the same thing in Luzon?'

'I believe the feeling is that you should not stay here, and that in any case guerrilla warfare will be easier to mount against the enemy from Mindanao.' He cleared his throat. 'That's if the other islands fall.'

'Then the best damn men for the job were those with me in Northern Luzon. They're natural-born guerrilla fighters.'

Skinny nodded. 'I see.'

'Leaving my men will be very hard, sir. I regard it as my duty to remain with them.'

'Orders are orders, son.'

Trap hesitated. 'But if I have to go without them, they'll think I've abandoned them, sir.'

Skinny made a rumbling sound in his throat. 'Rot. You know I'm a plain-speaking man. There's not a man jack on Bataan who won't vouch for you. That includes me.' Skinny's hand tightened on the younger man's shoulder. 'But I understand what you say and I reckon you should take the core of them with you. Makes sense.'

Trap looked hopeful at that. 'I'd really like to keep as many as possible; certainly my lieutenant and my Filipino sergeant.'

'Right, leave it with me, son. Those Patrol Torpedo boats only carry ten men and you've got to run the Japanese blockade, so it's not going to be a party. There'll be a driver and you, so that means you could take . . .' he paused in thought before going on, 'six or seven men, I suppose.'

'Don't you mean eight, sir? You said they hold ten.'

'They do, but that Englishwoman you found north of the Agno will be going along. Apparently MacArthur feels responsible for her. Didn't she have two orphan kids with her?'

Trap felt like he was drowning. He opened his mouth for air and after a pause answered, 'Yes, two local kids.'

'Right. I think they're going with you. They'll be airlifted out from Mindanao to Australia with General MacArthur.'

Trap made no comment. Those who knew him intimately, of which there were few, might have seen the telltale tightening of his cheek muscles confirming his displeasure. He straightened his shoulders before he enquired, 'Why is she with me, sir? Couldn't she go in one of the other craft?'

'No idea, son. I was told to inform you she'd be in your boat; that's all I know. Might be something to do with the fact you know her.' He gave a sudden shrug.

Trap grunted, obviously annoyed.

'General Sutherland says he'll tell you what you can carry with you, but I reckon it won't be much. Come on.' He headed back towards Sutherland. Trap walked behind him. When they stood together again, the Chief of Staff eyed Trap. 'Are you clear on it now?'

Trap's reply came slowly. 'Yes, sir.'

'Bring a small pack of items you want to take, no more than

ten pounds. Be in my Malinta Tunnel office by fifteen hundred tomorrow.'

Trap saluted and returned to Pugh and Dooley, who waited with expectant expressions.

'Well?'

Trap shook his head and both men gave grunts of affront. 'You mean you can't tell us?'

'That's what I mean.'

'Hell, must be important.' They looked surprised but said no more, and when General Wainwright joined them he slapped Trap affectionately on the shoulder as he passed by and, mounting the pier, walked swiftly along the damaged boards minding the holes. The three officers followed.

Dooley and Pugh were smart men, and they realised that what-ever had gone on, both the general and Trap had been very deeply affected by it.

In the launch going back to Bataan in the long grey swell, under a quickly filling sky of rolling cloud pushed by a rising wind, there was only silence.

As the day waned, and the distant cacophany of guns firing across in Bataan accompanied her, Lexi walked slowly uphill towards Topside. Trailing her came Jimmy, in his fist a single red flower which had been bravely sprouting through the rubble and charred vegetation at the wayside. Behind the toddler meandered Lessa, who still had not spoken a word since the death of her mother and grandmother.

Lexi had left the hospital in the Malinta Tunnel and come outside because one of the nurses had told her that the visitors from Bataan had gone on a tour of the island.

Her gaze roved left and right, and as they came to a break in the railway line which had been smashed in the heavy bombing of 29 December, she saw Donald Capinpin. He hurried across the broken track to her.

258

'Lexi, I can answer your question about Trapperton. He's alive, all right. Didn't have to radio Bataan. He was here on the rock this afternoon. I was hoping you would have run into him.'

She did not like his use of the past tense. 'Isn't he still here?'

'Afraid not. Saw him getting into a launch down at North Dock about two hours ago. He'll be well and truly back on Bataan now. So you didn't see him, then?'

The pit of Lexi's stomach felt like it was in her shoes. She tried valiantly to sound normal. 'Oh yes, I did . . . briefly.'

'Good. I'm glad.' He bent down on one knee and began to talk with Jimmy. The little boy handed him the flower and laughed.

Donald smiled. 'Why thank you, little man.' He ruffled the boy's crop of black hair and looked up at Lexi. 'How are the kids making out?'

'They're fine. They manage,' Lexi answered, though she felt deeply wounded that Trap had not come to find her. But then she knew he did not care at all, so why would he? She turned away from the soldier to Lessa, who stood watching, and hurrying over to her she picked her up, and added, 'Though my lovely Lessa still does not talk.'

The voluble Capinpin remained on his knees with Jimmy as he replied, 'Yeah. Well this isn't a place for kids, that's for sure. Lucky they've got you, Dr Robinson.' He touched Jimmy's cheek.

'Well excuse us, but we must get home before dark.'

Capinpin stood. 'I'll drive you back. I'm going straight to Malinta.' He pointed to a staff car on the far side of the track near the road.

Though Lexi's desire for walking had died, the last thing she wanted was Donald's effervescent company. She contrived a smile. 'Thank you so much, but I'd rather not. The children like to walk.'

Capinpin's mouth drew down. 'Right. Well, I hope to see you at chow-down.' She did occasionally eat in the officers' mess tent near the tunnel, and Donald ate there regularly.

'Yes, perhaps.' She moved quickly away, and as she rambled back down the hill her shoulders sagged as she remembered how Trap had walked right by her without even so much as casting her a glance.

A hundred yards from the tunnel entrance in the quickening dusk, Lieutenant Carmello, one of General Sutherland's staff, came trotting towards her.

'There you are, Dr Robinson. We've been looking for you. General Sutherland requests your company immediately in his office. He's got something important to tell you.'

Over on Bataan, the boat bumped up against the Marivales wharf and was tied up. The occupants climbed out to be met by Sergeant Hubert Carroll, General Wainwright's orderly, who had been waiting for them.

The constant rumble of guns was louder here. 'How are things?' queried Skinny.

'Japs strafed us about half an hour ago, sir. Other than that it's been quiet around here. Mind you, there's something big going on up there.' He pointed north-east. 'Lot of noise between fifteen and sixteen hundred.'

They climbed into the vehicle and on the ride back to the battered caravan which was still Wainwright's headquarters on Bataan, the small party continued in silence with their own particular contemplations.

That evening, as the dark shadows of night slid through the camp, Trap was called by Wainwright.

Skinny sat drinking a beer and pointed to a stool. 'We're getting low on everything. These are pretty much the last beers, son. Have one.'

'No thanks, sir, I'd prefer you drank them.'

Skinny gave an affectionate growl. 'Hell, Trap, take one. It'll be a good memory for me. Your father and I had enough together.' He smiled in reminiscence.

Trap picked up a bottle and sat. Skinny was quiet for a short time, just eyeing the younger man, before he put down his beer and wiped his mouth with his hand. 'You can take six of your own men with you, son. Good luck.'

Trap felt he had done as well as he could under the circumstances. 'Right, sir, thanks.'

'There's one more thing.'

'Yes?'

'It's felt that the officer in charge of the operation on Mindanao should be at least a half-colonel.'

'I see.' Trap swallowed a mouthful of beer. Suddenly he felt the whole thing slipping away from him. Why in hell had they recruited him for this if they were going to give it to a blasted colonel? He made himself reply in a self-contained manner. 'And who is that, sir?'

There was a pause while the general smiled. That really irritated Trap.

'You, son! Congratulations, Lieutenant Colonel Trapperton.'

Trap did not choke on his beer but he went close. He said nothing for a few seconds until he found his voice. 'Thanks, sir.'

'So when you finish your beer, go and pick your men.'

Trap found Caldo supervising the opening of two boxes of tinned meat. With the depleted food stores and strict rationing, everything had to be done with precision, scrupulously doled out and fairly handled. The big man, whose girth was diminishing to the point that his belt was now pulled in four extra holes, grinned, and his teeth shone in brilliant contrast to his dark face.

'When you complete that come and see me.'

Five minutes later Caldo appeared beside him. Trap motioned to two empty crates and they sat on them near a thicket of bamboo at the edge of the jungle, where he explained everything in temperate tones and succinct style.

By now there were a few fires alight. The Japs never attacked at night; there was no need when they could see so clearly without opposition in the daylight.

Sergeant Caldo found Trap's eyes in the red fire glow as a small colony of bats flew by overhead. 'Let me get this right, sir. You, me and five others are going to start a company of guys to fight the Japs guerrilla style down in Mindanao. And if the entire Philippines fall, we'll be taken off in a submarine.'

'That's the gist of it.'

'Shit.'

Trap forced a smile. 'Yeah, well, I knew that comment would turn up sooner or later.'

Caldo frowned. 'But the other boys, sir? I mean, what about leavin' them?'

'Yeah, it's a bitch.'

The sergeant drew his hand across his eyes beneath his green bandanna and just grunted.

'Now, let's decide who we take, and then go and get whatever it is they're calling chow for tonight.'

Trap did not mention Lexi. His brain was still in denial about that particular piece of information.

The following day, as the sound of combat grew closer, Skinny said goodbye. The general told Trap that he would explain everything to those of his men remaining on Bataan. 'They'll already be speculating, of course, but you leave it to me. I'll tell it personally to them the way it is.'

Trap knew he could count on the general. 'With your permission, though, sir, I'll say goodbye to Dooley and Pugh. They aren't stupid, they know something's up.'

Skinny grunted. 'Right. Do that. Then you and your boys better move out. The sunken road's under fire and you need to go through there. Hubert and Sergeant Morris are waiting in their jeeps. Good luck, son.' He held out his hand and Trap took it. 'How dearly I hope we meet again.'

Trap met Jonathan Wainwright's eyes. He knew this man was a brave and caring leader of men. He had shown it many times, and once more just a few days earlier. Skinny was a horse lover and had kept his handsome, spirited stallion, Little Boy, at Fort Stotsenburg, often riding the graceful animal across the heavy dew-laden grass of the early Luzon morning. The entire army knew how the general loved Little Boy. When the men of Bataan had been close to starving and the quartermasters could find no more native cattle to buy and slaughter, General Wainwright had ordered that they must begin to kill and eat the cavalry horses. He had chosen Little Boy as the first to die. Every man on Luzon knew how deeply that had hurt Jonathan Wainwright. It had simply cemented the soldiers' respect and affection for him.

Trap answered the general from his heart. 'Me too, sir. It's been an honour to report to you.'

Skinny swallowed hard, nodded and gave him a pat on the shoulder. 'I'll look forward to fishing back home with you.'

Now it was Trap who swallowed hard.

Later, he could not remember a word he said to Dooley and Pugh, but he knew they shook his hand and wished him luck. They were fine, brave men who knew that Bataan was doomed and themselves and the general along with it.

Williams, Ivat, Caldo, Clevelly, Eduardo and Cadee were waiting for him beside the two jeeps. Just as the vehicles pulled out, one of Trap's platoon, Neil Bannerman, came scurrying towards them carrying a box of ammunition. When he glimpsed the jeeps and the passengers inside, he pulled up sharply and stood there watching.

The vehicles rolled towards him on the muddy track as he waited motionless. He was young, not much more than twenty, a clean-cut conscientious kid.

Trap's eyes met Bannerman's as the soldier stood at the edge of the track, his cheeks spotty from insect bites, his forehead crinkled with interest, the box of ammo balancing on his left shoulder. And as they passed him, Trap gave a sharp nod and presented him with a faultless West Point salute.

The youth juggling the ammo, replied with a salute of his own.

Nothing was said. Bannerman knew he would not see them again. He knew they were going for good.

Trap and the boys with him refrained from looking at one another. It was bad enough knowing they would always have the picture of Bannerman, standing there fixed in their memories. Bannerman and the rest of them left behind on the enemy-surrounded Peninsula of Bataan.

Chapter Thirty-five

11 March 1942

Four-star General Douglas MacArthur recalled his first memory: the sound of bugles. At least that was what he told anyone who asked. Right from his birth in the Arsenal Barracks of Little Rock Arkansas and his baby and childhood, at Fort Wingate in northwestern New Mexico, he had been shaped by things military.

Another martial sound met his ears at this moment as he stood lost in thought on Malinta Hill, looking north; another he knew intimately: warfare, the sound of guns. The staccato refrain drifted to him across the water from remote Bataan.

And yet there was a sweet, harmonious melody wafting to him on the humid evening breeze: was it a piccolo? He believed it was; he knew there were some bandsmen on Corregidor, but he had never before heard them playing at this time of day. It floated to him, from where, he could not tell and the music from the unknown hand bestowed a massive significance upon the moment. He felt as if there were something almost supernatural about it.

The smoke from the big guns drifted in the air, the appeal of the island had long been demolished — it was a stark, ugly transformation, but yet he felt a connection with the very ground beneath him: a mystical attachment to the Philippines in a way ordinary men could not equate. His very first post had been here, ah, so long ago, the years of 1903 and 1904! Into his mind slipped a picture of the nurse who had administered to him when he caught malaria – a small delicate Filipina with topaz-coloured eyes who had wrapped him in blankets as he shivered in spite of a burning fever; what had been her name? He had not thought of her in decades. He had been only a boy really, twenty-four. And the singer at the Manila Opera House, where he had dallied on many a night: Tamara, was it?

He sighed, a long, loud breath. And after eighteen years away from these islands, and serving in the Great War in between, he had returned again. And he had kept returning ever since. The Philippines and all things Filipino had been in his psyche a long, long time.

Now he must leave once more, must leave his brave boys behind. He knew his detractors would make much of this departure, they would turn it into flight. Would they not see he was running the enemy blockade of the harbour? That alone was of enormous danger and there were no guarantees of success. It was a five-hundred-mile sea voyage down to their destination, the small port of Cagayan de Oro in Mindanao. He was attempting a unique and desperate mission to run the enemy lines and remove his key staff to another theatre of war to direct a new and intensified assault back upon the Japanese.

He turned full circle aware of the earth beneath his shoes as the tune from the piccolo insisted. It was one he remembered from long ago, hanging in the air, subtle in the haze from the guns, suggesting memories of a bygone time: his brother and himself at play, and his grandfather, Arthur MacArthur, a big-boned handsome man who had taught him poker. He was fourteen the last time they had played a hand and he had been elated as he threw down his four queens. 'There, grandfather, beat that!' And to his utter amazement his grandfather had shown him four kings!

'My dear boy, nothing is sure in this life. Everything is relative.'

Those sage words helped him now as he prepared himself for

266

the journey he must take. He was sixty-one years old. Yet at this minute, standing at the side of the grey slate house behind the Malinta Tunnel with the broken and blackened landscape around him and the incongruity of the piccolo music in concert with the gunfire, he was a boy again. His father, the youngest colonel in the union army, strode through his meditations, the man who had come to the Philippines during the Spanish American War and been made Military Governor. A truly military man who had taken a southern lady for his wife: 'Pinky' his mother.

Perhaps that was why he had ended up with Jean, another Southern lady. Momentarily the image of Louise, his first wife, wafted in his mind, quickly followed by Isabel: Isabel Rosario Cooper — his half-Filipina, half-Scottish mistress — who had been half his age. His mouth contorted into an ironic smile. There had been a lot of halves with Isabel. Even her affection for him had fallen definitely into the *half-hearted* category.

He dismissed the thought of her, recalling why he had come again to the Philippines in 1935 at Manuel Queson's request. To create a Philippine Army which was capable of defending the island commonwealth once it was independent. His task was underway when Japan attacked them.

The swift capitulation of most of Luzon and many of the other islands had shocked him, something he would not admit to anyone. In his heart he knew the locals were not ready, not trained. Perhaps he had overstated their capacity. He hated that his own predictions had been shown to be faulty. Standing in the decaying day of 11 March, looking out towards Bataan, he was in torment.

The mellow, sweet music gently persisted as he considered the 500,000 dollars Manuel Quezon had paid him before the Prime Minister had been evacuated from Corregidor last month. The bonus had been promised to him in 1935 and large sums of money also went to Sutherland, Marshall and Huff. He knew it was a controversial payment but the remuneration belonged to him, no doubt of it! He felt a hint of disquiet over the premiums paid to his aides but he brushed off that sensation. They were worth it, every penny.

The piccolo music stopped and the general's mind jolted into the present. He turned and walked swiftly to the house and across the porch to the door. 'Jean? It is time to go.'

Jean, followed by Arthur and Ah Cheu, the Cantonese amah, walked outside into the waning day. The women each carried a small suitcase with the ten-pound allowance in possessions inside.

Jean showed no sign of her inner feelings as she hurried with small steps behind her husband to the car waiting in the wide Malinta Tunnel. It was the general who turned in grave reflection to look back at the house as he entered the tunnel.

They drove without speaking to the dock.

Day faded as Lexi stood near the battered pier of the North Dock with Lessa clinging to her and Jimmy playing in the sand. It had been a strange twenty-four hours since General Sutherland had told her that she would be leaving Corregidor. It appeared that General MacArthur felt honour bound to her grandfather to take her with him. The PT boats would rendezvous in Mindanao and from there she and the children would be flown along with MacArthur, Jean, young Arthur and some of the general's staff to Australia.

It had all come as a surprise to Lexi, but she comprehended enough to know that she and the children were being offered a unique chance for passage out of the enemy's grasp.

Her heart told her she desired more than anything to stay near Trap, but he was on Bataan. It was expected of her to go, and for the sake of the children she must. She packed extra clothes for them, a single dress for herself, and added a cache of fruit and three tins of milk.

A number of servicemen milled around at the edge of the cement apron of the dock, watching events. They seemed to know what was about to happen and yet it was meant to be secret.

'Dr Robinson, this way!' A sailor waved to her. 'Bring the children and follow me. The main party is on its way here.'

Lexi and the children were helped aboard a battle-scarred torpedo boat seventy-seven feet long and introduced to 'Clicker' Quartermaine, the young driver. He grinned at Lexi, and greeted the children. Jimmy was dancing and smiling and enjoying the diversion, while his sister, as usual, remained silently adhering to Lexi's side.

Lexi's chest felt tight. She would probably never see Hank Trapperton again. She concentrated on the children as the haze of night swept across the harbour, and flashes appeared in the sky from enemy fire in the distance. The big guns of Corregidor began a diversionary action as Lexi lifted her head to see a group of men hurry along the pier and climb aboard. She recognised the hulk of Sergeant Caldo filling the space in front of her and her mouth opened involuntarily.

He nodded to her. 'Dr Robinson.'

Suddenly she saw the last man climb down into the boat. She heard the familiar sound of his voice, and watched him return Clicker's salute before he patted the man's shoulder and spoke, his voice calm and low. 'That's the lot of us, Sergeant. As soon as the Commander and his party embark in that PT forty-one ahead, we wait for him to leave. And once the other three proceed, we follow.'

'Right, sir,' answered Clicker as Trap's men spread themselves around the deck of the light, speedy plywood boat.

Ivat greeted Lexi and Cadee knelt down and spoke to Jimmy, but Lexi did not comprehend any of that. *He's here. Oh God in heaven, he's here in this boat . . . with me. I'm with Trap again!*

Finally he turned round to her. His action seemed slow, for her almost resembling the halting of time. She saw every detail: his shoulders swung in an arc towards her and his face was just a few feet away. She noticed how drawn his cheeks were and how tired he looked, and she felt sorry, wanting to lift her hand to touch and console him. And then his eyes met hers, and like a veil being drawn across his face, his expression became cold and his gaze distant and removed.

'Good evening, Dr Robinson. Try to keep out of the way on the voyage, will you?'

Chapter Thirty-six

Kathleen and Private Hyata walked over the damp ground, up the two steps and across the narrow veranda to enter the door under the ornate cornice to the shrill play of monkeys close at hand and the swish of the breeze through the dense foliage. Kathleen did not know where they were, but they had entered this mountainous jungle country a couple of days ago and they were closer to the battle front than previously, for a remote rumble of gunfire accompanied them.

She swept her fingers across her neck to wipe away the perspiration. The Philippine weather was similar to Hong Kong; it was not yet hot, but it was sticky and humid, worse here with the profusion of tropical plants and trees that formed an everlasting seal retaining the moisture.

They entered a dark foyer and were met inside by a soldier who was obviously expecting them.

Hyata's eyes found Kathleen's in farewell and she was escorted by the soldier down a dim and extremely long corridor with numerous doors, none of which they entered. Turning into a second and even darker hallway, they came at last to a door where she was ushered into the light of an extensive office. Blinking in the glare, Kathleen took in the four uniformed Japanese sitting at typewriters at four desks placed down the long, narrow room with wide-open windows on one side, allowing entrance to the torpid breeze. Outside she could see two trucks, one behind the other, parked close to the wall of the building, and beyond them grew the ubiquitous jungle of this area.

Papers lay in piles and trays in front of the soldiers, who rose in unison and left the room as a Filipina girl appeared and crossed to the newcomers. She handed Kathleen a wooden water-filled dish and small towel. Kathleen was used to this and she rinsed her hands and used the damp towel to wipe her face and neck.

The girl retreated and the soldier pointed to a chair near one of the desks, obviously expecting Kathleen to sit, but she ignored his gesture and moved past the seat to the window and looked out at the nearby trucks. The soldier made a frustrated sound, and said, '*Suwatte*' but Kathleen did not turn round, remaining facing away, looking out. He repeated the polite word for *sit*, '*Suwatte*' but she continued to disregard him.

She had been held by the enemy for many months now and she had begun to fight her own private war against the Japanese. Mute resistance was the major part of this undertaking. She had no other way to fight back, and while some might have dismissed her actions as useless and making no difference, that was not how she perceived it. Thus she was greatly rewarded every time she disobeyed or pretended she did not understand and saw a reaction of frustration, anger, disappointment or annoyance. The first time she had ignored a command she had expected to be slapped or chastised, or worse — beaten. But when none of these results had come to pass she dared to repeat her disobedience, until it became a daily source of enjoyment to her. And now as the soldier behind her repeated 'sit' and added '*onegai*' which meant *please* in a very pleading way, she leant on the window sill and ignored him still.

Suddenly a door in the far wall opened and she turned involuntarily to see Colonel Pig enter. Behind him came a man in horn-rimmed glasses. Kathleen had seen this man before. He was one of the colonel's staff.

Ikeda gestured for the soldier who had brought her to leave the office and for Kathleen to come towards him.

This command she did not disregard. She remained anxious in this man's company. She had seen him murder her friends in cold blood, and while he might have given orders that she was not to be harmed by his men, she lived in fear of being harmed by him.

As many as five or six days would pass without her seeing him, and then her Filipina maid would come and insist she was bathed and scented and given clean clothes to wear, after which she was ushered into his presence. Sometimes he would be eating a meal and she would be seated a few yards away. She would never be asked to join him, something she thanked God for, and when he had completed his food and drink he would lean back in his chair and regard her without speaking for some minutes. There were times he left the room for perhaps half an hour, and when he returned he examined her again before having her taken away.

On other occasions she would be brought to him as he worked at his desk in his headquarters. The same sort of eccentric procedure would occur and his conduct would be similar.

She always waited in apprehension, fearing something dreadful, but it never occurred. It was bizarre. Once he made her sit on a chair in the middle of the room and walked slowly around her, eyeing her, and on a more recent occasion he had told her to untie her hair and let it fall around her shoulders. Then he had simply seated himself and contemplated her for perhaps four or five minutes.

He was somehow fascinated with her and she wondered how long it would last before he treated her as he did the comfort women, like something to be abused. For she was positive the day would come.

As Kathleen crossed towards him over the bare floorboards between the desks, he turned away and led her through the door he had just entered. The man in the spectacles followed.

The adjoining room was smaller than the office; paint peeled from the walls and the high ceiling and it was empty but for one low table, an oblong seat and a koto. Kathleen knew of this traditional Japanese musical instrument. It was a type of zither, and when played well it emitted an evocative sound reminiscent of the Western harp or lute. Its thirteen silken strings were stretched along a soundboard of perhaps two yards in length made of hollowed-out timber.

The man in the horn-rimmed glasses proceeded over to it and placed an ivory plectrum on the thumb and first two fingers of his right hand, sat down behind it and began to play. A lovely haunting melody lifted from the koto as the man's left hand moved back and forth, applying pressure to the strings to vary the pitch. His head was down and he seemed lost in the dulcet sounds of his melody.

The empty room, the soft harmony, the bare floorboards, the warm zephyr drifting from the wide windows, Colonel Pig studying her again: it did not seem real.

Kathleen stood some feet apart from him. A film of perspiration covered his forehead and the top button of his uniform was open. But now, as the music filled the room, he fastened the button and removed his Samurai sword, which, due to his lack of height, hung dangerously close to the floor. He placed it almost reverently down on the table and walked back to Kathleen and took her in his arms.

She had half expected this from the moment the man in glasses had begun to play, but it still surprised her. It was the first time Colonel Pig had ever touched her, and she shivered as he placed his fingers upon the bare skin of her arms. He held her in Western fashion and began to move her backwards in slow dance steps.

He looked so grave and self-important as he circled her around the floor. He was a few inches shorter than she was and suddenly the whole performance was absolutely ridiculous to Kathleen. The preposterousness of it all forced a sudden unintentional laugh from her.

His face stiffened and he dropped his hands from her as if she were a firebrand. In one motion, he swung his right arm up and struck her hard in the face, the impetus of the blow making her fall back a step. He spun round to the koto player and screamed in Japanese and the man stopped playing and hurried from the room.

Kathleen held her mouth. The power in his fist had pushed her lip into her teeth and blood was running down her chin.

His eyes were pinpoints of fury and his eyelids narrowed until his black pupils all but disappeared in the folds of his skin. 'You do not laugh! If you dare to laugh again I will beat you till your mind is numb. You understand? I am Colonel Ikeda. You must show me respect. Respect! You hear me?' He screamed the words and she stepped another pace away from him.

'On your knees!' he hurled at her, pointing with his index finger to the floor.

She did not move.

'On your knees . . . now!'

She knelt, still holding her mouth.

He strode to her and knocked her hand away and grabbed her chin in his right hand, jerking her face up to him as he looked down on her. His fingers dug into the flesh of her face and her blood seeped across them.

'You are alive because I wish it. You live only because of me. Do you understand? Speak!' He screamed the last word.

'I understand.'

He released her chin and turned away.

She knelt watching him. *How I hate him! How deeply I detest him!*

He walked in short stomping steps to the far side of the room to pause beside the koto, and even though her terror of him was great, the depth of her enmity gave her the veriest feeling of defiance, and she began to rise. Even though she trembled, she would not stay on her knees in front of this animal!

He turned around as she slowly gained her feet and she waited for his wrath. But to her amazement he did nothing. He eyed her a few moments in silence and then walked four sharp, definite steps towards her but came no closer. They remained about ten feet apart.

He took out a handkerchief from his jacket pocket and wiped her blood from his fingers. 'Next time I dance with you, you will not laugh. Is this understood?' His voice was calm and controlled, his face stern and formal.

He waited. 'Well?'

Now was not the time to be defiant. Kathleen nodded. 'Yes, I understand.'

He threw the handkerchief on the floor at her feet. 'Wipe your mouth. You look like a Filipina whore.' He spun on his heel, strode to the table, took up his sword and left the room.

Minutes passed while Kathleen waited, dabbing her mouth with the handkerchief. Her heartbeat had returned to normal and she expected the soldier who had brought her here to return and take her away. But no one came. After five or six minutes she walked around the room and halted at the door leading back to the office.

Had they forgotten about her? Surely not. Perhaps everyone in the establishment had accepted that she would be a long time with Colonel Pig and had remained away from this part of the building.

She put out her hand and opened the door in front of her. The office was empty and the four desks abandoned; all was still. She entered, leaving the door open behind her.

She decided that Colonel Pig had gone; she had the feeling he was not coming back, and as the moments passed she became more calm.

Should she return down the corridor to find Hyata? Should she try to escape? And if she did get away, where would she go? As far as she knew, large sections of the Philippines were in Japanese hands. And if she were caught trying to escape? That would be bad.

She paused in uncertainty, still holding the handkerchief to her

276

lips, and as she did so she looked out of the window at the nearest truck, which was only a yard away from her. She could see into the vacant driver's cabin. Abruptly she realised that by stretching she could reach it, it was so close.

This sort of Japanese army lorry she had seen hundreds of times. They were used to transport troops and war supplies all over the place. She herself was mostly moved around in one. The canvas flap which covered the back was not down and she could see it was filled with what appeared to be dynamos, stacked in rows of three. She walked down the line of desks and observed the second lorry. Cautiously she leant across the windowsill and looked to left and right. The damp odour of the jungle loitered in the air and she could hear soldiers talking beyond the trucks, but there was no one in sight. She leant further out and reached for the canvas cover on the back of the lorry. Inside were piles of ground sheets and stacks of boxes of explosives and hand grenades. Her gaze flicked back to the familiar blue form lodged in the slot to the rear of the driver's seat. It designated where the truck was headed.

She could not speak any Japanese, but she could read and write a little, and occasionally when an enemy newspaper had come her way, usually via Private Hyata, she had tried to improve her reading skills. Hyata had been helping her. Her knowledge of the war had been gleaned from the enemy newspapers, even though she was aware much would be propaganda.

One thing she knew, for she had seen it many times. The drivers of these lorries were mostly chosen at random.

The contingent to which she and Hyata belonged had often been ready to depart a position and suddenly drivers would be designated at the last minute. Sometimes the men protested, for they could not drive, and then another man would be chosen. The driver would always go to the blue slip behind the driving seat and look at it to see where he was going. Rarely did they seem to know before they saw the form.

From where she stood she could read two words on the top

line of the form: *Ikisaki* and *Heisha. Destination*, she knew that word, and she thought she remembered *Barracks*. The third word she translated as *Lingayen*. Destination Lingayen Barracks! Underneath was a number, she thought it was 135. There would be more information below out of sight.

She spun back into the office, walked to the exit door and listened. No sound. She crossed back to the window and leant out again. Looking right and left, she lifted the blue form from the slot. Her hand shook a little and her pulse quickened as she hurried to the window where she could reach out to the other vehicle. She exchanged its blue slip for the one she carried.

Within fifteen seconds, both forms were on the wrong trucks.

Her cheeks pink from excitement, she hastened back past the line of desks and opened the door to the room where she had danced with Ikeda. Suddenly she heard a noise behind at the other end of the office. It was the far door opening! Hastily closing the one she held, she hurried to the middle of the room just before the soldier who had brought her entered.

She was offering a silent prayer in the hope he knew nothing and to her relief he simply signalled for her to leave with him.

Back through the office she was taken, not daring to look at the trucks outside the windows, and as they walked down the long, dim corridors they were passed by the four soldiers returning to their desks.

Hyata came to attention as they appeared, and she noticed the concern in his expression as he saw her mouth. She shook her head as if it were nothing.

It was later that night that Kathleen allowed herself to gloat. She had been driven many miles to a small broken-down hotel commandeered by the Japanese, where she found her usual Filipina maid waiting for her.

She stood looking out at wisps of cloud floating in streaks across the silver moon. Her mouth was swollen and sore but she

278

smiled widely. A warm, optimistic feeling ran through her; in a tiny way she had helped the Allies.

With a little luck there would soon be two very angry Japanese officers: one in Lingayen, the other in San Fernando. She visualised the one who had been expecting the dynamos shouting with frustration when he was delivered explosives and hand grenades; and the other who was in dire need of gunpowder and bombs staring in disbelief at a truckload of energy-makers.

Chapter Thirty-seven

Lexi woke. Her back was sore and she remembered where she was: on the deck of the PT boat.

It was Lieutenant Williams's voice which had disturbed her. 'Over there. I can see the shape of the wharf now, sir.' He held field glasses to his eyes and pointed.

Trap, who stood beside Clicker at the wheel, replied, 'Yes, we've got it in our sights too, but I can't see anyone.'

'No, me neither.'

The clouds lowered above them, rolling in dudgeon before the wind. They were days late for the final rendezvous of the PT boats in Mindanao.

As Lexi straightened, Jimmy's head came up under her nose. He had been asleep on her lap but had awoken with her. His hair smelt of sea salt and his small hands were clasped beneath his chin. At Lexi's side, with her feet tucked under the woman's knees, Lessa too woke and sat up.

They had begun the voyage from Corregidor as soon as General MacArthur arrived at the North Dock and boarded his boat.

Lexi noticed Jean, Arthur and Ah Cheu embark PT 41 while MacArthur had paused, and in the closing dusk, turned back to 'Topside' on the high point of the island where the guns of Corregidor boomed defiance in the falling night and black scars and scorched rock marred the hillside. Clusters of servicemen milled on and around the wharf watching as the general looked up and abruptly raised his Field-Marshal's white cap in a salute before he spun round and stepped aboard. It was at that moment that Lexi heard one of the soldiers on the dock ask, 'Sarge, what are his chances of getting through the blockade?' And the reply had been, 'Dunno. Maybe one in five. He's lucky.'

The small convoy of battle-scarred PT boats were hampered by lack of maintenance, congested with rust and armed only with 4.5-calibre machine guns and four torpedo tubes each. Lexi learnt later that MacArthur had thought they would have more chance of getting through in these speedier surface boats which could still manage thirty knots than in a submarine. The vessels were without armour or decent compasses, but these drawbacks were offset by the fact they were under the command of Lieutenant John Bulkeley who was known as 'that bold buckaroo with cold green eyes'. With speed and stealth he slipped them through the enemy minefield, and they all rendezvoused at the first point of Turning Bouy around 2000 that night. From there darting across the choppy water the tiny armada began to run the blockade of Japanese ships to Cabra island.

Lots of enemy lights were sighted on that part of the voyage, a sign that the Japanese knew an attempt to break through was being made. Lexi heard Clicker Quartermaine tell Trap that he was pretty sure their engines had been heard by the Japs, but he also said that the PT boat engines sounded like a bomber and it was hard to know the difference, especially at night.

A little later the seas had risen and visibility became difficult. The strain on Clicker's face became more apparent with the passing hours. Many times they saw lights from enemy ships in the distance above the waves, and waited, unbreathing, for the sound of a voice which would bid them identify themselves. But luck, or in fact the growing chop of the seas, hid the slender nautical shapes again and again as they followed Lieutenant Bulkeley, who constantly altered course.

The weather deteriorated, and the seas continued to grow. Lessa vomited and Jimmy complained and Lexi spent her time forcing herself not to be ill and to tend to them. At one point in the night, when huge waves were beating the small craft and the sea spray was hitting her face mercilessly, she thought of her existence of a few months ago, when she had worked at St Mary's Hospital and had servants to take care of her husband and her son, and when her life had appeared stable and calm. She recognised that her memories were an illusion, for Hong Kong was now in the hands of the enemy and life there would be hell, but she could not help but think of yesterday. She continued to reproach herself for having married Johnny. It had been wrong of her and unfair to him, knowing in her heart she loved another man. Over and over she murmured quietly to herself, 'But I never expected to see him again.'

She came back to the present as conditions degenerated. The boat seemed to stand on end and they slid along the deck, Lessa and Jimmy crying out as the little craft fought its way up what seemed to be a mountain of water and slid down the other side. The fear that she would be once more cast into the sea overcame Lexi, and as Trap leapt forward to grab the weeping children, it took her all her strength to keep herself from crying out in terror.

In the mighty seas the boats lost formation and separated. Trap spent the night rallying them all with words of confidence and Clicker drove the little craft with equal quantities of audacity and caution, finally bringing the boat into the relative calm of their dawn rendezvous at Tagauayan hours late at 1100 on 12 March.

'I see a boat,' Clicker cried, pointing ahead.

It was PT-34 riding at anchor. As the day wore on they waited until PT-32 and PT-41, carrying the MacArthurs, limped in around 1600, but the final craft did not appear. Now they were made aware that PT-32 had all but run out of fuel and its passengers

282

were divided between the others. Finally General MacArthur reluctantly gave the order to leave without the missing craft.

That second night of the voyage, a clear one but with continuing rough and gigantic seas, Trap's craft again became separated from the other torpedo boats, but they knew the route and continued. Once, towards morning, they saw the large black shape of a Japanese destroyer and Clicker instantly cut the engine and waited. Moments became minutes as it loomed over them, blocking out the stars while it crossed their path. They were bobbing up and down between the massive waves and to their relief the enemy either did not see them, or in the shadows mistook them for a Filipino fishing vessel.

When he was sure they were safe from the warship, Trap gave the order to continue the voyage, but now the engine stalled. An hour followed where Trap and Clicker and the soldiers tried everything to start it without success. Thankfully they were not out of fuel, and as dawn broke and the wind dropped and the seas lessened, they began to paddle towards nearby land to the north. Trap's fear was being seen, but their spirits rose when they found a small, deep cove concealed from the open sea and dropped anchor.

Trap and Clicker studied the charts. Their position was about 120 miles from their destination – the tiny port of Cagayan de Oro on Mindanao.

They hid from passing enemy patrols, their torpedoes aimed and ready for action, during which time Trap and the men dismantled the engine. Days passed, while they caught fish and ate wild bananas, until finally they had fashioned a broken part out of two spares and got the engine running. It was after midnight on the night of 17 March when they set out across the Buhol Sea in a small chop, and while Lexi and the children slept intermittently during the dark hours, the first moments of breaking day appeared as they sailed into the harbour which was their destination. The delicate grey light oozed up in the sky defining the collection of tents and hastily erected buildings along the shore.

And now as Lexi rubbed her back and stood up she heard Clicker say, 'There's somebody, look! I can see men now, sir, two o'clock.'

Trap found them. 'Yes, bring her in slowly, we want them to recognise us.'

'I'll wave old glory sir!' Caldo shouted.

As they drew into the port and half a dozen sentries of the Mindanao Force surged along the dock towards them, Lessa climbed over the ropes on the deck and, moving up beside Trap, tugged at his trouser leg. He looked down and she raised her arms to him, begging to be lifted. She still did not speak; the only noise they had ever heard from her since the death of her mother and grandmother was the sound of weeping.

For a moment Lexi saw the veil of annoyance cross Trap's features. Rebuff seemed inevitable; but as the little girl continued to hold up her arms to him, he hesitated. His hand went to his chin and he rubbed the scar beneath it before he bent down and lifted Lessa up while Lexi, clasping Jimmy within her own embrace, watched in surprise.

And that was the way Trap remained, standing tall in the bow, nursing the little girl in his arms, as Caldo's bulk beside him waved the flag and Clicker brought the PT boat and the weary inmates up to the wharf.

Hank Williams leant over the side. 'Colonel Trapperton's here to see General Sharp, and we have a lady and two children who are to join General MacArthur and his family immediately.'

The light frame of the boat gently bumped along the dock as Trap's boys jumped ashore and secured it to the bollards.

The nearest soldier answered. 'We'd given you up for dead. Thought you'd all bought it. General MacArthur's gone. He flew out last night in a B-17 bound for Australia.'

'Shit!' Caldo exclaimed, and turned sharply to Trap.

Trap's grasp on Lessa tightened momentarily. This was what had haunted him for all the hours of the recent days; this was

284

what he had been thinking about when he had been working furiously to repair the engine; when he had been short with Caldo and his boys because he did not want to imagine this exact flaming consequence – that MacArthur would have gone by the time they got here!

He had orders to remain in Mindanao and assess the logistics of continuing guerrilla warfare against the invaders. Perhaps to organise resistance. But the kids and the woman were to have gone with MacArthur! He had been going to be free of her at last. Trap told himself to look straight at the soldiers on the dock. Eyes ahead. *Don't look round at her. Don't do it!*

But as strong and tenacious as he was, he felt his body half swing in her direction, as if his mind gave way. He had not looked directly at her for all the days and nights they had been together. He had given instructions to her through Caldo or Williams, requests to her through Caldo or Williams, and no matter how strange his men had thought his actions, he had no intention of explaining himself to any damn one of them. And now, against his will, his gaze was wandering to her. He felt hot, annoyed. Control slipped and he turned right round and looked straight at her. She stood nursing Jimmy, with Ivat and Cadee on either side.

Her Virginia sky-blue eyes were on him, staring back at him.

He took two involuntary steps over the deck towards her, placed Lessa gently down and dropped his head. There in his eye-line were her feet in pale sandshoes. *Damn her*. He took a deep breath and, straightening up, looked hard at her, forcing himself to a frown.

He read her eyes, knew what they were saying, but he wanted none of it.

'Jesus,' he said, and turned his head away.

Half an hour later Trap and his men ate fried eggs with toast and drank mugs of sweet black coffee before Trap left with Major Paul Phillips, ADC to Brigadier General William F. Sharp to be escorted along a muddy thoroughfare. As they passed a blue-painted wooden building with a grass roof, Trap glanced sideways through the door. He knew this was where Lexi and the children had been taken.

Jimmy's raised voice greeted his ears and Lessa appeared out of the interior. Trap halted, as did Paul Phillips at his side. The little girl ran straight up to Trap and did exactly as she had on the PT boat at dawn – she lifted her arms in entreaty to him.

'Is she yours, sir?' asked the major at his side before he had time to check himself.

'Goddam it, no! She isn't!' Trap growled. 'Don't your eyes tell you she's a full-blooded Filipina?'

'Ah, sure. Sorry, sir.'

Lessa was holding the bottom of his tunic and Trap, with an exasperated sound, leant down and raised the child. He gave her a long-suffering look. 'Now listen, kiddo, this is becoming a habit. I can't have this, you know. Colonels don't go around picking up little girls in their arms. It isn't done.'

For reply, Lessa smiled at him and her smooth face gleamed in the morning sunshine. He could see she had been bathed and her hair neatly plaited, and as he stood there, the woman who had done these things appeared out of the dim interior of the house with Jimmy in tow. She wore a fresh dress; it was slightly tight and it adhered to her body in all the right places.

He looked away.

'Come along, Lessa,' Lexi said. 'Don't worry the colonel, he's too busy for us. He's got a war to fight.'

Trap could not help himself: he glanced sharply at her and glared as he returned the child to the ground and strode on with Major Phillips at his side. As they rounded the corner towards headquarters, Phillips remarked, 'Wow! Swell-looking dame ... real swell. Who is she, sir?'

Trap covered twenty yards before he acknowledged the query. The last time he had answered this question it had been asked by Caldo;

this time he gave a different response: 'A shipwrecked Englishwoman from Hong Kong. She's married to a guy I feel sorry for.'

'Oh, why's that?'

'Because she isn't good enough to lick his boots.'

Phillips brought Trap in to General Sharp, where he was surrounded by four others of his staff: Lieutenant Colonel Robert Johnston, Colonel Archibald Mixon, Lieutenant Colonel Howard Perry and a captain called O'Brien.

The general took off his glasses and drew his hand across his eyes. He showed signs of fatigue and coughed as he replaced his glasses and glanced around at his men. 'General MacArthur cannot continue to run things here when he's thousands of miles away in Australia. We haven't yet heard anything official from Washington, but we must hear any day now. My guess is that Wainwright will take over as commander-in-chief here in the Philippines. I just hope he understands our problems down here.'

He eyed Trap as he went on. 'When General MacArthur flew out of here at midnight, he was still hoping you might turn up. Up to now, my orders have been clear. If organised resistance becomes no longer practical, I'm to split my forces into smaller units and conduct guerrilla warfare from hidden bases on each island. Now, unless that order alters, you, Colonel Trapperton, can advise us, for we believe you're meant to be an expert in such matters. So I'm pleased to see you are not dead as we all believed.'

'Me too, sir.'

'Right, let's get down to business.' He leant over a map on the desk and ran his finger across the southern part of Mindanao. 'All of Digos is in the hands of the enemy ...'

The meeting lasted three hours and it was decided that Trap would reconnoitre certain northern parts of Mindanao which were not in enemy hands; that he would also go to the islands which the home forces still held and see where, and how, guerrilla armies

287

could be formed and maintained. Where he could, he would begin to recruit.

Finally, as the soldiers stood from the conference table, Sharp again took his glasses from his nose and wiped his eyes as he turned to Trap. 'Now, one more thing: this woman and the children who came here with you. I have no orders whatsoever about them. I know she means something to General MacArthur and his wife, for they were both distressed when they believed her dead, but it's not my fault that you weren't here on time for her to go along with them. I'm running an army, Trapperton, and there's a war on. Civilians just don't get a look in.'

'Sir, I can't take the woman and the children with me, surely that's obvious.'

The general spoke irritably. 'Yes, yes, of course it is. I'll make arrangements for them to be billeted with a Filipino family here for the time being, but it was made clear to me that you're working with a certain amount of autonomy. So I'm making it clear to *you* that the woman and the children remain your responsibility, not mine and not my army's. Understood, Colonel?'

Trap took a deep breath. 'Understood, General Sharp.'

Chapter Thirty-eight

Ten days later: 28 March 1942

John Drayton slapped at a mosquito as he stood near a group of soldiers playing cards beside a flagpole on the edge of the sand. He watched the horizon, bedecked with the colours of the dying day: brilliant reds, lavenders, oranges and pinks bedazzled the tall turrets of cloud in the western sky. His shoes sat on the sand behind him, and under his bare feet and between his toes he could feel the golden grains of fourteen-mile-long Cable Beach, which ran by the tiny Australian outpost of Broome.

They had been here four days, he and the survivors of the hellish voyage they had undertaken to escape Java. The powers that be, in the form of a very officious colonel in the RAAF, had half promised to fly them out to Brisbane at the first opportunity.

Broome had been bombed by the Japanese twice in the last three weeks. The local boys reported that seventy people had been killed and forty wounded. The town had been undefended but was currently undergoing swift fortification. Hundreds of servicemen – ironically dubbed John Curtin's 'ring of steel' for Australia, when many were underaged militia, – had been rushed in, and so John Drayton was not alone on the long, clean stretch of sand. Dozens of young men in khaki, mostly in shorts without shoes like himself, sat and lounged around the beach. Yet metaphorically John Drayton was certainly alone, isolated by his thoughts.

His wife and son were dead. He kicked the sand mechanically and walked forward into the foam at the edge of the Indian Ocean. He had finally accepted that fact on the long, weary and frightening days of existing in the open boat in the harsh elements of wind and sun. Much of that voyage he had believed he would soon join them, and he had come to acknowledge that if he did die, there was a correctness in it all. It would be fitting for the Whitby family to unite in death.

But he and Lieutenant Ron Howard, along with Smith, Ward and Bird, had made it home. Alec Marchant and Charlie Wiggers had died in the boat on the way south from Java; Alec during a strafing from a Jap Zero which had attacked them a few miles out from the Javanese shore just as a storm began. Doubtless the storm had saved them; they reckoned that otherwise the Jap would have come back for the lot of them. Poor Wiggers had died of starvation and exposure just prior to their rescue – when all of them were entering delirium and near death – by the British-Indian freighter *Jaipur*, bound from Madras to Broome and on to Perth which had found them bobbing in the choppy sea.

The bravery of his men in that open boat would live in his mind for always. He would forever be able to recall Howard offering the last of his water to the dying Wiggers, who waved it away, croaking his final words through swollen cracked lips: 'Save it. Don't waste it . . . sir. I'm going . . . west.'

Ward had been an inspiration, keeping up their failing spirits with his ability to see humour in the direst moments. He had been elected quartermaster and remained ever cheerful. His reliable sunny nature provoked them with phrases like, 'Now to breakfast, my dears. Here comes the bacon and eggs,' as he doled out a few slices of rotting cheese. He regaled them with stories of his perpetually comical family life with an overbearing mother and a monosyllabic father living in a suburb called Bundamba in Ipswich.

Just before they had all become delirious, they had grown philosophical.

Bird had lifted his gaunt form up into a sitting position and asked, 'Who said "War spares not the brave but the cowardly"?'

Ron Howard answered, 'Don't know, but from what I've seen so far it might be true.'

John Drayton thought of all his boys who had been alive just weeks and days ago, and now were gone. They had been brave men. He did not say anything; he just stared into the grey ocean.

Smith looked up from where he lay in the bottom of the vessel. 'Why is it each generation has to learn things for themselves? When you're young you think your parents are dills; then, as you get older, you admit how wise they actually were. So do you think that if humans lived to be, say, a hundred and fifty years old, it would make a difference? I mean, wouldn't they remember more and avoid rushing into wars so bloody quickly?'

Ward had scorned that. 'Wouldn't make a jot of difference, mate. You'd still have murdering bastards like Hitler and Tojo. Age would make no difference to them. Wouldn't matter if they lived to be two hundred, they'd be just the same.'

'But some people do repent,' Smith added.

'Not them,' Ward muttered with another tired laugh. 'Ya have to have some decency inside to repent, mate.' He sat up straighter and forced a grin. 'Now listen to this, you blokes, that just reminds me of an old mate of mine. He was a house painter who used to make his paint go a long way by thinning it with turpentine. Well, once he was painting a church and a mighty clap of thunder sounded and a downpour started. The paint was so thin it washed completely off the boards and suddenly a flash of lightning knocked him to the ground and he heard the voice of God booming, "Repaint! Repaint! And thin no more."'

Yes, once again Ward had managed to keep them smiling. By the time they were rescued they had survived a violent storm and

291

all were ill, with Ward the worst. John Drayton had submitted their names for Distinguished Conduct Medals.

The memory of the storm at sea made John Drayton shiver and he became aware of the cool water of the Indian Ocean flowing over his feet and ankles as the voice of Ron Howard at his shoulder brought him back to reality. 'There you are, sir, I've been looking for you.' Ron's nose and cheeks were still burnt and blistered from the days in the open boat. 'We've got a ride out, sir.'

'Where to?'

'Straight to Brisbane. Tomorrow morning at dawn.'

'Is Ken Ward well enough to travel?'

'He says he is, but I doubt it.'

Ward had been in hospital since they arrived; it appeared his liver was badly damaged and he was still fighting malaria.

As the sun met the horizon a corporal strode across the road and headed to the pole near them to lower the flag for the night. The banner stirred and lifted in the breeze, and at John Drayton's side Ron Howard spoke. 'Whenever I see the flag now, I can't help thinking of Harry.'

John Drayton pictured Harry Parsons lying beside him on the edge of the muddy stream in Java; the bullet hole in his forehead. He took a long, uneasy breath. 'Why's that?'

'Well, the kid used to brag about his uncle being one of the five joint winners who designed the flag in 1901.'

John Drayton had not known this.

'I think he said there were over thirty thousand entrants. He was mighty proud of that. Harry loved the flag, he did.'

'Don't we all?'

'Yes, we do.'

John Drayton shook his head, thinking of Harry and Marchant and Wiggers, Cassidy and Lewis and the thousands of others who had died to keep the flag flying.

And as if some universal conscience heard them speaking, the banner lifted and billowed high in the blazoned sky to reveal itself: the Union Jack and the Southern Cross and the Federation Star.

John Drayton eyed it silently in contemplation until finally he threw his arm around Ron's shoulder. 'Right, let's go and visit Ward, and then find a beer and toast our Harry and all of the others ... and our noble flag.'

Chapter Thirty-nine

The following morning John Drayton, Ron Howard, Derek Smith and Gavin Birch, without Ken Ward, lifted above the small outpost in an RAAF De Havilland Dragon transport and bumped through cloud to twelve thousand feet, where they saw the dawn gleaming ahead of them and felt a strong wind from the sea behind. It was a milk-run journey via airfields dotted across the immense dry continent, where they landed and refuelled. That night, Sunday 29 March, they spent in Cloncurry, a dusty, isolated settlement in north-west Queensland where B-17s of the 19th and 30th USAF Heavy Bombardment Squadrons had arrived that very day to line the airfield in a show of substantial security for all those who looked upon them.

The next day they landed at Archerfield Aerodrome in Brisbane, the capital of the state of Queensland. As the aircraft bumped along the runway lined with corrugated-iron Nissen huts, John Drayton was apprehensive. He had to tell Lexi's mother of the loss of her daughter and her sister. He looked out of the window at the Nissen huts as the transport rolled to a halt. He did not want to do it, but it was his duty and had to be done.

The noonday sun shimmered in zigzagging rays through the jacaranda and poinciana trees to light upon John Drayton wiping his forehead with the back of his finger. The fairness of his hair gleamed almost gold as he dropped his hand, his shoulders slumping in sorrow.

His stepfather-in-law, Jeffrey Bartlett, took hold of his arm. 'Oh God in heaven,' the older man breathed heavily. 'Lexine gone, baby Paul ... Jasper ... Della. Oh God, and Peter, Greg and Kathleen. It's hard to take in. I don't know how to tell Marlene. She'll be devastated.'

The young man nodded. 'Yes, I suppose she will.'

'Ah lad, it's a miracle you're alive from what you've told me. This bloody war is certainly taking its toll. And the Japs are having it their own way.'

'Yes, the little bastards.'

The two men fell silent for a few moments, the seriousness of it all weighing on both of them.

Jeff shook his head three times. 'So you went to Stonegate and saw Aunt Carly?'

Stonegate was the Bartlett home, an imposing house standing in a large block of land on Chermside Road on the eastern side of Queen's Park. John Drayton had left the train at East Ipswich station and walked up the gentle hill to 'The Fiveways' intersection, named because there were in fact five directions to be taken. He was soon at Stonegate. It had been Jeffrey's aunt who greeted him at the door with her deep, almost manly voice: 'You're Lexine's husband, I'd recognise you anywhere. I'm Carly Feathers, Jeffrey's aunt, and while I wasn't at your wedding in Hong Kong, I saw the snaps that Jeff brought home. What a lovely affair it was. Where's Lexine?' She took hold of his forearm.

John Drayton had not answered that. He was looking straight into her eyes, for the woman was at least six feet tall even though she denied it. He withdrew his arm from her firm grasp and told her he needed to speak to the Bartletts quite urgently. She indicated that it was Mrs Bartlett's day working as a volunteer at the All Services hut next to the War Memorial building down town.

'It's for the benefit of soldiers, sailors and airmen: they can buy cheap light refreshments and sit and relax in the shade of the trees. You can't miss it.'

John Drayton thanked her. He knew Ipswich, had been a pupil at the Boys' grammar school on the far side of the town. His home had been a property 400 miles away, so he had boarded there for four of his teenage years. On a visit to old school friends in 1935, he had met Lexi here. He was fond of the town and brimful of memories, he crossed to the peaceful haven of Queen's Park, nestling on one side of Limestone Hill. It was an easy half-mile walk into the business district and he was soon on the white cement road embedded with tiny chips of black stone which had been made during the Great Depression of the previous decade. Passing a smartly painted kiosk, he waved to a fair-haired little boy playing on the steps with a small black cat. The child stood up and returned the wave as three American soldiers in tailored uniforms crossed the road heading south towards their army camp on the far side of the park.

A fleet of American transport trucks drove by as John Drayton strode on along Limestone Street, where a number of slit trenches appeared in the front yards of houses. The business area began as he approached the stonemason's shop on the corner of Wharf Street, and it was a pleasant relief to be under the stand of shady trees along from the sandbagged front of the Country Women's Association hall. A hundred yards on, he arrived at Memorial Park on the corner of Nicholas Street, where was situated the All Services hut which had been opened by the Queensland Governor in January.

He recognised Jeffrey Bartlett climbing out of a utility truck. He called out and the man turned, surprise evident when he saw his wife's son-in-law in uniform approaching him.

Jeffrey Bartlett had come into town from his No. 3 coal mine to pick up his wife Marlene and drive her home for lunch. His amazement at seeing John Drayton had turned to sorrow and shock when he heard the news of the sinking of the SS *Fortitude*.

So preoccupied were the two men that neither noticed Marlene

Bartlett carrying a duster and a piece of chalk exit the small kiosk and walk across the veranda past three soldiers lounging on wooden chairs, to a small, neatly written sign:

Tea and coffee with sandwiches, biscuits, scones or cake: 3d
Cold meat and salad, bread and butter with tea or coffee: 6d
Bacon and eggs, bread and butter with tea or coffee: 6d
Soft drinks: 4d

She bent down, her plump figure and bright frock reminiscent of her sister Della, and she printed in chalk the words BACON FINISHED beside *Bacon and eggs*. Rising, she caught sight of her husband and soon came hurrying over to him. She was almost upon them before she recognised the soldier beside Jeffrey and she paused, a baffled expression on her face.

'What on earth are you doing here, John Drayton?'

Both men were caught momentarily off balance, but John Drayton rallied, taking Marlene's hands and lifting them to his lips. 'Hello, Marlene dear.'

'What are you doing here? Where's Lexi?'

Her husband drew her to his side and put a comforting arm around her. 'I think we should go straight home, darling.'

The frown on her brow deepened. 'This is about Lexine, isn't it? I had a cable from Pa. She was booked on a ship with Della and the rest of the family but I've heard nothing since and that was long before Christmas. I've been worried sick now for weeks.'

John Drayton forced himself to speak. 'Marlene, I'm so sorry, but the ship carrying Lexi and Paul ... all of them ... was torpedoed by the Japs. They ... that is, none of them ... survived.'

Marlene's high colour drained from her face. John Drayton saw it disappear, saw the grey hue spread over her cheeks and across her forehead. The muscles of her cheeks trembled and she stumbled over the words: 'All . . . of them . . . But . . . all of them. Oh no!' Tears welled in her eyes and she turned to her husband and sank into his arms.

Jeffrey hugged her close and kissed her hair as she sobbed, 'My Lexi and my grandson. I've never even seen him.' She focused back on her son-in-law. 'You mean Della too?'

He nodded.

'But what about Peter and Jasper?'

'Darling,' her husband hugged her again, 'he just told you. They're all gone.'

She was trying to cry quietly, not wanting people to notice, but her shoulders heaved and she could not retain the loud sobs breaking from her.

The two men stood helplessly, as Marlene wept; until Jeffrey tenderly moved her to John Drayton's grasp. 'I'll go into the kiosk and tell them you won't be back today.'

An hour later the two men sat on Stonegate's front veranda while Marlene rested in her pink bedroom after being administered a tablet by their family doctor.

John Drayton had given a brief summary of his experiences since he last saw Lexine. Jeffrey knew what he read in the *Queensland Times* and the *Courier Mail* but hearing about the fall of Java first hand was eye-opening to him, and he sat there shaking his head. 'It's a rotten time in the history of the world, son, that's for certain. We're lucky you made it through.'

He offered his guest a cigarette but John Drayton shook his head. 'No thanks, gave up when I married Lexi, she didn't like the smell of them.'

Jeffrey Bartlett being a mine-owner was a rich man by Queensland standards. He made instant judgements about people and was proud of the way he could size them up. He liked John Drayton and leant forward and touched him on the arm. 'I'm deeply sorry about your loss and to think that most of Marlene's family are gone. It's such an appalling thing. She'll take a long time to get over this.'

'Yes, sir, I'd imagine so.'

'I don't want to upset you more son, but what about Sir Brillard and Lady Helvetia? I gather they didn't get out of Hong Kong.'

The younger man had thought a lot about Sir Brillard in recent times. 'He wouldn't leave. Said as much to me the night of his ninetieth birthday. I'm positive he remained at Hydrangea even in the face of the Japanese invasion. That's the sort of man he was: an old lion who wouldn't run away. And that means only one thing: it was a bad ending for him and for his wife.'

'Oh hell.'

'Yes, *Oh hell*. Sir Brillard was a towering personality, a man to be reckoned with, and Helvetia . . .' John Drayton gave a sad smile. 'She was unique too.'

Jeffrey blew out a perfect smoke ring. 'You must stay the night here; in fact, knowing Marlene, she'll be wanting you to spend your leave here. Actually, that's a grand idea. We'd love to have you. After all, you're one of the family, and the way things are now . . .' He stopped short and his face wrinkled with sadness.

'Thanks, but I'm not sure, sir. I don't want to impose.'

'You won't be. In fact, it'll be the opposite. Now, stay here tonight and at least consider remaining with us for the duration of your leave.'

John Drayton knew the invitation was genuine, and the fact was, he rather liked the solid house with its wide verandas and the fiddlewood trees which grew in a straight row along the fence line and secluded it from the street. The park opposite was a tranquil place, and even the town itself was appealing. 'Thank you, sir.'

'Excellent.' Jeffrey liked John Drayton, thought the younger man a good type; had been drawn to him the minute he met him and he patted his shoulder as he sighed and rose to his feet. 'I'm going to pop inside and see if Marlene's asleep. I'm sure you won't mind a few minutes to yourself.'

John Drayton lifted grateful eyes to his host who moved along the veranda to a side door.

Left alone with the warmth of the day and his thoughts, John Drayton closed his eyes and leant back in the striped-canvas-covered chair, his brown hands grasping the wooden arms. He was picturing Lexine playing with Paul in their small exotic garden in Hong Kong. He saw the little boy crawl across the grass and heard the infant gurgles of pre-speech. Lexi was smiling and the day was fading . . . He pictured the night of Brillard's birthday party and saw Kathleen . . . lovely Kathleen who had been Lexi's friend, and his. He recalled the sound of her gentle voice on the telephone and the way she had cried at her mother's funeral. He felt sick. What had she said to him that night over the telephone? Something like: *I hope the good Lord watches over you and brings you through whatever's ahead.* He groaned and opened his eyes.

There before him, lounging against the veranda post, was a girl of about twenty in a tight green sweater. Her body was nicely rounded, even voluptuous; a Vivien Leigh face with a Betty Grable figure. Her eyes matched the colour of her sweater.

He sat up straight.

'What was the moaning about?' Her voice was far too brittle for her generous mouth.

He took a deep breath. 'I was remembering something.'

'Something awfully painful by the sound of it.'

He was about to ask who she was when she beat him to it. 'Who are you?'

'I'm John Drayton Whitby. And you?'

Her mouth opened in a dramatic 'O'. 'You aren't? Well I never! I felt I recognized you but how you've changed.' She gave a giggle. 'You obviously don't remember me.'

Abruptly Aunt Carly's deep voice carried along to them. 'There you are, Jane. We were wondering when you'd turn up. Lunch was over an hour ago. Not that anyone here ate much. We've had terrible news. Have you told her, John Drayton?'

The young man shook his head. He was looking hard at the girl in front of him. Jane . . . Lexi's little half-sister. The last time he had seen her she had been about fourteen, with pigtails and freckles, a flat chest and legs too long for her thin body!

Aunt Carly beckoned her. 'Come away from John Drayton. Leave him alone.' But the young woman stayed to enquire, 'What terrible news? What's happened?'

John Drayton stood up. 'Look, Jane, this is still hard for me to talk about, but . . . my wife – your sister Lexi – and our baby son were on a ship that was torpedoed by the Japs. They didn't survive and nor did a lot of your relatives.'

Jane's mouth trembled. 'Oh heck. Lexi? God!' Her eyes filled with tears. 'You poor thing. Who else was killed?'

Aunt Carly answered for him. 'Your Aunt Della and Uncle Peter, your cousin Greg and your uncle Jasper.'

John Drayton added to himself, 'And a good friend called Kathleen . . .'

Jane blinked; she was overcome by the number of dead. 'Oh dear, how's poor Mum?'

Aunt Carly shook her head. '*In extremis.* She's in her bedroom.'

Filled with sympathy, Jane put out her hand to John Drayton and stepped towards him, then quite suddenly she moved into his arms and hugged him. 'Oh, I'm so sorry, so terribly sorry.'

This action surprised Aunt Carly, but she supposed that after all it was understandable. Jane was young and demonstrative.

The girl began to cry quietly. 'How horrible for you,' she whispered against his tie and raised her damp eyes to his face.

Aunt Carly's large palm shot forward and gripped Jane's shoulder. 'Now come along. We're all upset.' She threw a glance to the soldier. 'I've given you the bedroom at the top of the stairs, first on the left. So any time you want to go up there, you can.'

Jane gazed at John Drayton and gave a small smile. 'Oh good.

I'm glad you're staying.' Then, with the brashness of immaturity, she added, 'Don't hold back. Talk to me about it whenever you like. I'll help you all I can.'

Aunt Carly looked skywards and led her away.

Chapter Forty

'Colonel? Colonel?'

Trap lifted his head from the grass mat where he sat eating a breakfast of bananas and melon and drinking coffee made from the last tin of the Javanese brew they had in the camp. The wide waters of Lake Lanao spread in his vision and the morning sun zigzagged through the tropical greenery on to his dark hair; his mind was far away in a grimy little place called Madura where he lay blissfully in the arms of an English girl.

The veil of memory lifted from his eyes. 'Yeah, Eduardo what is it?'

'Major Pugh on the wireless set.'

Trap had a bad feeling as he stood and followed Eduardo. This was not the usual day for communication. They never used the same frequency and did not speak long. So far they had avoided being tapped.

During his three weeks of reconnoitring parts of northern Mindanao, Trap had remained in touch with General Sharp's headquarters and with Johnny Pugh at the general headquarters on Corregidor. After MacArthur's departure General Wainwright had taken command of the Philippine military and naval forces and he now operated from 'the Rock'.

Johnny Pugh's dignified voice crackled over the line. 'Trap?'

'Yes, Johnny.'

'We've just learnt that General King over in Bataan is attempting to negotiate a peace for the peninsula with the Jap high command.'

'What's the old man got to say about that?'

'General Wainwright's instruction was "Do not surrender."'

'Then why did King . . .'

'He has no choice. His troops are starving and out of control; and now the Japs have taken to bombing the hospitals. Unbelievable. It's desperate over there. Two Corps are absolutely crippled and they're ignoring their officers and returning to the rear. Actually disbanding.'

'What about One Corps?'

'Still holding the line in the west. What about things with you?'

'Not good either. The Japs are on Cebu, but Brigadier Chynoweth is still holding out. Enemy pretty much all around, got a strong foothold in the south. I'm organising what future resistance I can, as fast as I can.'

The radio crackled with Johnny's voice again. 'One thing I do regret.'

'Yes?'

'MacArthur didn't tell the real truth about what was going on here. His reports to Washington were all rosy. He painted the Philippine army as invincible, when in the main it was raw, green and untrained. Not their fault, but a fact.'

'Yeah, the commander sometimes saw what he wanted to see.'

There was a strange silence, followed by Johnny Pugh coughing.

'You okay, Johnny?'

'Yes.'

Trap knew he wouldn't admit it if he weren't.

Pugh coughed again. 'History'll show that there was never a worse assignment than Wainwright's, but he'll continue to hold Corregidor and the harbour forts as long as he can. Oh, and to cap it all, we had an earthquake up here at midnight, like the blasted forces of nature are even giving up on us! Whole island shivered and shook.'

'Hope it shook the flamin' Nips.' Trap closed his eyes briefly as he tapped the receiver. 'Better finish, don't want the enemy to get a bearing ... Until next week, Johnny.'

'Roger. Good luck. Out.'

The radio went silent and Eduardo at Trap's side, hung his head and looked down at the palms of his hands. 'I guess we Filipinos just aren't cut out to be soldiers. We're tired, diseased and hungry, and getting killed. And the help promised us has never come ... and never will. We're all for it soon. There's no freakin' hope.'

'Don't be a flaming pessimist, Eduardo,' Trap spat. 'There are a lot of you guys who are top notch.' He slapped the man's arm. 'You just needed another couple of years to become a seasoned army. You were caught out by the Nips before your time. Look at Caldo and Evangelista and you, too, Eduardo. You're fine soldiers.'

The Filipino looked surprised at his inclusion. 'Well, we were trained by you after all, sir.'

Trap grinned broadly. 'Yes, that's true, son.' He pushed the soldier ahead of him. 'Now come on and we'll go back and finish that coffee. Can't afford to waste it.'

Trap strode confidently away to his lean-to, but he had to face it: Bataan was gone now. The boys he knew back there had been living on hope, and like a forlorn dying candle it had flickered out. His friend and mentor Jonathan Wainwright was in a dilemma few men had ever had to face. Wainwright, Pugh, Dooley, they were the best, the cream, and they were bereft of hope. With Bataan gone, the island of Corregidor was doomed.

He inhaled deeply and immediately wished he had not as the stench from the nearby swamp overcame him.

His part was to carry out his orders and then to report to General Sharp. There was an old saying, 'It never rains but it pours'; well, it was pouring here in the Philippines, pouring rotten Japs, and not a flamin' umbrella in sight.

* * *

305

Like Trap's metaphor, it was, in fact, pouring, in a typical tropical deluge, when some weeks later he presented Major General Sharp with a report on his activities to date. His preparations, recruitment and training, with the help of Caldo, Clevelly and Eduardo, had gone well.

He took the opportunity of being with the general to request medical supplies, stores and ammunition, and while Sharp could not afford to give him as much as he required, he had agreed to spare what he could.

William Sharp looked tired and worried. During much of the afternoon with Trap, reports kept coming in from all the fronts on Mindanao as he pored over a map of the southern Philippine Islands, a deep line permanently fixed between his eyes. He conferred with both Trap and Lieutenant Colonel Perry and fretted over the extent of the battle fronts his forces were required to cover. The need for reinforcements to hold Mindanao and the Visayans was vital, and they all knew the answer to that. Finally, as the dark, dank afternoon drew in and Trap moved to the door to depart, Major Paul Phillips entered and, saluting the commanding officer, announced, 'You wished to be reminded about Dr Robinson, sir.'

Sharp frowned, 'Yes, yes, thank you,' and turned to Trap. 'Now this situation with the woman . . .'

'What situation is that, sir?'

'Don't play games with me, Colonel. You know that I've had no orders of any kind about her. I've got to contend with two dozen nurses who've just been dumped on me. Evacuated here from Corregidor. God knows where I can send them.' He exhaled in a sigh.

Trap seized the opportunity. 'Couldn't Dr Robinson go with them, wherever it is?'

Momentarily the general closed his eyes in frustration and his voice hardened. 'They're army personnel, Trapperton. Now listen here. The only conversation of any kind I've ever had about Dr

306

Robinson was with Mrs MacArthur when the general and his party were leaving.'

'And what was it Mrs MacArthur said, sir?'

'That she was sorry Dr Robinson did not make it here, because her father or grandfather . . . or someone, had been a good friend of the general and she hoped that Dr Robinson would survive.'

'Can I make another suggestion, sir?'

Sharp's tone remained brittle. 'What is it, Colonel Trapperton?'

'That a message be sent to General MacArthur in Australia from your office informing him she's here and in your care.'

The general looked as if he might explode. 'I've told you before, she's nothing to do with me. Now I repeat, you and you alone are accountable for her welfare.' He searched in the papers on his desk and handed a memorandum to Trap. 'This gives you official charge of her. I've put it in writing and want no more of it. You take her with you when next you leave here.'

Trap's face clouded. 'Sir, I think you know what the enemy would do to a woman found with us, a unit of guerrilla fighters.'

General Sharp grunted. 'I do, but it's really out of my control. I told you my position on her before you left here the last time. Look, I'm aware you're important to people in High Command in Washington and I know about the submarine pick-up which will wait for you off these shores. You have the dates and the coordinates, haven't you?'

'Yes, I was given them in Corregidor.'

'Right, but I've had nothing official from MacArthur or any of his staff about the woman, so I'm instructing you to take her away and to include her in the exit party on the submarine when you leave.' He studied Trap for a few moments and grunted again. 'So I guess I can assume what High Command are assuming.'

'And what's that, sir?'

'That you won't get caught.'

Now Trap grunted.

Sharp shrugged. 'So you aren't enamoured with the situation,

Colonel, but I've got a host of my own pressing dilemmas.' He saluted, implying the interview was at an end, but Trap had one more thing to say. His voice now carried an edge.

'She's got a husband somewhere. He's in the AIF.'

Sharp paused in thought. 'In that case give Major Phillips his name and what you know about him and at some juncture we'll attempt to inform Australia she's with you. I make no promises. Meanwhile, goodbye, Colonel Trapperton, and good luck.'

The deluge continued as Trap strode out of the building and there, waiting under a grass-roofed shelter near the officers' mess, stood Williams and Caldo. He ran over, shook off the rain and growled, 'The old man is giving us what supplies he can spare, so get yourselves down to Ordnance and the quartermaster. But before you go, do either of you know where the female is?'

Both men knew what female that would be. Caldo shrugged and Williams answered, 'No, sir. Probably with that family she—'

Trap broke in. 'No probablies, soldier. One of you make tracks and damn well find out, and report immediately to me back here. I'll be inside nursing a glass of booze.'

He strode into the mess and 'Lady in Red' lifted from the gramophone in the corner near the bar.

'Goddam song,' he said aloud. 'Can't you play something else?'

An hour later, as the lamps glowed in the Baretta family's small wood and stucco house, Lexi sat beside the kitchen fireplace with Jimmy on her lap. The little boy had learnt some English words now and he often rattled off his entire vocabulary: *no, nana* for banana; *dink* for drink; *dark* and *soder* for soldier. He said one other word too, it was *Leky* and it was his name for her. Lexi had taught him to say it. She used to say Lexi to him and had laughed with delight the first time he used it, calling him 'such a smart little boy'.

He was playing with her hair and prattling to her, repeating Leky every now and then. Lexi realised that she treated Jimmy as if he were the reincarnation of Paul, but she saw no wrong in that. She liked to fancy that Kwan Yin, her beautiful Chinese bodhisattva, had given the children to her as her second chance. She kissed Jimmy's cheek lovingly as Mimi, the youngest daughter of the household, came running over the rattan-matted floor with Lessa behind her.

'Soder, soder,' Mimi called, pointing back through the house. *Soldier* was the one English word all the children knew.

Rain beat in staccato rhythm on the roof, yet through the flimsy walls Lexi could hear a man's raised voice and a shouted response from Danny Baretta, the owner of the house. Suddenly Jimmy jumped down from Lexi's lap and ran off, closely followed by Mimi and Lessa and the two older Baretta children. Jimmy's hoot of joy echoed back to the two women in the kitchen.

Lexi stood, swiftly straightening her skirt and pushing her hair back behind her ears. It was not unusual for the military to pass by and the children never ceased to be fascinated by them. But there was something curious in Jimmy's excitement which revealed the identity of this particular soldier to her.

She passed through the small rooms to the front of the house with Elvie, Danny's wife, close behind, and there, with the dark wet night as a backdrop, Jimmy danced in a little circle and Lessa clung to the legs of Hank Trapperton.

Danny was enthusiastically welcoming the colonel to his 'bahay' as Trap, uniform damp and cap dripping water, bent his long frame to pat Lessa's head, but she was not to be thwarted and she raised her hands high, begging to be lifted. He took some chocolate bars from his inside pocket and distributed them but Lessa continued tapping the side of his leg and holding up her arms in silent supplication until he gave in, and the little girl smiled with satisfaction as he raised her.

'Come in, please.' Danny Baretta ushered Trap past Lexi into the lamplit interior, where, because of the downpour, the rooms were blessedly free of insects.

Lexi observed the visitor. She had travelled five hundred miles through enemy-infested seas in his company on the PT boat, and watched as he used his skill and determination to fix the broken engine, hide them from the Japs, and bring them all through unscathed. She had witnessed the camaraderie with his six men and noted the care and thought he put into his actions. She had waited for one kind word or a sign from him that was not hostile, but none had come. He had not spoken a single word directly to her; it had always been through his men. At first she had been embarrassed, wondering what the men thought, but as time passed she became bolder and replied through them as if it were the normal way to communicate.

The only time he had even looked her in the eye that whole voyage was as they sailed into the harbour of Cagayan de Oro and then it had been merely to frown at her and to use the name of Jesus in vain.

Every day she relived the moment he had found her on the lonely road on Christmas Day. For those precious seconds he had acted as if he deeply cared. Without hesitation he had stepped forward and enveloped her and little Jimmy in a protective and tender embrace full of love. But since that day he had avoided physical contact, and when he lifted Lessa in his arms she hated herself for the pang of jealousy she felt.

He had not even said goodbye when he departed from here weeks ago. Instead he had sent Sergeant Caldo to inform her they were leaving on a mission and would be back in due course. When she had enquired of Caldo what that meant, he had tweaked his chin between his massive forefinger and thumb and blinked in thought. 'Well, I reckon it means we'll be back for you . . . when we can.'

'You mean I'm to wait here indefinitely with Jimmy and Lessa, not knowing when you'll return?'

'It's not like that, ma'am.'

'What is it like then, Sergeant?'

He shrugged. 'Aw, come on, Doc, don't make it hard for me. We'll be back for you, you can take my word for it. Over the last few months you and I have come to know each other. You've been through hell, I know that. And while the major . . . Ah that is . . . the colonel, treats you like you're poison . . . and maybe you are to him, I've got nothin' against you, ma'am. And the way you look after these two kids is real swell. You and Colonel Trapperton? Well, that's no business of mine, so let's just leave it at that.'

And now suddenly, on a doggedly wet night six weeks later it appeared that *due course* had arrived, for here in the cramped dwelling she shared with the Barettas stood the colonel holding Lessa in his arms. Finally he was facing her, looking straight at her, though the expression in his eyes was cold and remote.

He placed Lessa down and stroked her hair. 'Now run along, kids, I've got something to say to . . .' He gestured at Lexi.

Danny Baretta, taking the hint, beckoned to his wife, and as both adults herded the children from the room, Jimmy ran to Lexi's side. 'Leky, Leky,' he said and Lexi bent down and kissed him. 'Now you go with your sister and the others. I won't be long.' She tenderly pushed him to Elvie Baretta, who took him with a smile.

When they were alone, Trap stood stiffly in the middle of the floor for some seconds before he took off his cap, his black hair shining in the lamp glow. 'I've come to tell you we're leaving here the day after tomorrow.'

'We?'

'Yes. You, me, my men . . . *We.*'

'And what if I don't want to leave?'

He bit the side of his lip. It was an action of exasperation. 'Listen, Doll, you're my responsibility whether I like it or not. Top brass all seem hell bent on giving you to me, so don't make it harder than it is. I want you ready to leave here at sun-up on Wednesday.'

For a moment Lexi thought of her grandfather, imagined his

face and the strength in it, strength she believed she had inherited. 'I'm not going. You have no dominion over me. I don't care who says you have. Go away. The children and I will be all right.'

Trap flicked the droplets of water from the watch on his left wrist. He remained gazing down at it while a memory, painful, sweet and fragile, hovered briefly in his mind: this woman in the windy street of Hong Kong the day she had told him:

'I might never see you again. Yet I want desperately to see you all the time. Do you understand?'

That was the day she had told him her son was his and not Johnny's. That was the day he had wanted to take her, to love her and yet to kill her at the same time. Well, it seemed the poor bloody little innocent bastard who had belonged to both of them was dead. *Suffer the little children to come unto me.*

He drew his eyes from his watch, slowly, as if it were a physical effort to pull his head up to look at her again. Silently he regarded her as he straightened his shoulders in a deliberate action, the usual remoteness in his eyes replaced by the old anger.

She thought he was going to yell at her, but no, when he spoke his voice was steady, icy, yet his eyes still revealed his fury. He spoke as if she were one of his men, as if his instructions were not challengeable and while he talked his fists closed and opened like a boxer's might before he put on his gloves.

'This is the position, lady. We're surrounded by goddam Japs. This part of the Philippines is fighting back, but how long that can go on I've no idea. What you or I think about each other doesn't matter. I told you that once before and it hasn't altered. We're two little specks in the universal dust, Doll, so keep it all in perspective. General Sharp has told me unequivocally that he's not accountable for you and nor are any of his men. Hell, they're even going to send a blasted communiqué about you when they should be concentrating on battle strategies.'

He grunted in disgust. 'It's not what you want and it's not what

312

I want, but it's simple: be ready to go on Wednesday at dawn. Got it?

'Now those two kids you somehow managed to get in tow? Leave them here with the Barettas.' He pointed towards the door where the family had gone. 'They seem like nice people, I reckon they'll take them in. Where you're going is no place for kids.'

Lexi's jaw tightened. 'My God, it's all just simple to you, isn't it? You make assumptions and then hold them up as realities. You know so much about everybody! You think you can tell everyone what to do!'

Momentarily he cast her a long-suffering look. 'Don't try and analyse me, Doll, you'll swiftly get out of your depth.'

'I brought those children with me because they were orphans and because of the trauma they'd suffered.' Pink flooded her cheeks. 'I didn't abandon them then, so why would I abandon them now? MacArthur himself was going to take them to Australia, damn you.' Her eyes glinted and her voice had risen.

And now his anger subsided and he looked at her as if he spoke to a simpleton. 'Oh please. Listen, Doll, they were going to Australia in a B-17. Sure, they might have been shot out of the sky. Boom! Gone!' She flinched as he roared the last words. 'But they would have been gone in a wink. Where I'm going it's like another planet. We'll be crawling around in the jungle, scurrying from one hideout to another. Out in all sorts of weather and avoiding ambush and death. Kids don't have a place. Get it? They can get sick, bitten by something deadly or taken by the Japs. Be kind to them: leave . . . them . . . here!' He replaced his cap, strode to the interior door and called out to the Barettas, '*Salamat.*' As the family came flooding out, he moved with them to the veranda.

It was still raining, big solid drops, and as Trap gained the top of the steps Lessa pushed past her brother and ran out to him, arms raised. He paused and closed his eyes in frustration before he bent his knees and chucked the little girl beneath the chin. On straightening up he pointed his forefinger at Jimmy, gave a half-salute to the

Barettas and turned to Lexi who waited in the doorway, her gaze trained upon him. Abruptly, he gave her a nod and spun away, leaping down the four steps into the blackness and the rain, his words ringing back to her. 'Wednesday! I'll be here at dawn.'

The feeble grey glimmer of dawn kissed the streets and buildings of Cagayan de Oro when Trap appeared as promised at the Baretta bahay and mounted the steps to the veranda.

The door opened to reveal Lexi with the same cloth pack of clothes and goods she had taken from Corregidor.

Just for a moment he smiled inwardly. *Good, she's alone!*

He had taken a step forward, hand outstretched for her bag, when he glimpsed movement in the dimness of the doorway and a set of small feet appeared on either side of her.

'Jesus,' he exclaimed as Lessa ran to him and as usual beseeched him to lift her.

He ignored her as he took another step closer and jabbed the air in front of Lexi's face. 'Okay, Doll, I get it. But they're in your charge, just like you're in mine, understand?'

'I'm not in your charge!' Lexi bristled as he grabbed the bag from her and hoisted it over his shoulder. 'Once and for all, Hank Trapperton, I'm not in your charge.'

Bestowing an expression of pity upon her, he replied, 'Don't provoke me, Doll,' and his hand swept the air in a herding movement towards the children. 'Move, you two!' he growled, stomping over the veranda as the frail structure creaked under his weight.

Into the delicate glow of breaking day the little party of three hurried behind him as, with his gaze on the heavens, Hank Trapperton led them away.

Chapter Forty-one

Brisbane, 22 July 1942

General Douglas MacArthur, Commander-in-Chief of SWPA — the South-Western Pacific Area — set up in April 1942 and embracing Australia, New Guinea, the Bismark Archipelago, the Philippines and the Dutch East Indies, exclusive of Sumatra, stubbed out his cigar and drew his fingers over his high forehead where his hair, though still a healthy dark hue, receded. He tapped his cranium in thought, stood and crossed the shining parquet flooring to the first of the three tall windows which gave him a view of the city from the 8th floor of the AMP — the Australian Mutual and Provident Society Building — on the corner of Queen and Edward Streets. This was his brand-new GHQ. The majority of the shopfronts he looked down upon were partially concealed by sandbags, and the lack of vehicular traffic indicated the petrol rationing.

The city of Brisbane was a comfortable, attractive city of just over 300,000 clinging to the banks of the Brisbane River discovered by the English explorer John Oxley a hundred and nineteen years earlier. Douglas MacArthur liked it. From the sky with its straggling suburbs he thought it could have been mistaken for an American midwest city.

He was not animated by a knocking on the glass-panelled door behind him which led to the hall outside and General Sutherland's office directly opposite. He remained at the window until his chief of staff, who had escaped from the Philippines with him, opened the door and spoke. 'Douglas, there's a wireless message just in from Blamey.' General Thomas Blamey had been named commander-in-chief of the Australian Land Forces on 5 March; a controversial choice of a man who came with a chequered past and who had been widely disliked when he'd been the state of Victoria's police commissoner.

MacArthur turned and eyed his senior aide as the urbane and saturnine Sutherland; clever, haughty, many said *arrogant*, but always reliable, proffered the communiqué. 'It seems there's been a small enemy landing at Buna on the northern shores of Papua in eastern New Guinea.'

MacArthur grunted with exasperation as he took the message and read. 'Buna? Buna? Weren't we planning to extend the airfield there?'

'Yes, but it won't happen now. It appears Blamey's officers in New Guinea have some notion the Jap intention could be to push across the Owen Stanley range of mountains and attempt to take Port Moresby.'[1]

MacArthur read on. 'Well, Blamey doesn't give much importance to the landing in this message. Says it's perhaps one or two thousand enemy troops.'

Sutherland walked to the wall map. His uniform was immaculate, as was his companion's; as were the American uniforms right down the ranks. In fact the Australian soldiers in their heavy unattractive serge uniforms did not cut such appealing figures as their American partners. Sutherland pointed to the minute settlement of Buna. 'The airfield will be what the Japs are after.'

MacArthur was irritated. 'We should have realised when the enemy landed in Lae and Salamaua that this would happen. Get hold of Willoughby and Marshall, let's see what they think.'

An hour later the commander sat tapping the toe of his gleaming shoe, surrounded by members of his personal staff.

Beside him was General Charles Andrew Willoughby,[2] his Head of Intelligence, who had also escaped with him. Mystery surrounded this man's early years and he claimed to have had an American mother and a German Baron for a father.

It had been suggested in certain quarters that he was hardly competent but that he flattered MacArthur and so retained his position. Nevertheless, in this hastily called meeting he held an opinion. 'We in Intelligence are firmly of the conviction that this new landing at Buna is a minor force and that the enemy intend to establish an air base there.'

Brigadier General Richard Jaquelin Marshall, who had also escaped from Corregidor with the leader, asked MacArthur, 'If I might use your wall map, Commander?'

'Sure.'

'Major General Morris in Port Moresby seems worried about this.' He rapped the Owen Stanley mountain range with a white pointer. 'There's a sort of trail across here that goes up the mountains and over to a little spot called Kokoda. It's the middle of nowhere, as they say here, but there's flat land somewhere because there's an airfield, and this trail leads on from Kokoda; north to Buna and south to Port Moresby. It's meant to be pretty bad, almost impassable in places; it's a hundred miles of dense tropical rainforest, precipitous ravines, mountains, rivers, swamps and mud slides.'

MacArthur knew the place. 'Kokoda, yes, the Australian Thirty-ninth Militia Battalion should be there now.'

'Absolutely, General.' Marshall agreed, touching Port Moresby with the pointer. 'To be clear here, Morris's suggestion is that the Japs might use this trail to get overland from north to south to take the military base at Port Moresby, but it'd be tough going.'

Willoughby made a scoffing sound, lifting a monocle which had been hanging round his neck on a satin ribbon and appearing to study New Guinea. 'Those mountains are thirteen thousand feet high! Certainly a few militia might traverse it, but an army? I don't think so.'

MacArthur looked sceptically around his gathered staff as Colonel Roberts, the controller of the recently formed Australian Intelligence Bureau, broke in: 'I understand what you're saying, but the trail goes up and through a pass at around six thousand feet. It's feasible the Japs could be thinking of crossing it, difficult as it is.'

MacArthur raised his corncob pipe and Sutherland handed him a Zippo lighter. He puffed smoke into the air while his staff continued to put their points of view. Finally the fact that Willoughby and Sutherland, who often violently disagreed, both held this same opinion appeared at least to intrigue, if not re-assure, their leader, for MacArthur stood and, giving a typical flourish of his hand, proclaimed, 'All right.'

He began pacing back and forth in front of the wall map with dramatic steps. 'Wars are not won by being defensive. I face strategic challenges everywhere. I must be offensive. I need to mull this over.'[3]

Abruptly he halted and looked down his patrician nose. 'There's no point in sending any more troops to New Guinea for the present.' And waving his hand in another exaggerated gesture, he announced the meeting was over.

One week later Douglas MacArthur was angry. His face was florid as he paced again in front of Willoughby, Marshall and Sutherland. 'So the Japs didn't stay in Buna at all. They're pushing the Australians out of Kokoda. Right?'

'Well . . . yes, that's the latest we're to understand.'

MacArthur growled, 'Do we know current enemy numbers?'

Willougby's permanent frown deepened. 'Latest intelligence says perhaps five thousand have now landed near Buna and Gona, with more troop ships coming in.'

A westerly wind rushing down Queen Street from Victoria Bridge on the river rattled the windows as MacArthur waved his hands and halted in front of New Guinea on the wall map. 'Goddam it, so now we get a sense of what they're up to. None of you, including Blamey, gave this the attention it deserved. The Australians are falling back to Deniki to join some of the Thirty-ninth Battalion, and to cap it off I just heard that Owen's been killed.' Lieutenant Colonel William Owen was the Australian commander of the small garrison which had gone over the mountains from Port Moresby to the village of Kokoda.

Richard Sutherland looked unhappy. 'Yes, I'm sorry, Douglas. But look, we know there's a sort of an airfield at Kokoda. It might still be as we thought, that airfields are the enemy quarry.'

MacArthur paused and stared at his chief of staff. 'Nevertheless, we should be reinforcing the area. Whom can we send?'

Marshall answered. 'We'll need to speak to Blamey. I'd guess the Seventh AIF.'

'Well for God's sake let's get them moving. They won't be there for weeks even if they leave this minute.'

At this they stood and headed to the door as MacArthur announced, 'This loud-talking Australian politician Billy Hughes is criticising Prime Minister Curtin and his cabinet for not anticipating the enemy's movements. Now that's indirectly criticising *me*.'

'Take no notice of it, Douglas,' Sutherland replied, pausing as the other men departed. 'Your arrival in Australia in March has been the single most effective boost to the flagging Australian morale since the Japs entered the war. The average Australian reveres you. Remember that. No damage can be done to your image, you're too big.'

MacArthur bestowed a most appreciative smile upon Sutherland's back as the door clicked closed, and walking to the mirror hanging over a bureau on the far wall he struck a pose and eyed his reflection.

Suddenly the door reopened and MacArthur spun round to see whomever would dare to enter without knocking. The look faded at the cry of 'Papa!' and the four-star general opened his arms to his son, who ran across the carpet to him. MacArthur lifted little Arthur high in his arms. 'How's my boy?'

He bent to allow his tiny wife to kiss him. 'Hello, dearest. What a pleasant surprise to be visited by you two.'

'Yes, we're going for a walk in the Botanical Gardens and we *popped in* to see you, as they say here.'

The leader placed his son down and Arthur went immediately to the bureau with the mirror above and took down his father's gold-braided cap and put it on. The general appeared amused and eyed his two loved ones tenderly.

'Tea?' the little one asked. Since his arrival in Australia he had become fond of drinking tea.

MacArthur hated to deny Arthur anything but he did not have time to indulge his son today. He shook his head and Jean relieved the child of the cap. 'Now, darling, we must leave Daddy: he's very busy. We'll have tea together later.'

She stood on tiptoe and kissed her husband's cheek, saying gently, 'Bye bye *Father of the Year.*'

On 21 June he had been the first recipient of the 'Father of the Year' award from the American National Father's Day Council. He smiled and his gaze lingered tenderly upon his son as Arthur turned his head to call, 'Come home early, Papa.'

Left alone, he felt tired and his eyes strayed to the folded newspaper on his desk and the article, 'Lennons Hotel turned upside down for Supreme Commander of South West Pacific.'

Well, he had to admit, the headline was probably true but there was a war going on, after all, and in his position he had many needs to be accommodated. He, Jean, Arthur, Ah Cheu and his doctor were living on the fourth floor of Lennons' Hotel in George Street, the best that Brisbane had to offer. His staff were spread throughout the other floors. For a few moments he wondered what it would be like to live with his family in a real house with a garden and a fence.

320

The abrupt ringing of the telephone at his side brought him out of his reverie to hear that General Thomas Blamey had just arrived downstairs.

The shorter, stouter Blamey stomped into MacArthur's office and as MacArthur had foreseen, the topic under discussion was New Guinea and the battle going on at Kokoda. They both remained hopeful that the push by the Japanese as far as Kokoda was a feint, but they agreed to send General Sydney Rowell and the headquarters of the 1st Australian Corps, along with the 21st Brigade of the 7th AIF Division to Port Moresby forthwith. At the same time the 18th Brigade of the 7th Division would join the militia at Milne Bay on the eastern tip of New Guinea under the command of Major General Cyril Clowes.

Blamey left with the words, 'I remain confident that the Japs don't intend to advance further along this Kokoda trail. They'll get ahead of their supply lines if they do.'

No sooner had Blamey gone than the new commander of the air force, arrived.

The door swung back and in walked a stocky 5'6" New Englander who had had arrived at Amberley Aerodrome the prior evening after a long flight from San Fancisco via Hawaii, Canton Island, Fiji and New Caledonia. MacArthur rose from behind his desk and held out his hand. He had met Major General George Churchill Kenney twice before. 'George, I'm glad to see you, sit down. I've a lot to tell you about the disloyalty and shortcomings of the air force.'

Kenney took a deep calming breath. He had already heard a great deal on that very subject from Richard Sutherland who had given him a litany of complaints which Kenney had taken with equanimity, for he knew Sutherland of old from the days when they were classmates at Army War College in Washington.

General Kenney sat, giving no outward sign of being ruffled by this somewhat inflammatory opening statement from Douglas MacArthur.

Half an hour later Kenney had heard the commander's accusations and decided to reply forthrightly. 'General MacArthur, I flew seventy-five missions in the Great War and I know how to run an air force as well as, or better than, anyone else. If there are things wrong with the show here, I'll correct them. There will never be any question of my loyalty to you and I will demand the same of everyone under me. I've already got committments for the swift delivery of fifty 'F' model P-38s and three thousand fragmentation bombs[4] from War Reserve.'

Finally, as George Churchill Kenney rose to leave, he informed the commander, 'I'm flying up to New Guinea tonight. I need to see first-hand what to do up there.'

'You know, George, I felt tired before you came in here.' MacArthur was quickly sensing that he had indeed found the right man to rejuvenate his flawed air force. He surprised Kenney by striding over to him and placing his arm around his shoulders. 'But I don't now. I think we are going to get along together all right. As soon as you get back, do come and see me and we'll talk again.'

As the air force general left, MacArthur took out a Lucky Strike cigarette from a crystal container and lit it with the inevitable Zippo lighter. His voice was bright when he lifted the black bakelite receiver of the telephone. 'Get me that girl in the WAAF, the one who takes fast shorthand and types at a hundred and twenty words a minute.'

That night the scrambler phone in the stuffy basement of the GHQ building was in use.

'Prime Minister?'

'Yes, General MacArthur.'

'I'm a little worried about the situation in New Guinea. I feel it's possible we could be forced into such a defensive concentration that it could duplicate the conditions of Malaya. That is, if the enemy push further along this Kokoda trail.'

This was not what John Curtin wished to hear, for the Malayan campaign had ended in disaster for the Allies with the whole peninsula and Singapore in enemy hands.

MacArthur went on: 'We've also got to put an end to the rumours that the American servicemen are taking it easy here in Australia while the Australians do all the fighting.'

The Prime Minister cleared his throat. 'Really? Well, General, why don't you send some more Americans to New Guinea? That'll help.'

MacArthur stopped himself from retorting with an inflammatory reply. Hence his voice remained sober. 'I intend to do that as soon as I can, Prime Minister, but for now Blamey says he can spare your Seventh Division AIF who were blooded in North Africa. With your permission we'll get them shipped off immediately.'

'Yes, Blamey's already spoken to me about it.'

'We're all agreed on that, then?'

'Yes, General MacArthur, we are. Is that all?'

'Yes, Mr Curtin, for now. Good night.'

Douglas MacArthur returned in the lift to the eighth floor.

What a day of pressures it had been. But that was war! At least Kenney seemed to know what he was doing. At last he might get some air support to fight the enemy. The Japs were a hard foe; they fought tenaciously and fanatically.

He walked down the corridor and into his office recalling his son's words, 'Come home early, Papa.' Well, he would be late again, but the lovely Jean would be there to greet him.

He was sixty-two and still utterly confident of his military ability. Yesterday he had learnt a strange thing, his birthday was the same day as the birthday of this nation, the 26th of January. Arthur Phillip, the first Governor of Australia, had proclaimed it a colony on that day 154 years previously. Now that was not just coincidence. That particular fact was significant. For this was where he found himself: mounting the fight-back from Australia!

The heels of his shoes clicked on the parquet wood pattern beneath him as he took a final look at the wall map with its yellow markings for enemy-controlled territory. He studied it, lifting his eyes to the Philippines. A long, uncomfortable sigh racked him as he stared at the peninsula of Bataan, and a moment of unaccustomed self-consciousness ensued. He blinked uneasily, his eyes fixed, for he had imagined Jonathan Wainwright and remembered the fall of Bataan and Corregidor. This was what his nightmares were about; this was what haunted him! He wondered what it was like for Jonathan and the others over there: prisoners of the Japs.

Chapter Forty-two

The steamy heat rose from the damp ground beneath Skinny Wainwright's feet as he shuffled by Johnny Pugh and Brigadier General Clifford Bluemel, out past the feeble fence of the Tarlac Cemetery, half a mile north-west of the prison camp. The guard shouted to move them with as much speed as the starving men could manage.

The close of day was imminent, and as the burial party wended its way back, the shadows disappeared and the brief dusk developed to encircle them. They had just buried another of their comrades, who had caught a stomach infection and, suffering from lack of any medical care, had gradually worsened until, coupled with dysentery, he died.

'Have you still got paper?' Skinny enquired of Johnny, who returned to his side on the journey back to camp.

His aide knew why the general asked. He had drawn maps of all the burial places of the others who had died here in recent times. It was done in the hope that one day he could deliver the sketches of the sites to the families of the dead soldiers.

'Yes.' Johnny nodded. 'A couple of small pieces, and we can use the frontispiece or title page from one of the remaining books if need be.'

'Right, but don't tear up *Oliver Wiswell*, reading that is keeping me sane.'

325

Oliver Wiswell by Kenneth Roberts had been published two years earlier. It was a rare sympathetic view of the Loyalist side of the American War of Independence. General Wainwright who was a student of the Civil War and American History was losing himself in the life of the Yale student who sided with the British in this vivid and accurate work of historical fiction.

Pugh produced a smile on his thin, but still handsome, face. 'Yes, sure, I'll keep that book intact.'

As the motley group approached the gate of the prison camp, the stench of unwashed bodies and sweat from the hundreds of ill and emaciated men met their nostils. Skinny's gaze roved to the Japanese guards, rifles at the ready, watching from vantage points on rocks and higher ground. They had been prisoners of the Japanese since 6 May, 89 days, but it seemed like a lifetime: an accursed lifetime.

With a sigh he recalled the months prior: he thought of April and the continuous Japanese bombardment of Corregidor, the noise unrelenting, on and on. How the guns on Corregidor were systematically knocked out by the barrages and how the constantly damaged power plants needed daily repair. The majority of the motor transport on the island ended up as heaps of blasted metal, and those few which remained able to be driven became unusable because of the shell-holed roads. Casualties mounted and men and women continued to die.

Skinny rubbed his left ear as they passed the barbed-wire fences and entered the gate to the camp. His eardrum had been burst by the nearby explosion of a 240mm Jap shell on Corregidor on 28 April, and the same blast had impaired the hearing in his right ear.

The following day, 29 April, the enemy Emperor Hirohito's birthday, Corregidor underwent its hundredth bombardment since General King and the boys on Bataan had capitulated to the Japs. On that day the air and land gun barrage had been even more intense, lasting hour after hour, while the beleaguered defenders attempted to fight back. He would never forget the eerie moment the pounding ceased that day, the unnatural stillness under the drifting acrid fumes encompassing the island in a thick ashen blanket; the weary face of Johnny Pugh, helmet askew, looking round to him, hope ever lighting his eyes as he reminded him, 'Sir? The flying boats to evacuate the nurses and bring in the supplies are supposed to land at twenty-three hundred tonight.'

And land they had, in a spot on the water where two of the few remaining United States minesweepers had removed the mines between Corregidor and the small Manila Bay isle of Fort Hughes. Much-needed medical supplies and anti-aircraft fuses had been brought in and thirty-two nurses and sixteen officers had been airlifted out to Mindanao.

Yet that was all cold comfort, because by 4 May the battering had reached a record intensity. From 0700 to noon there was an all-time high for shelling: 500lbs of 240mm shells hit Corregidor every 5 seconds using 1,800,000lbs. The island was a graveyard. Skinny would never forget 2315 on 5 May when a continuous stream of the enemy: 2,000 in the first wave and 10,000 in the second, began their invasion of the island. The next day, 6 May, saw the capitulation of Corregidor. Mindanao and the Visayans followed, and by 9 June, all of the Philippines were in Japanese hands.

The general's dismal thoughts were broken into by Johnny Pugh's voice as they came to a halt inside the camp. 'I'll go and get that paper and piece of lead pencil for you.' Jonathan Wainwright watched his aide walk away across the dirt and mud. Johnny Pugh was an exceptionally brave man and had refused to leave Skinny's side, even though he had been given the opportunity to go. When the enemy had continued shelling Corregidor hours after the white flag had been hoisted, Johnny had returned to Malinta Tunnel through a massive bombardment to ensure that he, Wainwright, took some personal effects into captivity with him.

Yet there were so many brave men. Skinny was looking at them now as they lined up for the evening meal of a meagre bowl of foul-tasting grey rice. These had survived thus far when so many had died of maltreatment.

The general's reflections were mostly gloomy these days, and as he moved across to join the line he thought of the Bataan death march. He had learnt of this forced march of prisoners only after he had become a prisoner himself. In April, after Bataan fell and before Corregidor faced the same fate, seventy-six thousand Filipino and American prisoners of war, mostly without food or water and devoid of medical supplies, had been made to walk from Marivales, on the southern end of the Bataan peninsula, to San Fernando, fifty-five miles away. In the burning sun many of the prisoners faltered and grew delirious, and when they fell from exhaustion they were beaten to death or bayoneted. Some were forced to dig their own graves and some were even buried while still alive. Twenty thousand prisoners had died on that march, and thinking of it now Skinny closed his eyes.

He swallowed in bitterness: he could taste it. Why oh why had he ordered his men to surrender? A swift death with a bullet would have been preferable to the brutality which had followed. Ah, hindsight! He now believed he should have developed a guerrilla-based defence and severed the local commanders from his own mandate, allowing them to fight on, to take the chance of finding some dignity in a soldier's death . . . instead of like this! He sighed once more as he examined the faces nearest him, Brigadier General Lewis Beebe, Major General George Moore, Brigadier General William Brougher, all pathetic prisoners, and beyond them the silhouettes of once proud soldiers in the long, trailing line waiting for the tasteless rice and the possibility of an ounce of pork thrown in.

Skinny's eyes lifted to the gathering night beyond the barbed wire. He knew his soldiers did not blame him. Some had even said as much and he thanked God that they felt this way. He could not have borne the indignity of being a Japanese prisoner if they had held him responsible for their plight.

'Wainwright!' His name was called which sounded like: 'Rainrite!'

He shook himself out of his bleak thoughts to see a Japanese NCO waving at him. 'Come!'

It was Sergeant Fukuhara, an apprentice sadist whose name caused endless wisecracks amongst the prisoners. The man did not like to be kept waiting.

As skinny crossed to Fukuhara, he spied Johnny Pugh advancing across the yard and held up his hand for his aide to await his return.

The general saluted as he reached Fukuhara. All prisoners wearing headcovering, as Skinny currently was, with a cap, were required to salute all passing Japanese soldiers regardless of rank. And all hatless prisoners were required to bow to all Japanese soldiers regardless of rank. Strict disciplinary action was taken if this order were ignored.

General Wainwright rankled under this rule. He forced himself to contain his fury when he had to salute or bow. The first time he had been made to do so he had felt physically sick but he was now long past that sensation.

Fukuhara ignored the salute and asked, 'Are you Rainrite?' The Japanese NCO knew him well, but this perpetual game had to be played.

'Yes.'

'Forrow me.' And he strode away in haste past William Brougher's vegetable patch. Somehow that general had secured a few seeds and now the first tiny shoots of sweet potatoes, tomatoes and melon thrust their way above the sunbaked ground; it would be a miracle if they survived. Passing down a slope, the fumes from the latrines overwhelmed them.

Skinny knew the destination: the administration building, a long concrete block where he also knew the routine: he would be questioned again. Previous to being brought to Tarlac, he had been held in Manila, and there interrogation had been a daily occurrence, but here a blessed two and sometimes three days would pass between sessions. As they came into the interview room, Skinny was relieved to see, revealed in the sallow light thrown from a single light bulb, Lieutenant Koto. This young man was one of the kinder officers and occasionally handed out Lucky Strike cigarettes.

Skinny knew he could dare to be bold with Koto. When Fukuhara left and Koto motioned for him to sit, the general did not move. 'I have been brought here when the rice is about to be distributed. I will not receive my ration if I am here with you.'

'I will not keep you long if you answer my questions.'

'I don't believe you. I will lose my ration of rice if I stay here. I must go back to the line.'

'You will answer my questions.'

'I must go back to the line.'

Koto looked uncomfortable and after some internal deliberation crossed to a shelf and took down two tired-looking bananas and a can of milk and handed them to Skinny with the words, 'You can have these. Now you must sit and answer my questions.'

This was a coup. Skinny took them and sat.

'General, you still have not told us where you buried the silver currency or the paper money.'

The Japanese officer was referring to $140 million of Philippine monetary notes and $15 million in highly negotiable silver which General Wainwright had held on Corregidor. The gold reserve of the Philippines had been shipped to the United States not long after the attack on Pearl Harbor, but the silver and paper money had remained on the Rock.

Skinny shook his head. 'I've told you before, I've told every one of you who have questioned me, endlessly. The entire amount of government paper money was destroyed.'

'How?'

'I've told you over and over. We burnt it.'

'That's a lie. It is buried on Bataan. Tell me where.'

'It is not buried on Bataan.'

330

As Skinny parried the same old questions, the picture of Johnny and Tom Dooley executing MacArthur's orders filled his mind. They had sat at their desks night after night in the tunnel and copied the serial numbers of the bank notes. Once the mammoth task was completed, they radioed the list to the Treasury Department in Washington before cutting up and burning the money and destroying the list.

'Where did you bury the silver, then?'

'I do not know. I have never known.'

'But there was silver?'

'You say there was.'

'Where is the silver buried?'

'I don't know.'

The silver had been placed in strong wooden boxes, and on three successive nights barges had carried the boxes out into Manila Bay to a precisely surveyed position between Corregidor and Fort Hughes and dropped them overboard.

'You must tell me where the silver is.'

'I don't know. I have never known.'

'But we are sure there was silver and we are sure it was buried? Is it in Manila Bay?'

And for the thousandth time Skinny answered, 'I don't know.'

He was aware that there were prisoners far worse off than those here. Camp O'Donnell, a prison camp not far away, was known as 'the offspring of hell'. They had learnt that treatment of prisoners there was bestial and the deaths mounted. By comparison Tarlac was mild. Even though discipline was still severe, and men died from lack of food and care, like Carter they had buried today, there was the rare man like Lieutenant Koto who appeared to have a soul.

The sky was completely dark outside the window as the interview went on, exactly as it always did: the questions and statements from the Japanese officer and the denials from Skinny Wainwright.

Finally, Koto leant on his desk and stated as he always did about this time in the interview, 'You know you are our enemy and we will fight you and fight you – for a hundred years!'

Skinny had noticed time and time again the block in the consciousness of the enemy: they *could not* consider losing. It seemed to Skinny that they could conceive of no defeat for Japan; there might be setbacks in the war, but not defeat.

Suddenly Koto changed tack. 'What do you think of the calibre of Japanese troops?'

'What?'

'What do you think of the calibre of Japanese troops?'

Skinny could not cover a smile.

'What is funny?'

'Your question. What do you care what I think?'

'Answer the question.'

This was an unusual diversion. 'Well . . . Your higher command and senior staff officers are efficient, tenacious of purpose and possess a high degree of military education.'

This appeared to appease Koto and he wrote it down in what looked like a Western exercise book before he raised his head. 'And what about subordinate officers and soldiers?'

Skinny took a deep breath. 'Ah, they seem physically fit.'

'What else?'

'Well trained.'

Koto smiled. 'What else?'

'Not very good rifle shots.'

Koto's smile faded. 'You think that?'

'Yes. In fact, I'm pleased about it; a number of my men are still alive because of it.'

Koto blinked as if taking in the import of the words, but he did not write that particular piece of intelligence down. 'What else?'

'They appear vigorous, brave . . . Brave to a point that verges on fanaticism.'

This the lieutenant wrote down.

332

'What about our guns and equipment?'

'What about them?'

'What is your opinion of them?'

Skinny shook his head. 'By our standards most of your equipment looks crude. Your infantry rifle is too long, too small in calibre and too slow in action.'

Instead of the expected affront, Koto sat up with a frown of interest between his eyes. 'This is your viewpoint?'

'Yes, it is.'

Koto nodded and to Skinny's surprise recorded it, writing swiftly.

Skinny was warming to this line of questioning and he expanded: 'Even though I would throw out a lot of what you use, some of your equipment is doubtlessly efficient and you appear to be well provided with military supplies.'

As Koto lifted his pen the door opened and a corporal entered. After a short discussion Koto glanced to Wainwright and flicked his fingers at the door.

Skinny knew what this meant and he did not need urging. Clutching his bananas and tin of milk, the general of the United States Army exited the interview room into the wan electric light of the compound.

It was late that night, as insects buzzed around them and the night odours and noises from 180 men beset them, that Skinny sat on the barracks floor in the darkness talking softly with Johnny Pugh and Tom Dooley.

'That was an odd interrogation I had today. Koto asked me what I thought of the Jap army.'

Tom whispered, 'Good heavens. Why?'

'No idea.'

'Did you tell him?'

'Well, certain things. I attempted to remain mostly diplomatic.'

They all laughed quietly at that and Skinny added, 'He wrote ninety per cent of it down as if making out a report.'

Johnny had a point of view. 'Perhaps he's been asked to write a dispatch and thought he'd get a new, innovative attitude to put forward.'

'Could be.'

They laughed again, and as they fell silent Johnny Pugh sighed. 'You know, I often wonder what happened to Trapperton down in Mindanao.'

Skinny thought of the son of his old buddy from the Great War and spoke in a weary tone. 'I have to suppose he surrendered . . . or was killed.'

Johnny looked sceptical. 'The last time I spoke with him he was waging his own little guerrilla war with a few of the Twenty-sixth Cavalry and a couple of Philippine Scouts and local peasants, even though he had that woman from Hong Kong and two kids with him.'

'Weren't they meant to be airlifted out to Australia with General MacArthur?' asked Tom, hitting out at the insects that remained in unremitting attack.

Johnny nodded. 'Mmm, but they didn't reach Cagayan de Ore on time. Trap was out organising resistance the last time we spoke.'

Skinny grunted in thought. 'Well, Trap isn't someone who'd just roll over, but he would have had no choice when my general directive to capitulate came through.'

'I'm not sure about that, sir.' Johnny Pugh lifted his finger to underscore his reasoning. 'He was really answerable to Washington, wasn't he?'

'Now that's true.'

Johnny bent in to the others and whispered adamantly, 'Somehow I don't believe he surrendered.'

For the first time in weeks Skinny felt heartened. 'You know what? You might be right. And there was a submarine going to pick him up, wasn't there?'

'Yes, that's right. I believe . . .' The young major did a quick calculation, 'that was to be sometime soon. Sure, sir, Trapperton will still be free . . . and he'll come back here to liberate the goddam place, mark my words. They wouldn't have caught Trap! I'll bet on it.'

Skinny touched the damp cement of the floor beneath his hand as he looked around in the darkness at the cramped bunks and the outlines of the starving prisoners upon them, many of them without even a single blanket. Insects flittered constantly about them and spiders and cockroaches shared the walls and ceilings. It was a desperate landscape. Yet hearing Johnny's optimism and thinking of Trap, his tone brightened. 'Sure, Johnny, I reckon you're right. Yes I do.'

Chapter Forty-three

Trap sniffed. There was a noxious smell on the steamy wind again. The strong breeze carried an aroma across from the mangrove swamp nearby which grabbed at the nostrils and made them twitch. He spontaneously wiped his nose with the back of his fingers and looked over at Lieutenant Jake Williams sitting near him on the sand.

Williams grunted. 'Our numbers are still dropping.'

The constant reprisals against the relatives of the Filipinos made it difficult to raise and keep numbers; these days there were few new recruits. Whole families, men, women and children, had been rounded up and shot, and after the final attack on a supply convoy, twenty-one of his men had deserted in a single night.

'We can't blame them: terror is this world's foremost manner of persuasion. A lot of the locals are brave men but they can't stand by and see those they care for suffer so badly.'

'Yeah, I know, but Zotie says there's a guy called Fertig over on the other side of the island who's starting to rally men to him.' Zotie was their trusted Filipino guide, an ex-schoolteacher whose geographical knowledge of Mindanao was exceptional.

'Really?'

'Yes. Apparently he was an engineer working here when the Nips invaded. He was in the army reserve or something and now he's dubbed himself colonel.'

Trap grinned. 'I guess *Engineer*, doesn't have the same ring to it.

Anyway, good luck to him.' He considered a moment, then added, 'If I knew we were remaining here I'd make contact with him. But our orders are to get out on the sub.'

He looked up as he spoke and saw the Doll coming towards him from the next cave. He deliberately turned his head away: he did not need to see the rhythm of her legs beneath the men's trousers she wore and the tilt of her head as her body swung.

She had taken to wearing men's pants for ease of movement in this strange life they now lived; not that he cared what she wore. Oh, she was useful, he admitted that. Being a doctor, she actually made a big difference when men were wounded, and her expertise in swiftly removing bullets had given life to some who would be in the next world without her. They all called her 'Doc' as an affectionate term, though of course he did not; he tried to call her nothing.

Their medical supplies had dwindled and hence her healing skills were greatly diminished. It was a strange thing, but the flaming Jap bullets seemed to set a poison going in a man no matter where he was hit, and even a wound in an extremity had in recent times, without drugs, resulted in death.

He lifted his eyes up to the bunching clouds above. It rained most afternoons and today appeared no different. They must move on from this camp tonight. They could not stay in any one place too long. There were always informers who would reveal their whereabouts to the Japs, so they moved at night to new locations found by Zotie. He had made the difference between freedom and capture.

Yet the children were the least affected. They seemed almost normal, though the girl Lessa remained mute. They drew pictures with pencils and paper in the interior of the sea cave. Jimmy scribbled but Lessa's attempts at drawings could occasionally be deciphered. Trap had been furious when the Doll insisted on bringing the kids along, but even though he hated to concede it, she handled them with care and authority. She carried Jimmy in

337

a knapsack on her back and at times simply half lifted, half dragged Lessa along. It was as if the woman had resolved that she would be one hundred per cent accountable for them, refusing any help. She urged them along overgrown jungle tracks and hefted them in and out of vehicles, over fallen trees and across streams.

Trap could see in her face how tired and worn she was, but she never once let the kids know and spiritedly watched over them.

The weeks had passed and there had never been any good news. They had been in one of the hideouts in the hills of north-eastern Mindanao when General Wainwright had finally capitulated in May.

The coded message to Trap had told the story to him in patent particulars.

It had come from General Sharp:

I have been ordered to surrender all my Visayan-Mindanao United States and Philippine Forces by order of Major General Wainwright, the Commander-in-Chief of the Philippines. If I do not comply all garrisons and Harbor Forts in Manila Bay including Corregidor will be destroyed by Japanese aerial and artillery bombardment. This would result in the summary murder of thousands of men and women and in all conscience I cannot continue to resist under such circumstances. I intend to surrender forthwith. All organised resistance on these islands will henceforth end immediately. Officially I have no records of you or your unit's existence. So I leave it up to you to decide what to do on receipt of this message.

Intelligence confirms submarine pick-up waiting for you from twenty-three hundred to an hour before dawn on last three nights of August September & October. Pick up remains same coordinates intially agreed upon. If you do not make October pick-up it will be assumed you are prisoners or dead. Code-name for pick up remains 'Cuttlefish'. I wish you luck.

In the time since that communique Trap and his guerrillas had wreaked as much havoc as they could upon the enemy. During

April and May they had recruited and moved back and forth from hiding places near Lake Lanao and the spectacular Maria Cristina Falls south-west of Iligan City which were reported to be higher than Niagara. When Iligan had been invaded by the enemy on 25 May they had made their first successful raid and wiped out an entire vanguard of Japanese troops. This had been followed by other raids against enemy ammunition dumps near Cotabato on the coast where the Japanese had been ensconced since 29 April. In one of the actions six Filipinos had been killed and their wireless set had been blasted.

'Any luck with the wireless set?' Trap asked trying not to glance sideways to where Lexi was packing food in a knapsack ready for the night's departure to the new hideout. Zotie had been out reconnoitring yesterday and had come upon a Japanese patrol only a mile away. He had strongly recommended they move on to a safer position he had found, and Trap had agreed.

'No,' Williams replied. 'But we'll keep trying to fix it though it's probably gone west and that means no communication with the outside world.'

'Let's stay positive. Keep working on it.'

Trap was very aware of the woman coming their way. He did not look up as she reached them; he began counting his ammunition. It was Williams who put down the bayonet he was polishing, hit out at the flies and stood to greet her. 'Only another few weeks, Doc, and you'll be out of here.'

She nodded and smiled. 'Yes, we'll all be out of here.' She was conscious of Trap's desire to get his tiny group out safely; she was conscious too of what a burden she and the children were.

She gave a brief sidelong glance down at the top of Trap's head as she added, 'Cadee has peeled the mangoes and sliced the papaya. I've fed the children. Yours is ready.' She gestured back towards the cave she had exited.

'Right.' Williams half turned and called softly to Caldo, Clevelly, Ivat, Eduardo and the others who sat in a circle some yards away with the water of the small cove lapping the shore nearby. 'Boys, chow-down.'

They rose to their feet, boots crunching on the sand as they trailed after Williams.

Lexi remained beside Trap. She could hear the continuing tempo of the breakers beyond the reef round the point as he finally raised his eyes to her. These days he had taken to speaking directly to her, but his gaze was aloof and indifferent and his words were commands, questions or statements of fact, like the matter he referred to now as he rose to his feet. 'Make sure the children sleep this afternoon, for as soon as it's dark Zotie wants us to leave for the new hideout. It'll take us some hours to get there.'

She responded as she turned and walked away: 'I will.'

He delayed. His eyes, which had avoided looking directly at her until now, latched upon her, watching her body move as her boots left prints in the sand. He took in the swirling of her hair across her straight shoulders and stared at her taut back and the army-issue belt around her waist. He contemplated the swell of her bottom under the trousers.

His gaze remained fixed upon her until she entered the cave. He stood a few seconds more before he bent down and placed the rounds he held neatly upon the leather strip beside his feet. And picking up his Tommy gun, he wiped the sweat from his brow, straightened his shoulders and strode after her.

Chapter Forty-four

Night encompassed Ipswich town. An hour earlier, as the cold day dwindled and the shadows of the fiddlewood trees stole across the lawn outside the windows and a chill westerly wind buffeted the strong walls of Stonegate, Aunt Carly had put the finishing touches to a dress for Jane.

The young woman had watched with increasing excitement as her aunt ironed the gown, and now she swirled around in it and preened in the mirror, turning sideways and placing her hands beneath her breasts to smooth the material with her small fingers. 'Oh, I adore it.'

The masterpiece was copied from a dress by the famous English fashion designer Norman Hartnell. Jane had seen a picture in the *Australian Women's Weekly* and had prevailed upon Aunt Carly, who was a fine dressmaker, to reproduce it for her. It was made of green velvet, echoing the brilliance of her eyes. With a form-fitting bodice and daring décolletage, it featured tiny covered buttons running up from hemline to neckline. An embroidered bow was tied at the waist, and calf-length panels fell in glamorous swathes. Emitting a gloating sound of approval, Jane spun round on her heel as the door opened and her aunt entered.

'There you are, darling, John Drayton's just arrived. He's in the lounge room with your father and mother.'

'Good, I'll be right out. How do I look?'

'As pretty as a spring morning in the Ettrick Valley when the field daisies are aboundin'.' Aunt Carly and her sister, Jeffrey's mother, had been born in the southern Uplands of Scotland, and she rarely missed an opportunity to praise the place.

'I hope John Drayton thinks so.'

The older woman gave her niece a penetrating look. 'Do you really, darlin', or are you just flirting with him like you do with all the others?'

Jane scowled. 'Now don't scold, please. I want to have a nice night.'

'Yes, well, just remember he was your dear departed sister's husband.'

'Half-sister, you mean, and what difference does that make anyway?'

Aunt Carly tapped her foot in its black lace-up shoe. 'Now, Janey, behave. You're supposed to be in mourning for her, not acting coquettishly with her husband.'

Jane's pretty mouth pursed. 'Don't be such a prude, Aunt Carly.' She heaved a sigh. 'Anyway, I *am* sorry about Lexi.'

'I hope so; it was a dreadful thing an' all. I'll never forgive those Japs to my dyin' day. And if I'm a prude, as you say, I'm happy to be one.' She bent and picked up a matching stole from the bed as Jane brushed past. 'Don't forget your wrap, it's cold and windy tonight.'

'Pooh, I'm going in without it. I want him to *notice* the dress, not to hide it.'

Aunt Carly looked down her considerable nose at her niece. 'I just know in my bones your father will have a fit when he sees you. And I'm having second thoughts about making it, you're showing a deal of flesh there at the front. And on a cold night too.' She came up behind her niece and placed the green velvet shawl over the young woman's shoulders.

Jane shook it quickly off. 'Don't!' And she hurried out and down the hall.

In the lounge room before a fire, a luxury for Ipswich homes — where the residents simply had to wear more layers of clothing in the cold months of June, July and August — Marlene Bartlett reclined, feet on a stool and knitting a scarf for the Red Cross to send to the troops in cold climes. She was not over the death of her daughter and sister and spent a deal of time inside the house making items for the war effort. On the far side of the room John Drayton and Jeffrey sat in brocade chairs resting on an Axminster carpet.

Jeffrey tilted his head at his guest. 'The newspapers are full of the new landings by the Japs in New Guinea. A few places have been in the headlines. Apparently there's been fighting in . . . Buna, was it?'

'Yes.'

'And some other spots have been mentioned in the Owen Stanley mountains.'

'Probably Avala and Kokoda. They've had control of other north-coast villages for months.'

'That's right . . . and there we were all hoping that the battles of the Coral Sea and Midway had curtailed their expansion.'

John Drayton ran his hand across his clean-shaven chin. 'Well, they did as far as extending eastward by sea was concerned; no doubt about it. They've had major naval setbacks. As for New Guinea, sir, it's pretty tough going over the Owen Stanleys to the military base at Port Moresby, I'm told: rotten terrain. But if the Japs aren't stopped, it spells trouble for Australia.'

'Yes indeed. And I'm not sure how much our prime minister and his band know about warfare. Curtin's virtually untried at this point.'

'But operational control lies in the hands of General MacArthur.'

Jeffrey made a dismissive noise in his throat. 'Yes, son, and a lot of people think he's not worth a fig. The way he decamped from the Philippines, and now he's ... what is it? Supreme Allied Commander of the South Pacific?'

'*South-west* Pacific, I believe.'

'Yes, well, that's the bit we're in, so it's important,' Jeffrey stated emphatically as he stubbed out a Craven A cigarette in a porcelain ashtray.

John Drayton endeavoured to make a minor defence of the general. 'Lexi's grandfather knew him well; didn't seem to think he was a bad bloke.'

'Ah, old Sir Brillard, there's another military type for you,' Jeffrey grunted dismissively.

John Drayton said no more: he was well aware that MacArthur had moved his GHQ from Melbourne to Brisbane a few weeks prior. The fact was he was about to meet some of MacArthur's intelligence department. He had been instructed to report to the Allied Intelligence Bureau Headquarters in Queen Street Brisbane at 0900 on the coming Monday, though he mentioned nothing of this to his host, who was continuing to talk.

'And General Blamey. What do you think of him, son?'

The visitor looked at the ceiling. 'I'm in the army, sir, I'm not supposed to have an opinion about the commanding officer.'

Jeffrey emitted an amused grunt. 'The papers say they've sent the Seventh Division up to New Guinea now.'

'Yes, I saw that.'

'Well *I* say ... at last. I know a few blokes who were in the Seventh and my manager out at the Blackstone mines has a young cousin in it. There's going to be widespread fear if the Japs get it their own way in New Guinea, I can assure you of that.'

John Drayton nodded but said nothing. Common talk in the Redbank camp where he was stationed, was that the Australians had been pushed back and were retreating along what was becoming known as the Kokoda Trail.

'You know, a lot of my younger miners have volunteered.' Jeffrey gave his companion a searching look. 'When do you think you'll get your marching orders?'

'Any time, sir, any old time. I remain ready.'

Three weeks before, John Drayton had returned from Cairns, a thousand miles to the north. He had been sent there immediately after informing the Bartletts of the death of Lexi. His mobilisation had been due to the approach at the time of a large Japanese invasion force heading south towards Australia.

The Battle of the Coral Sea had resulted, the height of the battle fought on 7 and 8 May. As the Allies repulsed the Japanese on their route southwards, aircraft were launched by both sides from carriers, making the battle remarkable for the distinction of being the first sea battle in history where surface craft were out of range of each other and did not exchange shells!

The Allies' victory gave them heart and Australia and New Zealand were relieved of immediate threat by sea.

On John Drayton's arrival in Cairns on 1 April he was raised to the rank of major and had been pleasantly surprised to find two of the British commandos he had trained with in 1940 waiting for him: Special liaison officers, Captain Rupert Coalclark and Lieutenant 'Blinkers' Hervey. Between the three of them they soon chose fifty soldiers for their skills and athletic prowess, though John Drayton had taken Ron Howard, Derek Smith and Gavin Bird along as his own choices. The expectation was that in fourteen weeks they would turn the men into a viable jungle-fighting force.

He had been informed by a brigadier, 'You're to be a unit of secret service old man, given the somewhat curious title of "Z Special Operations".'

Approximately twenty miles north-west of Cairns, in the rain forests of the Atherton Tableland outside the humid green settlement of Kuranda, camp was made and instruction began. A month later the Allies gained more relief as they secured another great victory at Midway Island in the central Pacific. The Japanese were aggressively advancing on that small American territory and a mighty sea battle ensued. The Japanese Admiral with eight fingers, Isoroku Yamamoto — Isoroku meaning *Fifty-six*, the age his father had been when he was born — was defeated by the Admiral with nine fingers, Chester Nimitz — whose father had died prior to his birth.

This victory at Midway came about because of a major American intelligence coup which revealed the enemy's secret plans. The effect of this success on morale was far-reaching, and in the Atherton Tableland camp John Drayton's trainees absorbed their instruction with a new enthusiasm.

Months of day and night training brought John Drayton's unit to a slick jungle-fighting brigade. He had expected to be sent quickly into action, but instead he was transferred south to Redbank, where he currently helped form another intelligence unit. He was impatient to use his skills and take his men into action, but being a professional soldier he knew that the army moved in anomalous ways.

He came to visit the Bartletts as often as he could, and had taken Jane out twice previously. She was fun to chat to and to play gin rummy with on his nights off. The whole family continued to help him over the death of his wife and child and had written comforting letters to him while he was away.

John Drayton's parents were both dead, That had been one of the reasons he had joined the army and taken the exams for entry into Duntroon Royal Military College, Australia's Sandhurst or West Point.

He had always sought father figures. In Hong Kong it had been Sir Brillard; these days it was Jeffrey Bartlett. He was a brasher character than the knight, yet he was a figure of authority, had charisma and held sway over people, just as Sir Brillard had, and the fatherless John Drayton was drawn to such men. He felt comfortable with Jeffrey, to such an extent that, as they sat in front of the crackling flames of the fire, with Marlene engrossed

346

in her knitting, the soldier gazed down at his hands and, turning them palm up in his lap, disclosed a secret feeling. 'Dying an honourable death isn't a bad way to go, I suppose.'

The older man sat sharply upright but replied in an undertone so that his wife would not hear, 'Good heavens, John Drayton Whitby, what a hell of a thing to say. You're young, with life ahead of you. Of course you're liable to go into danger, you're a soldier, but you've come through before and will again.'

'It's not that I'm afraid of dying, sir, I'm not.' He thought of the men he had seen die. 'But there are good ways and bad ways, I reckon.'

Jeffrey suddenly understood that his companion was revealing something deeply important, and he bent forward and held the younger man's knee as his voice softened considerably. 'I'm not much for pretty words, son, but I know you aren't afraid and I'm sure you've seen things that can give you nightmares, but do try not to think about dying.'

John Drayton lifted his eyes. 'Mostly I don't, sir. It's just that war doesn't discriminate. All I mean is, if I die fighting aggression and evil, if I die fighting for freedom, well . . . so be it.'

Jeffrey glanced swiftly round to Marlene, but she was not listening. 'Look, son, I understand all of that, really I do, and I reckon you're a darn brave man. Indeed the ribbon on your chest confirms to me that you are, so no more sombre talk.'

The Distinguished Conduct Medal had been awarded to John Drayton for getting his men home from Java in the open boat. Ken Ward had been affronted on his behalf: 'You should have been given a damn Victoria Cross. They robbed you, sir.'

John Drayton fell silent and Jeffrey studied the younger man for some seconds before altering the subject. 'Do you know, I've been asked to double production at the Blackstone and Aberdare mines.'

The young man regained some spirit. 'Can you do that?'

'I'll jolly well try, son.'

347

There was a small cough and they turned to see Jane's entrance into the lounge. She did not exactly pose in the doorway but she paused just long enough to make an impact before she took a number of gliding paces towards her stepbrother-in-law as he rose from the armchair.

John Drayton's face creased in a smile but Jeffrey's face wrinkled in disapproval. 'What do you call that outfit?' he reproved, standing up beside the soldier.

Jane gave her parent a withering look. 'Oh Daddy, please.' Her eyes narrowed and a crevice formed in the smooth skin between her eyes. 'This is the latest fashion.'

But Jeffrey was not to be fobbed off. 'I can see your chest, an awful lot of your chest! If that's fashion, it's a disgrace.'

At that moment Aunt Carly came through the door behind Jane and slipped the stole around her shoulders. This time the girl did not resist. 'Daddy, we'll have to take your car, my hair will be ruined otherwise and it might rain.'

Jeffrey cleared his throat but answered agreeably, 'Yes, all right,' as his daughter's eyes met the visitor's.

'Shall we go?'

John Drayton smiled at Jane's parents. 'Good night. I'll have her home around eleven.'

'Yes, dear,' Marlene answered, rising and coming over to her husband. 'See you in the morning, then, for we shan't be up at that hour.'

As the two young people left the lounge room and walked down the hall to the front door, Aunt Carly called to John Drayton, 'You're in the same room as usual.'

'Did you make that blasted thing she's wearing, Carly?' Jeff rounded on his sister as the front door closed.

Aunt Carly blinked and turned to Marlene for support. 'Now please tell him Jane wouldna take no for an answer, or he'll be blaming poor me.'

Marlene took her husband's arm. 'Come on, darling, stop acting like an old fogey. Your daughter's turned twenty-one and you know what she's like when she's set her mind on something.'

Carly cast her sister-in-law a grateful look. 'Too right. Now let's go and have dinner and then a nice game of solo, shall we?'

Chapter Forty-five

John Drayton and Jane drove away in Jeffrey's Ford and considering that petrol was now rationed, the soldier thought it really quite generous of Jeffrey.

Jane took a quick sideways glance at her escort's shadowy profile as he turned right at the Fiveways and continued down Brisbane Road to Station Street in the suburb of Booval to the National Picture Theatre. The streets and highways were dark, devoid of any lighting, for 'brown-outs' were in operation in all Queensland towns situated on, or near to, the coastline. This meant the restriction of most exterior lighting, and it was a step back from a 'black-out' where no interior illumination was permitted to show to the street.

Jane inched marginally closer to her driver. 'I'm looking forward to seeing *Maytime*. I adore Nelson Eddy's singing.' *Maytime* was the third pairing of the singing motion-picture stars Jeanette MacDonald and Nelson Eddy. It had actually been made in 1937 but as usual American films took years to find their way to the Ipswich theatres.

They parked near a fibro house – a cheap material of bonded asbestos sheeting often used in place of timber – and walked across an open block of land to the theatre, which sat not far from the railway line. American servicemen in their smart uniforms hung about the foyer and dozens of the Ipswich girls were chatting to them. Jane cast her eyes across them and commented in her unabashed fashion, 'Some of these Yanks look really dishy. They certainly have classier uniforms than you do.'

John Drayton gave a sound of disapproval. 'And a lot more money.'

There were times when the average Australian soldier resented his American counterpart, for the locals perceived the well-dressed, higher-paid, better-supplied, servicemen from abroad as stealing their girls, and even though the Australians were deeply grateful in their hearts for the much-needed American help in fighting the Japanese, they envied the overt glamour of their confederates.

Minor skirmishes between American and Australian soldiers were not unusual, there were even odd occasions when they grew move serious, one disagreement becoming known as the 'Battle of Brisbane' where a soldier was killed and some others injured. But in the main the two armies 'got along' and admired each other and many true and lasting friendships between Australian and American servicemen were made.

And on this particular Saturday night the National Theatre was packed with both nation's servicemen and peace reigned. A newsreel ran after the interval showing the tides of war still ebbing and flowing in Europe and North Africa; some frames depicting the daring English General Bernard Montgomery with his troops in the current desert offensive. As the newsreel ended, Jane shivered and whispered, 'The soldiers are so brave,' and her companion leant over and patted her hand.

They had left the picture house by passing under numerous posters lining the foyer, all with war slogans and rousing messages.

Afterwards they drove home, and as they approached the Fiveways Jane touched her companion's arm. 'Let's go down to the Regal for a pie.' The Regal Café was one of the few which remained open late.

'All right, but we have to be back by eleven.'

They took the pies back to Stonegate's kitchen and Jane insisted they eat them in their hands: 'It's more fun than a knife and fork.' John Drayton drank a beer and Jane made a hot cup of tea and enthused about the 'flicks', as films were referred to in the vernacular.

At half past eleven John Drayton stood up, and reluctantly Jane followed him. As he paused in the doorway, Jane reached out and switched off the light. In the vague illumination from a lamp in the front hall she caught the soldier's arm and he turned to her. He was very close, his face above hers. She spoke with her mouth turned up to him. 'I know I'm poor Lexine's half-sister and I feel terrible and all about her, but don't you like me just a little bit?'

He could smell the pleasing heady aroma of her as she pressed against him to rest her body along the length of his. 'I'm cold,' she whispered. She was so tiny she was standing on her tiptoes, and he felt her lips on the side of his neck and her hot breath on his skin. Seconds later he was kissing her.

His head was swimming; the taste of her was so good, and she was murmuring sensually in her throat. Her mouth opened eagerly and he was losing himself in the warmth and nearness of her, his hands sliding down her body, her rounded breasts thrusting at him. Suddenly he pulled his mouth from hers and pushed her firmly away.

'What's wrong?'

'I shouldn't have done that. It was very wrong of me.'

She gave a little giggle. 'I thought it was very nice.'

He turned her by the shoulders and shoved her gently ahead of him. 'No you didn't. Forget we did that. It won't happen again.'

'Well I hope it does,' she mumbled in disappointment as she moved away down the hall where she paused near the lamp, glanced back at him boldly and disappeared into the darkness.

John Drayton rested back on the door jamb, feeling guilty. He was missing his wife and his son, missing Sir Brillard and all the family, missing Kathleen and his other friends and missing their life in Hong Kong. Kissing Jane had been foolish, spur-of-the-moment stupidity. Oh yes, she was attractive and her kiss had been quite ardent. He was reminded of kissing his wife, and compared the enthusiastic kiss he had just received. Why was it when his lips had been upon Lexi's that he sometimes felt she was simply going through the motions of loving him?

Surely he was wrong about that? Yet he could not help but contrast Jane's passion with his wife's temperate embrace. He became aware of the rain outside, the sounds of the drops spattering against the kitchen windows, and he inclined his head to let it rest on the cool wood as he was reminded of the dreary wet day of Kathleen's mother's funeral. He visualised Kathy clinging to him in the downpour at the gates of the cemetery. Had he stroked her cheek as she looked up at him through falling tears? He believed so. And now Kathy was dead. Kathy and Lexi – both dead. God! How he missed them.

He remained a little longer leaning there in the darkness listening to the rain before he shook himself out of his melancholy and, straightening his body, walked slowly along the corridor and up to his bed.

When he came into the breakfast room the next morning Jane looked meaningfully at him, and when he said his goodbyes before returning to Redbank an hour later she accompanied him out to his motorbike in the driveway at the side of the house while the rest of the family stood twenty yards distant on the veranda.

He mounted the Harley Davidson and Jane leant against his knee and met his eyes. 'That was a smashing kiss last night.' The sun was caressing the skin of her face, the unlined, smooth skin of extreme youth, and the pink on her lips glistened as she spoke. She looked pert and stylish in her pleated skirt and blazer and the expression in her gaze was tempting him to kiss her again. Yet even as she attracted him, he knew it was not Jane he wanted to hold.

For these moments while he regarded her he felt ancient by comparison. The fifteen years between their ages seemed to stretch

353

before him, and open up as if in a long parade of images: he saw the streets of Hong Kong and the thousands of Chinese refugees milling to and fro; he pictured Fort Stanley and the parade ground and Sir Brillard leaning on his cane, and Lexi snuggling her nose into Paul's face and Kathleen laughing, her calm eyes lingering upon him. And he could smell the jungle of Java and hear the sound of Jap bullets zinging by his ears as his fingers touched the hole in Harry Parsons's forehead while the boy lay dead beside the jungle stream. He felt the boat rocking beneath him in the infinity of the Timor Sea, day after day, with his men ill and dying and Ken Ward trying to cheer them.

He became aware of an insistent tapping on his arm and he blinked and refocused on the nubile child-woman in front of him with the sleek, immature face pushing into his vision as it spoke: 'John D, are you day-dreaming? You just ignored me! I asked you if you're coming back here next weekend. Are you?'

He hesitated before he answered. He knew what he should say, but instead his mouth formed the words 'I'm not sure.'

Immediately she groaned and her porcelain forehead contorted into furrows. 'But you must.' Her hand took hold of his arm. 'Say you will. Oh do say it.'

He relented. 'If I can.'

'Good. In that case, I'll let you go.' Her satin lips parted and she beamed at him, leaning in. 'Would you like to kiss me goodbye?'

'Good heavens, no! Behave yourself. Goodbye. I've got to call in and see a soldier who lives in Bundamba; he escaped from Java with me.'

'What's his name?'

'Ken Ward.' He edged the motorbike forward and after a few paces she let go of his arm.

'Well I don't like him because you could have stayed here longer.'

'Stop acting like a child.' He lifted his hand and waved to the family.

'Hope we see you soon,' Aunt Carly called as he rolled the bike through the open gate while Jeffrey strode down the steps to join his daughter and close the gate behind the departing soldier.

John Drayton rode away with arm raised while the older man latched the iron gate and placed his hand on his daughter's shoulder. 'He's a good fellow.'

'He's a dream,' Jane answered as a bicycle pulled up beside them at the gate.

'Good afternoon, sir,' the rider exclaimed, a young man of about twenty-two. 'Can I have a word with Jane?'

Jeff growled a greeting to the youth as Jane turned to the newcomer and gave him a haughty smile.

'Afternoon, Arthur.' She leant on the gate as the newcomer took off his cap and pointed with it after the receding Harley Davidson.

'Who was that?'

She gave him another smile which she hoped was mysterious. 'Someone.'

'Yes, well, I know that. But . . .'

'None of your business, Arthur Gilford.'

His mouth turned down, but at her next words it raised optimistically.

'But you can come in and have a talk with me on the front veranda if you like.'

Chapter Forty-six

Monday 10 August 1942

John Drayton arrived for his appointment fifteen minutes before the appointed hour. At 0900 a corporal in the uniform of an American marine found him and led him past seven industrious-looking WAAFs at desks, out into a corridor, up a flight of stairs and through a series of halls and doors. He was handed on to an Australian sergeant who finally delivered him to a room where all the windows were opaque, obstructing any view in or out, but allowing in light. As he entered, three men in Australian uniforms – a full colonel, a major and a lieutenant – looked round from where they stood in front of a glossy wall map of the Orient and South Pacific.

'Whitby?' enquired the colonel.

'Yes.'

The colonel introduced himself and the others: 'I'm Roberts of the Australian Allied Intelligence Bureau.' He inclined his head. 'Captain Darcy, Signals, and Lieutenant Toweel from our topographical department.'

There were handshakes all round, and as Roberts made to speak again the door at the end of the room opened and slammed back against the wall. Their heads all turned as a man in the uniform of an American brigadier general entered. John Drayton looked into a remarkably large face which tapered to a semi-sharp chin above deep lines etched from nose to the corners of the mouth. A pair of cold eyes, one under a monocle and both under a high forehead, regarded him.

'General Willoughby,' exclaimed the colonel to the newcomer, 'this is Captain Whitby. I told you about him.'

John Drayton realised this was Charles A. Willoughby, the controversial head of American intelligence for the South-West Pacific. He had heard it said by more than one of his superior officers that Willoughby was ill-equipped for his position and that while MacArthur kept him on, he took little notice of him, all of which did nothing to enhance Willoughby's reputation. But at this moment none of that stigma seemed to weigh upon the general, who strode forward with an aristocratic grace, nodding formally to John Drayton's salute. The general turned to Roberts.

'Have you told him?'

'Just about to,' the colonel replied as he took hold of John Drayton's shoulder in friendly fashion. 'Whitby, I'm going to take you down one floor to meet a group of radio operators. They've volunteered to go in behind Jap lines on a number of islands in the Bismark Archipelago, New Guinea and the Solomons. We'll drop them in by sub and they'll set up their radio transmitters in isolated well-hidden spots along the enemy shipping lanes and flight lanes and transmit immediate reports on hostile activity. We're dubbing them coast-watching stations. All brave blokes: and we also think you should know them because there might come a time when you and that jungle unit you trained will work with them.'

Roberts glanced over to Willoughby, who removed his monocle and let it drop on a black ribbon around his neck as he studied John Drayton.

'So, to get straight to it, Captain Whitby – and for the record, you're now a major with army intelligence – we're sending you and your boys to Milne Bay on the eastern tip of New Guinea. We want you in a position where we can dispatch you to remote places more quickly than we can from here. There's a highly secret fortification going on in Milne Bay at Gili Gili, an air, land and naval base, and with its completion we hope the eastern flank of our military hold on Port Moresby will be secure.' He turned back to Roberts with a questioning expression, and Roberts supplied the further information.

'Major Whitby, you'll leave from Amberley aerodrome in a transport aircraft tomorrow afternoon at eighteen hundred hours. Now we'll go over which of your men you take with you. You can pick them up in Cairns on your way to New Guinea.'

'Hello.'

'Is that you, Jane?'

Her voice melted. 'Ooh yes, John D, it is.'

'Can I speak to your father, please?'

'I think he's just walked in. But won't I do?'

'Jane, please. Put your father on.'

He heard her place the receiver down and call out to her father; a few seconds later Jeffrey's voice sounded down the line. 'Yes, my boy?'

'I'm off, sir, on active service. Sorry I can't tell you where.'

A brief silence ensued, followed by Jeffrey's clearing of his throat. 'Ah, I see. Well good luck, son. You'll be in our prayers.'

'I know that, sir. Thanks.'

'When do you go?'

As he answered, 'Tomorrow', Jeffrey retorted, 'So soon?' and John Drayton heard Jane call out, 'Oh no!'

'Sshh!' her father said and returned to the receiver. 'It's a bit sudden, isn't it?'

'Yes, that's the army. I'm given twenty-four hours' notice while some blokes have waited around for months and still nothing's happened.'

Jeff cleared his throat again. 'We'll write to you often, son.'

'Thanks, sir. Send them to Clearing House, AIF, Thursday Island. And please say goodbye for me to Marlene and Aunt Carly.'

'Of course. They'll be sad to have missed you. Just Jane here with me at present.' John Drayton heard another outburst from Jane before Jeff spoke into the receiver again. 'Good luck, m'boy, remember to come back to us ... and now Janey wants to say goodbye.'

He heard the muffled sound of the phone being transferred.

'John D? You're not going away?' Her tone was dismayed.

'Yes, tomorrow.'

'Oh no.'

'That's the army, Jane.'

'You'll be coming here tonight to see me then, won't you?'

'Jane, I can't.'

Now she sounded angry and hurt. 'But you must. You must say goodbye.'

'There's no time.'

'You have to.' She was almost crying. 'You must.'

He took a deep breath. 'Now Jane, listen. You need to understand something. I can't come tonight, and the fact is I might not come back at all. I want you to go out with boys your own age and enjoy yourself. I'll write to you.'

He could imagine her looking glum, and when she answered he could hear childish spite in her tone. 'Don't bother.'

'Now you don't mean that.'

'I do.'

'Jane, you're acting like a schoolgirl and why that should surprise me I don't know. So you be good, Goodbye, Jane.'

She sniffed and he heard a weak 'Goodbye,' followed by 'All right then, good luck.'

He replaced the telephone receiver in its holder and sat eyeing it with a tolerant smile. Jane would be over her infatuation for him in five minutes. She was unruly and wayward and used to having her own way: a spoilt child of wealthy and wonderfully generous and kind, but indulgent, parents. Yet she was not a bad sort of kid.

And the truth was, she had done one valuable thing for him. She had helped him through this strange, sad time and in some ways made him aware of what was important to him.

His fingers tapped the black bakelite of the telephone as he sat a few moments in thought until he felt the cold gush of air on his back and stood and moved over to shut the window against the westerly wind.

In the act of closing it he remembered a dream from the previous night. It had been of Kathleen, and she had been calling out to him. They were in a windy forest and he could not see her but could hear her voice shouting his name over and over. She had cried, 'help me.' And he stumbled around in the darkness unable to find her, until suddenly he had felt the ground caving away beneath him and had lost her completely . . .

He remained at the window considering the dream and imagining the lovely dead Kathleen. His expression softened into wistful regret. What a good friend she used to be to himself and Lexi.

His eyes locked and he stared into space. He was thinking of Jane again and her sensual kiss. He could not recall the last time his wife had kissed him like that. But it had been a good marriage, hadn't it? They had given life to little Paul. He recalled the night of Paul's premature birth and the dash to the hospital in the wee hours. And now little Paul was gone . . . and Lexi too.

A vivid picture of Lexi on their wedding night rose in his mind: her body blossoming out of the folds of the ice-white gown as it fell from her shoulders to her breasts and down to reveal her hips, before it descended to the floor; the smooth skin of her body inviting and irresistible. He remembered her momentary tremble at his touch before he brought his mouth down on hers.

His brow crinkled. Their wedding night was the very first time he had seen the odd look which was to cross her face in repose so often afterwards. That indefinable expression which used to come to his wife's face; reflective, even melancholy. That first night he had asked, 'Sweetheart, what is it? Is something wrong?' And the look had vanished immediately to be replaced with a tinkling laugh of merriment as she quickly kissed him. 'Wrong! Whatever would give you that idea?' And her laughter had bounced and danced like a love melody for his ears only. And so it had remained. When caught in that repeated moment of introspection there had never been acknowledgement, only Lexine's dancing smile and the effervescense of her laughter.

A gust of wind stung his face as he brought the window down and latched it.

Lexi was gone, so why did it matter? Yet the more often he was reminded of it, the more it troubled him. Such a short marriage. Had he known his wife? Truly known her?

Chapter Forty-seven

Lexi sat between the rocks sorting through the few medical supplies she had left in her knapsack. She was thinking of John Drayton, and as usual was experiencing regret and guilt. She should never have married him: it had been so unfair to him. He was a wonderful human being who had deserved real love, not the imitation she gave him.

When she had come back from Madura and realised she was pregnant with Hank Trapperton's child, she should have been able to stand up to the gossip and nasty talk that would have resulted in her unwed pregnancy. But then her grandfather had so very much wanted them to marry and everyone had expected it. She had been weak; she saw that now. But there was one good thing: she had given little Paul a name and he had not been stained a bastard for the fifteen months of his existence. As she thought of Paul, a great ache began in her body and she bent forward holding herself around the middle to regain control and stop herself from crying out.

A few yards away Trap stood with his back to her, gazing through the rain at the ocean from the hidden vantage point under a wide ledge which afforded them protection high in the cliffs. His men were cleaning and checking their weapons and ammunition for the coming night; except for Ivat, who maintained watch over the children sleeping on a blanket. Constant vigilance was needed against scorpions, spiders, snakes and crawling insects, and at night they kept a fire smouldering constantly in an area which could not be seen from below while one of them maintained watch.

Tension filled the air as they waited for nightfall, when they would travel to the pick-up point for the submarine at the designated coordinates in southern Illana Bay. This was the third and final night that the craft would be in the bay. If they did not join it tonight, it would leave without them. And that would mean they had to wait till next month for it to return when again the sub would wait the last three nights of the month. Trap did not care for himself: if they stayed he would continue to attack Jap outposts and hinder them where he could, and that went for his men too, who had become adept guerrilla fighters and would follow him no matter what. But it was not fair to the kids . . . or the Doll. He dearly wished to be rid of her for all sorts of reasons, the overriding one was if they were caught, she and the children would be shown no mercy. Now that particular fact played on his mind these days.

He had looked up the meaning of her name once, a long time ago: it meant *helper*, or *protector of mankind*. He had thought it inappropriate at the time, but these days he could see it fitted right enough: she was sure a protector and helper to the two little orphan kids.

Suddenly Eduardo spoke. 'Gawd, I hope we don't run into trouble again tonight.'

'Don't be such a defeatist,' Williams boomed. 'Zotie, you think we'll be okay, don't you?'

Zotie's head came up from where he was plaiting a rope seated on a rock. He was the only Filipino remaining with them. 'Yeah, sure. We told you the Japs had left the beaches when we were out earlier.'

The last two nights had brought complications. On the first night all the sea fronts in the area had been brimming with Japanese patrols. The same had occurred the second night. There were fires illuminating beaches and approaches to the sea, with enemy soldiers encamped. Zotie and Jake Williams had scouted ahead this morning and had found the beaches empty of enemy, so the hope was that departure would be made tonight.

Meanwhile Williams and Ivat had continued to painstakingly attempt to put back together the smashed wireless, but so far to no avail. So all they had to rely upon was the original pick-up time and place: that weather permitting, a sub would wait for the last three nights of each month from August until October, from twenty-three hundred to an hour before dawn. It was too dangerous for the submarines to remain longer.

Caldo moved across to the leader who was looking apprehensively at the sky. 'Hope the rain stops by nightfall. We don't want to be soaked before we have to be.'

'Well the sea's blessedly calm,' Trap replied, watching the gentle undulations as they rolled to shore. He was counting on getting the Doll and the kids out tonight. 'The inflatable boat from the sub will come in on the high tide but won't be able to get right into the beach. We must swim out to it. I'll carry Lessa strapped on my back, and you carry Jimmy.'

Lexi heard and stood up. 'No, I don't want that, Colonel,' she said, moving over to them and speaking as quietly and dispassionately as she could. 'I'll carry Jimmy. The one thing I am is a good swimmer. I saved my own life once by swimming like hell away from the Japs. And that was with machine-gun bullets to avoid. Tonight should be a snap.'

'If that's what you prefer.' Trap looked past her to his sergeant, who shrugged.

'Yes, I do. I'll take Jimmy as long as he's strapped on well with his head high up, near mine.' She turned and walked back to her kit.

Trap regarded her as she sat down again. He had never spoken to her about her escape from the Japs, though he knew about it through Caldo. The sergeant had furnished him with her story about the shipwreck and the wholesale slaughter of the survivors. And it had only been as recently as the other day when she had been wearing a torn shirt that he had seen the bullet scar on her back. Some hours later he had been annoyed at himself for allowing his curiosity to get the better of him when he had asked her about it. She had lifted her gaze to his, her blue eyes intensifying as she peered at him for a few seconds. 'It's my reminder that the Japs take no prisoners. Fortunately I can't see it, so mostly I'm allowed to forget.'

As evening fell, the weather complied and the rain abated; and in the last moments of the fleeting twilight drifting across the moss-covered earth between the rocks and the cliff face, while the clouds dispersed above, the leader stood in purple shadow facing his little band. Taking up his Tommy gun, he bent down on one knee, and Lessa, who knew what she was to do, climbed on to him piggy-back style while Caldo placed a piece of blanket over the child and bound her to Trap's body with thick leather straps.

Caldo's big hands worked speedily. 'I've actually convinced the Doc to let me carry Jimmy until we arrive on the beach, then I'll tie him to her.'

Trap glanced at Lexi and she nodded agreement. He showed neither approval nor disapproval.

'Leky?' Jimmy spoke at her knee and tugged her trousers, expecting to be lifted.

'No, my precious, I'm not carrying you yet, when we go swimming in the nice water I'll carry you.'

'Ca . . . wy you,' the little boy repeated her last words and she lifted him and kissed him and handed him across to the sergeant as Trap rose with Lessa on his back.

'Right, who's got the flashlight?'

Cadee held it high in the softly waxing night and handed it across to Williams, who took it and gestured with his other hand to Terry

Ivat. 'Private Ivat, follow Zotie,' he ordered and Eduardo, who always found the words *Private Ivat* amusing, sniggered nervously.

'Silence,' snarled Caldo thumping Eduardo in the back. 'Now move out.' In single file they hurried along the overgrown path which ran down to the shoreline and skirted the mangroves to pursue the rocky coast. Zotie and Ivat were the vanguard, leading Clevelly, Caldo and Jimmy, Lexi, Williams, Trap and Lessa, with Cadee and Eduardo as the rearguard.

It was hard to make speed at first, for the track was almost jet black, but later, as the moon rose to three-quarters full, occasional strands of illumination filtered though the massive trees. At times rustling in the undergrowth alerted them to the company of wild pigs, and once the shadow of colugos covered them: the flying lemurs with their arms like bat wings gliding from tree to tree.

When the overgrown sea path gave way to higher ground, the track rose and eventually came out of the jungle growth. They crossed a stream, remaining wary of the ubiquitous freshwater Philippine crocodile.

Beyond the stream they paused for a long time because Zotie knew there were enemy night patrols in this area. Eventually they moved on and came to a headland two hundred feet above the water.

Trap spoke softly. 'This is where we send the signal. It's deep water here so the sub should get close enough to see our light from this point. But we wait now till twenty-three hundred hours.'

He was highly conscious of the Doll standing next to him in the dark. He gave a quick involuntary glance in her direction as he asked, 'Someone untie Lessa from my back.'

'Sure,' replied Ivat.

'I'll take her,' Lexi announced, moving even closer to Trap as Ivat began to unravel the rope. Trap tried to ignore the warm touch of her hand on his back and the proximity of her as she took the child from him.

As she put Lessa on the ground Trap spoke to the child, 'Stay with *Babae*, now.' Babae was the title he used for Lexi when he spoke to the children. She knew it for the device it was. He never called her by name, he always cleared his throat or waved or grunted to get her attention. So, when speaking to the children he had *needed* a name for her, but something that allowed him to retain his aloofness, so he had come up with babae which meant *female*, *lady* or *girl* in most Filipino dialects.

He stroked Lessa's head before he strode away to Zotie and the lieutenant.

'Come, sweetheart.' Lexi took the little girl's hand as Ivat placed a blanket down. 'We'll sit with Uncle Caldo and Jimmy.'

The next two hours dragged, and the children were asleep when finally Trap stood up. The lieutenant took out the flashlight and he and Zotie moved closer to the edge of the cliff face carrying a black card to cover and uncover the beam of light.

Lexi gently woke the children as Zotie held the torch and Williams flashed a signal towards the ebony water. Anxious seconds passed.

Nothing.

'Shit!' proclaimed Caldo.

'Signal again, Lieutenant.'

Williams did so.

Nothing ... except the nervous shuffling of feet and a catalogue of tense murmurs from the little group who waited.

'We'll stay a while.'

'Shall I tie Lessa to you in readiness, sir?' Caldo asked.

'No, Sergeant, we'll wait until our signal is answered. We can tie the kids on pretty fast.'

Another two hours passed while the night breeze rustled the leaves of the trees, but there was never a reply from the inky black water. The children slept on the blanket and Ivat and Lexi kept watch over them.

'We'll give them a little longer.'

But when the light was beamed once more and there was no

answer from the bay, the sweat trickled down Zotie's temple and he spoke in a disenchanted tone. 'It too late. They not coming.'

Trap strived for optimism. 'Perhaps. But we'll wait a little longer.'

Zotie shook his head in the gloom. 'No, Colonel, we wait too long already. Take time to get back to hideout. Jap patrols out before dawn. We should not wait.'

The logic in this pronouncement was indubitable.

'Come, darlings,' Lexi said as brightly as she could, gently waking the children. 'We must leave this place.'

They both sat up and in his good-natured way Jimmy mumbled, 'Leky Leky,' as she kissed his cheek.

Thus, five minutes later, shoulders drooping as if carrying their disappointment like tangible weights, the weary guerrilla band sidled away down from the headland into the jungle, with Zotie in the lead.

Chapter Forty-eight

A Very light shot up into the post-midnight sky, spitting out its glow for long enough to reveal a mass of Japanese soldiers manhandling mortars and advancing across the swampy ground perhaps two hundred yards away. John Drayton was the senior officer holding the edge of Airstrip No. 3 where the Allied front line, including anti-tank guns, heavy machine guns and mortars, were skilfully sited to defend the area.

In a moment of stillness a voice rang clearly in the night. 'Ready to die? We come and get you now, Aussie boys!'

The colour sergeant opposite John Drayton shouted back: 'Oh yeah? Come on, you little bastards, try it and see what we've got for you!' And as the crew of the field gun beside him stood at the ready he yelled, 'Fire!' and the boom of the gun rocked the ground beneath them.

'Reinforcements coming up from the rear, Major.' Ron Howard spoke at John Drayton's side.

John Drayton smiled. 'Good! Move them forward on the left flank.'

They had been fighting the enemy in Milne Bay every day and night for a week. The first Japanese landing had occurred on the northern side of the bay on 25 August, followed by a night attack on 26 August at a plantation lightly held by Australian militia some ten miles to the east of Airstrip No. 3, where the current battle now raged.

John Drayton and his men had arrived in a DC3 Dakota transport on 14 August, the day after Australian Major General Cyril Clowes had taken command of this post, to find the defending forces dug in and ready for the enemy attack.

As the men around him reloaded and prepared to meet the enemy again, a messenger pushed his way through the gun emplacements behind and called to John Drayton, 'I'm confirming the intelligence report of earlier, sir. Enemy tanks are definitely stuck in the mud back near the village of Hionia.'

'You beauty!' John Drayton grinned and wiped the sweat from his forehead as he looked round to Ron Howard in the weird flashing lights from the explosions. 'That's the best news we could have. They'll have to manhandle all their equipment and field guns up here now.' He pointed to where the Very light had shown the oncoming enemy. 'It seems to me they're putting everything they have into it tonight and we've beaten them back every time.'

As another Very light went up, one of the soldiers on the nearest gun emplacement opined, 'The buggers like this night fighting, don't they?'

It was true, the enemy's main pushes had come at night.[1]

'Major?' The shout came from behind a pile of rubble and earth.

'Yes, Bird?'

'I reckon with a bit of luck we might soon have the ratbags on the run! Their attacks are thinning out.'

At this announcement earth and stones hurtled through the air, and the ground shook as the resounding boom of a mortar shell obliterated the last palm tree nearby. John Drayton coughed the dust from his throat and yelled, 'Keep up the positive thinking, Bird! And keep firing!'

*   *   *

Half an hour later a messenger came to John Drayton.

'Sir? The colonel requests you leave this position and report back to him.'

'Right.' He turned and shouted to Ron Howard: 'Take over here. I'll be back by breakfast.'

He followed the messenger to the rear through the lines of troops and field guns, with the eternal scream of mortars and crunch of howitzers being loaded and the nerve-shattering, never-ending explosions ushering them along.

'Nice morning, sir,' the messenger, a lance corporal, shouted as they bent double and ran.

John Drayton grinned. *The Australian sense of humour!*

By the dancing light of the night battle John Drayton and the lance corporal hurried past an evil-smelling swamp and after half a mile came out into an open mud-and debris-covered field where a waiting military vehicle stood in a dry area of track.

The corporal spoke with relief. 'Thank heaven Betty's survived, otherwise we'd have to walk.'

As they climbed aboard John Drayton felt hot and sticky and his jungle-green shirt clung to his body, even though there was a cool breeze blowing in the winter night.

Suddenly a hush enveloped them, and a stillness hung almost tangibly in the air as the blare of battle faded and three crisp bugle calls rang out behind them.

The lance corporal looked round at the senior officer as he pressed the button on Betty's dashboard. 'What's that, sir?'

A weary but joyous grin widened across John Drayton's face. 'That, Lance Corporal, I do believe, was the signal for a Japanese retreat.'

'Ah really, sir? Was it? Well now . . . Lovely sound, that.'

John Drayton climbed out of Betty as the first meek glimmers of dawn played on the horizon and, a hundred yards away, stood

371

the colonel on top of a slope on high ground with a pair of binoculars to his eyes. He looked round and smiled. 'Morning, Whitby. Can't see too much yet but I think we have the little monkeys on the run.'

'Did you hear the retreat call?'

'I did. And if we repulse them here it'll be inspirational to our fellows fighting over in the Owen Stanley mountains. They're having a bloody rough time of it.'

'Yes, sir, we're all pretty aware of that.'

'The old man was in radio contact with General Potts in Insurava yesterday; he's badly in need of reinforcements and it seems his boys are having to sit in the jungle and listen to the screams of their mates who've been taken by the Japs and are being tortured in an attempt to provoke our boys into attacking.'

His listener knew about the Japanese tactics. 'Yeah, they're one hell of an enemy.' He stepped closer to the senior officer, reminding him, 'You sent for me, sir.'

'Ah yes. General Clowes received a communiqué from SWPA headquarters about you. It specifically states that you are to remain in Milne Bay working with your squad of special operations intelligence types, or whatever they are. It states to keep you all out of the front line so you can get on with your brand of hand-to-hand jungle warfare training.'

John Drayton conferred upon the colonel a sceptical look. 'Do we know if they have anything specific in mind for us?'

'General didn't say, but he did say for you to stand by here for further orders. So you'd better get your men away from where they can be killed, right smartly.'

John Drayton raised an eyebrow. 'I'll do that, sir, but I'd say the worst of it's over. With the Japs on the run this morning, my boys should be out of danger for now.'

'Well get them back here anyway. I don't want General Clowes or MacArthur or Blamey on my back if any of your special fellows get hurt.'

John Drayton saluted and strode back down the slope. Typical of the army: *remove the troops from danger when the danger's over.*

The stirring strains of Reveille lifted on the dawn air and he paused to listen to the voice of the bugle. Another day had begun.

Chapter Forty-nine

Ioribaiwa, opposite Imita Ridge, New Guinea, 17 September 1942, on what was to become known as the Kokoda Trail

The heat haze lifted like steam from the ground behind him and black smoke reared up and loomed in the sky before him unimpeded even through the falling rain. Major General Tomitaro Horii took off his cloth cap, wiped his forehead and undid the remaining buttons of his tunic. It was hot here, hot like hell, and that was what his men were going through . . . hell. His black-booted feet were planted astride the track leading into what had been a cluster of grass huts, now razed to the ground with only smouldering debris representing them. Swarms of flies rose about the dead bodies, and for the present, the boom of guns and the whistle of shells and the tumult of battle were silent as a single Allied aircraft buzzed across the treetops to the west. The Australians had been strafing and bombing them this afternoon but thankfully had been ineffectual in the thick, unforgiving jungle.

Fifty yards away a log bridge was slung over a ravine, and his chief of staff, the squat Lieutenant Colonel Toyanari Tanaka, could be seen in the midst of a group of his soldiers pouring across it. General Horii was at the head of his army and they had suffered through, to his moment of jubilation. They were now halted on this ridge, in striking distance of Port Moresby. Only twenty-five miles from the military post and tiny administrative centre of this godforsaken land and the strategic position facing the Australian continent.

After all the hardship — hacking though the jungle with machetes, dogged by the rain and shifting mud; their supply lines breaking down along the narrow ridges and tracks of the mountain ranges and the days of virtual starvation; with the constancy of the Australians fighting like tigers and holding every village and ridge and ravine as they were slowly forced backwards yard by yard, mile by mile across the unforgiving Owen Stanley range through the swamps and mud — they were close at last!

The rain abated as quickly as it had begun. Horii would never become used to these tropical torrents of rain and he hankered for the cool breezes of Japan as he grumbled to himself and stepped over a filthy pool of water. Hundreds of weary soldiers flocked around him as he walked to a mound and climbed the few feet to the top, raising himself above them. Many rested on their shovels, specially made with holes in the blade, which they carried for clearing the mud away. They were all gaunt. Their rice rations were rotting. Sun and rain were all they had in more than sufficiency.

Horii noticed two of his colonels, Kiyomil Yazawa of his 41st Infantry, and Hori Hatayama of Intelligence, push through the dirty, wet and mud-covered men to stand below him as he lifted his hands for silence and addressed them.

'Men of the Japanese Imperial Army, we are close to our goal! We have kept the Australians off-balance. We bombarded them with our seventy-millimetre howitzers at ranges they cannot match. We crawled through moss forests and down ravines, we crossed steep torrents and rough passes. And now, at length, we have pushed the enemy to the last ridge above their armed forces base of Port Moresby!'

Cheers and howls greeted this statement and Colonel Hatayama held up his arms for quiet as the general continued: 'We have traversed the Stanley range; no pen or word can depict adequately the hardship we have suffered.

375

'We will strike a hammer blow at the military stronghold of Moresby!' He lifted his arms to the rising cheers.

'*Hai, hai, hai!*'

'However, ahead of us the enemy still crawls about. It is difficult to judge the direction of his movement, and many of you have not yet recovered your strength. I feel keenly that it is increasingly important to fortify our positions, reorganise our forces, replenish our stores and recover our physical fitness. When next we go into action, this unit will throw in its fighting power unreservedly!'

More cheers, more hais!

'Colonel Kusunose and the Hundred and Forty-fourth Infantry will soon arrive. We will send out detachments to dig up any native gardens around here to augment our rice, which is getting low. We will cremate our dead and take our well-earned rest.'

Horii again lifted his arms in a salute to the acclamation of his soldiers and stepped down to ground level, where Colonel Hatayama joined him. The two officers walked side by side as the general resumed speaking. 'I have spoken to the troops optimistically, but you and I know what the men do not. Since Commanders Hayashi and Yano and their marines were not successful in taking Milne Bay, our forces there have been evacuated. I don't think you know that Hayashi was killed and Yano wounded in that attack.'

Hatayama had not known, and his mouth turned down disconsolately. 'Then there will be no troops arriving here from Milne Bay to reinforce us?'

'Correct.'

'What about from the Solomons?'

Horii turned his sweat-covered face to his companion. 'Our men there in Gardalcanal are meeting strong naval and air attack, and Admiral Mikawa's initial naval victory is not being followed up. I'm told our troops are held down.'

'Then where are the reinforcements we so badly need to take Port Moresby coming from?'

Horii paused some moments before answering. 'I don't know. But my orders are to wait for reinforcements.'

'But our men are exhausted: this last twenty miles they've fought on spirit alone. We're now seventy miles from where we landed at Buna and the supplies are not getting through the mountains fast enough.'

Horii grunted. 'I know all that.'

Colonel Hatayama looked around. How he hated this place! Interminable disease-ridden jungle everywhere, relentless fighting, no alcohol for over a week now, no female company. He thought of the comfort women at their camps in the Philippines and longed for those easy times. A ripple ran though him as he recalled the girl with the thick, tasty lips; he had been so attracted to her. He used to draw her swollen lips in between his own and suck them as he flattened her ripe melon breasts with his body. Ah, how he craved that Korean. He closed his eyes momentarily, overcome with the sensuality of the recollection.

His eyes opened and he muttered with chagrin and regret. And now he was here . . . in this disgusting place. He was a soldier, he did not mind fighting, but this had been a relentless campaign; they had needed to wage war against the impossible terrain as well as the Australians. And there would be no women until they took Port Moresby. Once they succeeded there, it would be different. He took a little encouragement from that thought. Yes indeed, once they had the Australians where they wanted them, then they could stop awhile.

His face dropped again . . . but they would need reinforcements. It would be too hard to take the base without fresh troops. But Hatayama's tiny eyes grew wider with optimism at his leader's next words.

'There might be hope, Hatayama. I was alerted by communiqué that there has been a suggestion to gather a new army in Rabaul, under a new general.'

As Tomitaro Horii mentioned Rabaul, the Japanese stronghold

377

on the island of New Britain, four hundred miles to the north, he smiled. He had captured it, after the successful invasion of Guam, in January with these same soldiers he saw about him now, his South Seas Detachment; and it was from Rabaul that they had embarked in five well-escorted transports for this advance upon New Guinea.

'The message does not say exactly, but I have a feeling this new army will come to our aid.' He sighed. 'If we can hold on long enough.'

Relief flooded Hatayama's face as they walked on. 'Now that's good news.'

Six days later; 23 September

In his field headquarters south-west of General Horii's position, Australian Brigadier General Arnold William Potts,[1] Commander of the 21st Brigade AIF, stood fingering his fine moustache in contemplation, his head to one side watching the rain. He wore shorts, and sweat trickled down his back into his already stained dark green shirt. The new jungle-green uniforms had arrived at last and now the men wore a sensible camouflage colour for jungle fighting.

His men of Maroubra Force were spent: not one was without sore feet, and sickness and dysentery were rife. In one jungle battle after another in the treacherous mass of moving mud that they were calling the Kokoda Trail, they had been pushed back by the Japs, who overwhelmed them four to one. But his men were stubborn; he was often amazed at their endurance and he was damn proud of them. And there were positive 'angels' around like Salvation Army Captain Albert Moore who had ministered to more than his wounded men's souls. Potts had come to deeply respect 'the Sallies'.

He held no illusions: he felt he would probably be replaced, and

378

soon, as he was the leader of a retreating army. It was a shame, but he felt it was true, that the commander-in-chief of the Australian forces, Thomas Blamey, did not really appear to comprehend what the troops had faced in the Owen Stanleys.

They had even sustained a fleeting visit from General Douglas MacArthur the previous week. He had flown from Brisbane via Townsville into Port Moresby with the American air force general George Kenney. MacArthur had only been in New Guinea forty-eight hours: time to visit a few of the troops, address a gathering of newsmen and pose for photographs taken by a war correspondent called Parer. The American commander certainly had an air about him which was impressive; more than Potts could say for Blamey.

General Kenney seemed competent and had got things moving. Large numbers of American P38 aircraft were arriving daily from Queensland and there were now American troops being airlifted into Port Moresby to reinforce the Australians. Potts found this all reassuring, but a bit damn late for a lot of his boys.

He looked down at a message which had just come in. It informed him that the reinforcements of the 7th Division, 25th Brigade regulars they had sent up to Imita Ridge, had not helped and that the Australians had been pushed off the ridge near Ioribaiwa.

'Blast!' he said to himself, 'the poor bloody PBI.'

PBI was Australian slang for *Poor Bloody Infantry*. He muttered bleakly knowing that there had been so much hand-to-hand fighting these last few weeks that bayonet stabbings now counted for the majority of the injured.

Outside he could see Fuzzy Wuzzy stretcher bearers moving the wounded. The Australian soldiers referred affectionately to their New Guinea native allies as Fuzzy Wuzzys because of their tight crimped curly hair.

They could not have brought so many of their wounded back to the aid stations or received supplies without them. Bless them. Potts nodded solemnly to himself.

He felt odd, and hoped he was not coming down with malaria. His brow wrinkled with the many torments in his mind. In his enemy's place he would be gathering strength for a few days and re-forming.

He spoke aloud to himself. 'I suppose they'll burn their dead and dig in, build a sort of redoubt up there on the ridge. Once they've revived I'd say they'll come at us again.'

The next day; 24 September

As twilight fell in company with the incessant rain soaking the miserable little world of Ioribaiwa, General Horii's sturdy legs manipulated the mud-soaked track from the medical tent to his own. He was followed closely by his chief of staff, who attempted, with scant success, to keep the rain off his superior with a torn umbrella. Horii's face under his cap revealed signs of strain, and as he reached his tent a signal commander arrived at the same time.

'Message just in, sir, from Imperial General Headquarters.' He handed Horii a damp piece of paper.

As the general's gaze raced across the communication, his forehead puckered into a corrugation of lines and his face paled. Lifting his eyes, he spoke sharply to Lieutenant Colonel Tanaka. 'Get all my staff here ... immediately.'

Some minutes later the infantry commanders filed into his tent and Tomitaro Horii stood before them still holding the communiqué. Colonel Yazawa, who was suffering from malaria, found it hard to stand but he resisted help and remained unsteadily upright.

In dramatic counterpoint the evening was darkening quickly as Horii spoke. 'I have uncertain news. We have suffered a major defeat at Guadalcanal. Because of this we are ordered to make a strategic withdrawal across the mountains back to Buna and remain defending the beach-head until further orders. An army of reinforcements is

380

currently being marshalled in Rabaul, where one of our generals from the Philippines will take command and lead it to us in Buna. This will take some weeks, so our orders are to leave this position in the morning.'

The officers gazed around at each other in silence. They were staggered. Yazawa moaned and slipped down the canvas to the ground, as Seizo Okada, a war correspondent who was travelling with them, grabbed him and sat him against a tent pole.

Blotches of red rose on the face of Colonel Kusunose, and hardly controlling himself, he lifted his hands for attention. 'Sir? Why can't we make a thrust at Moresby on our own? We've come so far in hardship. The men have made it here on sheer pride. We cannot abandon our position. Moresby is so close. The Australian pigs are within our grasp. Let's attack on our own and take it!'

Loud mutterings of agreement met these words, and Kusunose and the other dissenters edged together. Even Tanaka eyed the commanding officer with an expression of approval at their stand.

Tomitaro Horii hesitated briefly before recalling the misery of the past weeks. He too was disappointed, but he had no alternative. He sighed before he growled in disapproval. 'Perhaps you feel cheated, and I understand it . . . but I lead no army of mutineers.' He came to attention, whipped out his sword and raised it. 'You are my officers. We will follow the command from Imperial General Headquarters. At dawn we fall back. I will hear no more.'[2]

Chapter Fifty

Mist rose above the steamy waters of the lagoon, lightning launched jagged knife edges of silver through the clouds on the far horizon, and the solitary form of Kathleen rambled under the palm trees, their fronds undulating above her in the rising breeze.

She was watched by two of her guards from the window of the decrepit *bahay* beyond the fringe of palms at the base of the incline towards the road. Corporal Hyata and Private Yomoko sat and smoked. Hyata had been raised to the meagre rank only a week before. The other four bodyguards were off duty. Two were away in the nearest village and two hung around outside the *bahay*, lolling on the long wooden seats, smoking, drinking Japanese beer and dozing intermittently.

Twenty yards from Kathleen's cheerless roaming in the haze of evening embracing the land, sat Dinty, her Filipina maid-cum-companion, who had now been with her since they had departed Luzon. Dinty had qualified as a school teacher a month before the invasion, and her parents and siblings had been killed in an air raid. The woman, round-faced and plump, waited, seated on a large palm frond clasping her knees. Her eyes, like Corporal Hyata's, did not leave Kathleen.

To these observers Kathleen gave the appearance of quiet meditation as she meandered along the stony foreshore, but her mind was brimful. She had not seen Colonel Pig since she had been brought here a week previously. The guards had intimated he had gone to Tokyo for a meeting with the high command.

Now that the United States and Philippine armies had capitulated and the populace of the Philippines were subdued, the resident army acted as watchkeeper. Ikeda had made his headquarters here on the island of Panay, though he travelled constantly to a number of the others. The Kempeitai, like the Gestapo in Europe, relentlessy sought out resistance of any kind and in particular hunted for the guerrilla bands which still roamed the hill country throughout the islands.

After the débâcle of that day when he had danced with her, she had not seen him for a month, and during his absence she had derived perpetual pleasure reliving her small personal effort for the Allied cause by redirecting the lorries to the wrong destinations.

Her four weeks of blissful solitude had ended when at last he had called for her, returning to the old way of having her bathed and scented and dressed and brought to sit in a room while he ate his dinner. Kathleen had been surprised when she had been handed a traditional brocade kimono for her attire. Dinty had simply said in her good English, 'He requires you to wear it.' That particular night after he had eaten he told her to stand and turn around. He indicated with his forefinger for a second rotation, and when she came to rest he eyed her for a long time before he stated, 'A kimono is the most becoming attire a woman can wear.' She had not argued and abruptly he had enquired, 'How is your mouth?'

'It is better.'

'You will not be impudent again?'

She shook her head.

'Say it.'

She complied. 'I will not be impudent again.'

Ever an enigma, he had smiled and his small black eyes had disappeared in the folds of skin. 'Now we will play chess,' he announced.

383

Kathleen was taken aback and she must have shown it, for he asked expectantly, 'You do play?'

She nodded. 'Yes . . . a little.'

Snapping his fingers, he rose and called for his chess set, and a magnificent marble board with jade and onyx chessmen arrived, carried in by two Filipino servants. And so they played the first of many games, none of which she had ever won.

She was thinking of their chess games now as she paused to observe the mist steal in silent wisps across the sea to her feet. The ritual of the beginning of the game never altered. Every time he leant back in his chair and surveyed her first before he asked, 'You do play chess?'

And she always replied, 'Yes . . . a little', before he snapped his fingers and rose to order the chess set.

At first she was no match for him, but as the weeks turned into months, sometimes the games went on over two sittings, and on occasion had gone to three. At the finish, after he was victorious, he would explain in detail where she had made mistakes and how she could have foreseen certain moves, and thus, slowly, she improved. Their play was, in the main, silent; he making his moves and she hers. Once recently during a game he had declared, 'Chess parallels battle and a soldier should be fighting. I tire of being in an army of occupation.'

Kathleen was well aware of his harem of Koreans and Filipinas, including Dinty. The young woman was no more than twenty and had confessed to her: 'I was a virgin before the colonel.'

For one period of six weeks on the island of Negros, Kathleen had lived in the same house as Ikeda, though now she was held separately. He often complained about the endless heat and sometimes left the door to his quarters open. Kathleen's room had been directly across the hall and she had not been able to avoid observing naked females in bed with him. He did not hide it and once had even called her to his bedside to speak with her. Kathleen had concealed her disgust as he rested on a pile of pillows, his arm around the naked Filipina's neck, pawing her breast.

She continued to be baffled. Why did he not use her as he used Dinty and the others? She wondered what aberrant game he was truly playing. She believed his toying with her must end in a frightening and fearful thing.

His cruelty did not wane. She saw him burn Philippine villages without compunction, and while she did not witness prisoners being tortured, she knew it was done time and time again on his orders. She realised one did not rise through the ranks of the Kempeitai without being carelessly brutal.

A month after the fall of the Philippines she had witnessed his beheading of an American who had been caught in a guerrilla raid. The horror of that atrocity remained with her. Ikeda had murdered the soldier in front of six hundred forcefully held villagers to terrify them. It had certainly terrified her. She had stood with Hyata on the veranda of a building a hundred yards away up a slope. As Ikeda lifted his sword above the blindfolded and kneeling man, her stomach turned and she shut her eyes and kept them closed. She shuddered, hearing the collective moan of the villagers, and remained head down until Hyata tapped her arm and whispered in a nervous voice, 'It's over. He comes now.'

Her eyes opened to see his short muscular form striding towards her, and as he came to within a dozen yards of the veranda a lieutenant ran after him to give him his newly cleaned sword. As the young officer handed it to the colonel it slipped and fell to the ground, and Ikeda in anger and affront slapped the soldier hard in the face. The lieutenant fell to his knees, retrieved the sword and handed it over with extreme care the second time.

Kathleen had seen military slapping before. At first it had astounded her, but as time passed she came to realise this was a form of discipline endemic in the Japanese army. Superior ranks slapped inferiors for perceived insubordination, neglect or infringement of duty. She had finally decided that if such were

385

the behaviour expected and accepted by the Japanese military, it followed that pity, compassion or mercy would not be shown to prisoners of the Rising Sun.

And so her own confusion and bewilderment continued. Daily Kathleen repeated the phrases which had become her personal and perpetual orison to Heaven, *Please release me from this horror. Please release us all from this horror. Why am I here when all the others were murdered? What does he want of me? How I hate him, how I despise him. How dearly I wish him dead. Help me, please, God. Help us all.*

She was repeating this softly now as she wandered across the pebbles lodged in the sandy earth of the lagoon foreshore, her gaze on the long-necked wading birds fishing in the shallow waters as the subtle sea mist gathered about them. How she wished she could be a bird . . . to beat her wings and lift off and fly away.

The sweet odour of musk borne on the breeze from a flowering vine in the jungle wafted over to her as she paused. The storm building upon the horizon would be with them soon. She watched the churning grey clouds and thought of John Drayton, as she did every day of her life, her oval eyes mellowing and closing in reminiscence.

'Missy! Missy!'

Kathleen spun round to see Hyata running towards her. Dinty jumped up from her resting place on the palm frond and Hyata called, 'Colonel . . . he comes!'

Kathleen hurried over to the soldier. 'Where?'

'His motor car has driven to the front of the house.'

'Thank you.'

Corporal Hyata took up position behind her, as if he had been there all the time, and they began to walk slowly along the foreshore in tandem as Dinty became rigid like a sentinel under the palm where previously she had sat.

They had gone perhaps ten yards when the human storm thundered noisily down the steps of the *bahay*, and shouted at them. They paused and turned, and there was Colonel Pig, his recognisable stamping stride bringing him down the slope towards them, his sword swinging at his side.

Momentarily Kathleen froze. The setting of the beach and Ikeda swaggering towards them had brought back the shipwreck and the aftermath: the Japanese soldiers crossing the sand and how he had appeared before them. She felt sick. How deeply she hated him!

Through the fringe of trees Private Teko appeared and saluted as Ikeda passed him accompanied by two of his staff.

'*Omae!*' Ikeda halted in front of Teko and prodded him in the chest. Kathleen could not hear what he said, but he flicked the soft field cap on Teko's head and yelled at him. She thought perhaps the head-covering had been crooked, for the private adjusted his cap and saluted again as the colonel left him.

Dinty's head was down, eyes on her feet, as he stomped by to stop a yard away from Kathleen. Behind him halted a lieutenant and Captain Funaki. They both carried black chevrons on their uniforms and displayed the white armband of the Kempeitai with the Japanese characters for 'ken' *law* and 'hei' *soldier* upon it.

Ikeda stared at Kathleen and announced in a formal tone, 'So I am here and you will come with me. We are leaving.'

This was not unusual.

'What about my clothes and things? They're in the *bahay*.' Kathleen gestured towards the house.

'You!' He pointed at Dinty, who remained head bowed. 'Pack her personal items immediately. We leave in ten minutes.' He pointed with his thumb back through the trees to the road. 'My staff car waits.'

'I will help Dinty,' Kathleen dared to say, though she did not move as Dinty hastened away.

Ikeda took a deep breath and looked up at her. It was then she noticed he wore a different insignia on his collar. She had not seen him for a week, and while she tried not to look at him if she could possibly avoid it, she had come to notice the insignia he usually wore on his collar: three silver stars on a red and yellow striped background. The majority of ranks in the Japanese army were denoted by stars. Today the small strip on either side of his collar carried yellow only, with a single silver star upon it. She did not know what it signified, except that he no longer held the rank of colonel.

He blinked and his head fell slightly to one side. 'If you must help her, then go immediately.'

She hesitated in surprise, for she had expected some sort of rebuke. His usual reaction would have been to scream at her or push her towards the waiting car. But no . . . he had *agreed* for her to help the servant.

She paused one second more, then waited no longer and hurried after the Filipina towards the house.

The sound of his laughter followed her as she caught up to Dinty. 'Why is he laughing?' queried the young woman as they hastened to the house.

But there was no answer to that; no answer at all. 'Damn him,' Kathleen said to herself. 'Damn him to hell.'

The small cavalcade left the lagoon house as torrential rain began to fall and the mounting storm surrounded them. Night fell and the flashes of lightning whiplashed the palms and wild banana trees tossing in the wind, while the tall bamboo leant across the dirt track above the vehicles and the thunder added to the pandemonium. Kathleen, eyes closed, sat stiff with fear, one hand on her mother's dragon pendant, which always hung around her neck: it gave her consolation just to hold it. Only inches away sat Ikeda in the back of his commandeered black Chevrolet which had been shipped from Manila. In the front beside the driver sat Funaki, and behind them in two lorries came the others.

It was as if the night protested at their departure and the elements had taken up the call.

Ikeda travelled in silence, which meant the other occupants did not speak. It was not until the water rushing across the windshield rendered the wipers impotent that Funaki spoke. The driver halted and they sat again in silence with the tumult engulfing them until, to Kathleen's relief, the storm abated.

They travelled slowly, for the dirt road was potholed and muddy, and eventually they reached a concrete road. Fifteen minutes later they arrived at an airfield. Ikeda spoke as his door was opened from outside. 'The flight will be of many hours duration.'

And now Kathleen risked a question. 'Excuse me, but where are we bound?'

He turned back in the seat towards her. She could see the glint in his narrow eyes from the ambient glow of the headlamps of the vehicles and the lights of the building nearby. 'What does it matter to you? You are going, wherever it is.'

The radial engines of the Kawasaki Ki-56 transport aircraft continued to hum as it thumped the ground and rolled along bumping and jiggling on the unlevel field and the two escort Zero fighters, fitted with under-fuselage drop tanks to extend their range, landed after it.

Kathleen glanced around in the burgeoning dawn light to meet Corporal Hyata's sympathetic eyes. He did not nod or smile and to anyone watching it would have seemed as if he simply looked ahead, but she alone saw the almost imperceptible change in his expression. It comforted her as it always did and she turned her head immediately to face forward, sensing that Ikeda was eyeing her. He was. They sat in two leather chairs which had been fitted in place behind the navigator. Her hands rested now upon the arms and she ran her fingers over the scratches and raised marks in the leather. The rest of the group accompanying them had positioned themselves on the forms which ran round the frame of the interior of the aircraft. Five had lain on the floor during the long night flight.

Kathleen came to the realisation that Ikeda had indeed been promoted when they arrived at the airport to depart the island.

389

There they were joined by a new officer called Colonel Kaneko Hosoda, who bowed low and called Ikeda 'my general'. So immediately to Kathleen he became *General Pig*.

He took her chin and turned her face to his, and his ebony eyes searched her features. There appeared no line of demarcation between his pupil and the iris, both melding into the blackness of one another like an oily blot on the white sclera of his eyeball. 'We have arrived in Rabaul.[1] Do you know where you are?'

'I'm not certain,' she answered.

He smiled. His smiles had the effect of chilling her. She could not help it, she read so much into them: cruelty, menace, malevolence. '*Konoshima wa watashitachi no mono.*' He said and immediately translated, 'These islands are ours.' His tone was replete with pride and ownership. 'They belonged to Britain but now they are a stronghold of our mighty Japan. The British are laughing on the other side of their faces.' Momentarily he paused and let go her face. 'Do you know that expression?' he asked abruptly.

'Yes, I've heard it before.'

With a smug delivery he repeated it: 'Laughing on the other side of their faces.' The narrow opening of his eyes grew wider as he warmed to his thought. 'And this island, which was theirs, is now *ours*, and incidentally, your new home. There is a special compound built already waiting for us, on a gentle rise, I'm told, with wide views. It was Hosoda's idea to remove us from the common soldiers; I like the idea. And from here I will mount an assault that will extend south from Buna in New Guinea and engulf everything between there and ... Hobart.' He stared into her eyes. 'Do you know where Hobart is?'

'I think so: in Australia.'

'Correct.' He made the word sound harsh and grating. 'The southernmost tip, with a harbour which could hold the whole Japanese fleet. The slow-witted Australians don't know that, but we do ... we do.'

She bowed her head as the aircraft came to a halt and the

engines died. One of Ikeda's aides left his seat; he lowered his head in the direction of the general before advancing across the aircraft to the rear door hatch. A second soldier rose and also bowed his head before helping the first unlock the door. The sound of voices outside reached Kathleen's ears and a flight of wooden stairs were pushed up to the side of the aircraft.

The aide looked back to Ikeda, who lifted himself up, moved to the opening and stepped out into the gleam of the morning. A brass band started to play as he descended to the ground, followed by the members of his staff, his chest swelling under his uniform as he strutted forward to inspect the two rows of soldiers at attention.

Kathleen followed into the morning air, and the smell of fuel wafted to her, for there, in row upon row beginning only yards beyond the troops that Ikeda inspected, were lanes of aircraft lined up like massive metal mosquitos. She eyed them in amazement: never before had she seen aeroplanes in such numbers. Men climbed on them and moved between them. She was to learn there were four more airfields here ringing the army base.

Behind her she felt the presence of Corporal Hyata, and as she stepped to the ground she knew he followed.

A minute later Ikeda completed his inspection and with a flourish of his hand over his sword strode away across the airfield towards some huts in the distance. Captain Funaki came hurrying back towards her, and indicating for Hyata to accompany her, he barked, 'Follow the general.'

Kathleen lifted her eyes above the aeroplanes to the emblem of the rising sun flapping in the wind. She shook her head: it repre- sented only misery and death to her. Her eyes blurred with tears because she perceived the red of the pattern as the spilt blood of her loved ones.

She almost stumbled as she swiftly wiped away her tears with the back of her hand and gazed beyond the airfield to the jungle-clad smoking mountain – obviously a volcano. Beyond it there were more;

North Daughter, Mother, South Daughter, Rabalanakaia Tavurvur and Vulcan rose from the earth all around. She watched *General Pig* striding away and as she moved after him, she heard Hyata's voice softly in her ear: 'I know there was a bad volcanic eruption here five years ago and another last year.'

Her reply was in an undertone. 'I don't care if one erupts right now.'

Chapter Fifty-one

Mindanao, 31 October 1942

It was a golden half-moon, and the stars peppered the inky sky above as the night cradled the seven adults and two children standing on the flat ground between the rocks and the bamboo of the dense jungle before them. Trap eyed his motley crew. They had lost Cadee a month ago. He had been mortally wounded by an enemy hand grenade on one of the missions the small guerrilla group had conducted. It had been one of the reasons they had not made the September pick-up. Cadee had still been alive, lingering on at the time, and the Doll had been loath to leave him. He had died on the final pick-up day, but that night had seen a torrential storm and no collection could have been feasible.

Williams and Eduardo had finally got the wireless working, albeit only long enough to advise Hawaii they were alive, and it had been confirmed that the sub would be waiting for them.

They all missed Cadee, not only because of his wide smile and stream of jokes but because he had been such an amazing cook. That man had been able to turn anything the boys came up with into tasty meals, and his wild pig stew had been a tour de force. Now they were relegated to eating wild fruit, fish and the occasional egg. Yeah, they sure missed Cadee.

They stood on the headland as the allotted hour came and went, faces to the sea filled with apprehension.

Lessa and Jimmy fell asleep, the little girl strapped on Trap's back, the boy in the arms of Ivat, who sat on the flat ledge of a rock complaining. 'Flamin' Filipino night life won't leave me alone,' he chimed soulfully as he slapped out into the darkness with a piece of cloth.

Lexi moved in and lifted Jimmy from Ivat's arms with the words, 'I'll take him for a time,' and as Ivat released him Eduardo spoke in a low, cheerless tone.

'Shouldn't we be signalling again, Colonel?'

A gloomy Clevelly, croaked, 'Same as August. We're not gonna get away. They ain't coming for us. I'm gunna die here. I know it.'

'Shut up, Clevelly, you're a goddam pessimist,' Caldo declared, but the soldier kept up his lament as Williams and Zotie, large flashlight and black cardboard in hand, moved towards the cliff-face and began the signal for the third time, as the eyes of the group scanned the black water.

Abruptly, like the evening star out there in the blackness, a series of flashes from a searchlight blinked in return.

Williams's voice was taut with emotion as he interpreted the letters. 'C . . . U . . . T . . . yes . . . Cuttle . . . fish. That's it. Looks as if the sub's about a quarter of a mile out.'

Trap called softly as he brought his arms round in a herding fashion for his band to gather: 'Move fast! If anyone else saw that signal we could have an unwelcome war party. The rubber boat from the sub will come in as close as it can, but we'll still have to swim out, so let's hightail it down to the beach.'

Zotie pointed in the night light. 'This way, cliff path not too steep, winds a bit. Stay together.' He moved off.

Four minutes later they were on the pebble-strewn beach and Trap whispered, 'Pants, boots and shoes off.'

While Caldo and Ivat strapped Jimmy high up on Lexi's back, Williams waved the flashlight again. An answering light, smaller and less intense than before, glimmered off-shore

Trap's tone was encouraging. 'Great, that's the boat coming in.

Head straight for it. Let's get into the water. You go first.' And as Jimmy woke up and began prattling, 'Leky, Leky,' he gently pushed Lexi with the palm of his hand in her lower back. It surprised her, for it was the first time he had voluntarily touched her since Christmas Day and both of them were manifestly aware of it. A shiver ran through her as he ruffled the tiny boy's hair and returned his hand to her back. She heard him say, 'Swim hard, good luck.'

She tried with all her might to answer in a normal voice but she knew she had failed. 'I will . . . thanks,' trembled from her and she turned and waded into the water with Caldo right beside her.

'I'll be with you all the way. Swim straight ahead to where the light was,' the big man encouraged, at the same time giving her a shove. And as the cool liquid enveloped her, Jimmy said, 'Leky, Leky, Dark . . . dark . . .'

'It's all right, my precious. You're safe with Leky.'

The others began to wade into the sea as Trap handed Zotie his revolver. The Filipino took it and tucked it inside his waistband. 'I keep for ever.'

'Sure. Now remember what I said. Get up the cliffs and high-tail it out of here. Understand? And good luck. You're one hell of a tough guy, Zotie.'

Zotie nodded. 'Thank you for what you have done to help my country.'

'Yeah, pity we couldn't have done more.' Trap could just make out the Filipino's eyes in the moonlight as he extended his hand and the man reached out to take it. Their fingertips had just touched when a scuffling noise broke the still night. Trap's head snapped round in the direction of the cliff path as a Japanese voice shouted an order and the sickening rattle of a machine gun erupted. Bullets spat in an arc across the beach, the stinging explosions on the rocks making ear-splitting blasts which echoed across the water.

Trap was yelling now: 'Move! Move! Into the sea!' as he pushed Zotie hard towards the water. He swung his Tommy gun up and rattled off a burst of twenty rounds in the direction of the enemy before dropping it and turning and wading with as much speed as he could into the bay. 'Come on, Zotie, come with us.'

'Jesus!' screamed Clevelly staggering a few paces. 'I've bought it!' and he fell face first into the murky sea as Lessa screamed in unison and Trap hesitated a second to roll Clevelly's body in the water. It was obvious he was dead, and rounding on Williams, who remained at his side, Trap shoved the lieutenant ahead of him, shouting, 'Everybody get going!' And he took a deep breath diving forward into the bay. But one man did not move.

Zotie turned back. He waded quickly to the shore and reached for Trap's Tommy gun lying on the beach. Bullets sprayed around and zapped into the sand beside him as with fumbling hands the Filipino picked up the weapon and began firing. He could make out the undersized black figures advancing down the beach towards him in the dim moonlight, and dropping down behind a rock he blazed away, all the while shouting curses at the Japanese and displaying the fervour and zeal that doomed men alone can muster.

Trap could not swim underwater: he had Lessa on his back holding him with a vice-like grasp of terror around his neck. Mercifully she was only a tot and could not choke him. He struck out with the strident noise of bullets on rocks in his ears. He thanked God that the Doll and Jimmy were ahead of him. They had entered the water first with Caldo. He thought he could see the shape of her making for the open water with clean, fast strokes. *Oh God, let the boat be there.*

Lexi swam in terror: *Not again! Not again! Oh please Lord in heaven, not again!* She reached out with every ounce of her strength and pushed through the water with the desperate adrenalin of fear and panic. The weight of Jimmy did not trouble her; it was the desperation of once again avoiding machine-gun bullets that numbed her mind. What if she were hit? They'd both drown! She sensed a spate of bullets cutting the water beside her and she prayed, *Oh please God, please help us. Swim, Lexi, swim. You know the boat is just up ahead.*

On she swam, arms delving fiercely in the sea and pulling her and her baby-burden away from the madness on the land. *Oh God, help Trap and Lessa . . . Help us all!* She could still hear the rapid, brittle cracking of the machine guns behind and terror urged her to even greater speed; then she saw it. A dark shape floating in the vapid light of the moon. She heard men cry, 'Over here!' and Caldo's voice answered them from some yards away to her left. And as she made for the craft she prayed for Trap and the others. She was only a yard away now from the black forms of men reaching out to her and she raised her arms and felt firm, strong hands lift her from the sea.

'You're all right,' a man's voice said in her ear, and as they eased her to the deck of the rubber boat she managed to say, 'There's a little boy strapped to me.'

'Yes, yes, we know.'

She was panting from the extreme exertion and for some moments she was not aware of anything except that they had cut the infant from her back and someone had dried her head and face and was now wrapping her in towels.

She heard a voice say, 'Oh no! Hell,' and then another cry out, 'Quick. Over there . . . Three more.' And men scuffled beside her to crowd forward to help the others in the water.

She lifted her face out of the towel and looked around in the wan moonlight for Jimmy. Burly mariners' bodies moved in front of her blocking her vision and then she saw him.

For some seconds she stared, resisting what her mind told her, disconnected from the reality. Jimmy, her surrogate son, hung like a broken doll from a big sailor's hands.

Her head swung as if detached from her body, her throat stung and she choked on words that would not come. As the boat tipped to one side she lurched to her feet and lunged towards the man, grabbing the child in her arms.

Finally the single word burst from her. 'No! No . . . no . . . no . . . no . . . no!'

'He's been hit, lady. I'm sorry, but the little fella's gone.'

Lexi did not hear the words. She slid to the decking holding the baby to her heart, pressing his tiny cold face to hers, her tears merging with the salt water on his cheeks.

Her chest heaved. She felt a terrible pain coming from somewhere, such pain as she had never felt before; it filled her head, her world, her universe . . .

She was unaware that she kept repeating, time after time, 'No . . . no . . . no . . .'

Shouting and gunfire drifted to Trap from the beach. He expected to be struck by a bullet every moment and it took him a little time to realise that someone had remained behind and currently held the enemy back. Someone had stayed fighting the Japs! And even as he thought of it, he knew. Zotie! It would be Zotie! As he pulled his way through the sea with all his strength, carrying the child on his shoulders, he sent praises on high for the bony little Filipino, short of stature but long on courage.

Trap saw the round black outline of a rubber craft ahead rising and falling on the sea. He was aware of his lieutenant to his right and he thought there was someone to his left. As the sailors in the launch called to them, the three swimmers reached the craft in unison to feel kind arms raise them from the water.

'Take the child from me,' Trap commanded, and a sailor took out his knife and cut the straps which held the little girl to the soldier. They were no longer amazed at what was coming out of the sea and they looked further to see if any of the others had children bound to them.

Trap's gaze moved beyond the sailors to the faces in the haze of moonlight: he saw the woman holding Jimmy, and Williams and Ivat and a sailor around her.

Beside him Caldo was comforting Lessa, and as the boat rocked the outboard engine kicked into life. He could hear the abrupt staccato blurting of machine guns again, and thought anxiously that if the Japs reached the water's edge bullets might stab the side of the rubber craft.

A sailor yelled, 'Here comes one more!'

Trap scrambled to the side of the boat. It was Eduardo, about fifteen yards away, and Trap leant out and urged the soldier on. 'Come on, man, come on.'

'Let's get out of here,' shouted someone, and Trap replied, 'No, wait!'

Suddenly Eduardo's arms flailed the water and he stopped swimming.

'Damn, he's been hit!'

Trap yelled to the driver, 'Spin to the left . . . we can still pick him up.'

As the driver swung the craft he answered, 'Where is he? Which way?'

'Keep spinning to the left, sailor,' a voice commanded, and the boat edged round in the gleaming black water.

'If a couple of bullets hit us right we'll deflate.'

'Yeah, we'll be goners.'

Trap's head was full of the noise of the engine and the sailors yelling and the caustic smell of the sea, but he realised Caldo was now at his side leaning out with him, reaching towards their comrade . . . and then they had him; even as he began sinking, they had him by both arms. As they heaved him up from the water, his body blocked out the moon and the starlight and he loomed up over them and into the boat even as it lumbered away and Trap heard a bullet zing by. He knew in his heart Zotie was dead now.

But they were fast sailing out of range of the shore and towards the waiting submarine.

'Well done,' Trap heard a sailor growl as he sat beside the drenched Eduardo, who managed a waterlogged grin.

'I'm okay, sir, just hit in the leg.'

A towel was handed to Trap and he wiped his face and eyes, and took a deep breath and looked around again. Lessa, her hair clinging to her face, was now in the mighty arms of Caldo, but beyond them he saw the tableau again, sitting on the decking, leaning against the side of the rubber craft, the woman holding Jimmy ... and around her, sort of hovering over her, Williams and Ivat and a sailor.

In that moment he understood.

Lexi's body shook with sobs and her face remained pressed into the infant. As time passed and the launch rocked she became half conscious of men's voices, gentle and consoling, but she still did not lift her face from Jimmy's. She could hear men shouting and she was aware that the engine coughed and started, but she continued pressing her lips to the cold little face; she did not even move when she felt the craft surge forward.

It was not until the hand grasped her shoulder and *his* voice sounded that she looked up. There, kneeling in front of her, was Trap, soaked and dripping as they all were. It was hard to see him in the wan night glow with the shadows of the men falling across them and the swinging movement of the craft ... but she could make out his eyes. She read sorrow, tenderness ... perhaps even more.

His mouth formed some words she could not hear; the engine blocked them out. He reached towards her and took Jimmy from her arms, and finally she released him. Slowly, gently, Trap raised the little boy and handed him to Lieutenant Williams while he remained kneeling in front of her.

She thought she recognised the battle going on inside him; thought she saw that he did not know what to do: that the mighty Hank Trapperton, who made decisions for all, was momentarily in a quandary.

She met his eyes and in that moment he took up her chilled right hand from her lap and turned it over, bent his head and kissed her palm, his mouth lingering on her skin. She felt the warmth of his breath. Seconds passed, then he shook his head and moved away.

The touch of his lips was as if life blood flowed into her. She inhaled deeply, looked around and saw Lessa in Caldo's arms and seated some yards forward. Rising and half crawling across the rubber decking, she moved up to them.

'I'll take her now, Sergeant,' she shouted above the engine's noise, her hair slapping around her face. Lessa slipped out of Caldo's grasp into hers and Lexi sank down, holding the little girl tightly within her embrace.

It was not long before the craft slowed down and the shadow of the dark hulk of the bull-nosed Porpoise class submarine *Pompano* loomed across and encompassed them.

Chapter Fifty-two

Once aboard the sub, Lexi lost sight of Trap. He had disappeared at speed through a maze of steel pipes and grey paint with the executive officer, who had been waiting for him. The sailors could not cover their amazement at finding a woman and child with the party, and for some minutes there was confusion about what to do with them. But organisation appeared in the form of a methodical lieutenant, and immediately Eduardo was taken to the sick bay and Lexi was led away by a seaman to be followed by Williams and Caldo with the sergeant carrying Lessa. Down a ladder they climbed to a small rubber-matted area where Caldo patted her shoulder and she turned to see his heavy brows coming together across his nose in a frown. 'Listen, Doc. Get some rest. You did more for that little kid than anyone else in this world could have done. Don't feel any guilt about it.'

He paused and Williams added, 'Yes, Jimmy was lucky to have you. To have all the love you gave him.'

Caldo was adamant. 'Yeah, for sure.'

Lexi looked from one to the other. 'Thank you both for saying that.'

The seaman had heard all this and he gently touched Lexi's arm. 'Dr Robinson, this way please.'

Jake Williams nodded to Caldo. 'You go with the Doc and Lessa; I'll see you later.'

The mariner led them through two compartments, and as she

followed him, Lexi walked as if stupefied, seeing a confusion of images: the damp, cold body of Jimmy in her arms, and the black night and the bullets whipping around her in the sea. She could hear Jimmy's voice in her mind saying *Leky* and could see his tiny brow puckering; then it was Trap kneeling in front of her, looking at her with such tenderness and sorrow. Her head dropped forward and she tried to blink back the tears, but they came anyway and her vision blurred as the sailor in front of her halted and a petty officer pointed to a section beside the forward battery compartment where he pulled aside a curtain. 'That's for the woman.'

The seaman answered, 'And the child?'

'What child?'

Caldo pushed his bulk past Lexi in the narrow space. 'This one.'

'Gosh, they didn't say anything about a little girl. It's a storage area that we've cleaned out, ma'am. It's a miracle of miracles we found a mattress and we've raised it on some timber and made a sort of bunk.'

'We can sleep together,' Lexi forced through her tears.

He pointed. 'That there's an intercom which connects you to the bridge, conning tower, manoeuvring room, control room, wardroom and torpedo rooms, ma'am.'

Caldo was bending in the tight space and still holding Lessa in his arms as he addressed the petty officer. 'As you can see, we're all a bit on the wet side. Dr Robinson will need some hot water for washing, and towels too and clean clothes for her and the child. She'll need food and drink quick smart and she should have a way of getting in touch with me if she needs me. Can we work this out now, Petty Officer?'

'Sure. I'll personally show the lady what she needs to know.'

Left alone, Lexi took off her own wet clothes and bathed Lessa, and the child submitted to it in her usual complete silence. As she dried the little one Lexi brought her emotions under control enough to gently explain, 'Darling, I'm not too sure how much you understand. I know you are very brave and have seen shocking things in your short life, but our little Jimmy is not going to be with us any more and we must both be strong and remember him with love. He's gone to Mummy and Daddy in heaven.' She could not hold back the tears, and the little girl hugged her, which tore at Lexi's heart. 'I'm all right, sweetheart, it's just that your family have taken . . . too much pain.' She kissed the girl's smooth cheek and heaved a sigh. She felt sure Lessa did not realise that her brother had been killed. Lessa was really only a baby herself: she had been three when Lexi had met her last December so the child could still only be four.

As Lexi finished drying the little girl she regained more of her composure and forced herself to behave as normally as she could. 'I know you don't speak, sweetheart, and I understand why, but perhaps one day you will.'

She put Lessa on the makeshift bunk and tucked her in and spoke in as bright a tone as she could. As the drowsy child closed her eyes Lexi bathed herself but the strain of the night had taken its toll, and she sank down beside the little girl. Suddenly she could hear 'Lady in Red' floating in her mind.

She sat up and looked around. No, it was not in her mind; it was being played somewhere aboard: softly in the distance but she could hear it. The song that had been on the gramophone at Henaro's in Madura the night she had fallen in love. She had not heard it since.

'Oh heaven,' she whispered, and sliding back down closed her eyes and slipped into a deep sleep of exhaustion.

In the mess hall Caldo and Terry Ivat sat eating pork and beans and drinking beers. Two packets of cigarettes, Lucky Strike and Camel, lay at Ivat's right hand. They had been shooting the breeze with a Motor Machinist's Mate before he had left to go on duty. The smell of the food hung in the close quarters around them

404

as Ivat leant over the steel table to his companion. 'I can't help thinking about Zotie and Clevelly. Poor old Clevelly was always frightened of dying, I knew that.'

Caldo grunted. 'Yeah, I reckon he was always a bit nervy. Pity he bought it at the eleventh hour.' His big shoulders lifted and fell. 'That was bad luck.'

'Yeah, and Zotie was a swell little guy. Gave up his life for us.'

'Yep, he did.'

'And that poor little kid, Jimmy.'

Caldo grunted affirmatively. 'Shit, yeah. He was nothin' more than a tot.'

'Doc took it hard.'

Caldo took a long swig. 'Yeah, she did. She's a woman, ain't she? And women love kids.'

Ivat nodded at the sagacity of this statement.

'She's a swell dame. The way she looked after those kids, just like they were hers. In the flamin' jungle and never a complaint.'

Ivat murmured in agreement. 'Well, I dunno what goes on with her and the Colonel, but don't tell me he ain't sweet on her, because he is. Oh yeah, he talks like he hates her.' He made a dismissive sound. 'But he doesn't fool me. You saw him tonight . . . kissin' her hand and everythin' . . . Don't tell me . . .'

'I ain't telling you anything, son. And it ain't your business.' Caldo paused, thinking of the morning of 27 December last year when he had come to say goodbye to the Doc in the shattered town of Bamban. He pictured her in the glow of early morning being brave and trying to smile as she confided to him, *When you see him, please tell him I said, I'll always remember Madura . . . All my life . . . He'll know what I mean.*

Well, he had kept his word and passed those words on as requested, and the look he received from Hank Trapperton when he did, told him never to mention Madura again. Not ever! And he never had.

Caldo shook his head to clear the memory as Ivat piped up

beside him. 'I know it ain't my business, Sarge,' he picked up another bottle of beer, 'but he still doesn't fool me!'

Abruptly the wireless set on the wall which was playing 'The Very Thought of You' crackled and the music stopped.

Everyone in the mess turned towards it as the dulcet voice of Tokyo Rose[1] sounded: '. . . onward east west north and south we come. Face the truth. There is no hope for you Yankee boys, so why don't you just surrender like nice boys? You can't win. Today you lost three cruisers to the might of the Japanese navy! They were completely destroyed. You have no hope of winning this war. You will all die if you don't surrender.'

'Stupid bitch,' yelled a sailor at the next table as 'The Very Thought of You' burgeoned back to drown out her voice, 'if you'd said *one* cruiser we might have believed you!'

Trap had grabbed a beer and visited the wounded Eduardo. A bullet was lodged near the tibia in his left leg. 'Your war's over for a while, son,' Trap remarked, and Eduardo groaned. 'I'm darn sorry to be knocked out on you like this, but it was a bit sticky back there, what with losing Clevelly and Zotie and the little kid too.'

'Mmm.' Trap shook his head and thought of the dead men, living or dying by the luck of where you stood on the beach. Clevelly had been a bit of a negative thinker but he had been a good soldier and Zotie had been what all truly brave men are: too good to die.

'Yeah, we've lost a lot of fine men, son, and it's too easy just to say we'll miss them.'

Eduardo nodded in silence.

'So,' Trap breathed noisily, 'you just get well and come back and find me somewhere.'

'Sure will, sir.' Eduardo grinned, lighting up a Lucky Strike.

Trap went from the sick bay to his other three men and saw them settled before returning to his cramped quarters beside the torpedo room where the torpedomen slept alongside their missiles.

406

As he left the sick bay, he could hear in the distance, probably drifting from the mess hall, the strains of 'Lady in Red' on the gramophone; he shook his head in disbelief.

'Goddam!' he said aloud. 'That thing haunts me.' He recalled when it came out on the hit parade. He had not liked it then and did not like it now! He did not need to be reminded of the Doll. He did not want to think of her just a few yards away somewhere aboard. No, he did not want that.

As he gained his quarters, a petty officer arrived with two dry uniforms, pressed and spruce, right down to the eagles on the collar. This was the insignia of a full colonel!

'Where did these come from, son?' he enquired of the young man.

'Don't know, sir.'

That seemed to complete that. 'What time is it, son?'

'Close to oh two thirty hours, sir.'

'Right then, I'll try to get some shuteye.'

'Go ahead, leave your wet clothes on the floor, sir, I'll come back for them.'

The sailor had just departed when there was a rapping on the metal side of the corridor nearby. 'Yes?'

A small, youthful, but already balding, figure appeared in the low light and Trap frowned as he surveyed the newcomer. 'Who the hell are you?'

'I'm Tommy Shibuyu, sir.' His English was impeccable and he wore a corporal of Marines uniform.

'What's a Jap doing aboard this sub?'

'I'm a Nisei linguist, sir, with Intelligence. Originally from San Francisco. I've been assigned to you.'

Trap frowned. 'Have you now?'

Nisei were second-generation Japanese who had been born in the USA and called America home. This generation was both Japanese and American in attitude and cultural heritage. First generation – those actually born in Japan who had migrated to

407

the USA — were known as Issei. After the attack on Pearl Harbor the Nisei and their parents, the Issei, faced a difficult situation. Fear of an attack by Japanese naval forces on the West Coast of the USA and worry about collaboration led to resentment against them particularly in Hawaii and California. Some people clamoured for those of Japanese ancestry to be removed into internment camps and certain numbers had been.

Trap had met a few Nisei in the Philippines, where MacArthur and Wainwright had used them for interrogation and translation, and those he had known had proven useful. To Americans and British the Japanese language was like an effective secret code in itself, and Trap knew that while some viewed them with suspicion, a good Nisei translator was a boon to have on your side.

'Why is that, Tommy Shibuyu? Why have you been assigned to me?'

'I'm not sure, sir. I thought you'd know.'

Trap was weary. He put his arm out and leant on the nearest set of pipes. 'I've got a pretty strong feeling I'll find out soon enough.' He studied the young man. 'Where are your parents, Tommy?'

'My mother is still in San Francisco, but my father is in an internment camp in Idaho.'

Trap studied him. He was about thirty, diminutive and thin but with an open gaze under very heavy black eyebrows. 'How do you feel about that, Tommy?'

Tommy was slow to answer. 'I hesitate because I wish to be unambiguous. My allegiance is to the United States and the Allied cause. I was born in California. I have never been to Japan, though I speak and write the language fluently. I know the fear that lives in some men's hearts so I understand the officially sanctioned discrimination which is internment, even though in many cases I think it's wrong.'

Trap knew that there were indeed fifth-column Japanese

sympathisers in the Nisei, as well as those who were one hundred per cent devoted to the Allied cause, as Shibuyu was claiming to be. The point was, proof only came with time. Claims were simply that – claims. Trap shot the young man a sceptical look. 'Very reasonable of you, Tommy.'

'Sir, I have been fighting in Guadalcanal.'

Trap nodded. He wanted this over with; his bunk was calling. 'All right, son. That's enough for tonight. I accept that you're on my team.'

'There is one other thing, sir. I know that in proving my loyalty, it will help my father.'

Trap needed to lie down; it had been one hell of a night up to now. He pointed to the way out. 'Right, son, no doubt you'll have plenty of opportunities to do exactly that. Good night.'

Shibuyu saluted and removed himself, and Trap climbed on to the bunk and lay there. His shoulders ached where he had swum carrying Lessa, and fatigue was overcoming him. Zotie and Clevelly had died tonight and Eduardo had been wounded; it had been a bad night all round . . . And then tiny Jimmy's death on top. He wondered how *she* was. The Doll had been heartbroken about the boy. In a way it was fortunate that she had Lessa.

His thoughts drifted, sleep began to blanket him, and he slid into a dream where he was kissing the mouth of an English girl with a lover's moon casting a silver trail across the rolling surf, while above, the whisper of forgotten dreams and promises borne on the breeze rustled though the palms.

Chapter Fifty-three

In the captain's cramped quarters, for there were no spacious areas on a submarine, Executive Officer Slade Deville Cutter, second-in-command of the vessel, sat under a framed photo of President Roosevelt and King George VI riding in an open carriage during the June 1939 state visit of the King and Queen Elizabeth to the United States. A visit of massive significance, for no reigning British Monarch had ever set foot on American soil before. It had been a marvellous success for the American people had responded with affection towards the King and Queen.

Cutter was clean-shaven, with a straight nose, and well-defined eyebrows. His open gaze was characteristic of that of a hero, which as the war advanced he would prove to be. Already, he had been a football hero at the Naval Academy in Annapolis in 1934, when he was responsible for the only score of the game by kicking the winning field goal to beat the heavily favoured Army team for the first time in more than a decade.

Opposite him sat Trap. On first introduction the previous night they had recognised certain qualities in the other which led to immediate respect. They sat now enjoying mugs of hot sweet coffee after breakfasting with Lewis Parks, the captain, who had brought Trap up to date with what had been happening in the south-west Pacific. He had told him of the Allied victory in the Guadalcanal battle in the British protectorate of the Solomon Islands, and also of what was going on in New Guinea. The commanding officer had subsequently departed, leaving the two men alone to talk, for Cutter served a second role aboard, that of intelligence officer.

Slade Cutter confirmed that Trap was now a full colonel and handed him the communiqué which made it official. 'Congratulations.'

'I wondered about the clean uniforms, thought they might have been a mistake.'

'Yes, we've been carrying them for some time. Seems your work in the Philippines impressed somebody.'

'Yeah.'

'Now to other things. The crew were given no idea that they would find a woman and child with you: that came as a big surprise!'

Trap frowned. 'I understood a message was sent before the fall of the Philippines from General Sharp's staff in Mindanao to General MacArthur in Australia informing him of the woman's whereabouts.'

Cutter shrugged his shoulders. 'Did you see it sent?'

Trap shook his head.

'Well it's my guess it wasn't. Because we sure knew about you and what you were doing, but I'd say that the fact Dr Robinson was with you got lost. You of all people know how everybody was pretty anxious and frenzied in those last weeks before the surrender.'

'Mmm.' Trap was thinking. His brow creased and he fingered the tiny scar on his chin. 'So where does that leave her?'

'At this point? Aboard us to Samoa, we're bound for Pago Pago and then Hawaii.'

Trap pondered a moment. 'Right. I suppose eventually she can get out of Samoa to Australia. She was on her way from Hong Kong to her mother in Queensland when the ship she was on was torpedoed by the Japs off Luzon.'

Cutter did not know any of her story except for the death of the little boy with her last night. 'Uh huh! That wouldn't have been any cakewalk.'

Trap took a gulp from his mug, pausing briefly. He pictured her in the inflatable craft the previous night, her face distraught

411

with grief. It had taken him all the strength he had just to kiss her palm and move away. He had wanted to crush her to him and hold her and take away her pain. But thank God he had pulled himself together and not allowed it to go any further. The moment they had climbed aboard the submarine he had made himself scarce, real fast.

This morning he had castigated himself for the damn weak blockhead he had been. Well he wasn't going to repeat anything like that. She was not his, she was Johnny's.

But he needed to tell Cutter a few things. He leant over and placed the mug down, speaking in a matter-of-fact tone. 'The death of the little boy last night shook her badly. She never talks about it, but her own baby son was drowned on the torpedoed ship. She sort of replaced him with that little fella who bought it.'

Cutter was sympathetic. 'Ah, I see. Was she travelling alone with her son when the ship was hit?'

'No. Actually she was with relatives who were butchered by the Japs.'

'Oh, that's too bad. She's really been through it, then?'

'Yeah.'

'What about her husband?'

Trap's head shot up and he answered a mite too quickly. 'What do you mean?'

'Well, she was travelling with her son, you said, so I'm guessing she's got one, right?'

Trap's delivery came back to normal as he replied. 'Yeah, she's got one. A soldier in the AIF; probably in one of their special operations units by now.'

'Why do I get the feeling you know him?'

Trap paused a couple of seconds. 'Because he's a friend of mine. We met in Malaya years ago.' His tone gained a businesslike quality. 'Look, Mr Cutter, the woman's a doctor, a pretty well-qualified one too, ran a hospital department in Hong Kong. Saved a number of my men in the jungle, and one thing I do know is, she's no slouch. She'd be a swell addition to any military hospital in Pago Pago. That way she could make a living and the surviving kid would be looked after. That is, till she can get home to Australia.'

Trap hurried on: 'Is it possible to transmit a message to MacArthur's headquarters in Australia and alert them she's alive? As you've pointed out, the first message doesn't appear to have made it.'

The executive officer shook his head. 'We're on radio silence in this area. But within a day or two we should be able to do that.'

'Yes, I'd rather not wait until Samoa. That's a while away.'

Cutter shot a quick glance at his guest. 'Well you couldn't do it anyway. You won't be there.'

'What's that mean?'

Cutter opened a file, took out a sheet of paper and handed it across to his visitor. 'This decoded message is for you. It's top secret. Came in from the Allied Intelligence Bureau in Brisbane. My codebreaker Lieutenant Burns and the captain are the only ones aboard who've seen this, other than myself.'

Trap flashed him a supercilious grin as he took the sheet of paper. 'Ah ha . . . I've been waiting to hear why I've been assigned Corporal Shibuyu.'

Cutter grinned. 'I guess things will get clearer from now on.'

Trap, expression impassive, raised the message. It was addressed to him and marked TOP SECRET as his companion had said. It read:

Hawaiian Intelligence intercepted Jap transmission revealing plans for recently commissioned Jap general arrive Rabaul New Britain: Indication is up to 15,000 troops for support army for new offensive on Papua New Guinea mounted from Rabaul. Intercepted transmission suggests November 28 embarkation Rabaul.

Approval from Washington and agreement SWPA Headquarters for

you and remaining Philippines' commando force join Allied co-action Rabaul.
Unit to be known as Commando Double. You in command: Objective:
kill general and cripple transports at anchor. You will meet allied commandos
at following co-ordinates.

The co-ordinates were listed, and there was more:

Code names within Commando Double x:
Operation Longtail: target, general
Operation Hornbill: target, transports

It was signed by Colonel Charles Willoughby on behalf of General
MacArthur. Beside his name appeared that of Colonel G. C.
Roberts, head of Australian Intelligence, but it was the other names
on the message which Slade Cutter remarked upon.

'I was surprised to see the Chief of Staff himself has signed,
with Donovan of OSS as well. While this is an Allied South-West
Pacific Area operation, it's got Washington's approval. Unusual.'

Trap grinned. 'Hell, now I'm responsible to everybody.' He
tapped the message. 'What's this OSS?'

'Ah, That's the Office of Strategic Services. I've been told to
inform you that it's now the principal US intelligence organisation in all operational theatres.'

Trap nodded. 'Got it. So MacArthur's cooperating with
Washington on this one. I thought he wouldn't agree to any intelligence operations connected to the local war effort in his theatre
of war unless the operation came directly under his command and
control.'

'Apparently he's making an exception in your case. You must be
one of the few who've impressed the great man.'

Trap laughed. 'And if I'm successful, they'll all love me?'

'Reckon.'

'And if I'm not, I'll have them all on my back.'

'Something like that.'

Trap glanced again at the message. 'End of November. So I need to get down to Rabaul.'

'You do. I reckon we can deliver you well on time. Should only take around six days, unless we run into trouble.' Slade Cutter was looking at Trap with admiration. It was not an operation he would choose to lead.

A rapping on the metal door broke into the conversation and it swung back to reveal a mariner with a sheaf of papers. 'Messages for you and the old man, sir,' he announced to the naval officer, handing them across.

Slade Cutter began to rifle through them as Trap moved to the charts which lay on a shelf at the side of the office. Thumbing through them, he found the island of New Britain.

Cutter glanced up. 'The only reason we have that chart is because some guy like you stole it from the Japs.'

'I'm grateful.'

'We're dropping you off in Atalikikun Bay.'

Trap found the bay as Cutter went on: 'It'll be a bit like the way you came aboard us last night, only the other way round.'

'Without the Nip war party, I hope.'

'Well for one thing you won't have to swim this time. We don't have much space, but we've brought light skiffs in pieces to assemble.'

'That's good.' Trap had just located the coordinates and tapped the chart in front of him.

Cutter moved to his side. 'Rabaul's a Jap fortress but there's an AIB Coast Watcher station hidden in the hills somewhere here near Pondo.' He touched a spot north of Open Bay. 'Through him we can radio your Australian contingent that you're coming.'

Trap grinned. 'I can make a guess at what a coast watcher station is, but enlighten me?'

'Ah. They're Australian guys with a radio transmitter who are dropped off like we're going to do with you. They do the things I reckon you're familiar with: clandestine operations behind enemy lines, sabotage, et cetera, as well as recruiting the natives in various areas to cooperate with us in fighting the Japs. They set up their transmitting stations hidden in the hills with a view of enemy shipping lanes or airfields. I've actually got a map for you of those already functioning in Papua and the Solomons.'

'Good.'

A metallic scraping sounded behind them and the airlock door opened again. 'Dr Robinson for you, Mr Cutter.'

Cutter turned and Trap moved hastily back to his seat, his mouth closing in a tight line as he automatically rubbed the scar under his chin.

'Ah, Dr Robinson, please come in.' The naval officer waved his hand at a bench along the bulkhead and Lexi sat. Cutter's voice was throaty, a mellow sound which reminded her of her grandfather; it caused her to feel kindly towards him.

The executive officer looked appreciatively at her. It was the first time he had seen the female guest. He had heard one of the lieutenants call her 'a looker' and she was.

'The colonel and I have been bringing each other up to date with things.'

Lexi, highly conscious of Trap three feet away, glanced at him but he was staring intently at the photo of the King, Queen and the President up on the bulk head.

'Firstly, Dr Robinson, let me say how sorry I am about your recent loss . . . The little boy.'

Lexi swallowed. 'Thank you.'

'None of us were aware of your existence before you came aboard last night. It's important for you to know that we're presently undertaking a long voyage and I have no orders whatever about you. It seems you're in no-man's-land, and therefore will have to accompany us to our destination.'

'Which is where?'

'Civilians don't usually receive this sort of info, ma'am, but in your case . . . The port of Pago Pago.'

416

'In the Samoan islands?'

'Yes.'

'What happens to me there?'

Cutter gave a friendly smile. 'Well, the colonel here suggested that at first you might be able to help out at the military hospital.'

She turned to look across at Trap, who this time made eye contact with her. He tried hard not to notice that she looked tired and sad as he expanded upon Cutter's statement.

'That's if you want to, of course. From there you should be able to get to Australia.'

She examined him. He wore that familiar look again, the removed and distant one. Her disappointment was reflected in her tone as she answered: 'If the Japs don't take the place.'

The executive officer shook his head. 'I wouldn't worry about that, ma'am. We're mounting strong defences there, and since we won the Midway and Coral Sea battles the Japs have been contained from expanding in that direction for a while. No, Pago will be a pretty safe place to be.'

Trap rose and at the same time tucked the secret orders into his inside pocket. 'Well thank you, Mr Cutter. I've got a wounded man I need to visit. Meanwhile, I await your summons any time. Good day.'

Cutter stood too. 'Sure. I'll find you later and we can go over that information again, Colonel Trapperton.'

'Okay,' Trap replied, straightening his shoulders as he departed. He did not glance in Lexi's direction again, though Cutter noticed her eyes follow him, and he inclined his head after Trap. 'Tell me to mind my own business if you like, but what gives with you two?'

The words rang in her head, 'What gives with you two?' For a brief moment she thought she would cry. She felt weak and pretty fragile. But glancing down at her hands and taking a breath, she lifted dry eyes up to the executive officer. 'We've been in each other's company . . . too long. I was an appendage he could have

417

done without. Having to fight the Japs with us ... that is, with a woman and children tagging along, wasn't too much fun for him.'

Slade Cutter was studying her now and getting a certain feeling about Dr Robinson and the colonel. 'Yet he spoke well of you.'

She looked uncomfortable. 'Did he? Yes, I suppose that's how he is: he's ... very fair.'

Cutter did not have a mind to go on with this. There was obviously some sort of a past with these two, but he had work to do and there was the Nip navy to avoid. It was nothing to do with him.

'Right, Dr Robinson, I just wanted you to know the state of play. The captain is particular about his vessel, so if you have any concerns or queries, call Petty Officer Jones; I think you met him last night. He'll lead you back to your quarters now.' He picked up the intercom and wound the handle at the side. 'Get Jones to come and take Dr Robinson home, will you?'

Lexi rose. 'So my understanding is, that Petty Officer Jones is assigned to me and the children—' She stopped short. 'I mean, to me and Lessa.'

Cutter stood as he answered: 'Absolutely right. He's a good man. Now one other thing I'll say is that we aren't used to having females or children aboard, so if you could keep the little girl away from the vital parts of the ship – bridge, engine room, torpedo room, mess, except at mealtimes – I'd appreciate it. Feel free to visit the galley. Potable water will be brought to your cabin to drink, and soda pop for the child. We'll present you with other water to wash in.'

'Thank you.'

Slade Cutter's gaze dropped across her. She was slender and attractive, with a soft vulnerability, even though she spoke with authority. He knew she had come through a tough time and he admired her resilience.

'Dr Robinson, I know Captain Parks wishes to see you later in

418

the day, but he's asked me to inform you that we operate differently to a surface ship so I'll just tell you a couple of things you need to know and let Jones do the rest. This is a long-range sub but we only travel short distances under water. Visibility becomes reduced below and we can only travel at about three knots because of the need to conserve the batteries: mind you, we can reach a maximum of nine knots down there for short periods. So, to cover extensive distances we travel on the surface. In fact we've been on the surface ever since you came aboard.'

'I thought that.'

He smiled. 'Submarines are in many ways simply surface ships that have the ability to dive. I guess there'll come a time in the future when they are pure underwater craft that have the ability to rise.'

She nodded in understanding.

'You'll hear a warning bell sound if we're going down. We can dive in thirty seconds to a minute. Get the little girl used to the alarms because sometimes we have to move fast and she'll find it odd when the floor tilts.' He gave her a sympathetic grin. 'But I'm sure you can look after her.'

'Yes I can. One thing I'll ask you now please.'

'What's that?'

'What did they do with Jimmy's body?'

'The little boy?'

'Yes.'

'I'll find out for you.'

'Thank you.'

'And I'll send the chaplain to you if you'd like.'

As Jones appeared at the door she replied, 'Yes, I *would* like that.'

'And I'll see you're settled in Pago Pago when we get there, so don't worry about a thing.'

Bestowing upon him a bleak smile she followed Jones away.

Chapter Fifty-four

2100 hours: 6 November 1942

The 300 foot 7 inch submarine, USS *Pompano* (SS-181) complement 5 officers, 45 enlisted men, christened on the 11 March
1937, cleaved its way through the liquid blackness which was
Atalikikun Bay on the north coast of the Gazelle Peninsula of
New Britain, in the Bismark Archipelago lying to the North West
of the Solomons. It had made splendid time from the Philippines,
though these waters were alive with enemy shipping and air traffic,
and stealth was paramount.

Caldo's tall, thick frame pushed though the cramped interior
and halted at the green baize curtain. 'Doc? Are you in there?'

Lexi knew that voice. 'Yes, come in, Sergeant.'

He drew the curtain aside and filled the tiny space as Lessa
slipped off the bunk. He lifted her in his mighty arms. 'Hello,
little Lessa.'

Lexi gave him a wan smile of welcome.

Caldo cleared his throat. 'I've been talking to the lieutenant and
Ivat, and they designated me to come and see you . . . to, well . . .
to say goodbye on behalf of all of us.'

'Goodbye?' There was a slight tremble in Lexi's voice.

'Yes, Doc. We didn't think you'd want all three of us in here
cluttering up the place.' He smiled. He had always liked the Doc,
right from the minute he saw her standing like some sort of

wonderful earth queen back there on that goddam road in Luzon on Christmas Day.

Lexi controlled her voice. 'Where are you going?'

'Sorry, Doc, can't tell you that.'

'Are *all* of you going?'

He knew exactly what that meant. 'Yeah, we leave the sub around midnight.'

Lexi could not hide the depth of her feelings, and he read them in her face as he placed Lessa back down on the bunk. 'Look, Doc, I reckon there's a lot I don't know, but I've guessed at it for a long time now. You're a swell lady, we all know that, none better . . .'

'Now don't make me cry, Caldo.'

'Nah, I wouldn't do that. I just want to tell you that whatever it is between you and the colonel . . . Gawd, I just hope it works out.' He looked self-consciously down at his feet.

'Oh Caldo . . .' Her voice broke and he brought his gaze back to hers with such an expression of compassion and sympathy, that tears welled in her eyes.

'Caldo . . . I want to tell you something.' She paused and he waited. 'You see it's that — I'm married . . . to a good man, a fine man. It's just that . . . Oh dear . . .' She faltered and now the tears came. 'I can't tell you the whole story, but I feel so guilty all the time. Trap is a friend of . . . my husband. It's all awful, but oh Caldo, I can't help but be in love with him.'

'Ah Doc, I've known that since the beginning.' The big man opened his arms and she stepped into them to weep against his chest. He could smell the clean wholesomeness of her as he hugged her inside his bear-like grasp.

'I met him in . . . Madura, years ago.'

Sergeant Caldo had guessed that one. No surprises there.

The big man had been under Trap's command for a single year, but in that short time they had shared more than many men who had known each other a lifetime; theirs was an attachment forged in torment and trouble, their fellowship nurtured by passing more than once through the valley of death. Caldo had witnessed many times his commanding officer's resolution, nerve and courage; Colonel Trapperton had guts! He came close to worshipping his leader, and if he could have chosen any woman in the world for him, he would choose this one here in his arms right now. And yet Doc had just revealed that she was wedded to someone else. Hell! Life was dumb all right.

She was pressing her face into his shirt. 'And now little Jimmy's dead. I just feel so . . . lost.'

Suddenly they were aware of Lessa's weeping. She was holding Lexi's legs, her small frame shaking with emotion. Lexi broke from Caldo's warm-hearted embrace and dropped to her knees to wrap Lessa's tiny frame in her arms. 'Darling, darling,' she consoled softly. 'There, there, little one. Now stop crying . . . Everything's all right and I'm not sad any more, see. Look at me.' She smiled as wide a smile as she could muster and wiped her eyes as the child slowly ceased crying. 'Now, see no one's crying. We're all happy. Uncle Caldo and you and me.' She looked up at the mighty frame above, meeting the man's eyes. 'I ran into Trap earlier today.' She managed a tepid smile. 'Can't really avoid seeing him now and then on a sub, can I? He didn't speak to me, but he picked up Lessa and nursed her as he always does. And you know how he always calls me *Babae* to the children . . . ?'

Caldo nodded. They had all noticed this affectation ever since they had left Cagayan de Oro.

'Well, before putting her down today he said to her, "Be a good girl and do as your *babae* tells you." And then he kissed her forehead. He's never kissed Lessa, not once in all the months we've been with you. But he did today, and now I know why . . .' Her voice trembled. 'He was saying goodbye.'

Caldo saw her eyes well with tears again and he felt so bad. Her hand came up to her mouth like a child's would and he wanted to hug her again and fix her sadness, but he saw her pull herself together for the child's sake. *She's something, the Doc, really something.*

Lexi took a deep sighing breath and kissed Lessa before she stood up. 'Please tell Lieutenant Williams and Private Ivat I wish them all the luck in the world.'

'You bet, Doc.'

With her right hand she drew Lessa's head in towards her side in a comforting manner as she added, 'And stay safe, Sergeant Caldo. You're one of the best there is. I'll truly miss you.'

'And we'll miss you, Doc.' He paused before he chucked Lessa under the chin. 'Bye, little girl.'

Their eyes met in mutual respect, and quite suddenly Caldo gave Lexi a beautifully executed salute and retreated through the green drape.

It was three hours later when Trap, with a studied expression, moved through the cramped interior to pause in the dim light before the same emerald curtain and stand there staring at it.

She was in there. Half of him wanted badly to say goodbye to her, but the other half knew better. At least now MacArthur would know she was alive and headed to Pago Pago. The message had been sent by Cutter to Brisbane GHQ. Trap reckoned that MacArthur would make sure she and the kid got out of Samoa and safely to Australia at some point. That gave him solace.

Every day since their pick-up from Mindanao, he had briefed Williams, Caldo, Ivat and their new recruit Tommy Shibuyu about their mission and they had talked over the little information they held. This evening they had gone over their departure from the *Pompano*, and they were all keyed up and ready to go. Williams, Caldo and Ivat had been suspicious of Tommy at first. Trap could not blame them – they were human beings and he had felt something like that himself – but gradually as the days passed and Tommy explained with fervour how he could aid their cause in enemy territory, toleration had blossomed and a degree of acceptance had taken root.

Contact had been made with the coast watcher station south of Rabaul and it had been agreed that their native guide would be waiting on the shores of the bay away from where any Japanese garrison was situated. Trap had informed his small group that this person who would lead the Americans to their Allied comrades was known as Raga, and the password was *gadfly*.

Yes, he would soon be ashore in New Britain, but at this moment he stood eyes fixed on the emerald screen in front of him. She was beyond it, probably asleep. He had seen her a number of times on their voyage here: inevitable on a sub. He had even come across her and Lessa this morning and he had not been able to stop himself from picking up the little girl and kissing her. The truth was, he would never see the kid again and she had grown on him.

Against all his instincts he allowed himself to think of the months with the Doll and the kids: the awkward primitive dwelling places; their rapid flights at short notice from hideout to hideout; being caught in jungle downpours and surviving in the relentless sticky heat; the insects unremitting day and night; the fear of standing on a reptile or meeting a freshwater crocodile when they crossed the streams. Yes, the Doll had stood up to it all, along with the ever-present danger of being caught by the Japs. She had saved the lives of some and helped others to die with dignity, and her demeanour had rarely altered. She had shown those kids only love and had won the admiration of all his men.

Momentarily, there alone in the dim grey world of the *Pompano* Hank Trapperton's face betrayed him. He closed his eyes and took a breath that rumbled from his throat.

The sub was moving cautiously on the surface in enemy waters. The drumming of the engines throbbed in his head. He opened his eyes and reached out and his fingertips almost touched the drape. *She's in there. Just the other side of this curtain, not two yards away.* His eyes were trained on the back of his hand; it inched forward and the pads of his fingers actually rested on the cloth. *Pull back the curtain, now. Go on. Do it! She's there.*

A moment later, his expression changed, his mouth formed the habitual hard line, his gaze became fixed and his hand fell back to his side as he spun round and walked away.

Night clung to the vessel. Captain Parks watched the officer of the deck, Ensign Roger Noah, a fair-haired, eager and smart young officer from New York City, as he turned to Slade Cutter standing with him on the bridge below the conning tower.

'Now, sir?'

The executive officer nodded. 'Yes, cut the engines.' The humming died beneath their feet and the vessel floated at rest.

Ozone drifted in the air beneath the clouds and there was a chop to the inky sea lapping the submarine's hull. The captain and the two officers with him could discern the land mass and they knew they were on the right coordinates.

Cutter pointed. 'Where's Colonel Trapperton? These sea lanes close to the coast can have enemy vessels day or night.'

As he spoke, an arm came up out of the entrance hatch in the deck and the night revealed the form of Hank Trapperton climbing through. Boots scraped on the metal ladder and he stood up.

The captain addressed him. 'Ready, Colonel?'

'Yes, Captain. Good night for a canoe ride.'

The Commander motioned down to the foredeck to the skiffs which had been been brought up from below and fitted together out in the open air upon the hull. They sat now in a neat row of four, paddles attached and held in position by five of the crew.

Behind Trap came Williams, Caldo, Ivat and Shibuyu, all dressed in black with dark berets on their heads. Every man carried a knapsack, the wireless set in Williams's, and all clutched Tommy guns and wore revolvers in their belts and bandoliers full of ammunition across their shoulders.

It was only in the last hour that the captain had informed his crew what was occurring. Until then only himself, Cutter, and his decoder Lieutenant Burns had known of this plan.

Captain Parks leant over and shook Trap's hand. Naval captain and army colonel were pretty much on the same level. 'Good luck, Colonel. We're right on the spot, so as long as you and your men row south-east, you'll hit the coast at the place where Raga should be.'

Trap gestured for Ivat to close the hatch. 'Don't need any extraneous light.' He lifted his hands to shade his eyes to view the shoreline. Suddenly he swung round to the captain. 'Can you hear that?'

'What?'

'Engines, I think . . . to the west. Sounds big, battleship or a cruiser.'

Everyone listened.

'Yes, I can hear engines right enough,' Ensign Noah agreed. 'We can't stay.'

Trap tried to find Cutter's eyes in the darkness as he did a mental calculation. 'Ten chances out of ten that's a Jap warship heading our way, and you can't risk being spotted.'

'Just get on with it,' Parks declared, and Cutter swung round on Noah. 'Flash the shore once only so they know we're here. Fast!'

Noah turned on the submarine lamp, and as Trap spoke his cool tone held a hint of excitement. 'Let's go. If Raga's waiting, he's seen our light, and if he's not, we'll have to make contact with the coast-watching teleradio when we get ashore.'

Williams studied the compass as the others said brief good-byes and clambered over to the skiffs on the hull while the commander of the vessel gave the order: 'Stand by to start engines.'

Noah turned. 'Hell! I reckon that ship's still coming this way.'

'Yes, I can hear it now,' remarked Cutter.

'Christ!'

'Things sound closer than they are at night,' Trap's tone was even as Slade Cutter met his eyes in the gloom.

'Good luck, Colonel Trapperton. I sincerely hope we meet again.'

426

Trap produced a grin. 'Who knows?' Then his face stiffened into seriousness. 'I'll ask you to do something for me if you will.'

'Sure.'

He proffered an envelope and the executive took it. 'Please give this to Dr Robinson for me.'

As the captain ordered, 'Start engines,' Trap flicked his hand in a quick informal salute to the submarine officers, climbed down the ladder and hurried across the sub's hull to his men in the waiting skiffs. Williams, who carried the compass, was in the lead and as their canoes were pushed off into the choppy sea they heard the engines rumble and the captain call, 'Good luck, Colonel Trapperton!' followed by Ensign Noah shouting, 'That ship's still coming this way. It sounds like a Jap heavy cruiser to me.'

'If you can hear them, they can hear us!' Cutter did a quick estimate of the distance. 'It's still out of range! It's deep enough here to dive, sir.'

'Stand by to dive!' shouted the captain.

Orders were relayed around the craft. All crew who weren't already on alert were tumbling out of their bunks as Noah hurriedly lifted the manhole and held it open.

The men needed no urging: they believed they could distinguish a black shape on course with them, and one by one they clambered down through the entrance hatch held open by Noah.

The submarine commander calculated the distance of the oncoming craft. 'Get inside, son. It'll be within range soon.'

Noah virtually leapt down, with Slade Cutter hard behind, followed by Captain Parks. He drew the hatch down above him as he shouted, 'Dive!'

And as the hatch was secured, the executive officer repeated the order 'Dive!' and followed the captain into the control room.

Lexi's eyes snapped open. What had woken her? Something was different. What was it? Then she realised.

The engines had stopped.

Day and night, on and on, the continuous whirring of the engines of the submarine had insinuated itself into her life. Always there, the constant unrelenting noise, the accompaniment to life aboard the submarine. And now? It had ceased. The silence had woken her.

She raised herself, switched on the wall lamp and looked down at Lessa. The child slept and the clock read midnight. Eyes towards the ceiling, she noticed her heart accelerate as she slipped her feet over the side into the men's bath slippers someone had given her a week ago. Standing, she moved to the curtain and drawing it aside took down the flashlight which hung beside it on the bulkhead. She believed she could hear movement all around and voices raised in the distance. There was low-level lighting in the outside compartment and a metallic echo reached her ears as she switched on the flashlight and bounced the beam along the series of congested grey pipes. The illumination revealed nobody, and she stood there in her naval-issue pyjamas with her tousled hair wrapping around her shoulders.

She thought of Trap and spoke aloud. 'You didn't even say goodbye.' Caldo, Williams and Ivat had thought to farewell her, but not him. A tear slid down the side of her nose and she sniffed and wiped it away. *He's gone, gone for ever . . . and he didn't even say goodbye.* A second tear slid down the other side of her nose as, abruptly, the internal speaker system crackled. 'Hear this! Alert! Man all stations! Prepare to start engines!' And a moment later, 'Start engines!'

The four diesel engines whirred into action and the craft vibrated with life again. Lexi took a deep breath. It appeared that whatever had occurred was over, and she pulled the cloth across and retreated, only to flinch as the intercom buzzed. Lessa awoke and sat up in the bunk rubbing her eyes as Lexi picked up the handset. 'Yes.'

'Ma'am, I'm Collins, one of the chefs, Petty Officer Jones told me to call you. I'm coming to you before the watertight doors are closed on each compartment. Don't worry.'

428

'What's that? What's wrong?'

'Prepare to dive!' bellowed through the speaker system, breaking into their conversation.

Fear tingled through Lexi as she replaced the intercom handset and clasped the wide-eyed child.

A voice rang out: 'Dive!' and the craft tilted down at an extreme angle.

'Oh God, what's going on?'

Suddenly there was a sort of *click*, followed by a rumbling sound and a throbbing from outside, or perhaps, from above. Lessa began to cry and the submarine lurched as a hellish noise erupted in the sea outside the hull and the curtain was flung aside and Collins materialised.

'Oh my lord!' Lexi's heart accelerated.

The *click* sounded again through the hull and the shock waves from an explosion in the sea beyond the metal made the craft shake and lunge sideways as Collins stumbled to the bunk and righted himself.

He patted Lessa's shoulder. 'Everything will be okay, little girl. Don't cry. This is just a funny sort of ride.'

Lessa eyed him in disbelief and Lexi, mouth dry, pressed the child to her body and kissed her hair. 'It's all right, darling, it's all right.'

'Yeah,' announced Collins, manufacturing a smile for Lessa in the wan illumination. 'We'll look after you, little Lessa.' He patted the child's hand as his eyes met Lexi's over her head. 'Reckon we're avoiding trouble, ma'am, that's all. Those were depth charges from above exploding.'

'Are we being attacked?'

'Reckon so. We must be getting down close to as far as we can go now. Around four hundred feet, that's the max, can't go lower.'

More shock waves battered the submarine and the three inmates heard heavy objects thump the vessel.

'What's that?'

'Not sure. But don't worry, whatever the old man decides will be best. Look, he might cut the engines; if so, don't worry. Being motionless could be our best chance.'

Lexi did not quite understand that point, but she was very willing to be a believer. She turned her eyes to his face, concentrating on his features to take her mind off what was happening. He was young, perhaps twenty-three, and a stubble of beard sprouted on his chin. His eyes were blue and his eyebrows were fair, not much of a defined line at all, a sort of haze of hair grew on the bridge of his nose. It was a kind face.

Suddenly the whole sub trembled so fiercely that Lexi thought it was about to rip apart. Again the craft lurched and two slabs of insulating cork fell down in front of them. Lessa screamed and Lexi wrapped her arms further around the little girl, pressing the child's face into her pyjamas. 'There, darling, there, there. We're all right.' She did not believe what she was saying, but it helped to utter the words.

'Our old man's the navy's best, and so is Mr Cutter. We're in plenty good hands, ma'am, you'll see.'

Lexi mumbled, 'Yes,' and closing her eyes hid her face in Lessa's hair and thought of Jimmy . . . and Trap.

Chapter Fifty-five

The breeze was sharpening, water washed over the front of the craft and the chop of the ebony sea threw spray into Trap's face as he paddled furiously towards the land. His eyes darted back and forth to the silhouettes round him: Williams in the lead, Caldo some yards behind and Ivat and Shibuyu forging along on his right side.

Abruptly awakening the night, loud splashing sounds rolled across the sea to them. Trap straightened his shoulders: he knew that noise. It was depth-charge canisters meeting the water. A boom followed, resonating across the mild swell behind them, and seconds later another boom reached them.

The *Pompano* had been seen all right and the oncoming ship had proven to be the enemy: around here it had no chance of being anything else. A sub fighting it out on the surface with a battleship had no chance; that was why Parks had taken the craft down. Thank God it was night.

Trap stopped rowing and the light craft began to bounce in the moving sea, but he was unaware of it because for the first time in his life, he knew fear: *fear for her.*

She was back there and the Japs were firing on the sub! A surge of emotion overwhelmed him as he shipped the oar and turned his head to look round.

The shape of the heavy cruiser was distinguishable in the night. If the depth charges hit the sub there would be an ensuing explosion and the sea would spurt high in the air.

She's back there and I'm here in a skiff eight hundred yards from New Britain. I can't do a goddam thing about what happens. Keep rowing, Trapperton. Get the Doll off your mind! Concentrate on what's ahead.

Ivat had seen Trap stop, and he too paused, their canoes rising and falling in the swell. Trap shook his head and yelled, 'Keep rowing, Ivat, that's an order. I'll be along.'

Ivat recommenced rowing but Trap remained motionless. If the sub were hit she would have no chance at all. He knew all the water on his face was not coming from the sea; he was sweating excessively and the exertion was not causing it. *If the sub's hit, she'll die.*

Trap's skiff floated, the oar in front of him lying across the tiny craft. *Get the Doll off your mind! Concentrate on what's ahead.* Yet still he did not move. He remained drifting on the liquid blackness. Another rumble of a detonation below the surface rolled across the water to him and he tensed. He felt helpless. He had never panicked, not in his whole life, but what he was experiencing right now might be akin to it.

Inhaling deeply, he blew out through his mouth and started talking to himself. 'Remember poor old Johnny . . . how she took him for a sucker. Sleeping with me and promised to him. And Johnny believed her lies about the kid. Think about that, Trap, old buddy.'

He saw the ebony shapes of his men disappearing in front of him and finally he shook his head. And with one lift of his eyes to the night sky, he picked up the oar, took another rumbling breath and rowed on, profoundly aware of the minutes passing. As he violently dug the water with his oar, he waited for the mighty explosion from beneath the sea behind him, but none came, and when the deep resonating booms from the depth charges floated to him no more, only the watchful night noticed his body relax and the relief spread across his face.

Lexi's short, nervous breaths kept coming as glass shattered somewhere nearby. She had not counted them but she believed that at least ten charges from above had ripped the sea and ocean bed outside the hull at about thirty-second intervals. And at some point the engines had been cut.

She was staring at Collins across Lessa's dark curls and he was staring back, continuing to reassure them: 'Stay calm, everything will be all right. This is the best way to avoid being hit. I've been through this before and we've always come up trumps.' He kept repeating, 'The old man's one of the navy's finest. He'll get us out of here.' He manufactured a grin. 'I reckon Captain Parks's got a straight connection to the Lord, so we won't worry. No, not at all.' He patted Lessa's arm and reiterated what a brave girl she was.

A minute passed without noise, and Lexi's heart began to slow its frantic pace. As another silent minute followed she imagined she could hear the rumble of a ship passing over them. Automatically she looked to the ceiling, still holding Lessa close as the seconds ticked by.

Collins sighed and patted Lessa's shoulder for the twentieth time, as the child moved and glanced up to meet Lexi's eyes. She kissed the girl's forehead and dared to believe they might have avoided the battleship. The last ague of rocking and wobbling had been many minutes previously, and Lessa had stopped crying.

Lexi eyed the chef. 'I thought the ship would break apart at one stage back there.'

He shook his head. 'No, she's a good sub is the *Pompano*.' Then he winked at her. 'I've gotta believe that, you know. Anyway, ma'am, let me formally introduce myself. I'm DeForest Collins, second chef on the *Pompano*, and we're all still alive.'

Abruptly a beeping sound reverberated through the submarine and Lexi flinched.

'Na, don't worry, that's the all-clear.' Collins interpreted for them.

Now the captain's voice gave encouragement through the loud-speaker, and in another few minutes they felt the throb of the engines starting up as DeForest stroked Lessa's cheek affectionately and stood from the bunk where they had all been tightly ensconced side by side.

DeForest Collins spoke encouragingly. 'Now, ma'am, see, what'd I tell you? We'll probably go topside again when the old man reckons it's safe, but meanwhile I'm gunna get you a nice cup of coffee and I'll bring a cookie for you, Lessa.' He grinned at the little one, who pushed her face into the side of Lexi's pyjamas and, revealing only one eye, gazed up at him.

Lexi managed a small smile. 'Thank you, DeForest . . . but do you make tea?'

'Sure I do. Wasn't my mother from Massachusetts, where they all drink tea? I'll bring you one real snappy. Milk and sugar?'

She nodded. 'Please.'

As he drew aside the curtain Lexi said, 'DeForest?'

He turned. 'Uh-huh?'

'We wouldn't have remained sane down here without you.'

He gave her a wry smile and winked. 'You did just fine, ma'am, just fine. Pair of first-rate mariners you two are, no doubt about it.'

Chapter Fifty-six

It was pitch dark now, for the moon was lost behind the overhanging branches and vines of the narrow stream. There was an odd smell drifting in the tepid sticky atmosphere and the beads of sweat on the rowers' temples had become rivulets. Mosquitos and other insects buzzed incessantly and occasional sinister shapes slithered into the water from the banks.

'Bloody hot,' croaked Ivat, hitting out at the insects. 'They always like me. That was one good thing about the sub, no flamin' bugs.'

'It's not just you, we're all being eaten by the little bastards,' Caldo growled, ceasing to row and striking the back of his neck. 'There's something inside my collar; it's big, whatever it is.'

Trap was immediately behind Raga, who, as expected, had been waiting for them when they made landfall. They had come into a rocky foliage-covered cove and at first found no one. After leaving Ivat and Shibuyu with the canoes, they had separated and moved both ways along the shoreline until Trap, who was alone, heard a whistle. He had halted as a voice spoke from the jungle in an undertone: 'Gadfly at night.' To which he had replied, 'Gadbee by day', and the undergrowth had parted to reveal in the vague night illumination an individual of average height. It was soon established that he was Raga and that he spoke passable English and chewed beetlenut.

The two could not see much of each other, but later it would be revealed that Raga had a not unattractive angular face atop a bony body and long thin arms, and included in this package, loyalty to the Allies and the heart of a lion. Trap and his new acquaintance returned to the skiffs, where they found the others, who had been halted by a swamp on the shoreline to the east and could go no further.

After the introductions Raga led them to a canoe of his own and the newcomers were surprised to see that his dugout craft dipped to the aft because an oversized battery-powered arc lamp sat in it. When they asked about it he brushed the question aside, saying, 'It broken.'

And to Trap's question on the whereabouts of the Australians, he replied, 'They inland, up river.' He gestured into the night. 'Better just me meet you. They wait.'

That corresponded with the briefing from Executive Officer Cutter aboard the *Pompano*: that Raga would be the one to lead them to the Australians.

Their guide appeared anxious to leave and he beckoned them to follow him. 'Stay close me. We go along coast then up river and streams.' And he climbed into his canoe and moved forward to balance the arc lamp. He surprised them by being able to row at speed from this position and they made fair time along the coast and up the river which later they would know as the Keravat. A mile or so inland they saw fires on the north bank and heard the echo of voices. Raga slowed right down and proceeded on by, hugging the far bank at a measured and cautious pace. Later he informed them that this was a village and an airfield where an enemy unit was stationed and that they had passed a number of deserted copra plantations.

Beyond that point they turned into a series of tributaries and pressed on for over half an hour until currently they had decelerated in virtual darkness under an overhang of jungle above the stream. Trap leant forward and spoke in a low voice. 'How much further is it?'

'Not far.'

Caldo grunted. 'That's what he said ten minutes ago.'

Trap guessed it must be later than 0200 by now. Another five minutes passed in the jet-black darkness before Raga enlightened them, 'Real close, round bend now.'

The overhanging branches and plants thinned out as Ivat declared, 'Jesus! A big croc just went by.'

Caldo grunted. 'Yeah right, thanks, Ivat. You should be used to them after the Philippines.'

'I'll never get used to them. Anyway, the ones I saw in the Philippines were a darn sight smaller than that thing.'

They turned at a sharp angle and immediately the stream widened and the canopy of jungle growth disappeared to reveal the light of a campfire ahead.

Drawing closer, the glow from a second fire delineated two huts. Raga brought his canoe nose into the bank and an Australian voice sounded out of the black night. 'That you, Raga?'

'Sure.'

'You bring the Yanks?'

'Sure.'

'You're a little trimmer, Raga.'

Trap followed the leader and edged his skiff into the bank in the firelight as the disembodied voice transformed into a soldier wearing the recent issue of AIF jungle greens. He wore a mosquito net over his head and carried a Martini-Henry rifle. He strode forward to help the newcomers, calling back over his shoulder, 'Give these blokes a hand, Davidson.' Another man emerged out of the night. He was more eccentrically clad in shorts, singlet and boots, but still with the mosquito net in place covering his face.

As Trap climbed out of the skiff the first soldier introduced himself. 'I'm Sergeant Major Lambert. Are you the colonel?'

'Yes. Hank Trapperton.'

'Welcome to New Guinea, sir. We were beginning to think you weren't going to make it. We've been expecting you for a fortnight.'

Trap was not quite sure what a fortnight was, but he did not

437

enquire as the warrant officer gestured back into the jungle. 'Our camp is inland and up a bit to get away from the water and the masses of insects down here. It's pretty well hidden too. Follow me.'

They did so in single file along an ebony path up a hillside and over a conglomeration of rocks which in the night were most difficult to traverse, until they emerged into a clearing where three more fires blazed. As they arrived, a snake, its skin gleaming in the flickering light, slithered past their boots into the undergrowth.

'Our commanding officer asked to be woken when you got here. So I'll pop along and get him.' Lambert hurried away to the furthest of the huts as the introductions to Davidson took place.

Davidson showed a missing eye tooth. 'I'll put the billy on the boil. We don't have any coffee but we do have some Billy Tea and some sugar. No milk, I'm afraid.'

'Tea'll do,' Caldo growled. 'It ain't no pep pill, but we need something after rowing half the night.'

'I've got plenty of bully beef. You can have as much as you like.' This was typical of AIF rations: 5 lb tins of unappetising salted beef which the soldiers had named Bully Beef.

The Australian camp was in a clearing surrounded by thick jungle alive with the clicking, croaking, rustling symphony of a thousand night creatures. In the fire glow Trap noted a stack of ammunition boxes and a tent with *Australian Imperial Forces* stamped on the flap.

Davidson pointed to a number of wooden crates. 'Sit down, fellas, while Raga and I make the tea.' Caldo, Williams, Ivat and Shibuyu were hitting out fiercely at insects when Davidson announced calmly, 'We've got a plague of bloody flying ants at the moment. But there seem to be fewer around the fire.' In a moment they were all ranged close into the flames even though their brows were damp with sweat. Davidson picked up an Arnott's biscuit tin from the top of a box of ammunition and brushed the insects off it. 'I think I've got something edible in here in case the bully beef doesn't interest you.'

The thud of boots on dirt sounded outside the ring of light and Trap turned as Warrant Officer Lambert strode back along the path, followed by a second man. 'Colonel Trapperton, this is our commanding officer.'

Trap remained still as the dancing gleam from the five illuminated the grin of genuine surprise on the Australian's face. It was only Caldo who noticed the momentary hesitation from Trap before he put out his hand to John Drayton, who took it enthusiastically.

John Drayton's grin broadened. 'You? I can't believe it. It's really you!' He remembered how in Milne Bay, when he had been told by the colonel that the leader of the coming operations would be an American, he had felt resentment, but now that he saw who it was, all indignation faded.

'Yes, Johnny, it's really me.' Trap remained holding John Drayton's hand. He was recalling Hong Kong and the night he had learnt that Johnny was married to *her*. He was also recalling that he had been called Chris Webster at the time.

But John Drayton did not show any discomposure at the name *Trapperton*. He had known this man in Malaya and met him again in Hong Kong, and both times had been under different incarnations, so for him to have a third name, albeit as he was to find out, the genuine one – caused no surprise. He squeezed Trap's hand as he remarked, 'Colonel Trapperton, I'm truly delighted to see you.'

Chapter Fifty-seven

The following morning the submarine surfaced well north of Trap's drop-off point. The captain had opted for safety and headed north, avoiding the danger of the narrow, busy enemy shipping lane which was St George's Channel. He intended to sail around New Ireland through the Ysabel Channel and into the open ocean, even though it added a couple of hundred miles to his voyage to the American Samoas.

A lookout was on watch for enemy craft in the air and on the sea, and at 0900 hours fresh air filled the grey passages of the *Pompano* while Lexi and Lessa sat in the presence of Slade Cutter. He had come and found them eating in the mess. At least Lessa was eating; Lexi had no appetite. Her thoughts were entirely of Trap. Her fears that he had departed the sub had been verified the night before by DeForest when he had brought her a cup of tea. She kept repeating in her head, *But he didn't even say goodbye*, and Cutter observed that she looked tired and drawn. He explained further what had occurred the night before and confirmed that after the departure of Trap and the others there had been an attack by an enemy battleship which they had fortunately survived.

He smiled. 'So our part has been successfully undertaken and we've dropped Colonel Trapperton and his men at the appointed place to go into New Britain.'

'Am I allowed to know why?'

'I can't officially tell you, Dr Robinson, but I reckon you can guess.'

'Some sort of guerrilla mission like the one he was conducting in the Philippines?'

'Yes, you could call it that. It seems he's a very good operator in enemy territory.'

Lexi agreed. 'True, Mr Cutter, I spent enough time with him to know that.'

Cutter nodded. 'And we've him to thank that you and the little girl are safely on your way to Samoa.'

A wistful expression crossed her face. 'Yes, we have.' Though in her heart she feared he had been right about the children: that she should have left them behind with the Barettas, where even under Jap occupation chances were they would have survived. Her heart ached for Jimmy and she looked down at Lessa as the little girl snuggled into her side. That gave her some consolation and she brought her eyes back to Slade Cutter.

The executive officer thought the time had come to pass over that which he carried. He reached into his breast pocket, took out the envelope and proffered it. 'He left this for you.'

The look on Lexi's face betrayed her inmost feelings and his eyes softened. 'Normally it would be my duty to read and censor a letter of this type. But . . .' He simply smiled gently at her, stood up and walked away.

Lexi left the child in the mess with DeForest, whom Lessa had taken to quite well, not surprisingly, for he had been wonderful to her. Down through the various compartments she moved, returning greetings from the crew until she entered her private area, drew the green screen behind her and walked to the bunk.

That had been two hours previously and she still had not opened the envelope. She was finding everything too hard to bear: the loss of Jimmy and now the loss of Trap. She had always known the day would arrive, but she had been unprepared. He had been close at hand for so long. Even his scorn had been acceptable because of the nearness of him. To be with him had been everything.

At times the guilt over how she had treated John Drayton rose inside her like a real thing. If only she could alter all she had done! She had been terribly wrong to marry him and to let him think Paul was his son; that had been so unfair, so cruel, she saw that now. And perhaps if she had never seen Trap again and this rotten war had not started, her life would have gone on calmly, but even as she thought it, she shook her head. She would always have loved Trap and that would have been cheating Johnny anyway.

She had lost her diamond engagement ring and her wedding ring somewhere in the jungles of Mindanao; she had taken that as a sign, but she still retained Silveria's wedding ring. She was glad of that, for one day she would give it to Lessa.

Three times she believed she had been witness to Trap's love for her: Christmas Day when he found her on the lonely road; the night they entered the sea to swim to the sub, and he touched her and wished her good luck; and the very same night when Jimmy had died. In those moments she had sworn his love was real. Why, the very touch of his lips on her palm in her heart-break over Jimmy had revitalised her.

She looked down at the envelope lying on the bunk. It had *Lexine Robinson Whitby* written on it in a flowing round hand.

Over the course of the morning she had picked it up and put it down half a dozen times. She heard the gong for noon chow-down and still she sat rigidly looking at it. But at last she overcame whatever held her back and with shaking hands she picked it up, opened it and read:

Nov 6 1942

> *Doll,*
> *I need to tell you a few things.*
> *1. Don't have any regrets about Jimmy, you were perfect on that*

442

score. He was a great little man and was going to be too damn good for this world anyway. You did all you could and a lot more. Yes, I mean it.

2. Lessa — she kind of grew on me, that kid. You do a fine job with her and she loves you to pieces. I reckon I was wrong when I told you to leave the kids behind. They were meant to be with you even though you might not think so just now.

3. You and me. You happen to be married to a swell guy so that's the beginning and the end of that. Yeah, I'll always remember Madura too . . . for what a mug I was.

It would be a good idea though if we could forget about it. Life will be better that way.

Trap

Lexi sat staring at the words as she heard footsteps passing in the compartment beyond the curtain, but she did not move. A tear fell and smudged his signature. 'You knew it would come to this, Lex,' she said aloud to herself, staring at the green baize. 'All along you knew it would come to this, so don't act as if you're surprised.'

She realised she was trembling and she grasped herself around the waist, crossing her forearms to suppress it. 'Buck up, Lexine,' she continued aloud. 'He's gone and you're on your own.'

Time passed and the spasm stopped. Slowly she folded the note and replaced it in the envelope, before she stood and slipped the letter into a drawer and moved across to the tin dish of water against the wall and splashed her eyes. Picking up a small towel, she wiped her face while she took deep breaths to compose herself, even as another ripple ran through her slender frame.

'No, Trap,' she whispered leaning over the basin. 'Life without you won't be better.'

Chapter Fifty-eight

12 November, 1942

The heavy humid odour of rotting flora sidled by on the breeze as a snake slithered down a tree trunk at Trap's right hand and melted into the obscurity of decay within the exotic green lushness.

Tommy Shibuyu had confirmed the sailing date for the enemy armada to Buna as 28 November by entering Rabaul disguised as a Japanese soldier. He had spoken to guards on the waterfront who believed him one of them, and had verified it. It was said that the Kempeitai general awaited the arrival of another commander thought to be General Hitoshi Imamura before he would depart. Trap's frown eased slightly thinking of Tommy: the young Nisei was beginning to prove himself very valuable. They now knew the name of the Kempeitai general: Ikeda.

But the limpet mines were not here yet. Trap would feel more confident when they were. Three of the Australians, Howard, Smith and Bird, had left today to travel the ten miles to the appointed spot for the drop. Their native guide, known as Cigs because of his insatiable appetite for cigarettes, had taken them. Cigs was a cousin to Raga, the native who had led Trap and his men to the camp.

Trap had been down to the river, and as he returned along the track to the camp he stiffened and halted on hearing Ivat's voice through the wall of trunks and vines.

'She was a great gal. Good doctor, too. Those hard-bitten guys came to think a lot of her, eh, Sarge?'

Caldo's deep tones rejoined, 'Yeah, she was somethin', was the Doc.'

'Where is she now?' It was an Australian voice.

'Back on the sub that brought us here.'

'Pity, we could have done with some female company.'

This statement was met by laughter. 'Yeah, too right.' Any woman would do right now, doctor included.

Ivat continued: 'She'd been shipwrecked, ya know, and she was a friend of General MacArthur wasn't she, Sarge?'

Sounds of disbelief issued from the listeners until Caldo enlightened them. 'Actually I think it was her grandfather who was the friend . . .' There was a certain reluctance in his tone, as if he would rather not give out this information, '. . . but for sure the general wanted to take her with him to Australia.'

'So why didn't he?' asked one them.

In the momentary silence following this statement, Trap peered through the hanging vines and tree trunks and made out the three Australian soldiers who were in conversation with Caldo and Ivat: Smith, Lister and 'Joker' Mayberry.

And now Ivat replied: 'Because she was in our patrol boat when we left Corregidor and we had an engine breakdown and missed the rendevous in Mindanao. When we got there, MacArthur had flown out so she was stuck with us.'

Lister gave a wide grin. 'Any hanky-panky go on?'

Caldo's retort was immediate and irritable. 'Shit, no. She wasn't a fast woman. She was a doctor, for Christ's sake. Be sensible.'

Trap did not hesitate any longer: he gave a loud cough and strode ahead, calling out as he came: 'Williams? Caldo? Anybody here?'

The men stood and it was Caldo who came thundering over the roots and foliage of the jungle floor as Trap burst into the clearing. 'Yes, sir, I'm here.'

*   *   *

Trap spent the rest of that day in unhappy thought, and as the afternoon receded into the regular downpour he sat in his tent staring at the rivulet of water cutting the living space in half as it emerged from under his bunk and streamed by his boots to the far side of the tent.

He knew he had to speak to Johnny about his wife. If he did not, it seemed certain that one of his men was going to innocently mention her in front of him.

None of his men knew Lexi was married to Johnny; she had been Dr Robinson to them, not Whitby.

Trap leant forward on the flimsy stretcher which he called a bed, holding his head in his hands, his elbows resting on his knees. He knew Caldo guessed a lot about himself and the Doll. Of course it stood to reason that right from the beginning Caldo and the boys with him would have suspected something: hell, on Christmas Day he had wrapped her in his arms when he had found her on that back road in Luzon. And it had been his sergeant who had brought the Doll's message to him a couple of days after Christmas, near Bataan; it rang now in his head as he gripped it with his fingers: *I'll always remember Madura . . . all my life*. He pictured Caldo delivering the message in a gruff tone and eyeing him, but he had terminated any further conversation with a dismissive salute.

The rain was becoming heavier; it pelted on to the top of the canvas and he lifted his head and watched it through the tent flap.

Yes, the big sergeant was aware right enough that there had been something of a past between him and Lexine Robinson, and of course his other men must at least suspect it. Ivat and Williams had seen the hand-kissing on the night of Jimmy's death; even if they had forgotten how he greeted her on Christmas Day. But none of them had an inkling that she was married to John Drayton Whitby . . . that was, unless Caldo knew something. He recalled he had told Caldo that she was married to a friend of his and she used to talk to Caldo a lot.

Every day since their arrival Trap had sought out Johnny to tell him that his wife had been with him and his men for the past eight months, and yet he had said nothing. Today, when he heard his men talking about her, he knew he could avoid it no longer.

When the rain eased and the short evening speedily enveloped the camp, Trap stode along the mushy track to pause outside John Drayton's tent. He bit the side of his lip, grimaced and lifted the flap. 'You in here, Johnny?'

'Yes, come in,' his friend laughed, 'into my waterlogged parlour.'

Trap bent and entered and squeezed in to sit on the end of the canvas stretcher. His friend sat at the other end with a set of papers spread out on the blanket between them. He had been about to light a kerosene lantern and the match was suspended between his thumb and forefinger.

The two men gazed at each other and neither spoke as John Drayton placed the metal lantern on a box beside the stretcher. The gloom, in its haste, was soaking up the final light of day inside the tent as he lit the wick and replaced the glass before turning towards his visitor. Trap was about to speak when to his astonishment John Drayton announced, 'Lexi's dead, you know.'

Trap was not sure he had heard correctly. 'What?'

'Lexine, my wife, she's dead. I've been going to tell you a dozen times since you arrived. It's not something I like to think about. I'm still fighting it.' He shook his head and made a sharp, sad sound. 'She's dead, and so is my son Paul.'

Trap stared at Johnny unspeaking, and Johnny, thinking his friend was saddened by the news he had just heard, hurried on: 'They were drowned, old man, on a ship which was torpedoed by the bloody Japs—' He broke off, overwhelmed, and hung his head as he added, 'I saw the manifest, there were no survivors. My relatives and . . . Kathleen Leigh died too.'

Trap looked at Johnny's head hanging down before him. It took him another moment before he spoke.

'Johnny, listen, your wife's not dead.'

John Drayton did not move, not one part of him. He remained

bent forward while Trap waited until at length his head inched up and turned. He did not blink, he did not seem to be breathing until the words exploded out of him: 'What are you saying to me? My wife's not dead?'

'That's right, Johnny.'

John Drayton's face transformed; a sequence of complicated expressions clouded his eyes. But now they narrowed enquiringly. 'How on earth do you know?'

'Because she's been with me. For the last eight months she's been in the Mindanao jungle with my band of commandos and Filipino freedom-fighters. She was on the submarine that brought me here.'

John Drayton was shaking his head in confusion, attempting to grasp what he had just heard. 'Thank God,' he whispered. But suddenly a change came over him and Trap noticed him gather himself in the lamplight. His expression was still perplexed but his voice was in control again. 'I reckon you need to bloody well explain all this, Colonel Trapperton, and start at what you believe is the beginning.'

Trap nodded. 'Sure, Johnny.'

'One question first: is my son alive too?'

Trap shook his head. 'No.'

John Drayton closed his eyes while silence ensued. After a long time he opened them and trained them on his companion. 'Right, let's have the story.'

The two men sat there in the lamplight for the many minutes it took Trap to tell Lexi's husband how he found her on Christmas Day last, and to relate the twists and turns, as he knew them, of her life over the past ten months.

Ivat came by to inform them chow was ready, but they did not move: they remained facing each other until Trap came to his ending and he cleared his throat and swiped at the insects around him.

He waited for Johnny to speak, but his friend just continued eyeing him the way he had during the recounting of the tale.

Rarely in his decades upon the earth had Hank Trapperton felt uneasy, but there was no doubt he did now. 'Look, Johnny, she'll be all right in Pago Pago. They'll be battening down against Jap attack, but she'll be able to get from there to Australia or even the States. She'll be safe. And listen, she never told me much about what happened to her with the Japs, but I reckon Caldo knows a lot. Certainly more about the shipwreck than I do; she used to talk to him.'

John Drayton blinked and shook his head. 'Why in God's name didn't you tell me all this the minute you got here?'

Although Trap had been waiting for this, he had no answer, his reply was extemporaneous: 'Hell, Johnny, I didn't know for sure what you knew. She was supposed to go to Australia with MacArthur. He might have been in touch with you for all I was aware. You've been in Australia, you might have found out. You didn't bring her up, so I didn't either. Jesus, none of this is easy.'

'What the hell does that mean?'

Trap brought his fingers to his chin and held it between them as he answered. 'It means there's a war on. We're all a bit crazy, I guess. Look, my boys only knew her as Dr Robinson; that's the name she gave them. I left it at that. They don't know spit.' Trap wished he were anywhere on the planet but here. He was looking at Johnny, his friend, and yet shouting inwardly: *Goddam, Johnny, I slept with her before she married you. The kid was mine, not yours. She's rotten . . . forget about her. You're too good for her; let me have her. I'm right for her.* He appeared to take charge of himself, eye to eye with his companion, but inside his head the voice went on: *Why do I like this man so much? If only I had hated you, Johnny, the whole convoluted mess might have been simpler.*

'Jesus, Johnny.'

John Drayton was watching the face of his friend. He had always thought of this man as a friend, even though he had never known his real name until a few days ago. He understood what Trap meant when he said the war made you crazy; yes, it did. He

449

thought of those who were dead who should be alive, and now suddenly Lexi was alive after he had thought her dead. Yes, that was the important matter: *Lexi was alive!*

His ambivalent expression faded and he shot out his hand. 'Lexi was lucky to find you. Thanks for looking after her, mate, I can't explain how deeply I appreciate it. Thank God she's alive.'

For a heartbeat Trap stared at the outstretched hand before he took it: what the hell else could he do? But now he suspected he knew a little bit about how Judas must have felt.

He eased his fingers from his companion's grasp and turned towards the tent flap. 'Hey, Johnny, that chow smells good, let's get some. We've got lots to do.'

They moved out together. And as they walked, swatting insects away from around their heads, John Drayton touched his companion's arm. 'So, I've still lost a son, but I've regained a wife.'

Again Trap wished he were anywhere else on earth but here. He did not turn towards his friend but kept facing straight ahead. 'That's right, Johnny, that's right.'

John Drayton spoke almost to himself. 'Well I'll have to get used to that again.'

Trap still did not look round at the man at his side, but a frown implanted itself on his brow. Now what the hell did that mean?

Trap and John Drayton were examining the chart of Simpson Harbour. Both had worry creases between their eyes because the limpet mines had not yet arrived. There were only three days left before the enemy troop embarkation for New Guinea, and if the contact mines did not arrive they would have to alter their plans. They would still go in and get the enemy general anyway, but abandon blowing up the ships. This did not sit well with them.

On the far side of the camp the voice of Lieutenant 'Blinkers' Hervey exploded: 'They're here, the limpet mines are here!'

John Drayton's head shot up and Trap turned to see Hervey

running towards them grinning, his excitement palpable. 'They're here at last. The limpet mines! Captain Howard, Smith and Bird have just come in with them.'

At speed the two men followed him through the camp to where a donkey laden with boxes stood surrounded by a host of commandos.

'Jesus!' Caldo exploded as he came running over to the soldiers surging around the newcomers.

The men parted to let Trap and John Drayton through to reach Ron Howard, who was now a captain, and who stood holding a donkey laden with the precious cargo.

'We're pretty pleased to see you guys.'

Lieutenant Hervey lifted up one of the magnetic bombs from a box strapped to the donkey, 'There's nothing stopping us now.' He handed the limpet mine to John Drayton, who turned it over in his hands and passed it to Trap while Hervey addressed the expectant faces all trained upon him. 'I know a lot about these little fellas and I've set more than a few in place in my time. They work wonders.'

Hervey was a naval underwater demolition expert and had worked with Major Cyril Vanderpeer Clark in military intelligence research back in England at the beginning of the war, on all types of underwater munitions. He looked lovingly at the limpet mine in the last moments of the fading day and smiled at it from under his handlebar moustache. 'Wish we could use these little trimmers on the bloody mozzies,' he opined, and a general rumble of agreement met his words.

Trap held up his hands for silence and spoke as the day began to wane through the emerald foliage. 'Right. We'll have a final briefing at nine hundred hours. Get a good night's sleep: tomorrow will be a long haul.'

451

Chapter Fifty-nine

Trap stood watching the men the following day at 0845 as a feeling of expectancy lingered in the steamy atmosphere of the camp. The commandos lined up to take their bi-weekly atabrine tablets; little yellow pills to help stop malaria. The Australian, Davidson, was just getting over a bad bout, even though they had been rigid with their discipline of administering the drug. At least no one was suffering from dengue fever or dysentery, though Shibuyu had a tropical ulcer on his arm which had formed from a scratch. Any careless soldier was likely to catch ringworm, hookworm, yaws or scrub typhus, and John Drayton and Trap diligently warned their men against the second unrelenting foe: disease.

After the administering of the tablets, the commandos wandered in twos and threes across to the southern side of the tents to cluster at the pencil-drawn map of Rabaul nailed to a banana palm.

John Drayton waited for the commandos to settle around him. He was thinking about the morning in Brisbane when he had met Colonel Roberts and the American General Willoughby. Roberts had told him, 'We understand you're a good swimmer and that you do the Australian crawl rather well. That could come in handy, so make sure you choose a few good swimmers in the platoon you take to Milne Bay.'

It had proved valuable advice, for they needed strong swimmers to place the limpet mines on the hulls of the waiting troop ships in the harbour.

As far back as the Kunundra camp in North Queensland, they had trained to hold their breath underwater in a clear patch of stream in the hills. The site of the camp here had been chosen specifically because it was well hidden and a mineral spring emerged out of the hillside to meet the river. A swimming pool was dug out of a section of the stream which ran below their camp. They had wired it off to keep out alligators while they trained at rehearsing how to fit the magnetic mines under water. In the real event they would have the added difficulty of being in darkness.

As he looked around the men, he mused on how this unit was top heavy with officers. But that was how it had turned out. These were all highly trained and right for the job, and there was a camaraderie between all ranks that he had never witnessed before. They were a cohesive team.

Rabaul, the enemy bastion currently estimated at some sixty thousand soldiers, was in a straight line only twelve miles away. There the enemy were quartered in every house and office, with tent camps stretching in all directions. The Japanese felt invulnerable in Rabaul even though Allied aerial attacks were becoming persistent. The assumption that the commandos made with the assistance of Raga, was that one of the reasons the Kempeitai general, here to lead the relief army, had built his small compound on the hill away from the overpopulated and barricaded entrenchment of Rabaul, was because of the air raids.

The local natives were anti-Japanese, and through them, and in particular Raga and Cigs, the soldiers were now aware of the construction by forced labour of a series of bunkers and underground tunnels, which ran for miles beneath the town.

John Drayton lifted his wooden pointer for silence as Trap sat down next to him on a log, and the men filtered around him for the start of the final briefing.

The leader's mind was not yet on things military, it was on the Doll. He hated the fact that he was thinking of her. He had left her the letter which unequivocally stated that she was out of his life because of this man beside him.

Trap had been analysing Johnny's reaction to the news that she was alive. He had mulled it over; fact was, it had kept him awake at night. If he had been in Johnny's place, he probably would have taken a swipe at a guy who had kept quiet for days on end about the fact that the Doll was alive. His friend had been annoyed, sure . . . but there was something in his attitude that Trap could not work out.

Johnny had said all the right things, and Trap knew for sure that he was happy for the Doll, glad she was still in the world, but there was something else. His joy had been tempered, not the true joy of a lover knowing his wife had survived. More like the happiness a mate would show, knowing his buddy had beaten the odds.

And he had said those words: *I'll have to get used to that again.*

Trap gazed up at his second-in-command. Sure, the guy was complex. Goddam, most people were, and the war just made things worse. Unconsciously he straightened his shoulders. Why did it make him itch all over thinking about the Doll? Why could she do this to him when she was thousands of miles away? Hell, it had been easier to ignore her when she was two feet away in Mindanao.

Lexi was sitting on a bench outside the operating theatre, breathing fresh air between cases. She gazed along the lush green Mapusaga Valley where Navy Mobile Hospital Number Three spread itself to the east of the sharp rising ground called Tau Hill in the tiny community of Mapusaga, on the island of Tutuila.

She could make out soldiers and gun emplacements in amongst the trees in the distance, and nearer to her, hospital staff came and went and ambulance vehicles and jeeps rolled by, but even with the activity all about she felt the weight of loneliness. The one bright spot in her life was little Lessa. It was not that she was

454

actually unhappy here, for working in the hospital brought satisfaction. It was that she could not help but live in the past, where each day she had seen Trap's face and heard his voice and been in his life, no matter whether he had acknowledged her or not.

The guilt still dwelt within her. She could not help that she loved Trap, but she hated that she had deceived her husband; she hated that she had been weak and married him when she knew it was wrong. She believed Paul's death was the penalty for originating the lie that John Drayton was his father. And the added death of little Jimmy only intensified what she regarded as punishment. These deliriums played daily on her mind even though, at the same time, she drew satisfaction from her work here in this tropical backwater.

When she had arrived in Tutuila aboard the *Pompano*, Executive Officer Slade Cutter had been true to his word and had taken her to meet Lawrence Wild, the local commander. He had found a billet for her with a manager at the coaling station and Lexi had tried to settle into her position at the hospital, where her experience and background were welcomed, but within a few days she had decided that Lessa would be happier living with the nurses in their quarters dubbed *Penicillin Row*. Luckily a room was found and the nurses treated the child with love and affection, which resulted in the little girl not always wearing the pucker on her brow. Lexi even began to think the child might talk, but that miracle had not eventuated.

She lifted her hand in a wave to a Samoan marine; he was the husband of Manuna, a woman with three small children of her own, who took care of Lessa during the day. He was heading across to the hospital ammunition dump.

Forty hospital buildings straggled along the valley under the coconut palms, and with the influx of wounded men from the Guadalcanal campaign, they needed every bed.

She heard her name called and, looking round, she saw one of the senior ward nurses beckoning her.

'I'm coming,' she answered, and stood up brushing the skirt of her uniform. As it was a military hospital and Lexine was a doctor, she had been given the rank of acting second lieutenant.

She headed back to the building housing the operating room, and as she walked, she slipped her hand in her jacket pocket and took out the folded paper. She carried Trap's letter everywhere. Lifting it, she held it to her heart for a moment and then replaced it in her pocket.

Even though what he had written at the end had cut her to her soul, she kept it because it was the only communication she had ever had from him, and it bore his signature. Every day she read Points 1 and 2. She had folded it so that she simply read one and two and then went straight to his signature. She knew it for the pretense it was but it remained the only comfort she had.

Trap was still musing on the Doll. If only he had known Johnny's connection with her when he ran into the damn woman. Hell! Literally ran into her, in that bar in Madura. What was it called? Henaro's? He would have avoided her like the plague.

That uncomfortable thought stirred him enough to make him stand up, and as he did so, a host of brilliant yellow and white butterflies rippled by, and Johnny slid his wooden pointer across Simpson Harbour as he announced, 'These transports are target number one.' He tapped the dots of the four battleships and one cruiser which were being used as transports for the twelve to fifteen-thousand-man army destined for Buna and the relief of the beleaguered Japanese in New Guinea.

As the leader stood, John Drayton's gaze rested momentarily on the small, delicate orchids growing at the feet of the ubiquitous palms. For some reason they reminded him of Kathleen, but he purposefully brought his attention back to the briefing.

The Australian, British and American commandos perched in various positions about him. They wore a motley array of garments: most were in shorts and singlets, but a few boasted the regular

456

issue of jungle greens with rolled-up sleeves, and one or two of them, a mixture of both army and civilian clothes. Caldo still maintained the bandanna round his forehead and adorned his chest with a bandolier full of cartridges. All displayed varying numbers of red marks on exposed flesh where the interminable mosquitos had bitten them. The Americans carried Tommy guns; the British and Australians Bren guns.

John Drayton continued to slide his pointer over the map to the red squares which marked the small Japanese enclave outside Rabaul town and camp. 'And as you all know, this is target two.'

They were listening carefully to the briefing even though they had heard it each day. 'There are two enemy generals here in Rabaul: we know for certain that Lieutenant General Hitoshi Imamura[1] has finally arrived here after a hasty journey by air from Tokyo via Truk, where he conferred with Admiral Yamamoto. Our own Corporal Shibuyu who has been into Rabaul, tells us that he has formally assumed command of the enemy 8th Area Army, and beginning soon he will establish his headquarters in the old government house on Namanula Hill which has been fortified for him with an air raid shelter and with the luxuries of a four poster bed, a bath and his own cooks and Korean *comfort women*, to use the Jap euphemism.'

A number of insults to Imamura ensued before John Drayton continued: 'But he is not our target. He was in Java when it fell and so was I, and believe me, that means I actually wish he were the target, because I've a few scores to settle with that bastard. But no, our target is Ikeda, who arrived here from the Philippines early in the month; the general in the Kempeitai – the degraded group who are brothers to the Gestapo.

'Ikeda and his staff officers are here to lead out the reinforcements to Buna. The coded dispatch which Allied intelligence broke, informed us that this army is to be used for a last attempt to reinforce the 18th army in New Guinea to bolster their hold on Buna, Lae and Salamaua, and to remount their New Guinea campaign. Our directive is to take out the general and his vessels, thus leaving the relief army headless and transportless.'

'Where does he live, sir?' asked Private Joker Mayberry, a thick-set individual with biceps like Caldo's and a cheeky grin.

'We don't know; but we do know he's in one of the six dwellings away from the tunnels and bunkers and airfields of Rabaul.'

'Perhaps Jap generals don't like to associate with each other,' joked Private Len Lister as a pitch black spider crawled by his boot and scuttled off into the undergrowth.

John Drayton's voice lifted above the ensuing comment. 'They do in fact associate, Lister, for the Kempeitai general met Imamura when he arrived here, and Raga confirmed that he went in to Rabaul again with his staff officers yesterday to see Imamura before he returned to his fenced-in compound. Which again, Raga informs us, has all the amenities of home with his mistresses and what seems a bizarre addition – a separate prayer room for the Kempeitai general alone.'

'Strewth,' commented Christopher Olsen, a nineteen-year-old Queenslander.

'We know Imamura is settling in, so it's a good time to strike. Rabaul might have been a gentle spot in the boondocks before the war, but we reckon near to sixty thousand enemy troops are presently here and if a fight starts, it'll be fairly one-sided. That means, get in fast and get out fast.

'In the exact manner Lieutenant Hervey has taught us, we'll attach the limpet mines, each containing two pounds of plastic explosive and an eight-minute fuse, and we set them and make ourselves scarce. As you have all heard before, our two operations are code-named Hornbill and Longtail. I'll lead Hornbill, and Colonel Trapperton will lead Longtail.'

A lock of his sun-lightened hair flashed in the sunlight as he raised his head and the map nailed to the palm trunk flapped in the breeze. Trap moved over to his side to the continuing accompaniment of a choir of bird calls from above, as John Drayton put down his wooden pointer. 'Colonel Trapperton will now go through the points of each raid.'

Trap then asked each man to explain in detail the role he would play.

John Drayton's team included the five best swimmers: himself, Lieutenant Hervey, Captain Howard, Sergeant O'Rourke, and Bird. Every one had a companion rower. The two-man teams would carry their canoes going in but would discard them on the harbour shore after the raid.

As the men recited their roles in the operation, Trap studied those who would accompany him. Caldo: he couldn't imagine being without Caldo, nerves of steel and big-hearted but brave to the point of recklessness. Williams: tenacious, and a thinker. Rupert Coalclark: the British captain schooled at Eton, and who, it was said, wore bespoke suits in civvy street. He had trained in North Africa with David Sterling and 'Paddy' Mayne, names which Trap now knew. They had formed a highly trained raiding unit known as the Special Air Service, the SAS. Coalclark had also been seconded to help train an American unit of commandos named Rangers the previous June. Yes, he knew his stuff.

The leader's eyes flicked to Joker Mayberry, the twenty-five-year-old ex-boxer from Gippsland in Australia, and to Shibuyu: he was gaining respect for Tommy and time would prove if that were wise or not. Finally his gaze rested on his last two: Sergeant Major Dan Lambert, a tough, never-say-die type, and Private Chris Olsen, who could slice a banana in two with his jungle knife at twenty paces. He did not believe there were seven better commandos anywhere in this goddam world, and that included the SAS and the newly formed Rangers.

The last commando to outline his participation in the raids was Shibuyu. He spoke well and his final words were, 'I will be dressed as a Japanese soldier; this way I go in first and ascertain which dwelling the general inhabits.' He supplied a short, sharp bow and sat down.

Trap knew that a lot of the men had a natural mistrust of the Nisei and he could not blame them for that. Anybody who looked Japanese was coming from behind the eight-ball with Allied soldiers; but so far he had found no fault with Shibuyu.

'Okay. Both routes in, avoid the heavily guarded Rabaul camp, though we do pass by airfields which we'll have to ignore, even though I'd dearly love to make a fast detour and send a few squadrons to high heaven as well.'

'Hear, hear!'

As the briefing drew to its end, John Drayton reminded them, 'The transports lie on the outer extent of the harbour, and when they blow and sink we hope to block the fairway. We reckon the first of the transport ships will explode at or around midnight. This will create pandemonium and confusion and most of the enemy soldiers will head to the harbour, thinking that an attack is coming from that direction. Searchlights will hit the water and every inch of the shore they can cover, so we'll just have to row like hell.

'When we all get back here we'll hightail it to the Allied coast watcher station forty miles south. Remain careful of the Molkolkol tribe down there. They're still warlike and continue their attacks on anything and anybody across the isthmus between Wide Bay and Open Bay. They made it hard for the boys of Lark Force when they were trying to escape the Japs earlier in the year. Once we're down there, we await instruction on our lift off this little bit of heaven called New Britain.'

Rumbles of laughter greeted this, and John Drayton sat down to Trap's closing statement: 'Get in, destroy your target, get out! And try to avoid shooting a female if possible. There'll be quite a few in the neighbourhood of the big brass, that's definite.'

Ivat scratched a bite on the side of his face. 'What if . . . something goes wrong and no one gets back here?'

Williams shot him a look of annoyance. 'Trust you, Ivat. I thought we lost the pessimist when poor Clevelly bought it.'

Trap took Ivat's part. 'It's a gloomy question, but needs to be answered. Raga and Cigs have spoken to Chief Innut of the local tribe, and he has promised to lead us out if neither of them get back.' The soldiers understood his meaning. 'So to answer your question, Ivat, if we're not all back by dawn, those who are here abandon anyway. Is that absolutely clear?'

General affirmative murmurs met this query.

Chapter Sixty

No breeze blew in Rabaul's sultry air. Colonel Yasute Nakayama bowed and exited the room, leaving the two Japanese major generals in sweat-stained uniforms sitting opposite each other.

'This is a terrible climate,' Imamura complained as he pushed aside a communiqué from Admiral Yamamoto, smudged and discoloured from the sweaty hands which had held it.

Ikeda grunted affirmatively, dipping a porcelain cup into a jug of water and drinking a mouthful. 'Yes, but until the glory is ours we must put up with it.'

'True. I can't help thinking of the old days in occupation in Manchukuo! They were the days, before we were generals, eh?'

'Yes, they were.' Ikeda sighed. 'The good times. Now we have real responsibilities.'

They spoke as old aquaintances. Imamura had been referring to their time together in the Kwantung army of occupation in Manchuria in 1936; when Imamura had been a Deputy Chief of Staff and Ikeda had been a major in the Kempeitai and responsible for *government shobun* which translated to government torture and punishment of the local insurgents. The Japanese had conquered Korea in 1910 and overrun Manchuria in 1931. The invasion of China proper had begun in 1937.

Imamura swallowed a mouthful of water. 'So, to your departure. Everything is ready for the day after tomorrow, I understand.'

Ikeda nodded. 'It is. We will sail at dawn. I expect to take two days to reach Buna, where I shall immediately land a shore party and assess the true situation for myself. We still hold that northern coast. I'm convinced that a surprise attack upon the Australians now, when they think they have us on the run after the battles in the Owen Stanley mountains, will have the desired effect, and we can secure Papua this time.'

Imamura gulped down a mouthful of water and wiped his brow. 'I hope it's that easy. The drowning of Tomitaro Horii there last month was a tragedy.'

Ikeda agreed: 'Yes, but the High Command now realise the retreat was a mistake. He was in sight of Port Moresby! Hence my mission to recapture Papua. Once that is achieved, we can begin again with our plans for southern expansion into Australia. We will continue to build up our numbers here in Rabaul and you can feed me the troops as I need them.'

'I will, and I hope your experience against the Australians is a more succesful chronicle than Horii's.'

Ikeda waved his hand enthusiastically. 'We will reclaim all that has been lost. My soldiers are fresh and keen. We still hold the Northern Solomons; we must regain our losses, and if we retake Papua New Guinea, who knows?'

His associate wagged his head in true conviction, and rested his plump face in his hands — elbows on the table — and altered the subject. 'By the way, will you be taking your mistresses?'

The Kempeitai general's heavy cheeks creased with a copious smile. 'Of course. A general in the field needs tender care.'

They both laughed, and Imamura remained holding his chin with his right hand and twisted the gold ring he wore on his middle finger as he casually enquired, 'What about the Eurasian?'

Ikeda's inky eyes locked with his colleague's. 'What about her?'

'You will take her too?'

'Of course. Why do you ask?'

Imamura licked the side of his mouth, tasting the perspiration. 'She intrigues me. I have heard it is said she is not one of your comfort women, that you simply like to ... *look* at her.' He began to chuckle. 'Well, you know what? I too would like to look at her.' His mirth compelled his rotund stomach to wobble under his belt.

Momentarily Ikeda's face dropped, irritation surfaced and he sat up straighter in his chair. He waited for Imamura's amusement to subside, and when it did his reply was cool and courteous. 'My *comrade* general, the Eurasian does hold a particular place in my ... shall we say ... *affections*? Therefore I suggest we wait until we have won the war, and then we will talk more of your desire to *look* at her.'

Across the peninsula during the same close, sticky afternoon, sunlight snaked through the trees and a wild pig grunted somewhere behind them as John Drayton wrote an entry in his diary and Ron Howard shaved nearby. They were to be partners tonight: and while the senior officer swam over to the *Shima Maru*, his selected enemy transport carrier, Ron would wait for him in the canoe.

Ron dipped the razor into a bowl of water and, looking into the broken piece of mirror he had lodged on a branch of a small *kamarere* tree, drew the blade down across his throat as he spoke confidentially. 'I know we can all recite the plans in our sleep, but I'm concerned about the timing of the fuses on the mines.'

'They're eight minutes.'

'Yes, I know. And as you've chosen to mine the furthest ship from shore, I reckon we'll still be out on that harbour when they start to blow. Eight minutes isn't very long.'

'Ron, what are you saying?'

The younger man paused and his eyes roved across to where two blue-eyed cockatoos screeched and danced together on a low branch. He stared at them, their yellow combs fanning out and then closing on their pristine white heads; they were a strikingly beautiful pair of birds and the blue rings around their eyes were particularly brilliant and easily observed, even from such a distance.

The young captain continued to watch them as he replied: 'I'm saying that the only ones who can possibly be back on shore for certain are Lister and O'Rourke, because they're mining the nearest ship to the shore. And they'll need to have rowed like hell to make it anyway.'

John Drayton glanced up and caught Ron's eye in the mirror. 'We knew all that from the start.'

'Yeah, well, it just hit home to me, I suppose.'

The senior officer put down his fountain pen and contemplated his companion. 'Ron? Are you going to worry about this? Would you rather be in one of the other canoes?'

Ron stopped shaving. 'Hell, no, sir. I just thought I'd point it out again. I sort of needed to say it out aloud, rather than simply think it. I hope you understand?'

John Drayton stood, moved over to his captain and put his arm around the younger man's shoulder. 'I do understand. I always think that if you can face a fear of any kind, it helps in a way to negate it. If you actually admit it exists within you, somehow it fizzles out a bit. Does for me, anyway.'

John Drayton sincerely believed in the advice he had just given. It had helped him a hundred times on the harrowing sea voyage from Java to Broome, when he had faced the fact that they all could die. That acknowledgement had lessened the terror of death for him.

He saw the soldier evaluating his words. There was a long silence before Ron Howard spoke. 'Yes, thank you, sir, I reckon that's true.'

The older man grinned 'Listen, Ron, as long as the bloody transports explode, I don't care where I am. All I want to hear is the sound of big bits of them shooting up to the sky!'

Ron laughed at that. 'Too right, sir.'

'And we know that by the time a patrol from either Rabaul or Malaguna reaches the point where we exit the harbour, we should be well on our way inland.'

* * *

Two hours later, the members of Operations Hornbill and Longtail stood in the firelight, their faces smudged with black, waiting for the two men who would lead them. Most were silent and deep in thought, the expectation of what the approaching hours would bring showing in their expressions. Caldo, his wide face rosy in the glow from the fire, counted his rounds of ammunition, and beside him Olsen sharpened his jungle knife on a piece of steel.

Caldo broke the silence. 'It's still stinking hot.'

Gavin Bird lifted his head and replied good-humouredly as he adjusted the harness holding his limpet mines: 'Well, a nice swim in the waters of Simpson Harbour will cool a few of us down.'

Jim Hanson joined the conversation as he looked up at the trees. 'Strewth, I think that wind's getting up a bit. Hope you guys will be all right.'

'Forget it, Hanson,' called Lieutenant Williams. 'You worry too much about the weather.' Williams was checking off the names of the operators on each raid. 'The wind's going to stay as it is; my old man was a weather expert.'

Ivat, standing beside him, scratched the side of his neck and looked up at the lieutenant in surprise. 'Jeez, I've been with you a long time now, sir, and I didn't know that.'

Williams merely sighed at this remark as Chris Olsen dug Caldo and asked confidentially, 'Sergeant? How many operations like this have you and the colonel done?'

Caldo's mind flashed back to Northern Luzon and the raids on the advancing unstoppable Japanese troop machine. He recollected the mad dash down the seaboard to the Gulf of Lingayen, only to hold off the enemy line by line in retreat and finally be pushed into Bataan. He remembered Mindanao and the series of raids on enemy installations, oil dumps and patrols, always running before the Japs and darting from one hideout to another with the Doc and the kids in tow.

He had been silent so long that young Olsen prompted him. 'So how many, Sarge?'

The sergeant stirred and swatted an ant climbing up his trousers. 'Listen, Olsen, the colonel has led me on more operations than you've had birthdays, and our numbers have dwindled to where it's just the colonel, Williams, Ivat and me.'

'Yeah, you guys sure are something.' The youth's tone was admiring.

Caldo made a rumble of acknowledgement in his throat. 'We just do our jobs, Olsen; we can all kill men with our bare hands, but the colonel can do it swifter, neater and quieter than any one of us. Once I asked him what made him so good at it, and you know what he said, son?'

The young soldier was completely absorbed, his oh-so-youthful eyes trained on Caldo. 'No, Sarge, what?'

'He said, "It's elementary, Caldo. It's because I've done more of it than any man I know. And if you don't get killed early on and it doesn't turn your stomach and send you scooting off to become a schoolteacher or a clerk or a blasted truck driver, then the natural result is that you get good at it, mighty good at it."' Caldo blinked in the firelight and focused on his young comrade. 'So, Olsen, *you* start getting good at it tonight. Do you reckon you're up to it, sonny?'

Olsen bristled. 'Jeez, Sarge, of course I am. You wait and see. I've got a lot of horse sense.'

Caldo grinned. 'Sure. And remember, you and I have been trained for one reason only: to stop the criminal expansion of the Japanese war machine. That's what the colonel expects us to do tonight.'

Olsen nodded his head. 'I know that.' He looked up to see Trap and John Drayton striding towards them. 'Look, here he comes now with Major Whitby.'

Trap could feel a sort of static tension in the atmosphere as the dark figures milled around like oversized wraiths in the firelight. Some of them would die tonight. It was hard being so sure about that.

He made eye contact with Johnny and knew he felt it too. Trap spoke under his breath. 'It's there every time, every time.'

As he spoke to himself they arrived beside the group of men.

'Now listen, boys, there's a fact we need to face. When Major Whitby and his party blow up the ships and we dispatch Ikeda, Rabaul will erupt like those damn volcanos over there!' He pointed towards them. 'Every man-jack of the tens of thousands of Nips will be after us. All roads, such as they are, will be blocked and small reconnaissance craft will search the environs of the harbour. Aircraft will lift off at first light to look for us and you can count on supreme outrage being the order of the day. The Japs will be screaming blue murder and they'll be mad – affronted that their safe harbour of Rabaul was infiltrated. They know they get bombed and strafed by Allied aircraft but they're not counting on any raid overland. I can't impress upon you enough to get back here and move immediately to the coast watcher station with all speed. We'll go to ground down there. It's in a pretty impossible place to find, thank God.'

John Drayton looked at his boots as he heard this. *There will be no mercy for anyone who gets caught; it'll be better to blow your own head off than be taken a prisoner.*

He lifted his eyes and saw Ron Howard standing in the glow of one of the fires looking straight at him. He made himself nod and smile confidently. A moment passed before his young captain replied in kind.

Fifteen minutes later Operation Hornbill was ready to move.

John Drayton held out his hand. 'Good luck, Hank.'

Trap took it. '*Hank?*'

'Yeah, well, I happen to like your name. It's nice to use it.'

'Jesus . . .' He paused. 'My mother liked it too . . . Listen, Trap will do fine.'

'Sure, Hank, see you back here.'

The leader grinned. 'Okay. Sure.'

John Drayton hesitated. 'And thanks for looking after Lexi.'

Oh no. Trap coughed and hoped like hell the night hid his uneasiness. 'Listen, she was the one who *looked after* everybody. She's a first-class doctor.'

'Yes, she certainly is, always was. How dearly I hope she's safe in Pago Pago. She'd be well and truly there by now, wouldn't she?'

His companion could not go on with this. 'Yeah, I reckon so. Look, you have to move out. See you back here later, old buddy.'

'Too right you will. Best of luck.'

Trap nodded, 'Good luck to you too, Johnny.'

Chapter Sixty-one

Kathleen shivered and the mosquitoes droned in the air around her. It was hot and humid and the soldiers moved in lethargy as the fleeting twilight merged into night. A strong, sultry breeze carried a fetid odour from the north as it stirred the endless fronds of the jungle undergrowth beyond the small compound. The air movement brought no relief, the atmosphere was oppressive, and yet still she shivered.

She had just witnessed General Pig slap Lieutenant Hioshi and he was now walking towards her with rage in his arrogant step. *'Kimi!'* he shouted at her and gestured with his thumb for her to follow him.

Kathleen rose from where she was seated under the overhang of her house, an area which passed for a veranda. Instinctively she clasped the jade dragon hanging around her neck; this made her feel as if her mother were near and that consoled her. Corporal Hyata had been standing near her wiping the eternal sweat from his forehead. His swift action of standing smartly to attention was ignored by Ikeda as he approached.

The general strode on by towards his dwelling followed by his chief of staff, Colonel Kaneko Hosoda. Kathleen fell in behind them, as did Hyata, and they marched in tandem across the grass to his front door. Ikeda halted as Colonel Hosoda slid the door open and two native women turned in fright from the table where they were placing the general's nightly bottle of rice wine and crystal glasses.

'*Mukouni itte!*' Hosoda shouted and they scuttled out of the room. Hyata halted and as Kathleen entered behind Ikeda and the colonel, the corporal shut the door after her.

The room was long and, like all Japanese dwellings, sparsely furnished. The walls were painted white and lanterns, already lit, hung from rafters above. On the low table beside the rice wine and glasses stood a bowl of fruit and beyond it was placed a single chair. Kathleen was inured to the routine and she walked over and sat down. A futon, with two buckwheat pillows and a down feather comforter, rested in one corner but it was not where the general slept. His bedroom was across a small hall.

The only decoration in the room was a large *byobu*, a six-panelled folding screen painted richly in gold and silver leaf with flowers, trees and herons, quite intricately depicted. It stretched across the room in delicate grace. Ikeda had told Kathleen that it had been painted in the sixteenth century and was worth millions of yen. She knew it well, for it had travelled throughout the Philippines with them. A stool rested in front of it as if someone often sat there to view it from that position.

Hosoda muttered something to the general and departed the way he had come. As the door slid closed behind him, Ikeda crossed to the futon. He took off his sword and threw it down before removing his tunic and dropping it beside his sword. He strode back to the low table and bending, poured himself a drink, which he swallowed in almost one swig. He glanced across at his lone companion and poured another, gulped it in the manner of the previous one and spoke in English: 'Would you like a drink?'

'No thank you.'

'I wish you to have one.' He poured it, stomped over to her and handed it to her. She took it but did not raise it to her lips.

'I am surrounded by fools,' he commented, pouring a third glass of the wine for himself.

Kathleen made no reply.

He walked to the window and stood there looking into the

471

fast-falling night as he drank again; when he had drained it he placed the glass on the ledge. 'I will be leaving here soon. Do you know that?'

'You have mentioned to me that you are to lead an offensive in New Guinea, that things have not gone well there and that you will bring the victorious relief army.'

He swung round, his narrow, tapering eyes enlarging with surprise. 'When did I say that?'

'Last week.'

He paused and his head dropped to one side as he smiled, and she shivered again. 'I must be starting to trust you.'

Without warning he turned towards the inner door and shouted, 'Maruta!' Kathleen started; her nerves were worsening by the day. His current favourite mistress came hurrying in and with hands together bowed in the doorway. These days Kathleen's maid Dinty was no longer in favour with him and did not share his bed; much to her delight.

Ikeda moved across to Maruta. She wore a kimono and he slipped his hand inside it to feel her breast. Kathleen turned her head away.

Ikeda grinned. He knew Kathleen's sensitivities and it entertained him to offend her. Drawing the slender Maruta over to the futon, he clasped her in his arms and kissed her in a noisy, carnal manner, but all the while he eyed Kathleen, who sat looking straight ahead at the outside door.

'Gochou!' He yelled and Kathleen flinched. The door opened and Hyata stood there at attention.

'*Omae!* Gochou!' The general rattled a spate of Japanese at him, and as Hyata nodded and bowed, Ikeda crossed back to Kathleen and pointing to the door growled, 'Go now!'

Kathleen placed the untouched glass of wine down on the floor and rose and crossed swiftly to the door as he added, 'Eat your meal and come back here at twenty-two hundred. Understand?'

On the threshold she took a deep breath and looked back over her shoulder. He had returned to his mistress and was bending down to her.

'Are you sure you want me back tonight?' she asked quietly from the doorway. 'Wouldn't you prefer to stay with Maruta and see me tomorrow?'

His face tightened as he turned on one knee towards her. 'Do not suggest anything to me, *Katleen*.' He rarely spoke her name and it surprised her. For a moment she expected his wrath, but he remained passive. 'Just be back here as you are told, and wear the white kimono with the peonies.'

'Yes,' she said as she closed the door.

At ten p.m., as Kathleen crossed the compound with Hyata to pause before the general's door, there was a stronger breeze scuttling across the compound, yet it remained clammy and hot. She disliked the kimono. It was too many layers to wear and even though it was of fine silk she perspired.

All was silent except for their footfalls on the pumice-stone layers of the ground as Hyata said softly, 'Kataleen, I wish to tell you something.'

She paused, pretending to study the night in case any eyes were upon them, and he too paused at her shoulder. 'Yes, Juni?' His first name was Junichiro and when they were alone together she called him Juni and he called her Kataleen: she was fond of the name.

His voice carried gently on the vigorous breeze. 'I am sorry for what you have had to see, for what you have witnessed these past months.' He expressed a tiny sound from his throat, sad and weary. 'I am not proud of the Japanese army, Kataleen and the Kempeitai are cruel beyond my understanding. I am often ashamed.'

An intense swell of emotion caught her off guard. Tears sprung to her eyes as she answered him, still without looking round. 'Ah, Juni, how kind you are. Thank you. It is because of you that I have lived through all this. You alone have sustained me.

473

You are . . .' she paused for the right word and it came to her in its purity and immense simplicity, '. . . good. Yes, you are good.' And as she said it, she knew that that was how she would forever remember him, as *Juni the Good*.

It had been this sort of empathy between them which had led to their friendship over the year of her imprisonment. He had confided in her: she knew he had been studying to be a teacher and hoped to open a school in the little village in the mountains where he had lived with the Shinto priest. She knew that while he would not hesitate to die for his emperor, he thought the war against the Allies ill conceived and not a true reflection of the will of all the Japanese people. He wrote verse and bore a poet's heart, and his thoughts held no resemblance to those of his military confederates.

He smiled and bowed his head in the darkness. 'I thank you, Kataleen, I shall always endeavour to be so,' he replied in tender formality, and they moved off again.

They crossed the small grassed area and stepped up on to the raised paved veranda outside the general's house. Juni took up a position beside a sentry as Kathleen knocked and Ikeda's voice responded.

She entered as ordered, and immediately she opened the door she knew he had drunk a lot of rice wine, for three empty bottles sat on the low table. It was not unusual for him to drink heavily at night, though he never appeared inebriated. Still, she could see that tonight he was what they would have called 'slightly tipsy' back in Hong Kong.

He was dressed in a loose fitting *yukata*, a type of simple casual kimono, and his mistress was nowhere to be seen. He sat on a cushion on the floor at the polished low table and rested his elbows on it as he spoke. 'Send in the gochou.' He gestured to the door and Kathleen returned to it, opened it and called to Hyata. The corporal entered and stood at attention.

Ikeda pointed his middle finger at the young man and abruptly announced, 'I know you two speak to each other in English.'

Both Kathleen and Juni showed their amazement.

The youth blushed and it was obvious as he answered the general in Japanese that he was caught off guard.

The general screamed at him and Hyata fell silent. And now Ikeda spoke in English again. 'I know all sorts of things.' He looked from one to the other. Neither of them had any idea what he meant.

'You, bakayaro!' He leant back, one hand behind him on the mat. 'As you speak English so well, we will converse in it. You are to go down to the camp and deliver this to General Hitoshi Imamura's secretary, Lieutenant Koizumi.' He took up a communiqué envelope from the table and threw it down near Hyata, who picked it up from the floor. 'You will spend the night there, for I want an answer first thing in the morning. Is this clear?'

Hyata answered in English: 'It is clear, certainly, General.'

This could have been construed as insolent and Kathleen was expecting a furious reaction from Ikeda, but no, as usual he confounded her by laughing. 'Do you wish to kiss her?' he asked, pointing with his thumb at Kathleen, and Hyata's flush of embarrassment deepened.

'No.'

'I am giving you permission.'

Kathleen looked at Ikeda in entreaty. 'Please, this is not funny.'

He waved his hand in the air. 'It is not meant to be. Gochou! I order you to kiss her.'

Hyata hesitated.

The commander's tone became threatening. 'Do as I say.'

The young man stepped forward and took up Kathleen's hand, kissed it and straightened, looking directly into her eyes; in his gaze she read what she knew he felt: regard, sympathy and concern. And as they stood together, Ikeda lifted himself from the floor and walked to the interior door, opened it and disappeared.

'What is he doing?'

'God knows.'

Kathleen touched her friend's arm. 'Shouldn't you set off for the camp, Juni?'

'I don't like to leave you with him; he's very odd tonight.'

Kathleen could not resist a feeble smile. 'He's always odd. Listen to me. I've been his prisoner for a year, he's never harmed me. Yes, he's slapped me a few times and once split my lip, and certainly he threatens me, but he never carries out his threats. I do not fear him now, Juni; he simply confounds me and startles me and mostly disgusts me.' She clasped his arm more tightly. 'I'd really like you to leave. He's given you his order.'

'Yes, but Kataleen, he did not release me to go.'

'For heaven's sake! I will tell him you went to carry out his command. Go, please.'

Hyata hesitated. She could see the confusion in him. 'Please, Juni, it is all right. I am not afraid, not at all.'

He gave her a tender smile and it comforted her. There was no sexuality in his gaze for they did not feel towards each other as lovers. The connection between them was platonic, but it was strong and earnest and very real. They conversed on many levels and shared much in the hours they were on their own. The mutual respect between them forging a band which both would remember for the duration of their days. She squeezed his forearm once more. 'Please?' she repeated. 'Juni, be sensible. You are a lance corporal, he is a general. You can do nothing even if you remain.'

As he delayed, the door swung open and Ikeda returned. Kathleen's hand slid from the soldier's forearm.

'So, the two who converse constantly in English are silent, it seems?'

To Kathleen's concern, the young soldier became bold. 'Shall I escort Miss Leigh back to her home before I go down to the camp, sir?'

'Why would I send her away when she has just arrived? No, it is you who go.' He waved at the door.

With an expression which revealed his desire to stay, Hyata

slowly backed to the door, but now that the general had dismissed him, he paid the soldier no attention. 'Come here, Katleen. We might play chess or we might just talk.'

Hyata halted as Kathleen met his eyes in a swift backward glance of encouragement to leave. Yet he continued to stand wavering indecision until she deliberately turned to him, her voice calm and mien composed. 'Goodnight, corporal.'

Juni gave in; bowed his head and departed. As the door clicked closed behind him, Ikeda asked, 'Are you in love with that soldier?'

'No. He is a kind and gentle man, that's all.'

The enigma who was Ikeda sniggered at that. 'Then he is a fool and will not rise in rank. There is no kindness in the military.' He pointed to the chair, but she remained on her feet. 'So you do not love him. Whom do you love?' He laughed. 'You notice I even say *whom*, I understand the English language so well.'

'I know you speak English grammatically. It has always been evident.'

'Don't equivocate. Answer my question.' His face dropped into a serious expression.

'Why? Why do you ask me?'

'Because I wish to know.'

'I don't want to say.'

He pointed to the chair again and snarled, '*Suware!*' She did as told and sat while at the same time, he lifted the stool from in front of the gilt screen and brought it over and sat opposite her, four feet away.

His tone was cold as he jabbed his middle finger back and forth at her. 'Tell me whom you love.'

In the forefront of her mind were all the nights they had played chess when he did not utter a word except to explain her mistakes at the end of the game. She thought of all the other nights she had sat in mute attendance and watched him eat his evening meal. She thought of the times they had travelled hundreds of miles in virtual silence and the evenings when he had danced with her, the

477

only sounds emanating from the koto and their feet upon the floor. She recalled that mostly theirs had been a relationship of taciturnity, that vocal communication had been a minor part, and yet tonight it was all talk!

She studied him. 'You might not wish to hear my answer.'

He leant in towards her. 'Katleen.' He used her name for the third time and it had the effect of baffling her. In the entire year she had been with him he had hardly used it at all, normally he called her *You*. He sighed in exasperation. 'You are being dull-witted. I would not ask you if I did not wish to hear your answer.'

'All right.' She spoke resignedly. 'I loved the people you *murdered* on the beach in Luzon. I loved them dearly.' She felt tears rising but she steeled herself against crying.

He watched her. 'Who else?' His voice was remote but his black eyes were riveted on her.

'I loved my mother.' As she said this, she reached up and clasped the golden dragon on her throat.

'Soo . . .' It hissed from his mouth. 'You loved your mother. That does not surprise me; your mother was worth loving.'

Kathleen had no idea why he would say that. It was doubtlesly the rice wine speaking.

'And the pendant you hold was your mother's, Elizabet's, yes?'

'Yes.'

'Indeed it was. It was hers.' He looked her up and down from head to toe with his black beads for eyes. 'Anyone else?'

She did not answer.

'Anyone else?' He repeated it. 'Do you love anyone else?'

Oh, how much she hated him! Her hate for him was like a living creature, it was so potent. She blinked in case he should recognise the loathing in her eyes.

'Answer me, Katleen.'

And now, for the first time in her life, she admitted to herself that she loved one other. 'Yes, I love someone else, a soldier, an Australian soldier.'

478

'What is his name?'

'What does it matter?'

He lifted his fat right hand as if to strike her. 'No insolence! Speak his name.'

She opened her mouth for air. This was all grotesque and yet she knew she should not be surprised; she had decided long ago that he was an inhuman monster. 'His name is John, John Drayton Whitby.'

He echoed her words: 'John Drayton Whitby.'

'Yes.'

'Is that everybody you love?'

She wanted to scream; she wanted to say she despised him and she despised this game he was insisting on playing, but instead she replied, 'I suppose I love my father, though I never knew him. He died when I was a baby.'

His unfathomable eyes flashed with sudden feeling and he stood and stomped two paces from the stool. 'Good! That is a good thing, to love your father.' His fat hands rested on the obi draped round his waist.

She was not alarmed any more. He was simply behaving irrationally, as he often did. He would come to the end of this aberrant game and then he would raise his hand in dismissal and she would leave him and exit his house and find waiting outside one of her bodyguards. The soldier would escort her to her quarters, and all this would be over for another night.

But it was not over yet.

'Your father. What do you know of your father?'

'I know my mother loved him very much.'

She saw him flinch, and that did indeed startle her.

'Did she say that to you . . . that she loved him?'

'Yes, many times. My mother was a missionary. She met him when she was twenty-five and she told me she loved him instantly, the minute she saw his face.'

To her amazement his head tilted sideways as if he were suddenly enthralled, and at the same time his voice softened. 'Tell me more.'

479

So to placate him she did. 'I know he was the same age as she was. They realised they had been born in the same month, July. She told me he was kind to his horse and that it was the first thing which impressed her. He was gentle with all animals and she said his smile reminded her of the gleam of the morning sun as it rose behind the mighty hills of the valley . . .'

Kathleen hesitated, for the general's high colour had drained from his face. His sallow skin had become almost ashen and his hands slid from the sash at his waist to clench at his sides. 'What else did she say?'

'He . . . he died a month after I was born. He was Chinese, the son of a landowner; he was called Lee Tain Sen.'

'He was not Chinese!' Ikeda screamed.

Kathleen's shock caused her to rise from the chair and take a rapid step away from him.

His face contorted and he shouted again, 'He was not Chinese, and that stupid name was not his name!'

Loud knocking on the outer door made the general spin towards it. 'Go away. I am all right,' he called, and revolved back to Kathleen. His eyes were spots of fury and the words flooded from his throat: 'I say he was not Chinese! Oh no, he was not!' He raised his hand and she sank away from him.

'Be silent and listen, Katleen, listen and understand. There was once a young officer in the Imperial Japanese Army, a young fool who saw the world through a naive cloud . . . He had been stationed in Korea and was sent on a delegation into China the year Emperor Meiji died.'

His voice dropped and his eyes lost their rage. His face remained drained of colour and he still rushed his words, but his expression became remote, as if he recounted a vision he saw in a far-off place. 'The delegation sailed from port to port and at length to Guangzhou in southern China, and for many months this youthful soldier travelled along the Xi river and into Yunnan province, and there in the land of the golden monkey he met a young woman missionary, a girl with light eyes and skin like alabaster whose hair grew in dark silken waves: a Christian girl who sang hymns and ballads in her sweet and lilting voice. A girl from a distant south-land far away beyond his ken. She told him she had lived there in a little hamlet where the summers were protracted, still and hot, but when winter came it fashioned chill winds and icy frosts; a place where rosy apples grew. She lost her parents in a terrible fire and had no family, none at all except the people of the mission there in that deep valley in China. The callow soldier listened to her and was entranced by her.'

Kathleen stood motionless as if mesmerised.

He lifted his clenched fist and opened his fingers to drape them across his forehead as he persisted with his vision: 'When the orders came for the soldier to return to Korea he left her, ah, so very reluctantly, with the promise to return to her, his love; but he and his comrades were set upon by Chinese brigands in the hills beyond the valley. The soldier escaped alive but was captive for two years: two harsh, merciless years during which he matured from innocent boy to adult man. And when at last he could keep his vow he returned to the valley for his Caucasian princess, but she had gone for ever from the place they had known together.' He stopped, and the disconnected, remote expression on his face died. 'No one could tell him where she had gone.'

Kathleen was now bewildered. She shook her head from side to side and opened her mouth to speak, but nothing came. When the words formed she hardly recognised her own voice. 'What game is this? Why do you tell me this story? How can you know these things about my mother?'

'How do I know?' he shouted, flinging his hands in the air. 'I know everything! Did I not give *Elizabet* the very pendant lying there upon the skin of your throat? The one you never take off. Did we not climb to Dragon Gate together and look down upon Dianchi Lake and the plains of Yunnan? And there, did I not place it round her neck with the kiss of truth and the promise

481

to love her always?' He made a guttural sound of derision. 'Always!' he spat the word. 'But no, she did not wait!' His head dropped forward and he repeated, 'She did not wait.'

He lifted his head and grunted at himself in scorn. '*Your father* was not a dim-witted Chinese. He was a *proud officer* of the Japanese Imperial Army!' He came to attention and his hands dropped to his sides, his body stiff and formal.

Kathleen's mind had ceased to work, though tears ran down her cheeks. The skin of her face blanched to the same ashen colour as his and she backed away from him until she hit the wall. 'No . . .' The horror she felt imbued the word with all the torment in her head. Her eyes were haunted and an expression of loathing etched itself into her face. Her innermost being was assaulted by his revelation, and even as she recognised it to be the truth; even as it all became clear to her why he had kept her with him, right from the day of the butchery on the beach, she denied it and at last her revulsion for him found words.

'You know nothing of love! The word sours when you use it. It isn't true, it's a vile lie. You're an animal, a brute. You're cruel and sickening and evil, you cannot be my . . .' Her chest heaved and all her revulsion for him rose up in her throat as she turned to the wall, fell against it and retched.

Chapter Sixty-two

John Drayton walked at speed behind the slender form of Raga, his every sense heightened in anticipation of what was to come. No moon glowed but the night was clear and the stars showed Raga's keen dark eyes all they needed to see. He was trusted and had proven himself many times. Before the enemy invasion on 23 January 1942, Raga had been a native policeman, loyal to Colonel Scanlon and the Australians, and been decorated for bravery during the volcanic eruptions in 1937. It was because of this allegiance that his wife had been raped and had her breasts cut off by the Japanese; it made for a strong incentive to aid the commandos.

The men carrying the skiffs were young and powerful and fleet of foot; they were moving faster than John Drayton had expected, no doubt from the same exhilaration he experienced. They had been travelling for over an hour, and every now and then he would call a halt and make sure the whole team remained together.

And as they travelled, he contemplated the profound news which Trap had given him: the news that Lexi was alive.

He had learnt extra details from Caldo when he had approached the sergeant after the final briefing on the operations was over. Amazement had spread over the big man's face when John Drayton told him he was Lexi's husband. 'The Doc? Your wife?' Caldo shook his head. 'But her name's Robinson.'

'Yes, that was her maiden name. She used it professionally.'

Caldo was looking at the major and hearing what the doc had

said to him on the submarine: that she was married to a man who was the colonel's friend.

Caldo cleared his throat. 'I understand, sir, thank you, sir.'

'What else did she tell you? Sergeant?'

Caldo blew air out of the side of his mouth and eyed the major before he answered. This information cleared up a lot of things, oh boy, did it ever. 'She didn't like to talk about any of it, but yep, she did tell me a few things. It was her uncle, someone called Jasper, who shielded her from the Jap bullets in the sea. She said he leapt in the air to cover her getaway and that she swam under water until her lungs almost burst.'

John Drayton remembered Jasper: the innuendoes about his sexuality; his apparent aloofness from the rest of the family. 'Are you sure it was Jasper who did this?'

'Yes, I'm certain.'

'Not Peter? Her uncle Peter?'

'No, it was definitely Jasper who saved her life.'

So, there had been a lot more to Jasper than met the eye. It appeared he was a very brave man. John Drayton frowned thoughtfully as the big man went on.

'Apparently her little boy had been drowned when the ship sank.' He coughed. 'That is . . . *your* little boy too.'

John Drayton emitted a soft, sad sound. 'Yes. Anything else?'

'A bullet grazed her back while she was escaping; she has a scar just below her wing bone. Oh! and she said when she came ashore on another island she was found by a Filipino family and it was with them that she travelled to San Fabian, a town on the Lingayen gulf. We met her somewhat south of there. The two kids with her belonged to that family, I'm sure, and I think the mother died in a Jap aircraft attack.' He paused. 'I guess that's about it. Sorry I can't tell you any more, sir.' Caldo had gazed with wonder again at John Drayton. He thought of all his own suspicions, now certitudes, about the colonel and the Doc! And now here he was confronted with the fact that the Doc was married to Major

Whitby. Well, Caldo was not here to judge the situation; whatever it was all about, one thing he knew, it sure wasn't simple!

He gave a shake of his head. 'How about that? The doc's your wife.'

Since learning of Lexine's survival, John Drayton had attempted to analyse his emotions. For the previous nine months he had believed her dead and worked hard to reshape his life: he had given himself entirely to the army, to his training of the commandos, to the order of things military and to fighting the enemy. He had wholly accepted that if he died in battle it was his fate. This attitude was given birth by the very belief in the loss of Lexi and all the rest of his close family.

To know that Lexine lived and was on her way to Pago Pago was like some sort of cataclysm inside his head. Certainly he was grateful and joyful in the knowledge that she had survived, and as he strode on avoiding roots and stones and dips and fissures in the track beneath his feet, he knew he thanked providence for returning her to him. Yet he was somehow numbed by the reversal of fate.

His eyes lifted to the star-filled sky and he recollected their marriage and what it had meant to him. And as he did his expression sobered, for he was again reminded of the frequency of those strange moments of introspection which came over his wife during their life together. With a feeling of discomfort he recollected them and how he had queried her repeatedly about them, only to be met by laughter and evasion. Surely Lexi had not kept a secret from him?

He frowned as Raga slowed down in front of him and halted.

'What is it?' John Drayton whispered.

'We must cross a road here.'

The message was transferred back down the line of commandos, and with infinite care and speed they hurried over the dirt track which passed for a road. Once in the jungle on the other side, the party began to descend an incline, and it was as they skirted the enemy camp in the area of Malmaluan that the leader's mind turned to Kathleen. He pictured the tender look in her eyes which he had seen so many times. He remembered what a good friend she had been to Lexi, and yes, also to him. He felt a sense of deep loss to think she had been murdered by the Japs. Yes, oh yes, he had a number of scores to settle with the enemy!

They were making good speed downhill and soon they would be at the harbour. He let out a long, noisy breath. He had lost Kathleen and her gentle soul, and his son, and others he cared about but he must take real solace in the fact that his wife was alive.

In the dark of night under the swathe of stars bestride the sky, Corporal Juni Hyata rode his bicycle on the uneven track down from General Ikeda's hill encampment towards the main camp of Rabaul. He knew the way well, but because the bike had no lamp attached he carried a battery-powered torch in his hand. As he bumped along and the beam of light danced over the irregular ground and washed the foliage at the edge of the path, he was thinking of Kataleen. She was like an oasis in the desert of his life. He could think of no better way to spend the war than to be one of her personal guards.

He had been concerned for her when he realised the general was more inebriated than usual tonight, but she had convinced him not to worry. The general drank every night but he did not harm her. Yes, Ikeda was eccentric and cruel and showed no humanity to the men, but with Kataleen much of his violent side seemed assuaged. For a reason which confounded all the men, he looked after her needs and kept her with him. Well, that suited Hyata; for in guarding the sweet Kataleen he avoided many of the soldierly duties which he abhorred.

He did not mind being a messenger either: this ride down to the main camp was pleasant; being away from his common confederates and out with the breeze and the night and the stars soothing his soul.

He knew he had not been fashioned for soldiering: he preferred to read; he had studied Japanese literature at university and many of the soldiers laughed about the slender well-worn volume of the ancient lyric poet Kakinomoto no Hitomaro which he carried with him. He would read it late at night when he was off duty and the others were sleeping, and he marvelled at how a man who had lived over a thousand years ago could touch a chord in his own twentieth-century heart. He was thinking of the poetry and began quoting aloud to the night:

'"At fair Kumano
Lilies on the beach
A hundred deep
My heart's yearning, but
Never will we meet"'

'Tomare!'

The word exploded in front of him, and hitting the brakes he lurched forward but swiftly regained his seat as his torchlight bounced off a soldier standing ahead in his path. Hyata slid his feet off the pedals to the ground, bringing his torch up to shine upon the uniform of a first lieutenant with the Imperial Japanese 8th Area Army.

He bowed from the shoulders. 'You were lucky, sir, I could have run straight into you!' Hyata lamented, dropping the beam to the man's boots.

'Yes, but you did not. Where are you going at this hour?'

The corporal moved the torch from his right hand to his left, and keeping the beam lowered, saluted. 'I'm taking a private communiqué from General Ikeda to General Imamura's office.'

'It must be important for you to be going there at this time of night.'

Juni nodded. 'I suppose it is.'

The lieutenant held out his hand. 'You are lucky for I'm on General Imamura's staff so you can show it to me.'

Hyata's confusion was apparent in the way he stuttered his reply. 'But, sir, I . . . I . . . that is, I have been ordered to hand it to General Imamura's private secretary, Lieutenant Koizumi, only.'

'Have you met Lieutenant Koizumi?'

'No, sir.'

The lieutenant laughed. 'You are looking at him, soldier.'

Hyata was amazed. 'Oh . . . I see . . . I am sorry, sir.'

'Yes, I often walk up here late at night after the stresses of the day. It does me good to be out with the air and the stars and away from the hordes of men in the camp.'

Junichiro empathised with that point of view. 'Yes, sir.'

'What is your name?'

'Corporal Hyata, sir.'

'So, Corporal Hyata, give me your torch and your missive.'

What could the soldier do? He thought it a bewildering co-incidence that of all the sixty thousand Japanese soldiers stationed in Rabaul, he had run into the very one he sought, but with due respect he handed both items to the lieutenant, who opened the seal and read the communication.

'Good,' he said. 'What were your instructions from General Ikeda?'

'To remain overnight in Rabaul, sir, and to return with the reply first thing in the morning.'

The lieutenant spoke in cordial fashion, stepping forward and grasping the handlebars of the bike. 'It shall be as you say. I can do what is requested of me in this communiqué and I shall have your reply waiting for you at eight hundred hours.' He tucked the envelope inside his tunic. 'Now, Corporal, General Imamura is thinking of sending some vintage wine up to General Ikeda tomorrow. Tell me which of the six houses is the general's.'

Hyata answered. 'The last one to the west, sir, the one built into the hillside with the trees around it.'

'Thank you. Now, off you go to Rabaul main camp and report to my office tomorrow. Where will you sleep?'

'My sergeant told me to go to the guardhouse in Chinatown, he said some billets are available there.'

'Is your sergeant still awake?'

Juni Hyata wondered what business of the lieutenant's this was, but he dared not say so. 'He was when I left, sir, but I should think he'll be asleep now.'

'Are there ten or fifteen of you up there with the general and his staff now?'

The young corporal knew he was looking at a lieutenant of the Imperial Japanese Army, and not only that, but a man who was the great General Imamura's own secretary; he also knew he was in the stronghold of Rabaul; otherwise there could have been reason to be suspicious of such questions. But there was no reason at all to be. So he answered: 'There are twenty-four of us, as well as the servants and the . . . women.'

The lieutenant laughed affably. 'Yes, of course. Now on you go, Hyata, I'll be ready for you at oh eight hundred hours.' He handed the torch back and turned and walked away into the black night.

Suddenly Hyata called after him, 'Where is your office, sir?'

The reply, muffled by the trees and foliage, was borne to him on the humid breeze. 'Ask anyone down there. They all know.'

Junichiro blinked and shook his head. He remained astonished at the coincidence of meeting Lieutenant Koizumi up here wandering around in the depths of night. But it was not for him to query the behaviour of officers.

He lifted his body back on to the seat of his bicycle and with a shrug of his shoulders and still mystified he rode on down the track.

Behind him in the trees, Shibuyu the Nisei hurried over to Trap and the others who had been watching from their hideaway. A smile widened on the young man's mouth as they gathered around him.

'So, Colonel, we now know Ikeda has a twenty-four-man guard.'

'Well done.'

Shibuyu continued, 'And we also know he lives in the last house on the hillside surrounded by trees.'

'Perfect.'

'What was in the message you took from him?' asked Rupert Coalclark.

Tommy Shibuyu removed the envelope from his tunic and held it up in the night. 'It requests one Lieutenant Koizumi, who is in charge of ordnance, to send Ikeda up four pounds of sugar and thirty eggs immediately, and states that the minute the supply ship arrives – which apparently from his note is due in the morning – he is to be informed, as he wants to pick his own frozen meats. It also mentions that all the food he chooses tomorrow from the supply ship is to be transferred to the transport ship *Hoto Maru*, which he is to embark upon, as we know, on Saturday.'

'Good,' exclaimed Caldo. 'So we had the right embarkation date. We're getting in just in time.'

Trap grunted and slapped Shibuyu's shoulder approvingly. 'Well done, Tommy, well done. So let's get on with it.'

They all moved off, with Cigs in the lead, and as they did so Trap looked back in the direction in which Hyata had pedalled away. 'The little monkey on the bicycle should thank his lucky stars. He gets to live because his commanding officer is a greedy bastard and sent him on an errand.'

Chapter Sixty-three

Purple blotches of fury smudged Tama Ikeda's face, his ebony eyes were ablaze with rage and he took five frenzied paces to Kathleen as she lifted her palm up to keep him away. But his fat hands caught hold of her and he pulled her violently around to face him.

'Treacherous one! What contumely you dare to speak. I will—'

Ikeda stopped in mid-speech as gunfire echoed in the night and his mouth opened in astonishment. He dropped Kathleen and she fell heavily to the floor as he spun round and ran to the door, swiftly sliding it open. There on the threshold was revealed a soldier with blood spurting from a dagger in his throat.

The general jumped sideways as bullets flew off the door jamb and thudded into the back of the bleeding soldier. Kathleen screamed and Ikeda slammed the door shut and locked it. His gaze flicked wildly back and forth across the room before he ran to the futon and hastily grabbed his sword, which lay in its scabbard on the mattress. Eyes wild, he took up the loaded revolver from the shelf beside it.

His mind raced as distant automatic weapon fire sounded, and as he paused momentarily, the inner door slid open and he whirled towards it, revolver at the ready, but it was only Maruta, Dinty and two other women. They eyed him with faces of fear as he pushed the revolver inside his obi and screamed, 'Where are my bodyguards?' But the women had no answer to that.

The boom of an explosion at the other end of the compound

shook the floor. Maruta and Dinty shrieked as Ikeda strode to Kathleen and pulled her roughly to her feet, shouting at the women, 'Get out and find my bodyguards!' but they backed into the corridor and stood there impotently.

Yanking the resisting Kathleen across the room and out of the door, he pushed by the females as the constant bursts of automatic gunfire continued outside. He was well down the passage when an explosion rocked the foundations of the building.

'They have blown in the door!' Dinty screamed.

'Shut up and find my bodyguards!' Ikeda raged, but terror kept the women stationary as the general reached an ornate glass panel in the hall and slid it open, hurling Kathleen inside.

She had never been inside the prayer room before, but now was not the time to marvel at the classic decoration or the glass fountain which trickled water over a number of smooth blue stones to a tiny pool in the floor. He slammed the panel shut in the faces of the terrified females as Kathleen pleaded, 'Leave me here!'

He renewed his grip on her arm. 'I have not kept you with me for an entire year to release you now. You are my daughter and you remain with me.'

'I am not your daughter and my mother would abhor you!'

'Shut up!'

To the cacophony of a battle echoing from outside he bundled his charge to the far wall and spoke agitatedly. 'Mistake to live up here! Mistake! I will boil Hosoda alive for suggesting it. In Rabaul we were safe . . . bunkered and reinforced. Why did I listen?'

As he spoke he whipped aside a huge ornate silk drape depicting a 'Sacred Grove' pattern, and it revealed a reinforced steel door about four feet six inches tall. He opened it and pushed his captive towards the dark interior.

'Stop! Stop! What are you doing?' She hit back at him but he smashed the sword handle down on her shoulder and forced her to bend her head into what she saw was a tunnel, and she immediately realised why the general's house had been built into the hillside: to enable this underground passage to lead away from it.

Ikeda grabbed a torch which was fitted to the wall and, switching it on, thrust the hunched-over Kathleen ahead of him.

His mind darted from thought to thought: thank heaven they had used the Korean prisoners and those Australians who had not been sent to Japan to build this escape route.

Abruptly, like the violent cracking of a hundred mirrors the glass door of the prayer room shattered. Kathleen looked back in shock, but at the same moment the general slid the steel door closed behind them and her view of the silk drape falling back into place was lost.

The torchlight bounced past her, and she bent her head in the damp and noxious-smelling passage.

'Hurry!' Her captor shoved her ahead of him.

In the rising wind the commandos of Operation Longtail moved stealthily towards the perimeter of the small compound. They were perhaps a hundred and fifty yards distant from their objective when Trap's hand went up automatically and the contingent paused. Through the foliage could be discerned a small fire burning and two sentries sitting on mats, smoking. This was obviously the forward guard post for the compound, but the soldiers appeared to feel completely secure, for their rifles leant on a stack of firewood at their sides and they chatted, one bending forward, elbows on knees. Beyond them the jungle was semi-cleared and through the trees a vague illumination was thrown from a single electric light attached to a pole above a fence which evidently surrounded the general's compound. They could not discern any other soldiers, but Trap knew there had to be at least one sentry on the gate. The sound of a dynamo motor rattled somewhere close; which no doubt fed the area with electricity. Dotted in the gloom beyond the fence they could make out the shapes of buildings.

Trap glanced around their faces in the feeble light. They all knew the plan intimately, and he and Caldo left the other six and walked forward cautiously in the darkness. Trap gave thanks for the endless night noises – insects buzzing, animal calls, the scuttling of nocturnal creatures and the croaking of frogs – for he knew their human footfalls in the blackness were not completely soundless.

Just outside the rim of the firelight they halted and separated, each edging along until both were as close as possible to the two enemy soldiers without being seen; then, abruptly, with split-second timing, they surged out of the darkness at the Japanese.

One soldier bounded to his feet, grabbing for his rifle, but Trap was upon him. The other actually emitted the start of a scream but it died like he did – from Caldo's knife thrust, up beneath his breastbone. His body lifted from the ground under the power of the big man's blow. By now Trap had seized the first soldier by the throat, and while the man's hands clutched wildly at the air he was held in such a way that he was near to fainting and could not scream.

Caldo's dead sentry dropped to the ground and the sergeant rapidly grabbed the other's flailing hands and subdued them as Trap's gaze darted in the direction of the camp. 'Thank God that dynamo's engine drowned the noise.'

'Yeah,' Caldo apologised, 'I'm slipping; he almost screamed.' And holding both wrists of the diminutive Japanese soldier in one of his hands, he wiped his knife on his trousers with the other and slid it back in the sheath on his belt.

The soldier was half choking in Trap's grasp, his eyes in the firelight glinting with terror as they easily pulled the little man into the shadows and Caldo took out twine from his pocket to tie his hands. Coalclark, Williams, Mayberry, Olsen, Lambert and Shibuyu clustered round. Just for a moment the eyes of the captive widened with relief, for he noted Shibuyu in the Japanese lieutenant's uniform. But his hope was immediately quashed when

Shibuyu spoke Japanese in hushed and sinister tones. 'If you make the slightest wrong move you will be killed instantly. We are going to relax the grip on you so that you can speak to us, but *very* quietly. Understand?'

The man's gaze rested on his dead comrade being dragged into the shadows by Olsen; he knew they meant it. He nodded and Trap loosened his grip.

'Ask him how many sentries are on the gate.'

Shibuyu did so.

'One.'

Trap knew a smattering of Japanese from his three-month stay in the country, and now he asked, 'Are you sure?'

'Yes.'

Trap met Shibuyu's eyes. 'Find out if there are any others on guard inside the compound.'

When Shibuyu asked, the soldier hesitated but Trap's hands tightened around his throat and the Nisei threatened, 'Answer or you die now.'

'Two bodyguards on the general's house. And a soldier guarding the woman Katleen.'

Trap followed the import of that sentence. 'Woman? Who is she.'

The Nisei translated the man's reply. 'I don't know who she is. She travels with the general, that's all.' Shibuyu shrugged at this and decided, 'Probably a reluctant mistress.'

Trap nodded. 'Find out where she is now.'

'She is usually with the general until the early hours. Then she is taken back to her own abode.'

Trap had one more query. 'Where are the barracks?'

The soldier showed reluctance to answer this, but once more Trap's hands constricted his throat and the information followed. 'To the left inside the main gate.'

Trap comprehended. 'Good.' He was feeling better. If this man were telling the truth, and he reckoned he probably was, then at least the majority of the guards were sleeping. He met Tommy Shibuyu's eyes. 'Now get him to call out and we can finish what we came for.'

Tommy bent forward to the captive. 'Listen carefully. I want you to shout out to the sentry at the main gate. Say there is a messenger here from Rabaul camp; that he has an urgent communiqué to deliver to the general.'

As the terrified soldier eyed them, Shibuyu added, 'Do it now or you die. If you do this successfully we will not kill you but gag and bind you only.'

The soldier's eyes rolled in disbelief.

'Do you wish to die instantly?'

He shook his head.

'Then do as I say.'

The others gathered around in the shadows as the sentry was hoisted to his feet. Shibuyu dug him in the side. 'Shout out now.'

He called in Japanese to the main gate.

No answer . . . only the throb of the dynamo in the distance and the nearby night noises of the jungle.

'Hey, Isago! You on the main gate!'

A few seconds passed and the silhouette of a man's head appeared above the fence and turned in their direction. 'What? Is that you, Nantio?'

'Yes.'

'What's going on?'

Shibuyu dug him again.

'There is a messenger here, come up from Rabaul camp . . . with a communiqué for the general.'

'From Rabaul, you say?'

'Yes.'

'At this time of night?'

Shibuyu jabbed him again.

'Yes.'

'All right, send him in.'

Tommy Shibuyu strode forward at speed towards the compound while Williams whispered, 'Do we kill him, sir?'

'No, we keep our word.'

Swiftly Williams and Mayberry gagged the already bound prisoner as the others stole after the Nisei, keeping to the shadows. As he hastened to the gate Shibuyu called out in Japanese: 'I'm coming in. I am Lieutenant Shibuyu from General Imamura. I've left my bicycle with the other guards out here.'

The compound fence was made of thick bamboo, without any barbed wire in sight, once again proof that all Japanese in this part of the world felt no fear from a land attack. The sentry walked to the gate; he wore spectacles and carried the newspaper he had been reading and his rifle. He was surprised that a lieutenant would be sent on this sort of assignment, which was more in keeping for perhaps a corporal. He was only a corporal himself and he spoke deferentially. 'I'm sorry, Lieutenant, but I cannot disturb the general. Give me the communiqué, please. I will see he has it first thing tomorrow.' He bowed.

The new arrival's tone became directive. 'No, I'll hand it over myself to the sergeant on duty.'

'He'll be asleep, sir.'

'What business has a sergeant on duty to be asleep?'

'Well, sir, I mean, not really asleep. Up here we don't have any callers. Well, not as a rule. He'll be resting.'

'Open up anyway. I wish to hand it to the sergeant myself.'

And using the same rationale as Hyata had, just eight minutes previously, the sentry saw no reason to mistrust his eyes and he unlocked the gate.

Shibuyu entered, and when the sentry turned his back on him to relock the gate the Nisei delivered a rabbit killer punch to the back of his neck as Trap and the others sprinted forward out of the shadows. The sentry sank to his knees, arriving in the next world four seconds later.

'Right,' Trap's tone was callous and his eyes were hard, 'close

497

the gate and drag this guy back into his guardhouse. Lambert and Mayberry, remain here and kill anyone who comes by, as silently as possible.

'Caldo, Olsen and I will get down to the general's house and dispatch the Kempeitai and his cohorts.' His gaze darted to the silent barracks. 'Coalclark and Williams, blow up the barracks in exactly three minutes from now and shoot out the electric lights. Shibuyu, stay here and back them up. We know there are workers and servants in the compound, so if any civilians come out, round them up and hold them till I return.' He looked at his watch in the feeble light. 'It's seven minutes to detonation time in the harbour.'

Trap, Caldo and Olsen ran on, keeping to the shadows. All was still and the buildings appeared as innocuous shapes in the midnight hour: there was only partial blackout here; occasional electric lights threw their glow from poles at fifty-yard intervals. Jungle grew close to the compound fence on all sides but the hill rose to the rear where they believed the general's house to be. As they ran through the grounds they could see in the moon- and starlight down the long incline to Rabaul town and camp, spreading along the harbour in the distance.

Trap, Caldo and Olsen slowed down when they saw the two structures ahead. From Corporal Hyata's description they decided the illuminated one was the Kempeitai general's house and assumed the other was that of his staff officers.

The leader's hand shot up and they halted. Three guards stood together quietly talking ten yards from Ikeda's door. Just as the sentry had said! Two for the general and one for the woman. Two rifles leant against the wall behind the soldiers and the third guard held his in his hands.

Slowly Caldo and Olsen began to edge towards the enemy from shadow to shadow. They were within twenty yards when the one who carried the rifle spoke and turned away, leaving the other two. He walked around the side of the house nearest the commandos, and coming within six yards of them, placed his rifle down and began to relieve himself. In an instant Caldo burst out of the night and repeated his execution blow. This time there was only a muffled sound of shock as the soldier crumpled to the ground. At the same second a burst of gunfire broke the silence from the other end of the compound.

Trap paused. *Something's gone wrong!* And in the same second the two guards at the front of the house twisted instantly towards the noise.

Trap hesitated no longer. 'Come on!' he shouted, taking two rapid steps forward and hurling his dagger. It carved lethally through the night to lodge in the throat of one soldier, who clutched at his neck and staggered in his death throes up on to the low veranda towards the door of the house. The second sentry dived back for his rifle as Olsen cast his knife, and at the same time his leader opened fire. The knife went wide but the soldier fell from the spurt of bullets.

'Shit!' Caldo came running round the corner of the house towards them while the noise of rapid fire continued from the other end of the camp.

In that second, the door of the general's house abruptly opened, but the Japanese teetering in the doorway hid the person inside, who immediately rammed it shut.

Trap was already running forward, Tommy gun spitting; the bullets slammed into the door jamb and the back of the dying soldier.

'Blow the door in!' he shouted as an explosion rocked the ground from the far end of the camp.

'The barracks!' Caldo looked round to the sound.

'At last. Now blow the door in!'

Caldo hurled a Mills bomb and the front of the house disintegrated with a boom. They had taken a step forward on the veranda when a spurt of gunfire hit the pillar beside them.

'Jesus!'

All three dropped to their knees behind a low wall to see two soldiers in sleepwear charging them from the darkened staff officers' dwelling, firing as they came.

'Christ! My gun's jammed,' Olsen shouted as the sergeant opened fire. One of the onrushing Japanese fell, but the other took shelter behind a stack of boxes near a stand of trees.

Two more Japanese darted out of the staff officers' door and joined their comrades shielded by the boxes, as another opened fire from a window and Trap and Caldo returned the barrage.

Suddenly Olsen began firing again. 'You beauty, it's working!'

Trap knew he had to move: the general would be aware of what was going on. He shouted to his sergeant. 'Cover me as well as you can, I'm going in after the bastard.'

So to the enthusiastic bombardment supplied by Caldo and Olsen, and the accompaniment of bullets spitting to right and left of him, their colonel leapt up and ran.

Chapter Sixty-four

Trap burst into Ikeda's burning front room.

Instantly assessing what was left of the room, he noted the single door in the surviving far wall and the broken remains of an elaborate gold and silver screen on the floor. Gingerly he crossed and looked carefully into the hallway. There he discovered Dinty, Maruta, and the two other women crying and hugging each other. He strode down to them. 'Where is the general?' he shouted in Japanese.

Dinty's hand shook as she pointed to a glass door. Trap ran to it and, spraying it with bullets, splintered it into a thousand pieces as the women screamed.

On into the prayer room Trap strode, firing as he came, but it was empty. He revolved three hundred and sixty degrees before he crossed the room to tear down the antique silk drape and discover the steel door.

'Blast!' He saw it would take more than a Tommy gun or a Mills bomb to get in there. He ran back into the corridor and, grabbing the terrified Maruta by the arm, pulled her into the burning front room. 'Where is the general?' His Japanese was good enough to ask this question, but Maruta burst into tears. He shook her by the shoulders. *'Where is the general?'*

Maruta was nineteen and from a poor family in Korea but she had lived well up here being a general's mistress; she was afraid of this foreign soldier but she carried more fear of the general's wrath.

'I know where he is!'

Trap abandoned Maruta and spun round to the speaker. It was Dinty.

'He's in the escape tunnel.'

'How long is it and where does it lead?'

Dinty recognised that this soldier was an American colonel. She spoke swiftly. 'I think perhaps eighty yards. It runs along inside the hill and comes out between two huge rocks. A track leads from there into the jungle and down to a bunker. I think that once you are inside it there are systems of tunnels leading over to Rabaul.'

'How do I get to the rocks and the exit?'

She pointed. 'If you jump the fence outside you'll land in a ditch and it will lead you straight there. I know because I walk along it when I gather wood.'

'Good girl!'

Beckoning him, she scuttled along the hall away from the burning part of the house. Reaching a side door, she opened it and pointed again to the fence which was revealed in the gleam from crackling flames. 'Go over it near the casurina.'

'Thank you.' Trap bounded from doorway to ground, where he paused, his body taut. The din of Caldo and Olsen's battle with the Japanese staff officers continued and he could hear persistent firing at the other end of the camp: it all concerned him but he could do nothing. If he hesitated and went to the aid of his men he would lose the bastard he had come for; he had no choice.

He ran towards the fence, and in the doorway behind him Dinty watched. Back in the Philippines her father had worked at Camp Stotsenberg in the military hospital; she had learnt her English at a military school there and she remembered her parents' admiration for the tall, thin general they had called 'Skinny'. She crossed herself and prayed that this colonel would kill the fat pig Kempeitai Ikeda. It gratified her to have been able to help.

Trap extended his stride, bounding over the sloping broken ground, avoiding small ruts and rocks and leaping across a straggling vegetable patch to scale the five feet of bamboo. He landed heavily, but still on his feet, and instantly began running as fast as the dark of night would allow along the trench. Suddenly he murmured aloud, 'Yeah, Johnny, yeah!' for, like the distant clash of a cymbal, an explosion lifted from the harbour. '*Now, Johnny, let me hear a dozen more!*'

He stumbled as his boot caught under a branch but managed to steady himself. This forced him to slow down a little. The trench floor began to rise and the jungle threatened from right and left, but his sense of direction led him up the sharp incline on to an open area, where, just as the woman had explained, two massive boulders loomed in ebony silhouette.

Cautiously he approached, and even as he rounded the nearest, saw the door half open in the wall of earth and plants between them. Ikeda had left the tunnel!

A second explosion rumbled from the harbour, followed by another and another. Red and yellow streaks of light surged into the night sky as he revolved in the open grassy patch, scanning the jungle for the path which Dinty had told him led away.

He spied it and ran, Tommy gun at the ready, hurrying in through the trees and ferns and vines as fast as he dared. Gunfire still rang out behind him and more thundering blasts reverberated from the harbour, but suddenly he became aware of scuffling sounds somewhere. He paused, uncertain from which direction they came, but a shout followed by a stream of screaming and what sounded like deranged yelling, oriented him. He moved on directly ahead, but now with care and stealth.

The beam from the torch fluctuated up and down as Ikeda prodded Kathleen forward with the butt of his sword and head bent, she stumbled ahead of him in the noisome underground corridor.

As he touched her she shivered with revulsion. He could not be her father. *He butchered Lexi and the others from the shipwreck.* She remembered how brave Jasper had been speaking up to him before

503

he died that unholy day. Their screams echoed in her head and she tried to pull forward from his hand as he urged her onwards.

Her heart thumped in the confining musty tunnel. No matter what happened to her, she prayed that John D would survive the war. She imagined him as she had last seen him, and even as she felt the pressure on her back again she prayed for him. Surely men such as this man behind her, could not win the war! *Deserve victory*, 'You must deserve victory,' she could recall Sir Brillard saying long ago. 'Be more honourable than your enemy; you must deserve victory.'

Her brain was reeling against what this cursed man had told her. How could it be that this creature pushing her could lay claim to her as a daughter? How could her beautiful, dignified mother ever have been with him? How could her mother have lied and lied to her year after year?

I despise him ... How could I have come from him? She felt ill, she felt unclean.

'Hurry!' he growled behind her.

Her head ached. Who was Lee Tain Sen? Who was the man in the photograph in the silver filagree frame? The man she had kissed every night from babyhood. How could her mother have done this to her?

The wavering beam from the torch Ikeda held hit the damp walls of the passage, divulging the way. 'There is a door ahead,' he barked and shortly afterwards they were upon it. He pressed her against the cold steel. 'Hold the torch!' he commanded, handing it to her before resting his sword on the side wall.

She did as commanded and he used both hands to take purchase on a metal nozzle protruding from the wall to their right side; wrenching on it he turned it round, and as he did so the door in front of her began to open, crunching and squeaking. When it was wide enough she moved quickly through, sighing with relief to be outside in the night air as he picked up the sword and followed.

'Give me back the torch,' he commanded, and she handed it to him. He now held the flashlight in his left hand and the sword in his right. The blade gleamed but the shadows of the night hid his inky-black eyes.

'This way.'

'Leave me here.'

She reeled back as he struck her across the mouth with the butt of the sword. And before she had recovered her balance he stepped to her and, transferring the flashlight to his sword hand, took her arm and pulled her across the open ground towards the jungle.

'You *will* come with me. I am tired of your insolence and shall have your tongue cut out if you don't accompany me silently.'

Even the sound of his voice sickened her. She fell silent and allowed him to pull her along. Her mouth throbbed and she touched a swelling on her upper lip. It was only luck that he had not knocked out a tooth, though she could taste blood. She was well aware that he was capable of doing exactly as he threatened. After all, she had seen him behead defenceless people without compunction.

Gunfire continued to echo from behind as they entered a track into the jungle. He was yanking and tugging her as she made a feeble, part-resistance, but they were still making fair speed over the rotting foliage beneath their feet.

Abruptly an explosion rose from the direction of the harbour.

Ikeda stopped short and his fingers tightened vice-like on Kathleen's arm.

What is going on? Attacks coming from everywhere! What if my ships are being blown up? What is happening? I must get to the bunker and the tunnel access to Rabaul.

He knew the entrance was manned by sentries. He would be safe there. He jerked her on, the ray from the torch darting through the heavy trees and the vines, reflecting the insects and the decaying ferns and the moody secrets of the jungle night.

In time Katleen will see sense. Yes, it is only a matter of time. He would

505

keep her with him, and if she did not comply then he might actually do what he had just threatened and cut out her tongue. Then she could not complain and insult him. Yes, he must tame her and could not abide any continuation of her offensive and uncivil talk. But she must remain with him. It was only fitting. *She should revere me! I am her father.*

A second explosion rumbled from the harbour, followed by a third and a fourth and a fifth.

The blasts infuriated him. 'We must hurry!' he shouted and began to speed up, but in his haste his foot caught beneath a vine and he winced as he slipped and his ankle twisted to bring him toppling to his knees. His left hand wrenched from Kathleen's arm and his overburdened right hand opened. Down fell the sword and the torch. In the arc of light cast between them Kathleen saw the revolver slip out of his obi and drop into a cluster of ferns.

She hesitated, but only momentarily, scooping the weapon up even as Ikeda recovered and began to turn and rise, shouting and grabbing out wildly for his sword.

The flashlight was lodged in the bracken close to her, and as he raised himself on one knee she snatched it and shone the beam of light upon him. 'I am not coming with you.' The gun shook in her hand as she backed away from him.

He gained his feet and blinked as the bright light hit his eyes. *You mean it. How dare you mean it! I am General Ikeda. I gave you life. You belong to me.*

He heard more explosions. Everything enraged him. Things were going wrong: the attack on the compound, the explosions, the actions of stupid Katleen; why was she shining the light in his eyes? How dare she?

'You hand me the gun now! You belong to me. I am your master . . . *I am your father!*' He whipped his hand around in the air in fury and he realised he was screaming and slicing the air with his sword, but he could not stop. A loud report sounded very close to his ears and a hammer blow thudded into his chest. He lurched backwards, his sword curving violently in the air and slicing a hanging vine.

Something hard slammed into his face and a hot, searing sensation flooded up from his heart, all over his head, all over his mind. He felt as if he staggered. His knees collapsed. He was falling . . . falling . . . down into a cold, black place. He was amazed.

How can this possibly be? I am General Ikeda. I am an important soldier of the Japanese emperor! I cannot die like this!

She has killed me. How dare she kill me? My . . . own . . . daughter . . . has . . . killed me . . .

Kathleen's shaking hands dropped the flashlight, and as it looped in the air and fell to the ground the ray of light hit the jade pendant round her neck; the dragon with its tiny rubies for eyes and the triangular ruby for the tip of its swirling tail gleamed like a beacon . . . just for a second.

Ikeda's mind carried that image as he entered the river of night.

Chapter Sixty-five

Kathleen could not control her trembling, and the thin beam of neutral illumination from the flashlight quivered upon the contorted body displayed before her on the jungle floor: Ikeda's sword caught in a branch so that it remained almost vertical in his hand. He was on his back, and blood covered his clothes and what was left of his face. His robe had opened to expose him and his fat leg protruded at a warped angle.

She moaned softly and the tears drifted from her eyes. Unable to truly take in what she had done, no thoughts came; her mind seemed separated from her body.

The noise of someone coming through the jungle did not rouse her. She remained facing Ikeda, her body quivering, gazing at him with staring eyes. For these moments she had given up caring about herself, and while she was half aware of somebody cautiously advancing upon her through the trees behind, she stood, shoulders drooping, the ray of light trained on the nightmarish Dada form, misshapen and ugly.

Water dripped on her from the branches above, and as she felt it run through her hair and down her neck, her mind began to function again: the fiend was dead. He would abuse no more women, he would torture and maim no more; he would sever no more heads. Two bullets, that was all it had taken to put an end to him and his swaggering madness: two small pieces of lead, cylindrical and pointed.

She did not flinch when a man spoke behind her in the encompassing gloom.

'Do you speak English?'

She nodded. If he were here to kill her, she hardly cared.

Trap came a step closer. 'Are you alone?'

She nodded again and the torch fell from her fingers.

Trap relieved her of the pistol and picked up the torch. 'Is this General Ikeda?'

Once more she motioned with her head, but this time murmured, 'Yes.'

Trap did not immediately take for granted that what the woman said was true. He ran on along the track for two hundred yards and paused and listened. Distant noises rose from the camp but all was quiet around him, no sound of anybody moving ahead. He was pretty sure the woman back there was in shock and had not lied to him. He ran back to her. She remained standing beside the corpse.

Trap shone the torch on the body: the dead man's face was mostly missing but his physique looked that of a Japanese man in his fifties which was definitely the right age. Shibuyu had learnt that Ikeda was of sturdy build with grey hair and that fitted too. He nodded to himself and grunted. So this tart had done his work for him. Good. All that mattered was that the target had been obliterated.

He held the beam of the torch down between them. It lit the bottom of her kimono and illuminated her Western shoes. She was shaking and obviously distressed to the point of distraction so he did not raise the light to her face. 'Listen, lady, I don't know where you want to go but I've got to get back to the compound.'

She did not reply.

'Look, I can't stay here.' He took hold of her arm. 'This man's dead. You've done a good thing, not a bad thing. Believe me, the Allies are grateful to you. He needed to be shot. So pull yourself together. You're a heroine, for Pete's sake.'

She did not reply but she appeared to calm somewhat, for her limbs stopped trembling and she shuffled her feet a little. He squeezed her arm for attention. 'I've got to leave you now.'

This stirred her and she lifted her hands to him. 'No, I must . . . come with you. Please take me back to the compound.'

'In that case, let's move.' He pulled her gently along for about ten yards. 'Listen, lady, we've got to pick up the pace and you've got to keep up if you're coming. I'll soon have every man Jack of the teeming blasted Japs on this island after my head.' He let go her arm and began to stride hurriedly away.

She watched him for a moment only before she ran after him. They moved fast, and while Kathleen's feet slid under her from time to time, she did not lose her balance and soon they returned to the clearing, where he accelerated and loped across the open space to slip easily down into the trench. He looked back once to see her skid down the slope behind him but she did not fall and he said, 'Good girl,' as he moved off and again she followed.

Trap was aware that the blasts from the harbour had ceased and so too had the firing in the compound. He was about fifty yards from the part of the fence he had scaled on his way out when he saw a figure he recognised coming towards him.

'Caldo?'

'Ah, there you are, sir. Wondered what had happened to you. Was just coming to find you.'

'Is everything all right?'

The sergeant eyed the woman with surprise but he answered the question. 'Yeah, but we lost Joker and Shibuyu's wounded. Apparently there was a patrol inside the camp that the little bastard we bound up *forgot* to mention. That was why we heard the gunfire before they blew the barracks.'

'Goddam.' Trap shook his head. 'Let's get back inside to the others.'

Caldo pointed along the ditch in the gleam from the still-burning general's house. In fact the whole of the compound was illuminated by the flames from it and from the barracks in the distance. 'Sir, there's a gate I blew open just along here; no need to climb the fence.'

'Right.' Trap strode on as he spoke. 'Let's find the boys and get going. We've got to make speed over the peninsula. The blasted enemy will be targeting us from all around, soon. We need to be on the track pretty quick smart.'

'Yes, sir!'

'How badly hurt is Tommy?'

After a moment's hesitation Caldo supplied the answer: 'He's taken a bullet in the gut.'

Trap said nothing and hurried to the hole in the fence. As they passed through, Caldo thought it was time to mention the woman who appeared to be with them.

'Who's the gal, sir?'

His colonel grunted. 'Ah, nobody. I think she was Ikeda's mistress. Did me a favour by putting a couple of bullets in him. Saved me the job. She must have tired of his—'

'I *was not* his mistress! Don't you speak of me that way, Mr Chris Webster! It isn't worthy of you.'

Trap halted sharply . . . but turned slowly.

Caldo's mouth pursed and his eyebrows rose. '*Chris Webster?*'

Trap strode back to her and peered into her face for the first time. 'Jesus, lady, let me get a good look at you.'

Kathleen peered back. Oh yes, she had finally realised who he was just a minute ago as they ran along the ditch. Once the confusion and bewilderment of killing Ikeda had subsided she had felt something was familiar about the colonel she was following. She had begun to recognise things about him and abruptly it had come to her. He was the American who had been at Sir Brillard's ninetieth birthday party in Hong Kong! How could she ever forget him? He was the one person in the world who had seen how she felt about

John D! She remembered exactly what he had asked her as he danced with her that night: *How long have you been in love with Johnny?*

In the glow from the blazes all around, Trap was shaking his head. Oh yes, he knew her now. She looked different with the swollen lip and wearing the costume, but he knew her. A conglomerate of thoughts tripped over each other in his head: *She's the best friend of the Doll. They were on the torpedoed ship together. She's in love with Johnny. Johnny thinks this woman is dead. How come she isn't?*

His tone became long-suffering. 'Yeah, right, Hong Kong. But weren't you with . . .' he hated to mention her, but he did, 'Dr Robinson . . . when the Japs murdered the survivors of the shipwreck on the coast of Luzon?'

'Yes.'

'Well what the hell are you doing in Rabaul with a Kempeitai general, for Christ's sake?'

She closed her eyes as if it were too much to answer and he spoke in a tone of dismissal. 'Listen, forget it. I can see it's going to be a blasted chronicle. Tell me some other time.' And he spun round and strode away.

Kathleen watched him; what he had just said hurt, but she could forgive his rudeness: he was fighting a bitter war and had little time for her predicament.

Beside her the sergeant shrugged and studied this Eurasian woman who had called the colonel Chris Webster. Caldo was no fool: he knew the colonel had lived divers incarnations in his restless existence, and had obviously met this dame in one of them. Then he remembered the talks he used to have with the Doc. Once she had actually mentioned a half-Oriental female friend from Hong Kong who had been on the torpedoed ship with her. Yeah . . . it was coming back to him now. She had been taken forcibly away from the other survivors on the beach by a Jap officer before he had the rest of them murdered. He recalled the Doc's words: *She didn't want to go; she resisted him, shouting out that she wanted to die with us, but he took her anyway. God knows*

512

what became of her. Well, Caldo reckoned he was standing beside her now!

How was it he and the colonel managed to pick up these dames in the middle of nowhere?

The woman waited, staring at him.

'Come on,' he said, and he strode away after Trap across the compound into the heat and crackling of the flames of the burning buildings. Sparks flew in the rising wind, the wail of sirens echoed up from Rabaul and the harbour lit up with dozens of glaring rays from searchlights criss-crossing in the distance.

Ahead of them a dozen Korean prisoners who were obviously labourers here in the compound clustered together. Caldo wished them luck. 'Get out of here while you can, you guys.'

Caldo halted behind Trap as he knelt beside Shibuyu. Sergeant Major Lambert had bandaged the wound as best he could from a first aid kit he always carried, but the ominous dark blood was already seeping through.

'Now listen, son, you've got to hang on. We'll carry you.' The leader glanced up at the rest of his band, who stood waiting. 'Caldo and you, Sergeant Major, carry Tommy.' His brow furrowed as he thought back to the briefing for this raid. That was when he had decided time would show whether to respect Tommy Shibuyu or not. Well, the Nisei had taken a bullet in the stomach for the Allied cause; that warranted one hell of a lot of respect. He put out his hand and stroked Tommy's glossy straight black hair. It was a fatherly gesture and the young soldier met Trap's eyes with a feeble smile.

The leader cleared his throat. 'You've done well, son.' He set his jaw and jumped to his feet, glancing round the faces of his boys, their eyes glinting in the glow from the fires. 'Okay, pick up your weapons. Let's go.'

'What about me?'

Trap looked around at the speaker; he had already forgotten about the woman. He mouthed, 'Blast,' as he eyed her.

Olsen, sweat trickling down his round darkened face, stepped forward. 'Who the hell is this Jap woman, sir?'

This inspired Kathleen to turn on him. 'I am not Japanese.'

'Well you're wearing a bloody kimono and you sure look like one,' Olsen snapped back.

'Shut up, Olsen,' Coalclark ordered, thumping him on the shoulder, 'and make ready to leave.'

One thing Trap knew for sure. This dame had no idea that the guy she was crazy about had set off all those searchlights and sirens. And he guessed that very same guy wouldn't exactly want him to leave this gal here to be dealt with by the Japs.

Kathleen began to panic about being left behind. 'I must come with you. I cannot stay. I was a prisoner here. I was with *him* against my will.'

'Listen.' Trap's tone was cold and his eyes were hard. 'It's simple, lady. You either keep up with us or you fall behind. We don't slow down for you no matter what the hell happens. Got that?'

'Yes, I understand.'

Trap shouldered his Tommy gun as he turned from her. 'We have no time to bury Joker. He'll just have to lie where he fell. I sure hope he understands.' And taking a deep breath he shouted, 'Move out!'

Rain began to fall as the small band mobilised: Trap in the lead and Williams at his elbow, followed by Coalclark and after him Lambert and Caldo with Shibuyu between them. Bringing up the rear were Olsen and Kathleen. They had not gone twenty yards when Kathleen felt a hand on her arm. She looked round into the face of Dinty.

'I'm coming too.'

Trap, at the front of the column and ten yards ahead, had not seen the Filipina join the party.

Olsen protested, jabbing his finger wildly at Dinty. 'She can't come with us, for God's sake. We're a raiding party not a bloody tea party. Why are these sheilas tagging along?'

514

But no one answered and Kathleen and Dinty simply fell in and followed them.

Trap strode at Cigs's shoulder. The downpour was heavier now and they were all soaked. It made them feel miserable but it might also have the added bonus of stopping the enemy patrols from spreading out. Nobody enjoyed being wet and wretched.

And he was lumbered with two women; and having Kathleen Leigh with him only made him think of the Doll and that did him no good, no good at all.

As the water began to trickle inside his collar and down his back, his mind took him back to Madura, to Maarten's on the sea front, to the room overlooking the water, to the low lamplight, the bed and her upon it in his arms: the feel of her skin beneath his fingers and the taste of her mouth on his.

'Goddam,' he whispered to the rain as he marched on with Cigs.

Chapter Sixty-six

Simpson Harbour was ablaze and alight. Searchlights streaked across the water, three burning transports emitted a fiery glow reaching skywards, and the frenzied lament of sirens rang from all directions. Sweat and sea water mingled on the brows of John Drayton and Ron Howard as they rowed at heart-pounding pace in the sturdy chop from the mounting wind. To their relief they heard two more successive detonations in the hull of another freighter behind them, belching red and yellow flames and sparks and pieces of metal in a mighty spout to the heavens.

John Drayton looked back and could not contain his jubilation; the glow from the blasts showed his eyes radiating with glee. His voice was high and stimulated. 'You beauty, that's the fourth!'

Exerting every muscle, they paddled on as fast as they could.

'Sir, I reckon I can see the wreck of the Catalina ahead.'

'Yes, I can too, Ron. Once past that we're in good shape.'

A Catalina flying boat lay where it had crashed into shallow water early in the war and its conspicuous broad body and broken wings had become a landmark about a hundred yards from the shore, Thus the rendezvous point for the commandos had been chosen exactly opposite it on the muddy mangrove-studded beach.

'Can you see any of the others still out on the harbour, sir?'

John Drayton's head cranked from side to side; the spray skipped from the choppy black sea to smear his darkened face as he turned, but he could see no canoes. If all had gone to plan, he and Ron were meant to be the last back to the rendezvous; the others should all be ahead of them.

'No ... and that's a good thing.'

Rain began to fall as searchlights probed nearer and nearer to them and a motorboat whizzed by about two hundred yards behind but did not deviate off course.

They were straining to keep up the pace when more explosions ignited the night sky.

'Ripper! I think that's five transports now.'

They drew within about thirty yards of the Catalina when a long burst of gunfire broke out to their west. Tensing, they looked sharply round but could see nothing. Suddenly a beam of light hit them and ran across the canoe.

'Strewth!'

'Do you think they saw us?' Ron Howard's question was answered when the streak of light wavered sharply around on the water and flashed straight back to them, sweeping across the craft and holding its brilliance upon them.

'Paddle like hell!' his companion yelled. 'Make for the dark side of the Catalina.'

The paddles gyrated in and out of the water and the veins in John Drayton's neck protruded with the ache of his massive effort as his young captain behind him grunted and groaned. Once they reached the wreck of the flying boat they would be hidden from sight.

Finding new strength, they pushed the canoe to more speed, but the searchlight lingered upon them and each moment they expected to be blasted out of the water by a burst of fire from an undamaged cruiser.

Abruptly, across the black water, they heard a motorboat revving.

'Where's that coming from?'

'I don't know.'

'I bet it'll be heading for us.'

'I'm afraid so.'

They continued heaving the paddles, their tired arms aching from the unrelenting exertion. Yet while the light remained on them, miraculously no firepower hit them, and ultimately they sped into the blessed concealment of the shadow of the crashed Catalina.

'We'll soon be ashore; stay in the cover of the aircraft.'

'I can hear that boat coming this way.'

They were panting, each breath racking their bodies, but adrenalin drove them to maintain their speed and a minute later arriving in shallow water the scraping of the bottom of the canoe sounded as they jumped out and heard the voice of 'Blinkers' Hervey in the mangroves. 'Who's there?'

'The major and I,' called Ron between loud quivering gasps.

Hervey's voice sounded relieved. 'Good. This way.'

The newcomers waded ashore and were greeted by the milling dark shapes of the waiting commandos. John Drayton looked at 'Blinkers' Hervey. 'Are we all here?'

'All except O'Rourke and Lister.'

'But they should have been back first.'

'Yes, sir, we know. Did you hear the rapid gunfire a little while ago?'

John Drayton had a sinking feeling about the gunfire he had heard back on the harbour. 'Yes.'

'We fear they might have bought it.'

The leader of the raid bent forward to rest his hands on his knees to regain his breath. Whatever had happened, it seemed O'Rourke and Lister were not coming back. There was no time for sorrow now.

Ron Howard was still fighting for breath as he pointed out to the Catalina 'We were . . . spotted back there.'

Hervey's tone was resigned. 'Yes, we thought so.'

Breaking the night, a shout echoed from Gavin Bird fifty yards away, watching the water. 'There's a patrol boat heading this way!'

The earlier arrivals had pulled their craft across the mud and hidden them in the foliage, but there was no more time for repeating that now as a searchlight beam hit the beach and ran its sinister feeler towards them along the shore. The men on the land dropped into the mangroves and those in the sea froze.

The ray of light came within a few yards of the figures in the water before it hesitated and reversed, and as 'Blinkers' Hervey handed John Drayton a Bren gun, he made a quick decision. 'Forget the skiffs, they know we're hereabouts anyway. Everybody get going!' He waved his arms in the darkness. 'That motorboat is getting too close.' And he left the inky water lapping his legs and waded through a break in the mangroves and reeds to run up the incline from the beach. Surrounded by his commandos, they hastened their departure as the shape of a patrol boat reached the Catalina and its searchlight combed the shoreline behind the soldiers.

At the top of the incline hidden in the trees they halted while the men from the canoes replaced their boots, which had been in the keeping of their comrades on the shore. As John Drayton led his men out, he realised that the thin man loping beside him in the darkness was Raga. *Good old Raga!*

A volley from a machine gun resounded behind them which John Drayton assumed came from the enemy patrol boat having noticed their two abandoned canoes and fired upon them. He clutched his Bren gun more tightly. The Nips would soon be ashore and following, and troops from Rabaul and Malaguna would spread out in a net. But if he and his men could keep this far ahead, along with Raga and his prodigious local knowledge, they had a chance.

'Sir?'

Trap looked back. It was Sergeant Major Lambert's voice calling him.

'Yes?'

'I think Shibuyu's dying.'

Oh Jesus.

He halted the column. They were on the track crossing the Gazelle peninsula between craters and leading round the rotting foliage of a swamp. It was a place where an enemy patrol could appear, at any time. Caldo and Lambert had dropped to the rear of the group under Shibuyu's weight, and now the leader moved back past his men and the two women to find Lambert and Caldo.

They eased Shibuyu to the ground under a banyan tree. Trap knelt beside him and felt his wrist, sensing a faint pulse. 'Tommy?'

Shibuyu made no reply.

'Tommy, listen, kid, can you hear me? You've got to hang on.' No reply.

Trap bent in close to Tommy's ear. 'Listen, kid, you did great tonight. You've proved everything you wanted to prove. You've helped the Nisei cause and set the name of Shibuyu high. Don't die on me now, kid . . .'

Someone switched on a torch and illuminated the young man. 'Shut that thing off!' It was Coalclark's voice.

The light flicked off.

Trap touched Tommy's hair and stroked it. It felt smooth and alive how could the kid be dying? 'Listen, son, we're over halfway back to the camp. Just hang on.' He bent in again. 'You're a brave man, Tommy. You can hear me, can't you?'

He believed he heard a moan from the young man and he glanced up to Caldo. 'Get some water. Can't we do anything more for the kid, for Christ's sake?'

Nobody spoke, and Caldo handed his Colonel a water bag, but Trap knew it was useless. He felt Tommy's throat: no pulse. He lifted his wrist again. *Nothing.*

'Damn.' His head dropped forward in the sticky air of the dark night. He thought of Tommy Mackim Denham, dead near the Luzon gorge. Boys called Tommy did not have a lot of luck around him. A few seconds later Cigs spoke softly at his side. 'He dead, Colonel Trapperton. We must go on.'

'Yeah, I know.' He hesitated another moment as his fingers

returned to the Nisei's head and he felt Tommy's hair against the palm of his hand again.

Abruptly Olsen spoke. 'What was that? I heard something . . . back along the trail.'

Everybody stiffened and listened.

Trap could hear nothing, but he paused no longer. He rose from his knees and with Caldo's help pulled Tommy's body off the jungle track.

'Right,' he called quietly, his face masking his feelings. 'From now on we keep a fast pace. Move out.'

Chapter Sixty-seven

In the inky night Ron Howard caught up to John Drayton and
fell in at his side.

'Sir?'

'Yes, Ron?'

'I just wanted to say that I feel pretty bad about what I said
to you earlier today.'

'And what was that?'

'About Lister and O'Rourke being the only ones who could
make it back to shore for certain . . . and now they are the only
two who didn't. I feel pretty terrible. Like I jinxed them or something.'

John Drayton understood but he knew he had to disabuse his
young officer of such thoughts. 'Listen, Ron, you know the outcome
of a raid like this is always uncertain. Whatever happened to them
could have happened to any of us. You didn't jinx them; you made
a perfectly sane observation. All I hope is that when we get back
to camp they're already there.'

The young man smiled and nodded in the dark. 'Oh sure, me
too, that'd be bonzer.'

'And if they aren't, son, it had nothing to do with you. We're
all taking the same chances. Got that?'

'Yes, sir . . . but what if—'

'Hit the dirt!' someone shouted, and the two men dropped to
the ground, followed by Raga and the rest of the commandos.

They were on a sort of road; there was no other path at this point in the return journey. Furiously crawling into the undergrowth, they watched the lights of a lorry appear out of the black night about two hundred yards away and trundle towards them along the dirt track.

John Drayton's face pressed into a pile of damp leaves as he held his Bren gun at the ready, peering through the grass. He was reminded of Java and the flight through the jungle when they had been betrayed by Dian, the Javanese, and ambushed. Ron Howard had been at his side then, as he was now. Tense and unmoving, they eyed the vehicle as it rumbled by. Just as they were about to rise, it halted and a bunch of Japanese soldiers alighted from the rear and milled about, their silhouettes delineated against the headlights.

'Christ,' murmured Smith on the far side of John Drayton, who turned his head and whispered, 'Steady . . . let's see where they go.'

A succession of orders were shouted and the Japanese formed a column and, to the relief of the observers, moved off in a southerly direction. The lorry drove on.

John Drayton stood and the others followed. 'That's what'll be happening all over.' He gestured in the direction the enemy had taken. 'And as we just witnessed, where there are no roads they'll send in patrols on foot. So come on, let's skedaddle. Under cover of night we've got a chance.'

Raga grunted in agreement. 'We go off road up here, close by,' he pointed his finger in the gloom, 'and head across country. I know way.'

'Thank Christ for you, Raga,' was the sentiment most favoured.

Hitoshi Imamura was awake and screaming, the muscles of his plump face taut with rage. His small, rotund figure in hastily drawn-on trousers and shirt advanced across the room to the far wall and swung round to his aide. 'I want them caught and brought here. Find them no matter what! And keep telephoning General Ikeda's compound. I must know what all that gunfire was.'

His aide was pale with concern. 'We are not raising them, sir. It appears that buildings are on fire up there as well.'

'*Shimatta!* What in heaven's name is going on? Get troops up there right away and report back to me.'

As his aide turned to leave the room, Imamura called out, 'Do we have a count on how many transport ships are damaged?'

'We think all of them, sir.'

Imamura's nostrils flared as he sucked in his breath. He could see the great hopes for the relief army to northern Papua fading into nothing. He closed his eyes and held his forehead. 'I will tear them into small pieces. I will skin them. Bring them here alive.' And as the aide hurried out, the general turned and smashed into the wall with his fist.

A lambency stole into the eastern sky as Trap paced back and forth in the small clearing where the briefing had taken place. They had arrived in camp an hour and a half previously, just as the rain ceased, and now he awaited Johnny and the men of Operation Hornbill. Johnny was overdue and his gaze kept flicking across the camp in expectation.

Trap's party had covered less distance, so being first back was expected, but now, with the imminence of daylight, anxiety showed on every face as the soldiers went about making ready for final departure. They had dug trenches prior to going out on the raids and now they were burying all they could not carry. If the enemy did find this place there would be nothing left of use to them.

Trap was aware, as they all were, that the whole of Japanese-held New Britain would be awake. This hideout was remarkable in its virtual concealment, for it lodged in a small valley hidden by rock formations in the jungle, but it was not impossible to happen upon. Also, Trap knew it was conceivable that the enemy could take one or two of Chief Innut's tribesmen prisoner and torture them, and then, even with their loyalty to the Australians and the Allies, the enemy would be led here. So they could not afford to wait longer than dawn.

Cigs had told him that the southerly route they were about to take through the middle of the island crossed swamps and jungle so dense that they would be safe, but Trap could not be sure of that. There were a lot of seasoned Japanese fighters here who would not be afraid of crossing swamps and hacking their way in and out of concentrated tangles of vegetation.

He looked round as he heard a noise behind him.

'Ah, Caldo. Any news?'

'No. I brought you some tea, sir. There's no coffee and Davidson says the tea's running out too.'

'Just when I was getting used to this Billy Tea business.' He drank some of the hot, sweet liquid; it felt good in his throat.

Caldo inclined his head to the sky. 'The major must come soon. I mean, we heard those transport ships blow. All of them went sky high.'

Trap nodded. 'That's true, we did.'

'Of course they might have run into trouble. They had to get by two airfields taking principal routes.' He paused, thinking of the danger there. 'Will you go without them, sir?'

Trap eyed the sky. 'I don't think we have a choice.' He drank the tea and handed the tin mug back to Caldo.

'Listen, in regard to the Eurasian woman, I want you to inform the captain, the lieutenant, the sergeant major and the others that I met her in Hong Kong when I was there last December. That her name is Kathleen Leigh and she's a nurse.' He cleared his throat. 'And she was a friend of Dr Robinson: you'd better apprise the Lieutenant and Ivat of that.'

'Yeah, I sort of put that together. I reckon the Doc spoke about her a couple of times. Said she was taken away forcibly by the Nip colonel who butchered the shipwreck survivors.'

Trap raised an eyebrow. 'Ah, I see. Well that answers why she travelled in Jap company. She mentioned that she'd been kept against her will.' Trap was still eyeing the eastern sky. 'Now listen, Caldo, there's one other thing I want you to know . . . just you, that is.'

'Yes, sir.'

'I'm aware you used to talk a lot to Dr Robinson . . .'

Caldo studied Trap and he could see the battle taking place in his colonel's mind. He dearly wished he could help him. 'Yeah, we talked now and then. She was a good person, the Doc.'

'Indeed . . .'

'Look, sir, if it's all the same to you. I don't need to know anything.'

Trap met the big man's eyes. 'This you *should* know. The Doc, as you call her, is married to Major Whitby.'

Caldo swayed from one foot to the other.

'What is it?'

'Well, sir, I know. The major told me.'

'He did?'

'Yeah. He came to me and asked what I could tell him about what happened to the Doc. Said you'd told him we used to shoot the breeze together.'

Trap was silent a few seconds before he grunted. 'I see. All right, Sergeant. I don't have many friends, but I do count Major Whitby one. We'll leave it there and you'd better bring Miss Leigh to me. I think she should be notified of Major Whitby's current whereabouts as she's acquainted with him. And ask the lieutenant to have the men make ready for immediate departure.'

Caldo saluted and turned smartly on his heel just as they heard Olsen shout, 'Colonel!'

The young commando came running across towards them from the campsite entrance, his boots making imprints in the soggy ground, his arms waving. 'They're coming in now, sir, the major, Raga and the others. They're here!'

Kathleen and Dinty sipped tea. It had been provided by a small, wiry soldier who had introduced himself as Private Ivat First Class.

On their arrival in camp they had been taken to a small tent where they had changed their soaked clothes and shoes for dry male equivalents and rested under blankets on camp stretchers, until after an hour a sergeant major had come and bathed and bandaged Dinty's feet. She had found the cross-country hike back to the camp very hard. During the last half-mile she had lagged behind in the torrential rain, and while Trap had threatened to leave her, he had not, and in the end she had made it. But not without tears; and complaints from Olsen, who had elected himself the vocal representative of the commandos.

Ivat had brought the tea and the tent had been dismantled, so now they sat on two bully-beef crates before a fire. Kathleen put down the tin mug and smiled sympathetically at the Filipina. 'Dinty, will you be able to continue? You know we must be leaving very soon.'

'Yes. My feet feel so much better now. He was nice and kind, the soldier who bandaged them. I like him, but the other one, the young one, he does not like me.'

'Now, Dinty, don't think about him. Concentrate on being determined to make the next journey. Be strong.'

Dinty looked down at the soldiers' boots she now wore and nodded earnestly. 'Yes, I will be like you, missy. You are always brave and strong. I will draw power from you.'

Kathleen leant across and briefly held Dinty's forearm. 'We will both be strong.' She raised her head to the awakening day and thought how amazed she would have been a year ago to hear anyone praise her for her strength. She had not even known she had any. How much she had altered since then: Kathleen Leigh of Hong Kong, the woman with the ordered existence, who spent her days in the hospital and evenings with her friends at clubs and restaurants; who dined and smoked and danced and drank a little; the Kathleen who had lived with her mother in complete acceptance of all the myths she had been force-fed since babyhood! She hardly recognised that woman; the one she had been.

Here she sat on a wooden box in a New Britain jungle after almost a year as captive of a dehumanised brute who had revealed to her a world which she could not have believed existed: a world where she had woken every day in fear; and yet, in surviving that world, she had altered for ever. The Kathleen Leigh of a year ago could not have killed Ikeda: that Kathleen would have been powerless. But this Kathleen *had* killed him, pulled the trigger on him and watched him die. She could always salve her conscience with the knowledge that he was flailing the air with his sword and could have struck her a mortal blow any second; but she did not need that excuse now. She had removed him from the earth. For all the evil she had seen him do, for all his victims, she had been the conduit. It was simply a fact.

That he had given her life remained grotesque: but that he had given her life had, in fact, allowed her to end his. *Deserve victory* ... The times she had heard Sir Brillard say that: and she had not taken any notice. She had simply heard it as an old soldier's motto: but now she understood it; absolutely, in the innermost corners of her soul she understood it. Ikeda had not deserved victory nor had he deserved life.

And so it was that dear Dinty held her in an esteem which she still found hard to believe.

She bent forward and her eyes wandered to the ground, where the sidling dawn light revealed hundreds of tiny frogs which had materialised after the rain. They were minute, perhaps half an inch long, and as the coming day showed them to her she realised each was tinged with gold: their bodies were brown but they were streaked down each side and on the tips of their heads, as if a paintbrush had stroked them with gold leaf. They were beautiful. She bent further forward to watch them, each with three tiny pads for fingers, translucent and exquisite. She thought of the thousands of infinitesimal creatures which must live in the jungle, all the unseen minutiae: ugly and beautiful side by side. She was wondering how long these tiny, delicate creatures lived as a voice broke into her thoughts. 'Ladies, prepare to move out.'

It was Private Ivat again, smiling encouragingly. 'I'll be back for you in two minutes.' He handed them four bananas. 'Now eat these. They'll give you strength for the next part of the journey.' He bent and picked up the empty tin mugs and disappeared.

Abruptly they heard a shout, 'Colonel!' Turning, they saw Olsen running by and calling, 'They're coming in now, sir, the major, Raga and the others. They're here!'

'Ripper!'

'Hurrah!'

In the rumble of excitement, the soldiers in camp moved in a body through the trees, but Kathleen's eyes were on a tall figure coming the other way . . . running through the grass and bamboo towards them. It was the colonel, and he came right to her.

'Look, I haven't had time to tell you, but I think you should be aware that it's Johnny who's arriving right now.'

Kathleen did not understand. She rose to her feet. 'What do you mean?'

As she asked the question, a mass of soldiers came swarming down the slope into the encampment as the waiting commandos surged forward in a wave to meet them.

'I mean Johnny, John Drayton; he's the leader of the harbour raid. They've just returned.' He left her standing there and strode away.

Kathleen felt dizzy. Her head began to swim, watching the colonel hurrying in the direction of the returning warriors. She observed them shaking hands and greeting each other, and there, in their midst, she recognized one who pushed through the body of men towards the commanding officer. Their hands met in a grasp and she saw his face: John Drayton's face, covered in dirt and grime.

She felt light-headed. A year ago she would have fainted, but now she walked forward, taking deep breaths to calm herself.

* * *

The two commando leaders clasped hands.

'We were hit once by a bloody Jap patrol on the way back. Raga and the night saved us, but it was only about two miles back. I lost Sudbury. Are O'Rourke and Lister here?'

'No, Johnny.'

John Drayton's hopes for them now faded completely. 'Then they must have bought it.'

'Ah, bugger. And I lost Shibuyu and Mayberry.'

'Oh no.'

They eyed one another in the slowly forming light. Both men knew the raids had been successful and that whether they were caught or not now, they had done what they had been sent here to do. But their expressions were bleak.

'Can't help but take it personally, can we?' John Drayton said with a grimace. 'Losing men you liked.' His voice became husky. 'It gets harder all the time.'

'That's right. Making friends in wartime is a rotten idea.'

'Ah, but we still do, don't we? It's what makes the world go round.'

Trap raised his eyes to heaven. 'Yeah, but every time we go into the slaughteryard it gets harder, Johnny.' Then he straightened his shoulders and made himself smile before he slapped his friend affectionately on the arm and pointed behind him.

John Drayton turned, and when he saw her, his face lit up. He moved out of Trap's grasp and hurried to her and took her in his arms. 'Oh God, Kathy, how can it be you?'

Her eyes sparkled and her face shone with life. 'It's me. It's really me.'

He pulled her close to his heart. She felt the strength of his body against hers. She was overcome with love for him and for these few seconds knew nothing else; until John Drayton said the words which brought her back to reality.

'Kathy, I thought you were dead and I thought Lex was dead . . . and you're not, you're both alive.'

Kathleen struggled to take this in: Lexi alive? How could she be? She had seen her die: all of them fall in the rolling waves . . .

Trap stood looking at the two of them. *Well, I always knew she was in love with him; but he sure seems mighty pleased to see her.*

He pictured the Doll, he could not help it, but he shook his head to rid himself of it and a moment later his voice ricocheted across the campsite. 'All right, finish up, and move out fast!'

Chapter Sixty-eight

The first weak shimmer of day slid over the sturdy banyan and kapok trees of the tropical forest guarding the Ancient Chiefs' Burial Ground and seeking further stole across the pillboxes along the seashore to brush Camel Rock and the gun emplacements and on to the sandbagged and fortified rows of stark grey military vehicles guarding the deep, natural and extensive harbour dotted with naval vessels riding at anchor.

The dawn revealed Lexi cranking the engine of her Chrysler utility truck which Lieutenant Lawrence Wild – the commandant of the naval station – had personally organised for her. It was a good smooth-running motor and started blissfully on the sixth revolution of the crank handle. She jumped in and headed out to the hospital.

Her route weaved along the seafront and into the tropical forest of the Mapusaga Valley.

She parked close to the X-ray unit – the pride of the hospital – and, alighting, strode past dozens of men and women in various hospital and service uniforms. The current flood of naval and marine corps personnel had increased the local population of this island from 10,000 in 1940 to over 18,000 now.

All of a sudden a dream from last night sprang into her mind. She had been in the garden at Hydrangea standing on the lavender carpet of flowers fallen from the jacaranda tree above; her grandmother and her family milling around her. In her hands she held

Kwan Yin and she ran her fingers over the sleek porcelain surface and looked down at it when it turned into Jimmy and then just as swiftly metamorphosed into Paul. She shivered now with the memory and shook her head to clear the images as a swell of loneliness encompassed her.

Rounding a stand of pepper trees she almost collided with Dick Fry. It was unclear whether he had been waiting there or whether he had just arrived. 'Good morning, Lieutenant Robinson.'

'Good morning, Lieutenant Fry.'

Doctor Dick Fry could not look at a woman without revealing his feelings. He was presently staring at Lexi appreciatively.

'Going to breakfast, are we?'

'I am,' she replied, passing by him. He fell into step beside her and squired her the rest of the way to the canteen where, uninvited, he sat down with her and made small talk:

'You know we've only been attacked here in Tutuila once, last January during the night. A Jap sub surfaced off the north coast and you know what?'

'What?'

'The very first shell landed on the only Jap store in town, old Frank Shimasaki's place. How's that for justice?'

'Amazing. Was anyone hurt?'

'Typical doctor's question.' He grinned. 'One casualty only and he was riding a bicycle. Actually a piece of shrapnel hit him in the knee: Commander Robinson, same name as you.'

Lexi gave a weak smile as he leant across the table towards her. 'So how about coming to the dance with me tonight?'

It was the third week in succession he had asked her to the medical officers' Friday-night rumba, as it was known.

The sun glinted on her fork as she toyed with her food. 'I was wondering when you'd get to that, I can't.'

Fry groaned in disappointment. Everybody was aware that Lexine Robinson had arrived here on a submarine with a little Filipina in tow. That had caused a bit of a stir! The talk around the island was that she had been involved in something top secret; that she had been a spy or something like it. Fry found her attractive, as did most of the men he knew. If anything, she was a touch on the lean side for him, but her breasts were big enough, not pimples like some thin women sported, and she had good legs; well, that was, what he could see of them under her doctor's uniform. He had never seen her in shorts or a bathing suit like a lot of the nurses wore on their days off.

Nobody knew her origin, though her accent was English; not uppity English, just easy on the ear. She had fine, clear skin that sort of shone with health. Her hair was thick and shiny and she had a kissable mouth. He was acquainted with a couple of other officers who had attempted to date her ... but no dice.

He put down his coffee. 'Listen, all work and no play makes Jack a dull boy; well it also makes Jill a dull girl. Come on, reconsider, say yes and make us both happy.'

A swell of misery shot through Lexi and quite abruptly she heard herself say, 'All right.'

He was on his feet, the whites of his eyes gleaming. 'You bet. I'll pick you up at seven.'

Once he had gone, she was sorry she had agreed, but she put it from her mind and left the canteen, passing the dispensary and taking a route under a stand of silk trees and into Ward Three to enter one of the only two 'private' rooms they had where the bare floorboards were wet from a recent early morning mopping.

Edward 'Eddie' Rickenbacker[I] was asleep. He had been the leading United States Air Force 'Ace' in the Great War and looked younger than his fifty-two years. Even his receding hairline did not diminish his appealing looks. Parts of his forehead still peeled from the exposure to the sun in an open life-raft.

He had been transferred here suffering from starvation and exposure after 21 days in the open ocean when his B17 had gone down.

She was about to turn away when he opened his eyes. 'Hello, Doc.'

She smiled. 'How do you feel?'

'After the mountains of fruit and gallons of fruit juice you feed me, I'm beginning to feel great.' He had been forty pounds lighter when he had been brought to the hospital.

Raising himself in the bed he smiled. His face had filled out. 'You're English aren't you, Doc?'

'Of English parents, I was born in Hong Kong.'

'Lucky you got out.'

Lexi was not going into all that. She nodded. 'Yes.'

'The war's going to be a long one, Doc. You know what? I was an isolationist. I was opposed to America entering this war, but I've changed my mind. Hitler and Tojo need to be stopped.'

Lexi met his eyes and replied slowly and adamantly. 'I always thought so.'

He took this well. 'Good for you, Doc.' He clasped his sizeable chin as he added, 'That fall into the drink is something I'll never forget, and thanks for what you've done to get me back on my feet.'

Lexi was warming to him. 'It's your own strength and will which did that.'

He grinned and his eyes shone with vitality; so different from the first day she had seen him.

'Four years ago I bought an airline – Eastern – if ever you're in the States you can fly free as often as you like.'

Now it was Lexi's turn to grin. 'I just might take you up on that.'

She left Rickenbacker feeling that special gratification which comes from helping to heal those who are ill and hurried across to the operating unit. It was exactly seven a.m. By one p.m. each day the operating room was abandoned, for even though it was fitted with overhead electric fans, all doors and windows had to be kept tightly shut to keep out flies and other insects, and consequently the heat built to excess.

Inside waited her assistant, Lieutenant John Donatelli, a doctor from Maine, and Nurse Hattie Enright. Hattie handed her the first case history. Lexi had read it the day before, but she glanced at the main items again.

Lister, Charles, Sergeant. 67th Fighter Squadron, United States Air Force. Wounded Guadalcanal.

Multiple wounds in chest. Shrapnel embedded lumbar region and opaque foreign bodies buried soft tissue left knee.

Two paragraphs of medical notes on the extent of the wounds followed.

John's tone was resigned. 'He's in bad shape. I think we should be reconciled to the fact that he probably won't make it.'

Lexi had been feeling buoyant after seeing Rickenbacker but this sobered her, she had lost men on the operating table before and while she did not like it, that was war.

'Right, let's scrub up and go in and meet the poor devil.'

Chapter Sixty-nine

Lexi approached the patient on the table. She had dealt with so many now: mostly American but occasionally a New Zealander — usually a flyer, or an Australian — usually a seaman, who had found themselves airlifted here from the Solomons and other war zones on the myriad islands in the South Pacific.

As she approached the operating table the patient turned his head and she gave a tiny gasp of surprise. Lister . . . of course! It had not occurred to her: Charles Lister was Chuck Lister, her sergeant who had done his best to help her in Luzon last December. Chuck Lister had been kind; he had carried Jimmy and insisted the other soldiers carry Lessa. He had attempted to persuade the lieutenant to airlift them out, but no, she and Lessa and Jimmy had stood alone on the airfield in the encroaching dusk as the transport aircraft rose into the sky filled with the grey clouds of twilight.

Lexi had never operated on anybody she had known before, and suddenly her hand shook. Taking a slow, deep breath she calmed herself and touched his arm. 'Hello, Sergeant.'

He was drugged and sleepy but he recognised her instantly. 'You? The girl from Hong Kong.'

Hattie Enright and John Donatelli glanced at each other.

'Yes, that's right. Now we're going to give you some chloroform. When the pad is placed over your face just breathe normally and you'll drift off to sleep. Don't worry.'

'Nah, I won't worry . . .' His bloodshot eyes met hers. 'Jeez, I can't believe it. You? A doctor?'

She signalled to Hattie and the nurse picked up the pad and covered his face. Lexi took some more deep breaths as the trichloromethane was poured on to the pad.

'You know this guy?'

'Yes, I do. I met him in the Philippines.'

'You okay to do this?' John's voice was sympathetic.

'Sure.' She had picked that up from Caldo and the boys. 'I'll be all right.'

Five hours later, she and John had done what they could for him and Chuck Lister was wheeled out.

They took a quick respite, drank water, changed aprons and washed again. There was one more short case: the setting of a broken arm.

As they re-entered the operating room, John turned to Lexi. 'The way you removed that piece of shrapnel near Lister's spine was masterful, Doctor. He was pretty battered but you gave it one hell of a try. Whether he makes it or not, I want you to know I was proud to assist you.'

Her gaze lifted to his. 'Thank you, that's kind of you, John, and by the way . . . *we* gave it one hell of a try.'

Lexi spent the afternoon on patient rounds and around four she took the damp, uneven path to the building where the danger-ously ill patients lay. She found Chuck Lister in an end bed surrounded by a curtain. She remained for a few minutes watching him as he slept. His face bore a yellow tinge and the skin around his eyes was a sinister grey-blue. She touched his right hand, which lay above the cover, and it twitched beneath hers even though he appeared to be in a deep sleep. The bandages around his chest were blood-stained. Lifting his wrist, she took his pulse and her mouth tightened in disappointment.

She walked swiftly to the tiny sectioned off area that was at the end of the ward. A nurse looked up from a pile of instruments and bandages on the bench in front of her.

'Who's in charge of the sergeant in the end bed?'

'Which one is that, Doctor?'

'Lister, Sergeant Charles Lister.'

The girl looked blankly back.

'He was operated on this morning.'

Realisation dawned on the nurse. 'Oh right, well there's no one specially attached to him, we—'

Lexi cut in: 'I want someone to watch him at all times. If he needs morphine I want it given. I want his pulse taken on the half-hour and I expect it reported to me if it alters. I need sulpha administered four-hourly and his bandages changed twice a day. He's dangerously ill, for God's sake!'

The nurse looked affronted. 'They're *all* dangerously ill in this ward, Doctor. We do our best for *all* of them.'

Lexi hesitated and blinked. Her shoulders dropped and she took a deep breath. 'Of course. I know you do. Look ... I'm sorry.'

The nurse was from a farming community in Kansas. She had volunteered for duty in the South Seas and had dealt with a lot of doctors in her time. Some were more demanding than others, and while she did not actually know this doctor personally, she received the feeling that she was a decent type: a lot of doctors never apologised for anything.

She smiled. 'I'll make sure that what you've asked for gets done. How can I be in touch with you if need be?'

'I'll be here in my office until six o'clock. I'm in Building Twelve. My name's Robinson. I'll come and see the sergeant before I leave. I live in the nurses' quarters in Fagatoga; if an emergency arises you can telephone me there.'

'Oh, I'm hoping to move in there soon; well, as soon as they have room for me.' The nurse smiled again, a genuine smile, open and sincere.

Lexi felt a swell of good feeling towards her. 'Right. Well, thanks, Nurse . . . ?'

'Jurgens, Juliet Jurgens.' She put down the bandage she held. 'And I'll go and read the sergeant's chart straight away.' She moved down the ward and Lexi watched her with a grateful glance to the nurse's back, where her long black hair was caught in a clean white bow.

As Lexi departed into the oppressive heat of late afternoon it was raining, and she paused under an awning, watching a group of marines rolling 44-gallon oil drums up a path by the baseball field. Beyond them in the middle distance, two orderlies carried a stretcher patient across from one building to another, hurrying and almost slipping in the rain. She felt annoyed: that was dangerous for the patient.

They had been hit by a mild hurricane four days before and leaks had appeared all over the hospital. A stream of water was finding its way down beside her now and she edged along the veranda to a drier spot.

A man was running towards her; she recognised Captain Mark Lane, one of the hospital administrators. He darted up to shelter on the veranda beside her. His reputation was that of a level-headed and fair manager. His uniform was wet and his face florid and he stuck his thumbs inside his belt, which fitted too snugly around his wide girth.

'Afternoon.'

'Hello, Captain Lane.'

'A message arrived regarding you this morning at Government House.' He took out of his breast pocket what was obviously a wireless communication. 'It's not top secret but it had priority. It's from General MacArthur's new GHQ in New Guinea. So you're well known to the famous Commander-in-Chief of the South-West Pacific Area, eh?' He gave a smile which invited her to confide in him.

Lexi eyed him steadily. 'It was my grandfather who was well

540

known to General MacArthur. Any interest he takes in me is because of him.'

Lane cleared his throat. 'Well, whatever you say, this communication regards you. General MacArthur appears to have believed you were dead until just recently.'

Lexi nodded. 'Yes, probably.'

He handed the message to her. 'Well, now that he knows you're alive, the suggestion is for you to leave here if you wish to and get back to Australia by Christmas. I don't know the detail of how it's proposed to happen, but you're to see the local commander in a couple of weeks. He'll get you a ride on something.' He gave her another smile. 'That is, assuming you want to go.'

Lexi did not reply. Her eyes dropped to the paper. The proposal was exactly as Lane had said. She folded the communiqué, considering the import of it. She suspected somehow that Trap had let South-West Pacific GHQ know about her; it had to be his doing . . . whose else would it be? She slipped into introspection, rapt in thought, faraway and absorbed.

Lane coughed. 'Acting Lieutenant Robinson?' The look on her face faded, she returned to the present as he said, 'Do you want to leave?'

'The message doesn't mention anything about Lessa, and I won't go anywhere without her.'

Lane nodded. 'There'll be a certain amount of paperwork in that, but I guess it can be organised.'

Lexi pictured her mother and her stepfather, Aunt Carly, and her half-sister Jane. There they all were across the Coral Sea in Ipswich, Queensland. She had only been there once, when she had met John Drayton; how long ago that seemed.

'The fact is, Captain Lane, I'd like to think about it.'

'Certainly, Christmas is a while away yet.' He nodded and walked on along the veranda.

She remained watching the rain, thinking of all the questions her mother would ask. How she would want details that Lexi would not want to give. All her relatives would be so sympathetic without having the slightest notion of what had truly happened to her. That was it. How could you explain horror to people who were cocooned from it?

Yet staying here was not the answer either. It might be better to be in Australia even if she did not go to her mother. There were hospitals everywhere desperate for doctors.

She lingered listening to the mesmeric sound of the rain on the corrugated-iron roof and staring into the wet day until finally the rain abated. She was sorry because she had hoped it might continue into tonight, then she could have avoided going out with Dick Fry.

Lexi twisted out of Dick Fry's arms as he tried to pull her back towards him.

'Come on, Lexi. What's the matter? Haven't you been kissed before?'

She put her hand up to hold him off. 'I said I'd come to the dance with you. I didn't agree to this.'

He gave a small laugh but dropped his hands. 'Come on. You're a good-looking woman: what'd you expect?'

Lexi leant back in the seat of the GP vehicle, the noise of the waves loud on the night air. 'What I expected was to be taken to the dance and driven home. I wasn't prepared for you to pull to the side of the road and kiss me.'

'You should be flattered.'

She looked round at him and his eyes shone in the night light. 'Take me home, please.'

He moved closer and slid his right arm around her shoulders again as his left hand came up under her breast. 'Be friendly, Lexi; just one more and I'll take you home.'

She pushed his hand down as she moved further away. 'Don't, Dick. I mean it.'

'What if I leave you here?'

She sighed. 'If you leave me here, you're nothing but a total creep and not worth a cent.'

This had a definite effect on Dick Fry. He emitted a long whistling sound and removed his hands from her, returning them to the steering wheel. A second later he got out and cranked the engine into life.

They drove to Penicillin Row in silence, and as he pulled up outside, the sounds of laughter drifted to them from Bingo's Bar two hundred yards away, and a utility in front disgorged three nurses into the night. There was a blackout in operation and no moon shone, but the night was clear and the stars gave a fragile glow to the world.

Dick came round the GP vehicle as his date eased herself to the ground. 'Look, Lexine, I'm not a creep. I appreciate women, yes, but I'm not a creep. I hope what I did won't stop you from coming out with me again. I'm sorry, honestly.'

The faint smell of fish was drifting on the breeze. 'Listen, Dick, forget it. We have to work together and we need to get along. The fact is, I was lonely; I *am* lonely. But don't ask me out again. That way we can stay friends.' She looked up at him, at the pale gleam of his eyes, before hurrying away along the path.

Lexi lay looking into the dark of night. She could hear the clock ticking and Lessa's breathing. A tear slid from her eye and she sniffed and wiped her nose with her forefinger. She pictured her grandfather and his infinite strength of character; at least it had seemed that way to her: she had always admired him. Had he ever wavered and felt alone as she did now? He had been a colossus in the shaping of her world view. He had taught her honesty and fair play; to give the benefit of the doubt and to treat all men the same way: as you desired to be treated. It was to him she owed most of her values. In her formative years, after her own father had drowned, she had transferred her affections to Sir Brillard: always sage, knowledgeable, reasonable and, to her, so kind. When

543

others had found him forceful, bossy and sometimes frightening, she had never been aware of it. He had always been the one she turned to for advice and help.

Now she had no one. In the depths of her heart she knew he was no more; the man who was Sir Brillard would not have gone quietly, submissively, into Japanese hands; he would have chosen death over servitude. She would probably never learn how he died, but she knew in her heart he had departed this mortal life defiantly. She could picture his vibrant old eyes, rebellious, yet replete with all the ideals he had taught her.

She wondered if a man like that could possibly ever have experienced indecision and fear like she did now. She felt inadequate and alone.

Help me, Grandpa; wherever you are, help me.

Immediately she offered up the prayer, she was angry with herself for being self-indulgent when so many had suffered and died.

She rolled over on her side, and as sleep stole over her Sir Brillard was there in her head: he sat on the wide front porch of Hydrangea in the first sweet breeze of the changing season when the days were bestowed with the hint of coolness.

Lexi was walking towards him, and as she drew closer, she noticed he wore his regimental jacket, its crown and pips sparkling. He stood from his chair, and there in the background behind him appeared her grandmother, close at his shoulder, almost as if they were joined. And as Lexi came up to them she fancied her grandfather smiled and spoke. 'I'm gone, darling, I can help you no more, but do what you believe is right and you'll find yourself again.'

At seven-thirty the following morning, Lexine entered the ward for the dangerously ill. The nurse on duty was again Juliet Jurgens and she smiled when she saw Lexi. 'He's slightly better this morning and his pulse is almost normal.'

Lexi felt a surge of relief as she walked the length of the ward. Chuck Lister was asleep and his breath came in short, unnatural intakes, but the waxen look of yesterday had gone. She picked up his progress report which hung on a hook at the end of his bed and read it carefully. What the nurse had said was so, his vital signs were stabilising. She felt his forehead but he did not wake.

Ten minutes later she presented herself to Captain Lane.

'It's funny, Captain, I thought it was going to take a long time to make up my mind, but it hasn't. I've been deeply proud to be a part of this hospital and the fine work being done here, but I must consider Lessa too, and what her future will be after this war's over.' She sighed. 'That is, if it ever ends. So yes please, I'd like to make an appointment to see the commander and we will take that ride out before Christmas.'

That night Lexi found the strength to write one of the letters which she had been putting off since arriving in Pago Pago. It was to her mother: a long letter telling as much of her story as she believed Marlene could comprehend. She ended with:

So the little girl and I are living here with the nurses and I'm working at the hospital. I'm sorry to shock you, for no doubt you thought me long dead and I can't really imagine how you'll feel receiving a letter like this.

I don't know what else to tell you other than I'm leaving here sometime before Christmas and heading in your direction. I might actually end up somewhere in Australia and if that's the case I'll contact you from there in the New Year.

I must write to Johnny too, so once I have a permanent address you can send his to me.

Your loving daughter,

Lexine

The letter arrived in Ipswich on a day when Marlene Bartlett was home alone decorating the Christmas tree. She heard the postman's whistle and walked down the neat path to find three letters, which she took back to the front veranda where the chairs were bathed in the morning sun.

Lexi's handwriting was unmistakable, and her mother ripped open the envelope hastily. After she had read it she remained a long time as if hypnotised, gazing at the fiddlewood trees which lined the front of the property. She did not open the other two letters, but rose a mite unsteadily and made her way inside. She knew where to find the bottle of brandy that Jeffrey had been saving for Christmas, and she opened it and poured a large glass ignoring the single nip measure which lay beside the bottle.

Marlene drank the brandy swiftly and poured a second, even though it had just turned eleven in the morning.

Chapter Seventy

Milne Bay, Eastern New Guinea, 14 December 1942

The damp air clung to Trap as he stood feet apart, hands behind his back, on the edge of the tented camp in the oppressive heat of afternoon as the sun disappeared and day transformed into dusk.

He was watching a Kittyhawk come in over the palms to land after having played its role in the continuing desperate resistance against the Japanese, its grey body blending with the twilight as its bull-nose bounced along the dirt strip.

Out of the trees and foliage a cassowary appeared and stomped a few yards. Even in the looming twilight its brilliant blue head and crimson wattle adorning its neck created splashes of colour that were easily identified. Mosquitoes hummed their endless melody and clouds of flies swirled in constant irritating attention to anything which moved.

Trap habitually flicked his fingers at the insects as he noticed two figures emerge a few hundred yards ahead on the far side of a row of tents. He straightened his shoulders as his gaze narrowed upon them. The petite figure of Kathleen and the larger wide-shouldered Johnny were easily recognisable.

Kathleen was due to fly out on the morrow to take up a nursing post in a military hospital in Port Moresby. Johnny had organised it by contacting the hospital himself. In August, nurses of the

2/5th Australian General Hospital who had been serving in Port Moresby had been evacuated due to concern over the battles on the Kokoda Trail; apparently against the will of the women, who strongly resisted. In the intervening months the nurses had been sorely missed. But now that the Allies had contained the Japanese in and around Buna and other sections of the north coast of Papua across the Owen Stanleys, General Blamey had agreed for nurses to return to Port Moresby, and thus Kathleen had been accepted. Dinty would leave with her. The Filipina was now so attached to Kathleen that there had been no thought of separating them.

The two women had shown a great deal of courage during the past month. At first the flight south of Rabaul to the coast watchers' hideout had taken all their reserves and determination. They had been followed by enemy patrols through swamps and over hills and across jungle-plagued valleys, but Trap and John Drayton had evaded them all and they had waited nine days for an Allied submarine to escape New Britain. At the time Trap had made the comment that they were 'getting used to submarine getaways'.

The commandos had said goodbye to the three brave Australian coast watchers in the hills above the shores of Wide Bay on the eastern coast of the island and slipped away in the night. In the middle of the Solomon Sea they had been transferred to the flagship of the Royal Australian Navy. This was the HMAS *Australia*, a County class battle cruiser, which had led the escort of the transport ships for the landing at Guadalcanal in August and had remained to support the Allied forces in the area. Aboard HMAS *Australia* the commando party had sailed south to within fifty miles of the western tip of Papua, where they had been transferred once more, this time into three patrol boats which delivered them to Milne Bay while the cruiser had returned to its duties in the Solomons.

During all that time Trap had not admitted to himself that he observed the way Kathleen and Johnny acted, but now, as the two halted and turned to each other in conversation, he found himself wondering what they might be saying.

Kathleen swallowed as she paused with John Drayton. She could not help but compare the rapture she felt in the company of the man beside her to her bleak days and weeks and months with Ikeda. It was as if the suffering and fear of the previous year were the penalty paid for the joy of this moment. The only time she could ever smile about the past was when a thought of Juni Hyata crossed her mind. She believed there must be others like him, and she truly hoped that the one gentle Japanese she had met would survive the war and live happily always. She liked to picture him reading from a book surrounded by small happy children at his knee in a little school in the mountains: *Juni the good.*

Yet she was not thinking of Juni now as she raised her eyes to her soldier's face and he pointed beyond the palms. 'The last time I was here in Milne Bay, the enemy were just over there and a battle raged.'

'You've survived so much.'

'So have a lot of people, you included, Kathy.'

'Do you have any idea where you are going after here?'

Her companion shook his head. 'No. But we're to meet with a representative of the Allied Intelligence Bureau who's flying in. Hank has an idea that he'll be wanted back in the States. And I was told this morning that Willoughby and his intelligence unit moved last month with General MacArthur's GHQ from Brisbane to Port Moresby. I hear there are plans for some of us to go into Dutch New Guinea.'

'I think there will be other dangerous assignments for you now, because you stopped the relief army from sailing.'

'I didn't do it alone, Kathy.'

'I know that.'

John Drayton was reminded of the ones no longer here: Lister and O'Rourke, and Sudbury and Mayberry and Shibuyu, and boys

549

he'd lost in Java. They all had been unusual men; war did that, sifted people out: pity it had to. A faint hope flickered for Lister and O'Rourke. He continued to believe they might somehow have got out and that they had not been taken prisoner.

Kathleen half lifted her hand towards him but thought better of it and dropped it back to her side. 'I suppose this is silly to say, but please be careful. I hope the good Lord watches over you and brings you safely through whatever's ahead.'

He grinned. 'Didn't you say that to me once before?'

And even though she knew she had, she replied, 'Did I?'

'Yes.' He thought a moment. 'It was in Hong Kong. You said the same words the night you telephoned from the hospital, shortly before I left.'

'Well if I did, I meant what I said then and I mean it now.'

He was staring at her and thinking how lovely she was: what a beautiful caring nature she had and how her soft dark eyes revealed the kindness in her soul.

'Kathy?'

'Yes?'

'I was in Port Moresby years ago, so I'll be able to imagine you in the hospital there.'

'Do you think you'll ever visit?'

'The hospital?' He chuckled. 'I hope not.'

'No ... I meant ...'

'I know. You meant Port Moresby.' He shrugged. 'I'm in the army. I go where they send me.'

'Yes, of course.'

'But who knows? At least you'll be nursing again; that'll help you. The war's interrupted so many lives. So many we knew are gone for ever. I thank whatever gods might be that you and Lex were saved ...'

She hesitated briefly before she said, 'I hope the people in Port Moresby will accept me.'

'Heck, Kathy, what do you mean?'

She did not meet his eyes.

'What do you mean?'

She paused again before meeting his gaze. 'Well, before, I thought I was half-Chinese; now I know I'm . . . not. Suddenly it's different. The people at the hospital, the soldiers . . . they might not accept me.'

He took hold of her shoulders firmly and brought her to face him as she went on: 'In Hong Kong, there were so many like me. Down here . . . it's not the same; they could regard me as the enemy.'

John Drayton's tone acquired a scolding edge. 'Dear Kathy, listen to me. You're a fine professional nurse. That's what you'll be doing, nursing. You have a lovely face and a nature to go along with it. Anybody who comes in contact with you cannot help but notice that. And if some make harsh, quick judgements before they get to know you, then that's nothing in comparison to what you've faced up to and lived through for the past year. Please see that.' His hands slid down her arms and took hold òf her hands and he lifted them to his lips and kissed her fingertips.

Her eyes glistened. 'Thank you.' What he had said made her remember the day back on New Britain when she disclosed to him what had happened to her. It had begun with his telling her about Lexi: how she had been the only survivor of the massacre when Jasper had saved her.

It had been raining that day, heavy, torrential rain as only the tropics can hurl upon the world, and she had needed to move close to hear him. Kathy had been aware of the jealousy in her heart as she listened, for now she had finally admitted to herself she was in love with John D; had always been in love with him. Sharing these last weeks with him had made it all patently clear to her. And yet she loved her friend Lexi, and this only led her to self-reproach and a sense of disloyalty to her friend.

How vividly Kathleen could recall the expression on John D's face as he recounted what he knew of Lexi's journey through

Luzon with the children and how they ran into Hank Trapperton. After he had completed it he said softly, 'So now she'll be in Pago Pago.'

Kathy had not taken her eyes from him. 'I thought they'd all been murdered.'

'Yes, of course you would. You know, Kathy, there was a sort of double, profound effect upon me when I realised you were both alive.'

It had surprised her when he leant forward and took up her hand and held it as he asked, 'Would you please tell me about the shipwreck and little Paul. I'd like to hear everything that's happened to you. But only if you can bear to speak of it.'

'Yes, I should tell someone. It's the one way I'll help to rid myself of it.'

The two of them had been in the coast-watcher station high in the overgrown verdant hills above Wide Bay. They sat on wooden crates at the back of the radio shack in a small lean-to where the rain drummed on the canvas roof and the steamy heat rose from the wet earth beneath and they shared the dirt floor with small armies of toads and lizards and beetles all escaping from the downpour. There Kathleen had recounted her story from the last time she had seen John Drayton at her mother's funeral to the dawn meeting with him in the commando hideout.

The rain had long ceased and evening was creeping through the jungle when Kathleen finally came to Ikeda's death. She had told her tale dispassionately until she revealed that Ikeda was her father. Her face and neck flushed and her words came quickly. 'He was slicing the air with his sword, screaming in rage. I thought he would slash me. His eyes were glazed . . . I think he had briefly lost his senses. I stepped away and holding the pistol straight at him I squeezed the trigger twice. The bullets hit him in the face and the chest. They knocked him backwards . . . he fell down dead.'

John Drayton's face wrinkled in sympathy. 'Oh my dear, my dear Kathy, how terrible for you.'

And now she surprised him. 'Yes and no, John D.' Her tone became decisive. 'Sometimes things must be done. I did it because it had to be done. He *needed* to die.'

He leant forward and rested his palm over her hand as it lay in her lap. 'Kathy, I'm astonished. It must have been a nightmare. You were so brave.' He shook his head. 'In fact, in telling me, you honour me too much.'

She looked down at his hand covering hers. 'It's all been strange, so very, very strange. I would wake some days and just for a moment I'd think it was all a dream. But it wasn't; it was grotesque, but it was real.' Suddenly her eyes filled with tears. 'Oh, you see, you have me crying and I am not sad, not at all.'

'You're a wonder, Kathy. You're brave and wonderful.'

'Stop saying such things or I really will be blubbering.' She withdrew her hand and wiped her eyes and, regaining her composure, took a deep breath. 'I just have not spoken of it to anyone, that's why I'm like this.' But in her heart she knew she was emotional because of him; because, of all the people in the world, she had told her ordeal to John Drayton Whitby; that was what had made her weep.

And now, as the shadow of coming night diffused across the airfield at Milne Bay, John Drayton asked, 'You'll be all right in Port Moresby, won't you? Please say you will.'

'Yes, I will, and I'll have Dinty for support anyway.'

'That's the girl.' He grinned.

'Though I shall miss you . . . oh, and the colonel and the others. These past couple of weeks I have felt . . . secure.'

Their eyes met and he thought again how striking she was: her fine features and delicate neck and body. She did not speak; she simply gazed back at him and at last he said, 'Kathy, the war makes a man see many things. Things which were hidden away become clearer. Please allow me to say I know you are very special; very strong, yes, and special.' He glanced away through the trees into the haze of day's end and cleared his throat before

553

he faced back to her. 'Look after yourself, and I do very much hope I get to Port Moresby sometime.'

She smiled. 'Thank you for everything. You've always been good to me. Perhaps, if you have time, you'll write?'

He nodded, 'I will,' and producing a small laugh took a step away from her. 'Come on, we'd better get over to the mess, it's almost dark.'

They moved side by side through the tents, where soldiers washed their clothes in dishes and finished their chores while others stood from their inevitable games of cards as night fell. With each step a terrible confusion spread in John Drayton's mind. He knew in all probability that his wife was safe in Pago Pago and he thanked God for that; but what had seemed right before had somehow altered. He knew for certain he would miss this woman at his side, and he admitted that in recent months when he had unquestioningly believed her dead he had begun to think differently about her. And *because she was dead* he had allowed his realisations to take shape, and in taking shape they had taken hold, inside his very self.

In being convinced that he had lost both Kathy and Lexine, he had permitted himself to examine his memories of them. When he thought of Lexi, what had begun as a ghostly suspicion flourished inside his mind: that his wife had hidden something from him. That she had a secret from him and that he had not known the real Lexine.

When he had thought of this woman beside him, he had remembered only her kindness and gentility. He looked sideways in the musty heat of gathering darkness and he felt the powerful, heady attraction to her; it overwhelmed him even though he hardly dared to acknowledge it. At the same time he knew he suspected his wife had never truly loved him.

But what if his mind deceived him after all? What then? Perhaps it was just the war. While degenerates like Hitler and Tojo held sway over so many, why wouldn't madness be abroad? It might just be the worldwide mayhem encouraging him to have wild thoughts. Was he simply sorry for Kathleen and his mind was misleading him with spurious charges against his wife?

With these considerations whirling in his head, John Drayton conducted Kathleen to the spacious tent that served as an officers' mess and in a haste which surprised her said good night and left.

Trap watched them disappear. He fought against the desire to speculate on what might have passed between them but he could not master it. He dearly wished he knew. When he had left the Doll on the submarine, he had convinced himself he would never see her again. That was that. He had been able to keep her at a distance all the long months of being together in the Philippines, so his hypothesis was that he would live the rest of his life, long or short, without her. But when fate had lumbered him with Kathleen Leigh and it remained obvious that she was still deeply in love with Johnny, it angered him; and when he saw more than friendship in the looks that Johnny returned to the Eurasian, it frustrated him.

He stepped out determinedly across to his tent and thumped his right fist into his left palm, talking to the twilight: 'Damn, what do I care? I don't care what they feel or think. I'll never see the Doll again. She's your wife, Johnny, and you can have both of them if you want them. Goddam, *I . . . do . . . not . . . care.*'

The next morning when Kathleen and Dinty flew out of Milne Bay on a transport aircraft bound for Port Moresby, John Drayton saw them off with what a disappointed Kathleen interpreted as official cordiality. He shook hands with her and wished her luck; though she took a small comfort from his statement: 'Remember what I said: you are strong, and you can face anything.'

At ten a.m. the two commandos met with Colonel Fry from AIB who informed them that what they had expected was correct:

Colonel Trapperton was to return to Washington and Major Whitby had orders to head first to Townsville and then in all probability to Dutch New Guinea.

The two friends left each other forty-eight hours later. The night before, the commandos had thrown themselves a beach party and all said their goodbyes.

John Drayton and Trap clasped hands.

'Look after yourself, Hank.'

'I've almost got used to that name coming from you.'

'Until we meet again.'

Trap nodded. 'You bet, until we meet again. Don't take any wooden nickles.'

John Drayton grinned at that. 'Listen, I'm not staying to watch you take off, so . . . goodbye. I'll miss you, Hank.'

'And I'll miss you, Johnny.'

They released their handshake and John Drayton waved once to Caldo, Williams and Ivat who waited at the edge of the airfield in the shadow of the Liberator before he strode away.

Trap watched him go. *She's your wife, Johnny. Nothing changes that; she's still your wife.*

Chapter Seventy-one

Lexi stretched her legs into the sun as she sat on a tree stump, her body in the shade of the semicircular Quonset hut, the American version of the Nissen hut. From under her straw hat she watched Lessa silently at play in the grass nearby. The child's eyes flicked back and forth from the rag doll she lifted in dancing motion up and down upon her knees, to Lexi's form in the shade several yards away.

They had landed in the B-17 from Suva two hours before at Ward's Drome, an airfield built by Australians and New Zealanders six months earlier and standing five miles outside the town of Port Moresby. A second parallel runway of 6,000 feet was currently being added and Lexi could see soldiers working with shovels in the distance. This field had been surfaced by American engineers; it was more substantial than most being used by bombers and heavy transports. Three DC3s squatted in the middle distance, four B-24s beside them and five Beaufighters perched nearer, a hundred yards away. The hefty B-17 they had arrived in sat on the nearside of the Beaufighters; one of the port-side engines was open and four mechanics were swarming over it.

They had departed Pago Pago in the morning and made good speed to Suva. From there, using the cover of night for safety as they were nearing battle zones, they had flown on to Bougainville.

557

As they approached the airstrip in burgeoning daylight at fifteen thousand feet, they had been fired upon by two enemy aircraft. Lexi had clutched Lessa tightly in her arms, recalling those previous times they had been in danger, and marvelled at the strength of her silent little girl and kissed her forehead and murmured words of love to her. The aircrew returned fire and the big craft slipped into a bank of cloud, and on emerging they were relieved to be unaccompanied in the sky and landed across a series of tents on the mortar-blasted island.

There, Lexi saw for the first time a platoon of Marine Raiders and their hard-working loyal dogs which were used for scouting and running-messages. As the soldiers marched by leading their dogs, Lessa ran forward to one of the animals and while Lexi shouted in fear, the big alsation cross-breed's reaction was to lick the child profusely which Lessa appeared to enjoy immensely.

To avoid harm's way, they had lifted off in the early hours of the following morning to fly into New Guinea. And as dawn's gold filtered up from the horizon, fate menaced them with a failure in the near port-side engine. They were half an hour out of Port Moresby when the engine stopped, but the captain, 'Junior' O'Grady, who was affectionately known as Jog, had brought the big bomber down unscathed. The crew and Lexi and Lessa all applauded him as the aircraft came to a smooth halt.

'We might have to remain here longer than we thought,' Jog told Lexi with a shrug, 'but we'll get you and the little one a place to stay.'

An American marine sergeant materialised who informed Lexi that he would arrange for her to be taken into the town. 'We'll find you somewhere to bunk down, ma'am. And if worst comes to worst there's the Papuan Hotel; at least the beds there are clean.' With a kindly grin he had told her: 'We'll get you some chow and I'll have someone come and drive you into town.'

They had breakfasted in the marine sergeants' mess on hot toast, tinned beans and eggs, and Lessa's small face had lit up with glee for she had taken a liking to canned beans; fortunately, as they were currently universal rations.

Now, as they waited outside in the shade of the dynamo hut for the next phase in their journey, Lexi elevated her gaze from Lessa's play and looked across their luggage, consisting of one small tin trunk and a khaki canvas US Army haversack, to see an army vehicle with a red cross on its side swing round the palm trees. It came past the Quonset huts to a stand still about fifty yards away outside a medical hut.

Two stretcher-bearers emerged from the building bearing a wounded man, and three people hopped out of the van: a male driver and two nurses. At that moment Lexi heard her name called and she turned away.

'Dr Robinson, Dr Robinson!'

She stood up and saw Jog and the marine sergeant pulling up in an open jeep. Jog leapt out and walked towards her.

Kathleen heard the shout, 'Dr Robinson, Dr Robinson!' She swung around from the wounded man on the stretcher and peered past the row of huts to see an airman alight from an army vehicle and stride towards a woman who rose from a log in the shade of one of the huts.

Kathy recognised the woman; she would know her anywhere!

But John D had told her Lexi was in Pago Pago.

Kathleen's heart pumped as a hundred conflicting thoughts both disturbing and joyful crammed her mind. She hesitated, uncertain, and as she waited the strongest feeling sustained itself and swelled up and endured as the others faded: *She's my best friend and I've found her.*

She spun round to Nurse Carol Raye at her side. 'I know that woman! Please hold on here a minute, I've got to see her.' And she began to run towards her friend, who faced the pilot striding over to her.

'Lexi, Lexi!'

Lexine froze. That voice? She knew it well.

'Lexi! Lexi!'

She turned around.

The sun was behind the female figure running towards her, she could not really focus for the glare, but she could see the dark body waving and shouting at her. The last time she had heard this voice was on the fateful beach in Luzon as Kathleen had been dragged away screaming and crying that she did not want to leave.

'Kathleen!'

For Lexi there were no uneasy thoughts connected with Kathleen, only jubilant ones that shouted of reunion. This was her life-long friend returned to her!

Jog and the marine sergeant watched in surprise as Dr Robinson sped from them, her arms wide open, and the nurse in the distance hurtled towards her.

Lessa jumped up, leaving the rag doll on the ground, and dashed after Lexi.

The two women were in one another's arms, laughing and crying.

'You?'

'You?'

'I knew you were alive, Lexi, but I didn't expect you here!'

'I didn't know you were ... I thought you were ... Oh God.'

'Isn't this wonderful?'

'Yes ... oh, yes. Kathy, oh heaven, oh God.' They kissed each other and Lexi stopped crying and picked up the little girl. 'This is Lessa.'

'Yes, I know.'

Lexi looked amazed. 'You know? How?'

The swift thought of John D momentarily marred Kathleen's exuberance, but her smile remained. 'I'll tell you, I'll tell you lots of things. Oh, there's just so much to say.'

They hugged again with Lessa held between them; the child smiling widely as she realised this was a very happy event.

560

'What are you doing here?' They said it in unison and began to laugh and cry again.

Lexi found her voice first. 'We're on our way to Townsville.' But abruptly she had an idea. She looked hard at her friend. 'Though you know what? There's no real reason to go there . . . none at all. I was simply heading to Australia because I had nowhere else to go.' She wiped her eyes with her free hand and the woman with her took it and kissed it.

'Lexi, darling, our boys are fighting up on the north coast, we get casualties all the time. We need doctors here.'

Chapter Seventy-two

Late September 1943

Australian Prime Minister John Curtin finished dictating the communiqué to his private secretary. 'Thank you, please type it up and bring it back for me to review before sending.'

He stood and walked to the window of his office. The single wattle tree he could see was just coming into bloom: it was early this year, the golden yellow buds emerging to bestow his view from Parliament House with its colourful umbrella.

He sighed.

The message he had just dictated was to South-West Pacific Headquarters in Port Moresby and addressed to General Douglas MacArthur. John Curtin took off his glasses and cleaned them with his handkerchief. In the communiqué he had suggested to the commander that the Australian Government needed to be given more information on deployment of troops and to be more active in making decisions in the South Pacific Area. He felt strongly that they were being passed over.

Curtin was tired of hearing about strategy and the movement of Australian troops second hand and was also tired of reading MacArthur's constant references to American forces. The general seemed incapable of recognising that there were Australians fighting in the Pacific too. In fact, there were New Zealanders and Fijians and South Pacific Islanders like Tongans and Samoans, as well as

New Guinea native battalions; and the British and Indian and Dominion troops along with the Chinese were fighting like demons on the Burma Road and the borders of India and China; but the most MacArthur was inclined to say was *Allied Forces*. This rankled not only with Curtin but with the Cabinet and the whole of Australian High Command, let alone the rank and file of the army itself. A soldier's spilt blood was the same no matter what the nationality of the body it coursed through.

Curtin and the War Cabinet did not resent the American soldiers; in fact the complete opposite was the case. They knew in truth that Great Britain was strained to the point of breaking with most of its resources used in fighting Hitler, and any troops, air support and ships that it could spare, spread across the world. Curtin recognised a long time ago that he had to put his 'eggs' in MacArthur's 'basket' to save Australia, and the American soldiers were good men doing exactly what they had been asked to do: to fight for freedom. But Australia was offended by Douglas MacArthur's apparent unwillingness to give credit to the other nations struggling in the Pacific. And while at times Curtin had begrudgingly come to admire the egocentric patrician soldier, he knew MacArthur for what he was: one who loved the limelight for himself and thus he was seeking public recognition for his own troops almost exclusively.

So finally Curtin had written a brusque communiqué: not about MacArthur's language – he would say that to him first chance he got, face to face – but about his high-handed way of conducting combat in this theatre of war.

Douglas MacArthur sipped his afternoon coffee and puffed on his corncob pipe. He had just returned from speaking to a group of war correspondents and a look of pride and gratification spread across his face as he gazed at the citation which had accompanied his award of the Air Medal.

Earlier in the month, while the 9th Australian Division of El

563

Alamein fame launched an attack on the enemy-held town of Lae on New Guinea's northern coast, MacArthur had accompanied the flight of the United States 503rd Parachute Regiment into the first major jump of the Pacific War. This had been to seize the pre-war airfield of Nadzab in the Markham Valley. MacArthur had insisted on joining General Kenney who was going along. The award of the Air Medal had followed.

Douglas placed his coffee cup down, stood and moved across to the antique bureau he had brought with him from Brisbane. Honours and medals and citations from many nations! He eyed the letter from Prime Minister Winston Churchill when he had been bestowed with the British Order of Chivalry: the Grand Cross of the Bath. That had particularly gratified him.

Yes indeed, Douglas MacArthur felt satisfaction, pride, achievement: he was back to taking the initiative in the South-West Pacific Area. He mused on the great militarists of the past: Alexander, Caesar, Cromwell, Wellington, Marlborough, Napoleon, Grant, and as he did so, he stood tall, catching his reflection in the glass of the window as the rain pelted down outside. Under his leadership they had now won battles: Kokoda, Milne Bay, Bouganville, Lae and Salamaua, and the fight continued. They were cutting off Japanese troops in enclaves without hope of rescue all over Dutch New Guinea and the islands of the South Pacific.

Admiral Nimitz's ocean war against Japan was also gaining momentum. MacArthur had hardly dared to admit it to himself but in 1942 he had felt dejected, dreading that defeat would be his final disgrace. He knew he had hidden it supremely well from the public and even from most of his command. But now at last, he dared to hope that he would be triumphant after all.

Douglas considered the past six months with a smile. The enemy were losing battles and experiencing setbacks; one significant reversal being the loss of their commander-in-chief of the Japanese combined fleet, Admiral Isoruku Yamamato. The transport aircraft carrying him had been shot down. It was still top secret, and the pilot – Captain Thomas Lanphier – was as yet an unsung hero.

The SWPA commander eyed the rivulets of rain on the glass. He had moved his headquarters from Brisbane to Port Moresby last November to this attractive, rambling building on a hill in Kaevaga, north of the town and overlooking the harbour. Government House was perhaps a touch rundown, but it was the most stately dwelling in the whole of New Guinea, with a splendid view out over the Coral Sea. Past the hills beyond, a large station hospital and an Australian military hospital had been erected, where Sutherland had informed him he had run into old Sir Brillard Hayes's granddaughter, Lexine.

He was considering whether he should invite her to dinner one night soon and find out how she had ended up here. The last time he had heard of her she had escaped from the Philippines with Colonel Trapperton and his boys. The Philippines! He honestly could believe he might have a chance of being back there to liberate it within twelve months. A wide smile creased his face at the thought of that. It had been his compulsion behind many an act! Ah! then they wouldn't dare sing, *Dougout Doug!* How he detested that coarse, offensive ditty!

Abruptly his mouth tensed. In remembering the Philippines he had remembered Jonathan Wainwright. 'Damn,' he whispered to the rain. He did not want to think of Jonathan right now.

Skinny Wainwright stood looking down. His nickname now described his condition in defined detail for he was truly a mobile skeleton. He was actually smiling at his feet for his bony ankles projected out of a pair of heavy British army shoes that had miraculously arrived in some depleted South African Red Cross stores which the guards had inexplicably let through. He and the prisoners with him had gladly dispensed with the Japanese clogs they had been wearing and Skinny saw the humour in feeling joy at possessing such unattractive items.

A noise behind him made him turn, and there stood Colonel Sasawa, a member of the staff of the commander of the Formosan Army. As his roly-poly body stepped into the small eight-by-ten-foot room he screwed up his mouth before he spoke and Skinny made unflattering comparisons to primates he had seen. This was one of the general's ways of mentally fighting back in his continuing frustration and situation of impotence. Sasawa was a regular visitor to the prison camp of rough pine board which sat on a hill above a valley of rice fields near the small Chinese village of Muksaq.

From the first prison camp, at Tarlac in Luzon, Skinny had been sent here to Formosa along with twenty-six other high-ranking officers. They had been transferred from the Philippines in a leaky, filthy, cramped coastal ship, where they had spent the night's crossing jammed in a hold thirty-five feet by nine wide.

The prisoners had spent seven and a half months starving in cruelty in the prison camp of Karenko. There had been gathered the largest and most distinguished group of prisoners held anywhere in the world: the British contingent including Lieutenant General Arthur Percival, and Sir Mark Young, the Governor of Hong Kong, and General Merton Beckwith-Smith; and the American Generals King and Sharp from the Philippines as well as top-ranking Dutch officers. Also included was a startling array of governors and generals and chief justices from all parts of the Orient. These men were all skeleton-like and carried whatever precious possessions they had been allowed to keep.

Skinny recalled an officer from Hong Kong arriving at Karenko with a highly polished teapot under his arm, a poignant and pathetic sight, yet somehow uplifting to them all, for it was a symbol of civilisation and a statement of the officer's dauntless spirit.

After Karenko they had been shunted on around Formosa to another camp at Tamazato, and then in June they had been brought here to Muksaq.

Sasawa cast his eyes around the small space. He was not a

favourite of the prisoners, for he had killed the camp's only pet, a duck called Donald, and had eaten the bird on what he had termed a 'picnic' for the prisoners.

'General Rainright.' Sasawa's high voice sounded as he revealed protruding teeth between his plump lips. 'What is it you would like most in the world?'

Skinny paused, deciding how best to answer before he spoke. 'I would like to see the war successfully terminated and get back home to my country.'

'Exactly,' the colonel replied. 'And I know a way you can do that.'

The general's eyebrows rose in speculation as he waited for the revelation and at the same time he followed the progress of three enormous cockroaches slithering down the wall behind Sasawa.

'If you will write a letter to your President Roosevelt and tell him there is no use carrying on this war any further—'

'I decline!' Skinny growled, attempting to sound deeply affronted. 'I decline to discuss this any further with you.'

To the general's surprise Sasawa took this in good spirit and laughed. 'You have no chance of beating Japan. You listen to me.' He pointed his forefinger at Skinny. 'It took *twenty thousand* Americans to defeat two thousand Japanese soldiers on Attu Island. Ten to one! There are one hundred million people in our Japanese Empire; therefore it will take *ten times* that many soldiers to defeat us. You could never raise such an army. It would take generations of people and you will not live long enough.' His thin voice rose to screeching. 'None of you will live long enough!' He spun on his heel and stomped out.

Skinny shrugged and went back to admiring his shoes.

Douglas MacArthur blinked to clear his mind of Jonathan Wainwright and turned away from the deluge as a knock sounded on the inner door.

'Come in.'

Richard Sutherland entered. He looked hot, and his brooding good looks were marred by a deep crease of concern. 'What do you want to do about the message that came in yesterday from John Curtin?'

Douglas frowned: his good humour had faded altogether now. The Australian Prime Minister had sent a communiqué which smacked of pique to Douglas MacArthur. He had suggested that the Australian Government needed to be given more information on deployment of troops and to be more active in making decisions in the South-West Pacific Area.

MacArthur released a noisy breath. 'Damn it. I'll have to go to Australia to see him. It needs to be handled in person. I've become almost fond of old Curtin, though on first meeting him I never would have dreamt it. Organise it, Richard, will you?'

'Of course.' The chief of staff nodded and departed.

Chapter Seventy-three

Sister Muriel Abbott tapped Lexi on the shoulder. 'Dr Robinson, there's a soldier, an officer, waiting to see you out on the side veranda.'

So he had come at last. For months now she had suspected he would arrive if he could manage to get leave. She knew that having written him only two letters in almost a year could not help but motivate him to confront her, and she had needed him to come, to say what had to be said, looking one another in the eye. Even though she dreaded it.

She felt her heart speed up as she walked along the white-washed corridor and out on to the wooden veranda, and there he was: her husband, John Drayton, whom she had not seen since he boarded the aircraft at Hong Kong airport almost two years before.

The rainy season had just begun and a deluge was currently in progress over Port Moresby and as she drew closer to him, she saw the wet stains on the shoulders of his jacket and the shining droplets clinging to his hair. He looked so handsome, standing in his uniform, holding his cap in his hands, and suddenly a great sad place inside her welled up. He appeared older, more mature, and as she halted in front of him she noticed a few strands of grey hair at his temples. Somehow that caught her off balance: the young man had gone.

'Hello.' The word caught in her throat.

'Hello, Lex.' He looked her straight in the eyes. 'I'm stationed not too far away, in Dutch New Guinea, so finally I managed to get a couple of days' leave. I hitched a ride on a B-25 . . . and here I am.'

She looked down and noticed that his boots were wet too. 'Johnny . . .' She faltered.

And to her genuine amazement he made it easy for her. 'Listen, Lex, I've come to say this, and so here it is. I've had two letters from you in a year. I've got boys in my unit whose wives write to them every week, some *every day*. My wife sent me two letters in a year, letters that said very little . . . and yet they said it all. You're not the sort of person to write goodbye in a letter, but you might as well have.'

She began to speak but he held up his hand. 'No . . . You need to hear me. I came here to say what I've felt for a long time. Hell, if the truth be known, I've felt it from the beginning, from our wedding night. You weren't happy. I don't know what it is, Lexi, and I don't need to know, but something's been eating at you from the start. Look, war's the worst thing that can happen to anyone and any country, but perhaps it makes you see what otherwise you might never see. Without the war I would have floated along in our marriage, kept the illusion . . . possibly for ever.'

'Johnny, let me—'

'No, Lexine, let me complete this.' He stepped nearer. 'I've had a lot of time, in a lot of jungles, to analyse you and me, and what I came up with is this. I reckon you don't love me. When we first met you seemed to, but something altered along the way. And why you married me is still a mystery.'

She could not help it: a tear slipped down the side of her nose. She raised her hand to him, but thinking better of it let it fall to her side.

And now he actually astounded her.

'And you know what, Lexine? It's all right. I don't mind.'

'You don't?'

He took a pace towards her; he was only two feet away now and he dropped his cap on a cane bench nearby and took hold of her hands. Suddenly she could not curb her tears and they broke from her eyes as she gazed down at their hands clasped together.

'Don't cry, Lex, it's all right.'

'But it's not all right!' She wept and her conscience disgorged the anguish and suffering she had held inside for so long. Her face twisted as the torment in her soul gave voice to her guilt. 'I've been terrible to you. I married you . . . when I shouldn't have. I told you lies, I let you think I was good, and I'm not. I *should* love you, you're fine and strong and brave and kind. But I . . . oh, Johnny, I'm not worthy of you. Forgive me, please. I never wanted to hurt you. I just can't help any of it.'

He gave her a smile, a strange, tender smile. 'Lexine, Lexine. Listen to me.' And he stepped in and took her in his arms and held her close and spoke into her hair. 'Stop talking rubbish. I'm a big boy and I accept that we're probably better apart. For heaven's sake, I'm not an angel. I've altered too.' He tilted his head back and looked into her eyes.

She took a noisy breath. *It's now or never. I have to tell him.* 'Paul, little Paul, he wasn't yours . . .'

She felt him flinch, and his hands slid down her arms, releasing her.

He was slow to speak. 'Ah, I see. Well that hurts, Lex.' He frowned and stepped away.

'But please understand, if you can. They all expected us to marry: Grandpa, Mummy, all the family, all our friends in Hong Kong, everybody. I was promised to you. I'd given you my word. I didn't know what to do. If I hadn't married you there would have been gossip, mean talk, censure . . . God, the indignity of it all. I just couldn't face up to it – the shame.'

'So you married me instead.'

She nodded, and more tears flooded down her cheeks. 'Yes.'

'Hell, Lex, that was bloody unconscionable.'

'I know it was. I've died a little bit every day because of it.'

His eyes flared and he jabbed his index finger at her as he spoke. She could hear tears behind his words although they did not fall. 'I . . . wish that Paul had been mine. That at least would have been one thing which was honourable between us.' He made a fist as if he wanted to hit something but, instead, sharply pushed his hand into his trouser pocket, and looked down.

To see him so hurt rent her heart. 'Oh God, Johnny, I had to tell you, don't you see? I had to. Otherwise . . . it would have been too much to bear. It's like lead in my heart now. I've lived with it for long enough.'

Slowly his eyes lifted. 'Lex, I don't mind that you don't love me. It's taken years, but gradually I've realised I'm not the same man who married you. I need other things too. Losing you frees me. And that's probably what I want.' His voice broke again, the sound of the unshed tears clouding his tone. 'But how dearly I wish Paul had been . . . ours.'

She tried to smile but it did not happen. 'I wish it too.'

The rain rose to a new intensity and they stood looking at each other. 'Can you please . . . forgive me.'

He turned away and taking his fist from his pocket, clasped the railing, as the rain hit his hands and the arm of his jacket. She watched him silently until his hands were completely soaked, then she drew him away from the railing and brought him round to face her.

'John Drayton, we can't alter any of it, and I'd change it all if I could. Just please forgive me. If you leave here and I know you go away forgiving me, I can go on. I had to bring you here, you see. It was the only way.'

'Who is he, Lex? Does the man have a name?'

She had feared this moment for a long time. She moaned softly as she answered: 'It's Hank Trapperton.'

For some seconds John Drayton was utterly still; even his eyes did not move. It was as if he were transfixed. Finally he began to nod his head in a measured way, biting the side of his lip and looking out into the drumming rain. When he brought his eyes around to hers, she could not read anything in them. His vapid expression matched his tone. 'Ah, Jesus Christ, why is it I'm not surprised?'

'But he doesn't want me; he has no respect for me, because of what I did to you.'

John Drayton made a sneering sound. 'Oh, really?'

'It's true. The last time I saw him was when he left the submarine to meet you in Rabaul.'

'I assume Kathleen told you about that?'

'Yes.'

'Did she tell you anything else? About me?'

'What does that mean?'

'Ah, Lexine, can't you see it all smacks of swapping bloody partners?'

Lexi shook her head. She blushed. 'You . . . and Kathleen?'

'Don't jump to conclusions. Your friend has been just that . . . your friend. She has never by word or deed been anything else.'

'Then what are you saying?'

He paused for a moment as the rain subsided. They could hear explosions in the distance. Port Moresby had been mostly free of air raids for months, but blasts were coming from somewhere and the war came flooding back into both their minds.

He spoke first. 'I came here to let you know you're free of me if you wish to be.' He glanced in the direction of the booms which seemed to be somewhere down the coastline. 'Look, Lex, who the hell knows if we'll survive the war? It's all complicated enough. You're correct in naming Kathy, but I'm not truly sure how I feel about her.'

'God, what does that mean?'

'Nothing, but I spent a month with her at pretty close quarters. She's a nice, decent person.'

573

'Oh, please . . .'

'Don't say any more, Lexine. I need time to think things through. It's not just you who's altered. I told you, I have. And it's about time I examined my own feelings. But getting things straight with you is what I want right now.'

She murmured in acknowledgement. 'Then I need your forgiveness, Johnny, I truly do.'

John Drayton pictured Paul. He saw him in their house in Hong Kong, in Nintuck's arms. He heard his gurgling baby laugh and thought of the times he had hugged and kissed and comforted the child. Paul was not his; he had belonged to Hank Trapperton. *God in heaven, what a mess.*

He searched the face of the woman in front of him. She was no longer his wife. But there was no hatred for her; how could there be when there had been a time of great love for her. And grudges were pathetic, certainly while this bloody war raged; any one of them could die any time. But there was something he had to know.

'When was it, Lex? When did it happen?'

She did not hesitate. 'In Madura, only once. He had no idea I was engaged to you. I didn't know I carried Paul until I returned to Hong Kong.' Her eyes pleaded, brimming with tears: a tiny nerve beneath her right eye twitched involuntarily.

He looked past her along the wooden veranda and down the hill, where the trees and undergrowth had been cut and removed to build the hospital. Long grass had grown up and a number of straggling trees remained; an ambulance wended its way up the slope past a line of tanks. He watched the vehicle advance though the diminishing rain while Lexi watched him. Ultimately he drew his gaze back to the woman beside him. He felt old, very old. 'Listen, Lexine, if we survive this damn war, we'll . . . get divorced.'

Again tears broke over her lids and coursed down her face. 'I suppose so.'

He stepped back in to her and lifting his right hand brushed her cheek. 'Goodbye, Lexine.'

She stared at him as he turned away, picked up his cap and strode slowly along the veranda. She studied his firm, definite paces. The explosions continued, though the rain had ceased and the clouds parted briefly to let a crack of sunshine through.

She felt drained and deeply sad, but for the first time in years she felt unfettered, her conscience assuaged at last. She had looked John Drayton in the eye and told the truth and he had released her from the mountain of pain she carried. She would always love Hank Trapperton, but what that meant or did not mean she could not guess; and if she were fated to carry her love for him without hope of having it returned, then that would have to be the way it was. She had made her peace with her husband; that was enough for now.

She continued to study him striding away along the wooden planks towards the steps leading down into the yard, and suddenly she saw Kathleen emerge in nurse's uniform out on to the veranda in front of him.

Lexi had known Kathy since babyhood; they had grown up sharing secrets and working together. They had lived side by side now for a year, and as time passed they had divulged their grim experiences to one another. Kathleen had been slow to reveal the truth about Ikeda and the dreadful months in his company, but once she had, the tale of being saved by Trap and Johnny in Rabaul followed. In return Lexi had imparted her own gory anecdote of survival and the months in the Philippines with Trap and the children. One night some months previously, Lexi had finally disclosed to her friend her true feelings for Trap. At the time Kathleen had listened silently and simply said, 'I'm sorry if you love him so much and it's not returned.'

And Lexi remembered she had replied, 'I just hate hiding all this from Johnny.'

575

And now, only now, Lexi knew why Kathleen had replied, 'John D is an exceptional man; he's not a fool and it would be best to be honest with him.'

Lexi contemplated the two of them standing together in the distance along the veranda. She had lost John Drayton because she had wanted to; she had been the motivator. Yet it seemed an odd trick of fate to make her closest friend her successor. She could not quite shake off the sense of betrayal she felt.

Lexi would always care enough about the man she had married to want him to be happy, but as she observed them together she could not hold back the words that slipped softly from her mouth: 'How inscrutable you've been, Kathleen Leigh.'

When Kathleen appeared in front of him, John Drayton halted.

'Were you going away without seeing me?' she asked in her gentle, melodious voice.

He nodded. 'Yes, Kathy. I've had my fill of emotional episodes today.'

'It does not have to be emotional with me.' She stepped closer to him and he did not move away. 'Though I would have been hurt to think you did not care to see me.'

'It isn't that. I've learnt a lot today. I need time to adjust to it all.' He placed his damp cap on his head and brushed past her, but quickly turned back to catch her eye. 'Give me time, Kathy, please, just give me time. I'm full to the brim. Please understand. It's important that you do.'

'I do,' she replied immediately. 'I just wanted you to know that my fears . . . about how they would react to me here?'

'Yes?'

'Almost everybody has been wonderful. And as you said to me, those who aren't don't bother me.'

This really did please him. 'Good girl.'

'Come back . . . I'll wait.'

He nodded and gave her a brief half-smile before he walked away down the steps.

Both Kathleen and Lexi remained where they were and watched him until he disappeared downhill along the muddy road past a row of tanks.

Chapter Seventy-four

The two women remained stationary until John Drayton vanished behind the armoured vehicles, and, catching one another's gaze, held it momentarily, before Lexi spun round and went inside.

Kathleen waited a little longer before she too retired to her duties. They did not see each other for the rest of the day and their shifts ended at different times.

When the battered lorry dropped a bunch of nurses off near the row of small buildings which were additional temporary hospital quarters built to the north of Port Moresby, the brief twilight was fast receding into night. All the nurses except Kathleen entered the small, square cement buildings, but she stepped along the path running by them and heading up a slope. In the end hut, the thatch-roofed communal bathroom which they often shared with rats, lizards and sometimes even snakes and spiders, she could hear through the thin walls the sweet voice of Jacque Murphy as it lifted in tune:

'Toora Loora Loora, Toora Loora Ly, Toora Loora Loora, That's an Irish lullabye . . .'

Kathleen's shoes made no noise on the ever-damp dirt path which led up the small hill to the two-roomed hut, built of bamboo, cement and agarwood, which she, Lexi, Lessa and Dinty shared. It was separated from the other medical quarters by a cluster of palm trees and had been erected as an office, so it had its own water tank and its own slit trench out the back for a latrine.

As she neared the dwelling she heard a noise, and looking round, saw Lexi step forward from the moody darkness beneath the palms.

'You've been waiting for me?'

'Yes. Lessa's with Dinty in your quarters. I'd like to talk with you.'

'All right.'

Lexi opened the door to the room she shared with Lessa and they moved inside. 'I'll light a lamp.' She took out a box of Lucifer matches, lit a hurriane lamp, placed it on the low table between the single beds, and motioned to the two cane chairs between the cots and the wall.

Kathleen lifted Lessa's rag doll from one of the chairs and placed it neatly beside her handbag on a wooden box decorated with a lace doily, before she sat and raised her eyes to her companion.

Lexi met her gaze. 'Why didn't you say something?'

Kathleen knew exactly what that meant. 'What would have been the good? How could I tell my best friend I was in love with her husband? What sort of person does that?'

'Oh Kath, we were so close.'

'Exactly.'

'When did you know?'

'That I loved him?'

'Yes.'

'I suppose the first time I saw him in Hong Kong.'

'God.' The word was replete with despair.

Kathleen closed her eyes and held the bridge of her nose for a few moments as if she were in pain. 'When you told me who it was you'd been with in the Philippines all those months, and when you revealed to me how you really felt about him, I remembered your grandfather's birthday in Hong Kong. *He* was there. And that night in the middle of the party you became ill, so ill you talked about leaving, but you didn't; you stayed. I began to think about things and it led me back to Madura. Back to Henaro's

579

bar that night. It was supposed to be forty-eight hours before we left the place, but suddenly the next morning you found me at the hospital and rushed us off the island on the noon clipper. You told me a story about some Japanese barbers threatening you the previous night and *an American* saving you from them. I now realise it was cock and bull. You said we had to leave fast and so off we went! Come on, admit it, that American was *the American*. It was Hank Trapperton, wasn't it?'

Lexi lifted her hands in a despairing action. 'All right, yes, I slept with him that night.'

'I knew it.' Kathleen clutched her own hands in an agitated way and her tone dropped into sarcasm. 'I always wondered about the seventh-month-baby!'

Lexi jumped to her feet, her face rosy in the lamplight. 'Well, now you know. And little Paul's gone.' She closed her eyes and groaned.

'How could you do that to a wonderful man like John D?'

Lexi's head spun back and her voice rose. 'Now don't you start being contemptuous. You've coveted another woman's husband for years.'

'Don't say that.' Kathleen rose beside her. 'I never did anything wrong. You're the one who cheated and lied.'

Lexi caught her breath and her eyes hardened. 'Ah, so now I know how you really feel.'

Kathleen's hand went out to grab her friend's arm. 'Stop. I'm sorry. We've been close since we were tiny. I don't like this.'

But there was no stopping and Kathleen's hand was brushed aside. 'Today I lost my husband, and in all probability to you . . .'

'But *you* don't want him.'

'This is too hard, it's all too hard. You stand there in judgement. How dare you? Hell, you're getting John Drayton, for God's sake. What have you got to be holier than thou about? The man I love finished with me before he damn well started.' Tears sprung to Lexi's eyes.

Kathleen turned from her. 'Stop! Please be quiet. Dinty will wonder what's going on in here.'

'Oh damn it, what do I care?' But Lexi did care, and she realised that perhaps Dinty and Lessa might hear, so she dropped her voice, though the anger remained. 'I think you're mean and you're twisting everything to suit yourself. I'm going out for a walk. It'd be far better if we tried to avoid each other for a while.'

'Suits me.'

'Me too.' Lexi grabbed an umbrella from beside the door and looked back. 'I suppose it's too much trouble for you to take Lessa down to the mess hall and see she gets some dinner?'

'Don't be pathetic. Of course I will.'

The door slammed.

Kathleen was shaking. She had never had a real argument with Lexi in her life: the closest had been minor disagreements long ago in their teens. This was awful. She wiped away a bitter tear, slowly picked up her handbag and walked over and blew out the lantern flame. Once outside, she composed herself and hurried the ten yards down to her own door. Knocking, she entered.

Dinty and Lessa's heads came up from the book they had between them. Lessa stood and ran over to the newcomer and held her around the knees as Kathleen bent down and kissed the top of her head.

She struggled to sound normal. 'Come on, Dinty, and little Lessa, let's all go and have some nice supper.'

Chapter Seventy-five

*Outskirts of Hollandia, north coast of Dutch New Guinea, seven months later.
End of June 1944*

The smoke-filled room of American General Walter Krueger's
Sixth Army headquarters on the beach at Hollekang in Humboldt
Bay was peppered with South-West Pacific Area's High Command.
They were in the heart of territory previously held by the Japanese
and there remained pockets of enemy troops in the surrounding
hills. In April, air, land and naval forces of SWPA, had, in Operation
Reckless, taken both Hollandia and Aitape one hundred and eighty
miles east. Hollandia was now being rebuilt by the Allies, though
it was yet a tent city.

General MacArthur had flown in from Port Moresby with
General Sutherland. This was a top-secret meeting: the generals
were only here for twenty-four hours and many of their staff officers had not known their destination when they saw them off on
the aircraft which had brought them here.

The gathered generals believed that the Hollandia area would
prove an excellent air, naval and logistic base from which future
operations in Dutch New Guinea could be staged and from which
a large part of the force assembled to invade the Japanese-held
Philippines could sail.

MacArthur's desire to free the Philippines had become his main
objective; some were quick to call it his main obsession.

The meeting was drawing to a close and coffee and tea had been provided for the fifth time to the assembled galaxy of generals who now informally chatted as they sat, stood, lounged or smoked. Beside MacArthur sat the dutiful Richard Sutherland, exercise book open on his lap, writing notes in it with a maroon and gold fountain pen.

MacArthur graced one end of the room and General Blamey, the communist-hating stocky ex-Commissioner of Police from Victoria, who ran Australia's defence, the other.

Between them paraded a notable array: General Walter Krueger, the host of the meeting, was in company with such noted Air Force and Army tactitians as: Generals, George Kenney, Ennis Whitehead, George Henry Decker, James Frink and Robert Eichelberger. The navy was represented by Admiral Thomas C. Kinkaid. The single Australian who had accompanied Blamey, the Royal Australian Air Force Commander Air Vice-Marshal William D. Bostock, completed the powerful party.

The ratio of American generals to Australian ones reflected the might of the American forces in the Pacific.

The SWPA commander was holding forth to General Kenney as Richard Sutherland placed down his pen and bent over and whispered something in the leader's ear. MacArthur grunted affirmatively, and as the star-studded group looked to him to break up the meeting he placed his pipe down. 'Gentlemen, we're all looking forward to whatever sort of dinner Walter is able to supply.'

An amused muttering met this comment.

'But there's one more thing we haven't quite covered, though we touched on it briefly earlier. That's the consolidation of the guerrilla forces in the Philippines. We want resistance in specific areas prior to the landings, and that means organising the Filipino freedom fighters.

'Through Ultra we've learnt a lot about where the concentrations of enemy units are located.' Ultra was the name given to top-secret intelligence resulting from decryption of enemy

583

communications. 'We're already in touch with certain guerrilla groups in operation on some of the Philippine islands, but in the main they are simply disorganised Filipino patriots. So I've requested from Washington the return to us of a man who was a most successful guerrilla fighter and commando. He stayed behind in Mindanao for many months after the capitulation, did a lot of damage to the enemy in Rabaul and then in the Gilberts. More recently he's been in the European theatre and earlier this month he was in an airborne assault in Operation Overlord, the beginning of liberation for Europe. He'll be here tomorrow.'

He paused, and in the moment of silence General Blamey cleared his throat and spoke. 'General MacArthur, I assume you're speaking of Colonel Hank Trapperton, and I understand from AIB that his co-commander will be our Colonel John Drayton Whitby. We at Australian headquarters are under the impression that the Australians, Americans and British officers who worked with them previously have been brought in again. Is that correct?'

MacArthur raised his eyebrows to Sutherland, who nodded.

'Yes, that's so,' MacArthur rejoined sharply. 'What's the point, Thomas?'

'My point is, Whitby's remarkable. He's been running a viable intelligence operation throughout Japanese-held New Guinea from our outpost at Merauke. My understanding is that he's requested several of his former commando team to join him for this run, and that Trapperton will bring with him the three remaining members of his original commando unit.'

'So?' MacArthur's eyebrow rose.

Blamey cleared his throat. 'We . . . er . . . see it as a co-command.'

The SWPA commander's expression soured and Richard Sutherland leant forward and spoke consolingly to the Australian. 'It's General MacArthur's decision to keep Whitby and Trapperton together. The two of them had remarkable success and we

584

acknowledge the part Whitby played ... very, very able, but it's never been in any doubt that Trapperton leads.'

MacArthur waved his hands in mitigation of the subject. 'That's it, Thomas, let's leave it: Trapperton's in charge. Darn fellow is an outstanding commando, spy, infiltrator of enemy lines, call it what you will.' He inclined his head to Sutherland. 'Remember, Richard, when we first met him? I recognised his ability immediately, didn't I?'

Richard Sutherland did indeed remember that meeting. It was actually one he preferred to forget. Trapperton had claimed that a Japanese fleet was headed into the Pacific to an unknown destination. 'Of course you did, of course you did, Douglas.'

The commander stood up, signifying the meeting was over. 'Then, gentlemen, I suggest we adjourn for dinner, as the sun is setting.'

Two hours later, four hundred miles directly south, the hum of mosquitoes, flies, beetles and other airborne insects permeated the night air, while fleas, chigger and fire ants and leeches, snakes, spiders, toads, centipedes, alligators and the myriad creeping jungle creatures, abounded in the slime-covered roots and swamps around Merauke. Inside the half-wood, half-canvas construction which was the AIF officers' mess, Trap and John Drayton sat on duckboards at a folding table and ate their meagre evening meal of bully beef by hurricane lanternlight.

Trap had not noticed anything different about John Drayton except that he now wore the insignia of a colonel. They spoke as old friends do who have been away from each other for a time, speculation on their coming assignment being the main theme of conversation as they swatted those insects which had discovered a way through the netting.

They had not seen one another since Trap left for Washington. John Drayton had remained in New Guinea and had worked with various intelligence units and travelled back and forth to Australia as required. He had been in Merauke now for six months.

There was an energetic air about Trap and his tone was light. 'When I went back to the States I was lent to General "Hap" Arnold, he's our fairly enlighted Chief of the Army Air Forces.'

'Isn't he the one who brought in women pilots within the USA to release more males for combat duty?'

'Uh huh, the same. He's pretty far-sighted and the airborne commandos have been one of his pet themes. I managed to keep Williams, Caldo and Ivat with me and finally off we were sent to England to help train our boys for Operation Overlord.'

'Were you in that?' John Drayton was very aware of the successful D Day landing.

'Uh huh.'

'I often wondered just what you were up to.'

Trap thought he heard an edge in Johnny's voice, but he decided he was mistaken. He shrugged. 'Well, Johnny, fact is I wondered about you too. So when they brought me out of France to reunite with you, I was kinda glad.'

It had been two weeks earlier when John Drayton had been alerted that the old Commando Double X, as they had been known, was to re-form for something big. Ron Howard had remained with him, but he had immediately requested through his intelligence channels to be reunited with as many as could be found of his old troop. Agreement was given, and Rupert Coalclark, Derek Smith, Gavin Bird and Chris Olsen were found. They had been seconded from their current units and flown north straight to Hollandia, where they presently waited for orders. John Drayton had also asked for Sergeant Major Dan Lambert and Digger Hervey, but Hervey had returned to a British unit in Europe and Lambert was missing in action.

Five hours previously, Trap had flown into Merauke during a short cloudburst. John D had been waiting at the airfield to see him arrive in a Beech C-45 Expeditor, and when Williams, Caldo and Ivat climbed out behind him toting their haversacks, he had shouted, 'You beauty!' and hurried forward in the rain to greet them.

Tomorrow another aircraft would deliver the commandos the four hundred miles north to Hollandia for the briefing on their coming top-secret raid.

As Trap sat eyeing his colleague, he felt glad to be reunited, and kept pushing aside the thought that being with Johnny was reminding him of the Doll.

As 2100 approached, the steward found a bottle of malt whisky which a major with the 11th Brigade AIF helped them consume. When he departed an hour later, the two friends remained and moved across the duckboards to a quiet corner where they sat on canvas chairs while a corporal brewed them Billy Tea and they chased away the insects which continued their forays under the netting.

It was edging towards 2300 when John Drayton leant forward, elbows on knees, as the gleam from the lanterns smoothed the planes of his face. 'I saw my wife last November.'

Needle-like pinpoints tingled though Trap's frame, even though outwardly he merely raised an eyebrow. 'Oh?' He hated himself for his interest.

'She reached Pago Pago on the sub just as you told me in Rabaul, but she wasn't there long. Sometime before last Christmas she moved to Port Moresby; that was where I first heard from her. You remember Kathleen, don't you?'

Oh Trap remembered her all right. 'Mmm.'

His companion leant back in his chair. 'She went to Port Moresby, you'll remember that too . . .'

'Yeah, Johnny, I do.' Trap straightened his shoulders and cleared his throat.

'You probably know Lexi and Kathleen have been friends since they were toddlers, so apparently when Lex landed in Port Moresby and ran into Kathy, that was it, she stayed. Now they're both working in the same hospital.'

How cosy. But where the hell is this leading?

John Drayton put his tin cup on a wooden crate and looked

hard at his comrade. 'I know I'm getting a bit sozzled, but I reckon I need to be, so that I can say what I have to say.'

'What does that mean, Johnny?'

'It means I liked you the minute I first saw you back in Malaya in thirty-nine. But I mightn't have, not if I'd known what you were going to do.'

Jesus, what's this? Trap's body tensed beneath his uniform. 'What's on your mind, Johnny?'

'Hell, Hank, why did it have to be you?'

Trap had the feeling he did not want to hear what was coming. He tried to gain time. 'Why are you the only person in the world now my mother's gone who ever calls me Hank?'

This was dismissed with an irritated grunt as John Drayton trained his bleary eyes on his companion. 'I know about you and Lex. Yeah, Hank, old boy . . . I know. Though I didn't know. Uh-uh.' He shook his head again. 'I didn't know any damn thing, though at times I suspected a lot; but you know what? It never dawned on me it was you, my best mate. All those times she slipped away from me and went into that brown study, call it what you like, I knew she had a secret, and guess what?' He poked his index finger across the space between them. 'You were that secret.'

'Johnny, this isn't helping.'

'Helping? I don't care about helping. I've become enlightened, that's all.'

'Listen, Pal. I don't know what your wife told you, but I can tell you what happened is—'

'Don't, mate.' John Drayton twisted in his chair and held up his hand. 'I don't want to hear it, because she told me it only happened once and I really want to believe that. I want to believe it because she was my wife and you were my friend.'

'Jesus, Johnny, I am your friend. What she said is absolutely true. I didn't know who the hell she was. She was some dame I met in Madura who got under my skin. Since I found out who she was I've avoided her like the plague. Listen, no offence, but

I've got no time for her. She's nothing to me.' Trap's face slipped into dark, sombre lines and his mouth hardened.

He had said it with such conviction that his listener hesitated, falling silent and pursing his lips in thought. Suddenly he looked around. They were the only two officers remaining. He lifted his hand to the steward, who came over. 'Yes, sir?'

'Any more of that whisky left?'

'Another couple of nips.'

'Well I'd like one: not much water.'

'You, sir?' The steward turned to Trap.

'Yeah, I reckon I'll have one too.'

When the man moved off, John Drayton asked, 'So she's nothing to you, huh?'

Trap did not reply. *This day was bound to come along, and here it is, Trap, old buddy.*

'Christ, Hank, she might be nothing to you, but I can tell you, you're something to her. You know she actually said that to me ... she said you didn't want her.'

Trap felt the pit of his stomach churn.

'Listen, I've changed. *Know thyself* ... I've learnt that right here in Merauke from a friend of mine. And I'm trying to do just that. You know what, Hank old mate? Learning to know thyself leads to all sorts of profound understandings. First about you, then about others, and on and on ...' He gave a sad, strange smile. 'That includes you, old man. Look, I know I'm sort of drunk, but I'm not the bloke who reported for duty to Fort Stanley every day in Hong Kong either. I'm bloody different all right, and at last I'm beginning to know who I am and how I really feel.'

Trap decided to comment on that one. 'Good, Johnny, I reckon that's a good idea.'

The steward returned with the whisky and John Drayton took a quick swallow. 'Yes, I'm beginning to see myself with the help of a major here in intelligence. He told me about Socrates ... smart old Socrates.'

Trap thought that now Johnny was beginning to ramble. 'Yeah, sure, buddy. Socrates, Greek, clever guy.'

'You're bloody right there. Listen, I've got a lot on my mind tonight. I went and saw her, yeah . . . cleared it up; made our peace. What do you think of that?'

Trap was trying not to think anything.

'One thing I have to accept is that the kid I thought was mine was yours. That part hurt, yeah, it hurt at the time. But I'm used to it now.' His eyes locked with Trap's as he added, 'And I want to believe it was only . . . once.' He straightened his shoulders and tugged at his shirt collar as if to loosen it.

Trap needed to get out of here; he had heard enough. 'Look, buddy, I reckon I'm a bit plastered myself. But for the record, yes, it was only once.'

'I believe you.' John Drayton finished his drink in one gulp and placed the metal container down with a thud. 'All I want to say is, I'm all right now. I've promised Lex a divorce, and hell, in learning to know myself I've admitted that I care about Kathy. Bloody hell, maybe I always cared about Kathy.' He jabbed the air with his index finger. 'So none of us need to get emotional.'

Trap thought that one a bit far-fetched.

John Drayton rose and wobbled a little as he put his hand on Trap's shoulder. 'You know what? You're my old mate. My old mate's got to go to Hollandia tomorrow . . . and after that, God knows where! We've got to rely on one another. Completely rely on one another, big thing that.'

'Yeah, pal, that's the truth.'

John Drayton chuckled. 'Socrates was right, we need to know ourselves; big messes wouldn't happen if we all knew ourselves, see, that's the point . . . strong point that . . .'

Trap was beginning to feel a bit light-headed and philosophical himself. He rose up beside his friend. 'Sure, sure . . . that's the point, Socrates was right. Better go and drink some water . . . not the hemlock.'

They gazed into one another's eyes and abruptly John Drayton began to giggle. 'Atta boy. Drink water, not *hemlock*.'

Suddenly Trap started to laugh too and they stood there, face-to-face, their mirth ringing in the night, before moving off arm-in-arm to steady each other, across the duckboards. John Drayton cupped his hand and whispered loudly in Trap's ear, 'Jesus, Hank, you and I've got to stay pals.'

'Sure have, buddy, sure have.'

'Got to forget about the women . . . got to rely on one another.'

'Sure have, buddy, sure have.'

Side by side they made deliberate but wavering progress towards the tent flap as the steward rushed over and lifted the net for them to emerge into the multitude of jungle noises that made up the Merauke night.

Chapter Seventy-six

Twelve hours later, the humid air of noonday wafted around Trap, who sat elbows upon knees on a crate of 5lb-tins of bully beef, the Arafura Sea lapping the shore in the distance. He held his head in his hands as the muggy breeze invaded the tall grass beyond to carve furrows between the stalks. He was feeling somewhat hungover and gazing down at a trail of black ants making their way past his boots and heading on to Merauke's single-runway dirt airfield. Perhaps it was thinking of the alcohol he and Johnny had consumed last night that made his mind slip back to 1925 when prohibition was at its height and bootlegging flourished. His father thought it 'a ridiculous law' and railed against it saying it encouraged police corruption.

He was remembering the day prior to his father's departure on the fishing trip which was to end his life. They were walking a forest path which later became part of the Appalachian Trail back in the Old Dominion State under a cerulean sky where wisps of cirrus clouds laced high above. Trap was home on leave from West Point. His father's laugh had been hearty and exuberant and it sounded that day as he looked forward to the Alaskan trip with his old buddies from the Great War.

A week later the news had come via the local sheriff: William Trapperton and his three friends in the flying boat had all disappeared in fog over Kodiak Island. Trap had immediately placed a trunk telephone call to Jonathan Wainwright for he had been meant to be along on that fishing trip.

Skinny had taken Trap under his wing and in the years following, Trap spent many furloughs with the Wainwright family becoming friends with Skinny's son Jonathan M. Wainwright V whom Skinny called 'Jack'.

He visualised Skinny now, hoping like hell he was still alive. Skinny had been fifty-nine when he had been captured and while Trap knew the general's willpower would remain intact he was unsure how his constitution would stand up to the horrible deprivation that he undoubtedly was suffering.

Trap remained, thinking of the past, staring at the solid line of ants and he pictured his mother, Christine, who had collapsed on hearing of her husband's disappearance. She had always been frail and a year later she had simply faded away and died one hot afternoon, while bees buzzed in the host of flowers in the window box and white-tailed deer meandered down the hillside through the woods beyond and cardinals fluttered their wings and kissed each other in the branches of the maple trees. Her son was quite aware she had died of a broken heart.

The picture of her gentle pallid face transmuted into another – the Doll's. He gave a grunt of emotion as his eyes snapped open and he sat up straight.

On the far side of the airfield John Drayton strode across the mud between the tents in the camp, a battered leather suitcase in his grasp. His head was fuzzy today, but he had put in a good morning's work and left his section of the department tidy and orderly. Beside him strode a brother intelligence officer, Major Chambers of the 62nd Battalion AIF. When the 22nd Motorised Battalion had arrived in Merauke in February this year, the 62nd had moved out, but Chambers and a few other intelligence officers had remained.

With much of New Guinea back in Allied hands, Merauke

was rarely bombed these days, yet the trenches remained and the sandbags were still piled high around the camp.

'It was a different story a year ago,' Chambers said, pointing to the disused trench they were passing. 'The Japs bombed us almost every single day in forty-three. Sometimes they flew so low we could see them waving at us.' Chambers had come to say farewell. He was an able intelligence officer and a layman philosopher, the man who had introduced John Drayton to Plato and Socrates, and in particular, to Socrates' guiding counsel, 'Know thyself', which John Drayton had been expounding upon to Trap the night before in the mess.

John D's baptism in philosophical thought had occurred when the two of them were alone crossing a swamp to rejoin a patrol five months earlier. The subject of being away from home and family had arisen and the fact that Chambers read the Greek philosophers to liberate his mind from the environment of the jungle came into the conversation.

Major Chambers lifted his Tommy gun over his head as he waded into the thigh-deep slime of the overgrown marsh, and turning his body slightly back to the other man declared, '*Learn to know thyself*, it's over two thousand years old, sir, but it remains an excellent admonition for man or woman. It's of eternal significance. When one begins to explore such a dictate it leads to profound understandings about self. It can make unhappiness, fear, sadness, doubt, and all the negative emotions meaningless.'

That had definitely got John Drayton's attention. 'Tell me more of Socrates.'

'His method of enquiry is known as the Socratic approach or method of elenchus. It's to do with finding truth by eliminating that which is not true.'

And the major went on to explain that Socrates had left no writings of his own but that two of his famous disciples, Plato and Xenophon, had, and that Aristotle too, had referred to Plato many times.

John Drayton had been so intrigued and uplifted by the dialogue in the strange environs of mud and foul water and slime that he continued to seek out the major and they had often sat for long periods in discussion on all sorts of topics. There was a deal of comfort in it, the major was seven years the young man's senior and became another father-figure to him.

He began to challenge his own value system and to analyse things which before he had simply accepted as true. He had borrowed one of the major's collection of books on *Early Greek Philosophers* and read it enthusiastically. And as the weeks passed he attempted to see himself and after that, Lexi and finally, Kathleen.

Side by side the two men halted at the edge of the airfield, smiled and shook hands.

'Goodbye, John Drayton, and good luck.' Chambers took the book which he was carrying from under his arm and handed it to the younger man. 'I'd like you to have this.'

John Drayton was taken aback. It was the major's most precious book, though battered and mildewed from its days in the jungle: an eighteenth century-edition of Plato's *Early Socratic Dialogues*.

'I think you'll like this, because this is where Plato seeks to define bravery.' The major smiled. 'Stay in touch, and you know my home address.'

John Drayton studied the man in front of him, looking deeply into his strong face and solid blue eyes. 'I know the *true* value of this gift. Thank you for all you've done for me.'

He watched the soldier withdraw between the tents, the back of his slouch hat revealing the large human eye painted upon the crown. It had been an idea Major Chambers had devised to trick the local Kia Kia natives who were headhunters, into believing the eye could see, after a couple of Australian soldiers on patrol had been attacked from behind by Kia Kias. John Drayton thought it quite ingenious and worthy of the philosopical soldier, and a number of the troops had copied it and now wore 'hat eyes' as well.

As Chambers disappeared in his jungle greens, the young man

blinked to hold back his emotion, and into his mind slipped a picture of his real father.

Perhaps losing the company of Major Chambers had reminded him of his dad. He had come to rely on the major over the months of being here in Merauke. He had found many similarities between his father James Whitby, and the major. They had both fought in the Great War in the Battle of the Somme in France, they were self-educated, deep thinkers and hard-working men who had been born in England and married Australian girls.

John Drayton had been seventeen and a boarder at Ipswich Grammar School the last time he had seen his own father. These days he was becoming aware that losing him at so impressionable an age had conditioned him to seek out surrogates.

Home had been a cattle station west of Roma some two hundred miles away. He recalled standing together on the playing field down the short hill from the white turreted building which was opened as a school in 1863. 'What do you really wish to do?' James Whitby asked, looking keenly at his son in the over-bright Queensland sun.

'I'd like to join the army, Father, I'm thinking of applying for Duntroon.'

The picture of his father walking away from him that after-noon was etched in John Drayton's mind: the glare of the Queensland sunlight, his father's gait particular to himself, each stride with the veriest of rolls to it, as if he had been a sailor not a soldier.

John Drayton felt the unshed tears sting behind his eyes even now as he thought of it. Both his parents died in a motor car crash ten days later.

Drawing his fingers across his eyes he came back to the present as three Kia Kias, decked in feathers, issued out of the jungle ahead of him: stone-age men with short spears. Upon spying him they receded from view, melting into the trees as if they had never appeared.

Passing the spot where they had vanished he drew close to Trap and saw his friend raise his head and sit bolt upright. John Drayton strode in, placed his suitcase and book down, and motioned into the distance. 'Here come your boys, and I reckon this'll be our transport as well.'

A tired-looking Beechcraft transport flew in over Caldo, Williams and Ivat, who were marching across one end of the airfield. It rumbled along to halt about thirty yards away, exhibiting a painted tiger on the fuselage. Out jumped a man who pushed back his goggles, took off his helmet and looked around. He wore a sergeant's uniform and came running over. He was a few yards away when John Drayton noticed to his surprise that the flyer was an Australian Aborigine. He nodded to the man's salute, 'I didn't know any of you blokes were in the air force!' and the pilot smiled. He was a most handsome youth, about twenty, with high forehead, sleepy eyes, sleek dark skin and a generous bottom lip.

'Reckon I'm the only one, sir,' he replied. 'Len Waters at your service. I usually fly Kittyhawks, but I've been commandeered in the Beechcraft today to pick up Colonel Trapperton and Major Whitby and Co.'

Trap stood. 'In that case, we're your cargo.'

John Drayton wore an intrigued expression. 'Where are you from, Waters?'

'Born in northern New South Wales but mainly from Saint George now, sir.'

Saint George was a tiny town about a hundred and twenty miles directly south from where John Drayton had been born.

'Queensland, eh? Good. I hail from near Roma.'

Len Waters beamed and his dark eyes shone. He liked this officer a lot; many were certainly not as friendly. 'I'm honoured to fly you, sir.'

As the soldier reciprocated the smile, the Aborigine added, 'My brother Don's with the Ninth Division AIF.'

'Good for him, another volunteer. Well done the Waters family.'

Trap bent to his knapsacks. 'Okay, let's make tracks.'

The pilot hesitated. 'I need to refuel, sir.'

'Right. Make it snappy.'

Half an hour later, Len Waters lifted them off into the clouds, and after a bumpy flight of close to three hours, but without incident, they came down on sections of perforated steel matting hooked together, which were safer for aircraft landings than the rough dirt strips of the jungle airfields.

They thanked Waters and John Drayton asked, 'What were you in civvy street, Sergeant?'

'I suppose I was a shearer, sir.'

'Well you're a darn good flyer now.'

Len Waters presented John Drayton with another smart salute and the commandos piled into a jeep and were driven to General Walter Krueger's advanced command post on the beach at Hollekang. There they were reunited with Howard, Coalclark, Bird, Smith and Olsen. Before they had time for reminiscence, John Drayton and Trap were ushered outside by a lieutenant and shown to a recently built cement building into the company of General Richard Sutherland.

He smiled in recognition of Trap and John Drayton was introduced. Both Trap and Sutherland recalled the darkening evening on the wharf in Corregidor when they departed in the torpedo boats, but neither mentioned it and the general went straight on: 'I have here top-secret outlines of what we expect of you.' He handed both men a file. 'Don't let these papers out of your sight and read them tonight. Tomorrow there'll be detailed briefings.' He turned to the noise of the rain hitting the window and made a disgusted sound. 'I'll never get used to this freaking tropical rain, and this is the dry season.' He motioned for them to sit at a folding wooden table and took up position opposite.

'Now, gentlemen, we're all aware that the Allies have regained many significant islands and our next major advance will be upon the Philippines.'

The two commandos caught one another's glance. *Now why aren't we surprised about that?*

'We want you you and your men in there on the ground. Reason: the need to coordinate the local freedom-fighters into cohesive units so that you can pave the way for strategic Allied landings.'

Jesus, that sounds easy.

As if Sutherland read Trap's mind, he leant forward and announced, 'Easy to say, yes, but obviously complex and dangerous.' He grinned. 'But then that's what you two are meant to be experts in: the complex and the dangerous. You'll be meeting with our GHQ Intelligence in the morning at oh seven hundred.'

Trap looked first at his companion and then at Sutherland. 'My understanding is that the guerrilla bands in the Philippines are less effective than their British and American-led counterparts in Burma because of their constant contention with each other and the wide separation between them on isolated islands.'

'Yes,' Sutherland nodded, 'I'd agree with that. That's one of the reasons why we want professionals like you back in there to lead them, so to speak. You're going to the Lingayen Gulf area. A group there is led by two locals called Gomez and Ramez.'

'Sounds like a vaudeville act.'

Sutherland chuckled. 'Yes. We can give you more on them. And there's a guy called Volkmann still organising resistance in northern Luzon. We finally received a radio message from him just three days ago. And a guy called Fertig doing the same in Mindanao, your old stamping ground, Trapperton.'

'Yes, I remember him.'

'We've broken a number of Jap codes recently which lead us to think an initial Allied landing on the island of Leyte is preferable. Followed by Mindoro, which is the ideal jump-off point into the Lingayen Gulf and southern Luzon.'

John Drayton asked, 'When is it proposed we go in?' as the door swung back and in swept the commander of the SWPA. He had a lighted Lucky Strike cigarette perched between his teeth and he gave an unceremonious return of salute to the commandos, who rose from their seats. Behind him in the corridor stood a number of officers of his general staff. He closed them out and proffered his hand.

'Trapperton, good to see you again.'

'Thank you, General MacArthur.'

'I knew your father.'

'Yes, I believe so.'

'I assume you're Whitby.'

'Yes, sir.'

MacArthur glanced at Sutherland, who gestured to the files on the table. 'I've given them the rough idea. They'll read the files tonight and meet with Intelligence first thing tomorrow.'

'Good.' MacArthur struck a pose, one foot in front of the other, as if he held forth to a hundred instead of three. 'The proposed landings are in the pipeline. Hence the need to get you boys in sooner rather than later, eh, Richard?'

Sutherland smiled, his white teeth glinting against his sun-browned complexion. 'Very much so.'

The commander warmed to the topic. 'You two will play a grand part. We're still code-naming your unit Commando Double X.

'We now have SWPA troops with firm holdings here in Dutch New Guinea and the Admiralties, Wakde and Biak. Central Pacific troops are in the Gilberts, Marshalls and the Marianas, so now we can go ahead with parallel drives converging on the Philippines and Formosa.' He waved his hand for emphasis. 'After that it's on to enemy-held China and ultimately Japan.' He beamed widely at the thought of it and looked keenly at the two commandos.

'One of the purposes of the coming Philippine campaign is to liberate the Filipinos; but keep in mind they won't understand liberation if it's accomplished by indiscriminate destruction of their homes, possessions and lives. Humanity and our moral standing throughout the Far East dictate that destruction of lives and property in the Philippines be held to a mimimum whilst still destroying hostile effort against us.'

John Drayton looked sharply across at Trap and raised his eyebrows. So many towns and settlements in New Guinea and the other islands had been razed to the ground, completely smashed, so he found this statement at odds with what MacArthur had done in other places, and at odds with warfare. Was there something more special about Filipino property and life than a New Guinea native's? MacArthur's long and close relationship with the islands was known to all.

A compulsion to reply to MacArthur rose inside John Drayton. 'General, that's a tenet we all understand. We're not indiscriminate civilian killers and slaughterers of babies like our enemies. We never have been. We'll take precautions to try and do what you ask, but we can make no promises. We're being sent in to do what we know how to do: to wreck as much of the Japanese war effort in the Philippines as we can and pave the way for our Allied landings. We can't be shackled or we won't accomplish what you're expecting of us.'

MacArthur's face clouded and he brought his feet sharply together, terminating his theatrical stance, as Sutherland's surprised intake of breath sounded on the air.

'Listen here, son. You're speaking to me! Didn't you hear what I just said?'

Trap responded immediately. 'General MacArthur, what Colonel Whitby means is this: we don't know the fine detail of what's required of us yet, and while General Sutherland has given us a broad understanding, nothing truly specific has been said. Once we read the files we'll be in a better position to judge all sorts of things, and yes, while sometimes it's difficult not to destroy civilian property, we'll be as careful as we can. We understand perfectly what you're saying, and as soon as we meet with Intelligence we'll know exactly where we're going and what we'll be doing. That's *actually* what Colonel Whitby meant.'

The affront which had waxed in MacArthur's eyes waned marginally. He did not like bold opinions contrary to his own, and he did not accept insubordination, but he knew the value of these two soldiers. He looked keenly past the speaker to John Drayton. 'Is that what you meant, Whitby?'

John Drayton opened his mouth to answer in the negative, but the sharp pressure of the heel of Trap's boot being planted on the toe of his own altered his mind. He managed to check himself and reply dispassionately, 'I reckon so, General MacArthur.'

The commander grunted. 'In that case, best of luck.' But he had heard enough from these two *cowboys*, and he rocked around on his heel, swung the door open and departed.

Sutherland watched the door slam. Rarely, if ever, had he heard the commander spoken to in that way. He looked with new eyes at the Australian as he coughed to cover his confusion. 'Right, er . . . read the file and I'll see you here at oh seven hundred.'

When the two friends found themselves outside in the falling rain, Trap grabbed John Drayton's arm. 'Colonel Whitby, what the hell were you trying to do in there? Get us court-martialled?'

'Of course not. It's simply that since I've read Plato and Socrates and Aristotle, I'm looking inside myself and I'm aware of what is truth for me.'

'Hell, buddy.' Trap grinned. 'Throw those goddam books away pronto.'

Chapter Seventy-seven

Lexi looked up from the desk and the letter she was writing to her mother, to glance through the window of the doctors' rest room. She immediately put down her fountain pen, stood up and walked away.

Outside, Kathleen, who carried a tray of instruments along the veranda, saw Lexi's behaviour, gave a grunt of exasperation and hurried past the open window.

At first, after Kathleen's admission of her long-standing deep feeling for John D and the upset which had followed, she had believed that because Lexi loved Hank Trapperton she would see the futility of her attitude and relent. Kathleen had expected that all the years of closeness would count for something.

But when a week had passed since their argument and she returned home to Dinty one day to learn that Lexine had moved herself and Lessa to a room which lay vacant on the other side of the hospital quarters, she realised that the matter was grave.

Kathleen appreciated that Lexi's overriding emotion was the feeling that her closest friend had betrayed her by falling in love with her husband. And while it smacked of childishness to Kathleen, she began to comprehend how a woman who seemed to have no hope of ever having the man she loved, could maintain her stance.

Dinty still took care of Lessa while the two women worked, and because she had been a teacher she attempted to help the silent little girl to learn, but Lexi made sure that in the handover of the child each day she avoided meeting her estranged friend.

Kathleen walked quickly on along the veranda and down the steps past the two ambulance vehicles with the stark red crosses on their sides and on by the dynamo and the water towers to enter the operating unit. She placed the instrument tray down and took off the cover as Nurse Jacque Murphy came through an inner door carrying a foot tub filled with Lysol.

Kathleen began to place the instruments in the disinfectant. 'Where's the alcohol?'

Jacque smiled. 'I'm just going back to get a tin.'

After the Lysol soaking they washed the instruments with alcohol.

'Can you finish the soaking for me? I'm alone in here at the moment.'

'Certainly.'

Left alone, Kathleen continued with the job until the door opened and in came one of the ward nurses, Arlene Duckworth, who carried the obvious nickname of Ducky.

Ducky looked hot. 'Oh there you are, Nurse Leigh. We need you in here for the rest of today. Bella Lansky's gone off sick and two operations are scheduled. The first one at eleven o'clock and you're the only nurse on duty over here with operating-room experience.'

Kathleen looked up at the wall clock. It was 10.40 p.m.

'Right, I'll just go and let the nurses in with the scrub typhus patients know that I'm commandeered, and I'll change my uniform and scrub up.' She was moving back to the door when she had a sudden strong feeling of dread. 'By the way, who's performing the operations?'

'Dr Robinson, with Dr Fellows assisting.'

As Lexi hurried away from the window to cross into the corridor she felt a headache coming on. She could ill afford it, for she had to operate in less than half an hour. *Pull yourself together, Lexine.* She halted and returned to the doctors' rest room, took an aspirin and went about her preparation.

By the time she crossed the yard she was calm. It was the middle of the wet season and she leapt along the duckboards and perforated steel matting laid across the mud where a few brave gerberas, planted by the hospital staff, accorded a line of colour to the outside wall of the operating room. As she opened the door to the anteroom, the first person she saw was Kathleen, standing beside Nurse Murphy and Dr Frank Fellows. Lexi's face hardened. 'Where's Nurse Francis?'

Jacque answered in her soft brogue. 'She's gone home sick.'

'Why wasn't I informed? I prefer to choose my own nurses.'

The Irish girl shrugged. 'Sorry, Doctor, Head Nurse Duckworth made the decision.'

Jacque was one of the few nurses aware of the cool relations between the two women, and she looked sideways at Kathleen as Lexi brushed past to face Frank Fellows.

'Have you read the cases?'

'Yes, and the first one's ready.'

Lexi glanced back to the two nurses. 'Come on, it's all right. The wounded soldiers waiting for us are more important than who assists.'

Jacqueline raised her eyebrows at Lexi's back and then turned to Kathleen. 'Don't mind her, we'll be all right.'

For the first minutes in the operating theatre Kathleen could feel the veil between her and her alienated friend. But as time passed and Lexi applied herself to the removal of the bullets, the opaque atmosphere in the operating room cleared.

Three hours later, as Jacque mopped the doctor's brow with a cloth, Lexi dropped the second bullet into the tin dish Kathy held and looked to Lieutenant Frank Fellows, assisting her. 'You can sew him up please, Doctor. Thank you all for a job well done.' She smiled as she left.

In the anteroom, she took off her blood-stained apron and washed her hands, dropped the clothes into an open cane basket, and put on a new apron.

She moved outside into the hot, sticky air to await the second case, and stood staring at the few straggling gerberas: normal things in an abnormal world. She bent and picked one.

She felt odd today.

Buck up, Lexine.

She breathed deeply and returned inside.

It was after five when Lexine completed the second operation. The soldier had lost his hand; they could not save it, though the two nurses and Frank Fellows had toiled staunchly along with her to prevent the amputation of his whole arm: at least they had achieved that.

She washed up and changed and made a quick visit to three of her other patients in the intensive care unit before she left the hospital and strode out to the west side, where staff gathered to wait for the six o'clock bus to deliver them back to their quarters.

She did not walk down and join the others, who milled about talking at the side of the dirt road under palm trees. Instead, preferring not to make small talk, she paused beside some tall grass near a wild persimmon tree about twenty yards away.

Day was fast dwindling when she realised that someone stood next to her.

'Oh, it's you.'

'Yes.'

Lexi heard the sigh that followed Kathleen's word but she said no more. They simply stood side by side.

The hospital sat in a clearing inside a ring of low hills and they both watched the ridge in the direction of Fairfax Harbour where the sun had sunk as twilight seeped down the hills and across the lowlands towards them.

Minutes passed until Lexi moved and faced round to her disaffected friend. 'You're a good nurse. I'd forgotten.'

'Thanks.' Kathleen's voice dropped. 'Today's John Drayton's birthday.'

Oh God, so it is. 'Of course. I'd forgotten,' Lexi answered.

In years to come, Lexine would wonder where her next statement came from. 'I don't know when Trap's birthday is. I've never known. God, I wish I did. That would be something for the long years of nothing.' She felt the same old churn of her stomach as she said it and her hand slipped into her pocket to feel the folded paper she carried.

Kathy's voice trembled with emotion as she replied, 'I wish you did too.' Then, to cover her feelings, she rummaged in her handbag and removed an Ardath cigarette and lit it. Knowing Lexi's preference for not breathing smoke, she moved away.

To her amazement, Lexi stepped after her. 'No need to move.'

Kathleen looked round, eyes widening, but she did not speak.

'The bus is late.'

'Yes.'

'When was the last time you heard from him?'

'John D?'

'Yes.'

Kathleen sighed and thought a moment or two before giving her reply. 'Lexine, I've only had three letters from him since the day he was here with you, though I write to him all the time. God knows where he is, for in the last letter he said not to expect to hear from him for a long time.' She hesitated before adding, 'And that was months ago.'

And now Lexi could not help herself. 'Kathy, did he ever mention Trap in any of the letters? You know they worked together in Rabaul, so I . . .' She trailed off.

'No. All he wrote in the last one was that he was in training for something with a unit he had been in before. You know how it is: they can't say anything much really.'

'*A unit he'd been in before* . . . Well, that could have meant with Trap, couldn't it? I mean, it really could have . . .'

'Yes, I suppose it could, at that.' She dropped the cigarette and stood on it. 'Here comes the bus.'

Lexi felt a well of disappointment as Kathleen hurried forward and joined the group.

They sat four rows apart on the bus, and when it pulled up outside the quarters, they all disembarked into the night air and Kathleen walked away in the direction of her own room. Strangely, after the heat of the day, the air was almost cool; a breeze wafted up from the port and quivered in the palm fronds, making a crackling sound.

She was past the last hut and gaining the slope when she heard, 'Kath?'

She turned round in the darkness. She could see the shape of her estranged friend following her along the path.

'Wait.'

Kathleen waited. Lexi came right up to her and halted a foot away. She did not speak; she just stepped in and took Kathy in her arms.

Instantly they were both in tears, the pent-up emotions of the long months of division freed at last.

'Forgive me, Kathy. Please forgive me.'

'Oh darling, you were so hurt. I'm sorry.'

'No, no, I was stupid.' She began to sob violently and Kathleen was kissing her.

'There, there.'

'I love Trap . . . so much. I hated that Johnny seemed to want you . . . Oh God, Kath, I was such a mess . . .' She broke into another flood of tears and her friend held her close.

'It's all right, Lex, I understand. Honestly I do.'

'I knew in my heart all the time that you were my . . . friend.'

'Darling girl, I've never been anything else.'

'And I want you to have Johnny, I truly do. It's just that . . .

608

Oh God, Kathleen, I want Trap so much . . . I was just being a fool.'

'Hey, what's going on up there?' It was the Irish lilt in Jacqueline's voice flowing up the slope.

Kathleen called in answer, 'Nothing, Jacque, it's Lexi and I, we're discussing life.'

'Really,' came the disembodied voice. 'Does that mean we'll see you *both* for chow tonight?'

'Sure does!'

'Ah, thank the good Lord, that's wonderful.'

The two women turned and hurried up the path, and when Kathy knocked on the door of her quarters and entered with Lexi at her side, Dinty could see by the light of the kerosene lantern that they had both been crying and swiftly understood.

As Lessa jumped off the bed and ran forward to greet them, Lexi said, 'We're a family again,' and while Lessa didn't understand any of it, she felt the warmth and forgiveness in the air around her, and laughed quietly as the two women picked her up between them and kissed her, and Dinty stood arms akimbo, nodding in approval.

Chapter Seventy-eight

18 October 1944

Trap eyed his wristwatch as Caldo completed setting the charge.

His head came up. 'Done.'

They ran, doubled over, back along the dirt road and up the hill through the trees and tall grass to where the others waited.

'The Japs should be here any minute.'

It was dusk and the eyes of the black-faced commandos flicking back and forth glistened white in the shadows of falling night.

Four minutes later Bird called softly from his elevated position up a palm tree: 'Here they come,' and he swiftly scaled down the trunk and joined his confederates.

The enemy lorries trundled slowly up the hill, and as the first one gained the centre of the stone bridge and the second rolled on to the edge of it, Trap's hand dropped from its raised position. Ron Howard plunged the handle on the detonator and the charge ignited.

The lorries blew to pieces and the bridge disintegrated in a loud explosion, scattering rocks and cement high into the twilight.

'Let's get the hell outta here!'

In single file Howard, Bird, Caldo and Trap departed their cover and ran west along the track through the ubiquitous nipa and banana palms to their bicycles. Bounding upon them, they rode away even as the Japanese in the succeeding undamaged vehicle vaulted to the ground and began firing indiscriminately into the palm trees.

A-Day, 20 October 1944. The first step in the Allied liberation of the Philippines took place when the largest number of naval assault carriers and warships ever massed in the Pacific sailed confidently into the Leyte Gulf. For forty-eight hours prior to A-Day Rear Admiral Oldendorf had used six battleships to soften the Japanese shore positions, their shelling supported by aerial bombardment.

The troopships expelled their cargo of soldiers into the surf to charge ashore, where they met resistance from pockets of the enemy.

In the third assault wave Douglas MacArthur chose to go ashore. Wearing his sunglasses and his braided and laurel wreath decorated, Philippine field marshal's cap, with the American eagle rampant, he transferred from his command ship the heavy cruiser *Nashville*, lying two miles out, into a landing craft, and once close enough to the beach, waded through the surf. Richard Sutherland accompanied him on his left, President Sergio Osmena, the successor to Manuel Quezon, on his right, and they were followed by General George Kenney and a number of staff officers. The party came ashore near the town of Palo on a muddy beach-head designated Red Beach where the 24th Division had landed and had worked their way inland about 300 yards. Photographers and cameramen who had previously disembarked stood in the sea to record the historical event.

With the smoke from burning palm trees in his nostrils and the pulsing *crump crump* of naval shells exploding and the shouts of the soldiers and the staccato rattle of small arms, MacArthur gained the shore and wandered briefly over fallen logs for about a hundred yards or so. As he paused to study three Japanese dead, he pointed to them and turned to Sutherland. 'I recognise the insignia of the Sixteenth Division, my old enemy Homma's ace unit.'

A brief tropical rainstorm began and the general returned with his officers to a quickly raised tent, where a mobile broadcasting station had been assembled. Out at sea a kamikaze suicide bomber smashed into the cruiser HMAS *Australia* as the SWPA commander picked up the microphone and spoke to those Filipinos listening who had managed to keep radio sets:

'This is the voice of freedom. General MacArthur speaking. People of the Philippines: I have returned . . .'

5 December 1944

Trap looked across to John Drayton and around the faces of his men gathered along with the band of local freedom-fighters and their leaders, Juan Gomez and Luis Ramez. Gomez had his arm round his girlfriend Louisa, and in the background other women moved around the camp. When they had joined up with the resistance group the two commando leaders had attempted to talk them into forgoing their women until after the Allied liberation landings had taken place here in Lingayen Gulf, but to no avail. The women were here to stay.

The humid winter breeze meandered up from the Agno river to ruffle Louisa's long hair as they gathered under the nipa palm roof in the centre of their hideout in the foothills of the Zambales mountains.

Trap held up his hands for silence. 'We have received a radio message that the Allies effected a successful landing on the island of Mindoro today to minimal ground resistance from the enemy, but heavy attacks from the air. General Willoughby's intelligence unit has informed us that target day for the Allied liberation landings here in the Lingayen Gulf is still January ninth at oh nine thirty, and that code names remain S-Day and H-Hour.

'Currently the enemy have seventy known airstrips in the Philippines and continue to bring in air power from Formosa and

Hainan, so we expect significant enemy air raids and sorties on S-Day itself.'

The commandos glanced at one another and Louisa pressed herself against Gomez and whispered in his ear. He grunted and squeezed her closer as Trap continued: 'Seventy-two hours prior to the H-Hour landings, minesweepers and hydrographic craft will begin sweeping the gulf, followed by bombardment of shore defences. Fire support groups with anti-submarine patrols will enter the gulf. Aircraft from the Escort Carrier Group will strafe and bombard shoreline defences.'

Olsen whistled. 'Jeez, sir, that doesn't help us any. The Japs are going to be mighty bloody aware of what's coming next.'

Trap grinned. 'Yes, so be careful.'

A ripple of laughter greeted that.

John Drayton, who sat a yard from Trap, stood up and held up a chart. 'So to be clear, we'll go over our operation again. Our job on the early morning of S-Day is to clear the beaches as completely as possible of remaining enemy resistance so that the landing parties can come in virtually unhindered.'

As he opened the chart and smoothed it under his hand, Caldo bent forward and strategically placed three pieces of coconut to hold it down.

'Thanks, Sarge.'

The men surged round to study the chart and Louisa's black eyes sparkled as she turned again to Gomez. 'It's only ten days to Christmas: let's all hope this is the last Christmas of the war.'

'Yes, my flower.' Gomez planted a loud kiss upon her lips.

Chapter Seventy-nine

Christmas Day 1944

The afternoon waned in Port Moresby. Lexi, Kathleen and Dinty sat on a blanket on the slope below their rooms and watched Lessa playing with Lily Belle, her rag doll, in the diminishing golden light of evening. It bathed the child's face as she lifted the doll high in the air. Dinty had stitched the toy for her and Lexi had painted a face upon it and named it, and while the little girl remained mute, she seemed happy and content and that brought some sense of achievement to Lexi.

They could see the water of Fairfax Harbour in the distance as the sun set over it. It was quite a cool day and blessedly almost free of insects, though a few had found them now that the day was waning. Dinty was filing her nails. She was off to a gathering at the barracks of the 1st Filipino Regiment, who were in training and waiting to return home to their islands with the armies of liberation in the near future. At her side lay two baskets she was weaving. She had made dozens for the Red Cross.

At Kathleen's side rested John Drayton's eighteenth-century edition of Plato's *Early Socratic Dialogues*. He had sent it to her for safe-keeping. She did not know where it had come from because the censor had scored out his address, but it had been wrapped in brown paper and the note inside told her it was very special to him, that he was going somewhere he could not take it, and asked her to hold it for him. In the same message he had alerted her that she would not hear from him for some months. He had signed that letter with the words *Lovingly, John D.* Now that had made all the difference. She rested her hand on the book. To her it embodied the man she loved, and she saw it as a talisman.

'We'd better get ready,' Lexi reminded them. A small Christmas function was to start in the nurses' quarters in an hour and they had agreed to go along and take Lessa just for a little while. They refrained from calling it a party while the war continued.

They stood up and Kathleen whispered, 'I don't really feel like going when so many are still suffering. It doesn't seem right. We're so lucky to be here. It's impossible to explain what being in captivity is like.'

Lexi took up her hand. 'I understand. We won't stay long.'

The same day

Skinny Wainwright's hands were wrapped in pieces of rag for warmth as he wrote in his diary, while a bitter Manchurian wind rushed through the cracks in the ill-made building. The diary was a collection of flyleaves and title pages from the three books he had treasured and read and reread over the years of his imprisonment: Kenneth Roberts's *Oliver Wiswell* and *Northwest Passage* and Stewart Edward White's *The Long Rifle*. His precious chip of lead pencil ran across the paper:

What a travesty on the day. Christmas, hell! I only hope my dear ones at home are happier than I am.

He eyed the two inches of lead pencil which he sharpened with the razor he kept honed by using a tiny concave-shaped razor hone willed to him by Master Sergeant James Cavanaugh before he had died of starvation in the hell-hole camp at Karenko. The pencil had been given to him in Karenko by British General Merton

Beckworth-Smith, a former commander of the Coldstream Guards, a first-class gentleman and soldier.

He was another who had died in Karenko. There were no good memories of that place. General Beckwith-Smith had given a salute to a minor Jap officer who for some reason had not thought it good enough and had punched the general repeatedly in the face. It had not been long after when Beckwith-Smith died of malnutrition, strep throat and the beating. Tenderly Skinny placed the two treasured gifts of pencil and razor hone back in their hiding place, along with the pages.

Brutality had been the daily occurrence at Karenko; he too had been beaten but he had survived. Although he did not doubt that his time in captivity had weakened him.

When he had been a prisoner on Formosa, Skinny and his group of senior officers had been shunted from camp to camp until October 1944. At that time they were moved on a seemingly aimless journey via Kyushu and Fusan to Sheng Tai Tun and finally to this prison near the little Manchurian village of Sian on 1 December.

And now he was enduring another Christmas Day in captivity. He badly missed Tom Dooley and Johnny Pugh, his aides who had been with him until they had been left behind in Formosa. Life was very different without their support.

How he longed for home! He imagined Adele, his wife, in the family home in Skaneateles, New York. He pictured her in her neat woollen suit and sweater with pearls at her throat, as he had seen her a thousand times. God, he missed her!

He looked around the room that he and General 'Ned' Edward King shared. Today was icy, for while the long, low building was fitted with steam heat, it kept breaking down for days, and even weeks, at a time. There was no hot water and he could not recall the last time he had seen a piece of soap. Sometimes the temperature dropped to forty-five degrees Farenheit below zero. Men had died from the cold and the count was rising.

His mind slipped into meditation as it did every single day, meditation on the surrender of Corregidor. Yes, there had been many reasons, but the most compelling had been that there was no aid in sight. He had known they would have all been slaughtered on that island if he had not surrendered. He hoped as he did constantly that history would judge him kindly.

He sighed, unsure of that very point, as a rattling on his door sounded and it opened to reveal Lieutenant Marui behind his spectacles who had arrived for his daily inspection. He had handed out to every one of them an extensive list of instructions on where all items in every area had to be placed or 'punishment would follow'. Certain articles of clothing or bedding had to be on certain shelves in exact position; fire bucket in precise place, down to the need for small tins and metal eating plates to be set with meticulous accuracy. Skinny thought during every inspection how badly Marui needed a psychiatrist.

Amazingly enough the Japanese hurried through and his check took half the time of the usual. Delighted, Skinny saw him off and Marui gave him the habitual departing order, 'Refrain from thinking evil thoughts about Nippon.'

Marui would not have liked the thought which ran through Skinny's head as he bowed and closed the door.

Skinny was shivering when half a minute later there was another rattle upon his door and in walked Private Johnny Kroeze, Netherlands East Indies Army, and Private First Class Lloyd Kelly, United States Army, holding between them a chair.

'Happy Christmas, General. We know you don't have a chair and we reckoned you'd like one.'

Skinny beamed. 'Like one? It's wonderful.'

No prisoner in the entire camp had a chair.

They placed it down and Skinny admired it. It had arms and a sort of shelf on the right-hand side to place a book. The article itself was wooden but the seat was made of canvas.

'For heaven's sake, how did you make this?'

Kelly grinned, his youthful eyes gleaming with the pleasure of giving. 'We found an old cot down next to the latrines. No idea how it got there, but we hooked it.'

Kroeze explained, 'We've been working on it for weeks, sir. The Japs have seen us and at first we felt sure they'd confiscate it, but for some reason they've ignored it.'

Skinny shook hands with them and thanked them. 'Marvellous gift, boys, you've endeared yourselves to me for life.'

That made them laugh.

He eased himself down into the chair and murmured appreciatively. 'My old bones feel good in this, boys. Merry Christmas.'

As they grinned and exited, the general called, 'Let's hope by the grace of God we'll be home for the next one.'

'You bet, sir.'

Skinny sighed loudly to himself. The joy of giving: even in these conditions. 'God bless you, boys,' he said softly as he leant back in his chair.

Same day: Ipswich

Aunt Carly had supplied them with as fine a Christmas dinner as the rations would allow, and they sat at the rosewood dining table while Jeffrey said grace, and finished with the words: 'We pray for all those who have so little when we have so much. And we pray for an end to this terrible war. Amen.'

After they had eaten the small piece of roast beef and before Aunt Carly sliced up the Christmas cake which she had made without raisins or nuts, for there were none to be had, Marlene took an envelope out of her pocket and put on her horn-rimmed glasses, announcing, 'I saved this letter to read until we were all together. It came in Saturday morning's post and it's from Lexi.'

She began:

Dearest Mum and Jeffrey, Aunt Carly and Jane,

Well, here we still are in Port Moresby, and Kathleen and I prevailed on one of the 'walking wounded' at the hospital to cut us down a small tree, so at least our rooms feel a bit like Christmas . . .

As the letter went on, it kept its high-spirited tone and it seemed clear to the family that Lexi was comfortable with her life at the military hospital and happy to be with Kathleen.

It was as she turned to the last page that Marlene paused and took a deep breath and said, 'This is the important bit.'

No doubt you are wondering when you'll see me, and to be truthful I'm not sure. It looks like in Europe the Allies are winning the war and that's how it seems here in the Pacific too, thank God. The war has altered all our lives for ever and it would be too much to contemplate if the other side were winning.

I might stay here in Port Moresby indefinitely, or I might come to North Queensland. I don't think I'll ever return to Hong Kong, too many memories there and all of them so hard to bear. Fortunately, I'm a doctor and work seems to fall my way.

Now, I want you all to understand some important things: Johnny and I were never suited. He is a marvellous man, but he's not for me. He feels the same way about me so don't you all start feeling sorry for him. Please Lord he survives the war, he's a real hero from what I know, but if he does, I reckon he'll be returning to my friend Kathleen Leigh and not to me. That's the first thing. The second is I'm keeping Lessa. She's my child after all we've been through. I will always mourn the loss of my two little boys — yes, that's right, two! Lessa had a brother called Jimmy who was the light of my life after my darling Paul was drowned. So you see, I've got a child to bring up and work to do.

Yes, we'll come down and see you sometime and tell you all sorts of things that'll raise the hair on the back of your necks, but that could be a long while because it will be after the war is over. But please under-stand I've got to choose the time, it has to be right for me.

I truly loved a man I'll never see again. I will love him throughout eternity. There will never be anyone else for me. His name was Hank Trapperton and he took my breath away. Someday I might be able to tell you about him.

That's it. I love you, Mum, and you too, Jeffrey, and I send hugs to you, Aunt Carly, and one to my little sister Jane.

Yours lovingly,

Lexi

Marlene lifted her eyes from the page as tears welled over her lids and dropped to the tablecloth, and Jeffrey leant over and took her hand. 'There, there, darling, we should be happy. She's told us the truth at last.'

Aunt Carly sniffed and commented, 'The war's to blame.'

Jane jumped from the table. 'That's lovely, Mummy. But I'd just better hurry now and change my dress and brush my hair. Dennis is due soon.'

Dennis Knap was Jane's new beau.

She swept out of the room.

'Now,' said Aunt Carly, rising, 'let me clear the table and we'll have a nice game of solo. I'm sure the Lord won't mind us playing cards on his birthday.'

Jeffrey kissed Marlene's hand and smiled.

Chapter Eighty

9 January 1945

'Boom! boom!' Explosions to the left and right spat sand and earth and parts of a Japanese gun emplacement towards the overcast sky as John Drayton dashed along Orange Beach near Lingayen town. Dogfights were plentiful in the sky and kamikazes raced through the air, but the beach seemed deserted now but for their own boys.

Throwing a quick glance over his shoulder, he saw Trap and, to his amazement, an enemy soldier who had appeared out of nowhere and was dropping to his knees to take aim at him. As John Drayton stopped in his tracks, sand sprayed from his boots, and he brought his Tommy gun round and fired. The Japanese toppled forward into the sand as Trap raced up to his friend and halted beside him. He shouted above the booms: 'Thanks, buddy. Where the hell did he come from?'

'Don't know. It's pretty much clear of Japs now.'

John Drayton pointed towards the ditch where he had seen Caldo and Ivat heading. 'Some of the boys are over there, come on.'

They strode rapidly up the beach and slipped into the gully beside Caldo, Ivat, Olsen and Coalclark.

'Where are the others?'

'Back towards Lingayen town.' Caldo pointed his thumb.

John Drayton grunted. 'Good. The rendevous point with Gomez and his boys remains the same. We're to join up at oh ten thirty.'

They were on an elevated section of land overlooking the pebble and sand beach and could see mortar boats riding the swell and barges unloading troops from the 40th Division, XIV Corps of the United States Sixth Army, into a strong surf. Japanese kamikazes strafed the disembarking troops, and in turn, dogfights took place and warships returned fire. It was 0930.

Trap sounded satisfied. 'Well done. From the explosions I'd say we've annihilated any opposition right along the beaches from Lingayen town to the mouth of the Agno. The gun emplacement that just went up was the last one round here. There'll be virtually no resistance when the troops land.'

'Yep, sir, so far so good.' Caldo waved his hand down the beach.

'Anyone hurt?' John Drayton asked.

'Ramez and one of his boys; Ortago, I think,' Olsen answered, wiping sweat from his brow with the back of his hand. 'Ivat and I saw some of his blokes carrying Ramez to safety, didn't we?'

'Yeah, dragged him away, back of the marsh. But Ortago bought it.'

Trap looked at his second-in-command. They both knew the orders: Trap was to remain on the beach and make contact with General Brush of the 40th Division, and to lead an advance platoon along with a mortar unit in a safe direction to the Agno river. John Drayton would join up with Gomez and his group of Filipinos at the rendezvous point near Lingayen town and lead the second wave of 40th Division troops south from the beach to the airstrip and beyond.

Trap lifted his binoculars just as an enemy aircraft flew low over them and they all ducked. 'Shit,' announced Caldo, 'That bandit nearly took our heads off.'

The leader again raised his binoculars and gazed out to sea. 'I reckon General Brush won't come in until he's sure we've got a totally secure beachhead. Could be hours yet, even this afternoon.'

He put the glasses down on the side of the ditch and turned to John Drayton. 'Listen, I'll wait here with Caldo and Olsen. You, Coalclark and Ivat go on to the rendezvous with Gomez.

'As soon as I've made contact with the general and we know what's what, I'll get a wireless message to you and we can join up later.'

'Right.' John Drayton hesitated and caught his friend's eye. 'Can I have a private word with you before I go?'

'Sure, buddy.' They stood and moved off a few yards.

'What's up?'

'Look, I know you think I've gone troppo now that I'm reading the Greek philosophers.'

Trap simply opened his hands palm up and winked. 'They have their place, Johnny, they have their place.'

'Well I reckon they've sure shown me a few things. So I'm not leaving you now without telling you this; it's been hovering on the tip of my tongue long enough.' He took a deep breath. 'When the war's over I've agreed to divorce Lex, you know that. I haven't seen her for a long time, but I know that what she felt for you was lasting; she's in love with you permanently, my friend, but that doesn't mean you won't lose her. No one can wait for ever.'

Trap glanced skywards, showing the whites of his eyes.

'Now listen to me, just for once listen to somebody else and forget the pose. I'd say she loves you more than anyone or anything. I saw how she was the day she told me about you. She told me that unless I forgave her, she couldn't go on. I forgave her, mate, and it's about time you did.'

Trap groaned. 'Jesus, Johnny.'

'Well that's all I have to say.' He put out his hand and Trap took it. 'Be careful, Hank.'

'Sure, Johnny, sure, you too. See you tonight. We'll have some of that rum Gomez's been hoarding.' He lifted his arm to Caldo and Olsen and they all strode off down the ditch to the west.

As Trap stamped away, hoisting the strap of his Tommy gun

over his shoulder, he stared ahead. Yeah, sure, he knew what Johnny had just told him was true. But forgiveness did not come easily to Hank Trapperton. It was not the same for Johnny: he was that way inclined, to see the good side, to forgive, to read the goddam philosophers . . . Jesus.

A picture of the Doll appeared in his head, as it did every damn day: the night in the rubber craft in the cove in Illana Bay, when little Jimmy had drowned. He saw the anguish on her face and what she was going through. That had got to him right enough! He remembered the moment of kissing her palm to help her through it . . . *not because I love her, but to help her through it. Goddam!*

He looked round at Caldo right behind him, who was looking straight back at him as if he were reading Trap's mind. Even Caldo had championed her.

'Come on, let's move.' With the same customary action of straightening his shoulders, he marched on at speed.

John Drayton watched them go and with a grunt of frustration turned back to Coalclark and Ivat. He raised his head and gazed through the murky atmosphere of swirling smoke from the explosions. There was still a long-range enemy gun firing on them from somewhere.

He thought momentarily about the last letter he had written to Kathy, telling her she might not hear from him for a long time. He had sent it with the book Major Chambers had given him. The letters he had written previously he had signed, *Fondly, John Drayton*, but in that last one he had signed, *Lovingly*. He was glad he had done that. Thinking about it now made him feel good.

'Okay, fellas,' he said, exhaling loudly, 'let's move out.'

At noon Trap spoke to General Brush on a wireless set brought in to the beach from one of the warships. The general told him it would be hours before he would come ashore and assume command but he approved that Trap take an advance platoon and three mortar teams overland to the mouth of the Agno river and set up an observation post.

'When you return, report to my command post, Colonel.'

After that Trap spoke to John Drayton on the same set and told him that it would probably be late that night before he, Caldo and Olsen would return to Lingayen and rejoin them.

Around 1600, as heavy clouds clung to the gulf and beaches, Trap led the advance unit of troops in sight of the wide Agno river, a number of small islands littering the delta mouth in the distance.

They made their approach through a rice field and up along solid ground through a stand of palms and knee-high talahib grass to within ten yards of the soggy cliff bank of the river. One of the boys with the 40th ribbed Olsen, 'So, *old Pal*, how long have you been with this Allied commando unit or whatever it is?'

'I just joined it this morning, "*old Buddy*",' Chris Olsen retorted, bringing eyes of fire round to the speaker. 'Amazing how the colonel taught me so fast to clear the bloody beach and pave the way for you, isn't it?'

The soldier laughed. 'Don't get hot under the collar. So where do you guys all come from? You look like a chequered lot.'

Trap answered for Olsen without looking back, his eyes scanning the river. 'It's like this soldier, our commando includes five Aussies, seventy Filipinos, one Brit, and three of us Yanks; and Caldo here who's half-and-half.' He grinned and unclipped his binoculars from his belt and put them to his eyes while he added, 'And both halves are all warrior!'

'Yeah,' grinned Caldo, 'we're a regular little group of mixed metaphors, whatever that is.'

Trap surveyed the river and attached his binoculars back to his belt. 'All seems clear.' He moved gingerly along the edge of the river bank.

At that second there was an explosion to their right and bits of palm trees flew into the air. 'Hit the deck!' They all dived to the ground.

'Where's it coming from?'

'Not sure.'

'From behind, I think,' Trap shouted, hurriedly calculating the distance to the ruins of a collection of nipa huts and one half-demolished cement wall further along the bank where he knew he could take cover and reassess what was going on. 'Get the mortar teams up here pronto. Let's make for that section of wall. Come on, Caldo, Olsen!'

The three-man mortar teams ran forward carrying their guns and ammunition as another blast went off behind them and two of their number stumbled and fell.

'Shit!' Caldo yelled. 'There, look!'

Down the slope beyond the palms they saw four Japanese: one about to hurl another grenade.

Trap got off a burst of Tommy gun fire, as did Caldo at his side, and the enemy soldier with the grenade crumpled.

'Let's go,' Trap shouted and charged towards the partly standing wall. He was ahead of Caldo by about six yards and the mortar teams and Olsen were making good time behind them, followed by the soldiers when the bank of the river in front of Trap exploded. Kaboom! Blue, red and orange flames vaulted up and out in blazing streaks of light! Clumps of dirt, fragments of palm trees and chunks of rock hurtled into the air, reaching high towards the lowering clouds.

They all fell headlong into the dirt, and when Caldo raised his eyes the entire section of river bank in front of him where Trap had been running – some eight yards long and five wide – had caved in and hurtled into the river, where the free-flowing Agno was fast flooding into the created opening.

Caldo was on his hands and knees and his head spun to the river, his eyes rotating, searching wildly for a sight of the colonel. 'Shit, no . . .' Two palm trunks swirled out towards midstream, and for a moment of brain-tingling hope he peered at them but they swivelled in the fast-moving current, stood end up and disappeared.

His head swung, upstream, downstream: nothing. Only the river churning and flowing at speed towards the gulf.

The colonel, *his* colonel, had been right there, right there in front of him, not six yards away, running and alive and yelling at them to follow!

The ground had gone, their leader had gone.

He crawled a few feet, hefted himself to his knees and looked around in amazement, his eyes wide and mouth open. Olsen was rolling over, covered in dirt, two yards away; the mortar teams were sprawled out beyond him and the rest of the boys were raising their mud-covered heads and beginning to scramble unsteadily to their feet.

'Jesus!' exclaimed Olsen, whose scalp trickled with blood. 'That was close. Let's get down to that bloody shelter quick smart so we can get our mortars going.'

They all rose and ran on but Caldo did not move. He was still on his knees staring at the spot where Trap had been.

Olsen, who had dashed forward a few steps, suddenly realised who was missing and halted and turned back.

'Oh God!'

Caldo did not speak; he knelt there shaking his head. A wound on his massive right bicep was beginning to ooze blood, but he was oblivious to that. Behind him in surreal stark relief half a palm trunk was burning and sparks discharged into the air.

Olsen ran back to him. 'Oh God, mate, come on.' He began tugging at the big man's good arm. He saw the tears running down Caldo's cheeks. Olsen would never have believed that the sergeant could cry. He was staggered: the colonel gone, blown apart, Caldo on his knees, weeping!

'Shit, Sarge, come on. You know he'd want us to.'

Caldo jerked his arm free and continued to kneel, shaking his big, craggy, dirt-covered head.

Olsen was panicking. 'He wouldn't want us to die too, I just know he wouldn't.' He pulled again at Caldo, the rock, but it made no impression.

By now the mortar teams were down behind the standing section of the ruined building and had a line on the enemy. They began firing.

The ground shook with blasts as Caldo's eyes lifted to the smoke-filled darkening sky. His voice broke. 'But he . . . can't be gone. Not the colonel. Not after living through hell a hundred times . . .'

'But he *is* gone. Come on, mate, please.'

'You go.'

'No, not without you.'

The mortar boys were shattering trees down the slope and aiming at a spot near the rice field. Pieces of trees, dirt and stone were shooting upwards in the distance and gunfire was still rattling through the palms and talahib grass. Fires burnt all around.

'All right, we'll both stay here and get *shot dead.*' Olsen sat down heavily on the ground and put his gun on the dirt.

'Shit,' Caldo whispered, closing his eyes briefly before his mountainous body shuddered into action and he staggered to his feet. He looked once more out into the river in disbelief and grunted in anguish.

Olsen picked up Caldo's Tommy gun and handed it to him. 'Come on, Sarge.' And side by side they trotted along the bank into cover.

Trap was spinning through red and yellow and blue and purple flashes; dancing, blazing lights all around! The noise was unbearable. There was pain somewhere, bad pain, and yet he somehow knew his arms and legs were flailing in the river. He struggled madly . . . his mouth was filling with water. He thought he might black out when he felt himself pulled sharply at violent speed through the water as if a giant hand had snatched him and dragged him along. *Jesus Christ, what's that?*

His face was above water! He gulped in the sweet, precious air of life and immediately he was underwater again. What was going on? He spun around and swirled in the current at an enormous rate.

His senses were blocked; all he knew was the gushing speed of his transit underwater in the river and he pushed and twisted and gyrated to try and free himself from whatever force it was that held him. His head burst up above the surface again and in the second he sucked in more air he realised he was attached to a tree trunk. He pulled and jerked as he went under again, and *snap!* The power slackened. He was released. The mad ride ended.

He could not feel his body now, just throbbing somewhere, yet he knew his head was above water and he knew he was still being compelled by the current. But he had the air on his face and he was loose of the trunk and was not going to drown.

Relax into it. Just stay above water. Let it take you wherever the hell it's going.

Caldo and the boys soon established that one pocket of Japanese in a pillbox was responsible for most of the mayhem, and after getting a line on it they mounted a mortar attack and charged it, blowing it apart and relieving the area of invaders.

By nightfall on 9 January, the 40th Division of XIV Corps of General Krueger's Sixth Army had secured a beachhead which ran from the mouth of the Agno river to Lingayen town with a depth inland of approximately three and a half miles, including the possession of Lingayen airfield. Beyond the town the 37th Division had been similarly successful all the way to Dagupan. It had been the same triumph for I Corps all along the southern side of Lingayen Gulf.

And even though there appeared to be a gale brewing for tonight, satisfaction reigned. As rain began and the breeze gained momentum and dark of night oozed over Luzon, the soldiers of liberation put up their tents and found billets in disused buildings, and slept victorious.

Chapter Eighty-one

The voice of Jake Williams called, 'Colonel Whitby, message coming in for you.'

They had set up their wireless transmitter in a front room of a rambling hotel called *Maribago* on the west of Lingayen town near a salt-water stream. The smell of the mangroves wafted through the glassless windows as John Drayton mumbled, 'About time,' and strode down the candlelit corridor and over to the wireless set standing on a dusty table.

'Thanks, Sparks,' he joked, taking the large microphone from Williams, and placing his right boot up on a wooden stool, balanced on the edge of the table with his free hand. 'Whitby here.'

'Yes, Colonel, Thirty-seventh Division Headquarters here. I've got a message in from a forward platoon bivouacked in Section P.'

John Drayton knew Section P was at the mouth of Agno river where Trap and the boys were. 'Yes, go ahead, over.'

'The message is that Sergeant Caldo will make the rendezvous point as soon as possible tomorrow.'

John Drayton frowned. 'Are you with him?'

'No, sir, I've taken a wireless message only. Over.'

The Thirty-seventh were on the far side of Lingayen town to the east; how had they become involved? John Drayton frowned. 'Is that all? Over.'

'Yes, sir, I'm doing a favour by relaying it. Over and out.'

John Drayton pursed his lips in thought as he returned the microphone to Williams, who shrugged. They both thought it odd that Trap had not reached them himself; but still, there was a war going on!

They headed back to the boys, the sound of their boots echoing on the mosaic floor as they returned down the wide corridor which at one time must have been beautiful. For even now the murals on the walls retained a certain amount of colour and the gold beading along the edge of the mosaic floor, though chipped and dirty, spoke of former glory. The owner, a slight fellow with broken teeth, and called Arroyo had begun selling the soldiers and freedom-fighters liquor from his well-hidden, obviously bomb-proof cellar. John Drayton could see into a room ahead where Gomez and his boys were enjoying the landlord's hospitality by candlelight. Two or three Filipinas had appeared from somewhere and were dancing to the clapping hands of the freedom-fighters who had pitched tents outside, across a cobbled street on the bank of a stream. All seemed set for the night.

The commandos were sharing this hotel with a company of Engineers. One wing was damaged on the western side and John Drayton had commandeered a sizeable room at the back that contained a cot in it and was reasonably clean. Most of them had been able to have a bath and clean clothes had been supplied to them by the quartermaster corps set up under a tarpaulin on the edge of town. As Ivat explained, 'The quartermaster sergeant took pity on Bird and me and gave us clean duds even without requisition forms.'

They had eaten well, for two cooked fowls had been sent over to John Drayton, compliments of Marine Colonel Leopold Jackworth. The birds had gone beautifully with the rice and beans which the cooks from C Company had supplied. At least they would go to bed with full stomachs.

The expectant faces of Coalclark, Howard, Ivat, Bird and Smith lifted towards them as they entered the small annexe where the commandos were seated on boxes drinking beer.

'The others are coming in tomorrow morning; something's delayed them. I'm going to turn in.'

Williams sat down as Coalclark stood up beside John Drayton. 'Me too, I'm for the sack.' They said their good nights and both picked up their Tommy guns, slung their leather magazine pouches over their shoulders and wandered outside into the cloudy dark night.

John Drayton took out his torch and shone a beam of light for them to make their way across the cement yard over hunks of rubble and debris as a drizzle of rain began. Coalclark pointed back over his shoulder with his thumb towards the clapping and shouting. 'Don't think we'll get much sleep for a while.'

'It won't make any difference to me, I'm pretty weary.'

'I'll come in and light your candle,' Coalclark offered.

'No thanks, I've got some matches.'

They wished each other a good night's sleep and parted.

Inside his room, John Drayton lit the candle and took off his tunic and boots. Ivat and Bird, who had become the unofficial quartermasters, had supplied blankets, and at least the landlord had mattresses on the beds. He was pleased to have clean clothes. Their own uniforms were back in their hideout across a ford of the Agno in the foothills of the Zambales mountains, and he doubted he would ever see them again.

Musing on the nonpareil of a clean shirt and trousers, he lay down and fell asleep.

He awoke not long after dawn. The winter air was cold and humid but at least the window pane was not broken so the rain was kept out. He splashed his face with cold water to wake himself. The wind was making crying noises. He tilted his head to listen as it gusted again in another whine. Was it only the wind? Or was that a human sound?

He pulled on his boots and buttoned up his tunic. The wind dropped momentarily, but he could still hear something like sobbing. He opened the door and the strong breeze carried the smell of food cooking. Great! The good old cooks were making breakfast somewhere.

Out on to the cement of the yard he strode. It was a drab, chill morning, and he paused listening. *Somebody was crying somewhere.* He followed the sound in the falling rain along the narrow alley at the side of his room and halted in front of five steps down to a door which appeared to be the entrance to a cellar immediately underneath the room in which he had slept. The door was half open and he strode down the steps and pushed it aside.

Three sets of eyes lifted to him in tear-stained faces grubby with dirt; the children huddled together on a piece of filthy carpet. They had obviously been abandoned. One was only about three; he was doing the crying. The other two, who were clinging to him, were a boy of about five and a girl of perhaps nine.

'Well hello.' It was not an unusual thing; displaced children would be one of the world's biggest problems for the foreseeable years. He had seen many in the islands of the South Pacific. Some local adult usually helped out, but not always. A soldier had to harden his heart, but at least he could feed these three, and perhaps Gomez or the landlord would take them to someone who would care.

'Come on.' John Drayton lifted the youngest and urged the other two ahead of him out into the rain. The smell of the food took him over to the eastern side of the courtyard, where he met Ivat and Bird.

'What have you got there, sir?'

'Three Filipino kids, obviously abandoned. Let's get them some grub.'

The cooks, three corporals and a private, made grumbling noises, but they dished out some bacon and tinned beans for them all the same, and the children's eyes widened in their dirty faces as they eyed the food with wonder and began to eat it with their hands.

'No, stop that! Here ...' Ivat handed the two older ones a spoon each and began to feed the baby himself.

'Jeez,' Bird grinned, 'you're a regular little mother, Corporal.'

'Ah, shaddup.'

Ivat's nose twitched. 'These kids need a bath worse than us,' he commented as the children wolfed down the food, their eyes constantly roaming back and forth in amazement at the soldiers and the activity around them.

'What time do you think the colonel and Caldo and Olsen will be here?' Bird asked John Drayton.

'If they've managed to commandeer a vehicle, I'd say any time. Colonel Trapperton and I have to see top brass here this morning. Find out what's required of us now.' He looked around. 'Where are Gomez and his boys?'

Ivat pointed to the rear of the establishment with the spoon he held. 'Getting ready to leave, sir, behind the hotel. They're all a little worse for wear after last night, but Gomez said they were off to make plans for killing some more Japs.'

John Drayton stood up. 'Listen, you two, bring these kids along now. I reckon I might be able to get Gomez to take them to Louisa.'

Ivat dolloped a last spoonful into the baby's mouth and the little girl took another piece of toast in her hand as they hurried to follow John Drayton. 'Come on.' Ivat lifted the littlest in his arms as Bird herded the other two.

The rain had ceased, though the sky still maintained the threat of another downpour, and behind the Maribago sure enough, across the cobbled street in a muddy field of nipa palms, Gomez and his infantry were mounting their bicycles on the bank of a shallow stream which ran out into the mangroves of Lingayen Gulf.

'Hey, Gomez?'

The Filipino turned his moustached face, one thin leg hung over the bar of his bike. He wore muddy black boots, grimy white trousers, a bullet-filled bandolier across his chest and carried a .3 calibre semi-automatic MI Garand rifle, which had been supplied by the Allies in an air-drop two months before. A tattered red scarf around his neck danced in the wind and completed the picture. 'Hey, Colonel, we return to our place.' That was Gomez's euphemism for the hideout.

He raised his MI in the air and chuckled. 'You will remember your promise.' He spoke with an American accent, his vocabulary was wide and he often referred to his *personal guro* when he was growing up, giving those who listened to believe he had the advantage of wealth and a private tutor. But Gomez's bearing and manners belied his claim; he possessed all the trade-marks of a peasant and brigand, but he had learnt exemplary, almost accentless English, somewhere, and his intelligence was never in doubt.

Gomez fell perfectly into the mould for a resistance fighter. The fact was that the large percentage of Filipinos who had collaborated with the Japanese were the upper classes of the political and financial elite, ordinary and low-class Filipinos had remained true to the struggle against the violators of their country.

'When you talk to the general today, hey? Tell him we want Tommy guns, mortars, jeeps and vehicles, so we can keep damaging the Japs. This is very important to us and to you, Colonel, yes? You'll do this for me, huh? Remember how we have helped you.'

'Sure.' John Drayton smiled. Gomez would probably turn his grandmother in to get guns and ammunition. It was uncertain just what the partisan leader would do when peace came, but the one thing he would not be was a law-abiding citizen. Yet he had been very handy to have on the Allies' side for the last few months. Ramez, his partner, was a softer character, but he had taken a bullet in the stomach.

'How's Ramez?'

'He's been taken back to our place. Not sure, might be bad.'

'Listen, Gomez, see these three kids?'

'I do.'

'Well, I found them in a cellar on their own. God knows who they belong to, but their families sure aren't here now. Probably got separated when they moved out ahead of the Allied landings. Will you take them to your girlfriend? She'll know somebody who'll look after them.'

Gomez grunted. 'What do I want with three kids? Forget it, Colonel.'

'Come on, Gomez, where's your heart? The army can't keep them. They're Filipinos like you and just abandoned little kids. Louisa has family, friends. So do your boys. Somebody you know will take care of them.'

Gomez's eyes narrowed. 'How much?'

'Jesus, Gomez! Have a heart.'

The Filipino looked straight into the soldier's eyes. 'That's your weakness, Colonel. Too much heart. I have seen it. The other one, Trapperton, he is colder, no heart.' He waved his MI. 'Answer me, please, Colonel. Will you requisition more guns and ammunition and mortars and jeeps like I need?'

'You know I can't do that. I have no real authority here. I'm in a commando, for God's sake, not the regular army!'

'Then go to your friends the Americans; they have authority.' Gomez mounted his bicycle.

'Find somebody else, old friend,' the Filipino called, and began to ride away along the bank of the stream.

John Drayton looked at the three waifs: dirty hair, filthy faces, ragged clothes, bare feet. He wished he had left them in the cellar. After all, there were thousands of deserted kids, for one reason or another, all over war zones. Gomez did not care about them. But damn it, he *had* taken the little buggers out of the cellar and he felt responsible for them. Plato and Socrates had taught him about truth and moral value in all actions. 'Damn! Why did I read you Greeks?' he said aloud, before he shouted, 'Gomez! Wait on!'

Gomez stopped and climbed off his bicycle and so did his

men, who all proceeded to take out and light Lucky Strike cigarettes which the soldiers had supplied to them the previous night.

John Drayton strode up the muddy track to the partisan chief. 'Listen. I'll have to find the right ordnance officer, it'll take a while, but if I promise to do that, to request the guns and ammunition—'

'And the mortars?' Gomez grinned.

'Yes, and the mortars.'

'And the jeeps?'

'Jesus, Gomez, I think that might be pushing your luck. Look, I'll do it. I'll ask for what you want. Now please, take the kids.' He gestured back to them.

Gomez shrugged. 'I trust you. You will do as you say.' He turned to his men and spoke in Tagalog. Three dismounted their bicycles as Bird and Ivat took the children along the bank of the stream to make the handover.

Each of the three partisans hoisted a child up on the bar of his bicycle, and as one of them lifted the middle child – the little boy of about five – he overbalanced. The bicycle fell on to his leg; he yelped in pain as his comrades burst out laughing, and the boy dropped to the ground and tumbled down the four-foot bank to land unceremoniously face first, in the shallow running water. The troupe of men guffawed as the man cursed and rubbed his leg and regained his bike, while the child lifted himself up out of the stream and stood up shivering and began to cry.

John Drayton stared down at the child. The current had rinsed the boy's face and hair. He was fair-headed and now his face was clean, he did not have the olive skin of a Filipino but was light-skinned. As he climbed up the bank whimpering, John Drayton could see his eyes were not dark; in fact they were blue.

Gomez was the first to comment. 'Hey! That kid's got fair hair! He's not pure Filipino, must be a half-caste offspring of Big Boss General MacArthur!' He laughed loudly at his own joke and slapped his thigh as those of his men who spoke English hooted with mirth.

The child, still sobbing, wiped his eyes, looking warily up at them, and the guerrilla fighter meant to carry the boy seemed to have lost interest in him and moved away.

Gomez yelled, 'Who's going to carry the kid?'

Another shouted that he would and began to wheel his bike back through the throng.

'Come on, son,' John Drayton announced, and bent to lift the shivering child across to his new keeper. The little fellow raised his arms, and in that second he exposed the inside of his wrist . . . revealing a diamond-shaped brown birthmark.

John Drayton felt slightly light-headed as he raised the child and held him. He turned the little one's arm around to view the mark again. It was undeniable. He had only ever seen such a distinctive birthmark on one infant in his life. It had been on Paul's wrist, the baby he had called his own, the baby who had been drowned when the *Fortitude* sank; went down at the mouth of the Lingayen Gulf approximately four years ago!

The boy in his arms was exactly the right age. God, now he studied him, he could even see a resemblance to Hank, and the blue eyes? Yes, they had Lexi's expression in them.

Lord God in heaven, this is Paul!

Gomez was screwing up one eye and squinting at him. 'Hey, Colonel, you look bad. Your face is pale. Aren't you feeling well?'

Bird and Ivat wondered just what the devil was going on.

'What's wrong, Colonel?' Gomez queried again.

'Would you ask the girl about this child, please? Ask her if he is her brother. Or who he is.'

Gomez wiped his nose with the back of his hand. 'Colonel? Colonel? First you desperately want us to take the kids away and now you waste my time by asking questions about them.'

'Just do it, Gomez, go on.'

The Filipino grunted and swivelled on his bicycle and spoke

638

to the girl. When she replied he nodded and turned back. 'She says yes, he is her brother. Now can we go?'

John Drayton did not release the soaking boy; his mind raced. 'Ask her where he came from.'

Gomez sniggered and retaliated, 'From the same place we all do, Colonel!' The men who understood English hooted loudly.

'Don't play games, Gomez. Just ask her where he came from.'

Gomez wanted the military supplies badly, so he shrugged his wiry shoulders once again and did as requested. This time the girl's answer elicited a croak of surprise from the freedom-fighter as he gazed back at John Drayton. 'Ah, now this is truly odd. She says *he came from the sea.*'

John Drayton looked steadily at the boy in his arms; the child was wet and trembling with cold but he had stopped crying. Gomez's men had fallen silent, all interested to see what happened next.

As he spoke again, John Drayton's voice sounded distant and thin. He spoke very slowly. 'Yes, I think so . . . from the sea.' And now he amazed his listeners. 'I'm keeping this boy, Gomez. So you only have two to find homes for. Explain to the little girl that I know who this boy really is; that yes, he did come from the sea just as she says and that I know his real mother and must return him to her.'

Gomez was out of his depth now. This was a most peculiar turn of events. 'What the hell's going on, Colonel? You say you know who he is?'

'I do.'

'Mary, Mother of God.' He crossed himself. 'From the sea?' But he recovered quickly and holding his MI high announced loudly, 'Don't forget the weapons, Colonel, and the jeep! You've promised!' And with that he sped off on his bicycle, followed by his men.

John Drayton handed the boy to the perplexed Ivat to hold while he took off his clean tunic, and wrapping the boy in it, retrieved him and walked away. The child looked around almost happily from his eyrie in the soldier's arms. This was all strange and exciting to him, and while he was but very young, he somehow felt the importance of what had occurred and had some sense that this man who bore him along was doing something wonderful just for him.

Passing down the alleyway, John Drayton strode by the cellar where he had found Paul and entered the cement courtyard accompanied by Ivat and Bird, who were speechless.

A mud-covered jeep swung through an opening in the concrete side wall and pulled up beside them. It contained Caldo and Olsen, and as they scrambled out of the vehicle, Williams, Coalclark, Howard and Smith exited the courtyard rooms where they had slept.

'Hey, good to see you,' called Howard, while Williams shouted, 'Where's the Colonel?' And Coalclark enquired, 'Who's the kid, sir?'

John Drayton did not speak. He was still trying to contend with what he had discovered, still grappling with the truth of what he held in his arms so that when Caldo answered he did not really understand it.

'Colonel Trapperton was blown up yesterday. Grenade exploded and ripped the whole area he was standing on apart.'

Nobody moved. It was like a communal holding of breath. The dripping of water from the slate roof plopped over-loudly and too emphatically into the open tank beside them as John Drayton came back to reality to see the commandos' faces: appalled, stiff with disbelief.

'What? What was that? I did not hear.'

Caldo's voice broke as he managed to say it a second time. 'Colonel Trapperton was blown up yesterday. Grenade exploded and ripped the whole area he was standing on apart.'

Chapter Eighty-two

Hank Trapperton gone? John Drayton felt a hazy pain begin in his head. No! Hank had marched through life, a gargantuan personality; God! he had marched through John Drayton's life. Even in his disorientation he could not help but see the irony in that thought. He looked at the child in his arms. The little boy's face was within inches of his own; the child he had held and cuddled as a baby, the child he had believed was his. A swell of sadness overcame him.

Hank Trapperton was gone and his son was found!

> The glories of our blood and state
> Are shadows, not substantial things;
> There is no armour against fate;
> Death lays his icy hand on kings . . .

He realised a light rain had begun to fall and he became aware of the commandos standing around him, all talking over each other, except for Williams, who had moved away from the others and stood apart looking up at the lowering sky. Caldo's and Olsen's shoulders drooped as they were inundated with questions.

It was Rupert Coalclark who brought some order. 'Come on, lads, we're all in shock. Let's get inside out of the rain and let Caldo and Olsen tell us what happened more calmly.'

John Drayton shook himself and rallied. 'The captain's right; come on.'

In the small hall which Landlord Arroyo called the Vestibulo they listened as Caldo began. When he got to the aftermath of the explosion he stopped speaking and hunched forward in despair. Olsen completed the account.

John Drayton stood in front of the sombre assembly and placed Paul down on the floor. He had partly regained his equanimity, and as the men muttered he spoke firmly to them. 'We're all devastated by the loss of Colonel Trapperton, but we've got to pull ourselves together, to rally ... for him. Hell, think of what he would want us to do, hard as it is.

'I must go to see the general this morning and we'll find out what's what. Until then there isn't a lot we can do except clean our guns and check our ammo, and you all remain here at the Maribago for my return.' He glanced at Caldo. 'Oh, and hang on to that jeep, it'll come in handy. And somebody should bath this kid and clean him up.' He looked at Ivat and Bird. 'You blokes should be able to do that.'

Paul gazed up from his seat on the floor; even after being deserted and soaked he appeared resilient, for he was playing with a ball of cotton he had found under a chair. *How typical of a son of Hank Trapperton to come through this as if it were all normal.*

John Drayton motioned to him. 'I happen to know for certain that this kid was a survivor from a civilian ship which was torpedoed at the mouth of the Lingayen Gulf by the Japanese in late 1941. It's not speculation. I recognise him by the diamond-shaped birthmark on his wrist, and the fact that he's the right age and Anglo Saxon-looking.

'So let's break up now. We can't help by going over the loss of the colonel any more.' He nodded to Caldo. 'A word, Sergeant, please.'

Caldo followed him to the side window, where the rain streaked the window pane as they conversed. 'Sergeant, you're the only one here who is aware of the complications which surrounded Colonel Trapperton, Dr Robinson and myself.'

Caldo nodded. 'I didn't make it my business, sir, it sort of unravelled bit by bit.'

'Yes, I suppose it did and it's all right, Sergeant, it's just that I think it wise for you to know a little more about this boy I found; in case anything happens to me. He was with Dr Robinson ... my wife ... aboard the SS *Fortitude* when it sank. It would appear he's been with Filipinos ever since, but now I must return him to her. She's in Port Moresby at a military hospital.'

Caldo's eyes widened. 'Shit.'

'Yes, indeed.' John Drayton paused a moment. 'I also deem it best that you are aware the child's name is Paul and that he's Colonel Trapperton's son, not mine.'

Caldo's mouth opened. He was suffering badly from the death of his colonel and not much was making sense to him, but to hear this was staggering. Involuntarily he turned to look at Paul, who was being carried out to be washed by Ivat. 'Oh, shit.'

'Yes, Sergeant, exactly.' John Drayton took a long, deep breath and eyed his companion. 'So we must ensure that he's returned to his mother. You're Filipino, so you at least belong to this country and can see that the right things are done for the child, if need be.'

Caldo's voice came softly out of his cumbersome frame. 'It's like some morbid dream. And now the kid ...' He was incapable of saying any more. He was thinking of all that had occurred, of all he had been through with Trap and of how he had hoped that one day the colonel might see sense and return the love the Doc carried for him. He studied the man in front of him. He respected and liked John Drayton Whitby. He could not really know the ramifications of what must have gone on, but he had seen this man in all sorts of situations; seen him act with care towards his men and seen his strength and his capabilities. Colonel Whitby was quite a man in his own right. 'I will do whatever needs to be

643

done, and thanks for paying me the honour of telling me, but nothing better happen to you, sir, because I don't intend to be around. So I sure as hell hope you deliver the little guy safely to his mother.'

'What does that mean?'

'I know you'll be seeing the top brass soon, and God knows what they've got in store for us. But if it's nothing, if there's no operation planned for us straight away, do you think you could get permission for me to stay here?'

'In the Philippines?'

'Actually here. I want to go looking . . . I *need* to go looking . . . Well, fact is, I badly want to get back down to the mouth of the Agno.' His face crinkled and he let out a long breath. 'I want to mosey around, sir, mosey about.'

John Drayton's expression softened. 'He's dead, Caldo.'

Caldo shrugged. 'Yeah. But I've got to go back there. To the spot. To really look around. It's like a . . . ?'

'Pilgrimage?'

'Yeah, that's right, Colonel, that's the word.' He moved awkwardly from one foot to the other. 'But it's not just a pilgrimage, you see, sir. I just don't believe the colonel's dead.'

'Oh Caldo, don't you realise that's hope talking and not reality?'

'It might be, but it's something I must do. To go and look for him; to look and to find out if my feeling here inside is either right or wrong. We all know how many men have died in this goddam war, but I have to be absolutely sure about this particular one.'

'I'll do what I can.' John Drayton looked at his watch: it was only 0730 hours. It seemed like such a long time since he had risen from bed. He noticed Caldo's arm was bandaged. 'Bad wound, Sergeant?'

'Nah, sir, a scratch. I just wish I could have traded places with the colonel.'

The senior officer's face showed his thoughts. Caldo was not a man for idle talk, but he did not know any man who would swap places with a dead one. He examined Caldo's eyes and his rugged brown face, and there amongst the lines and crevices he saw the depths of feeling: the pain of regret, the sadness of loss and a strength of belief like the truth the ancient Greeks wrote about. To find any of that in Sergeant Caldo's face, the face of the archetypal commando, was confounding to him. It reinforced the meaning of true friendship and honour.

'Yes, I believe you do wish that, Caldo. The colonel had a rare friend in you, Sergeant, he truly did.'

By 0800 that morning an eight-foot surf, kicked up by the strong winds, accompanied the rain and made it impossible to unload to the beaches from the transports anchored in the gulf. Valuable vehicles, equipment and the material for Bailey bridges were needed, but the troops still pushed on inland and a new landing area for the supplies was found in the mouth of the Dagupan river.

It was an hour later when a message came for John Drayton, informing him that his meeting with General Brush was now a meeting with General Walter Krueger himself, in the Capitol Building in Lingayen at 1100 hours.

Howard and Williams took him in the jeep, rolling down the byways past the numerous fishponds of Lingayen and the hardy nipa palms which still stood in the badly damaged town, much the result of the Allied liberation forces' bombardment of the previous days. They pulled up outside the sandbagged front of the dominating Capitol Building. Many of its graceful ionic columns along the façade were smashed and the roof on the domed front had gone completely. Only one section of rooms overlooking the airfield remained intact. This had been taken over by General Krueger's staff.

Williams and Howard dismounted with John Drayton and waited outside while he was passed from officer to officer until at last he fell into the hands of Colonel Kenneth Pierce, Krueger's deputy chief of staff, a good-looking man in his thirties with a pleasant smile and abundant bottom lip.

'Follow me. The old man's just returned from inspecting the beaches. He's in here.'

They found the general with his head down perusing charts on trestle tables and drinking coffee and smoking a cigar. He lifted his clean-shaven face to the newcomer.

'Colonel Whitby? Come in.' He had a sharp, unequivocal way of talking and, one suspected, a sharp mind as well. He beckoned the newcomer to his side. They shook hands.

'After a conversation with General Brush I've heard what happened to Trapperton. Bad, very bad. Result? I've asked my staff to make some enquiries about what to do with you and Commando Double X, as you're in my sector.'

John Drayton was grateful. 'Thanks. The men are still recovering from the loss. Things aren't ever going to be the same for them without Colonel Trapperton.'

'Yes, understandable. He had a pretty unusual reputation. Some people seemed to think he was invincible.'

John Drayton shook his head at that, momentarily closing his eyes.

'Colonel Whitby, you've gained a pretty fine reputation yourself. Truth is, I wanted to take a look at you close-up. That raid you and Trapperton made in Rabaul is becoming legend.'

John Drayton did not know that. 'Thanks, sir. Though it's soured now, without Hank around.'

'Hank?'

'Colonel Trapperton.'

'Oh, right, how true. He'll receive a posthumous Medal of Honour, no doubt about it.' His old man would have been proud. I knew Bill in the Great War. Fine guy.'

John Drayton blinked. Trap would not care about a Medal of Honour: he had a chestful of medals that meant nothing to him

646

as it was. But he decided this was not the moment for truth. 'Yes, I suppose so.'

The general puffed on his cigar while the wind charged through the open areas and rattled the few remaining pieces of glass in the windows. 'What we've done is sent off a message about you to the cruiser USS *Boise*. General MacArthur's aboard; he's sailed up from Mindoro on it. You come directly under his command.' He looked to Pierce. 'Any news on that?'

'Not yet.'

Krueger asked, 'How many of you are there?'

'Nine of us now Colonel Trapperton's gone. We're a motley crew, Australian and American, and one British officer. I also have Sergeant Caldo with us; he's an ex-Filipino Scout.'

Suddenly a siren screamed and the three of them hit the tiled floor together and ended up side by side under a trestle table. An explosion shook the foundations and some plaster fell from the remaining walls. Through the babble of voices outside they heard, 'A single Jap bomber, came out of nowhere!'

The general looked into John Drayton's eyes under the table and chuckled. 'Bugger must have known we're having difficulty bringing our big guns ashore in that swollen surf!' They rolled out from under the table as the all-clear sounded.

'You nearly didn't get to your birthday sir,' commented Pierce as they rose.

Walter Krueger smiled, picked up the dropped cigar and climbed to his feet. 'That's one thing General MacArthur and I have in common, same birthday.' He laughed, a brusque sound. 'But I'm a year younger.'

He dusted his uniform. 'We're leaving combat units all along the shore; we don't want any enemy attacks on our flank as we move south. Whitby, you can share billets and messes, quartermaster stores and ordnance with any of them for as long as you're here.'

'Thank you very much, sir.'

'Does the commando have its own wireless transmitter?' Colonel Pierce asked.

'Yes, we do.'

'Then give me your frequency and we'll get General MacArthur's intelligence on the *Boise* to contact you without going through us.'

John Drayton felt the interview was drawing to a close, so he asked for the weapons, ammunition and jeep for Gomez. 'He and his men have put up a good fight for us, sir. He's got his own intentions but he's on our side against the Japs, that's for sure, and you've got his help until it's no longer needed.'

Krueger grunted. 'Okay. Colonel Pierce will see he gets the mortars and the weapons and ammunition, but we can't run to a jeep.' His hand shot out to John Drayton, who took it.

'Thank you, General Krueger.'

'Glad I met you, Colonel Whitby. Sorry again about Trapperton. He was amazing and as professional as they come. Good luck.'

As it happened, MacArthur did request John Drayton to report aboard the light cruiser USS *Boise*.

It was evening on the 12th when he took a PT boat out to the ship and met with General Richard Sutherland, who offered General Willoughby's apologies for not being there. He, after all, was MacArthur's head of intelligence, and John Drayton had expected to see him. Sutherland took his visitor down to the ward room and there, over a brandy, revealed in a manner as diplomatic as was possible that Commando Double X was to be disbanded.

'It appears there's been some disagreement inside the Allied Intelligence Bureau as to who would take over now that Trapperton's gone. These things are always complicated, particularly when it involves people like you in special units. You'll understand that, Whitby. Whatever the reason, it seems preferable to the AIB that we demobilise the unit.'

John Drayton was aware that this meant American Intelligence did not want him to take command and Australian Intelligence did. More than once he and Trap had spoken about the jealousies between Allied commands. He could hear Hank in his head: *Pettiness, Johnny, it's everywhere from High Command down to the foot-sloggers. Let's not have any of it. We're all fighting the same war.*

John Drayton felt it could stem from MacArthur himself. He knew he had certainly incensed the general at their one meeting in Hollandia. He smiled wryly in recollection.

He focused on Sutherland, who was still talking '. . . So General Willoughby preferred me to inform you, bit awkward for him, wasn't his decision.'

John Drayton made no reply and Sutherland kept on speaking.

'So, Whitby, congratulations on all your successful missions to date. Please pass on General MacArthur's personal compliments to your men. There'll be citations in it for all of you, have no doubt.' Sutherland's hand lifted to the steward to pour him more brandy as he continued. 'You've all played your part in the success of the landings here. The battle front is moving south into Bataan and central Luzon. We have great expectations. We hope to liberate Manila in a few weeks.'

'Yes, I understand, but back to the commando, sir. It's being disbanded, so what happens to us now?'

'You'll leave for New Guinea once I can get you a ride. The AIB office there is expecting you. They might pass you on to Townsville, but being a colonel you can probably make your own choice on that. There'll be a certain amount of furlough for all of you.'

'I see. Then regarding Sergeant Caldo, I'd like to ask you something.'

'Shoot.'

'He has requested permission to remain here in the Lingayen Gulf.'

'Really?'

'He's the best of men, General Sutherland. Fine soldier, fine commando. None better. He's not asking for a discharge. He's

649

asking for permission to remain here. As you just said, we'll all be getting leave, so call it that. He sure deserves it. The others will be happy to accompany me.'

Sutherland squeezed his lips between his thumb and forefinger as he considered the request.

'He's been an exemplary soldier, sir. In fact I'd recommend him for a commission. He's outstanding.'

'Yes . . . but at present he's AIB-controlled.'

John Drayton knew he had to push this home now. 'If AIB really decide they want him, they can get him. As the highest-ranking officer in the commando, I'm recommending to you and General Willoughby that he's given extended furlough to remain here.'

Richard Sutherland was not a man who did favours, but even he was impressed with Commando Double X's operations. These men had helped to make MacArthur's decisions on intelligence operations look good, and that helped make all MacArthur's personal staff look good, including himself. His saturnine features broke into a smile. 'All right, Whitby, I'll fix it.'

They finished their brandies and shook hands, and a petty officer accompanied John Drayton to the main deck to disembark. As he climbed down to the PT boat, he was swamped with memories of Trap. They had truth between them and had made their peace. Hank Trapperton had told him, looking in his eyes in Merauke, that he had never touched Lexi after that first night. John Drayton believed it absolutely and had gone on loving Hank, yes loving him, just like Caldo did. He thought of Plato and Platonic love, the perfect purity of it.

Spray skipped off the bouncing waves into his face and hair as he stood holding one of the .50 calibre guns mounted near the bulwark of the torpedo boat speeding across the grey waters of the gulf to Lingayen town.

God, how strange to think that the last time I saw Hank on the beach I was the one to ask him to forgive Lexine. He shook his head at that thought.

Hank had been the damned hardest of men, and too the bravest man he had ever known.

He felt sad for Lexi. What had she said about Hank that day on the hospital veranda in Port Moresby? *He doesn't want me; he has no respect for me, because of what I did to you.* Yes, that was it. Obviously she had lost hope of Hank returning her love a long time ago. And now? Now he could take Paul to her, and at least she would have Hank's son to love in his stead.

As the boat slowed and his eyes drifted across Lingayen harbour, his fair hair floated back from his forehead in the breeze. So he would soon see Kathleen, hear her gentle voice and feel her long, smooth fingers. How did he feel about that? He smiled. It made him feel good inside.

Chapter Eighty-three

Three days later

Kathleen held Lexi's hand tightly as they walked down the gentle slope past the grey trunks of the tall palms to Ela Beach behind the little settlement of Port Moresby.

'It will be all right, darling. I know it will.'

'Oh God, Kathleen, I'm all atwitter.'

'Naturally, you haven't seen him for over three years.'

'He can't possibly remember me; he was only fifteen months old.'

'Don't worry about that. You're his mother; he'll know that soon enough.' She squeezed Lexi's hand. 'He'll love you to pieces.'

'I'm so hot. I'm perspiring with fear not just from the heat.'

Kathleen noticed the two figures edging out on to the beach fifty yards ahead. 'Oh, there they are.'

'Oh Lord.'

'Listen, darling, I'll wait here. You go on.'

Lexi looked round into her friend's smiling face. So much had happened in the last six hours. At nine that morning Kathleen had come to her with her eyes shining and clasping her hands in front of her in an excited way to tell her John D had turned up at the hospital.

'He's here in Lieutenant Finlay's office. He's just flown in from the Philippines. He was so pleased to see me. Oh God, Lexi, I'm so happy. Now he wants to see you; he's got things to tell you.'

Kathleen had pulled her along the corridor to the office, where John Drayton turned from the window and removed his cap and came forward to them across the sparsely furnished office. He took Kath's hand tenderly and kissed it and asked her to wait outside, and she had left them alone.

'How are you, Lex?'

'Not so bad, John Drayton, not so bad.'

He had told her immediately how Trap had been blown up and she just stood there listening and yet not making a sound. Surely she would have known if Hank Trapperton had left this world? Wouldn't she have felt a part of her heart separate from the rest? *Oh sweet Jesus, I only had those few tiny moments when he seemed to love me, those few tiny perfect moments.*

'I'm so sorry, Lexi.'

Tears ran down her face and she found her voice. 'Thank you for bringing the news to me, Johnny. I know how hard it must be for you to tell me about him. You're a wonderful man.'

He had scoffed at that. 'Ah forget it, Lex. I'm in pain too. Hank Trapperton was all sorts of things, but he was my friend.'

'Yes, I *know* he was.'

He stepped to her and took her in his arms, and it helped just to be held by him.

He kissed her forehead. 'Lex, I have other things to say. First, Caldo. He's remained in Luzon to search for any sign of Hank. Look, don't get any hopes up, please. It's futile. But that's Caldo.'

She felt a minute pulse of hope kindle in her soul. *Caldo is looking for a sign . . .*

He released her and held her hands.

'But if Caldo thinks—'

'Ah Lex, please don't hold out any real hope. It might only cause you more pain in the long run.'

She shook her head and wiped her eyes. 'I'd rather hold out hope than not. Even if he doesn't want anything to do with me, I still want him to be alive.'

He thought how pathetic that was, the sort of thing a child would say. 'Ah Lex, he valued certain things, did Trap, and he wasn't always right. But don't set yourself up for more anguish, that's all.'

Now his voice hardened slightly. 'The AIB disbanded my commando unit, so the other boys including Ivat and Williams are here with me. They want to see you, of course, but we'll wait until you're ready, there's no rush.'

Lexi tried to smile. 'How are they?'

'Just the same.'

She was thinking of Caldo, dear Sergeant Caldo, the Atlas with a heart as big as his muscles. She had always felt close to him; how she hoped one day she would see him again. *He's searching for a sign; he must believe there is some hope if he's searching for a sign . . .*

'There's one other thing, Lexi.' He drew her across to a chair and sat her down. She looked up at him.

'I found Paul in Lingayen Town in the Philippines.'

A chill ran through her. 'Paul? What? I'm not understanding you.'

'I found him; little bloke was with the Filipinos. Must have washed up on shore in Lingayen Gulf somewhere. He's here with me now; I've brought him to you.'

Startled, she looked around wide-eyed.

'No, dear girl, not right here. He's with the boys, but I want you to have him as soon as possible.'

Into her head flashed an image of the ship sinking, with the noise and confusion, the screaming and the uproar, and she recalled the way Uncle Jasper had taken Paul and methodically strapped him into the life jacket. *Oh Uncle Jasper, wherever you are; wonderful Uncle Jasper, thank you.* Her eyes brimmed with tears again. 'I'm afraid it's all too much for me, Johnny. Just all too much.'

He pulled her to her feet and hugged her again.

'I want him so badly and yet I'm so frightened.'

'Now come on, that's not like you. The sooner the better. We'll meet you somewhere away from people. I know! The beach at the back of the town. Kathy tells me both your shifts end at two today. We'll meet you on the beach at three.'

She felt as if she were being engulfed; she was panicking. As she gazed at him, he saw her dismay. 'Come on, Lex,' he said, patting her hand. 'I know it's all overwhelming, but you have your son back. If he stays any longer with me, he'll think the wrong one of us is his parent.'

That statement hit her and new tears came. 'Oh Johnny, I'm so sorry.'

But he smiled and shook his head. 'Don't be. I didn't say it for that. I said it because he needs to be with you.'

'How can you be so ... good to me?'

'Lex, you've been through hell. I'm over any anguish I had about us. I admire you, for heaven's sake. If I have any bitterness it's not towards you; I'm a soldier, it's for the enemy. Now you just get yourself together and meet us at three o'clock.' And as an after-thought he added, 'And bring some chocolate bars.'

And now, on the sand of Ela beach with the straggling settlement which was yet a garrison town behind them, Lexi squinted in the sunlight as a B-17 flew over them. 'All right. Here I go.'

Kathleen smiled encouragement as she let go her friend's hand and Lexi walked across the yellow sand towards her son. Suddenly into her mind shot a memory of Nintuck muttering her incanta-tions over Paul. Surely they meant nothing in Hong Kong? Yet whatever it was that had saved him for her was a miracle. *Dear Nintuck, how I hope you survive.*

Her gaze was locked on the small boy along the beach as her shoes sank in the sand with each step.

As she came closer, John Drayton squatted down and spoke to Paul, and she was overwhelmed by the irony of the three of them being together again.

She walked up to them and went down on her knees beside

her son. 'Hello, sweetheart.' She caught her breath as she looked into Paul's face. He was a miniature Trap, and when he smiled at her, she was overcome with love.

Lessa had run straight to Paul and hugged him; it was as if she thought he was her new little brother. That first night they shared the same cot, Lessa at one end and Paul at the other.

The days passed and turned into weeks and they heard more and more of the war in Europe. The liberation armies drove onwards; Mr Churchill's voice came over the short-wave radio, and as April opened, the immense events on land sea and in the air had the Allies pushing on into Germany itself. They heard and read of the millions facing starvation in Europe and were grateful for the little oasis called Port Moresby, military base though it was.

Lexi took great joy in seeing Jake Williams and Terry Ivat again, and meeting the other commandos who had risked their lives so often in the long fight for freedom against the Japanese.

Each day Lexi woke and looked at her children: the beautiful mute Lessa with her black eyes and hair, and her fair Paul with his father's wavy hair and her own blue eyes.

Paul spoke more and more English as time passed, and the miracle of having him and Lessa caught at her heart. Paul was her living memory of Hank Trapperton and the Lord had blessed her after all, by returning his child to her.

But as day waned and that time arrived when the sun was behind the hills and the haze of eventide faded into night, a sadness drifted into Lexi's soul and she placed her hand beneath her breast, where her heart lay, to feel it beating as she whispered, 'Where are you, Trap? Are you gone from this world? Or are you still here?'

Chapter Eighty-four

15 August 1945

Trap sat under the awning of interwoven nipa palm leaves. His cane rested on the arm of the bamboo chair and his bad leg was up on a padded stool. He took the beer from Caldo as he switched off the short-wave radio set.

'At last, Colonel Trap, the war's over and Hirohito has conceded defeat. Although didn't the announcer say that not once was the word '*surrender*' used by him in his speech?'

Trap nodded. Talking still needed effort, but his voice was coming back. 'Whatever Hirohito said meant the same thing.' He raised his glass. 'To Johnny and the boys of Commando Double X, wherever they are . . . And to you and me, Caldo. For freedom.'

Caldo lifted his glass. 'For freedom.'

They both drank and sank back into their bamboo chairs.

Trap continued to have bad dreams about drowning and being thrust along underwater by the *monstrous hand*, and crawling through the mangroves and across the field of talahib grass to the dirt road.

He had drifted in and out of consciousness and could hear the sounds of big guns in the distance, and as time passed the noise faded away so he knew the battles were moving ever further from him. He did not know how long he was in the dust before the two Filipino peasant farmers on bicycles arrived.

The men made a palm-frond litter and pulled him to their *bahay*, where their wives attended him. He was aware that his left side was badly damaged; the pain was, at times, so intense he suspected both arm and leg were broken in many places. He did not realise it but he had suffered many surface wounds from the explosion and the top of his left ear was missing; and as there were no hospitals in that area of Pangasinan he knew that all they could do for him was to use their herbal remedies and pray.

In his conscious moments he saw the same woman on her knees offering prayers on his behalf. Prior to this time in his life he would have told her, 'Forget it, lady, don't waste your goddam time', but now? Hell, why not let her? He needed all the help he could get.

At first he did not see well out of his left eye, and one day as the sun set and the short golden glow of dying day sat on the bamboo of the windowsill, he could feel his left side throbbing so badly that he was slipping into unconsciousness when he heard a voice he knew well and he opened his eyes. Through the blur he saw a man who remained indistinct until he bent over him. 'Am . . . I dreaming?'

'No, Colonel Trap, this ain't a dream. It's Caldo. I've found you at last.' Trap saw the tears cloud Caldo's eyes; that had made him overcome his pain and concentrate on the face of Caldo, his sergeant and his friend. He read all that John Drayton had seen: and he felt as John Drayton had felt.

Caldo had gone away and brought back with him a Filipino doctor who set Trap's arm but could do nothing with his leg.

'You're a lucky man not to have gangrene. I cannot move you and it is so badly fractured that I cannot set it. That you are still alive is a tribute to your extraordinary physical strength. We've had no supplies for all the years of the Japanese occupation, and morphine is hard to get even on the black market, but I can provide you with some dried marijuana leaves to smoke when the pain is unbearable . . . if you want.'

Trap raised an eyebrow. 'Pity I don't smoke,' he replied.

The doctor departed with the words, 'It will take many months, perhaps six, seven, or even longer, but with a strong will, you might be mobile.'

Caldo's tone of voice had been unconditional as it sounded from the end of the bed. 'He will be mobile.'

After the doctor departed, Caldo came to Trap and eased his frame down on to a stool. A candle burnt on a shelf nearby, the wax which had melted over time covering the shelf like a robe. Insects flickered around its flame as Caldo spoke. 'Colonel Trap, what do you want me to do? I'm on extended furlough, no need to report to anybody, but you? They all think you're dead.'

A long time passed before Trap's reply came. It had been almost impossible for him to talk at that early stage, for the wound on the left side of his throat had not healed, but he croaked out his reply, which Caldo waited patiently to hear: 'Then let them think it for a while longer.'

'But I could go and appropriate a jeep somewhere and take you to a military hospital. They'd have the right drugs.'

'No, Caldo ... the goddamn army ... doesn't need to know I'm alive.'

'But what about the boys? Shouldn't we let them know?'

Trap sank back on the pillow and thought of them all, Johnny and the others. But Hank Trapperton was a broken thing and they all knew him as he was before. He was aware of his powerful pride. *Jesus, I'm looking at myself. Johnny would be proud of me.* He made a decision. 'No, Caldo, not yet.'

Caldo had purloined a radio set from somewhere and they had followed the course of the war. In May they had celebrated the end of the war in Europe and drunk the intoxicating coconut wine known as 'tuba' and toasted Winston Churchill and the late President Roosevelt. One of the Filipinos brought in a grubby, well-read *Manila Post* newspaper with a photograph of King George and Queen Elizabeth and Winston Churchill on the front, which they read and re-read.

After that, the war in the Pacific endured; the Allies made gains but the Japanese refused to end the fight. On 26 July, the Potsdam Ultimatum – the final appeal to Japan to surrender – was sent from the Allies. It ended with: *We call upon the Government of Japan to proclaim now the unconditional surrender of all the Japanese armed forces, and to provide proper and adequate assurances of their good faith in such action. The alternative for Japan is prompt and utter destruction.* These terms were rejected by the military rulers of Japan. Leaflets warning of intensive air bombardment were dropped on target cities and the decision was made in Washington to drop the atomic bomb to avoid a bitter and prolonged invasion of Japan itself. The result had been the capitulation of the Japanese.

Caldo watched Trap as he leant back and closed his eyes. In the beginning it had grieved him every day to look upon his colonel, but as the weeks and months passed he had seen his spirit holding steady, his determination to walk again build, and Caldo had become more positive.

Trap's long hair kissed his shirt collar. He had lost ten pounds in weight, and though Caldo was aware he experienced continuing shooting pain down through his shattered left side, the sight in his left eye was improving and he knew Trap's old energy was back.

Now was the time: 'Colonel Trap?'

Trap opened his eyes to his friend. 'What's that, Caldo?'

'I've said nothing before, because it's taken this long for you to get yourself back together.'

'Hardly together, Sarge. I'm a bit too beaten up to be described as *back together*.'

'Yes, well, I meant soul as well as body.'

Trap closed his left eye and squinted at his friend. 'Explain that, old buddy.'

'I'm not good at expressing myself, Colonel Trap, but here goes . . . I used to think this was none of my business, but I reckon it

660

is now, you see. There's a girl ... no, a woman somewhere; well, last I heard she was in Port Moresby, and she needs you badly and her name's Doc Robinson. I saw it time and time again: she loves you and nobody else.'

Trap shook his head and his wavy hair moved on his collar. He had lain here day after day and thought of her. But the Doll had loved the old Hank Trapperton, and that man was no more.

He gazed at Caldo, who was frowning. 'We can't just go on living here for ever in this nipa hut, Colonel Trap. It ain't right.'

Trap swallowed the last of his beer. 'Listen, Caldo, the truth is ...' He gave a brief smile. 'I'm sounding like Johnny, damn it. The truth is, I've been waiting for you to bring her up. And you might be right about not being able to go on living here ...' He cast his gaze around to where the farmer's children played in the long grass, and Maria, the wife who had prayed for him, drew water from a well near their hut, 'Though it's been what I needed, as it turned out. A place away from everything I know, to reassess.

'I needed to be blown up to start to look at myself and get a few things straight, so maybe the explosion was the essential bit.' He gave a grimace which turned into a grin.

'So let's talk of the Doll, as you've apparently been so goddam patient up to this point.'

Caldo thought this was promising. 'You treated her badly, Colonel, you know you did.'

'Okay. I know I painted her a tart and a deceiver, and I did that because of my blasted pride, my conceit. I slept with her in Madura and I blamed her for leaving me. I blamed her for being with me when she was engaged to another guy. I blamed her for getting pregnant by me. I blamed her for marrying the man she was promised to when she had no other blasted alternative. I blamed her for having my son. Everything was her fault and none of it mine.

'Johnny told me they called it quits because they'd both changed, but no, I hung on to my illusions.

'The truth? I couldn't get over the fact that she actually walked out on me: me, Hank Trapperton. How could any woman do that? As long as I looked down on her and called her a tramp, my ego remained intact. Well, that particular self-deception was blown out of me when I hit the Agno river head first.'

He stopped talking and looked down at his leg on the stool. 'And you, my Caldo, my good, amazing, true companion who brought me back to life, have waited all this time to hear that. Look, I know exactly how I feel about her. But it's no good, old pal. Oh, I've thought of finding her, sure. But what for? To offer her half a man? No, that's where I've got just enough of my goddam pride left; it's just a teeny bit but it's lodged solidly here inside, and it's enough to keep me from asking her to nursemaid me through the rest of my life. She deserves a whole man, a real man. She deserves a darn sight better than me.'

Caldo took a long breath and blew it out of the side of his mouth. He leant forward and held his chin in his hands and then he sat up and wrung his hands in his lap before he spoke. 'I've never spoken to you like this in my life. But you're wrong, Colonel Trap, dead wrong. You've got to see sense. That woman loves you with a love I've never seen in anybody. You're it. Half a man, quarter of a man; God, she'd want you if you were in a coma. Jeez, listen to me: don't be selfish enough to spoil her life because you've still got some silly pride left. Damn your pride, think of her for once. You never have before.'

He had said his piece and he bit the side of his lip.

Trap met Caldo's eyes. He looked away, then looked back. He gazed for some seconds down at his bad leg and finally back at Caldo. But he did not speak.

Caldo stood up and walked three paces out into the air and stood a minute on the dark earth before he swung round and came back. He had yet another revelation for his colonel. 'This is a hard one to tell you, but here it comes. The kid? Your kid with the Doc? Paul?'

Trap edged himself up straighter in his chair.

'The little fella was found by Colonel Whitby, here in Lingayen. He said he knew he was Paul because of the diamond-shaped birth-mark on his arm. And I saw the kid: he's the spitting image of you. Last I knew all those months ago was Colonel Whitby was taking him back to the Doc in Port Moresby.'

Trap could feel a sudden bad ache starting in his leg. 'Jesus.' He bent forward and rubbed his thigh. He felt light-headed but it was not from the beer. Caldo came over and massaged his leg with his big hands and Trap watched the hens and roosters in the yard as if they were the most interesting creatures he had ever seen.

Abruptly he asked, 'So has she still got Lessa?'

'Gawd, sir, I don't know. But I'd reckon she does. She's not the sort to abandon her, no way.'

Trap grunted and jabbed his finger at his companion. 'Just never call me *sir* again, all right? You saved my life. Even this Colonel Trap business is a bit much. How about Trap?'

Caldo smiled up at him from where he knelt. 'Look, *Colonel Trap*, don't change the subject.'

Trap's eyes lifted skywards and he concentrated on the interlaced palm leaves overhead, until after another lengthy silence, he spoke steadily. 'I've heard all you said, every word. Let's leave it there for tonight. My leg feels better, thanks. Now how about another beer? We've got to toast the end of the war again.'

Chapter Eighty-five

Port Moresby, 1 September 1945

It was Saturday afternoon and the sun was beginning to slip down on the other side of Fairfax Harbour as clouds raced across the sky chased by a zephyr breeze.

Lexi and Lessa and Paul and Kathleen were sitting on a blanket in a dip in the slope under the tall palms where a frangipani tree grew, and from where they could look down to the road and across country to the water. They spent most Saturday evenings this way until rain or insects forced them inside.

At present they could smell the sweet fragrance of the white flowers above them. Lessa was lying on her back looking up at the azure sky. Paul sat very close to Lexi, his small left hand on her skirt and his right hand clutching a blue bunny rabbit which Dinty had made for him as her parting gift before she returned to the Philippines two months prior. He had blossomed in the months with Lexi.

John Drayton had arrived back in Port Moresby two days ago, much to the delight of Kathy. Lexi felt sure they would make a happy marriage after she and Johnny were divorced. He had been exemplary in that too, saying he would take the blame. She supposed one day there would be no need for a guilty party in such dissolutions, but that was not yet. She had been embarrassd about it, but he had prevailed upon her. John Drayton, the finest of men, and he would always be important to her. Yes, Kathy was a lucky woman.

They were waiting for him now. He was taking Kathy to a regimental dinner out at Murray Barracks. Kathleen was already dressed for the affair except for her evening shoes.

Lexi turned to her. 'I wonder how the commandos will take to civvy street once they're demobbed.'

'With difficulty, I think. They'll all be restless; I feel sorry for them. It's not like being a normal soldier. They're elite, special, and have been for a long time; there's a sort of magic in it for them, even though the dangers were constant. I know I'll have to be patient with John D. I even think perhaps he should stay in the army for a while; it would help him to segue from being a special operator to being a civilian.'

Lexi nodded. 'That's so sensible. You know it'll be different for all of us, lots of adjusting to do. I suppose they'll close the hospital sooner rather than later.'

They fell silent, each with their own thoughts.

'Kath?'

'Yes?'

'Do you feel angry about what happened to you?'

Kathleen hesitated a few moments, looking up to the heavens before she replied. 'Sometimes. When I have nightmares. I suppose we'll all have nightmares, all of us who were victims of the Japs. I guess we'll have them as long as we're alive. That's our legacy for surviving.'

Lexi sighed. 'Yes, it'll be hard to forget, perhaps even impossible as you say, but we must try.' She rested her hand on her son's head and he looked up at her and pushed his rabbit into her lap before he rose and walked over to Lessa, who sat up as he perched beside her. 'At least we can try to make sure our children never suffer the trauma we did.'

Kathleen sighed. 'I'd like to think that's true. But it seems to me that good and evil walk hand in hand.'

Lexi groaned. 'Oh Kathy, I was trying to be optimistic.'

'Well, take my mother. She was so good, so kind, so benevolent to people, and yet she'd been a consort of that thing who was my father.'

Lexi took Kathleen's hand and squeezed it. She had not said anything like this before. 'Oh, darling, please. Don't say that. Bess was with him so long ago, he must have been different then. You know he must have or she would not have cared for him.'

Kathleen shivered. 'I suppose you're right. But he had corrupted completely. Some of the things I saw him do . . .'

'Ah, darling, don't do this to yourself.' Lexi made herself brighten. 'Now listen to me. Don't think of that man or anything bad that happened. Whenever you find yourself thinking of the terrible past, stop and think of John D and the future. Please will you promise me?'

Kathleen gave a wan smile. 'All right. I'll try.'

'No.' Lexi said it so firmly that Kathleen started. 'Don't try, Kathy; you must *do it*. It's the only way. It's what I practise and I want you to as well. Whenever I start recalling the ugliness I saw, I make myself think of you and me, swimming in Repulse Bay in the golden afternoons, and I concentrate on Grandpa and the happy stories he told me in amongst the sweet drifting scents and the orchids in the gardens at Hydrangea . . . and I remember Kwan Yin and all the light-hearted days we had in your mother's curio shop when we were growing up. It works, I promise you.'

Abruptly Kathleen spun round on the blanket and hugged Lexi close and kissed her. 'Oh Lexi, thank you, yes, you are right, so right. Whenever I think of *him*, I'll remember John D and happy things and *Juni the good*, that will make me smile.'

'Who is Juni the good?'

'The guard I told you about, the one I became close to: he was gentle, with a poet's heart.' In her mind she heard his voice calling her *'Kataleen.'*

'Now that's more like it,' Lexi said, as she noticed John Drayton

666

pull up in the jeep down past the nurses' quarters. 'Your beau is here.'

The two children turned to watch the adults, and Paul began to laugh when he saw the soldier bound out of the vehicle and stride up to them. He looked so military and handsome in his dress uniform as Kathleen rose to her feet and kissed him.

'Hello, Lex, hello, kids.' He bent down on one knee and hugged the children.

'I'll go and put my good shoes on and touch up my lipstick and get my evening bag.' Kathleen hurried away.

The sun was hidden now and a red glow shimmered in the sky as John Drayton sat down on the rug with the children between him and Lexi. Paul handed him a pack of cards, calling him 'Uncle Johndy.'

At first Lexi had been embarrassed about the use of that name, but John Drayton had insisted. 'Lex, it's better, and I want him to think of me as a relative, so Uncle John D is what it should be.'

He ruffled Paul's hair. 'He's a remarkable little boy, he's irrepressible; has been since the minute I found him. He's Hank's son, no doubt about it.'

Tears sprang to Lexi's eyes. 'God, Johnny, that's just too generous of you to say that.'

He shook his head. 'No, love, it's true. Important to see what's true, Lex. I face lots of things now that I didn't before the war. I'm not talking about you and me, I'm talking about growing inside. This war was another wicked blot on the record of humanity, and the suffering doesn't end now, it goes on for decades one way and another. And if we don't learn from what happened, then all those great boys I knew ... and all your relatives and friends ... died for nothing. Can't have that, wouldn't be right. So we have to concentrate on what's relevant and what's valuable, for their sake. We're the lucky ones. We made it through.'

Lexi studied him. It seemed perfectly normal to sit here side by side talking as friends, and it warmed her soul to hear him talk.

'I still miss Grandpa.'

He nodded. 'You always will. Your dilemma is, you cannot help but love men who cast long shadows.'

That brought a small smile to her face. 'Yes, well, you were one of them.'

He leant over and patted her hand. 'You know what? We discuss more now than when we lived together.' He lifted her hand gently. 'You realise you and Kathleen might be called as witnesses at the war crimes trials, don't you? Being survivors of the massacre.'

'I hadn't thought about it, but yes, I guess we could be. Oh God, that'll bring it all back.'

He squeezed her arm in understanding as the strains of 'Waltzing Matilda' echoed up to them from the dirt road beyond John Drayton's jeep and an Australian brass band came marching along.

The children jumped up and clapped their hands in delight, and as it passed John Drayton said, 'I love that tune. It's the heart of Australia.'

Lexi grinned. 'I agree, it's so evocative of the country, the people. It's very moving.'

He gave a good-humoured grunt. 'Perhaps you're Australian after all.'

She laughed at that but as the band disappeared her mood altered and she turned gravely to him. 'What do you think, Johnny? All these months gone by. No one's ever heard anything of Caldo. What do you truly think?' She put her hand in her apron pocket as she spoke and took hold of Trap's letter.

He knew exactly to what she alluded. 'Oh Lexi, I don't know. Hank was unique right enough. He inspired and influenced all the men who ever knew him and he lived through more danger than I could ever explain to you. He was lucky so darn often. But to hold out any hope now . . .'

As he said these words, Lessa walked off the blanket and stood staring down the slope into the falling twilight.

'Come here, darling,' Lexi said. 'We'll have to go in now.'

Kathleen's heels clicked on the pebble path as she returned, and noticing Lessa she called to her, 'Do what Mummy says, darling, come back.'

But Lessa did not come back. She started to walk down the slope, and suddenly she astounded them, for she cried out a word that they thought was 'You!' And she began to run swiftly away from them.

Lexi jumped to her feet and so did John Drayton.

And in that second Lexi saw what Lessa had seen, down there in the moody dusk on the side of the road coming slowly towards them.

A strangled joyous, heartrending sound issued from her throat as she sprinted after the child, while John Drayton and Kathleen watched in amazement, for now they also had seen.

Paul cried out as he watched his mother and sister running, and John Drayton picked him up in his arms. 'Your daddy's here,' he said softly to the little boy as they watched Lexi racing recklessly downhill with her skirt flapping and the wind lifting her hair high behind her.

Lessa reached him first and lifted her arms to him. He handed Caldo his cane and Caldo supported him as he bent and raised her up in his arms. 'It's . . . you,' she said, and she kissed his cheek.

'Yes, it's me, little Lessa,' he answered as he passed her to Caldo and stood waiting for Lexi, who slowed to a halt a few feet from him.

She could see, even though the shadows of night were enfolding them, and what she could see broke her heart. 'Oh my love,' she whispered. 'Oh my love.'

'I'm not the man you knew, Lexi,' he said, 'But if you'll have me, I'll try to be.'

The tears were streaming down her cheeks, her eyes were awash, she could hardly see him as a sob of love burst from her. 'Oh Trap, you called me *Lexi* at last. I love you so. I always have, I always will.' And she threw herself into his arms as he winced in pain and kissed her tears and her face and her mouth.

She was laughing and crying and kissing him. She was home, she was in Hank Trapperton's arms!

And now, pressing her to his heart, he knew it did not matter that he was not the Hank Trapperton of before. He had the true love of the only woman he had ever wanted, and she was here.

Suddenly Lexi realised that Caldo stood there beside them holding Lessa, just as she had seen him do a hundred times in the Philippines. She smiled at him through her tears and looked back up the hill to John Drayton and Kathy, and then back to Trap. 'Oh how wonderful it is, we're all together,' she said.

'Yes, and let's stay that way.' And he kissed her again and asked, 'Shouldn't I meet my son?'

Epilogue

Sunday 2 September 1945, Tokyo Bay, Japan

It was a surprisingly cool slate-grey morning on the deck of the the Third Fleet flagship USS *Missouri* when the Japanese formally surrendered and the historic documents were signed. General Douglas MacArthur and the emaciated Generals, Arthur Percival and Skinny Wainwright, stood together near Admiral Chester Nimitz and a host of Allied generals, air marshals and admirals, including Walter Krueger, George Kenney and Thomas Blamey. The deck was crowded with representatives from Britain, Australia, America, New Zealand, Canada, France, China, the Netherlands, and Russia who had declared war on Japan just one week before Japan surrendered.

The Japanese delegation of eleven men was led by its two plenipotentiaries: sombre Foreign Minister, Mamoru Shigemitsu, in frockcoat and stovepipe hat, white gloves and his ill-fitted wooden leg, who would later be sentenced to seven years imprisonment for war crimes; and General Yoshijiro Umezu who would subsequently be charged as a Class A war criminal and sentenced to life imprisonment.

But it was Douglas MacArthur who was centre stage. Beneath the big guns packed with servicemen he made a short eloquent speech and moved dramatically to the table to sign the duplicate surrender documents with six fountain pens. The first one he used, he handed to Skinny Wainwright. The second one he used, he handed to General Percival. Everyone on the deck of the warship was touched by these gestures, but none more so than the recipients. The last pen he used was small and red-barrelled, which he took out of his pocket: it belonged to his wife, Jean.

The representatives[1] of the other gathered nations followed and signed on behalf of their countries, and photographers and newsreel cameramen recorded for posterity the highly dramatic, unforgettable event which ended with a giant airborne armada thundering over the *Missouri*.

As Skinny looked up at the thousands of Allied aircraft, he was very aware of his stalwart aides, Johnny Pugh and Tom Dooley, amongst the hundreds on the crowded decks behind him and of Arthur Percival who had heard of the end of the war along with Skinny in the freezing hell hole of Sian in Manchuria.

Skinny could not help but remember those he had seen beaten to death and those he had seen die of starvation and lack of medical help. He had already heard horror stories of prisoners in some camps who had been slaughtered immediately the enemy had known they were beaten. For a few moments he could not look at the delegation on the far side of the table, but then he caught Arthur Percival's eye as the multitude of aircraft droned above. They both knew exactly what the other was thinking.

They were here on this momentous day, free men again, after the years of unbearable tension and servitude. They were out of purgatory: what unutterable joy it was to be free. Skinny rolled his shoulders to cast off the desolate thoughts, and to allow those of grace, civilisation and kindness to flourish in his head.

An hour later, after the generals and admirals and air marshals had partaken of coffee and doughnuts in Admiral Bill Halsey's quarters, MacArthur offered Skinny a lift back to Yokohama in the destroyer *Buchanan*. A number of them were to fly on to the

Philippines that afternoon for the formal surrenders there the next day.

On the voyage across Tokyo Bay Skinny went down to the cabin set aside for MacArthur's use. They talked briefly and Skinny commented on things which were amazing to him, like the new uniforms and helmets and present-day aircraft, and even current terms he had never heard like 'GI' for the American soldier.

During their conversation, MacArthur generously offered to organise a reunion between Skinny and his son Jack immediately Wainwright returned to the USA.

At that point the Commander lit his pipe and surveyed his companion with an odd expression. 'Now, Jonathan, I've heard it said you've already been offered money to write your memoirs?'

Skinny nodded. 'Yes.'

'Bully for you! You do it, then once you've written them, send them straight to me and I'll look them over for you and I'll send them on to the War Department.'

Skinny smiled. He did not say yes, he did not say no. But he knew for certain he was not going to let Douglas MacArthur get his hands on them. Skinny admired MacArthur, but he knew the true ilk of the man. His story would remain Skinny's story, without any alteration of the events by the SWPA Commander.

And so it was that '*General Wainright's Story: The Account of Four Years of Humiliating Defeat, Surrender and Captivity*' appeared on sale in 1946 and was told by Skinny and no one else.

Endnotes

Chapter Eight

1 On 7 December 1942, the Japanese Ambassador and Special Envoy in Washington, instructed by the Japanese Government, had requested and been alloted a 1 p.m. meeting with Cordell Hull, the Secretary of State. This meeting was to read to Hull the reply to his 26 November communiqué from Tojo, the Japanese Prime Minister: 'Outline of Proposed Basis for Agreement between USA and Japan'. History records this meeting was postponed to 2 p.m. East Coast time by which hour Hull had received Admiral Husband E. Kimmel's message from Hawaii: 'Air attack on Pearl Harbor. This is not a drill!' Given the independence of the Japanese Military Forces, it is possible that the Japanese Diplomats in Washington, while doubtlessly cognizant of Japan's pending war plans, were not informed of the date of the strike.

Chapter Nine

1 Brigadier John Kelbourne Lawson fell in action defending Hong Kong on 19 December 1941.

2 Both Maltby brothers were to be captured by the Japanese: Air

Vice Marshal Paul Maltby and Major General Christopher Maltby. They would both be incarcerated in Japanese POW camps and they would meet up in captivity and after years of maltreatment both brothers would survive and finally be evacuated from Camp Hoten, Mukden in Manchuria, on the same day: 27 August 1945.

Chapter Eleven

I The Japanese attack on Kota Bharu was made at local time: 12.25 a.m. on 8 December. This was Greenwich time 4.55 p.m. on 7 December and thus local Hawaiian time 6.25 a.m. on 7 December.

The air strike on Pearl Harbor occurred after the Kota Bharu invasion. It was an hour and a half later, just prior to 8 a.m. on 7 December, local.

Chapter Thirty

I Darwin Bombing 19 February 1942:

180 Australian and and American servicemen lost their lives in this raid. Seven ships in the harbour were destroyed and two north of the harbour. The *Madura*, the hospital ship, though taking a direct hit, survived.

The total of 252 deaths in all on the 19th is the accepted number.

Japanese Air Raids on the Australian Mainland and Horn Island during World War II, in alphabetical order from the Australian war memorial, were:

Location	Number of Raids	Date
Broome (WA)	4	During period 3 March 1942–16 August 1943
Darwin (NT)	64	During period 19 February 1942–12 November 1943
Derby (WA)	1	On 20 March 1942
Drysdale (NT)	1	On 27 September 1943
Exmouth Gulf (WA)	4	During period 21 May 1943–16 September 1943
Katherine (NT)	1	On 22 March 1942
Millingimbi (NT)	3	During period 9 May 1943–28 May 1943
Mossman (QLD)	1	On 31 July 1942
Onslow (WA)	1	On 15 September 1943
Port Hedland (WA)	2	During period 30 July 1942–17 August 1943
Port Patterson (NT)	1	On 28 August 1942
Townsville (QLD)	3	During period 25 July 1942–28 July 1942
Wyndham (WA)	2	During period 3 March 1942–23 March 1942
Horn Island	9	During period 14 March 1942–18 June 1943
TOTAL	97	

2 The main aerial battle over Java was fought and lost on 19 February 1942.

3 The Battle of the Java Sea was fought from 27 February to 1 March, 1942, during which Admiral Doorman himself was killed in action when Dutch light cruiser *De Ruyter* and all the main ships of the ABDA were sunk.

677

Chapter Thirty-two

1 Late in January 1942, a 1.1-in quadruple mount, automatic weapon, formerly intended for the U.S.S. *Houston*, was turned over to the Harbour Defences by local authorities, together with several thousand rounds of ammunition. A special concrete base was constructed atop Malinta Hill on which the weapon was mounted and taken over by the Anti-aircraft Defense Command. Each round of ammunition was tracer type.

Chapter Thirty-four

1 Written by Frank Hewlett, War Correspondent, in 1942. Hewlett and two other war correspondents, Clark Lee and Dean Schedler, escaped from Corregidor in April 1942 in a tiny Philippine liaison aircraft flown by the courageous Air Corps Major Bill Bradford who flew into, and out of, the island at night for weeks under most dangerous circumstances.

Chapter Forty-one

1 Port Moresby was the administrative centre for the Australian territories of Papua and New Guinea.

2 Charles Willoughby was possibly born Karl Tscheppe-Weidenbach in Germany on 8 March, 1892. Close scrutiny of any birth records would cast suspicion upon the assertion that he had a baron for a father. He certainly took an Anglo name on his arrival in the US and he joined the United States Army around 1910. He fought in the First World War against his original native land and rose through the ranks.

3 General Douglas MacArthur was smarting over a couple of recent rejections: having his idea of attacking Rabaul – the

Japanese stronghold on New Britain north-east of Papua New Guinea – turned down and being overlooked to lead the coming offensive by the United States on a small virtually unheard of island in the British Solomon Group – the British island of Guadalcanal.

4 Fragmentation bombs were 25lb-bombs with parachutes attached for low-altitude attacks where the parachute slowed down the descent while the aircraft had time to get out of range of the fragments from the exploded bomb.

Chapter Forty-eight

I Commander Shojiro Hayashi, the early leader of the attacking Japanese marines from the 5th Kure Special Naval Landing Force and the 5th Sasebo Special Naval Landing Force, was a stickler for night fighting. During the Battle of Milne Bay a new commander took over from Hayashi. He was Commander Minoro Yano, though the night attacks continued.

During the daylight hours Royal Australian Airforce aircraft from the 75th and 76th squadrons flying P 40 Kittyhawks played an important part bombing and straffing the enemy where the jungle was broken enough to allow it.

The Battle of Milne Bay was significant because it was the first land battle won by the Allies against the Japanese. 8,000 Australians mostly from the Australian 7th Division defended Milne Bay with the support of 1,300 United States combat and service troops.

Chapter Forty-nine

I General Thomas Blamey sacked General Potts on 22 October just as the Japanese were coming to the end of their offensive strength. Many of his men wished to resign when they heard the news. But in war resignations are not accepted.

2   The spirit of General Tomitaro Horii's army was broken by the command to withdraw. When they moved off in retreat the following morning the thousands of men soon began to flee. The soldiers who had forced themselves to fight their way across the Kokoda Trail now turned into a rabble, taking flight and running before the Australians who pursued them through the unrelenting New Guinea jungle, hills and swamps.

General MacArthur was now determined to seize the initiative and he sought to establish his Australian and American armies on the North Coast of Papua New Guinea by overland march and air transport. During October as the Japanese retreated in disarray, north coast landings were carried out by the Allies and many of the decamping Japanese who reached the coast were surrounded and routed. Allied fighter aircraft, under the inventive command of George Churchill Kenney, cooperated with ground units and strafed the enemy positions.

However, some stands were made and battles ensued into November.

When the fleeing Japanese survivors reached the flooding Kumusi River which flowed to the sea near their Gona-Sanananda-Buna beachhead, many of them plodded laboriously along the left bank towards the sea but some made make-shift rafts to sail dangerously down it. When General Horii first heard the distant sounds of heavy mortar fire in Gona where he knew a battle was going on, he decided to speed his progress by riding one of these rafts to the mouth of the river and then paddling along the shore to the Buna area. Both he and his aide made the treacherous journey to the mouth of the Kumusi safely but during the relatively short trip in a native canoe along the shore towards the Japanese headquarters in Buna, a squall came up; the relatively light craft sank, and Major General Tomitaro Horii and his Staff Officer were both drowned. Most historical accounts reveal General Horii's death from drowning but the exact detail given here I discovered in *The Reports of General MacArthur: The Campaigns of MacArthur in the Pacific, Volume 1.*

The Japanese troops who did return to Buna, dug in and held it until the Battles of Gona and Buna December 1942–January 1943.

CHAPTER FIFTY

1 Rabaul:

After World War I the island of New Britain became a mandated Australian Territory. Rabaul was the administrative centre. A small Australian military detachment known as *Lark Force* was stationed at Rabaul with companies on Bougainville and the Admiralty islands.

The first Japanese bombs were dropped on Rabaul on the morning of 4 January, 1942. The initial attack was followed up and air-raids became constant until the seaborne invasion on 23 January.

Lark Force was swiftly overcome and the island fell into Japanese hands.

The order which is rarely given, 'Every man for himself', was, in fact, given on 23 January by Colonel J J Scanlon when he realised the overwhelming strength of the enemy.

Pre-war Rabaul was a charming tropical settlement with tree-lined streets, a few thousand in its native population, a community of Chinese and approximately a thousand Europeans.

During the Japanese occupation it became a massive garrison which at its height numbered nearly 100,000 Japanese troops.

CHAPTER FIFTY-TWO

I Tokyo Rose was the sobriquet given by the Allied forces in the South Pacific to any of what is now believed to have been several English-speaking female broadcasters, of Japanese propaganda. However, the name is usually associated with Iva Toguri D'Aquino, a Nisei stranded in Japan by the war. She was born in California in 1912 and had travelled to Japan in 1941 to visit an ill relative. She was harassed and coerced by the Kempeitai and the Tokko (an organisation of secret police, called Tokubetsu Koto Keisatsu, or Tokko for short), and finally she became a propaganda broadcaster until the end of the war. She was arrested in 1945 by US Counter Intelligence Officers but was released after a year in prison. Iva was arrested again in 1948 and tried in San Francisco in 1949. She was found guilty of one of eight counts and served a prison term until 1956. In 1977 Iva Toguri D'Aquino was granted an unconditional pardon by Gerald Ford.

CHAPTER FIFTY-NINE

I Lieutenant General Hitoshi Imamura was Commander of the Japanese 16th Army which invaded the Dutch East Indies in December 1941. He became the Japanese Military Governor of Java and Madoera on 10 March 1942, thus being the highest authority. He remained in this position until he departed on 11 November 1942 to return to Tokyo before taking up his command of the 8th Army in Rabaul.

When the Allies in Java capitulated to the Japanese on 8/9 March 1942 over 200 Allied soldiers, mostly Australian and British, escaped into the hills near Malang and formed themselves into resistance fighters. With the overwhelming numbers of Japanese soldiers and the fact that the Javanese often collaborated with them, they were all captured by Imamura's troops in April. The Allied prisoners were forced into three-foot-long bamboo pig-carrying baskets and transported in lorries to a rail siding where they were transferred into goods wagons to the Java coast. There they were carried in their cages aboard boats which sailed out into waters off Soerabaja, where sharks were known to be present in large numbers. Still enclosed in their cages the Allied soldiers were thrown overboard.

After the war, in a Netherlands Court, Hitoshi Imamura was acquitted of this atrocity for lack of evidence; but an Australian Military Court found him responsible for other crimes. *'For permitting his subordinates to commit brutal atrocities against the Australians and Allies in New Guinea'* he was handed down a ten-year sentence. He served eight.

Chapter Sixty-eight

I   Edward V. 'Eddie' Rickenbacker, America's leading 'ace' in World War I had scored 26 victories in his Spad XIII. He was released from the U.S. Navy's Mobile Hospital No. 3 ('MOB 3') in Mapusaga in late November, 1942.

He and his companions spent 22 days in a raft after their aircraft, a Boeing B-17E Flying Fortress, went down, on a tour of the Pacific theatre. They were rescued by an aircraft and a PT boat near Funafuti, in the Ellice Islands, were treated there, and were then taken to Samoa for more extensive medical care. Rickenbacker wrote that wartime Tutuila was: 'alive with all kinds of military activities; and from being one of those so-called island paradises of the South Seas it was fast becoming an ocean fortress. The scenery is wonderful, and in many other respects the South Seas is the most attractive place in the world to fight a war. But the region has its drawbacks. The rainy season had just begun, and you have my word for it, it doesn't just rain out there – the ocean tilts up and swamps you.'

1   On the Surrender Documents the two Japanese signatures of Mamoru Shigemitsu and Yoshijiro Umezu appear in acceptance of the provisions set forth at Potsdam on 26 July 1945. The signatories for the Allied Powers' are in order:

(General) Douglas MacArthur: Supreme Commander for the Allied Powers

(Admiral) C W Nimitz: United States representative

(General) Hsu Yung-Chang: Republic of China representative

(Admiral Sir) Bruce Fraser: United Kingdom representative

(General) Kuzma N Derevyanko: Union of Soviet Socialist Republics representative

(General) T A Blamey: Commonwealth of Australia representative

(Colonel) L Moore-Cosgrave: Dominion of Canada representative

(General) Jaques P LeClerc: Provisional Government of the French Republic representative

(Admiral) C E L Helfrich: Kingdom of the Netherlands representative

(Air Vice-Marshal) Leonard M Isitt: Dominion of New Zealand representative

Bibliography

Bauer, Lt Col. Eddy: *World War II*, Vols. 1–6, Orbis Publishing Limited, London, 1972

Beck, John Jacob: *MacArthur and Wainwright, Sacrifice of the Philippines*, University of New Mexico Press, USA, 1974

Belote, James H., and Belote, William M: *Corregidor: The Saga of a Fortress*, Harper & Row, NY, 1967

Bicheno, Hugh: *Midway*, Cassell & Co., London, 2001

Birch, Gavin: *The Wartime Jeep in British Service 1941–1945*, Jeep Books Limited, UK, 2004

Churchill, Winston S.: *The Second World War*, Vol 1–6, Cassel & Co. Limited, London, 1951

Costello, John: *The Pacific War*, Rawson, Wade Publishers, Inc., New York, 1981

Courtney, G. B., MC: *Silent Feet, The History of 'Z' Special Operations 1942–1945*, Slouch Hat Publications, Australia, 1993

Darman, Peter: *Uniforms of World War II*, Blitz Editions, UK, 1998

Decker, Malcolm: *On A Mountainside, The 155th Provisional Guerrilla Battalion Against the Japanese on Luzon*, Yucca Tree Press, USA, 2004

Dunlop, E. E.: *War Diaries of Weary Dunlop, Java and Burma 1942–1945*, Penguin Books Australia Limited, 1990

Dyess, Lt Co. W. E.: *The Dyess Story*, G. P. Putnam's Sons, USA, 1944

Edgar, Bill: *Warrior of Kokoda, A Biography of Brigadier Arnold Potts*, Allen & Unwin, Australia, 1999

Forty, George: *Japanese Army Handbook, 1939–1945*, Sutton Publishing Limited, England, 2002

Goodwin, Dr Bob: *Mates and Memories, Recollections of the 2/10th Field Regiment*, Australia, 1998

Goodwin, Michael J.: *Shobun, A Forgotten War Crime in the Pacific*, Stackpole Books, USA, 1995

Gordon, Richard M., with assistance of Llamzon, Benjamin S.: *Horyo, Memoirs of an American POW*, Paragon House, USA, 1999

Groom, Winston: *1942, The Year That Tried Men's Souls*, Atlantic Monthly Press, USA, 2005

Hammel, Eric M., and Lane, John E.: *76 Hours, The Invasion of Tarawa*, Tower Publications, Inc., USA, 1980

Kenney, George C.: *General Kenney Reports, A Personal History of the Pacific War*, Office of Air Force History, United States Air Force, Washington, DC, 1987

Krueger, General Walter: *From Down Under to Nippon, The Story the Army in World War II*, Combat Forces Press, Washington, DC, 1953

Lamont-Brown, Raymond: *Kempeitai, Japan's Dreaded Military Police*, Sutton Publishing, Stroud, England, 2002

LaVo, Carl: *Slade Cutter, Submarine Warrior*, Naval Institute Press Maryland, USA, 2003

Lindsay, Oliver: *At the Going Down of the Sun, Hong Kong and South East Asia 1941–1945*, Hamish Hamilton, London, 1981

MacArthur, General Douglas and his General Staff: *Reports of General MacArthur, The Campaigns of MacArthur in the Pacific*, Vols. 1 & 2, Government Printing Office, Washington, DC, 1966

MacArthur, Douglas: *Reminiscences*, McGraw-Hill Book Company, USA, 1964

Manchester, William: *American Caesar, Douglas MacArthur 1880–1964*, Dell Publishing, NY, 1978

McDonnell, Leslie: *Insignia of World War II*, Silverdale Books, UK, 1999

McEwan, John: *Out of the Depths of Hell, A Soldier's Story of Life and Death In Japanese Hands*, Leo Cooper, Yorkshire, 1999

Miller, Col. E. B.: *Bataan Uncensored*, Military Historical Society of Minnesota, 1991

Morton, Louis: *The Fall of the Philippines, The War in the Pacific*, National Historical Society, USA, 1995

Mueller, Joseph N.: *Guadalcanal 1942*, Osprey Publishing Ltd, UK, 1992

Naval Submarine League: *United States Submarines*, Barnes & Noble Books, NY, 2004

Perret, Geoffrey: *Old Soldiers Never Die*, The Life of Douglas MacArthur, Adams Media Corporation, USA, 1996
Soldiering On, The Australian Army at Home and Overseas, Australian War Memorial, Australia, 1942

Public Record Office, England, *SOE Syllabus, Lessons in Ungentlemanly Warfare, World War II*, St Edmundsbury Press, UK, 2001

RAAF, Directorate of Public Relations: *RAAF Saga*, Australian War Memorial, Australia, 1944

Schultz, Duane: *Hero of Bataan, The Story of General Jonathan M. Wainwright*, St Martin's Press, Inc., NY, 1981

Special Operations Warrior Foundation: *US Special Operations Forces*, Hugh Lauter Levin Associates, Inc., USA, 2003

Stone, Peter: *Hostages to Freedom, The Fall of Rabaul, New Guinea 1941–1945*, Australian Print Group, Australia, 1995

The Army Historical Foundation: *The Army*, Barnes & Noble Books, NY, 2001

The Australian Military Forces: *Jungle Warfare with the Australian Army in the South-West Pacific*, Australian War Memorial, Australia, 1944 The War, Years 1, 2, 3, 4, 5, 6. Odhams Press Limited, London, 1940

Wainwright, General Jonathan M.: *General Wainwright's Story. The Account of Four Years of Humiliating Defeat, Surrender, and Captivity*, Doubleday & Company. Inc., Garden City, NY, 1946

Whitcomb, Edgar C.: *Escape from Corregidor*, Henry Regnery Company, USA, 1958

Willmott, H. P., and Keegan, John: *The Second World War in the Far East*, Cassell & Co., London, 2002

Wright-Nooth, George, with Adkin, Mark: *Prisoner of the Turnip Heads, The Fall of Hong Kong and Imprisonment by the Japanese*, Cassell Military Paperbacks, London, 1994

None But The Brave

Joy Chambers

'We belong to a special branch of the armed forces. We're interested in people who speak foreign languages and who are young and fit. We could be trained in hand-to-hand combat, to jump out of aircraft, scale walls and who wouldn't mind doing things which come under the heading of dangerous.'

John Baron Chard, orphaned as a baby and brought up in Australia, is unaware that the family he loves is not his own. When his life is thrown into turmoil, he leaves for England to join the RAF as war looms over Europe.

Samantha Chard, young and headstrong, is a pioneer woman photographer. When she cannot have the man she loves, she marries Cashman Slade – a union with disastrous consequences.

Cashman Slade, charismatic and arrogant, discovers an easy way to live in style when his father squanders the family's wealth. But nothing is free, and as Cash flees from his past he is forced to make his stand in the world's greatest conflict.

NONE BUT THE BRAVE sweeps these three courageous people into the battlefield as it travels from France to Great Britain to the Australian bush and back again in a gripping insight into a fascinating period of our past.

Praise for Joy Chambers' novels:

'An epic saga and meticulously researched: this is an understatement. It is both these things and more . . . History skilfully combined with fictional characters' *Daily Telegraph*, Sydney

'Joy Chambers has written a real blockbuster' *Best*

'Brimming with drama and intrigue' *Publishing News*

'Written with an ease of style and sophistication' *Liverpool Echo*

978 0 7553 0521 6

headline

Vale Valhalla

Joy Chambers

In the 21st century the men who fought in the Great
War have all but faded away, and only the memory of
their sacrifice will be preserved. Between 1914 and
1918 soldiers from all over the world converged on the
trenches of Belgium and Northern France: from
Australia and New Zealand, Canada, England, India,
Ireland, Scotland, South Africa, Wales and the far
reaches of the British Empire they came to fight
alongside the Belgians and the French.

VALE VALHALLA

traces the lives of a group of Australians through the
years prior to, and during, the First World War, and
reveals how they were forever altered by their
sufferings in that singular and relentless conflict. The
result of many years of research, VALE VALHALLA
cleverly melds fact and fiction and is a compelling epic
novel from the bestselling author of MAYFIELD and
MY ZULU, MYSELF.

'An epic saga . . . meticulously researched . . . history
skilfully combined with fictional characters'
Daily Telegraph, Sydney

978 0 7472 6088 2

headline

My Zulu Myself

Joy Chambers

Darlengi called out, 'John Lockley! Is it you?'

'Oh dear sweet Jesus!' John Lockley shouted. 'Yes, yes, Darlengi, I'm here!'

There was a moment of pure elation as they rushed forward to each other. Then they were in each other's powerful arms; hugging, laughing, shouting for joy, clasping each other like the treasure they thought lost for ever . . . Even the moon shone more brightly.

From the moment John Lockley saves the Zulu boy, Darlengi, from drowning they almost believe they are true brothers; born on the same day, never knowing their mothers, they spend their formative years together sharing a deep and abiding love for their country of South Africa. But when love intervenes in the young men's lives, tragedy appears, and all they hold dear is threatened as they fight to maintain a relationship across cultures and a deeply divided nation.

978 0 7472 4859 0

headline

Now you can buy any of these other bestselling
books by **Joy Chambers** from your bookshop.
or *direct from the publisher*.

My Zulu, Myself	£5.99
Vale Valhalla	£5.99
Mayfield	£6.99
None But the Brave	£7.99

TO ORDER SIMPLY CALL THIS NUMBER

01235 400 414

or visit our website: www.madaboutbooks.com

Prices and availability subject to change without notice.